THE PRICELESS COLLECTION

Books 1–3

THE PRICELESS COLLECTION

Books 1–3

DAVIS BUNN

HENDRICKSON
PUBLISHERS

The Priceless Collection

Hendrickson Publishers Marketing, LLC
P. O. Box 3473
Peabody, Massachusetts 01961-3473

ISBN 978-1-61970-701-6

Florian's Gate © 1992 Davis Bunn.

The Amber Room © 1992 Davis Bunn.

Winter Palace © 1993 Davis Bunn.

This edition by arrangement with the copyright holder.

First Hendrickson Edition Printing — October 2015

FLORIAN'S GATE

THE
PRICELESS
COLLECTION

Book One

THIS BOOK IS DEDICATED TO MY WIFE'S
FAMILY AND TO THEIR POLISH HERITAGE

Tę książkę pragnę dedykować Rodzinie mojej żony.

Tylko dzięki Wam mogłem napisać tę opowieść, tylko dzięki
temu co Wy przedstawiacie—tylko dzięki Waszej niekończącej się
gościnności, Waszym doświadczeniom, którymi dzieliliście się ze
mną, Waszej mądrości życiowej i Waszej miłości dla mojej Iziuni.

Otworzyliście przede mną swoje domy i swoje serca i pokazaliście
mi ten inny świat, który dane mi było poznać tylko przez Was.
Tylko dzięki Wam pokochałem Wasz jakże piękny i jakże tragiczny
Kraj. Dzięki Wam Polska będzie zawsze częścią mnie samego.

"And I said to the man who stood at the gate of the year: 'Give me a light that I may tread safely into the unknown.' And he replied: 'Go out into the darkness and put your hand into the hand of God. That shall be to you better than light, and safer than a known way.'"

MINNIE LOUISE HASKINS

Quoted by King George VI in his annual Christmas address to the British nation in 1939, on the eve of World War II.

AUTHOR'S NOTE

All antiques mentioned in this story do indeed exist. Prices quoted are based on actual sales or market estimates at the time of the original writing.

Jeffrey Sinclair swung around the corner to Mount Street in London's Mayfair district and greeted the wizened flower seller with, "It looks like another rainy day, Mister Harold."

The old man remained bent over his rickety table. "Too right, Yank. Mid-June and we ain't had a dry day since Easter. Don't do my rheumatics no good, s'truth."

"How much for the white things up there on the shelf?"

"What're you on about now?" The man straightened as far up as he was able, shook his head, and said, "Chrysanthemums, Yank. Chrysanthemums. Didn't they teach you anything?"

"I can't say that before coffee. How much for a bunch?"

"A what?" The man squinted at Jeffrey's double armful. It was an Edwardian silver punch bowl, chased in gold and sporting a pair of intricately engraved stags locked in mortal combat. It was filled with disposable diapers. "Got old Ling in there?"

"Yes."

The old man snorted. "Better bed'n I've ever seen. How much that thing worth?"

"It's priced to sell fast at seven thousand pounds." About twelve thousand dollars. "Maybe your wife would like it for her birthday."

That brought a laugh. "The old dear'll be getting' the same as last year, a pint at the pub. You're a right one, walkin' 'round these streets with a silver jug for a birdbath."

"It's not a jug." He spotted Katya walking toward them and felt his heart rate surge by several notches. She was sheltered within a vast gentleman's anorak, which she wore to hide the fancy clothes required for working in his shop. The hood framed a pixie face.

She greeted him with a smile that did not reach her eyes and said, "Good morning, Mr. Harold."

"Hello, lass." Wizened features twisted into a delighted smile. "Been keepin' you waitin' again, has he?"

She shook her head and said to Jeffrey, "I'm doing research at the library this morning, and I need a book I left at the shop." She peered into the vessel, asked, "How is Ling?"

" 'Ere, let's have a look." The old man's blackened fingers peeled back the upper layer, exposing a baby bird about three weeks outside the egg. "Blimey, he's a runt. What you figure him for?"

Jeffrey knew at a glance that he would have to reply. Katya had a way about her on days like this. She moved within an air of silent sorrow, a shadow drawn across unseen depths. Jeffrey could do little more than watch and yearn to delve beneath the surface and know the secrets behind those beautiful eyes. "Katya thinks it's a robin, but we're not sure."

The bird was sleeping, its gray-feathered body breathing with the minutest of gasps. Its wings were nothing more than tiny stubs covered with the finest of down. It looked far too fragile to live.

"What's he eat?"

"The vet said we ought to buy this special formula, but we couldn't find it anywhere. So Katya's mixed up baby food with bird-seed and some mineral drink. Ling eats enough of it, that's for sure.

"The girl's right, Yank. Never did trust them doctors." He reached out one finger and nudged the little body. Immediately the bird leapt upright, its tiny beak opened just as wide as it could, its scrawny neck thrust out to a ridiculous length.

"Look what you did now." Jeffrey's exasperation was only half-faked. "He'll drive me crazy until I can get the shop opened and his formula heated."

The old man remained bent over the tiny form, a smile creasing his unshaven features. "Reminds me of how my littlest one, Bert, used to go on. Lad could eat a horse. Mind you, he made a lot more noise than this runt, Bert did."

"I've got to go now, Mister Harold." Jeffrey said, and started down Mount Street. "Bring a bunch of those white ones by the shop, okay?"

"I would, Yank, if I could figure out what in blazes you're goin'
on about," the old man replied, turning back to his table. "Around
these parts we sell flowers by the dozen."

The bird kept up a continual high-pitched tweet the entire way
down the block. Jeffrey handed the bowl to Katya, fished in his
pocket, drew out and inserted the round ten-inch strong-box key
in the special slot. He turned it once, punched the four numbers
in the alarm box set in the red brick wall, turned it a second time,
and sighed with relief when the locks unsheathed with a loud click.
A year on the job, and he still got the jitters every time he had to
open early.

Nine months previously he had forgotten the numbers, and
while he was fishing around in his wallet and trying to remember
what different sequence he had written down—subtract one, add
two, do the first last, whatever—the sky had split open and the
gods of war had been set loose. Alarm bells shattered the quiet of
the six o'clock street, lights flashed, and a loud wailing began to
slide up and down the scale. The racket caused him to drop his
wallet into the slush of yet another half snow, half rain that had
turned his first winter in London into a seemingly endless grayish
hue. Heads popped out of louvered windows to scream abuse. The
police raced up with yet more flashing lights and wailing sirens, and
it was only after another half hour of browbeating from all sides
that Jeffrey managed to break away, slip inside, and begin another
day at the office.

That morning all went as it should, except for Ling's endless cry
and Katya's silent distance. Ling had been named by Katya, who
had said The Ugly Duckling was too long for something that tiny.
Katya was his sort-of girlfriend. The sort-of was from her side, not
his. As far as he was concerned, today would have been a fine time
to set up house. This morning, in fact. Right now, not to make too
big a point of it. But he couldn't—make a point of it, that is—since
Katya made it perfectly clear that she wasn't interested.

Hers was not a lighthearted attraction, but rather one which
remained surrounded by walls and hidden depths even after seven
months of their being together. Her hair was very dark, almost

blue-black in color, and cut very short in what used to be called a page-boy style and what now was referred to as functional. It was very fine hair, and it framed her face with a silky aura that shimmered in the light and shivered in the softest breeze. Her eyes were wide and grayish violet and very expressive, her mouth somehow small and full at the same time. Hers was a small, perky face set upon a small, energetic body. He loved her face, loved the quiet fluidity of her movements, loved the way she smiled with her entire being—when she smiled, which was very seldom. Katya was one of the most serious people he had ever met.

Only once had he seen the seriousness slip away entirely, when they had gone to Hastings for the day and spent an unseasonably hot early May afternoon on the beach. After a laughter-filled swim in absolutely frigid water, she had toweled her hair and left it salt-scattered, happy enough to be warm and wet and in the sun for a while. From behind blank sunglasses Jeffrey had examined this strange woman in her brief moment of true happiness, and wondered at all that he did not know of her. Her mysterious distance was a crystal globe set around the most fragile of flowers, protecting a heart from he knew not what. And as he looked, he yearned to come inside the globe, to know this heart, to taste the nectar of this flower.

That time on the beach remained one of the few moments of true intimacy they had ever shared. And even then Jeffrey had almost managed to mess it up—without intending to, without understanding what it was he had said, without knowing how to make things better.

They were lying on a shared beach towel after their swim, enjoying the rare day of summer-like heat that warmed away the water's chill. Katya sat supported by her arms, with her head thrown back, her uplifted face and closed eyes holding an expression of earthly rapture. Jeffrey lay beside her, turned so that he could watch her without her seeing him, knowing that he should understand her better to feel as he did.

She opened her eyes, squinted at the sky, then pointed upward and said brightly, "Look, that's where God lives."

"What?"

"Over there. See the light coming through the clouds like that? When I was a little girl I decided that it happened when God came down and sat on the clouds. That's why they lit up with all those beautiful colors. And that big stream of light falling to earth was where God was looking down at people to see if they were behaving."

"Do you believe in God?"

She turned and looked at him with clear gray-violet eyes that gave nothing away. "Don't you?"

"I used to. I used to feel as if God was around me all the time."

"He is."

"Maybe so, but I couldn't ever seem to find Him when I needed Him." Jeffrey settled his hands behind his head. "I guess I stayed really religious for about three years. Then when I was seventeen I started going through some bad times. I ended up deciding that if God wasn't going to help me more than He was, then I needed to stop relying on Him and learn to help myself. So I did. I didn't mean to let religion slide, but I guess it has. No, I know it has. It just never seemed to matter very much to me after that."

She looked down at him for a very long moment. "That is the most you have ever told me about yourself."

You're not the most open person either, he thought. "I guess I've never had anybody seem all that interested before."

She kept her solemn eyes on him, and for a moment Jeffrey thought she was going to bend over and kiss him. Instead she turned her face back to the sky and said, "I ran away from home three times when I was six. That's what my parents called it, anyway. What really happened was I went running over to where God was looking down. I wanted to ask Him to make the bad things go away. But I never could get there in time. Sooner or later the light would go out and I knew God had gone to watch other people somewhere else."

He lay and looked at the still face, with its delicate upturned nose and upper lip that seemed to follow the same line of curve. Her chin, too, rose just a little bit, as if carefully planed by a gentle artist. "Did you have a lot of bad times as a kid?"

She lay down beside him, her breath causing her breasts to rise and press against the suit's flimsy fabric. Jeffrey decided he had never seen a more beautiful woman in all his life. "I didn't have anyone to compare with," she replied. "It seemed pretty bad to me."

"Do you want to tell me about it?"

She met him once more with that same level gaze, as though searching inside him for something she couldn't find. "I don't think so," she said. "Can I ask you a question?"

"Sure."

"Have you ever thought about giving God another chance in your life?"

"No," he replied honestly.

"Why not?"

"What for?" He turned his face to the sky. "Why should anything be different this time?"

"Did you ever think that maybe you'd understand why you had to go through what you did, if you'd give Him a chance to explain?"

"Why didn't He explain it then?"

"I don't know, Jeffrey," she said, her voice as calm as her gaze. "Maybe you weren't listening. Or maybe you were listening for something that He didn't want to tell you."

For some reason that struck a little close to home. He countered with, "What about you? Did you find all the answers you were looking for when you were little and hurting and went looking for God?"

"No," she replied. "But I kept looking, and now I do."

"You mean you found an excuse." Her certainty irritated him. He sat up and said, "You went looking for a reason to believe in a God who let you be hurt when you were a little defenseless kid. So you found one. If I wanted to, I could come up with a thousand perfectly good reasons. But it doesn't mean God exists."

She raised up to sit beside him. "You don't understand."

"You're right."

"I found understanding because I let God heal the pain. That's when it started to make sense, Jeffrey. So long as I was still hurting, I couldn't see beyond my pain. But when the wounds healed and the pain left, I was able to see the real reason. The only reason. You can too."

"You really do believe, don't you?"

"With all my heart," she replied simply.

He shook his head, turned to face the sea. "Crazy. I thought I'd left all that stuff back home."

She rose to her feet in one fluid motion. "I think I'm ready to go now."

"Why?" He looked up at her. "There's another two or three hours of sun left."

"I'm going home, Jeffrey." She began slipping back into her jeans. "Would you please take me?"

======

Jeffrey entered the shop and watched Katya walk to the back, retrieve her book, and leave with the fewest of words. He stood for a moment in the center of the shop and felt the vacuum caused by her silent passing. He sighed, shook his head, and carried Ling's bowl back to the cramped office space behind the stairwell. He set the bowl carefully on a Queen Anne rosewood table and turned on the hotplate. While he prepared the formula and washed the eyedropper, he occupied himself with a rundown of the week's activities.

It was going to be busy, with a major buyer over from America, one of his paintings up for sale at Christie's, the Grosvenor House Antique Fair getting under way, and his boss coming in that Wednesday from goodness-knows-where. A buying trip, that much he knew. Probably from somewhere on the Continent, but he wasn't sure. Where Alexander Kantor bought his antiques was the best-kept secret of the international antiques market. Not to mention the basis for endless speculation and envy.

The most likely rumor Jeffrey had heard was that over the years Alexander had maintained relations with the Communist leaders of Eastern Europe. Now that they were out of business, he was making the rounds as a staunch supporter of the new democracies. Yet not the minutest bit of proof had ever been unearthed. The only thing known was that Alexander Kantor, the sole and rightful owner of the Priceless, Ltd antique shop of Mount Street, had more formerly unknown treasures to his credit than any other dealer in the world.

Jeffrey Allen Sinclair, former consultant with the McKinsey Group's Atlanta operations and currently Alexander Kantor's number two, filled the eyedropper and began feeding the mixture into the pitiful little mouth. Ling took it in with great swallows that wrenched his entire tiny frame. After five mouthfuls, he slowed down, pausing and weaving his little skull back and forth, then coming up for one last gulp before collapsing.

Jeffrey slid his hand under the fuzzy little body and was rewarded with a rapturous snuggle. Ling loved to be held almost as much as he loved to be fed. Jeffrey smiled at the trembling little form cradled in his fingers, extremely glad that nobody back home could see him right then.

He had taken in the bird the night they found it, since Katya had class the next day and didn't want to leave it alone in her own flat that long. He had kept it because it brought Katya over to the shop every afternoon. No question about it, the bird was a much bigger draw than he was. For the moment, anyway. Jeffrey had big hopes for the future.

By the end of that week Jeffrey was hooked on the bird and wouldn't have given Ling up for love or money. If Katya wanted the bird, she'd have to move in—or at least that was what he was planning to insist on if she ever asked, which she didn't. Katya had an uncanny sixth sense that steered her clear of all such uncharted waters.

When baby was fed and burped and packed between pristine sheets, Jeffrey set up the coffee brewer, then started opening for the day. He flipped the switch to draw up the mesh shutters over the main window, turned on the shop's recessed lighting, and began opening the mail.

Just as the coffee finished perking, the front doorbell sounded. Jeffrey walked forward with a smile of genuine pleasure and released the lock. "And a very good morning to you, madame."

A visiting American dealer named Betty greeted him with, "Does it always rain here?"

"I seem to remember hearing somewhere that Boston's weather wasn't always that nice."

"Maybe not, but we get breaks from it. The sun comes out to remind us what's up there."

He led her toward the back of the shop, asked, "Did you sleep well?"

"I never sleep well in London. My body is not accustomed to being under water. I need to breathe air that doesn't smell like the inside of an aquarium. I'm growing webs between my toes. Next comes oily feathers so the water will roll off."

He helped her off with her coat. "Some coffee?" he offered.

"Thank you. I'm beginning to understand why you make it stronger than my nail-polish remover. It's intended to warm your bones on days like this." She handed him a heavy plastic bag. "A little offering toward your continuing education."

She always brought a stack of recent U.S. magazines; he always played at surprise, but his gratitude was genuine. They were those she worked through on the transatlantic flight, and passing them on to Jeffrey was as good a way as any of tossing them out. But he had been in the business long enough to know that having a buyer perform anything that even resembled a courtesy was rarer than genuine Elizabethan silver.

He leafed through them in anticipation of a slow afternoon's pleasure. There was the *Architectural Digest*, at five bucks a pop; *Unique Homes*, filled with full-color full-page ads for the basic sixteen bedroom home and rarely showing anything valued at less than a million dollars; *HG*, the restyled *House and Garden*, struggling desperately to attract the yuppie reader; *Elle Decor*, basically concentrating on the modern, but just snooty enough to give him the occasional sales idea for a piece that wasn't moving; and a variety of upscale magazines to teach him what there was to know about the slippery notions of American taste—*House Digest, Southern Accents, Colonial Homes, Connoisseur Magazine*.

"These are great, Betty. Thanks a million."

Betty shook a few drops of water from her short-cropped gray hair. "I've been here eight days now. No, nine. This miserable misting rain hasn't stopped once. Or correct me if I'm wrong. Perhaps I blinked in the wrong place and missed the glorious English summer."

"It has been pretty awful. But we had a few days of beautiful weather back in May. Hot, sunny, crystal blue skies. I even went down for a day at the beach."

"Impossible. I refuse to believe that London could have had sunshine. It would have made the front pages of every paper around the world."

He smiled. "Come on downstairs, there's something I'd like to show you."

He led Betty down the narrow metal staircase to the basement. It was a simple concrete-lined chamber, void of the upper room's stylish setting. The floor was laid with beige indoor-outdoor carpeting and the low ceiling set with swivel lamps on long plastic strips.

"I've been saving this for you," he said, reaching up to turn a lamp toward the space beneath the staircase.

The light shone on a gateleg table, one so narrow that with both leaves down it was less than eight inches across. It was simple oak, burnished for over three centuries by caring hands until the original finish glowed with fiery pride.

Betty ran a practiced hand over its surface, bent and inspected the straight-carved legs, pronounced, "Definitely Charles the Second. Late Jacobean."

"I thought it might be."

"No question about it." She raised up, her eyes lit with undisguised excitement. "I know just where this is going."

"You're not supposed to let it show, Betty."

"You don't have any idea just how special you are, do you? I've never seen so many twisted definitions for honesty as I find in this trade." She walked back over, patted his cheek. "Did you know you're already gaining a reputation?"

"Who says?"

"One the other traders would kill for, I might add. Of course, they treat the concept of honesty as something they can buy." She chuckled, shook her head, turned back to the table. "What a true work of art. It deserves to go to a home where it will be appreciated, don't you think?"

"I wish I could afford to keep it," he confessed.

"Don't worry. That too will come."

"How can you be so sure?"

She did not look up. "Less than a year in this game, and already the word's getting out about you. Just be patient and don't give in to greed when the opportunity arises. How much for the table?"

"Five thousand. Pounds."

She gave a single nod. "High, but fair. Set to allow me an honest profit, no need to argue or bicker or stomp around in pretended rage. And you don't carry another Jacobean piece in the entire shop, do you? No, of course not. You really were holding it for me, weren't you?"

"The minute I saw it, I knew you'd flip."

"I'm too old and set in my ways for any of that, I'm afraid. But I do love it and you are a perfect sweetheart to think of me." She gave him a from-the-heart smile, another rare gem in this trade. "Now how about some of that coffee of yours? Still making it too strong?"

"I'm trying to get it to where it'll take the tarnish off my spoons," he replied, leading her back upstairs. "I'm not quite there yet. The last batch melted the silver."

"It's difficult for me talk about antiques without talking about my love of antiques," she said, once they were back upstairs.

"You always say that when we start talking."

"Well, it's true." She accepted her cup, took a sip, made a face. "Good grief, Jeffrey. You're going to melt my inlays."

"Too strong?" he asked politely.

"Pour some of this out and fill it halfway with milk. Maybe I'll keep my stomach lining."

She watched him doctor her cup, took another sip, gave him a nod. "I do believe I'm going to be able to drink this batch without gagging."

"Coming from you that's real praise."

Betty settled back and began what for them was the favorite part of their time together. As she sat and sipped her coffee, he sat and drank her words.

"When you think of antiques in the United States, you have to ask yourself how the pieces got here. Some of the early items were brought over by wealthy families. We tend to see all of our ancestors as having arrived in rags, packed into the holds of sailing ships like cattle. For many, many people this just was not true."

She stopped to taste her coffee. The cup was one of a set of Rosenthal, so delicate the shadow of her lips could be seen through the porcelain. On the outside was painted a pastoral scene in the tradition of the early Romanticists; with either excellent vision or a magnifying glass one could make out genteel ladies under frilly parasols watching gentlemen in spats lay out picnics while being watched by smiling cows and prancing horses. In the background was a mansion in the best Greco-Italian-fairytale style.

"In most instances, the wealthier families traveled over with their own craftsmen. They intended to build their homes, you see, and skilled workers were as hard to find then as now. Once the main house was completed, these craftsmen would begin to make furniture."

They were seated in the little office alcove behind the stairwell. Between the banister and his desk Jeffrey had set a nineteenth-century screen, whose three panels were inlaid with ebony and mother-of-pearl in a European parody of a Japanese garden scene. His desk was a real find, an eighteenth-century product that appeared to have been carved from one massive piece of fruitwood. Its front was curved to match the wood's natural grain, with the two drawers made from the panels that had been cut from those very places. The legs were slender and delicately scrolled, matched by four short banisters that rose from each corner of the desk top. They in turn supported thin panels no more than two inches high, carved to depict a series of writing implements—quill pens, inkstands, knives for sharpening, miniature blotters, tiny books.

"You have to think of American antiques in terms of where people settled, moving from the East to the West, and adapting as they went along," Betty continued. "The same is true between the different settlements in the North and South. In the North you had Chippendale, you had Sheraton, you had craft shops where you found so-called manufactured pieces. These were mostly copies of styles originating in Europe, usually from either France or England, but lacking many of the really intricate details. American craft shops tended to go for higher quantities, you see. And there were fewer people with the really refined tastes who would be willing to pay the outrageous sums required for delicate inlay work."

At the front of the shop, beige lace curtains formed a backdrop that allowed in light, but also restricted the view of passers-by to the lone semi-circular sideboard standing in solitary splendor on the window's raised dais. The remainder of the shop was designed to create an air of genteel splendor. Pieces were placed with ample room to breathe, as Alexander Kantor had described it to Jeffrey upon his arrival. Recessed ceiling lights were arranged to cast the sort of steady glow that was normally reserved for art galleries, with their hue and brilliance individually set so as to best bring out the wood's luster. The whole shop smelled vaguely of beeswax polish and wealth.

"The big southern plantations occasionally had craftsmen so talented that pieces could be identified by their quality," Betty went on. "If you hear of such articles going on the market today, they are usually sold as collectors' items or works of art. The prices would place them in your range, which for American antiques is very rare."

The two back walls of his office space were decorated with original steel engravings, the prints so detailed as to almost look photographed. Beside his desk stood a set of antique mahogany filing drawers, probably used in the director's office of an old shipping company, as each drawer was embossed with a brass anchor and the sides had carvings of a compass face. In the ceiling corner above the filing cabinet swiveled a miniature video camera, which piped its continual picture to a security company located down the street. An enclosing barrier had been erected to the side of Jeffrey's writing desk in the form of mahogany bookshelves. They stood a full nine feet high, and were fronted by a series of miniature double doors, each the height of two shelves and containing hand-blown diamond-shaped glass set in brass frames. The shelves contained Jeffrey's growing collection of books on antiques.

"Most of the affordable fine pieces came from the northern craft shops, since many were manufactured in lots and not as single pieces. This meant that as the professional class developed, their front hallways and living areas had tables and cabinets and sideboards imported from somewhere up north."

Set in the ceiling corner across from his office alcove was a round convex mirror, through which Jeffrey could watch the entire shop while seated at his desk. Keeping half an eye always on the store was by now old habit, although the front door—the shop's only entrance—was always double locked. Entry during office hours was possible only once he pressed the release button by the banister, then walked forward to personally throw the latch and open the door. Even with all the smaller items safely locked in the pair of Edwardian glass-fronted jeweler's cabinets, unless it was with a very trusted client like Betty, Jeffrey never sat down with a customer in the store. Never.

"When I was a little child my mother used to take me on what she called her buying trips. I was the only girl, and I had four older brothers. When we went off together like that it was the only time in those early years when I felt as if I could just enjoy being a girl."

Betty talked with a soft southern accent which had been gradually whittled away by years of trading all over the East Coast. Her shop had been located on Boston's Beacon Hill for more than three decades, but her work took her from Texas to Canada and back several times a month. Her shop was the source of only a fraction of her income. Auction houses called on Betty to identify unknown pieces. Interior decorators in ten states had her on retainer to seek out antiques that would fit into the residences and executive offices and fine hotel lobbies they were hired to adorn. Wealthy households would ask her to keep a look out for something to fill an empty space. Something elegant, they would often say, not knowing themselves what they wanted besides the status of owning an almost-priceless one-of-a-kind. Something expensive. Betty had a way of listening that bestowed respect upon such a customer, and that was what many wanted most of all. Respect.

"I was raised in Virginia—I believe I told you that before. My parents were what you would call middle class, and there were not a lot of antiques that had been handed down. When my mother and I went off to buy, we were looking for pieces that would go into our own home. Those were some of the happiest days I have ever known, getting up early and traveling off to some country antique store or a market somewhere, just me and my mother, eating in nice restaurants and talking girl-talk. Very precious memories. My love of antiques started right then and there."

Betty was a smallish woman who carried herself so erect that she appeared much taller than she was. She dressed with an artist's eye, conservative in color and extravagant with materials. Today she wore a midnight-blue crepe-de-chine silk dress with a matching cashmere jacket, and for a necklace had a small antique pocket watch hung from a gold rope chain.

"My mother did not have a lot of money. Most of what she spent on antiques she saved from her weekly shopping, putting it in a little pewter sugar bowl until it was full, and then off she'd go. Back then there were not many antique shops. This was back in the mid-thirties, just as the Depression was lifting. Times were very hard, even for a relatively well-off family like mine, and this was really her only diversion.

"A lot of black people in the rural areas had been given furniture and cut-glass bowls and even some crystal from the homes where they had worked. Back in the twenties, as people became wealthier, they wanted to discard these old things and buy something new and store-bought. That was what it was called in the South, although most of the rural families purchased from catalogs—store bought goods.

"My mother was a very sweet person, and during the very hard times had organized a church group to help the poorest of these families with food and children's clothes and medicine. People remembered her kindnesses, and now that she had some money and wanted to buy these old things, they would try to help her. So she would drive down these country roads, often nothing more than dirt tracks, and someone would come out on the front porch and say that so-and-so had a pretty piece of pressed glass or a chiffarobe or flow-blue, which was a special kind of pottery china with a pretty blue design on it, and they needed money and wanted to sell it.

"I bought my very first antique in that way. It was a little blue chicken of hand-blown glass that you could open up and keep candy in. A woman let us go up into her attic and go through a trunk filled with old glass wrapped in old newspapers, and she let me buy that chicken for twenty-five cents. It had probably taken me six months to save up that many pennies—money was still very hard to come by, especially for a child. I still have that piece. It sits on its own special little shelf in my kitchen."

The phone gave its querulous demand for attention. "Excuse me." Jeffrey picked up the receiver, was greeted with distant hissings and pops. "Priceless Limited." There were a couple of crackling connections. "Hello?"

"To whom am I speaking, please?" The voice was cheerful and heavily accented, the words fairly shouted.

Jeffrey raised his voice in reply. "This is the Priceless antique shop. Can I help you?"

"Jeffrey?" The gentleman's unspoken laughter called above the line's crackling. "Do I have the pleasure of speaking to Jeffrey Allen Sinclair?"

"Yes." Jeffrey tried to place the voice, came up blank. "Who is this?"

"Ah, an excellent question. Who is this indeed?" The laughter broke through, a most appealing sound. "I fear you will have to ask that of our friend Alexander. How are you, my dear boy?"

"I'm all right," he said, giving Betty an eloquent shrug.

"Splendid. That is absolutely splendid. Alexander has spoken so much about you I feel we are already the best of friends."

"He has?"

"Indeed, yes. Has Alexander arrived?"

"Not yet." Jeffrey was almost shouting the words. "He's supposed to be here the day after tomorrow."

"No matter. Please, Jeffrey, do me the kindness of passing on a message to Alexander. Would you do that?"

"Of course."

"Splendid. Splendid. Tell him the shipment is ready. Do you have that?"

"Got it."

"Excellent. And now, my dear boy, I bid you farewell. I do so hope that we shall have an opportunity to meet very soon. Until then, may the grace of the Lord Jesus Christ, and the love of God, and the fellowship of the Holy Spirit be with you always."

Betty watched him hang up the phone and said, "That sounded curious."

Jeffrey scribbled busily, replied, "I get all kinds of weird calls a week or so before Alexander arrives. I've stopped worrying about them."

"Or wondering?"

He stripped out the page and stuffed it in an already bulging folder. "I don't think I'll ever get that casual."

She handed back her cup and motioned toward the lead-paned bookshelves. "Do you mind?"

"Not at all." He opened the desk drawer, fished out his key ring, inserted the miniature skeleton key and opened the top set of doors. "These are my most recent purchases."

She slipped on a pair of gold-rimmed reading glasses and began examining the titles. "Is Alexander bringing in a lot of jewelry these days?"

"Just five pieces, but they were all Russian, and all really special, and I didn't know the first thing about them. I've been playing catch-up."

"So I see."

All the books were of the tall, oversized variety favored by publishers of high-priced, richly photographed volumes. The titles made an impressive list: *The Twilight of the Tsars; Russian Art at the Turn of the Century.* Von Solodkoff's *Russian Gold and Silver.* Bennett and Mascetti's *Understanding Jewelry.* Abrams' *Treasures From the Kremlin.* Von Habsburg's *Fabergé.*

She pointed to the book entitled *Das Gold Aus Dem Kreml.* "Do you read German?"

"No, a little French, that's all. But the pictures in that book are the best of the lot, and I can sort of figure out what they are talking about in some of the captions."

"Can you really." She peered over the top of her glasses. "You really must tell me the next time Alexander comes up with one of his little surprises, Jeffrey."

"I thought you dealt only in furniture and paintings."

"I do not intend it for the market." She waved a hand at the other shelves. "Open up and let me see, please."

The books represented an awkward dipping into various wells, spanning centuries and styles and markets with breathtaking speed. There were beginner's guides to identifying the otherwise unseen, such as the well-known *A Fortune in Your Attic*. The remainder were fairly indicative of what Jeffrey faced within Alexander's shop—a need to catch whatever was thrown at him, and speak of it with relative authority.

"Do you mean to tell me you've read all of these?" Betty asked.

"There are a lot of slow days in this business. You ought to know that." Jeffrey found it difficult to describe, even to Betty, how fascinating his study had become. "It gives me something to do while I wait for the bell to ring."

Without turning around, she asked, "Do you ever come across the really singular piece, Jeffrey?"

He thought of the item that had first taken him to Christie's, replied, "Sometimes."

"I was not restricting my question to furniture."

"I know. I wasn't either."

"I'd very much like you to remember me the next time something comes up." Betty reached over and traced her finger along one Moroccan-leather binding that bore the title *Russian Embroidery and Lace*. She kept her voice casual as she said, "I have a number of very rich customers. Very discreet. They would be most willing to pick up a truly singular item and effectively make it disappear." She turned to him. "Do you understand?"

"I'm not sure."

She patted his arm. "How utterly precious. Just promise me that if something comes in that takes your breath away, you won't forget to call me, all right?"

Jeffrey's arrival in London had marked the beginning of changes on every level of his being. From an emotional perspective, it was the first time since a brief fling with faith at an early age that Jeffrey really *felt* anything besides a rising frustration. Before his departure from America, he had recognized his lukewarm attitude toward life and accepted it as the price paid for playing the part. Now, there was an emotional dimension to his life. Everything that registered in his consciousness registered in his heart as well.

His father was the quintessential mild-mannered, soft-spoken man, an electronics engineer turned production administrator and corporate vice-president. Jeffrey had inherited a full dosage of both the emotionless demeanor and the quiet ambition that lurked beneath his father's bland surface. Yet a young life spent witnessing the price his father paid during his corporate rise left Jeffrey wondering what on earth to be ambitious *for.*

Jeffrey adored his parents. It was more than just a bonding of filial love; he truly *liked* them. They were good, genuine people who had struggled through a life of hard knocks, and finally achieved a success they fully deserved. They set about enjoying their definition of the good life with hard-earned determination and their elder son's blessings.

Jeffrey had seldom complained as their lives' course wound through seven states and eleven homes in as many years. He had not felt a need to complain. He was happy with his family. He loved his parents and he trusted them. Early in life he developed a skill at building new friendships and growing new roots deep in strange soils. He fashioned a detachment and a maturity long before most young people were even aware of what the words meant.

As he entered high school, he looked around at his fellow students and saw people who were simply not up to dealing with the torments that life threw their way. They sank into throes of boredom or empty cliques or drugs or casual sex or fanatical devotion to sports. They tried as hard as they could to escape from the fears and pains that kept boiling up inside them.

Jeffrey felt comfortable with himself, and marveled at how seldom that appeared to be the case with others. If his ability to float through turbulent times was a product of being uprooted and replanted every dozen months, so be it. He knew the constant shifting of his life had helped him tap some unseen, ill-defined well inside himself. For this he was truly grateful. He also knew that his father's path was not for him, yet he admired the man for knowing so clearly what he wanted.

Jeffrey was proud of the fact that the furious cross-currents of a life lived without a settled family and familiar surroundings had forged unbreakable bonds between his parents. It had also drawn the three of them more closely together. In the dismal early days of a new home full of boxes and vague smells and other people's histories, they huddled together for warmth and love and comfort.

They learned to laugh at the repetitiveness of problems that drew a sameness into every new city—streets that took them away from where they wanted to go, doctors and electricians and plumbers and bankers who had no time for newcomers, impersonal name-takers who tried to chill their very bones with a total lack of friendliness as they adjusted to new schools and new rules and new lives. The warmth and healing of close friends they found among themselves, and with each move became more intimate, more reliant upon each other.

But not Jeffrey's younger brother. With every move, his brother had fallen a little further away from the safety of their tightly bound trio. And with each new year, his brother had also fallen a little more apart. His increasingly demented behavior tore at the fabric of Jeffrey's life in ways that no move, no transition, no earlier trauma had ever prepared him. He found himself faced with the specter of hating his brother, hating him for the pain he caused to himself and to their parents. He was unable to respond with the compassion shown by his parents, terrified of having his protective bland exterior pried away; so he took the only other alternative he found open to himself. He decided that he no longer had a brother. He wiped the slate clean. And in doing so, he lost the need to hate.

With his move from university into corporate life, Jeffrey found a new reason to drown in negative emotions. The corporate world clutched at his very existence, calling him to give his all to some nameless company that offered vague promises of reward somewhere further down the line. Jeffrey responded by becoming a consummate actor, playing the ambitious go-getter to all the outside world.

If anyone had ever bothered to ask Jeffrey Allen Sinclair what it was he wanted most out of life, he probably would have replied, a calling. But no one ever did. He wore the yuppie mask far too well for anyone to think he sought more than just to be on top.

Four years with McKinsey in Atlanta had left him bereft not of ambition, but of goals. He burned with a desire to succeed, to achieve, yet he had no idea what to aim for.

The senior partners had one common thread running through all their lives: they were grimly, determinedly, daily dissatisfied. He searched their faces with anxiety, just as he searched his own heart. Why had they spent their lives struggling for the title and the income and the five-acre colonial spread if all it gained them was ulcers, bad backs, divorces, kids who hated them, and eyes that lit up only at the thought of yet another big deal?

Jeffrey was too aggressive and too full of energy to quit when he saw behind the charade. He would have gone crazy without some channel, some direction, even if the direction made no sense. Instead, his life simply became a theater. He knew the lines and spoke the part well, but in his heart of hearts there bloomed a yearning desire to be elsewhere. To do more. To live life with more gusto than was offered by a padded chair in a carpeted glass-lined cell.

Jeffrey was of slender build. Just over six feet tall, he had a supple strength without appearing overly muscular, and played a number of sports with disinterested ease. He found little on the playing fields that tempted him to give his all, so he played whatever his group played, and only so well as to not draw attention to himself.

Jeffrey's features helped enormously in making the theatrics a success. It was a strong face, full of the sharp angles and long lines of a determined success story. His hair was turning prematurely gray, but only in the most dignified manner. There were brushstrokes of silver at each temple, and faint pewter threads woven through a full and virile crop. To everyone except Jeffrey, it lent him an enviably distinguished note. For him it was the makings of his worst nightmares.

He had dreams of standing in front of his mirror and watching the aging process carry him through all the stages of decrepit decline. He would wake up in an empty-hearted sweat—not because he feared growing old, but because he feared a growing void where life's purpose was supposed to reside.

In his walks to and from the McKinsey offices in downtown high-rise Atlanta, Jeffrey would catch himself staring at the men and women who were barely visible to his fellow high-fliers. He watched their faces, this cadre of underlings, the hordes who trod their way daily through jobs that held little interest and less hope. The older faces chilled him to the bone, their empty exhausted gazes foreshadowing what might befall him if his act were ever uncovered.

Then, fourteen months ago, the invitation to lunch with Alexander Kantor had arrived like a lifeline tossed into a dark and stormy sea. Jeffrey had not seen it as such at first, however; in fact, he had almost avoided the meeting entirely.

━━━

They met for lunch at his father's insistence, during one of his infrequent visits back to Jacksonville. A lunch with an unknown relative was positively the last thing he wanted to do on a sunny Saturday afternoon, especially when his friends were headed for the beach. But when he told his father that he was going to skip the meeting, his father shook his head and said, I'm not sure that's a good idea. It wouldn't surprise me to hear that he wanted to talk with you about your future. Jeffrey snorted, you mean a job? I've never even met the man before. His father replied, Alexander has his own way of doing things, and he's always seemed to know more about our lives than we have ever known about his.

So Jeffrey went. Angry that he was not at the beach, but he went.

He arrived at the restaurant hoping to find some way of shaking the man's hand and making polite conversation and then leaving. Jeffrey figured a five-minute meeting would be enough to satisfy his father. But Alexander wasn't there. Jeffrey sat in the nicest restaurant in all of north Florida, and smoldered.

The longer he sat there, the more grotesque his picture of the man became. Alexander Kantor. What a name. He probably fit in perfectly with all the interior decorator types an antique dealer had to work with. Jeffrey toyed with the ice in his empty water glass, saw the man take form before his eyes—slender as a beanpole, dressed in skin-tight canvas pants with buttons, liked deck-shoes without socks even though he got seasick at the sight of a boat rocking at anchor. Poorly fitting toupee and a mechanical sunlamp tan that left him looking like an underdone lobster. Yeah, Jeffrey could see him, all right. The black sheep of the family, the one nobody'd even heard from in ten years, the one who'd never married. All they knew was that he had a fancy antique shop in London. Right. That wasn't so easy to check up on from five thousand miles away. The guy probably dealt out of the back of an old van, a battered white one with bald tires—

"My dear boy, I'm terribly sorry to have kept you waiting." A deep, heavily accented voice boomed from beside him, making Jeffrey jerk upright. "I do hope you haven't been here long."

Jeffrey banged both knees in his scramble out of the booth. The gentleman extended a hand and said in his cultured voice, "Alexander Kantor. At your service."

"Ah, nice, that is, Jeffrey Sinclair." His hand was taken in by well-tanned fingers covered with the loose skin of an older man, then squeezed with a strength that made Jeffrey wince.

"You most certainly are. You would not know it, I am sure, but you are the mirror image of your maternal grandfather as a lad. Piotr was my father's brother; you might have heard that from your family. When I was a young boy I positively worshiped the gentleman." He gave a polished, even-toothed smile. "This lunch has already started off well, wouldn't you say?"

He was every inch an aristocrat. His hair was a burnished silver, cut to perfection. His eyebrows bushed upward at an angle that on a lesser man would have looked ridiculous; on him they simply fit. Beneath their jutting arrogance, gray eyes peered at him with frank inspection. His face was fleshy, but held from looking overweight by a ponderous jaw. His nose was a veritable eagle's beak. His dark suit was double-breasted and clearly hand-tailored. His tie was a mellow silk that matched his pocket kerchief, his shirt a crisp gray pinstripe with white collar and cuffs. His watch, ring, and cufflinks were a matching design of woven white and yellow gold.

The waiter appeared at their elbow, beating the maitre d' by half a stride. The two of them hovered about Alexander Kantor and played the roles of imperious restaurant manager and bustling server. The old gentleman paid them no mind, clearly accustomed to this sort of attention. All around the restaurant heads turned, brows furrowing in concentrated effort to remember where they had seen him before. There was no question about it, Alexander Kantor exuded a magnetic presence.

"So." He waved aside the waiter's ministrations, snapped open his napkin. "What is the family saying about me these days?"

"Ah, I don't believe—"

"Come, come. I used to be their favorite topic of gossip; don't tell me I've been forgotten. It never ceased to amaze me how they came up with some of the notions they did."

"All I know is that you have an antiques business in London and live, ah . . ."

"Yes, go on, my boy. This is where it tends to become interesting." At last he deigned to notice the maitre d'. "I'll have what my young guest is having."

"Sir, thus far your young guest has made do with six glasses of water and a dozen breadsticks."

"Is that so? Well then, in that case I should compliment the young gentleman on his graceful manners, don't you agree?" He settled the maitre d' with one frosty glare. "It was most kind of you to wait like this, Jeffrey. It really was."

Jeffrey watched his plans for a quick getaway fade into the distance. "My pleasure."

"We have quite a bit of business to discuss. Perhaps we should dispense with the head-fogging ritual of aperitifs, don't you think?"

"Fine with me."

"Excellent. Now tell me," he said, turning back to the maitre d'. "Does your wine menu extend as far as the fair fields of France?"

"It does indeed, sir."

"Splendid. With this heat, I believe we'd be wise to stay with fish, don't you, Jeffrey?"

"Sure."

"Then let us have a bottle of your finest Pouilly Fuissé," he said, pronouncing it correctly. He waited while the maitre d' made his bowing exit, then turned back to Jeffrey. "American waiters are all either college students with too much smoke between their ears or actors who never made it on stage, don't you agree?"

Jeffrey decided to try a dose of honesty. "You aren't anything like what I expected."

"I'm not the least bit surprised. When the family is not painting me out to be a mock prince sporting around one of his three dozen castles, they have me living off the crumbs from some rich heiress's dining table."

"Something like that."

"Well, there's more than a bit of truth in both of them. I do have several residences, although none of them are quite grand enough to deserve the title of palace. And anyone in the antiques trade lives off the rising and falling fortunes of others. An antique is nothing more than a used bit of life's flotsam and jetsam that someone or another has decided is worth a king's ransom, either because it's old, or because it's pretty, or because it has belonged to someone they deem to be worthy of remembering. Whatever the reason, one thing you may always bank upon—another backside has rested in that chair before you."

As the meal progressed Jeffrey found himself becoming captivated by the gentleman. Alexander's strong Polish accent added an alien burr to his polished speech, and came to represent the two sides of his character—the gracious international businessman on the one hand, and the mysterious relative on the other. Jeffrey sat and ate and listened and slowly came to the decision that he genuinely liked the man, mystery and all.

"Jeffrey. What a positively American-sounding name. I suppose all your friends call you Jeff."

"Not if I can help it."

Alexander Kantor showed genuine alarm. "Don't tell me you've been turned into a Jay."

"Good grief, no."

"Thank heavens. I'm certain I couldn't bear the strain of having a Jay skulking about."

Jeffrey started to ask, skulk about where. Instead he replied, "I don't skulk, and nobody's ever called me Jay twice."

"Do I detect a note of steel beneath that bland American exterior?" Alexander Kantor inspected him frankly. "Well. There might be hope yet. Tell me, Jeffrey. How have you spent your time since university?"

"I've worked with McKinsey Management Consultants out of their Atlanta office for the past six years."

"Really." The jutting eyebrows raised a notch. "In Europe a man hired from university for a consultant position is considered to be one of the best. Is that the case here?"

Jeffrey shrugged. "There were about four hundred applicants for each person hired."

"How interesting. I suppose you must find the work tremendously stimulating."

"Not really."

"Oh? Why is that?"

"Do you prefer honesty or corporate diplomacy?"

"I have always put the highest value on honesty, young man," Alexander replied. "Carry on."

"The pay for the lower grades is lousy. There's an endless back-stabbing battle to see who is going into one of the senior slots. Partners go out to the client companies, make the presentations, and leave us behind to do the trench work. Because of the competition, people on my level spend ridiculous hours doing research, poring over figures, writing out stuff that nobody in his right mind is ever going to read. Justifying the fees charged by the partners, basically."

Jeffrey leaned back, allowed the waiter to collect his plate. "Working there has been like joining a secret order or fraternity, with the partners coming by our cubicles every once in a while to pat us on the back and tell us to keep at it, because look how wonderful it's going to be once we hit the jackpot. But only less than one in ten actually make partner. The rest suffer from severe burnout and drop by the wayside."

"And which are you to be?" Alexander Kantor asked gravely.

"Burnout, most likely. I lack some of the basic ingredients, like an overriding desire to go for the jugular. Sometimes I pull back and wonder what in the world I'm doing there. It all seems so silly, chasing after an ulcer, a heart attack, and an early grave. But every time I put on the brakes I see all the others start pulling ahead, so I dive back down in the trench and keep on digging."

"I take it, then, that your present occupation does not grant you the satisfaction of having found the purpose for which you were placed upon this earth."

Jeffrey laughed a rueful no.

"Let's see. This would put your age at twenty-six, is that right?"

"Twenty-seven. I took a year off to travel before graduating."

"Ah yes. I recall a card or letter to that effect, saying that I should expect to find a bedraggled and no doubt bearded young man on my doorstep, and that I should not set the dogs on him. You were to be fed and allowed to wash your drawers. I believe your dear ones also included a request to have the doctor check you for lice and other horrors before placing you on the plane home—as though there were European strains of bacteria designed to attack visiting American college students."

"I think it was more a fear of where I had been sleeping."

"No doubt with good reason. In any case, I was quite disappointed not to have heard from you."

Jeffrey sipped at his water, recalling the impressions he had carried with him to Europe. Somewhere in his backpack had been a series of three or four addresses, enough to seem as if there was at least one place in each country he had visited belonging to this unknown uncle. Only he wasn't really an uncle, and no one in the family could bring themselves to speak of him without a smirk and a shake of the head.

Jeffrey had dutifully carried the addresses around with him for a year, along with a mental image that kept shifting between a crotchety old man with too much money and something a little more swish. Upon his return, he had made some vague excuse for not having called the mystery relative, and nobody had seemed very concerned.

"Why do they talk about you as they do?" he asked.

"Who, my long-lost American kin?" Kantor made a regal gesture dismissing the waiter's offer of anything further. "That is quite simple. Anything that is not known becomes shrouded with supposition, Jeffrey. It is one of life's unwritten rules. With time, the supposition becomes reality. It is much easier to believe nonsense than to search out the truth, and most people are either too lazy or too comfortable to look for truth any further than their front gardens." He cast a careful glance Jeffrey's way. "I do hope I've not offended you."

"Sounds to me as if you know them perfectly. The family never visited you, did they?"

"Not in years, although I must admit that I have not made an effort to visit your clan since Piotr's untimely departure from this earth. I tried to keep in touch, in my own feeble way, but your own family seemed to hop across the nation at such speeds that I would receive the latest address only to learn that you had already moved elsewhere."

"Yeah, that was Dad's life. When I was a kid I thought for a while that he was paid to move."

"Another of the prices for being an American executive. He was with IBM, I believe."

"Still is."

"Of course. Well, enough about the various kinfolk, as you say. Tell me more about yourself, Jeffrey."

"Like what?"

"Well, perhaps a bit more about your work."

Jeffrey leaned back in his seat and took a moment to gather his thoughts. Alexander Kantor offered a sense of immediate intimacy. He invited a frank discussion by offering the gift of intense listening. Jeffrey found it immensely satisfying to have this chance to speak with someone who *understood.*

"When I started out, the work at the big consulting groups was already shifting—only I didn't know it then. We went from helping companies identify problems and learn better management techniques, to simply growing bigger faster. Mergers and acquisitions became the name of the game in the eighties. Those words alone are enough to start a consultant salivating."

"Change is inevitable," Kantor said. "Why should you be disturbed by an altering of direction within the consulting industry?"

"Mergers tend to wipe people off the map," Jeffrey replied vehemently. "It brings out the worst trait of business, lack of concern for the little person. And even the people who are left after the firing squads have worked their way through the companies—which was one of our jobs—still end up feeling either left out or squashed down. People are so shaken by this change in their working life that they forget about other people. I only see it inside the businesses, but I'll bet it happens in their families, too. They don't have time anymore for other people's feelings, fears, ambitions—anything but their own skin. I hate what it does to people, and I hate the misery it causes for everybody but the handful of top executives who skim off the cream. It's become about seventy percent of our business, the most profitable section. If you're a trench worker like me, the best way to make it to partner is to get yourself attached to an

M and A team. You can always tell who they are, too. They're the ones walking around with blood on their hands."

"How remarkable," Kantor murmured. "A businessman with heart. Tell me, Jeffrey. Do you like dealing with people?"

"I've always thought so. That was why I got into management consulting work in the first place, so I could deal with a *lot* of people and a *lot* of issues. Maybe somewhere up the ladder that's the way it is, but right now I spend so much time in my little cubbyhole, I'm not sure I even remember how to be cordial."

"You're doing quite well, I assure you," Kantor said. He reached for an inner pocket, drew out a slender metal tube, and unscrewed the cap. He drew a cigar from a paper-thin screen of wood. "Do you mind?"

"Not at all. My grandfather used to smoke them."

Kantor smiled. "He most certainly did."

"I love the smell; I just can't stand the taste."

"Tell me, Jeffrey." He brought out a polished key chain and grasped a gold-plated guillotine the size of his thumb, an apparatus with a springblade and circular opening to clip off the cigar tip. "What would you say is your strongest point?"

Jeffrey thought about it, replied, "That I'm hungry."

"I beg your pardon?"

"Not for money. Well, sure, that too. But it's not number one. I want to learn. And do. And expand. I'm not sure that makes any sense."

"On the contrary, it makes very good sense. It is always difficult to put matters of the heart into words. You wish to stretch the limits of your experience."

"That's it exactly."

"A most commendable trait." He rubbed the cigar back and forth between thumb and forefinger, asked with deceptive casualness, "And what would you say is your greatest failing?"

"As far as your business goes? Simple. I don't know the first thing about antiques. Or furniture. Or interior decorating. Nothing."

"It is indeed an issue, but not an insurmountable one. You clearly have the aptitude for learning and have expressed a willingness to adapt." He fastened upon Jeffrey with a gently penetrating gaze. "Besides this, then, where is your greatest weakness?"

He did not need to search very far. Feeling very exposed, Jeffery replied, "I'm so frustrated and impatient with my life I feel as if I'm going to explode sometimes. I get incredibly angry at everyone, at life, especially at the people close to me, because I feel so trapped. I don't know which way to turn to get out of the bind, and that gets me even angrier. I'll start thinking about it sometimes without even realizing it, and then all of a sudden I'm so furious I'm shaking."

Alexander Kantor eyed him for a very long moment. "Your candor is most admirable, young man. You certainly did not need to consider that one very long."

"My girlfriend broke up with me last week because of it, so it's still on my mind a lot. She said she was tired of trying to make a go of it with someone who was never satisfied. I tried to tell her that the problem wasn't with us, but it didn't make any difference. Not to her, anyway."

Kantor released a long thin plume of smoke toward the ceiling. "If it is any consolation to you, young man, I learned a lesson about dissatisfaction some time ago that has brought me great consolation over the years. Shall I share it with you?"

"Sure."

"It is quite simple really. Dissatisfaction tends to lift one's eyes toward the horizon. Those who are comfortable rarely make the effort to search out something better. They may yearn for more, but they do not often receive it. They are too afraid of losing what they already have, you see, to take the risk. And there is always risk involved, Jeffrey. Always. Every major venture contains a moment when you must step off the cliff and stretch your wings toward the sky."

Jeffrey watched the man across from him and was suddenly struck with a feeling so solid it arrived in his mind already cemented into certainty. *He wanted that job.* There was no question, no need to doubt or consider his possibilities or salary or benefits or anything. Every mundane detail paled into insignificance beside the utter appeal of working with such a man as this. He *wanted* that job.

"A moment ago I mentioned a need to adapt," Kantor went on. "This cannot be stressed too highly, young man. The greatest failure of most intelligent people is a false confidence in what they already know. If you are going to succeed in this game, you must begin by assuming that you know nothing. Nothing at all. It is essential to your success."

Struggling to keep his eagerness from touching his voice, Jeffrey replied, "I understand."

"I am not sure you do," Kantor responded gravely. "I am not speaking solely of your knowledge of antiques and the related businesses. That in itself is only a small part of what is required. You must begin by assuming that you know *nothing*. Not how to dress, nor how to stand, nor how to greet a client, nor what to read, nor in some cases even what to think."

Kantor paused to draw on his cigar and gauge Jeffrey's reaction. He in turn kept his face carefully blank as he felt the words sink deep.

Clearly pleased with this silent response, Kantor went on. "You are about to enter an entirely different world, young man, one totally alien to anything you have ever experienced before. It has rules all its own. To assume that all people everywhere are basically the same, and thus you can get by on what passes for etiquette or correct prejudices or current wisdom here in your American existence, will doom your efforts to abject failure.

"This does not mean that you must affect a false attitude. I personally loathe the catty pettiness that pervades such people's lives. No, what I mean is that you must learn to adapt while remaining true to yourself. Do you understand?"

"I think so," he replied solemnly.

Kantor examined him carefully, and in time appeared to reach a decision. "Splendid. Now tell me, Jeffrey. What would you think of a ninety-day trial period in my London business?"

Resisting the urge to jump up, run screaming around the restaurant, kiss the frowning maitre d', he responded with a simple, "That sounds fine." Then he gave the game away with an enormous face-splitting grin.

Kantor replied with a small smile of his own. "Excellent. Ninety days will grant us ample time to see whether or not you have the ability to learn the required lessons and adapt to the new world, I am sure. Now I think it would be proper to offer you a small gesture of congratulations for this decision. Have you ever flown first class?"

"No, but I'm sure I could adapt to it very quickly."

"No doubt. It doesn't make long flights enjoyable. Nothing could go quite that far. But it does enliven the time considerably. When can you leave?"

The grin would just not stay down. "I have to give a month's notice."

"And I must take care of a few items in Canada before returning to Europe, then travel on the Continent for a week or so before arriving in London. Let us say that I shall expect you on the first day of June. That gives you fifty days to prepare. Is that sufficient?"

"Great. Just great."

"Splendid." He reached back into his coat pocket, extracted two folded sheets of heavily embossed paper, handed them over. "I prepared these in hopes of finding you a worthy candidate. On the first sheet you will find various addresses and telephone numbers for my residences and the London business. I must tell you, however, that when I am on a buying trip I am rarely in a position to be contacted. The second sheet contains a list of books I would like you to commit to memory before your arrival. There are fifteen in all, and should give you a basic overview of some of the more important areas in which my business trades. You will find them quite expensive. They are all extensively illustrated with color plates, which should assist you in understanding the finer points. Bring the receipts with you. At the bottom of the page is the name and address of my New York travel agent. He will be sending you a plane ticket and the address of your temporary London residence."

Jeffrey looked up from the pages and said gravely, "Thanks a lot, Mr. Kantor."

"You are quite welcome, young man." He signaled to the waiter and rose to his feet, extending his hand to Jeffrey. "I shall look forward to seeing you in London. Until then, good afternoon."

As Jeffrey was ushering Betty back through the front door, the phone rang. It was the assistant chief of Christie's furniture section. "Sorry to bother you like this, Jeffrey, but I've had a rather strange call this morning."

A year in the place had not diminished Jeffrey's enjoyment of the tony way Britain's upper-crust spoke, though it left him feeling the uncouth country cousin. "No problem. What can I do for you?"

"It seems that we have an official from the German government coming in for a bit of a snoop."

"The chest of drawers?" Jeffrey guessed.

"Precisely."

"It sat in our front window for almost a month, you advertised it all over the world and then put it on the front cover of last week's auction brochure. Why do you think he's shown up now?"

"If the German bureaucracy is anything like our own, perhaps because they just heard of its existence," the Christie's man replied. "In any case, I understand you were planning to attend today's auction. I was wondering if you might be willing to pop by afterward."

"Why me? The piece is sold."

"It appears that this chap has the power to block the sale, or at least make trouble for our buyer. You are aware that it is a German industrialist who placed the high bid."

"I was at the auction."

"Of course you were. Well, it appears that our caller intends to apply some rather crude pressure. Tax reviews covering the buyer's previous five generations, or something of the sort. Very nasty, really."

"So where does that leave us?"

"From the sounds of it, this chap intends to claim the high bid as his own. I suppose from our perspective, it's not quite so important as it will be for our industrialist friend. At least somebody will be paying us." He hesitated, then went on. "The gentleman asked some rather pointed questions. I thought it might be nice if you would help me clarify the matter."

"There's not a lot I can say besides the fact that Alexander found the piece and brought it here."

"Yes, your man Kantor does attach a great deal of mystery to most of his pieces, doesn't he? Still, it would be nice if you could come in and meet this chap."

Jeffrey glanced at his watch. "My assistant should be here in about fifteen minutes. I'll need to leave immediately, as my painting is one of the first lots. When is this guy showing up?"

"In about two hours."

"Why don't I meet you upstairs as soon as my item has sold?"

"Splendid. That really is most kind."

He hung up the phone, and reflected that it would not be difficult to keep the antique's origins a secret. Jeffrey knew very little about Alexander Kantor and even less about where his furniture came from. Almost nothing, in fact. Yet the mystery was somehow part of the man, and he liked Kantor intensely.

And the freedom—he liked that too. It was the sort of freedom that he would have dreamed of back when he had been working for McKinsey if only he had been able to imagine it. He had known several friends who had made the major move, risked it all and gone out on their own. They had all spoken of yearning for a freedom they did not have and *could* not have so long as they worked for someone else. Jeffrey had nodded and agreed and secretly envied them.

In the evenings spent watching traffic speed by in endless urgent streams beneath his high-rise Atlanta apartment window, Jeffrey had wished that he too had possessed the money and the ideas and the *desire* to go for broke. But nothing had called to him with an urgent tug of the heartstrings, challenged him sufficiently, or spoken to him with that sense of utter certainty, *this is it*.

Nothing, that is, until now. He did not own the business, but in many respects was already coming to claim it as partially his. Especially when Alexander took off on one of his unexplained tours.

The first such disappearance had occurred nine months before. After three months of working virtually day and night with Alexander, the gentleman had announced that he was leaving the next day on a buying trip.

"For how long?" Jeffrey asked.

"It is terrifically hard to tell about these things," Alexander had replied. "But I would guess about three weeks."

Three weeks alone. Jeffrey looked around the shop. The retail value of their stock at that moment was approaching four million dollars.

Alexander showed his usual perceptiveness. "It's all yours."

"What does that mean?"

"This will not work if I give it to you only halfway," Alexander replied. "Clients will refuse to close a deal with you. They'll assume you won't have the authority to set prices. And three weeks is too long to leave the business without a signatory present."

Jeffrey felt as though he'd been pushed over the cliff-edge. "What if I do something you don't like?"

"If I felt there were even a slim chance, I would not be making this journey," Alexander Kantor replied. "But if the unforeseen does occur, I assure you that it will only happen once."

———

Jeffrey spent the time waiting for Katya to arrive, going through the morning mail, dusting furniture, doing anything to keep from thinking about the mystery that surrounded this strange young lady.

Katya had begun working at Priceless about a month before, when the regular shop assistant was called away by a family emergency. Jeffrey remained delighted with the arrangement, yet found it to be an exquisite torture. He loved the hours they spent alone together in the shop—she with her classwork, he with his catalogues and books—loved teaching her the rudiments of his newfound passion and profession. But it was so difficult being so close to her for so long, and having to resist the constant desire to hold her, caress her, tell her the thoughts that continually ran through his mind like a never-ending song.

He had met Katya on a bitter-cold November night, in the student's canteen beneath the University of London's central library. He had been granted temporary access through providentially meeting a librarian whose passion for antiques had known no bounds. In return for occasional guided tours of his shop and invitations to all the major antique fairs, Jeffrey had been given a visitor's card—a boon slightly less common than a passkey to the Tower of London's chambers for the Crown Jewels.

Jeffrey was not permitted to check out books, but within the library's confines he had virtually unlimited access to a treasure trove of reference materials. He spent many a happy hour lost in richly pictured tomes, tracing the development of patterns and styles and inlays and jewelry and art.

That particular evening he remained hunched over his book on early Biedermeier furniture for so long that it had taken both hands to unclench the cramp in his neck. His kneading and silent groans were stopped by the realization that two of the most beautiful eyes he had ever seen were holding him fast.

Her face was formed around cheekbones so pronounced and upraised as to give her eyes an almost Oriental slant. Yet the eyes themselves were a startling grayish-violet, with irises whose depths seemed to invite him in, drawing him further and further still, until before he knew what was happening he was on his feet and walking over to her table.

She greeted his approach with neither smile of welcome nor frown of refusal; rather she watched him with a look of utter vulnerability, a helplessly open gaze that had his heart pounding by the time he stopped and looked down and said, "May I join you?"

Her voice was as light as a scented summer breeze. "I was just going back upstairs."

"May I walk with you?"

"To get my things, I mean. I have a bus in fifteen minutes."

"I've been sitting too long anyway. May I accompany you?" He sounded so formal, so silly to his own ears. His usual well of casual banter was sealed off by this unblinking gaze of vulnerability. He had the impression that if he held out his hand, this strange young woman would have been forced to take it, a victim of whatever left her unable to hide her heart. Instead he was content to stand above her, gaze down into the endless depths of two star-flecked eyes, and know that he was lost.

They left the smoky student din behind them, stopped to pick up her coat and books, and entered the startlingly crisp coldness of early November dark. From time to time Jeffrey searched a blank and empty mind for words and came up only with the fear that once they reached the street, this spell would be broken, this moment lost, this woman forever gone. His heart hammered with a fury that left his legs weak and his tongue stilled.

Just as they arrived at the curb a black London taxi rum bled by, its 'vacant' light glowing. Jeffrey's arm shot up automatically, leaving him faced with the dilemma of either telling it to go on or going himself.

Instead he turned to her, and found the same achingly open gaze resting on his face. He said, "You've really got to let me take you home."

She neither replied nor hesitated, but rather gave the driver a Kensington address and climbed in the back.

It was enough to open the gates. "You have an accent I can't place," he said. "Are you British?"

"American." Her voice was so soft he had to lean closer; she did not shy away. "I've lived here since I was nine."

"Here in London?"

"No, Coventry. Do you know it?"

"Not well. I attended an auction there once." Coventry was about an hour from London, one of countless industrial British towns with all the charm of a construction site on a rainy day. Virtually demolished by German bombers in World War II, it had been rebuilt in hasty uniformity as a settlement for factory workers.

Its endless rows of semidetached houses looked like products of a second-rate production line.

"What kind of auction?"

"Antiques. I run an antiques business."

"Here in London?"

"Yes."

"Then you're not a student at the university?" She seemed disconcerted.

"No. Why, is that bad?"

"I don't know," she replied. "I don't even know what I'm doing here."

"Sharing a taxi," he replied. The taxi stopped in front of a nondescript row-house in dire need of better care. A long metal plate of buzzers indicated that the three stories had been split into a rabbit-warren of tiny student flats. "Listen, there's a cafe across the street. Can't we go in for a couple of minutes?"

"I really don't think I could stomach another coffee just now."

"The drink is incidental. I just want to talk a little longer."

She gave the tiniest hint of a smile. "All right. But just a few minutes. I have a lot of work still to do tonight."

The place was cramped and cluttered and smoky as only a poorly ventilated London cafe could be. Jeffrey led her to the only free table and went back to the counter for a couple of teas. He said on his return, "You don't have to drink this."

Their conversation flowed more smoothly. She had a way of asking the smallest of questions, and then listening with such absorption that he felt able to tell her anything. He found himself talking at length about his family, Alexander, his departure from America.

"So," she said, absently stirring her cup, "did you leave a lady pining for you back in America?"

"I had a girlfriend in Atlanta," he confessed, wondering what there was in those unfathomable gray-violet eyes that invited an honesty he had not known with some girls even after months together. "But she ditched me, not the other way around."

"And how long have you been separated?"

"Personally about seven months. Now that I look back at it, though, I'd have to say we were emotionally separated since the second day I knew her."

She showed no reaction whatsoever. "Wasn't it hard, going out with someone you didn't love?"

"As far as I knew at the time, everything was fine. It hadn't occurred to me that there could be something more." He searched those unreadable eyes. "Not then, anyway," he said.

"That is so like a man," she said quietly. "So sure the next pretty face is his dream come true, the girl designed to fulfill his every wish and give him perfect happiness."

"I can always hope," he replied, thinking to himself, I've never felt like this before in my entire life. "What about you? Have you been someone's perfect happiness before?"

"You'd have to ask them. I could never tell you that myself."

"So there've been others," he said, hating them all.

"Other what? Other men? Look around you. The world is full of other men."

"You know exactly what I meant," he said sharply.

She turned contrite. "You're right. I should not have said that and I'm sorry. I've always had difficulty talking about myself."

"Does that mean I shouldn't ask?"

The hint of smile returned. She shook her head. "You just need to hide behind something after you do."

He made a motion as to duck behind the table. "So I'm asking."

"About other men?" Her eyes blossomed like petals of a flower made from violet gems and purest smoke, opening and revealing depths that Jeffrey could only wonder at.

"Somebody has hurt you very badly." It was not a question.

A little girl within her eyes cried to his heart. "Yes," she whispered.

"Do you want to tell me about it?"

"It wasn't what you think," she said, her voice a fragile wind blowing words and sadness through the gaping wound in his heart. "It wasn't a lover. I haven't, I've never . . ."

The sorrow filled him with a selfless compassion he had never known before. He reached across the table, took her hand in both of his. She looked down, studied it with eyes that spilled their burden over both of them. "It wasn't a lover," she repeated.

A jangle of boozy laughter from a nearby table shattered the moment. They both started back, pulling away from the shards of emotion that sprinkled around them. She looked at him and was comforted to find a smile waiting for her.

They left the cafe and walked the short distance to her doorway in silence. She hesitated at the bottom step, reluctant to go inside.

"I'd really like to see you again," Jeffrey said. "Could I invite you to dinner?"

"If you like."

"I'd like very much. How about tomorrow?"

"All right. What is your name?"

"Jeffrey." The openness of her gaze left him aching to hold her. "And yours?"

"Katya."

Then she was up the stairs so fast that his words, that's a beautiful name, were said to empty space. He watched her enter the door without a backward glance, and wondered why his heart suddenly felt such exquisite pain.

———

Jeffrey heard Katya's gentle tap on the front window only because he was listening for it. He walked toward the front door, where she stood laden down with a half-dozen books. He opened the door, asked, "Are you planning to move in for a week?"

"I thought I would work on my research if there was any free time."

He took the books from her and carried them back to the alcove. "I bet you didn't stop for lunch. I left an extra sandwich in the fridge for when you get hungry."

Katya followed him with solemn eyes. "Thank you, Jeffrey."

"Here, let me take your raincoat." He pointed to the silver serving dish. "Baby's just been fed and changed."

Katya bent over, touched the tiny form with one gentle finger, cooed softly.

Jeffrey watched her, smiling at the way Ling cuddled to her finger. "Who would have thought there could be so much love in a little bundle of fluff?"

"I was thinking about our little bird in church this morning," she told him. "But now I wonder if maybe I wasn't thinking about myself."

"What do you mean?"

"When you're hurt, you think you have to protect yourself against everything."

He set the bowl down on a satinwood side table. "Who hurt you, Katya?"

"Such a little bird," she went on quietly. "He must have been so scared when we tried to help him. He didn't know who we were or what we were doing."

Jeffrey reached up and stroked the silken hairs at the nape of her neck.

"But we made him feel safe, and he's learned to trust us."

"Who hurt you?" he repeated.

"That doesn't matter now. You didn't know who or what hurt this little bird either, but you still helped him."

"I need to know."

She looked at him with desperate appeal. "I can't tell you just now."

"When you trust me enough," he conceded, and wondered if the time would ever come.

———

There were only three Rolls Royces and one Bentley parked outside Christie's when Jeffrey arrived—it was still a little early. The porter stood as always, dressed in his formal gray uniform, facing the entrance with his back to the street. Within the portals, all was elegant light wood and beige carpet and discreetly armed security guards. Overly thin women wearing too much jewelry spoke in tones of cultured snobbery. They were accompanied by men with tony voices and diction that made them sound as though they were speaking around a mouthful of marbles. Jeffrey counted seven double-breasted navy-blue blazers in the front foyer alone.

Just prior to Jeffrey's arrival in London, the bottom had dropped from the high-end art and antique markets with a speed and force that left the art world shell-shocked. Although a recovery was currently under way, this instability made Jeffrey's pricing and sales decisions doubly difficult. Alexander left him with such sweeping powers that on some mornings he entered the shop wondering if at the end of the day he would still have a job.

His biggest problem came from the enormous variety of pieces they handled. In-depth study was impossible. There was no predicting from where the next piece would originate—what era, wood, country, or style. Most of their business came from furniture, yet a significant portion covered virtually the entire spectrum of antiques—from jewelry to crystal, plates and watches, boxes and lace and chests. It was easier to predict what the next incoming piece would *not* be.

They handled no guns or weapons of any sort. Alexander viewed such items with a genuine loathing, and referred to weapons specialists as historians of murder and mayhem.

There were few world-renowned painters among the art that they either sold directly or placed under the hammer. Most of the works they handled were from second-level painters, those often found in museums yet not known outside a relatively small circle. Jeffrey either used a professional evaluator for setting the prices of those which he chose to hang in the shop, or passed them on to Christie's.

Occasionally an etching or sketch or watercolor or pastel arrived that took his breath away. The first items he took to Christie's—the first time he had ever entered an auction house in his life, for that matter—were six hand-sized studies of the same woman's face. They were drawn with an astonishing minimum of line and shading, yet were vivid in their portrayal of pensive sadness. The agents at Christie's confirmed that they were by Monet, and treated Jeffrey with the utmost of practiced respect as they pried his reluctant fingers free.

The Priceless shop sold no sculpture at all. There was nothing from genuine antiquity—ancient Greece, Rome, Phoenicia, or Egypt. There were few tapestries, almost no crystal, and nothing at all from the Far East.

In short, Jeffrey had almost nothing upon which to base a valid guess as to where their stock originated.

Other dealers dubbed their shop the "West End Jumble Sale," and stopped by often to search and wonder and ask the occasional indirect question. Jeffrey found it easy to offer the dealers a blank face in reply.

Everyone wondered at Alexander Kantor's sources. It was only natural; so did Jeffrey. He had been around enough of the high-end shops and auction houses to know that variety and quantity was almost never combined with quality. An entire estate sold through a single dealer was such a rarity that word spread far and wide long before the last item was sold. Yet Alexander Kantor had continued to handle quality most dealers could only dream of. He had done so for four decades, and no one was the wiser.

Especially not Jeffrey.

On slow days, Jeffrey would find himself cataloging the room and the items he had placed elsewhere, and wonder at their incredible diversity. French Napoleon III vied with Italian Rococo, Russian icons with German Romance paintings, rosewood with oak, satin finishes with gilt—and almost all of it of exceptional quality. There was no possible way that one estate could have contained such a diversity. There was no logical explanation as to how Kantor could disappear for weeks or months at a time, leaving no phone number or forwarding address, and return in total secrecy time after time with such antiques.

═══

The Christie's auction chamber is not particularly impressive—a long high-ceilinged hall with wooden floor and cloth walls of an unremarkable beige. There are padded folding seats for perhaps a hundred and fifty, most of which that day were full. The auctioneer's dais is placed very close to the first row, and raised so high that the auctioneer, a bland gentleman as gray as his suit with a permanently fixed smile and a two-tone voice, has to lean over the ledge in order to focus on the closest patrons. He holds a small handleless wooden stamp with which he smacks the dais smartly to close a sale.

There was a constant silent scurrying behind the dais as Jeffrey entered and seated himself. The lobby-sized back chamber was filled to overflowing by canvases neatly stacked and numbered and turned to face the closest wall. At the rear of this chamber, a door opened to a vault-room used to house paintings not on display. The austere main hall itself was lined with pictures too big to be carried to the bidding table. With the smaller pictures, one of the innumerable red-aproned assistants would hoist the painting onto the baize-covered table set to the right of the auctioneer, and hold it in utter stillness until the bidding ended. Larger pictures were indicated by an assistant standing beneath its place on the wall.

A board set high in the corner beside the auctioneer gave each bid in five different currencies. The moneys listed were determined by those being bid for a particular piece; if a telephone bidder was working with a Danish client, then one listing would be in kroner. If a visiting bidder from Italy made himself known as he entered, then all prices would be listed in lira. A woman at a desk directly beneath the auctioneer's dais typed with the new bids and the currencies required into a computer hooked to the board. When the bidding came fast and furious, the numbers moved in a continual blur.

The hall contained a fairly typical mixture of bidders for a second-level Christie's auction. A first-level, or major auction, was scheduled on an annual or semiannual basis, and attracted museum directors and gallery owners from across the globe; the type of person who would travel only if a ten million dollar-plus purchase was being considered.

Today, several yuppies up on long lunch breaks from the City were looking for bargain investments and eyeing the ladies. The number of yuppies at such auctions had dwindled rapidly as the banking industry had bit the bullet, let them go, and forced them to fill the local used-car market with their Porsches. There was one effeminate Arab with his boyfriend. Beside him was a rock star whose presence anywhere else would have caused a minor riot; here he was just another addition to the scene.

Two contingents of professional agents and gallery owners were present. The ones there for the long haul were seated and reserved and extremely attentive. Some held portable phones and smug expressions, announcing with silent satisfaction that they represented a confidential bidder. The second group congregated at the back of the hall, whispering quietly among themselves and offering cynical comments on the state of the market. They were around to bid on one specific item, or keep tabs on the market, or pretend that they needed to. Their shops were generally second rate, their comments acid, their faces twisted by a determined effort to get the better of everyone.

Jeffrey preferred to sit up front. It gave him the feeling of being at the heart of the fray. He was not comfortable with the clubby atmosphere at the back. The way they offered their single token bid of the day, waving a casual hand and then turning away with a smile and a spiteful word when someone else bid higher, left him certain that they would taint the joy and the thrill and the genuine love he held for this new profession.

Today marked the eleventh time Jeffrey had offered pieces for sale, and the first time he was recognized by a number of the staff as he entered—including the auctioneer. The gentleman gave him a minutely correct smile and bow from the dais as Jeffrey settled himself. He found that just being recognized raised his stock a great deal. The women—and there were many of them, most of them beautiful—watched him with a speculative eye.

Along the side wall, beginning close to the auctioneer's dais, ran a long table holding thirty phones. Telephone sales assistants discreetly came and went, depending on which languages were required by the bidders who had requested calls in advance of a particular sale.

Even after eleven visits it remained incredible to Jeffrey how fast the whole business moved. Bids were entered at the rate of over six a minute. The auctioneer handled the crowd with a surgeon's precision, squeezing the price up at an electric speed, his crisp politeness never slipping.

After several further paintings by artists Jeffrey had never heard of before, his own picture came up—a Musin boat scene. Even before the auctioneer's attention moved from the register where he noted the previous sale, Jeffrey's heart was racing. All fourteen standing telephone assistants were immediately on the phone, some handling two or even three lines and in as many languages.

"And lot fifteen, an exceptional Musin," the auctioneer chanted, looking around and spotting the assistant with his hand in the air. "Ah, thank you very much. Showing at the back wall, being pointed out to you. Lot fifteen. Starting the bidding at fifteen thousand pounds. Fifteen thousand is offered. Seventeen thousand."

After the opening bid was accepted, a price already bid was rarely mentioned. The exception was when the auctioneer chose to identify the bidder and place him or her momentarily in the spotlight. Otherwise attention was immediately drawn on to the next upward move by pointing to the bidder and then stating only the next asking price.

"Sixteen thousand. Seventeen thousand. Eighteen thousand. Twenty thousand. Twenty-two thousand. Twenty-four thousand pounds. It's with you at the very back, madam, at twenty-four thousand. Twenty-six thousand. Thirty thousand."

The next bid increment was set by the auctioneer and offered as a statement, not a question. Never a question. There was no doubt in his voice, no hesitation shown as the size of the jump increased as the bidding price escalated.

"Thirty thousand, thank you. Thirty-two thousand. Thirty-five thousand. Thirty-eight thousand. Thirty-eight thousand pounds. The bidding now stands at thirty-eight thousand pounds."

Initially the bidding was fast and furious and came from all over the room. At thirty thousand pounds the storm abated, and at thirty-five there was a moment's hesitation. The lead bid came from a gallery owner named Sarah, with whom Jeffrey had placed several works. From the light in the woman's eyes, it was clear she knew she was walking away with a steal. Thirty-five thousand pounds for such a painting was a rare bargain, caused by the recession that had wreaked random havoc throughout the art world.

"Thirty-eight thousand. Am I bid thirty-eight thousand. Ah, thank you, bid from the phone for thirty-eight thousand. Forty thousand."

A new opponent had appeared, an invisible bidder whose presence was announced by a heretofore silent telephone operator raising one hand and accepting the thirty-eight thousand bid. Jeffrey watched the gallery owner's excitement turn to brassy defiance. Sarah accepted the forty thousand bid with an angry gesture. The auctioneer recognized the beginning of a battle with a smugly satisfied smile.

"Forty-two thousand. Forty-five thousand. Forty-eight thousand. Fifty thousand. Fifty-five thousand. Sixty thousand. Sixty-five thousand. Seventy thousand pounds."

A light hum rose from the room as the bids began rising at increments of about eight thousand dollars. Sarah continued to make counter-offers with furious jerky gestures of her card. The card had a number, assigned to her prior to the auction's start, and was utilized by habitual buyers to both ensure no confusion over purchases and reduce the need to be identified and fill out forms while the next lot was being offered. The steely grip with which the gallery owner continually thrust her card upward gave her fingers the look of talons locked in a death grip.

The young lady manning the phone read the newly accepted bid-value from the computer board, and relayed it into the telephone with a voice pitched too low for Jeffrey to catch the language she spoke. With each new bid from Sarah and subsequent price-rise offered by the auctioneer, she would whisper, wait, then lift her eyes and nod to the waiting auctioneer.

"Ninety-five thousand." Another pause, this one from the gallery owner. Jeffrey kept his hands still by clenching the auction catalog in his lap. "Ninety-five thousand against you at the back. Thank you, madam. One hundred thousand. Am I bid one hundred thousand pounds. Yes, from the telephone. One hundred and five thousand. At the back one hundred and five thousand pounds is bid. One hundred and ten thousand. One hundred and ten, thank you. One hundred and fifteen, yes, thank you, madam. One hundred and fifteen is bid at the back. One hundred and twenty thousand pounds."

The telephone assistant spoke the bid, waited.

"Am I bid one hundred and twenty thousand pounds."

The girl spoke again, waited, then looked up and shook her head with an apologetic smile. The entire room finally took a breath.

"A valiant try," the auctioneer said to the telephone assistant. Then with a smack of his gavel he said, "Sold for one hundred and fifteen thousand pounds to you, madam. Buyer one-eight," he intoned as he wrote, naming the number on Sarah's card. "Congratulations, madam. A lovely acquisition."

The sale had taken less than three minutes.

———

Jeffrey raced up the stairs to the larger auction hall, where last week's furniture sale had taken place. The assistant chief of their furniture division was a young man by the name of Trevor with a decidedly Oxbridge accent. He brightened immensely at Jeffrey's arrival.

"Ah excellent, excellent. Mr. Sinclair, may I take this opportunity to introduce Professor Halbmeier from Bonn."

The man did not offer his hand. "I would like to know where you obtained this piece."

"I don't know," Jeffrey replied, bridling at his tone. "And if I did I wouldn't tell you."

"Yes, well, perhaps we might just have a look at it ourselves, shall we?" Trevor exposed a bland peacemaking smile to all and sundry. "The professor was just telling me that he was not familiar with the item."

"How could I be? There was no record of anything from the Kaiser's palace having survived."

"Yes, it must be quite a shock. Shall we?" He drew the professor over and ran a hand along the top. "This is actually something we sold last week, as I told you on the phone."

"That remains to be seen," the professor replied ominously.

"Yes, well." Trevor cleared his throat. "In any case, it's by perhaps the greatest German cabinet maker, certainly the greatest neoclassic cabinet maker, a fellow by the name of Johann Gottlieb Fiedler. There are very, *very* few pieces by him still around. Wars and such, you know. Bombs tend to have a rather lasting effect on wood.

"So far as we know, there are three pieces by Fiedler in Berlin, one in the Wallace collection, and this particular piece that literally sprang to life before our very noses. Quite a bit of conjecture about where this one came from. Gave our verifications people quite a time, I don't mind telling you.

"What's most interesting about it is the top, of course," the young man went on. He ran a casual hand across a fitted stone block that had been made to sit on the chest's upper surface as though growing from it. Its face was a geometric mosaic, designed from hundreds of thousands of tiny multicolored flecks of marble.

"A lot of these are marbles that haven't been known since antiquity. We think many of them were probably carved out of ancient columns, but our people have been able to come up with absolutely nothing certain. Quite frustrating, really. This bit in the center appears to be one piece, perhaps lifted from some early Roman vessel, and the rest was then designed around it. But it's all conjecture."

The mixture of colors on the face was almost psychedelic—rich hues belonging more to semiprecious stones than to modern marble.

"In any case, we do know that it was made around 1780," the young man continued. "Most probably for the Crown Prince of Prussia, Friedrich Wilhelm. The precise date hinges around whether one thinks he was arrogant enough to have it made before his uncle the Kaiser died."

The German official was not taking all this very well. In fact, he appeared to be building up a full head of steam.

"Our man said the fellow positively wouldn't have dared commission it unless he was already the Kaiser," Trevor blithely continued. "It was just so grand, you see. And there was no evidence that his uncle ever owned such a piece. It would have been a real case of one-upmanship, something he certainly couldn't have afforded until the crown was already in his grubby little hands."

Trevor was too caught up in the tale to realize the effect his words were having on the bulbous gentleman beside him, who had begun to take on the shape and rigidity of a beached blowfish.

"At first we actually thought the top might have been put on in England. It was just the sort of thing the early nineteenth-century English grand tourers might have done, you see. They'd been in Italy, we thought, and bought themselves this magnificent top, and then either had this bottom handy or puttered around the Continent until they came upon a piece that would fit it. But then we decided the two pieces were set together too snugly to have been made separately, and also the top's thickness suggests that it was actually designed by a German craftsman."

The man made a sound like a strangled bulldog. Trevor missed it, having bent over to roll out one of the drawers, and went on. "As you can see, there are three central concave-fronted drawers set on the most remarkable roller system. Feels light as a feather, but I would imagine each must weigh close on a hundred pounds. Solid as a rock. Immaculate construction, really. The frieze here is in walnut, but so heavily inlaid it is difficult to tell in places. The waved apron here is also heavily gilded, remarkable work. Scrolled legs, all hand carved. The gilded bronze flanking the corners here was a way of framing the work, of course. Must have been spectacular when it was new. These lion-faced handles here are a bit of a mystery, I must say. The only parts that we don't think were actually made in Prussia. In fact, they were probably bought by mail order, such as it was at the time, from England. The English were masters at the art of making these lion masks."

Despite the gentleman's growing fury, Jeffrey could not help but become caught up in the specialist's enthusiasm. "How can you be so sure that it was not done by the duke?"

"Simply because it is the grandest of its type." In contrast to many of his fellow antique specialists, Trevor clearly relished having someone around who shared his fascination. "He was a real style leader, this chap the crown prince. And the king, you see, his uncle, was never really interested in the whole subject. When Crown Prince Friedrich then became Kaiser, he carried his involvement along with him. Stayed right at the center of the whole style thing throughout his reign. Even retained this fellow Fiedler as his own personal cabinet maker. That of course doesn't mean his furniture was all Fiedler did, but it does make it highly unlikely that he would risk challenging his uncle in such a way before rising to the top of the heap, as it were."

The gentleman demanded, "How did it come to be here?"

"Well, there you are," Trevor replied eagerly. "The thing about all such articles is that with time they become unfashionable. This particular item was eventually given to the Russian ambassador, that much we've been able to piece together from the archives in Germany. It was later sold by his widow, some thirty years after. By then, of course, it had become so unfashionable it was probably used to store dirty laundry in some minor bedroom of their secondary palace."

"Disgraceful," the gentleman rumbled.

"Yes, I suppose so," the young man replied. "Of course, there just is no accounting for taste."

The gentleman rounded on him. "I mean that it is disgraceful for such a piece of German heritage to ever have left German soil."

"My dear fellow," Trevor replied. "This particular piece has never set foot in Germany. When it left the Kaiser's palace for parts unknown, that stretch of earth was still proudly Prussian."

The gentleman ignored him. "And to wind up in a London showroom. Outrageous."

"Yes, well, we have tried our very best not to soil it over much," Trevor replied, winking at Jeffrey.

"It could have been bought by just anyone," the gentleman went on. "Lost to the German people forever."

"Oh, we shouldn't have allowed that, I don't think. Not without a struggle, in any case. As a matter of fact, it appeared that all top five bids were from Germans."

That took the wind from his sails. "They were?"

"Indeed yes. Several museums showed quite a bit of interest as well."

"Which ones?"

"Oh, it wouldn't do for me to pass that on, now, would it? Discretion and all that."

The man gathered himself and said, "I am authorized to offer a substantial amount of money for this piece."

"Yes, well, it would have to be, wouldn't it. The winning bid was the highest price ever paid for a piece of German furniture, which I suppose isn't saying much since the level of prices up to now wasn't particularly staggering."

"You can forget that bid," the man snapped. "He has decided to retract it. Or rather, to grant the German government the right to this property."

"What a pity," Trevor said, not the least put out. "Still, I suppose we'll have to wait and hear that from the gentleman in question, won't we?"

"The final bid was for one hundred and eighty thousand pounds, was it not?"

"That is correct," Trevor replied blandly. "Quite understandable, really. It is a remarkable find."

Jeffrey watched the young man's face, wondering if he would ever reach the point of being able to say the price for a chest of drawers was three hundred thousand dollars without bursting into hysterical laughter.

"You may speak to the former high bidder at your convenience. This article now belongs to the German people. A check from my ministry will be in your hands tomorrow." The professor wheeled around to face Jeffrey. "It is a disgrace that a piece of national heritage has been treated in such a manner. You, sir, will be hearing from my solicitors."

When he had stormed out of the hall, Trevor smiled and said, "I think that went rather well after all, don't you?"

"I guess so. Do you think there's anything to his threat of legal action?"

"Not unless it was stolen." Trevor eyed him carefully. "It wasn't, was it?"

"I hope not."

"Alexander keeps you in the dark about his sources, then, does he?"

"Sorry, I can't answer that."

"No, of course not. Still, if you're going to keep on digging such treasures out of holes in the ground or wherever it is he comes up with them, you're going to have to expect the odd complaint now and then." Trevor extended his hand. "And do keep us in mind the next time something like this turns up, won't you? We always do enjoy a good mystery. Especially one where there's money to be made."

Jeffrey knew very little about the Polish side of his background. His mother, an only child, seldom spoke of her father's homeland. Jeffrey's own father came from a large family of good Scotch-Irish stock who proudly referred to themselves as hybrid American mongrels. There was a vague sense of uneasiness among his parents and uncles and aunts whenever the topic of his grandfather's birthplace arose.

Once he had asked his grandmother why her daughter, his mother, did not know more about her father's heritage. She had shown a rare moment of regret and said, "Your mother was tutored in Polish by a neighbor starting at the age of six. At thirteen she refused to take further lessons and promptly forgot everything she had learned. All she wanted was to fit in, to be a part of her own little world. A Polish father and a pride in a country other than this one simply did not fit. Her father and I did not have the heart to insist."

"Did it bother you when Mom married so young?" Jeffrey's mother was seventeen when she married and eighteen when Jeffrey was born.

"Of course it did. I was immensely distressed. But your grandfather felt otherwise. He said when he met me he could not have waited another week to be wed, and sensed that same urgency in the way your mother felt about your father."

She smiled in fond remembrance. "I argued with him until he told me that his greatest regret was that we had not met earlier. Let them marry, he said. Give them the joy of the twenty extra years together that we shall not have."

Jeffrey's grandmother looked at him, and went on, "Someday when you have children of your own you will also be faced with problems that will leave you wondering for the rest of your life if you did the right thing. It is the way of the world. All you can do is hope that you tried and acted in their best interests, not in your own."

An immigrant from an Eastern European country that most of his relatives could not even place on a map simply did not fit in with their proper scheme of things. So everyone referred to that Polish aspect of his heritage with a shrug, a wink, a smirk, a glance at the heavens. Only his grandmother's reaction differed from the family norm. Whenever anyone asked, she would reply, yes, my husband was a true Pole. There was so much pride and love in her voice, even after living as a widow for twenty years, that Jeffrey never ceased to wonder at why no one else showed his grandfather's heritage some of the same esteem.

His grandmother was a doddering old lady now, shrunken to teacup size and bent to match the old rocking chair that was her permanent daytime residence. But her eyes were still bright, and she loved to talk of the man who was no longer.

She had been a career secretary, working for the United States Embassy in London on a five-year contract toward the end of World War II. Approaching thirty, facing a worldwide shortage of available men, she had consoled her move to spinsterhood by taking the battery of exams and winning the coveted London post. Her second month there, the impossible had occurred and she had fallen in love.

Piotr, or Peter as he soon came to be known, was penniless, almost homeless, and twenty-three years her senior. To her co-workers and few friends, he was just one of the countless thousands of displaced people who flooded every government office in Western Europe, all with tragic tales of wrongs unrighted and estates lost forever. Some of these stories were even true.

At the time of their meeting, Piotr had barely a nodding acquaintance with the English language. His rough speech, his formal old-world manners and travel-worn clothes, all were a source of endless amusement to the other embassy staff. They called Piotr a clown. But even then, at the very early stages of their blossoming relationship, she knew better. Love granted her the power to see beyond the shabby exterior and realize that this graying man with his strong face and handlebar moustache and weary eyes truly held a heart of gold.

So they were married, and while she worked at the embassy Piotr studied English and continued his profession as a watch-maker and jeweler. When her five-year stint was completed they returned to the United States with their baby daughter, where the first of Peter Kantor's three jewelry and watch stores was soon up and running.

———

The year Jeffrey graduated from university, his grandmother fell and broke her hip. While she was lying immobilized, her only child—Jeffrey's mother—finally convinced her that the days of liv-ing alone were over. By the time she was released from the hospital, her home had been sold and her most treasured possessions had been moved into his brother's old room—the same brother who for Jeffrey was no more.

After that, going home took on a new meaning for Jeffrey. His first year with McKinsey, he logged more trips from Atlanta to Jack-sonville than he had during his entire four years at university. His grandmother loved to talk, but few in the family were interested in hearing about the past. In all honesty, Jeffrey cared little for the old days, but he loved this sense of connection with a family that had been shattered beyond all recognition by time and events.

Although her hip was pronounced fully healed, it bothered her to move. She preferred to spend her days in the rocker set by the room's large window. Jeffrey found it immensely reassuring to just come and sit with her. Evenings when his parents were out, grate-ful for the freedom his presence gave them to take a deserved break alone, he would often bring in his weekend workload, spread it out on her vanity, and sit and work. They spoke little in those times, content to enjoy the silent company. It also helped him enormously to gradually replace the memories of what the room once had been to what it was now.

The Saturday afternoon following his acceptance of Alexander Kantor's offer, he returned to find her resting where she always was this time of day, her rocker set so that sunlight fell on her lap and not her face. His mother had recently redone the room in new wallpaper, one with tiny rosebuds blooming in perpetual profusion. The old lace bedspread covering her miniature four-poster bed was matched with new lace curtains and lace doilies over the two side tables. The whole effect was cozy and feminine and very fitting to the old lady.

"I wanted you to be the first to know," Jeffrey told her, pulling up a chair and sitting down, "I'm going to London to work for Alexander Kantor."

The crystal-clear gray eyes showed a momentary glimpse of deep pain, then returned to their normal calm. "You have certainly been unhappy at work."

"How did you know?"

"I may be old, but I still have eyes. Sometimes I see things more clearly now than I ever did before." Her voice had the toneless quality of the truly ancient. "I shall miss your visits, Jeffrey."

"I'll miss you too," he replied, and realized that he might be seeing her for the last time. The awareness seared him; before him sat the strongest link he had to the family of his youth.

"One thing you should do before you go," she told him.

That was enough to draw him back from the brink of real sorrow. "Don't say it," he replied coldly.

"Make peace with your brother."

"No."

"Please. For me."

"I don't have a brother. Not anymore."

"So much like your grandfather," she said softly. "Stubborn as an ox."

"I wish I'd known him better," he said, relieved to be back on more comfortable ground.

"He would have been very proud of you," she said. "And he would tell you the same thing."

"I can't," Jeffrey said simply. "Can we please talk about something else?"

She nodded her head, a single tiny motion, and said, "Your grandfather thought the world of Alexander. He would be pleased to know the family was staying together in this way. Very pleased."

He had not thought of that. "Is that why he offered me this job?"

"Who knows what Alexander thinks?" she said. "He is a bachelor, always has been. There has always been a little touch of the mysterious about Alexander. And a bit of the mystical about his cousin Gregor. You have never met Gregor, have you?"

Jeffrey shook his head. "I really don't know much about him. He's the one who escaped to England and then went back to Poland, isn't he?"

"That's correct. Gregor was always a religious person. A very gentle man with a wonderful sense of humor. I always felt good around him. He had a way of cheering everyone up, no matter how troubled they might be. He called it his spiritual gift." She looked at him. "You mustn't be concerned about the whys behind Alexander offering you this job."

"Your vision is perfect," Jeffrey admitted.

"Rest assured, if Alexander keeps you, it will be for one reason, and one reason only—because you are good." The old eyes rested gently on him. "Which you are."

"Thank you."

"One thing I know for certain. Alexander Kantor cannot abide mediocrity. Not in antiques, not in houses, not in clothes, and certainly not in people."

Jeffrey settled back. "Tell me about him."

"Well, with a man like Alexander it is sometimes difficult to separate truth from legend."

"I've noticed. What I've heard about him sounds almost like fairy tales from a children's storybook."

"Yes, the family has certainly done him an injustice. But this is the way people often deal with a character who is larger than life. And Alexander certainly is that."

"Why do you let them talk about him like they do?"

Fragile shoulders bounced in a single silent laugh. "Since when does anybody listen to what I have to say?"

"I do."

"Yes. You have been a great comfort. I will certainly miss you."
He pushed the renewed pain away. "So what was he really like?"

"When your grandfather first began courting me, Alexander
was a sort of ghost around the apartment. They call them flats in
London, don't ask me why. His family all lived there, or rather
all of those who had escaped with him. There was your grandfather Piotr, which is Polish for Peter—I soon had him change it
to something I could pronounce, I assure you. Then there were
Alexander's parents—your great-uncle and aunt. Then there was his
cousin Gregor and Gregor's wife. She died soon after their arrival in
London; perhaps you knew that."

"I didn't even know he was married."

"He's not now. That is, he never remarried. They were clearly
very much in love, and apparently he was able to love only one
person in all his life. But you asked me about Alexander. Well, as I
said, he was rarely there in those early days of our courtship."

"I love that word," Jeffrey told her. "Courtship. It sounds so
formal."

"That's why I use it. Your grandfather was a very formal, courtly
person. He had the finest manners of any person I have ever met,
except perhaps Alexander. But where Alexander acted with such
polish, my Peter acted with heart."

She wiped at the wet spot in the corner of her mouth with a handkerchief as delicate as the hand that held it. "Whenever I visited Peter's
flat—which was a ghastly, crowded affair, I assure you—Alexander was
never there. His things were on the bed beside Peter's, and next to his
in the closet. But the man himself was never around. Never. I did not
actually meet him until after Peter and I became engaged. I don't know
what I expected, but I was shocked at what I found."

"I can imagine."

She looked at him. "He still cuts a handsome figure, does he?"

"Very."

"I'm so glad. Our heroes should have the right to age gracefully.
Back then, Alexander was undoubtedly the most dashing man I
had ever met."

"Why did you call him a hero?"

"Well, first of all because of their escape. From what I recall it was quite an adventure. I'm afraid I don't remember the details. But there was much more than that. Much more. He financed your grandfather's first jewelry store here in America. Ah, I see you did not know that. Yes, and a home for us. And Gregor's education in London—that is, until he decided that he was called back to Poland. That was the way Gregor always described it, that he was *called*. Alexander never accepted a penny in return from anyone. He refused to even discuss it. He called such talk a dishonor." She smiled into the distance, repeated, "Your grandfather thought the world of that gentleman."

"Why was Alexander never home? I mean, when you used to go over there."

Her eyes twinkled mischievously. "Because he was out gambling."

"What?"

"I only learned the truth after Peter and I returned to America. In London they simply wouldn't discuss it. Such a thing was horribly incorrect. His family were old aristocrats, you see, and had a lot of trouble accepting the fact that the war had left them penniless. You cannot imagine how destitute they were when we first met. Your grandfather had one jacket, two pair of trousers, and two shirts to his name. That was all. Still, the idea of Alexander earning the money to pay for the lion's share of their living expenses with cards was simply not to be discussed with anyone. But he was so successful at it that they dared not complain. They couldn't afford to, you see."

Jeffrey leaned forward in his chair. "Successful."

"Incredibly. So successful that he was eventually banned from some of the gambling clubs. Gambling is legal in Britain, you see, but only inside licensed clubs. Yes, Alexander only played blackjack and poker and bridge, games where his amazing ability with numbers gave him an advantage." She was clearly enjoying herself. "You didn't know that either, did you?"

Jeffrey made do with a slow shake of his head.

"He trained as a mathematician in Poland. No, I take that back. Something else. Something to do with calculating odds."

"Statistics?"

"Thank you. He had just started his studies, I seem to recall something about being quite young, so young that he could not enter university and was being tutored privately. Then the war broke out and everyone's life changed for the worse."

"Amazing," Jeffrey said. "A professional gambler."

"Not just, young man. Not by any means. He took courses at the university and worked a daytime job loading trucks."

"And gambled."

"Almost every night, sometimes until dawn if he was in a private game. Peter was very envious of Alexander's ability to live on two or three hours of sleep a night, rarely more."

"I bet I can guess what he did with the money," Jeffrey said.

"London was full of refugees, or displaced persons as they were known then. Many were quite wealthy, or had been. Most had something to sell—jewelry or silver or rare boxes, perhaps a small painting, anything that could be easily carried as they made their escape from wherever they had come.

"They were terrified of the London dealers, and rightly so. They were offered pennies for treasures that had been in their families for generations. There was so much being sold, you see, and so few people with money to spend. So Alexander began seeking these people out, and when he found something he liked, he would buy it for twice, three times, sometimes as much as ten times what the dealers were offering.

"He bought only the best and tried to pay a fair price. An honorable price, was the way he put it. He was building friends as well as a collection, you see. That has always been his way. And these friends remember him still, him and his honesty and the respect he gave them when they had nothing and were no one. Those who are still alive come to him even today, to buy or to sell. And their children. That, Jeffrey, is the measure of Alexander Kantor."

"So what did he do with those first pieces?"

"Alexander was a man with vision. He knew that prices would eventually rise, especially if he dealt only in the very finest. So he rented a bank box and placed all his purchases in there for safekeeping.

Then the box was replaced with a larger drawer, then two, then three, and so on." Her eyes shone with remembered pride. "I can still recall the first time he showed me his collection. It was the day before my wedding. He took Peter and me to Claridge's for lunch—you must go there once for me, Jeffrey. Promise me you will."

"All right."

"Thank you. Yes, then after lunch he took us down into the bank vault and opened up all five of these great drawers that he and a guard pulled out of a wall of locked boxes. He opened them up and said that we were to pick out whatever piece we liked the most as a wedding present.

"You should have seen the treasure. When I collected myself, I told him I couldn't possibly do such a thing. So he gave me an emerald necklace, pressed it into Peter's hand because I refused to touch it, it was all too much for me, I had only met him once before. I still have it over there in the rosewood box on my vanity. I intend to give it to whichever of you boys marries first. I do so hope I'm still around to see that day."

Jeffrey leaned back in his seat and said softly, "Incredible."

"Yes, that is the perfect way to describe Alexander. He is an incredible man. Always a gentleman, always generous and gallant. Yet always a loner, preferring to go his own way. All his life he has held who he is and what he does out of sight from the rest of us. I truly believe that is why he decided to remain in London and set up his business there. Because he preferred to be alone."

"I have to go." Jeffrey rose his feet, leaned over to kiss the withered cheek. As he raised back up he asked, "Why doesn't he ever come to see you?"

"Because it is his nature," she replied simply. "You will discover with time, Jeffrey, that people do not always act in a logical manner. Alexander loved my husband. He has not been to see me since the funeral. Period. I could become angry and destroy the affection I hold for him, or I can accept what is beyond my power to control. He writes me with unfailing regularity, at Christmas, on my birthday, and again at Easter. He never fails to mention how he misses my husband. I do not agree with how he chooses to deal with Peter's absence, but I will not allow this to come between me and the memories of a man my husband adored. I simply will not allow it."

As he was leaving, his grandmother called after him, "Jeffrey, please. Do it for me."

He stopped, felt the old familiar tug-of-war begin inside himself. His hand gripped the doorknob with white-knuckled intensity.

"Think of it as a last request from one who has loved you all your life," she pleaded. "Go and see your brother."

He nodded, not trusting his voice, and left.

———

Jeffrey's Tuesday morning began as usual. The trash men and the builders arrived at half-past seven, banging dustbins and racing heavy diesels and trading curses in broadest Cockney. Jeffrey swung out of bed, checked the weather by craning and locating the one patch of sky visible in the corner of his bedroom window. He decided to skip his morning run through Hyde Park and instead take breakfast in Shepherd Market.

Even in early June there were mornings when low-lying clouds clamped themselves firmly over the city, a lingering reminder of winter's steel-gray cold. But if the air was dry, as it often was, by midmorning the clouds would lift away, leaving an afternoon of breathtaking beauty. On such days lunch hours were stretched to include lazy strolls through Mayfair's numerous parks and squares. Every bench was full, ties were cast aside, blouses opened another notch. Every possible square inch of sun-starved skin was exposed to spring's gift.

Scattered among these weeks came days when the air took on a jewel-like clarity. Heavy winds and heavier showers scrubbed the air to a newborn brightness. London's buildings and parks and monuments positively sparkled. Dawn runs through Hyde Park became mystical exercises, each breath a perfume-laden draught.

South Audley Street, where Jeffrey's minuscule apartment was located, ran from Grosvenor Square and the United States Embassy to Curzon Street. It was by London standards a broad and smooth-running thoroughfare, one long block removed from Park Lane and Hyde Park. So many films and television programs had used its thoroughly Victorian facades as backdrops that the equipment required for a full-scale shoot caused more irritation than excitement.

His neighborhood was flanked on all sides by the lore of centuries and filled to the brim with wealth. South Audley Street was a ridiculously posh address, made affordable only because the American who owned the flat was a friend and client of Alexander's. In the late sixties—back before London's property boom had pushed Mayfair prices into the stratosphere—he had purchased it both as an investment and a holiday flat. He let it to Jeffrey half as a favor to Alexander and half as a security measure; in recent years thieves had taken to marking down all flats not regularly occupied and robbing them at their leisure.

According to the agreement, Jeffrey had the flat fully furnished for eleven months a year. In July the owner and his wife flew over from California to spend a month doing the London social scene. For that month Jeffrey moved into rooms at his club. The arrangement was ideal. It brought a tastefully furnished Mayfair flat down to an affordable price, and allowed Jeffrey to savor the experience of making the heart of London his home.

By American standards, the flat was only slightly larger than a moving crate. The living room looked down on a busy city street and was just big enough for a glass-topped dining table, an ultramodern sofa, two matching chairs, and an unadorned Scandinavian corner cupboard. The bedroom, whose tiny window overlooked an alley, was much too small for its American-size bed. Jeffrey had to do the sideways shuffle to arrive at his clothes cupboard. Dressing took place in the front hall.

The bathroom was down a narrow staircase that was both steep and dangerous, especially after a round of local pubs. The kitchen was an afterthought, an alcove so narrow that two people could not pass each other.

The monthly rent was more than his father's mortgage for a four-bedroom house on one of Jacksonville's main canals. Still, Jeffrey was enormously glad he had followed Alexander's urging to accept the offer. The Grosvenor House Hotel, which was half a block behind his flat, charged four hundred dollars a night for a standard double room. A furnished studio flat two doors down from his was advertised for rent at more per week than he was paying per month. And the location suited him perfectly—two blocks to his shop, one to Hyde Park, and three from the fabulous English breakfasts in legendary Shephard Market.

Shepherd Market was a collection of narrow winding streets and tiny cottages more suited to a quiet country village than the heart of London's West End. Tradition had it as the gathering place for drovers bringing their flocks to market, back seven or eight hundred years ago, when London-Town was still confined to its original walls. In those early days, drovers slaughtered their flocks behind local butcheries, and put themselves up in cramped little rooms above the local pubs.

By the time Queen Victoria began her reign in the nineteenth century, the drovers were no more. Yet Shepherd Market survived the centuries and the transitions, retaining its reputation as a gathering place for the less genteel, and gaining a name as having the largest selection of courtesans and streetwalkers in all England.

Jeffrey's walk to breakfast was for him a stroll through a living museum. At the Hyde Park end, Mayfair was mostly brick and stone festooned with an abundance of Victorian foppery. Queen Anne cottages stood cheek-and-jowl with more recent construction, yet to Jeffrey's unabashedly biased eye, the charm had been preserved. In the relative quiet of his early morning walks, he imagined himself transported back to a time of top hats and morning coats and ballooning skirts and hansom cabs.

Jeffrey was in love with Mayfair. All of London held him enthralled; for that matter, the fact that he slept and ate and worked and played on an island perched at the upper left corner of Europe filled him with sheer explosive delight. But he *loved* Mayfair.

To Jeffrey Allen Sinclair, Mayfair had all the makings of a magical land. There were so many hidden nooks and crannies and tales and characters that he could spend a dozen lifetimes within its confines and never drain the cup of adventure.

Jeffrey crossed over Curzon Street, walked the narrow foot passage, and entered a collection of streets never intended for car traffic. Shepherd Market lanes were fifteen feet wide or less, and lined with tiny cottages housing a variety of cafes and shops and pubs and restaurants. Jeffrey's own favorite was a corner cafe with hand-drawn glass panes, warped as though pebbles had been dropped onto their still surface and then frozen in place. The cafe's ceiling and walls were plaster framed by ancient uneven beams, its tables set so close together that a diner who ate with elbows extended was simply not welcome. Jeffrey had long since learned to fold his morning paper into sixteenths.

═══

Once Jeffrey returned home for Ling and arrived at the shop, he barely had time to settle in before the electronic chime announced his first visitor of the day. From the safety of his office alcove Jeffrey glanced up, smiled, tucked the little bird into its new bedding, put on his professional face, and walked forward.

He swung the door wide with a flourish. "Good morning, Mr. Greenfield. Morning, Ty."

"Hullo, lad," Sydney Greenfield said. "I've always wanted to be your height when I walk into a bar. Isn't that right, Ty."

"Gets him proper switched on, it does."

"Come in, gentlemen. Come in."

Sydney Greenfield, purveyor to the would-be's and has-been's of London's Green Belt, entered with his normal theatrics. Behind him walked Ty, his shadowy parrot. Jeffrey did not know him by any other name, did not even know if he had one. Ty he had been introduced as, and Ty he had remained. Jeffrey truly liked the pair. They were a part of what made the London antiques trade unique in all the world.

The Green Belt was an almost-circle of suburbs and swallowed villages that stretched through four counties. They were linked to central London by an extended train service and road system, allowing those who could afford it to live surrounded by a semblance of green and still make it to work more or less on time.

Sydney Greenfield described himself as a contact broker extraordinaire, and survived from the hand-to-mouth trade of bringing buyer and seller together. He had somehow attached himself to Jeffrey and the shop during Jeffrey's early days. They had actually brought him one sale, albeit for the cheapest article in the shop at the time. Nonetheless, following that maneuver Sydney Greenfield had treated Jeffrey and the shop with a proprietary interest, as though their own success were now inexorably linked with his.

Sydney Greenfield was a florid man with thin strands of gray-black hair plastered haphazardly across an enormous central bald spot. Even at ten in the morning his cheeks and nose positively glowed from the effects of too many three-hour pub lunches and liquid dinners—an integral part of the finder's trade. He wore a tailored pinstripe three-piece suit made from a broadcloth Jeffrey had long since decided came from the inside of a Sainsbury's chocolate box, it was so shiny. Beneath it bunched a wilted white starched shirt and an over-loud tie. A large belly strained against his waistcoat.

"With regard to the cabinet," Sydney Greenfield said. "We've been broaching the subject with Her Royal Highness the Princess Walrus. How long has it been now, Ty."

"Nigh on seven weeks, it is."

"Yes. Long time to be weathering Her Royal Highness' storm, seven weeks is. And I must tell you, your asking price for that cabinet has created quite a storm, hasn't it, Ty."

"Right stood my hair on end, she did."

Jeffrey fished out the key ring for the glass display case. "I think you'd better sit down," he said.

Sydney Greenfield clutched at his heart. "You're not meaning it."

Jeffrey raised up a crystal decanter, asked, "Perhaps a little brandy?"

Greenfield sat with a low moan. "You promised me first call. Didn't he, Ty."

"Stood right there and gave his solemn word, he did."

Jeffrey handed over a crystal snifter holding an ample portion, replied, "I told you I'd hold it for seven days. Which I did. And that was almost two months ago."

Greenfield downed the snifter with one gulp, breathed, "Details, lad. Mere details."

"I had a buyer who waited through that seven-day period, then paid the price I asked."

"Seventeen thousand quid?" Greenfield waved the goblet for a refill. "Paid up without a quibble?"

"Didn't even blink an eye."

"Tell me who it is, lad. There's a couple of little items I'd like to show a gentleman of means."

Jeffrey shook his head. "Seventeen thousand pounds buys a lot of confidentiality in this shop."

Greenfield drained the second glass, smacked his lips. "Well, it's water under the bridge then, right, Ty."

"No use crying over milk the cat's already drunk."

"Did I ever tell you why I call him Ty, lad?"

"Only every time you come in."

Greenfield ignored him. "It's after the *Titanic,* because the fellow goes down like a bolt at the first sniff of the stuff. Never seen the like, not in this trade."

Sydney Greenfield recovered with the speed of one accustomed to such disappointments. He pointed an overly casual hand toward one of the few English pieces that Jeffrey had kept for their own shop. "We've done quite a bit of analyzing the market for that other little item."

It was a chest of drawers made in the William and Mary period, and was constructed in laburnum wood, a tree whose seeds were deadly poisonous. The wood had been cut transversely across the branch, creating a swirl effect in the grain which reminded Jeffrey of the inside of oyster shells. The inlay was of darker holly, which traced its way around the outer edges of each drawer; the carpenter had used the inlay to frame the wood's pattern, rather than smother it. The piece was probably constructed somewhere around 1685, given its similarities to other antiques that Jeffrey had been able to identify and which had more established provenances.

Establishing an antique's provenance—its previous record of ownership—added significantly to an article's price, especially if there were either royalty or unique stories attached. One part of the mysteries attached to Alexander's antiques was that they almost never had any provenance whatsoever. They were therefore sold on the basis of their beauty, condition, and evident age. Jeffrey's own education had shown that the more valuable the antique, the more often there was a fairly clear indication of lineage. To have no provenance whatsoever with antiques of this quality suggested that Alexander was intentionally hiding the records in order to protect his sources.

The cost of the chest of drawers was twenty-six thousand pounds, or about forty-five thousand dollars.

"We are on the verge," Sydney Greenfield announced. "Yes, lad, we might actually be pouncing on that one tomorrow. We don't have her signed, mind you. I'd be lying if I said that, and as you know I'm a man of my word. But we're close enough to see the whites of her eyes, aren't we, Ty."

"Close enough to steal a kiss and bolt."

"Yes, that is, if anyone could actually bring themselves to kiss the old walrus. Mind you, I'd probably take the plunge myself if I thought it'd get the old dear to part with her brass."

Katya chose that moment to arrive at the front door. She leaned up close enough to see through the outside reflection, tapped her fingernails on the glass and waved at him.

At first sight of her, Greenfield sprang from the chair as though electrocuted. "Who's that, lad? Not a customer. Life's unfair, I've known that for years, but it'd be stepping out of bounds to hand money to looks like that."

"My new assistant," Jeffrey replied, opening the door and ushering her in. "Katya Nichols, may I present Sydney Greenfield and his assistant Ty. I'm sorry, Ty, I don't believe I've ever learned your last name."

Sydney Greenfield displayed a massive grace as he sidled up and bowed over Katya's hand. "My dear, if this were my shop, I'd have raised the prices ten percent the instant I signed you on."

Katya had compromised over taking salary from Jeffrey in a way that was uniquely her own; she spent it all on clothes that she wore when she was working at the shop. Today she had on one of his favorite items, a high-collared blouse in gray-violet silk the shade of her eyes. It had little cloth buttons and an Oriental design sewn across the left breast and up both sleeves. It was gathered at the waist with a leather belt of almost the same shade, and worn out and draped over a knee-length skirt of midnight blue. Jeffrey thought the color of the blouse made her eyes look positively enormous.

Katya responded to Sydney's compliment with her unshakable poise. "It's very nice to meet you, Mr. Greenfield, Ty. Has Jeffrey offered you gentlemen coffee?"

"He was obviously waiting for you to arrive, my dear. Knowing as he would that it'll taste twice as good coming from your hand, won't it, Ty."

"Like nectar, it will."

"How do you gentlemen like it?"

"Ty likes his straight up, seeing as how it's the only drink on earth he can stomach in pure form. I'll have mine with a touch more of the amber, if your boss here will relax his death's grip on the bottle."

Sydney watched Katya vanish into the alcove, murmured to Jeffrey, " 'Truth, lad. I wouldn't get a dollop of work done with that in the shop."

"I have the same trouble," Jeffrey replied.

"Where on earth did you find her?"

"In the London University library."

Sydney made round mocking eyes. "You mean she can read, too?"

"She's an honor student in Eastern European studies."

Greenfield rolled his eyes. "Oh, you wouldn't catch me studying them places. Or going there, for that matter. Would you, Ty."

"Rather marry Her Royal Walrus, I would."

"What do you mean?"

"Communists, lad. Communists. Stands to reason, doesn't it. What, you think all them card-carryin' pinkos just up and vanished, poof, in the blink of an eye and all that?"

"From what I've read, the Communist parties have either been banned in those countries or have lost so much support they're not really a factor anymore."

"Wrong, lad. Dead wrong you are." Sydney lowered his voice to a brandy-soaked whisper. "There's Commies everywhere, and this time they're mad."

"I rather doubt that."

"Out for blood, aren't they, Ty."

"Worse than Dracula coming off a diet, far as I see it."

" 'Course they are. Been in power for donkey's years, and all of a sudden they're out on the street, nowhere to go, nothing to do but find a capitalist pig and roast him."

"Thanks for the advice."

"Not to worry, lad. There's always more where that came from." He leaned closer. "And here's another morsel for good measure. Latch onto that one, lad. She's one of a kind."

Jeffrey bit off the thought that came to mind and said as Katya came back into view, "I've got to be getting over to the Grosvenor House. You gentlemen will be all right here with Katya, I take it."

"Right you are, lad." Greenfield performed another little bow as he took the proffered cup. "Run along and see to your business. We'll suffer on here without you."

The Grosvenor House Hotel dominated the stretch of Park Lane approaching Marble Arch and Oxford Street. Originally built as the city palace for Sir Richard Grosvenor, the then owner of all West Mayfair, it was a modest red-brick affair of two wings and four hundred rooms.

In 1920, when the palace became a hotel, its downstairs ballroom was converted into an indoor skating rink that could accommodate as many as five hundred people at a time. Those days were long gone, however, and now it was home to some of the largest events of London's social season, including the most exclusive antique show in all England.

Jeffrey entered through the hotel's back doors, passing as he did a taxi rank filled to overflowing with Bentleys and Jaguars and Rolls Royces and stretch Mercedes and several dozen bored drivers. He circled the lobby, showed his dealer's pass to the uniformed attendants, and joined the flow entering the double doors.

There were a number of dealers with whom the Priceless, Ltd antique shop placed pieces. Part of the reason was simply volume—when a major shipment arrived, which took place as often as four or five times a year, there was no way they could stock all the items, much less market them properly. Moreover, there was also the issue of quality and style. They did not handle much English furniture, for example, and did not seek to build a reputation in that area. They turned most such items over to dealers who had made it their life's work—as was the case today.

Visiting the fair was a daunting experience for Jeffrey, though nothing like the year before. He was beginning to know his way around, and did not feel like such a silent idiot when talk turned to pieces and dealers.

A hodgepodge of languages greeted him as he stepped into the fair proper. Around him he saw elegant women kissing cheeks and laughing over snide asides, languidly flickering jeweled wrists to accent their own verbal thrusts. Jeffrey skirted around them, extremely grateful that his own shop had never become a gathering place for the overly rich and overly bored.

"Hello, hello, what do we have here?" A dealer named Andrew stepped back from a clubbish circle of dealers and waved Jeffrey over.

"Not half bad, that." This voice belonged to a dealer named Jackie, a short feisty man with a reputation for provoking fights and accepting goods no one else would touch. "Take a stroll from the shop, whisper a word in the right ear, steal an honest bloke's customer, sneak on back, pick up a few bob. All right for some, I suppose."

"Shut up, Jackie," Andrew said, his gaze still on Jeffrey. "How are you then, lad? All right?"

"Yes, thanks. I was just—"

"Oh, we know all about that. Never a minute free for a bit of idle chatter, our lad. What's brought you over, then?"

Trying to match his casual tone, Jeffrey repeated a remark often heard among dealers: "Just wanted to see if you had anything I could use to dress up the shop."

Andrew shook his head. He was a cheerful, solidly built man who had worked his way up from extremely poor beginnings to the management of a very successful Kensington High Street antiques shop. Jeffrey had placed pieces with him on several occasions, and found him to be both honest and shrewd. "No, nothing for you at the moment. Stop back in a couple of days, though. I'll let you have whatever's left for a song, long as you haul it away and save my aching back the trouble."

"Sounds good, thanks."

"Just give us a shout, we'll have us a look around, all right?" Andrew turned back to the group, asked, "Everybody here's met Kantor's whiz-kid, have they?"

There were a few greetings, a couple of genuine smiles, several calculating looks from very hard eyes. Jeffrey replied with a hello and a blank smile, and looked forward to getting away.

"Have you ever been into their shop?" Andrew asked the clan.

"Never had the pleasure," a dealer in old silver replied.

"Generally they have this huge great mixture," Andrew said. "Everything comes in, from the most darling little post-Impressionist etchings to great hairy stuffed baboons."

"I missed the baboon," Jeffrey said.

"Did you really? Probably before your time. Gave me such a fright, that one."

"Must be quite the place," Jackie sneered.

"'Tis, yeah. Sort of a flea market for the Bentley crowd, you might say."

"More like a garage sale put on by the British Museum, from the sounds of it."

"It's all right for some," Jackie said. "We're sure not seeing the like."

"No?"

He shook his head. "We're down forty percent on our takings this year. Watched three of our best customers go under the same week. Left me with this lot of paper and a letter from the bank saying I'll stand in line with the others to get paid. What rot."

Most dealers made complaining about business a singular art form, but there was the ring of truth about what the tough little man said. The recession was hitting the antiques and art trades much harder than anyone expected. According to recent figures, the recession was biting into British business at the rate of nine hundred and seventy bankruptcies every *week*.

"Tough times, Jackie."

"It is, yeah. Might have to pack it in."

"You're joking."

"I'm not, I tell you. Another year like the last one and we'll be back to peddling from a pushcart. I'm glad the old man didn't live to see the day. Wish I hadn't."

"It's tough for all of us," the silver dealer said. "Well, the wolf's at the door. If you'll excuse me, I'm off to make an honest quid."

"Me too," Jeffrey said, nodding to the group.

"Here, lad," Andrew said. "Mind if I join you?"

"Who's tending the store?"

"Got me an old dear, must be eighty if she's a day. Better with the clients than I'll ever be. If they try to talk her down, she grabs her ticker like the shock'll do her in. Shuts them up every time. What's brought you over, then?"

"I've got a chest here with a dealer."

"Want to hear him do his pitch? That was a wise move, lad."

One condition Jeffrey placed on dealers who wished to work with him on a regular basis was that he have the opportunity to hear them describe his piece to a potential buyer. It was one of the best possible learning tools, he had found. Some dealers hated it bitterly, accused him of trying to steal their customers. No one accepted it without a fight, and several had taken it up with Alexander. Jeffrey had been gratified to find the gentleman back him on something so totally unorthodox.

"So why did you complain when I asked you?" Jeffrey demanded.

Andrew gave a casual shrug. "Automatic, wasn't it. Anything to do with negotiations, you don't give in without a struggle. You should know that, lad."

The dealer Jeffrey was to visit today was a leading authority on early Chippendale. He had accepted Jeffrey's condition as he would a dose of castor oil, then compromised by allowing Jeffrey to listen in while he was being interviewed by a magazine reporter. Jeffrey did not object. His goal was simply to hear how someone else described a piece for sale. Who the pitch was made to was immaterial.

The reporter was already there when he arrived. Jeffrey stood just outside the stall, pretending to be a buyer who was simply stopping for a gander. Andrew took the silent hint and stepped back a pace, greeting the stall owner across the way. The pair of them moved up behind Jeffrey, far enough back to be unobtrusive, close enough to hear what was going on.

The dealer ignored them entirely. He was a tall aristocratic man in his late fifties, with ruddy features and a patronizing tone of voice. "It is very difficult, this process of locating the right sort of antiques," the dealer was saying. "One is forced to travel all over the world. There are just so few pieces available of the quality our clients demand."

"He's laying it on over thick, don't you think?" a voice behind Jeffrey muttered.

"Not a bit," Andrew whispered in reply. "The dear's just asked him where his stuff comes from, and he's telling her it's none of her business. Quite right too, if you ask me."

The reporter was a fresh-faced young woman whose interest appeared genuine. She pointed to a tall piece with wood the color of a burnished red sunrise and asked with an American accent, "And what about that piece? Is that a sideboard?"

One of the men behind Jeffrey snickered quietly.

"Ah, no, well, that's a bureau cabinet, really." The man's snootiness inched up another notch. Jeffrey kept his features immobile and recalled the time, three weeks after he had started working with Alexander, when he had asked a dealer with a blessedly short memory if a cherry-wood table wasn't eighteenth-century French. The man had looked at him as though he had just grown a second head, replied that it was a brand-new reproduction of an English Sheraton piece, and asked him if he had ever thought of taking up a different profession—accounting, perhaps.

Jeffrey leaned forward slightly, as the piece under discussion was his. It was also clearly the finest article in the man's collection.

"It was made in England in about 1760," the dealer went on. "George the Third, which makes it of the Chippendale period, of course."

"Of course," the cowed young lady repeated, scribbling furiously.

"It's got a lovely color, I'm sure you'd agree. And wonderful architectural pediments."

"Pediments?" she asked.

"Yes, pediments. Quite rare for a piece of such age, actually."

Jeffrey understood both the reporter's confusion and the dealer's refusal to explain himself further. Like most professions, the world of fine woodworking had a technical vocabulary all its own. And like most such terms, it was difficult to explain one point without referring to other unknown factors. Jeffrey had several times approached the point of giving up and burning his books before it all began to fall into place.

A cabinet's pediment was the ornate carving above the cornice, the molding that framed the top. If the antique rose above the level of simple furniture and sought to be a work of art, as was the case here, the cornice often rested upon a horizontal section, called a frieze, which was either inlaid or carved or both. Thus an elaborate item might be crowned in stages, rising from the upper framework, or carcase, to the frieze, then the cornice, then the pediment.

Jeffrey had spent over a week memorizing the more than two-dozen most common styles of pediments. These were most important to a dealer, as they were oftentimes the first indication of where and when the antique was made.

The Chippendale period was usually identifiable by what was called a broken pediment, which basically looked like the roofline of a house with a chunk bitten out of the middle peak. Ornate articles often had pierced carvings rising from this central gap.

"This item still has vestiges of the maker's label inside the top drawer," the dealer was saying. "Not enough to identify it, unfortunately, but enough to establish in our mind that it was made by a man of importance who prized his work enough to put a label in it."

This, Jeffrey knew, was pure conjecture and would not hold water with a serious collector. For all they knew, it was a fragment of an old map or will or anything else important enough to be varnished into a safe and relatively secret place. But it sounded good, and the young lady ate it up.

"This also has all the original cast brass handles and features. Very nice fitted interior. Newly lined in silk."

"What kind of wood is this?"

"Mahogany. One of about two hundred kinds, actually. Cuban or Honduran, we have decided. It was used quite a lot in that period by the better English cabinetmakers. Excellent quality, I'm sure you'll agree."

"And the price?"

"Thirty-eight thousand pounds."

The young lady gaped. Jeffrey bit back a smile. That was the litmus test of a raw beginner—inability to disguise shock over prices.

"What is very difficult for some people to understand," the dealer said, somewhat testily, "is that this piece is exceptional precisely because of such details. The pediments, the original handles and cleats, all these add tremendously to the value."

"As does a good case of the blarney," muttered the voice behind Jeffrey.

"What happens if a piece comes in that has been refinished?" asked the young lady.

"You buy it for a song and then you lie," the voice offered quietly.

"Ah, well," the dealer replied. "If a piece is ruined, then that is it. Once an article like that has been stripped and repolished, no amount of work will ever restore the color or the surface patina."

"Lucky for us there's a world of fools with money to burn who don't know the first thing about patina," the voice murmured.

"It's very difficult to make a generalization, though," the dealer continued. "It depends on the damage to the article. I mean, some things can be restored and some can't. If you don't know what you're doing, you can spend a lot of money on restoration and have absolutely nothing to show for it."

Jeffrey decided the talk was winding down. He nodded to the dealer, who continued to ignore him, and turned away. Andrew followed him. "There's a few of us gathering at the Audley tonight, lad. You ought to stop by."

"What for?"

Andrew smiled at his directness. "You're getting to be known as a real mystery man. Couldn't hurt to show the face now and then, let people know you're actually human."

"I feel as if I'm under attack every time I meet these people."

"Yes, I suppose you are. No more than the rest of us, though." Andrew patted his shoulder. "Give it a thought, lad. If you're going to make this lot your own, it might be time to widen your circle a little." He gave Jeffrey a friendly nod and wandered off.

The remainder of the afternoon was spent preparing for Alexander's arrival the next morning, dealing with the occasional customer, and knowing the exquisite frustration of Katya's silent presence. When they were alone like this, they shared the cozy shelter of the little back office. Katya set her work on a small satinwood table beside his bookshelves. He sat at his desk and compiled notes, made calls, carefully went through his accounts for the past month, and rewarded himself with glances at her.

He yearned for the chance to tell her that her silence appealed to him, that somehow it created a tenderness in him that he had never known before, an awareness of her fragility that seemed to cry out for his protection. But he could not speak of it because she would not let him.

At a dinner together two weeks before, Jeffrey had almost admitted defeat. He had sat across from her, and wondered if perhaps it wasn't time to let her go. Six months of futility was enough.

Katya chose that moment to look up. She sensed the change within him, and reacted with a look of real fear before saying, "You've never told me about your family."

"I've tried," he replied. "Several times. You never seemed to care."

"I'm listening now."

He started to tell her, that's not what I said. Instead he replied, "My family revolved around my father's business life. I was what you'd call a product of the American corporate culture. The way my father told it, Old MacDonald was president and chairman of the board of the E.I.E.I.O. Corporation."

"Oh, stop it."

"He had his Moo-Moo Division over here, see. And the Oink-Oink Division over there. And the Quack-Quack Division was stuck out back by the lake because they never could get out of the red."

"Did your family belong to a church?"

"For the last eleven years my family has lived in Jacksonville, Florida. That means I'm Baptist. Back home, either you're a retired

Yankee or you're a Baptist or you're dead. And if you're dead, then you're a dead Baptist."

"My mother and I belong to an Anglican church," Katya said. "It's sort of like the Episcopalian church in America."

"I've always thought of Episcopalians as sort of Catholic lights. You know, all the fun but only half the guilt."

"There's a real revival going on within the Anglican church in this country," Katya persisted. "It's really meant a lot to me, being a part of this upsurge in the Spirit."

Jeffrey nodded, worked at keeping a casual tone. "So when were you saved?"

She looked deep at him. "The same time as you, Jeffrey. About two thousand years ago."

"We used to have this preacher, a professional auctioneer during the week. I never heard anybody talk so fast in my life. He'd take ten minutes to get cranked up, like a jet engine winding up before take-off. His face would get all red and swollen, then he'd blast off, and all we'd see was a trail of fiery smoke in the sky. He'd start in Genesis and fly right on through to the maps. In an hour. Every week."

Her gaze remained steady and searching. "Why do you make a joke out of everything?"

Because I love to see your smile, he thought, but could not bring himself to make such a confession. "Maybe because the truth is so boring."

"Try me."

"You sure?"

"If I wasn't I wouldn't ask."

"Okay." He took a breath. "The truth is, I don't even know where to say my family is from. My dad was with IBM. I remember when I was six years old he came home one day, and he and my mom got all excited because he'd been put on the fast track. I didn't have idea one what they were talking about, but I still remember how happy he was and how proud my mom got. From then on, we never spent two full years in one place.

"I've lived in eleven different cities in seven states. I went to four junior high schools. We finally settled in Jacksonville when I was seventeen, and we've been there ever since." Another deep breath. "We had to stay there. My brother got . . . sick."

"I thought you told me you didn't have any brothers or sisters." His face was set in rigid lines. "I don't."

Her eyes rested on him in silent watchfulness. "And you want to start a relationship with me."

"This has nothing to do with it."

She slid from her seat, rose to her feet, and said, "I think it's time you took me home, Jeffrey."

"Why?" He did not try to remove the harshness from his voice. "Because I won't talk about things that don't matter?"

"Are you going to take me home or should I walk by myself?"

He paid and guided her from the restaurant. On the street he realized that he faced a final farewell, and he found himself unable to raise his hand and flag a taxi and open the door and say the words and watch her leave his life. Instead, he took her arm and led her across the street to where the thinnest tip of Hyde Park separated them from a pair of monstrously modern hotels, the Hilton and the Inn on the Park, which in turn backed up onto the Shepherd Market corner of Mayfair. He realized he was simply putting off the inevitable, and that as soon as they left behind the park's leafy confines and reentered the rushing nighttime traffic, she would step into a waiting taxi and be gone. No matter how ready he was to end the futile struggle, the thought left him helplessly wounded.

She appeared to enjoy the evening's cool mist, and walked beside him in a silence of her own. Then she gave a little cry, slipped off the path, bent down and crooned at something he could not see. Jeffrey started to make some comment about the elves of Mayfair when she straightened and lifted cupped hands toward him. He leaned forward and saw it was a baby bird.

Because it was the closest refuge, they took the bird back to his apartment, a five-minute walk. It was the first time Katya had ever agreed to come up.

She gave a cursory glance to the apartment's pastel carpets and glass-topped dining table and light-stained Scandinavian furniture and garishly expensive mirror mural on the living-room wall. "This is not at all what I expected."

"I rented it furnished." He pointed toward the kitchen. "Bring the bird in here."

"Do you think it will live?"

"I don't have a lot of experience with baby birds," he replied, looking down at the shivering little form and the wide-open up-thrust beak. "What do we feed it?"

"Maybe just a little warm milk to start." She rubbed one finger along the blind little body. "He can't be more than a day or so old."

Jeffrey lit the stove and set down a pot with a smidgen of milk. He thundered down the stairs to his bathroom, reappearing a moment later bearing a eyedropper. He washed it thoroughly, filled it with warm milk, and dropped a bit on his wrist. "Feels okay."

"You do that like a real professional."

The baby bird liked it immensely. Jeffrey dropped the milk in as carefully as he could, but the body did not have strength to keep the head steady. He chased the tiny weaving body around and in the process painted its entire form with a warm white covering. Finally he managed to get three drops on target, enough to turn the gaping little mouth into a tiny white lake. The bird took the milk with a swallow that shook its entire frame. There was a moment's pause; then the head raised back up and again begged for more.

The baby was gray and covered with a dusting of scraggly hairs over wrinkled yellowish skin. Its wings were mere nubs of featherless quills, its head a skull covered with translucent skin, its beak bigger than its head. Its claws were feathery wisps that could not close. It trembled continually, even after it accepted the last convulsive swallow, then curled up in Katya's palm and breathed in little gasps that shook its entire meager form.

Jeffrey went out and returned with a pair of clean dish towels. He lined a cereal bowl, then guided Katya's hands over and helped settle the tiny body. He watched her coo and caress the form for a moment. "Katya, I'm not sure it's going to last the night."

She replied with a nod, refusing to take her eyes off the baby. "We have to try," she said. "What will we do with him? I can't take him to classes, and I can't get back home to feed him every hour."

"I'll keep it with me here and take it to the office," he said, and amended silently, if it survives. "You can take care of it there."

She raised her head and gave him her vulnerable look. "You still want me to come in and work with you?"

"I wasn't so sure earlier." He fought to keep his voice calm. "Katya, I care too much for you to be able to go on like this."

"You've got to be honest with me," she replied.

He nodded. "But I need the same in return."

She lifted one hand up from the bird and stroked his cheek with a feather-soft touch. "It's been difficult for you, hasn't it?"

"Horrible."

Her gaze turned inward. "I wish I knew what to do," she murmured. "It's all so confusing."

"What is?"

She focused on him, real fear in her eyes. "I'm trying, Jeffrey. I really am."

"What is it that makes it so hard for you to open up with me?"

She started to say something, then changed her mind and dropped her eyes back to the little bird. "If I tell you, it won't work."

"I don't understand, Katya." He refrained the urge to pull out his hair by the roots. "If you don't tell me, how am I supposed to figure it out?"

"I don't know," she said to the sleeping little bundle. "But I pray that you will, Jeffrey. Every night I pray."

━━

The Audley Pub stood on the corner of South Audley and Mount Street and maintained a charm reminiscent of a Victorian gentleman's library. Leather-lined booths ringed both the bar and the smaller, more stately saloon. Windows with diamond-shaped panes were set in the polished-wood walls. A trio of crystal chandeliers reflected the cheery light from the saloon fireplace. The clientele came from every walk of society; taxi drivers rubbed shoulders with city gents and foreign tourists avoiding the scalper's prices of West End hotel bars.

The first person Jeffrey spotted upon entering that night was Sarah, the gallery owner who had acquired his Musin boat scene the day before. He sidled up next to her. "That was a nice painting you picked up yesterday. I'll miss having it around."

She turned around. "Oh, hullo, Jeffrey. That was yours, then, was it? Pity about the masked bandit on the phone. Thought I had myself the buy of the century."

"So did I."

Her gaze turned penetrating. "That wasn't just a bit of fancy footwork on your part, was it?"

Jeffrey's shock was genuine. "I'd never do that."

She searched his face a moment longer before permitting herself a hard smile. "No," she replied. "You wouldn't, would you?"

"I don't even know who that other bidder was. Honest."

"Honest, yes, that's such a pleasant word." She patted his hand. "The world needs a few more like you, young Jeffrey. Come on then, you can use a bit of your honest killing and buy me a drink."

When Jeffrey entered the circle of dealers, Andrew gave him a smile of approval and the words, "You must be celebrating something special to be out on the prowl like this."

"He most certainly is," Sarah replied for him. "He made an extra eighty thousand pounds off me yesterday by the skin of his teeth."

"Sounds like a good story, that," Andrew said.

The venomous little trader named Jackie slid from the booth, "I don't have time for such rubbish. Some of us have to work for our living."

"Don't be daft, Jackie. It could have just as easily been you."

"What rot." He tossed off the last of his drink, gestured angrily at Jeffrey with the empty glass. "He's got a handle to the royal family, gets them coming and going, buying and selling the royal seat warmers. By rights it ought to stay in British hands."

Sarah turned to Jeffrey. "Seen much of the Queen Mother lately, dear?"

"Not since I stopped by the palace for tea last week," Jeffrey replied.

She turned back to Jackie. "That eliminates your little theory, Jackie."

"Rubbish. You don't think he'd tell us, do you? Nobody's that daft. Not even a Yank." Jackie wheeled around and stormed from the bar.

"Rude, if you ask me," Sarah said. "Sorry, Jeffrey. Guess I'll have to apologize for him."

"It's okay."

"He's right in a way," Andrew said mildly. "That's basically how all Mount Street got its start, you know. Catering to the carriage trade during the social season. Word was, a visit to the Kensington High Street shops would mean too long a time between martinis."

"Jackie's losing his shop," grumbled a dealer Jeffrey knew only by sight. "You can't expect him to pat this successful young lad on the head and say, 'Well done.'"

"He's dug his own grave, Tim," Andrew replied. "I'm sorry to say."

"No you're not," Sarah said. "Sorry, I mean. You positively loathe the man and always have."

"That may well be, but it's beside the point. If he'd had the slightest shred of business acumen, he'd have spent more time building allies and less ripping off anyone who came within arm's length."

"And I suppose you've always handled your affairs with white gloves."

"Don't be silly. Of course not. But what I mean to say is with Jackie you were positively certain that he'd do his level best to turn a dirty trick whenever possible."

"At least you knew where you stood with him," Tim replied.

Sarah set down her glass. "I didn't see you leaping up to help him in his hour of need."

"I don't deal in his sort of goods, though, do I."

"Jackie's problem," Andrew persisted, "is that he's like a chess player who can't see but one move ahead. He's only interested in making an extra quid, honest or dishonest, regardless of who might be hurt. I told him that, too. Quite a few times, actually."

That raised eyebrows around the table. "I never thought Jackie would allow anyone to tell him anything," Sarah said.

"Oh, he always denied it."

"He would."

Jeffrey asked, "Why did you bother?"

"Because, lad, Jackie and his kind hurt us all. It serves no one in the end, especially not Jackie."

"What did he do?" Jeffrey asked.

"Yes, Andrew," the stranger drawled. "Do be so kind as to give the boy a few pointers."

"We'd have to turn him over to you for that," Sarah replied acidly.

"Nothing that a thousand other dealers haven't done," Andrew replied. "Passing rubbish off as authentic antiques, disguising repairs with a new coat of varnish, calling it a genuine article and pricing it accordingly."

"Buffing new silver and stamping it with an old mark," Sarah added.

"Jackie's problem was that he did it too much and too openly," someone else offered.

"He cut his own throat," another agreed. "Drove off all the good dealers, and couldn't get his hands on any decent wares."

"A visit to Jackie's store was like a trip to Alice in Wonderland," Sarah added. "You were certain that nothing you saw was real, and everything Jackie said was utter nonsense."

"And all the while he'd be doing his level best to convince you it was a steal."

"That reminds me of a good one I heard the other day," Andrew said. "Seems a chap read in the local paper up in Glasgow that there was a genuine Louis XIV commode going for a quid."

That brought a laugh. A commode was a sort of ornate chest on legs, much like what in America would be called a dining room sideboard. The going rate for an authentic Louis XIV commode would have been at least thirty thousand pounds.

"The local dealers had quite a good chuckle over that one," Andrew went on. "Strange thing, though. Nobody actually bothered to check up on it but this one chap I know."

"You're not expecting us to believe this," someone said.

"This is the truth, I tell you. No one even bothered to ring up the number."

"I'm not the least bit surprised," Sarah told him. "I can just hear it now. You give them a ring and find yourself chatting with a fellow recently imported from Sicily. At no extra charge the lucky buyer finds, stuffed inside the commode, a body in perfectly good working order, save for quite a small hole in the middle of his chest."

"That wasn't it at all," Andrew replied. "Anyway, this chap I know called and the woman on the other end said, yes, she had this commode for sale, and yes, the price was one pound. So he figured it was worth at least driving by. Which he did. And the lady was quite correct. The article was both authentic and in mint condition."

"Someone's putting you on."

"They're not, I tell you. It was exactly what she said it was."

"For a quid."

"One pound exactly," Andrew agreed.

"Go on, then. What's the catch?"

"There wasn't one. Well, not for the buyer. It turned out her husband had recently passed on, and left instructions in his will for the commode to be sold and all proceeds to go to his secretary. The trouble was, you see, his wife knew all about the little affair he and his secretary had been having."

"You're putting us on," someone breathed.

"So she sold it for a quid," Andrew continued. "And passed the money over, just as the will instructed."

"I still don't believe it."

"Stop by the shop sometime," Andrew replied with a grin. "I'll be happy to make you a special offer."

Jeffrey spoke up. "The other day I had a French client tell me how she'd visited an auction house in Paris. She was leafing through the catalog and saw a marble-topped Empire table just like her own. She thought it would be wonderful to have a matched pair, so she spoke to the dealer, who gave her a really attractive price. She examined the page more closely, just to make sure there were no visible flaws in the piece, and recognized the painting on the wall above the commode. It was the painting from her own living-room wall."

"So what did she do?"

"She immediately placed an order for the table, paid a cash deposit, gave a friend's name for her own, and pressed the dealer for an early delivery date. Then she went straight to the police. They staked out her house, and tapped the dealer's lines. The woman went around making noisy plans for a big trip. The night she left, the thieves arrived and the police busted a ring. Turned out they were working all over France, paying a photographer to break in and photograph pieces, then not stealing anything until a buyer had been found. Kept them from needing to have the stolen goods around for long."

"Is that how your Kantor gets his hands on all those goods?" Tim's voice was taunting. "You telling stories on your own boss?"

"Oh, do be quiet, Tim."

"Absolutely," Andrew agreed cheerfully. "Even if you were right, our lad here wouldn't let on, now, would he?"

Tim subsided behind his drink. "All I know is, it's uncommon strange how he keeps turning up with these little gems nobody's ever heard of before."

"It's because Alexander keeps his nose to the grindstone and not to his glass," Sarah countered. "Isn't that right, Jeffrey?"

"It sure is," he replied, rising to his feet. "And you'll have to excuse me. His plane arrives first thing tomorrow morning, and I've got to go out to Heathrow to meet it."

"Where'd you say he was coming in from, lad?" Andrew asked.

"I didn't," Jeffrey replied. "Good-night, everybody."

Jeffrey arrived at Heathrow Airport half an hour before the flight was scheduled to land. He sat in the Rolls' front seat, somewhat embarrassed by the stares of passersby. The driver was new, but he came from their traditional car-hire firm, and had clearly been warned in advance of Alexander's abhorrence for small talk.

The chauffeur eased the massive car in front of the arrivals gate, then spoke for the first time since greeting Jeffrey at the shop, "I'll be in the VIP lot at the terminal side, sir. I'll have to ask you to come out to let me know if the plane's been delayed. I can't sit there but a few minutes."

"Right." The door shut behind him with a satisfactory thunk. It was one of the Rolls' trademarks; all the pieces fit together as though designed to last several generations.

Jeffrey stood by the doors to baggage claim and found himself growing excited. He had not seen his boss in almost a month, had not spoken with him for over three weeks. The distances between Alexander Kantor's visits to London were growing longer, the periods when he was lost and gone and out of contact easier to bear.

Large metal doors pulled back and permitted a slightly dazed Alexander Kantor to walk through, followed by a porter carrying three Louis Vuitton cases. Jeffrey stepped forward and took the matching briefcase from Alexander's limp hand. Flying always left his boss exhausted.

"Ah, Jeffrey. You received my fax."

"Over this way," he said, grasping Alexander's elbow and pointing toward the far doors with his free hand. "I confirmed the fax the day it arrived."

"Did you? When was that?"

"Last Friday. Are you sure you want to talk about this right now?"

"Quite right." He rubbed a weary brow. "Why on earth did they do away with shipping liners? Allow a body to arrive in proper style."

"You can't get to London from Geneva by liner, Alexander. The Alps are in the way." Kantor now had his only residence in Geneva. All the others—London, Monte Carlo, Sicily, Montreal, a flat on Copacabana in Rio—had been gradually sold off over the previous twelve months. The only explanation he had given Jeffrey was that the cost of keeping servants on three continents was becoming ridiculous.

Kantor shot his assistant a peeved look. "You are positively enjoying yourself. I had no idea you had sadistic tendencies."

"It's just that you are so seldom in less than top form." Jeffrey allowed Kantor to pass through the exit before him. "Did you have a good trip?"

"Don't be ridiculous. There is no such thing as a good trip on an airplane."

"I've always thought flying was great," Jeffrey replied, signaling to their driver.

"Flying is never great. You can have a ten-course meal, watch the finest film since *The Maltese Falcon,* be served by a matched pair of angelic hostesses, and your flight would still not be great. Interesting, perhaps, but never great."

"You're slurring."

"Of course I'm slurring. I always try to nap on a plane, which makes me more tired than I was before I started, and I always slur. Where is Roger?"

Roger was Kantor's driver of choice in London. As far as Jeffrey could tell, his entire vocabulary consisted of three words: very good, sir. "With a trio of golfers in Scotland. Gone all week."

Alexander replied to the driver's murmured greeting with a nod and allowed himself to be guided into the Rolls' leather backseat. Jeffrey supervised the loading of the cases, tipped the porter, and climbed in beside Kantor.

"Claridge's, driver," Kantor said.

"Sorry, Alexander," Jeffrey said. "We don't have time."

"What on earth are you talking about?"

"Count di Garibaldi is waiting for us at the shop. He is on his way overseas, and he insists on speaking to you personally about a certain item."

Kantor let out a groan. "I positively do not have the strength to deal with that man."

"You always say that when you arrive, and in fifteen minutes you're always fine."

"Am I really?"

"Always." Jeffrey reached over to the front seat, retrieved his briefcase, extracted a thermos and a pair of embossed mugs, and said, "Would you care for a cup?"

"My dear boy, how thoughtful. I have no idea what they serve on those planes, but it is most certainly not coffee."

He handed over a steaming mug, sweetened as Kantor preferred. "You always say that, too."

"Am I becoming so predictable in my old age?" He took another sip and color began returning to his features. "Your coffee is improving."

"Betty accused me the other day of trying to dissolve the roof of her mouth."

"Americans declare anything stronger than old dishwater to be dangerous." He took another sip. "Yes, I do believe I will survive after all."

They sped down the M4 until the morning traffic backed up and reduced their progress to a crawl. It took them over an hour to arrive in Mayfair, by which time the thermos was empty, most of the papers in Jeffrey's briefcase had been covered, and Alexander's traditionally alert good nature had been fully restored.

He rewarded his assistant with an approving look. "You have done well, Jeffrey. Remarkably well."

"Thanks. It's getting to be a lot of fun."

"I'm so glad to hear it. A business like ours requires that sort of attitude. Otherwise it is next to impossible to close a sale." He studied Jeffrey a moment longer. "And you are weathering my absences well?"

"Easier each time. I do have the odd moment, though, usually late at night after you've been out of touch for a couple of weeks. I wake up in a sweat, wondering what I'd do if you didn't show up again."

Alexander Kantor turned toward the window streaked with misting rain. "There has been a method to the madness, I assure you."

"I figured there was."

"Yes?" He turned back around. "And what did you suppose was the purpose?"

"To test me."

"Obviously. But in what way?"

"To see if I could be trusted when there was no way you could be looking." Jeffrey took a breath. "To leave me with no set rules, no real parachute, a lot of opportunities to sell at one price and record another, buy and sell on the sly, that sort of thing."

"Quite right. You've done very well, I might add."

"I thought you had some of the customers in there, you know, watching and reporting back to you."

"Of course I did." He reached to the burl table which folded out from the driver's seat-back and lifted the sheaf of ledger pages. "But the real evidence is right here, Jeffrey. Not only are you scrupulous in your record-keeping, you have done an exceptional job in researching our pieces, presenting them in the best possible light, placing them at auction houses when appropriate—basically, in coming to master the various facets of your new profession. I am indeed pleased."

Jeffrey felt his face flush with pleasure. "I've tried to be careful."

"You've been meticulous. I shall return to these compliments under more conducive circumstances. Now tell me—" He leafed through them to the section labeled *Miscellaneous Expenses.* "You have several items here for salary. I take it this is not for a raise you have given yourself."

"No." Jeffrey tugged at his ear. He had thought this over several times, was still not sure how to handle it. "It was one of those judgment calls I had to make myself."

"Go on."

"I needed someone who could help in the shop when I was out at auctions or seeing out-of-town buyers or visiting another business. Somebody pretty much available to work only when I needed them."

The smoky gray eyes gave away nothing. "And how long has this person been employed, may I ask?"

"About four weeks."

"Since just after my trip began, then. And why did we not discuss this on the phone?"

Yes. That was the clincher. Jeffrey swallowed. "It's a little hard to explain."

The Rolls turned onto South Audley one block up from Mount Street. Alexander leaned forward. "Find some place to pull over and park, please, driver."

"Right you are, sir."

"Go on, Jeffrey. I'm all ears."

He took a breath. "She is more than just a shop assistant."

"Ah." Kantor was visibly relieved. "I understand. You did not wish to discuss your personal situation on the phone with me, and you did not want to discuss hiring her without telling me everything."

He nodded, immensely glad to have it out in the open. "If I knew what our personal situation really was, maybe I wouldn't have such a tough time talking about it."

"We can leave that for later. Perhaps I shall be able to help you see the situation more clearly. For now we shall focus on the business aspect. And I must say, Jeffrey, your judgment call, as you describe it, was not the optimum one. You should have felt obliged to tell me about this young lady immediately. You have entrusted the shop and all its contents to an unknown. That simply will not do."

Jeffrey nodded miserably. "It started off as an emergency. I had to go out to Sussex to see the Countess Drake. You know what she's like. She called up and said it was now or never, and it was that Florentine dresser you've been talking about with her for as long as I've been with the shop. I had a buyer from Spain who had telephoned for an appointment that same afternoon. And Mrs. Grayson had been called out of town the day before. Her daughter went into labor with Mrs. Grayson's first grandchild."

Mrs. Grayson was a mild-mannered old dear who had been with Kantor's shop for years. She did little more than mind the store when everyone else was away, but she did this with honest diligence. Her courtesy and genuine friendliness ensured that customers returned to learn more details or conclude a transaction with Alexander or Jeffrey.

It had taken several months before Mrs. Grayson would give Jeffrey her approval, for she was fiercely loyal to her oft-absent director. Yet once it was granted, it was done with the wholehearted warmth of a proud mother. She made no bones over her dislike of the previous three assistants Alexander had brought in, none of whom had lasted a year. Jeffrey had known an inordinate amount of pride over his acceptance into Mrs. Grayson's fold. During his boss's long and silent absences, it was the only signal he had received of a job well done.

"So I asked Katya to come over and cover for me," Jeffrey finished, mightily worried.

"Katya," Alexander murmured. "A lovely name."

"Yes, sir." He swiped at his brow. "Anyway, the next week I had this group over from New York, fourteen people in the shop at once, and Mrs. Grayson let me know that even if I threatened her with dismissal she was not coming back. It seems there's been some kind of health problem with her daughter. Mrs. Grayson is staying in the Midlands until everything is okay. Anyway, with the tour and a lot of other things going on right then, Katya came over and worked three more afternoons. And then there was something the week after that—I don't remember what. I had a terrible time just getting her to accept a salary; we had a real argument over that one."

"Did you really. How remarkable."

"By then it was already sort of a done deal. I started to try and call and tell you, if I could track you down. But like I said, I honestly didn't know how to describe our own situation. So I left it. I'm sorry. I realize I messed up."

"Indeed you did. So. Consider yourself chastised, Jeffrey. And see that it does not happen again."

He realized that it was over. "Thanks, Mr. Kantor. It won't."

"Alexander, please. Fine. Now that's behind us. So tell me about this Katya. Is she as lovely as her name?"

Jeffrey nodded. "It fits her perfectly."

"An attractive woman who works well with customers is quite an asset. You obviously trust her; I do hope it is not based solely upon your emotions."

"No, sir. She's very religious, and her honesty is something that I've never had to concern myself about. She's one of the most honorable people I've ever met. I don't think it would even occur to her to steal."

"Is she English?"

"American. Her father was from the States. But she's lived here in England for over ten years."

"Her mother is not American?"

Jeffrey's brow furrowed in concentration. "Katya doesn't like to talk about her past all that much. Her mother is from the western part of Poland—I've forgotten the name. She told me only once."

A new light entered Kantor's eyes. "Silesia perhaps?"

"That's it. Silesia. Her mother came from there to the West some time after the war."

Kantor nodded slowly. "And what does the young lady do with the remainder of her time?"

"She's a third-year student at the University of London. She's in East European studies, specializing in the German and Polish languages."

"How remarkable." He straightened and spoke to the front seat. "Thank you, driver. You may proceed now."

Kantor remained silent and pensive as the Rolls cruised up the block, waited at the light, turned down Mount Street. Jeffrey let himself out as the driver held Alexander's door, then followed his boss into the shop.

"Ah, at last." Count Garibaldi rose from the chair that he had pulled up close to Katya's. "My good friend Alexander, you have saved me from disaster. If you had arrived just two minutes later, I would have been swept away by this lovely face and proposed.

You know my heart. It leaps forward with little concern to this frail body. I would have lost our wager for sure."

"But what is the value of a wager in comparison to a new love?" Alexander extended his hand. "It is wonderful to see you again, Ricardo."

Count Ricardo Bastinado Grupello di Garibaldi prided himself on being a man of few illusions. He had grown from an unknown immigrant of doubtful heritage into one of London's leading property developers, and his title and courtly manners were as false as his teeth. He did not care who knew it, did not care what was said about him behind his back. He considered the manners and the title and the polish all a part of the game of being rich. Count di Garibaldi had been both rich and poor, and anyone who believed it was better to be poor was a certifiable fruitcake in the count's book.

The count was a dried-up old prune who was so sure he would outlive his friend Alexander that he had insisted they wager on it. His nose was the only feature that had withstood the ravages of time. It was an aristocrat's beak, a craggy mountain that could nest eagles in each nostril. It was a very useful nose. He could raise his chin about one millimeter and snub the world down its double-barreled length. It gave a deceptive sense of strength to an otherwise shriveled frame.

All the count had to live for was his collection of antiques and his seventeen children. His five ex-wives no longer spoke to him. All seventeen children idolized him. They had to. The count demanded it. But he could not control his ex-wives because of what he considered to be the most pestilent of modern inventions—alimony. They had more than they would ever need, so they delighted in scorning him and calling him foul names. His children, however, were a different matter.

In return for seventeen most generous monthly payments, he demanded peace with him and peace with each other. Anyone who let a spoiled nature run wild within the family was swiftly stripped to a bread and water diet. A couple of months without petrol money for the Ferrari, and the worst of them learned to stew in silence. The count did not demand love; he was too realistic to insist on the impossible. He was quite happy to settle for peace.

The count stretched his bloodless lips in a smile of genuine pleasure. "You are well, Alexander?"

"Perfectly."

"No morning aches and pains?"

"I would never permit myself such an indulgence."

The count's smile broadened as he clapped his more virile friend on the shoulder. "You don't stand a chance, Alexander. I'll beat you by ten years."

"This is one wager I do not look forward to winning," Kantor replied. "Which I shall."

The bet was for fifty thousand pounds. On the day the other died, the lawyers for their estates were instructed to issue a check—providing the survivor still had the strength to drink a glass of single-malt whiskey neat, then dance a jig on the other's grave.

"I must compliment you on your choice of assistants," the count said.

Kantor turned to where Katya stood toward the back of the shop. In the soft lighting reflected from the highly polished surfaces, her features glowed. "I confess this arrangement was not of my choosing," Alexander replied. "But she certainly meets with my approval. How do you do, my dear. I am Alexander Kantor."

She walked forward and presented her hand with a poise Jeffrey found remarkable. She stood so erect as to appear regally aloof, a dark-haired vision with eyes the color of heavens seen through the smoke of a winter's fire. "Katya Nichols. Jeffrey has told me so much about you, Mr. Kantor."

"Has he really." Kantor did a stiff-backed bow over her hand, then said something in a tongue Jeffrey assumed was Polish. Katya responded with cool grace in the same language. Her remark caused Kantor's eyes to broaden momentarily. They exchanged more words; then Alexander repeated his formal bow. He returned to English, saying, "This is indeed an unexpected pleasure, Miss Nichols."

Jeffrey thought his heart would burst with pride.

"My dear Alexander, if you would kindly return your attention to the business at hand," the count said sharply. "You may be interested to know that I was not referring to the young lady. I have already been informed as to how she came to grace your establishment. I was speaking of your young man here. I am not sure you realize what a find you have under your roof."

Kantor's eyes lighted upon Jeffrey. "I am well aware how fortunate I am."

"Nonsense," the count snorted. "How could you, since you are scarcely ever here? Now listen to your good friend, Alexander. The only passion left to me is my collection. I would not joke over something as important to me as my passion, you know that. There are few dealers with whom I consider it a genuine pleasure to do business. If you know what is good for you, you will do everything in your power to hold on to him."

"I intend to," Kantor replied. "And now that you have thoroughly embarrassed the young man, shall we get down to business?"

"Very well." The tone turned lofty. "I had thought to purchase that rather poor example of a writing desk you have propped up there against the back wall. But your young man must have misplaced the proper price tag, and I therefore wanted to take it up directly with you."

"The price is correct."

"You have not even asked him what he quoted me."

"I don't need to. You have just told me what an exceptional find he is. I am quite prepared to stand on whatever price he quoted."

The piece in question was a seventeenth-century *escritorio*, a narrow cabinet with a fold-down face used for writing and fronted by as many as two dozen small drawers. In this case there were twelve, forming an upside-down *U* above and around a central door. When opened, the door revealed yet another door, this one opening only when a tiny switch elegantly concealed inside one of the drawers was pressed in just the right manner. The drawers and central door were inlaid with a mosaic of mother-of-pearl, brought in at enormous cost from some mysterious island on the other side of the globe by a wooden ship flying flags and as many as thirty-six sails. Jeffrey had spent long hours fantasizing about what the world had been like when pieces such as this had been created, and the stories connected to their centuries-long journeys to Mount Street.

The price on that particular work of art was seventy thousand pounds.

"Preposterous," the count complained. "No writing table on earth is worth that much money, especially not one which made its debut in the back room of some second-rate counting house."

Jeffrey cleared his throat. "Perhaps I should mention that we've received another offer."

The count paled. "When?"

"Yesterday. A gentleman from Canada. I told him I would have to wait until this morning, as you had been granted first refusal."

The count's bluster dropped immediately to weak relief. "Bless you, young man. That was truly kind."

Jeffrey ignored the fact that Alexander's approving gaze rested upon him. "I knew you were interested in it, Count. It would have been incorrect not to allow you a chance to make a counter offer."

The count glanced at Alexander, then turned to Jeffrey, "Shall we say seventy-five?"

"Perfect," Jeffrey replied. "When shall I have it delivered?"

———

Since selling his Belgravia flat, Alexander had made Claridge's his London residence whenever he was in town. That evening he and Jeffrey departed the hotel for the *Ognisko,* the Polish club on Prince's Gate, one block off Hyde Park. It was a holdover from the time when post-war Polish refugees with money and status all gathered and lived in the vicinity. With the passing of time, rents in that area grew from high to vicious and on to levels that were affordable only by the super-rich and by corporations seeking headquarter addresses. Yet the Polish club lingered on, secure in its distinguished position because it was a freehold property.

The Polish club had a simple brass plaque on the pillar outside the entrance, announcing in a most understated way that the entire building belonged to the *Ognisko,* the Polish word for hearth. In days gone by, it was a haven for strangers forced by war's uncaring hand to leave behind home and beloved country, and begin again in a strange new world.

The club was open to all who wished to enter, and served excellent Polish dishes at what for London were extremely reasonable prices. In the seventies and eighties, however, as families had moved on and others had died out, attendance slowly dwindled to a handful of old faithfuls.

"Thank you, driver," Kantor said as he allowed the chauffeur to hold his door. "We shall be several hours, if you would care to dine and come back."

"Very good, sir."

Jeffrey waited until Kantor had started up the stairs before turning back to the driver and saying in a low voice, "It'd be a good idea if you'd stick around for half an hour before taking off. We might not be staying as long as he thinks."

"Half an hour it is, sir."

"Thanks."

They stepped through the wide double doors and were immediately awash in a flood of noise. Alexander Kantor hesitated, then stepped into the foyer and bade the two ladies staffing the front desk a good evening. One immediately went into the bar and returned with the club manager, a crusty old gentleman. His features were a series of jagged lines and caverns, carried on a body held stiffly erect despite the weight of seventy-some years.

"Welcome, Mr. Kantor, welcome." The man grasped Alexander's hand and gave a formal bow. "It is always an honor to have you join us."

Alexander glanced over the man's shoulder into the bar. It was wall-to-wall people, loud music, and thundering noise. "Sigmund, what on earth is happening?"

"Ah, Mr. Kantor, it's just awful." The man showed tragic concern. "We've been discovered!"

"I beg your pardon?" As was his habit, Kantor continued to speak in English so long as Jeffrey was in listening range. Even with clients who stubbornly insisted on remaining in the old tongue, Kantor would politely continue to respond in English. If furrows appeared around the client's brow, Jeffrey would normally get up and leave the room. The only exception was when Alexander was dealing with someone whose English was not good; he then went to great pains to translate and include Jeffrey in even the most mundane of discussions.

"It was the Sunday *Times*," the old man said, his voice almost a wail. "Their restaurant writer was brought here by Polish friends, or so the article said. Then some awful magazine called the *Tatler* came by, and since then it's been nonstop."

"It's like this every night?"

The old man nodded. "You should see it on the weekends, Mr. Kantor. Simply dreadful."

"I see. Any chance of a table?"

"Oh, Mr. Kantor." It was clearly what the old man had feared hearing. "If only you had called ahead."

"Of course, Sigmund." Kantor gave the old man's shoulder a conciliatory pat. "Don't let it trouble you."

"I could perhaps have something around midnight if you'd care to wait."

"I think not." Kantor grasped the old man's hand in both of his, gave it a warm shake. "We shall return another night, old friend. Rest assured of that."

"Early is best, Mr. Kantor. It's not so bad before seven."

The driver sprang from the car as soon as they appeared. Alexander asked Jeffrey, "You told him to wait?"

Jeffrey nodded. "I thought maybe it would be better for you to see that for yourself."

"Quite right. I suppose we should travel on to Daquise, then, don't you?"

"Fine with me."

"Number Twenty Thurloe Street, driver," Alexander instructed. "Near the South Kensington Tube Station."

"Very good, sir."

Daquise was another holdover, but from a decidedly different strata of transferred Polish society. It was a single long room set in a block of other small, slightly seedy shops.

South Kensington was a district in perpetual transition. Daquise was located in an area at the scale's lower end; the Rolls' arrival stopped traffic and turned heads a half block away. The restaurant's tables were linoleum-topped, its vinyl-covered booths and seats too old to be truly comfortable. But the food was excellent, and its clientele immensely loyal.

"The old menus looked like choir hymnals from a bankrupt church," Kantor said once the manager had greeted them, led them to a choice seat, discussed the menu, and left to give their order to the kitchen. Kantor's good humor had revived considerably. "They were enormous padded red-leather affairs, and battered as a third-rate French hotel bed."

"You've told me," Jeffrey said, nodding his thanks to the waitress who set down their fluted glasses of steaming tea.

"I realize that," Kantor replied. "Now you will wipe that long-suffering look off your face and play the politely interested employee."

Jeffrey cocked his head to one side, made round eyes, asked, "How's that?"

"Ridiculous. It's not often I indulge in reminiscing."

"Just every time you come over," Jeffrey replied, thoroughly enjoying himself.

"Which is not often enough by the look of things."

"This is the best quarter the shop has ever had."

Kantor waved a casual dismissal. "I dread to think what we could have accomplished were I daily at the helm."

"Bankruptcy?" Jeffrey kept his smile hidden. "Public shame? Fire-sale signs on Mount Street?"

Their evenings together became times of ever-deeper discussions and ever-greater pleasure for the young man. It was only recently, one evening after receiving Kantor's arrival fax, that Jeffrey had wondered if perhaps the old gentleman was lonely.

Kantor gave him a frosty glance. "Remind me why I put up with your over-active tongue."

"Because it doesn't detach. And because I'm good at my job. And because I'm honest."

"Are you now."

"Totally."

"Yes." Kantor's eyes creased upward. "I suppose you are at that. So where was I?"

"Goodness only knows."

"The menus. Thank you. Yes, the prices were all written by hand and in a shaky Polish script, then rubbed out and redone so often no one could read them."

"Which is why they finally purchased these awful plastic things," Jeffrey finished for him.

"Do I truly bore you that badly with my little stories?"

"Truly?"

"I would not ask if I did not mean it."

"Then truly, I look forward to your visits more than I like to admit even to myself."

Carefully the old gentleman sipped his tea, his face immobile. "Why is that, do you suppose?"

"The truth again." Jeffrey took a breath. "I have never met anyone like you. Never. You are a genuine individual in a carbon-copy world. Neither age nor success nor wealth has ground you to grayness."

"You've obviously given this quite a lot of thought."

Jeffrey nodded. "I've wondered if I'd ever have the chance to tell you. Or the nerve."

"I see." Kantor seemed momentarily nonplussed.

"You're one of the few people I've ever met who is never boring. And with all the changes you've pushed me toward, there's always been a perfectly good reason. I've never felt as if I'm being forced to fit some egotistical role."

"I'd rather try to reform the Rock of Gibraltar."

"You don't know how rare that is," Jeffrey replied. "And I'm more grateful than I'll ever be able to say for your giving me a job that I love. Truly."

"Well." Kantor was clearly at a loss. "I say, Jeffrey, I do believe you're blushing."

"It comes with the confession."

"No doubt, no doubt."

They were saved from further embarrassment by the arrival of their dinner. They ate in comfortable silence until Jeffrey laid down his fork, pushed his plate back, and said, "I come here a lot."

That brought another start. "When I'm not in town? Do you really?"

"I like the food."

"How fascinating."

"A lot. And the people." He motioned toward an old crone nodding in the corner. She was nursing a glass of tea, drawing out a nightly ritual, staving away the loneliness of an empty flat. She wore a blue velvet turban and an ancient diamond tiara. Her face was a mask of sagging folds, her nose a beak. "Everybody in here has jumped from the pages of a Tolstoy novel."

"Mmmm." The old woman noticed their eyes. Alexander gave her a grave seated bow, murmured a greeting in Polish. She responded with a regal nod, replied with a voice made ragged from disuse, and returned to her own internal musing.

"The correct term is *staruszka*. It means little old lady, but only in the nicest of terms. The word for old in Polish is *stary*, a term I'm coming to know on a too-intimate basis."

"I've never thought of you as old."

"How kind. Yes, if truth is to be the evening's main course, then I must confess that my years have become a burden. You must experience the weight of years for yourself, Jeffrey, before you can really understand."

"You've had a good life."

"That I have, in part at least. Too good to leave it willingly behind. But for the first time since the war, I feel as though I can look ahead and see death's door. It's not that far away anymore. Just around the next bend."

Jeffrey felt the room grow chill. "You've seen a doctor?"

"Many doctors. They all say the same thing. I am fine. I have some good years ahead of me. There is nothing wrong. They have leeched more money from me than even I thought possible, and tortured me with so many machines and needles I have begun to cringe every time I pass a hospital. They with all their modern wisdom have found nothing. But I know, young man. My body does not lie. We have passed more than sixty-five years in each other's company, and come to like one another quite a lot. I heed its voice as often as I can, gracing it with comfortable beds and sensible foods and adequate rest. It in turn permits me the foibles of an occasional cigar and a third brandy on a cold night. In all the years since the war, it has punished me with nothing more serious than a stuffy nose."

"And now?"

"And now. And now it says it is growing tired. It no longer willingly rises when I ask, nor responds to simple pleasures. Food has begun to taste flat, wine bitter, cigars stale. Worse still are the whispers of what is yet to come. Lingering illness. Pain. Embarrassing moments. Lapses of memory. The prospect of growing old distresses me more than anything has since the war."

"I would really like to hear about your escape from Poland if you ever feel like talking."

"Another time, dear boy. I couldn't discuss the escape without referring to what came before it, and to speak of that and the loss of my faculties all in the same night would simply be too much. I will tell you of this, I assure you. I can see your interest is genuine, and I will honor it. There is no need for barriers between us. Honesty becomes a lie if it is doled out in half measures. But not tonight."

Jeffrey nodded, hurting without knowing why. "You look great to me."

"Thank you. I feel it, too. This small dose of truth between friends has done me a world of good, more than all the doctors I have visited over the past months. But the whispers I hear are not vague, and my time on this earth no longer appears as endless as it once did. What's worse, I have begun to question my life. A most uncomfortable pasttime, I assure you. But with this unmarked door up ahead, it suddenly becomes much more appealing to turn around and look back. Only I cannot do this with the same comforting blindness with which I lived the moment. I am finding my own innate honesty has become a finger pointing at flaws and errors I have managed to ignore for a lifetime."

Jeffrey hoped his voice would not betray him as he said, "I think you're one of the finest men I've ever met, Alexander."

"Thank you, dear boy. That means more to me than you will ever know. But I fear my own selfish blindness can protect me no longer from the failings of this life I have been privileged to call my own. Not, that is, if I am going to continue to find solace from the future by looking back. There are few things that I shall be able to change, I recognize that. Age and my own disposition makes change at this late date most unappealing. But there are a few wrongs that I shall attempt to right in my remaining days. And a few of my better actions that I must endeavor to anchor against the unforeseen. Which brings us to the matter of our trip."

Jeffrey sat up straight. "Our?"

"Not in here. I may have been lured into a public confession, but I shall not discuss confidential business in a public place." He signaled to the waitress. "Come along. It's time for a quiet glass at your club."

———

Jeffrey's club was around the corner from Berkley Square, where the nightingale sang no more—and even if it did, no one situated farther away than the next tree limb would be able to hear the melody. Nowadays the square was awash with an unending toneless symphony of blares, hoots, revving motors, angry shouts, jackhammers, squealing brakes, snarled traffic, and construction turmoil. Berkley Square had been transformed from a relatively quiet alcove to a focal point for Piccadilly-directed traffic, compliments of London's one-way road network. The constant man-made storm had not affected rents, however. People paid staggering sums for the Berkley Square address, long after all charm had evaporated in a cloud of diesel fumes.

The club was a short half block up a street as nondescript as the club's entrance; a gray portal opened in a gray building on a gray street that shrugged its way around a corner and ended quietly in an alleyway. Inside, uniformed porters guarded the entrance with respectful vigilance, offering members a properly subdued greeting. Jeffrey had chosen the Landsdowne Club because it was close to his home and to the shop, had an excellent sports hall, and because it was available. Many of the London clubs granted membership only to those with title or wealth or renown, and very rarely at all to foreigners. Admission to the Landsdowne had been Alexander's gift at the end of Jeffrey's probation. As far as he was concerned, it was the perfect fit.

Jeffrey had once seen an etching, made in 1811, which vividly displayed the rural atmosphere of the region. At that time, the Landsdowne mansion had stood within several walled acres of garden, and had been surrounded on three sides by open fields.

By the onset of the twentieth century, the gardens were long gone, the fields no more. A road expansion decreed by the London government in the thirties rudely demolished the Landsdowne manor's front forty feet, taking with it a good many of the most beautiful chambers. But as far as Jeffrey was concerned, those that remained were more than adequate.

In a sitting room by the bar, Lord Shelburne, Prime Minister under King George III, had signed the declaration that ended the Revolutionary War and granted the United States its independence. The main hall, a vast affair with a seventy-foot arched and gilded ceiling, was once a central locale in the busy London social season. Jeffrey loved to dine on the club's traditional fare of roast lamb or beef, stare out over the heads of nodding elderly members, and strain to hear the echoes of violins fill a room lit by vast candelabras.

Nowadays the room was seldom more than a third full, and was a most comfortable place to come and sit by the roaring fire and read undisturbed, the chamber's huge dimensions a welcome change from his cramped apartment.

Jeffrey allowed Alexander to lead them to a set of comfortable chairs near the fire and well removed from the few other occupied tables.

"You know the basis for these clubs is to duplicate the atmosphere of the British school system," Alexander said as they took their seats. "The surroundings are grandiose, the food inedible, the furniture tacky, and the rooms frigid even in summer."

Jeffrey saw no need to tell him how impressed he was by his surroundings. "What was the first club you ever went to?"

"Let's see. Ah yes, that would be the Carlton. Every Conservative prime minister since Peel has belonged."

"Even Margaret Thatcher?"

"Oh, most definitely. They made her an honorary man. Some of those members who put her name forward said she was the only member of her cabinet who deserved to wear trousers, so in their eyes it was not breaking with the all-male tradition."

A waiter appeared at his elbow; Alexander ordered brandy for them both. When they were again alone, he said, "I must tell you, Jeffrey, that I am vastly impressed with your young lady."

"I'm not sure she's my anything."

Alexander waved the comment aside. "What you have not seen is the way she looks at you when you are not watching."

"You're kidding."

"About matters of the heart I never, as you say, kid. Although I do not know her yet, I am coming to know you and trust your judgment. You have chosen well, Jeffrey."

"And if she doesn't choose me?"

"Give it time."

"That's easy for you to say."

"Yes, it is indeed easier to view such matters from a painless distance." He gave Jeffrey a comradely smile. "But if an outsider may be permitted to add his ten pence worth, I think your chances are perhaps better than you think. The tenderness in her gaze touches even this crusty old heart of mine."

Jeffrey gave him a sidelong glance. "Are you sure we're talking about the same girl?"

"It is a good thing to find someone with whom you can share your work, Jeffrey. The antique trade has clearly become a passion with you, and this pleases me enormously. It is one of the essential ingredients of success in our profession. Yet a passion is either the strongest bonding force possible within a relationship, or a barrier you will fight against for all your days."

Jeffrey nodded his understanding. "Is that why you never married? You never found someone to share your passion?"

Kantor took a long time to reply. "I lost my love in the war."

"Oh. I'm really sorry." Jeffrey hesitated, then added, "Nobody back in the States ever said anything about you losing somebody before coming to the West."

"That is not what I said," Kantor replied solemnly. "My love died in the war. What happens to the bodies after such an event is inconsequential."

After a moment's silence, Alexander went on. "As a matter of fact, Jeffrey, there may be a way of my assisting your own affairs. It has to do with the purpose of this little discussion. You don't speak German, as I recall."

"No. Some French, that's all."

"But Katya does."

"Fluently, so she says."

The waiter approached their isolated corner, set down two linen napkins and upon them a pair of heavy crystal snifters containing ample portions of aged amber. Kantor paused to swirl the brandy under his nose, sipped, breathed out that first heady aroma, and said, "For a shop like ours, to sell well is only half the game. Some would say even less. I do not mean to belittle your responsibilities, however."

"But we've got to have something to sell," Jeffrey agreed. The excitement of possibly being partner to one of the antique trade's best-kept secrets added its own flavor to the evening. "Finding the right product at the right price is what separates the men from the boys."

"Precisely. We have no guaranteed source of supply in this game, you see. Nor do we know from whence our next piece will come. There is only a limited number of quality antiques available, and a veritable fury of sharks seeking them out. All the major auction houses right the world around, shops who compete with ours from Tokyo to New York, many of our own customers who seek to lower their purchase price with a direct buy; they hunt for the same items as we do."

Kantor lowered his silver-gray mane, and sought answers from the swirling brandy. He said to his goblet, "There are times when a risk must be taken in order for life to progress. But knowing that the time has arrived and actually taking the step can be two quite different matters."

Jeffrey sipped from his own glass and held back on the dozens of answers that came to mind. No amount of pushing would help here.

"There are a few things which I have shared with almost no one. Were I to include you in this very small group, Jeffrey, the only gratitude I wish to receive from you, the only thanks, the only show of respect, is that you would keep my secret and guard it well."

"I understand."

"Excellent. It so happens that I have a supplier who has disappeared, leaving me with several unsold pieces—some quite remarkable antiques, really. All on consignment. Besides that, there is the matter of the money I owe him for those which have already been sold."

Alexander paused as a pair of slow-moving elderly gentlemen ambled by their table, then said quietly, "Something over eight hundred thousand pounds."

One and a half million dollars. Jeffrey gave a low whistle.

"This sum has been collecting in a special account for over a year," Alexander said. "I have heard nothing from him since the one and only shipment was received."

Jeffrey waited, decided it was time to ask the one impossible question. "Where did it come from?"

Alexander eyed him over the rim of his goblet. "You are aware of what you are asking."

"Yes."

"I see that you are. Very well, I agree. It is time to tell you." Alexander sipped his brandy, then went on. "About two years ago I was approached at an auction in Geneva by a man I had never seen before. Which is a surprise, I assure you, especially considering the quality and the number of articles he had to offer. Were we speaking of only one or two antiques, it could be entirely possible that I was meeting a dealer new to the realm in which we operate. But he showed me photographs of over thirty antiques. Thirty, Jeffrey. All of them absolutely first rate, I assure you. It was an astonishing collection."

Jeffrey understood Alexander's surprise. The number of dealers at such levels was quite small. It was part of any professional's job to know all the major players. Thirty world-class antiques was for any house an immense number; coming from a total unknown it was unheard of.

"The man told me he was an arts and antiques dealer from Schwerin," Alexander said. "Have you ever heard of the place?"

"No."

"It is the capital of Mecklenburg-Vorpommern, the northernmost state in what previously was East Germany. This contact came about two months before the Wall collapsed. Already there were rumblings, with street demonstrations and so forth, but no one imagined it would all move as swiftly as it did. In any case, I found it astonishing that a perfect stranger from such an unstable region would approach me with such an offer."

Jeffrey snapped his fingers. "King Freddy's drawers!"

"I beg your pardon?"

"The Kaiser's chest of drawers. That's how I always thought of it. Putting a nickname on a piece like that helps me not to get overawed by how much money we're talking about."

"How remarkable. Well, it so happens you are correct. That was indeed one of the pieces included in this little collection."

"We had a little trouble with the sale," Jeffrey said, and related the story of the professor's arrival at Christie's.

"I am most sorry to hear of the hue and cry," Alexander said when Jeffrey was finished. "Although I suppose it is not overly important who in the end acquires the piece, I thoroughly detest strong-arm tactics of any form. You must find me the name and address of the industrialist, Jeffrey."

"You're going to offer him something at cost, aren't you?"

"I must seek to make amends. It is the least I can do." Alexander eyed his assistant. "Why are you smiling?"

"No reason. You were saying about the East German dealer."

"Precisely. I was most concerned that I not become involved with a thief. But his documents were impeccable, Jeffrey. Flawless. He had papers declaring him to be the director of Schwerin's official antiques store, which of course would make him a member of the Communist Party, but I have managed to do business with such people in the past. Never from East Germany, however. I had no contacts there whatsoever."

"Which made it all the more suspicious," Jeffrey added.

"Indeed. But he said that I had come highly recommended as a man whom they could trust. Honesty in these matters was essential, I was informed. In any case, he also had official export documents, and permitted me to telephone both the East German Embassy in Berne and the Department of Arts and Antiques in East Berlin to confirm who he was."

Alexander waved his empty snifter in the direction of an attentive waiter. "What was more, the antiques were already in a bonded warehouse in Hamburg, waiting for me to pick them up."

"Did he tell you how he had obtained them?"

"An excellent question. One, I might add, which is not always possible to ask. However, in this case I positively insisted on being informed. It appeared that a number of very senior officials within the East German Communist Party had read the writing on the wall, and were seeking to unload items that they hoped would help ease their own personal transition to a new capitalist empire."

"Amazing," Jeffrey breathed.

"Indeed so, but also most believable. And an explanation which could not be checked up on, I might add. My calls resulted in nothing but confirmation of everything that the man had told me—everything, I hasten to add, which could be confirmed."

"And you want me to go find him."

"Or find out what has happened," Alexander replied. "There is always the risk that our gentleman has been swept away in the tide of change. If that is the case, then we must try to find which of the actual sellers is still around and seeking his due.

"You should not need to stay for more than two days," Alexander continued. "If it requires more time than this, you will need to return later. There are some pressing matters that cannot wait, a shipment which must be seen to. Do you think Katya could mind the shop for a week by herself?"

"Without a doubt. There's a lot she doesn't know, but she is very honest with the clients, and is careful to write down their questions for me to answer. Sometimes it actually works out better that way, because we then have their addresses on file, and the clients like her a lot. Her classes are over for the summer, so I don't think it'll be a problem, but I'll have to ask." Jeffrey felt like dancing on the table. A shipment. He was going to be taken along on a buying trip.

"Then I want you to pack for a week's voyage," Alexander instructed him. "Longer, perhaps. It is hard to know before we arrive. I will meet you at the airport in Hamburg after you have checked on this, and we will continue on from there. But you must not under any circumstances take more than two days for this Schwerin business."

He nodded, resisted the urge to ask where they were going. It was Alexander's secret, and he would have to choose the time. "Why won't you go yourself to East Germany?"

"You are no doubt aware that World War II began with the Nazi invasion of Poland. After five years of Nazi occupation, Poland then suffered the tragedy of the Warsaw Uprising, where the Soviets stood across the Vistula River and watched almost eight hundred thousand Poles be massacred by the Nazi forces. Once our own forces were decimated, the Soviets then rolled into Warsaw and took up where the retreating Nazis left off. We suffered under their iron grip for over forty years." Kantor paused while the waiter returned with a new drink. "Wild horses could not drag me to Schwerin. A land that is both Communist and German is a land with one devil too many."

"They're not Communist anymore."

"The shadow still lingers across the land, I assure you. No illness that grave can vanish overnight after having been around for forty years."

Jeffrey waited, and when nothing more was forthcoming, said, "I'm not sure I understand."

"No," Alexander Kantor sighed. "I suppose not."

He reached into his coat, extracted his wallet, and drew out a yellowed black and white photograph. He handed it over. "This was my sister."

Jeffrey examined a lively smiling face who missed being truly beautiful by having a little too much of Alexander's strength. There was no doubt of their being related. "I didn't know you had a sister."

"Svetlana was much older than I. In 1939, after the Germans invaded Poland, she and her husband started a clandestine anti-Nazi newspaper. They were caught." His voice took on a toneless drone. "He died in a concentration camp. She was imprisoned. Unfortunately she was three months pregnant, and the prison guards beat her badly. Svetlana gave birth in her prison cell to a crippled baby boy. She died nine months later, spending her time until then trying to keep her baby alive within the prison."

Alexander reached over and extracted the photograph from Jeffrey's numb fingers. With slow, deliberate motions, he inserted the picture back into his wallet. "To travel to a Germany frozen for five decades, occupied by the same Russian invaders who have stifled my homeland since 1945—" He shook his head. "No, my good man, that combination is simply too much. This trip you and your young lady will have to take on your own."

CHAPTER 7

Katya asked, "So the two of us would be traveling to Schwerin together?"

Late afternoon sunlight spilled through the shop's front window, turning the gauze curtains surrounding the dais to burnished gold. Alexander had left to take care of some personal business, and to let Jeffrey broach the issue with Katya in solitude.

"Alexander will take care of the shop. He doesn't want . . ." Jeffrey hesitated, then decided it was Alexander's secret. "He can't come with us. It's not possible."

"So you're saying you want me to go off with you for a sort of long weekend?" She shook her head. "I don't think so."

"I need you, Katya," he insisted. "Alexander says almost nobody speaks English over there. The second language is Russian, the third Polish or Czech. And I have to take somebody we can trust." He softened his voice. "I trust you."

"It just wouldn't be proper."

"What is there to be proper or improper about? We really need your help on this. I need it."

"Just a business trip?"

"Well, yes and no," Jeffrey was flustered. "I wouldn't be honest if I didn't say how much I'd like to do this with you."

"So this is a business trip and you want to enjoy my company."

"This is a special time in Germany, especially in the East. You're studying about it. I'd have thought you'd leap at the chance to take an all-expense-paid trip over there."

"It's not the trip."

"I want to understand what's going on over there," he persisted. "I can't do that without you."

She was silent for a long moment. "For how long?"

"Two days. We leave together, have one night in Schwerin, then you come back to mind the shop while I travel on with Alexander."

"When?"

He took a breath. "Tomorrow. Alexander says there is another trip which he and I have to make immediately afterward."

"What about Ling? Who will take care of him?" Then she answered it and gave her assent at the same time. "I'll ask Mama. Will you come with me this evening?"

He was already up and moving. "Let's go. I just closed up."

=====

Coventry was a charmless town located about an hour from London. Katya's mother lived there because of the company that bought her ceramics. Katya refused to discuss the ceramics, which left Jeffrey to imagine that her mother made bowls and sold them on the sly, supplementing what was probably a meager monthly relief check.

Magda lived in a run-down council house attached on both sides to two equally drab tenements. Her neighbors were a rainbow coalition of Indians and Pakistanis and Africans and Arabs, with the odd white face thrown in for good measure. The view from her front porch revealed block after oppressive block of red-brick council houses, whose crumbling facades and dirty windows and peeling woodwork exuded an air of tired resignation.

Magda had the face of a shrew and looked twice her age, which Jeffrey guessed to be something over fifty. A long bony nose thrust from an overly pointed face. Her thin lips sagged under the weight of pasty-colored cheeks. The first time he met her, Jeffrey had the impression of a spoiled child grown into a perpetually unhappy adult. The only color to her face was in her eyes, which peered from sunken burrows with surprising light. Her gray hair was perpetually unkempt and looked hacked with garden shears. It was only partially trapped in place by dozens of bobby pins.

She was always suffering, and each pain had its own signal. When her arthritis flared, she kept her hands close to her stomach and rubbed them constantly, one with the other. When it was her back, she walked bent at what Jeffrey thought a ridiculous angle, teetering from one chair or other support to another. When it was her shoulder, she stooped inward, as though only one side of her body were whole.

Her expression was one of silent suffering. Jeffrey would sit across from her, searching for something benign to say, imagining her doing a quick check in the mirror before opening the door to greet her daughter. Then he would look up and catch those piercing eyes watching him steadily, and wonder if she could also read minds.

Katya always responded with loving sympathy and heartfelt concern. Always. This transformation from cool and distant beauty to attentive daughter never failed to give him a severe pang of jealousy.

Jeffrey had continued to go with Katya on her regular weekly visits because he had little choice. It was either that or miss seeing her on Saturdays. As it was, he held his breath through the two-hour ordeal, and was rewarded with the pleasure of her company during the train rides and with an evening together afterward.

During his first visit, Jeffrey had been severely stung by Magda's total indifference to his presence. She had inspected him briefly, ignored his smile and outstretched hand, and turned back to her daughter with a painful grimace. He had stood there, as hurt by Katya's silent acceptance of her mother's rudeness as he was by Magda's actions, then turned away. Two could play at that game.

He opened his briefcase and brought out a book he had taken along for the voyage, a text on identifying types of wood. Within a few minutes of sitting down in the farthest corner from Magda's padded chair, he was lost in his work. He registered the musical tone of Katya's voice and Magda's querulous replies, but they did not intrude on his concentration. It was more than half an hour before he felt eyes on him, looked up, and found Magda watching him with a measuring gaze, as though she were seeing him for the first time.

Today it was her feet. Jeffrey watched her open the door and greet them with a little teary-eyed smile that never slipped, never changed, always crying for attention better than words ever could. Jeffrey pasted on what he hoped was an expression of concern, entered the cramped and cluttered living room behind Katya, watched Magda walk forward with little steps that swayed her body from side to side like a ship at anchor. Every chair, every stool, every low table wore a cushion for a hat.

He stood in the middle of the cluttered room and watched Katya settle her mother back in her customary chair and set the baby's box in her mother's lap. She left Magda crooning over the bird while she went around picking up and setting the room in order with swift little motions. She returned and plucked the shopping bags from Jeffrey's arms and carried them into the kitchen. He started after her, then decided against it. There was barely room in there for one.

Magda finally greeted him with a very tired, "How are you, Jeffrey?"

"Excited," he said, refusing to play the false sympathy game.

"Ah, how nice." She settled down farther into the thick padding, raised her legs one at a time with her hands underneath the calves, handling them like hand-blown glass. When both feet were safely on the cushion, she pulled up her cheeks in a long-suffering smile. "And what do you have to celebrate, young man?"

"The director of my store is increasing my responsibilities."

"A promotion." She picked up the lace prayer shawl she always wore when Katya took her to church, and laid it across her lap. "How nice for you."

"It's not a promotion," Jeffrey said, mentally gripping his teeth to keep his voice casual. She barely seemed to be listening to him. "Well, not in the sense of a raise or anything. I am going to start traveling for him as a buyer."

"All young people like so much to travel," she said, her eyes following Katya's movement in the kitchen. "And where will you be going?"

"East Germany. And perhaps Poland."

Her eyes snapped around. "Is that so."

Katya's voice called out from the kitchen. "Jeffrey's boss is Polish, Mama."

"Is he now. And why haven't I heard of this before?"

Katya returned from the kitchen, drying her hands on a towel. "Why should you be interested in who Jeffrey's boss is?"

Her gaze held a strength that belied her ailments. "Because he is your young man, is he not?"

Katya gave her mother a startled glance and vanished back into the kitchen.

"It is remarkable that your little bird has survived this long," Magda went on. Her speech had a rough-edged quality. "Why did you bring it here?"

"I have a chance to go to Schwerin," Katya said from the kitchen alcove.

"With Jeffrey?"

"On business. Just for two days."

Jeffrey held his breath, wondered if Katya was mentioning it in hopes that her mother would object.

"Some questions have come up about a supplier," Katya went on. "Jeffrey needs me as an interpreter."

"That sounds like a wonderful idea," Magda replied. "I traveled there once after the war. There are some truly beautiful lakes in that city."

Katya reappeared in the kitchen doorway. Her face mirrored Jeffrey's astonishment. "You want me to go?"

"You have to see if the old Strand Hotel is still there. It was quite a place in my day."

"That's where the travel agent has placed us," Jeffrey said, and added hastily, "in separate rooms."

"It's such a romantic place," Magda said, looking at her daughter. "At least it was."

"Then you don't mind me going?" Katya asked.

"Oh, Katya. You're a big girl now. It's a wonderful opportunity to apply your studies. I always told you the German would come in handy, didn't I?"

Katya entered the room and pulled up a straight-backed chair beside her mother. "Sometimes you surprise me, Mama. I thought it would worry you."

"Katya Maria, you are an adult woman. You must make your own decisions. I can tell by your eyes that you really want to go." Her tone sharpened. "Were you hoping that I would say no and give you an excuse?"

Katya remained silent.

"Go," her mother said. "Have a good time. Be sure to take an extra sweater. It gets quite cold at night by the sea. Don't worry about your little bird. What do you call him?"

"Ling," Jeffrey offered.

"I've had tougher assignments than this in my life." She turned to Jeffrey. "You will be sure that she takes her extra sweater along."

"All right."

Her wrinkled features took on a hint of a smile. "You think I am acting out of character, young man?"

He started to nod, checked himself just in time.

"The fact is, young man, you don't know my character. Not at all. To you, I am an old sick woman living out her days in a little English town. But I have lived in many places, and lived through many things, that have made me what I am."

Magda's eyes remained on him. She demanded, "Are you my daughter's boyfriend?"

"I wish I were," he replied bluntly. "I'm not so sure about what she thinks."

"Ah, an honest answer."

"It's what I feel most comfortable with."

The gaze sparked. "Do you, indeed?"

"Leave him alone, Mama," Katya said quietly.

"It's all right." He then said to Magda, "I've never met anybody like you before."

"And what is it that makes me so special, may I ask?"

"Mama," Katya stood and resumed her activities. "That's enough."

Your eyes and your illnesses, Jeffrey thought. They don't match. "I haven't decided."

"I see. And will you tell me when you do?"

If I'm still around, and feel like committing hari-kari with our relationship. "I don't know."

Magda seemed pleased with the response. She turned toward the kitchen. "Why don't you show your young man my workshop."

"He's not interested in your ceramics, Mama."

That stung him. "Why don't you have the courtesy to ask me before you say what I do and don't like?"

Both their reactions surprised him. Katya immediately turned sheepishly apologetic; her mother clearly approved. Magda repeated calmly, "Show him the workshop, daughter."

With the motion of a little girl, Katya gestured for him to join her in the kitchen. Mystified, Jeffrey stood and walked over, and was surprised to see that the house did not end with the kitchen as he supposed. Through the window of the back door he saw a glass-walled addition, one originally intended as a greenhouse.

"That atelier is why I chose this house," Magda said from the front room.

Katya led him forward and opened the door but refused to meet his eyes. Jeffrey stepped into an artist's atelier. Shelves lined both side walls and contained an immense variety of ceramic shapes. Very few of them were exactly the same. All wore the bone-white coloring of once-fired clay. Beneath the shelves stretched thick wooden slabs, standing on legs about waist-high—tables set either for standing or sitting on a stool. A number of flexible lights stood at varying degrees, and beneath them rested paints, jars, pallets, rags, cans, magnifying glasses, several unfinished works, and some of the thinnest brushes Jeffrey had ever seen.

He bent over one work, a double handled loving cup. It stood perhaps ten inches high, and had a delicate peaked cap set to one side. The cup's base was formed like the foundations of a Doric column and was gilded a shimmering gold. The cup's background began as a delicate cream coloring at the bottom and rose to deep sky-blue. At the center-point of the transition, a gathering of clouds was back-lit by a sun whose light burst forth in a radiant circle. Set in the center of the clouds was a lamb bleeding from a wound in its side.

"You may pick it up if you like." Jeffrey turned to find Magda leaning heavily against the doorjamb. Her expression was lacking all the pain he had come to think of as permanent. "It is all right. Just use the handles."

"You did this?"

She nodded and said simply, "It is my life. This and my daughter and my faith. It is all I have." She smiled for the very first time, a bare flickering that did not register below her eyes. "Sometimes it is almost enough."

Jeffrey examined the cup more closely. "This is fantastic."

"Thank you, young man." She searched his face with a gaze that bit deep. "This is to be your first visit to the East?"

"Yes."

"Perhaps when you return you'll understand better." She thought it over a moment, gave a decisive nod. "Perhaps."

———

They sat across from each other on the train ride back to London, a linoleum-topped table between them. Jeffrey watched the final remnants of a glorious cloud-flecked sunset beyond the train window and thought about what Magda had said.

At last he turned to Katya. "You've never told me anything about your father."

"That's because I don't remember a lot about him. He left home when I was seven."

"I'm sorry." Subdued, he still did not want to let the moment of rare candor go. "Was the divorce tough on you?"

Her eyes remained fastened on the train window. "I didn't say they were divorced, Jeffrey. I said he left. And yes, it was hard."

"You mean he just walked out on you?"

"Can we please talk about something else?" Katya asked the window.

"Sure, we can. Only I really would like to know more about your past."

She faced him then, her gaze steady, the distance between them vast. "Why?"

What came to mind surprised even him. "Because I want to share the hurt with you, Katya. Not just the good times."

The look of utter defenselessness that had pulled him close their very first night returned, and he yearned for something stronger between them, something that would allow him to say what he felt and feel what he dreamed.

Katya said, "My father was an American soldier in Germany after the war. A private. He was in the Occupying Forces. Germany was split up into different zones, each one with a different military government."

"I knew that."

"My mother and her older sister were raised in Poland, but wound up in Germany at the end of the war." She gave him a help-less look. "This is a very difficult story, Jeffrey. And complicated. I'm not sure I can tell it."

"Try," he urged.

She was silent for a moment, then said, "My grandmother was Polish and her husband was German. They lived in a village in Upper Silesia, not far from the German border. My grandfather became active in anti-Nazi activities. Towards the end of the war he was caught and shot. My grandmother feared that the family would be arrested, so she sent my mother and her sister to my grandfather's family. They lived in a town in Germany about a hundred and fifty miles away. I am sure they expected to be re-united soon, but it never happened.

"At the end of the war, the town where my mother and her sister lived was declared part of the Russian Zone, what later became East Germany." Katya's soft voice carried a determined note. "The border with the American Zone was only twelve kilometers to the west, but it might as well have been on the other side of the world. There wasn't any hope for returning to Poland, or going anywhere else. Travel was very tightly controlled, even between cities within the same zone.

"My mother was very good at languages, and even though she was still just a teenager, she went to work in an American military base called a *Kaserne*. She crossed the border between the two zones every day with a special pass.

"The American Zone was better off than the other areas, and because of her job on the base she and her sister always had enough to eat. But there were enormous problems everywhere in Germany, and every morning more old people would be found dead from cold and hunger and no medicines for their illnesses. A lot of people became sick and died because there was no treatment. My mother's sister was one of them.

"Soon after her sister passed away, Joseph Stalin died. His death sparked off riots all over Eastern Europe, as the people he had oppressed began fighting against the occupying forces and demanding their freedom. The Russian soldiers guarding the border with the American Zone started harassing people who were passing through every day. One night after work she saw a group of Russian soldiers club a man with their rifles. She suddenly turned and fled back towards the American Zone. It must have been a very frightening experience for her. She could hear the Russian guard-dogs snarling and barking to be released as the soldiers yelled for her to come back. But the American patrol came to her aid. The Russian soldiers got into a big shouting match with them, but the Americans would not send her back. My father was one of those American soldiers.

"They got married a couple of months later. It was a big problem, because the American military didn't like soldiers to marry local girls. They called these local women gold diggers, the ones who tried to get an American boyfriend. A lot of them were, I suppose. Anyway, when my father's tour of duty ended, my parents went back together to the United States."

Jeffrey waited, and when he was sure nothing more was coming he asked quietly, "Where, Katya?"

"Baltimore."

"And that was where you were born?"

She gave the window a small nod.

"And you lived there until your father left?"

"'Put it in park, sport,'" Katya said softly. "I can remember my father saying that a lot. 'Put it in park while you still can.'"

She looked at him, her eyes two pools of sadness. "Isn't that a strange thing to remember about your father?"

"Do you remember what he looked like?"

Her forehead creased with concentration. "He was big, I remember that. And his hair was dark. He had big hands, strong hands. He was a mechanic in a factory, and his hands were hard and strong. When he would come home, I would run to him and he would swoop me up and over his head. I would squeal, and he would give me this big booming laugh. Sometimes he would make a muscle for me, and I would try to push it down. It was like trying to crush a stone with my hands. He liked to roll his shirt sleeves up so you could see his muscles, I remember that." Her face had the look of a little girl's, wide-eyed and open and yearning to be sheltered.

"And then he was gone," Jeffrey said, aching for her.

"I didn't understand it. Why would he leave like that? I spent *days* looking all over the house for a letter, a note, anything. How could my daddy have left me without saying goodbye? What had I done that upset him so badly?"

"Nothing," Jeffrey said quietly.

She came awake with a start, spent a moment faltering over what she had said. Then she turned back to the window. "I don't want to talk about it anymore."

He reached across and took a small warm hand in both of his, then held it the rest of the way to London.

From the outside, Claridge's was easy to mistake as just another row of expensive apartment buildings. There was no sign with flashing lights, no ornate marquee announcing its presence, no break in the turn-of-the-century red-brick decor. Claridge's did not advertise. It did not need to.

Claridge's, like its sister hotels the Connaught and the Berkley, did not accept groups. Even visiting kings and presidents were requested to arrive without a large entourage. There was no check-in desk at Claridge's; instead, an arriving guest was ushered into a small sitting room to one side of the main foyer. Quietly efficient staff in starched white shirts and dark formal wear filled out the various details before personally escorting guests to their rooms.

The style throughout the hotel was Art Deco, the fittings worth a fortune. The entrance hall was tiled in marble, the chandeliers all gilt and silver, the furniture antiques that Jeffrey would have been delighted to display in his front window. Passages from one room to the next were tall and arched and flanked by marble pillars, with liveried footmen stationed at discreet intervals. One suite that Alexander had previously used held a Regency display case filled with silver-framed photographs of royalty who had stayed there, including Czar Nicholas and Queen Victoria. Another had a sitting room large enough to contain the grand piano used by Sir Arthur Sullivan to compose the Savoy Operas. All the suites enjoyed working fireplaces, which a butler would stoke at the press of a button.

Jeffrey's favorite room, however, was the main restaurant. Even at breakfast it was an artistry of massive floral arrangements. Cream silk wall coverings and beautiful Art-Deco mirrors lined the chamber. It was laid out on two levels, with an upper terrace where Jeffrey enjoyed sitting and watching the arriving guests and scuttling waiters. Alexander vastly preferred having breakfast in his room, but knew from experience that Jeffrey would put up a struggle to be able to sit downstairs and watch six waiters serve his table. Six. For a dawn breakfast.

It was the morning of their departure for East Germany, and as instructed, Jeffrey had packed for a longer voyage. To where, he still did not know.

"It is vital that you do not take more than two days in Schwerin, Jeffrey," Alexander began, once their breakfast dishes were cleared away and coffee cups refilled. "These other matters simply will not wait."

He nodded. "But why send me now? I mean, it's waited this long, if this other stuff is so urgent, why not put it off until later?"

"An excellent question." Alexander Kantor paused to sip from his cup, went on. "Last week I received a telegram to my Geneva address asking me to call a number in Schwerin. It took me a surprisingly short time to place the call. I suppose the West Germans are managing to improve things after all. In any case, a woman answered—someone I've never heard of before. A lawyer—at least that's what she said she was. She did not speak English, and I speak no German, but I had anticipated the difficulty and had an interpreter available. Through this individual she told me that she had heard I was an honest man."

"Just like the dealer."

"The exact same words," Alexander agreed. "But if it was meant to be a code, someone failed to tell me about it."

"So what did you say?"

"In all my years I've never known how to reply to something like that. I asked her how the weather was."

"She must have loved that."

"It did give her pause. Eventually she came back and said she had a most urgent matter to discuss with me. Something to do with several of her clients."

"Plural?"

"Yes, that disturbed me too. I asked if she referred to the dealer, and she said only indirectly. He was not the client to whom she referred.

On that point she was most clear." Alexander Kantor toyed with his coffee spoon. "She said it was absolutely crucial that we speak together immediately, before the matter was brought before the courts."

"What matter?"

"I haven't the faintest idea." Alexander Kantor replied. "But the idea of being taken to court in East Germany is most appalling, I assure you."

"That stuffed shirt from Bonn, the one who made all the trouble at Christie's over the chest of drawers, threatened us with the same thing."

"I want you to go and find out what has happened to this dealer," Alexander instructed, "and what on earth this lawyer is concerned about."

"I won't let you down," Jeffrey said.

"Of course you won't." Alexander reached to an inner pocket, drew out a neatly printed page, went on. "The dealer's name is Götz. He runs the official antique store on the central market square."

"Can you describe how he looks?"

"Mind you, I only met him once, and that was two years ago. He was a smallish man, certainly no higher than your shoulder. Pale features. I don't recall the eyes save that they were most unfriendly. Bad teeth, yes, I recall that vividly. You will no doubt see a great deal of that in your travels, but his were exceptional. My impression when he smiled was of looking at more cavities than teeth."

"Strange for a man who's got eight hundred thousand pounds waiting in a London bank."

"Perhaps, perhaps not. Many a village child in Poland after the war had his or her teeth worked on without the benefit of a painkiller, simply because there was none available. I have no doubt that such a memory would keep many people from returning to the dentist chair for a lifetime."

Jeffrey scanned the page, mispronounced the name.

"Götz is pronounced Gertz, because of the umlaut. Gertz."

"I thought you didn't speak German."

"There was a time in my past when a little German was forced upon me, but we shall not go into that just now. His shop is part of the National Antique Association, and like most shops in the East, it has no further name than that."

Jeffrey read down the page, tried the lawyer's name on for size. "Renate Reining."

"Almost there. The last name should rhyme with the river Rhine. Reining."

His eyes still on the page, Jeffrey asked, "May I ask where it is we're going after this?"

"It is almost time for your departure, so if you will permit me I will wait and give you the details upon meeting you in the Hamburg airport. Is that acceptable?"

"I suppose I can wait," Jeffrey replied. Barely.

"Splendid. There is no harm, I suppose, in telling you our destination. It is Cracow, the medieval capital of the Polish Empire."

"Our family is from there."

"Indeed they are. We will be speaking of all these things in greater length, as I have said. But from the very outset I wish to impress upon you how vital it is that you do not discuss any of this with others."

"I understand."

"Whenever you make travel arrangements from London, you must always have as your destination a city in Western Europe. There is a travel agent I use in Zurich, a most confidential sort of individual. I will give you his name. Use him for booking everything in the East."

Jeffrey took the information as it was intended, an assurance that he would be told everything, and that this was not to be his only trip. "Thanks, Alexander."

"I thank you. This affair is long overdue for a conclusion, and it is good that you will be representing us. As I said, it is one trip I would avoid like the grave."

"I mean, thanks for trusting me."

"You have earned it, I assure you." He pushed back his chair. "And here comes your lovely young lady."

Jeffrey felt only relief as Katya entered the restaurant. Alexander noticed his expression. "You look as though you didn't expect her to appear."

Jeffrey waved her over. "With Katya I'm never sure about anything."

"In my youth we would have called that a woman's prerogative," Alexander said, rising to his feet.

"Nowadays we call it infuriating."

"That, my boy, is both universal and constant. Unless you intend to make a life for yourself as a celibate, you must accept the burden of patience."

Katya approached their table and said breathlessly, "Good morning Mr. Kantor, Jeffrey. Are we ready?"

"You look positively splendid this morning, my dear." Alexander glanced at his watch. "I suppose you had best be off. You have a plane to catch, and I a store to open."

He extended his hand first to Katya and then to Jeffrey. "You will take care, and you will call me."

"This evening, as we agreed," Jeffrey replied.

"Excellent. I wish you both a splendid trip, and all success."

Jeffrey's nerves pushed to the surface. "What if—"

Alexander stopped him with an upraised hand. "There is no need to anticipate trouble. I know you will do well, Jeffrey. I am sure of it. We will discuss what you find as you find it. Have the same confidence in your abilities that I do." He patted his assistant on the shoulder and repeated, "I know you will do well."

═══

The flight from London to Hamburg took just under an hour. Continuous turbulence made it seem like five. They arrived to the darkness of a heavy thunderstorm, rented a car, and worked their way through snarled traffic to the autobahn for Berlin.

After an hour and a half of monotonous highway driving, the shadow of a tall brick tower appeared through the pouring rain.

"The weather certainly is appropriate," Katya said.

"It looks ghostly," Jeffrey agreed.

Vague skeletal shapes rose from the gloom and took on the form of high metal watchtowers, barbed-wire fences, and concrete-lined trenches. The autobahn went through a violent burst of bumps and uneven strippings, then the former East German border was upon them.

A vast expanse of asphalt stretched out to either side of the highway, now cordoned off with makeshift fencing. Beyond the inspection area loomed multistory brick and glass buildings. Structures with mirrored glass walls rose from their roofs, reminding Jeffrey of airport control towers.

All around this compound, and down the barbed-wire fencing as far in each direction as they could see, rose tall prison watchtowers.

The border-control buildings were thoroughly trashed. The lower windows were all smashed in with a violence that had torn many of their frames from the walls. Huge chunks of the buildings themselves had been hewn out, leaving gaping holes and corners that looked gnawed by a raging giant.

The entire border area was gripped in a deathlike stillness. Nothing moved. Nothing at all. There must have been a dozen buildings in all, with no sign of life anywhere.

"Where is everybody?" Jeffrey asked.

"Trying to convince anybody they can find that they had nothing to do with anything," Katya said, her voice very small.

He glanced over. "Are you all right?"

"Drive on, Jeffrey. I don't want to stay here any longer than I have to."

By the time they reached the turn-off for Schwerin, the worst of the storm had passed and the sky was clearing. It was a good thing; the road leading to the capital city of Mecklenburg-Vorpommern was little more than a rutted country lane. Ancient cobblestones vied with sloppily poured asphalt, and the covering of rain hid potholes of bone-jarring depth. The road passed through tiny villages of unkempt houses, their front doors just inches away from the stumbling traffic and clouds of diesel fumes. Trucks loomed up from time to time, slowing for no one, demanding most of the road as their right; Jeffrey reduced his speed to a crawl, hugged the curb, and hoped for a safe passage.

They passed a sign identifying the Schwerin industrial estate, a series of factories with dirt-clouded windows and filthy facades. Then they became thoroughly lost in a Schwerin housing development—scruffy multicolored high-rise buildings that dominated a hill on the edge of town. Three sets of directions finally took them through a tiny forest and down to the edge of one of the city's lakes.

The sun was forcing its way through the scuttling clouds as Jeffrey turned onto a narrow road that ran alongside a dirty sand beach. A number of heavyset people in shapeless sweaters and rolled-up trousers were making their way down to the lakeside, eager to soak up whatever meager good weather they were granted. Jeffrey pulled up in front of an attractive white-stucco three-story building with yellow trim, bearing a small sign announcing itself to be the Strand Hotel.

The woman staffing the reception desk was as heavyset as the beach-goers, and gave them a dubious look when Katya confirmed that they wanted two single rooms. She led them upstairs and showed him cramped chambers barely large enough to hold the narrow bed and small corner desk. He dropped Katya's bags off, went to his own room, opened the window, and spent a few moments looking out over the lake to the distant skyline of Schwerin.

When he came back downstairs, Katya was on the hotel's only phone, speaking in what he assumed was German. He walked out and sat down on the hotel veranda.

Now that the sun was out, the weather was balmy. Every veranda table was taken, the people talking softly and gazing out at the lake. The body of sparkling water was wide enough for its farthest shore to be beyond the horizon. Its border was mostly forest, except for where Schwerin rose to his left. The people walking along the narrow beach and seated on the veranda seemed all cut from the same mold—overweight and pasty-skinned, older than their years, wearing clothes of muted colors and clunky shoes.

"I tried to call the numbers you gave me," Katya said as she appeared on the veranda. "There wasn't any answer. They must be taking a late lunch."

Jeffrey had a fleeting sensation that at the sound of Katya's English every face turned their way, then just as swiftly ignored them. A lifetime habit, he supposed. "Why don't we have a bite to eat here?"

The waitress watched with half-hidden curiosity as Katya explained the German menu to him, took their orders, gave Jeffrey another of those fleeting glances, and left. He turned back and found Katya watching the other tables.

"Why are you smiling?"

"This is a holdover from another era," she replied.

He reached over and took her hand. "Tell me what you see."

She looked down at his fingers covering hers. "This is supposed to be a business trip, remember?"

He left his hand where it was. "Tell me, Katya."

She looked back out at the veranda. "Those ladies over there have been coming here for forty years. They come to breathe the good sea air—that's what they would call a lake this big, an inland sea. Their doctor once told them it was good for the lungs, and they still believe it. Their husbands all died during the war. And the one real pleasure left in life is to get in a bus and come to the Strand Hotel once every summer."

"And the rest of the year?"

"Life in a little gray village, somewhere unmarked on any map."

The waitress returned with their food. Jeffrey waited awkwardly while Katya bowed her head for a moment. No matter how often she did that in public, it did not become easier for him to endure. When she lifted her eyes he pointed toward a distant table and said, "My grandmother used to have a hat like that one. A straw boater lacquered with white enamel and a couple of fake flowers on one side."

"Don't point."

"Why not? Nobody's looked our way since they heard us talking English."

"Yes, they have. They've seen we're foreigners and that's all they need to know. They have a lifetime's practice of not appearing to look where they're not supposed to."

"But that's all gone."

"The reasons for it might be," Katya agreed. "But it's one thing to say it and another to relearn habits so ingrained they are instinctive."

Jeffrey looked around. "There's more gray hair here than I've ever seen in one place."

"Clairol's campaign for youth in a bottle didn't reach to the East," Katya said. "People look a lot older here than Westerners of the same age. They don't think about looking chic. They can't. They struggle too hard just to arrive at being comfortable—or at least as close to comfortable as they can ever come."

She tasted her food, then went on. "They wear orthopedic shoes and use canes when they're in their fifties, twenty years earlier than in the West. They'll never think it strange or embarrassing, though. Look at the people on the street when we go out today. You'll find eyes that slide over to one side of their head and bad scars and worse teeth. All products of a system that lifts the welfare of the state above all else."

"I thought the state was for the people."

"Don't be sarcastic. Many of these older people believed that with all their hearts. It has been extremely difficult for them to accept that the basis for a Communist society was nothing more than a lie."

When they had finished eating, Katya went to try the two numbers again. A few minutes later she returned and reported, "There isn't any answer at the antique shop. But I did reach the lawyer, Frau Reining. She will meet us at the Café Prague in one hour. Do you want to leave now and go by the shop first?"

———

The city of Schwerin was a jarring mixture of old and new. Jeffrey's progress was slowed to a crawl by the surrounding traffic; plastic-looking cars bearing names like Trabant and Moskovite and Lada puttered by in clouds of blue smoke, smelling and sounding like poorly tuned outboard motors.

Their way took them back by the new section—the apartments were nicknamed *Arbeitersschliessfächer*, Katya said, or filing cabinets for workers. From a distance they loomed in irregular patterns of multicolored brick and pastel concrete. Up close Jeffrey saw that the yellows and blues and pinks were gutted and peeling and shabby. The roads were scarred and potholed, the sidewalks pitted. Weeds grew everywhere in unruly clumps, giving the entire area an atmosphere of abandonment.

Forty thousand families lived in the housing project, Katya said, reading from a pamphlet she had picked up at the hotel. The buildings stood like tired bastions to a forgotten dream. They were crammed one against the other, balconies strung with laundry and old flowerpots and frayed curtains.

"This looks like the punishment block to an inner-city housing project," Jeffrey decided, looking around as he drove.

"In East Germany," Katya told him, "the average waiting time for an apartment in these developments is five years."

"You've got to be joking."

"At least they have a bathroom for each family," Katya said. "And indoor plumbing. And running water in the kitchens. Most of the time, anyway."

Farther along, the road leading to the city center was lined on one side by the Russian military compound and on the other with the dilapidated Russian officers' apartments. Both were encased within concrete walls and razor-wire and metal gates topped with bright red stars. The stars were the only recently painted item along the entire mile-long stretch.

They parked their car at the outskirts of the city's old section and walked, soon coming upon a vast eight-story palace—the former residence, according to Katya, of the Dukes of Mecklenburg. The castle dominated an island situated in one of the city's lakes. The island was connected to the city proper by a narrow bridge, its surface paved with cobblestones and its sides decorated with ancient sculptures and gas-lit lamps. Everything, from the street to the carvings to the palace itself, suffered from a severe case of neglect.

The city was no different. All but the main streets were laid in uneven cobblestones. All but the tourist areas were lined with buildings buried under decades of soot. Ornate facades protruded at odd intervals from beneath layers of filth.

The antique store stood on the central square. According to a small card taped to the door, it was owned by the central East German Ministry for Art, Subsection for Paintings and Antiques. A fly-blown sign tilted against the front window announced that it was closed, and from the looks of the dust blanketing every surface, Jeffrey could see through the window it had been for some time.

He stepped back from the window and scanned the square and connecting streets. The shop was a couple of businesses removed from what appeared to be the newest and gaudiest store in town; flashing lights surrounded a sign announcing that it sold pornography. A line of customers waited patiently by the door, gawking at the relatively conservative display in the windows.

Many of the stores were undergoing radical innovation, with bright new displays gracing the windows of tired gray buildings. Katya followed his eyes. "Under socialism," she said, "all the shops had names given to them by the department that ran their section. They were all generic names, like grocery, watch repair, and so on. These buildings you see around here, the old ones with the sort of shadow writing above the store, are all left over from before the war. They probably haven't been painted in forty years, since they were all nationalized and placed under central control."

Jeffrey nodded distractedly, then pressed his face to the antique shop's window and spent several minutes carefully scanning the room.

Katya watched his expression, asked, "What's wrong?"

"Something doesn't add up," he said, using his hands to shade his eyes from the sun's reflection. "I can see almost the whole shop."

"So?"

"There's nothing in there that I would even think of having in our shop. It's all second-rate stuff. Worse. Some of it's barely above junk. Not even antiques at all, just used furniture."

Katya moved up closer. "It stands to reason that a shop like this would hold its best pieces and send them out where they can get better prices. And Western currency."

But Jeffrey wasn't satisfied. "This is a state-run store. The guy who spoke to Alexander had all sorts of documents saying it was official state business. Nowadays they could get Western currency selling goods directly from the store, couldn't they? I mean, they're using the German mark here now. So why isn't there at least one piece like the stuff he sent us? It's a completely different collection. Worlds away."

"What are you suggesting?"

He turned away. "I don't know. It doesn't add up, that's all. Come on, let's go meet the lawyer."

===

The Café Prague was a recently remodeled little gem across the street from one of the central ministries. The ceilings were thirty-five feet high and supported by a series of pillars. The upper windows were arched and set with lead-lined stained glass; the lower windows were broad and high and cast a lovely light through the interior.

They had been at their table only a few minutes when a bird-like woman came up, inspected them with sharp nervous eyes, then leaned over and said something in German.

"She wants to know if we are the ones from London," Katya said.

"Yes," Jeffrey replied, standing and extending his hand. "Nice to—"

The woman seated herself and spoke again in the same abrupt manner.

"She wants to know if she can trust us."

Jeffrey lowered his hand and sat down. "She should have already decided that before asking us to come all the way here."

"I can't tell her that. And you behave."

"If she can be rude, why can't I?" Jeffrey turned to the woman. "Yes."

"Good," the woman replied in English. She extended her hand. "Frau Renate Reining. Excuse. Few words English only. Russian, yes. German, yes. Czech, some. You speak Russian?"

"No."

"No. Nobody speak Russian. A new world. People speak Russian last year. This year, all forget. World change."

The lawyer was a tired dark-haired woman in her middle forties who clearly gave little concern to her appearance. Her fingernails were chewed to the quick, her gestures nervous and as abrupt as her words. She wore a pair of dusty double-knit pants, an unironed white shirt, and an open sweater with two of the buttons hanging by raveled threads.

She stood and motioned for them to follow her. "You come."

She led them out of the cafe and around the corner to a door whose stone and mortar frame was decorated with half a dozen brass plaques announcing various professional offices. They climbed five flights of circular wooden stairs that bowed and creaked with their passage. The center of each step was worn to a cavity of bare splintered wood.

On the fifth floor, they walked down a long dusty-smelling hall on a strip of moth-eaten carpet. Bare ceiling bulbs illuminated flaking paint and warped wood. Frau Reining produced a set of massive pre-war skeleton keys and opened a door with a cracked plastic sign announcing the law offices of three partners.

The office was one room crowded to absurdity with three desks, a kitchen table for conferences, and floor-to-ceiling wall cabinets. She waved them toward the table, shrugged off her sweater, and spoke to Katya.

"She says this costs nine hundred dollars a month now. Before the Wall came down it cost eighteen. It's all they can afford."

"It's, well, functional," Jeffrey replied.

"Sit, sit," Frau Reining said. "Business."

"Business," Jeffrey agreed, seating himself in an unyielding wood-and-metal chair.

The lawyer lit an unfiltered cigarette, leaned back in her chair, and began speaking rapid-fire German in a low drone. She smoked as she talked, the words rolling out in a cloud of smoke. The longer she talked, the larger grew Katya's eyes, the more pallid her complexion.

"What's she saying?" Jeffrey demanded, alarmed by her expression.

Katya replied with a single upraised finger. Wait.

"Minute," the woman said. "One minute still." She continued on in German, stopped, and gave Katya a hard-eyed inspection.

"Well?"

Slowly Katya turned his way. "Something's gone horribly wrong."

"With the furniture?"

"Not exactly." Katya brushed distractedly at the hair on her forehead. Her hand trembled slightly. Jeffrey shot a glance at the lawyer. For some reason Katya's reaction seemed to please her.

He leaned forward. "Tell me what's wrong."

"The antique store director has been arrested."

The discomfort he had felt on the street before the closed shop solidified, became reality. "Tell me," he repeated.

"They arrested his assistant too. She's agreed to give evidence in return for a lighter sentence—I forget what it's called."

"Plea bargaining."

"Yes." Katya's eyes had a lost look. "According to the assistant, the dealer came to you—Alexander, I mean. They came to him because they heard he was honest. The dealer they used before knew what they were doing and started raising his commissions."

"What they were doing was illegal," Jeffrey said. It was not a question.

"Illegal," the lawyer agreed, nodding her head vigorously. "Everything illegal. That man breathes, it is done illegal."

"Frau Reining represents some of the lawful owners of the furniture. About forty. In one . . . I can't think of the word—"

"Consolidated claims," Jeffrey suggested.

"Yes. Thank you." Katya took a breath. "She says most of them are out of prison now."

"Prison," Jeffrey repeated.

Katya nodded. "Those they can find. Some have disappeared. She's representing their families."

"Poof," the lawyer said, blowing her fingertips open. "Dust in wind. Story of Communist life."

"Jeffrey, they were finding people with antiques and just putting the owners away." Katya's expression mirrored the pain in her voice. "Stealing all they had, forcing them to sign documents saying they were sold for money the people never received. If they complained they were just locked up. No trial, no rights, no word to their families. Nothing."

"I don't understand," Jeffrey said, struggling to hold on. "The antique dealer was doing this?"

"Stasi," the lawyer corrected. "Secret police."

"He was a front," Katya said. "There were people involved right up through the Party hierarchy. They don't even know how high it went."

"High," Frau Reining confirmed. "This much money, maybe top."

"It was millions, Jeffrey. Millions. They still don't know how much, or how many people were hurt. Frau Reining says all but two of her clients were imprisoned, some with their families, even little children. Some were tortured." Katya pleaded with him. "Why did this happen? How could they do this to people just for pieces of furniture?"

"Not furniture," the lawyer interrupted. "Money. Much money. In East, before Wall, one dollar like one hundred dollars in West. People do much for millions here. Anything."

Alexander didn't know anything about this, Jeffrey kept repeating to himself. For the old man to be caught up in something like this went against everything he stood for. Still, the niggling doubt remained; had he been sent over in Alexander's place to sniff the wind? Had the story of his sister been a lie?

"Jeffrey?" Katya asked softly.

"I—" He felt the lawyer's eyes on him. "Tell her I'm sorry. We didn't know. Nothing." His words sounded feeble in his ears. "All the documents, everything, it was all correct."

The lawyer searched his face, then nodded abruptly and reached forward to grind out her cigarette. "I believe."

"Alexander even called Berlin to verify." The whispers of doubt laced painfully across his mind. It couldn't be. Alexander wasn't involved. Jeffrey shook his head to clear the fears away.

The lawyer misunderstood his gesture. "No. Means nothing. Documents all correct, but all false. Correct for law, false for man. Old Communist story. Big lie."

She started rushing through another flood of German. Katya nodded in time to the words, then turned to Jeffrey and said, "Frau Reining says that she believes you knew nothing about all this. You and Alexander. The dealer's assistant was very clear. She says you mustn't blame yourself.

"She has studied the law," Katya went on. "There is no redress permitted them, since the export documents and the sales were all done legally, and were done in another country. She will give you a notarized letter to that effect. But she would like to know if you can give them an idea of how many pieces you handled."

"Alexander said something like thirty, I don't know the exact number."

"She would like to know if you can give them either a picture or a description of the pieces you sold. It would help a lot in the court cases."

"We photograph every piece we sell," Jeffrey replied. His voice sounded dead in his ears.

The lawyer smiled for the first time, showing crooked and yellowed teeth. "She says that is excellent," Katya translated. "Could they please have copies?"

"I'll ask. I think so."

"She wants to know if any are still unsold."

"A few. Not many."

"She doesn't think the people will want them back." Katya's voice gave a slight tremble. She cleared it, went on. "She says they would probably be too much of a reminder of things they will want to forget. If Alexander could send pictures of them also, she will try to track down the owner and see what they say."

Katya surveyed him with wounded eyes. "This is horrible, Jeffrey."

"A nightmare." He had difficulty bringing his thoughts together. "Tell her I'm not sure how long we can keep pieces that aren't for sale. Our shop is really small. We can put them in storage, though."

"She understands. She'll come back within the week with instructions. Is that okay?"

He nodded. What would Alexander say? He pushed himself to his feet. "I have to call Alexander." His body weighed a ton.

"We meet tomorrow," the lawyer said. "Have more talk." She turned to Katya, fired off a rapid flow of words.

Katya translated. "There are a couple of important things she wants to discuss with you. Alexander explained the time limitation to her in their conversation. But she really has to speak with you again tomorrow early." Katya looked at him. "Are you all right?"

"Not really."

The lawyer went to her desk and started rummaging in a drawer, talking all the while. Katya said, "She has something she wants to give us. She was invited to a piano concert at the castle tonight. She has to meet with a client and can't go. She wants to know if we would like the tickets."

Jeffrey struggled to focus his thoughts. "I don't know."

Katya's expression held concern for him. "Maybe it would be a good idea, Jeffrey."

"Yes. All right." To the lawyer he said, "Thank you. That's very kind."

She nodded in her short, sharp way and handed over the tickets. "No blame," she said.

CHAPTER 9

The telephone line hissed and popped as though Jeffrey were speaking with darkest Africa. "I have some bad news and some incredibly worse news. Which do you want first?"

"A trip of extremes, I take it." Alexander paused, asked, "Is the very bad truly so earth-shaking?"

"Worse. What's stronger than awful?" Jeffrey spoke from within the hotel manager's office, where he had been permitted to pull their phone after Katya had pleaded with her for almost twenty minutes.

"I'm sure I don't know. Perhaps you'd best ease me into it before plummeting over the cliff."

"The dealer Götz has been arrested." Jeffrey worked at keeping his voice level. "We are not implicated in any way, however. In fact, it appears from his assistant's testimony that he came to you specifically because we have a name for honesty."

"So our integrity remains intact. Good. That is very good. I am sorry to hear about Götz, but I cannot say that I am all that surprised. Tell me the details."

"That's part of the plummet."

"I see." The voice turned brisk. "Very well, Jeffrey. You may now deliver the blow."

Jeffrey told him the story in its entirety, from finding the shop closed to what the lawyer said. When he finished he sat listening to the line hiss and sputter, his heart hammering a frantic beat.

"Alexander?"

The line emitted a hoarse groan. "Blood money."

"Alexander, are you all right?"

"I've dealt in blood money." The man sounded totally spent, broken in body and spirit.

Jeffrey felt a flood of relief sweep away every last vestige of doubt. "She knows we were not aware of what we dealt in," he said, sinking into a nearby chair, his body trembling slightly. "She's giving us a notarized letter tomorrow saying that her clients will not seek reparations. She asks if we would be willing to give her photographs of the pieces we handled from Götz, and store the unsold pieces until she identifies the rightful owners and learns what they want to have done with them."

Jeffrey waited, strained, heard what sounded like a series of low moans in the distant hissing background. "Alexander? Do you mind us giving her copies of our pictures?"

"Do what you think best." The voice was so feeble as to be almost inaudible over the constant crackling.

"I'm sure she'll wait until I'm back, then if you'll tell me which ones, I'll make the duplicates and mail—"

"Give it back to her," Alexander said, his voice low.

"What? Give back the unsold antiques? She doesn't want—"

"The money. Give it back. All of it. Tell her she can have every cent."

"The eight hundred thousand pounds?"

"More. She is to have all the interest and my commissions as well. I refuse to taint myself by living from blood money."

Jeffrey's heart surged with pride and affection for the old gentleman. "What about setting up a fund to help all those who have suffered, maybe to help with legal costs or something?"

"Do what you think best. I'm sorry. I . . . I must go. We will speak at the airport tomorrow. I . . . Do what you think—"

The line went dead.

===

When he appeared on the veranda, he found Katya sitting in the far corner, reading intently from a small book in her lap. He walked forward and looked over her shoulder. It was a New Testament. She raised her head at the sight of his shadow, studied him intently.

"You're feeling better," she decided.

"Much."

"Talking to Alexander helped you a lot, didn't it?"

He nodded. "Really took a weight off my shoulders."

She closed the book. "In Polish, you say that a stone has dropped from your heart."

"That's exactly how it feels, too."

She waited a moment, then, "Did you think that Alexander was caught up in all this?"

"I didn't really think it. Nothing that strong. Just afraid that it might be true." Terrified was a better word, he decided.

"And now you're not."

"He didn't know. I'm sure of it now."

"I never doubted you," she said solemnly. "Not at all."

He felt himself falling into the violet depths of her eyes. "Thank you, Katya."

"I couldn't," she replied. "There wasn't room in my life at that moment for doubt."

———

The Schwerin Castle was a six-story behemoth crowned on one corner with a knight riding rampant on a two-story steed, and on the other three angles with eighteen spires and turrets. As Jeffrey and Katya joined the crowds passing through the palace's main gates for the concert, they watched a variety of punts and rowboats and paddle skiffs flow in the slow-moving water that surrounded them.

The throne room, where the piano concert took place, was extravagantly gilded. Scenes were painted in the shape of shields around the ceiling, each depicting with timeless clarity the nation-state ruled from this one room for over three hundred years. Marble pillars supported an ornate fresco of smiling gold cherubs and detailed scrollwork. The throne, gold-over-precious wood, sat empty and regal beneath a royal blue and gold canopy.

The sound of Mozart lilted in harmony with the room's elegance. Jeffrey sat and listened and looked out through the tall windows that flanked the polished grand piano. The windows were open to permit the gentle breeze entry. He was borne on the music out to the water that flowed in constant peaceful silence just beyond the palace grounds. The melody, soft and coaxing, carried him away from the questions and the problems and the issues and the worries. Its purity spoke to something deeper, beyond the turmoil that had buffeted his world. He closed his eyes and saw the furniture he had studied so carefully, not as items to be evaluated and sold, but as works of art. In that moment, the price tags and the buyers' greed and the dealers' cynicism and the business competition were all swept away.

He listened, and visualized the pieces that had come to be his own personal favorites, savoring the artistry and the loving craftsmanship that had gone into their creation. He listened, and felt the world to be split in two—the creation and the craftsmanship on one hand, the greed and the material desire to have and to hold and to possess on the other. He listened, and saw himself balanced on the fulcrum, teetering to either side, not knowing where he belonged.

Jeffrey reached over, slipped his hand into Katya's, and waited. Sometimes when he did that she reacted as one trained to be polite even when faced with something repulsive. She would sit and let her hand rest there with the cold limpness of a dead fish, then a few moments later extract it softly and pull her body slightly away. It always left Jeffrey tremendously hurt and afraid to try again.

But this time she *enfolded* it in both of hers with the calm movement of one giving him his rightful place. She too was caught up in the music and the mood and the flowing waters and the evening's perfumed breeze. Jeffrey felt his heart grow wings as she drew his hand farther into her lap, where she could better nestle it with one hand and softly stroke the hairs of his wrist with the other.

At intermission she sat for a long time, not looking his way, not letting his hand go. Finally she stirred and sighed gently. "Shall we stretch our legs?"

They joined the crowd drifting through the adjoining rooms, inspected paintings and gilded adornments in silence, too shy over this newfound closeness to face each other directly.

At the sound of the bell, Jeffrey followed the crowd back into the throne room, only to realize upon his arrival at their seats that Katya was no longer with him. He returned back through chamber after interconnecting chamber, and breathed a silent sigh when he found her in the very back room, what once had been a formal library. He walked toward her, then faltered when he saw the tears on her face.

She stood before a statue of a young woman, a girl probably a year or so beyond puberty. She was nude save for a long shawl draped over her head. Her arms were tied behind her back with the same rough cord used to bind her ankles. She remained on her feet, yet crouched down so that she could cover much of her naked body with the shawl. There was an air of tragic submission, of utter fear, of helpless fragility about the girl.

"Katya?"

She turned and looked at him with brimming eyes. "She's going to be put on the block and sold into slavery. Did you know that was the story? It's written here in German. It happened all the time in the Eastern lands, Jeffrey. All the time. The Tartars or the Cossacks or the Mongols or the Turks would come marching through, and all the girls young enough and pretty enough were stripped and shackled and counted as loot. This wasn't a thousand years ago, and it wasn't on the other side of the earth. This was yesterday. And today, somewhere else on this earth. Some girl is trapped and scared and helpless, some father has been taken away without reason, some mother is no longer there to take care of her. This is what they've done to these people, Jeffrey. Enormous evil for the sake of greed."

Jeffrey swept her into an embrace. He stroked her hair, and shushed her gently, feeling for her own pain, wondering if this was what it meant to be in love.

"Why is the world so cruel, Jeffrey? Can you tell me that? When will it ever end?"

The next morning Jeffrey and Katya returned to the lawyer's cluttered office. "She wants to know if you were able to speak with Mr. Kantor," Katya translated.

"Yes. He was very upset by the news. Extremely upset."

Frau Reining nodded as though expecting nothing less. She spoke in a torrent of German, which Katya translated as, "Not half as upset as the people I am representing. I would like to hope that such horrors are behind us completely, but the times have taught me nothing if not caution."

Jeffrey took a breath, then announced, "We have decided to give back the income from the sales of Götz's antiques."

The words were greeted with silence. Frau Reining turned to Katya and demanded a translation. Reluctantly Katya turned her eyes from Jeffrey, told her what he had said, then asked him, "Is it true? That's what you and Alexander discussed?"

He nodded, keeping his eyes on the lawyer. "All of it."

Frau Reining said sharply, "You no must."

"We're going to do it anyway."

She appeared not to hear him. She stood and went to her desk and returned to the table with a letter which she handed to Katya.

"This is a notarized document," Katya translated, pointing to the official seal and signature at the bottom. "It says that they are relinquishing all rights to prosecute or request restitution."

"You no must," the lawyer repeated.

"Yes, we do," Jeffrey replied. "Tell her that there is a difference between what the law says we must do and what is right. We are giving it all back. Commissions included."

The lawyer's sharp gaze bore into him as she listened to Katya's translation. Then she asked, "How much?"

"I don't know the exact commission we charged, but I would guess the total to be around nine hundred and seventy thousand pounds."

The gaze continued to rake him for a long moment. Then she reached for her pack of cigarettes and lit one with trembling hands. She said with the first gulp of smoke, "Million pounds."

"Give or take some change," Jeffrey agreed, and told her what he had spent sleepless hours mulling over. "We want you to set up a trust to help cover the damages caused to everyone you can find. We will draft a letter of instruction, but it is important that you offer us any suggestions you may have as to how the money should be spent."

He was startled to find Katya's hand slide over his. He glanced her way, but found the gaze too inviting to pay it any mind just then. He went on. "We want to remain very flexible about how the money is to be used, so that it can be matched to individual needs. Since this is not legally required as repayment, I think we would prefer not to have it all go back to the people who owned these particular antiques. You can give them something; we'll work out a figure. But not all of it. There are too many others in need."

When Katya had translated, the lawyer nodded agreement. She said with Katya translating, "It now looks like the German government will provide compensation to the victims of these crimes if we can successfully prove our case in the courts. But this will of course take much time. Your money will help a great deal to cover their needs in the meantime."

"Much needs, much help," the lawyer said in English, approval shining in her gaze. "Thank you. For all families. Thank you."

"You're welcome."

She stubbed out her cigarette and stood. "Come. We go."

They followed her down the stairs and out of the building. She set a brisk pace over the cobblestone passages. Katya walked between Jeffrey and the lawyer, never letting go of his hand for an instant.

She paused before a block-long building topped with the watch-walk of an imitation medieval castle. Miniature turrets rose at each corner, far too small to be more than pillars intended to hold up the sky. Despite its finery and broad windows and fresh white paint, there was an air of isolation to the place. No one walked along that side of the road—all crossed over to the opposite side, all refused to look at it. No one entered or left through the high central portals.

"Stasi," the lawyer announced. "Secret police. Before, not now."

"The place of children's nightmares," Katya said quietly.

The woman spoke rapidly. Katya translated. "When the protest marches began the week before the Wall toppled, there were forty thousand the first night, and eighty thousand the second. Out of a population in Schwerin of one hundred and twenty thousand. That left the Communists, the grandfathers, and the babies at home. We all walked down to this building, and set eighty thousand candles into the stonework at the building's base. Then we stood and held hands and sang. Toward dawn we went home smiling, because that night we knew we had won."

She set off once more at her brisk pace, talking all the while. Katya translated in breathless snatches. "When we all marched on the streets, we were truly one Volk. One people. It was this spirit of community we had to build up in order to survive. If it had not been there, the Wall would never have come down.

"It's all gone now, put to sleep by greed. Nowadays everybody hears that they can have everything they want, buy all they desire, if only they go out and work and earn more money and don't give it to anyone else, just keep it for themselves. This new greed isolates us. It makes us more conscious of being alone. And overnight the feeling of pulling together was lost.

"People are diving headfirst into consumerism, and don't understand that there are rocks beneath the surface. Nothing in their lives has prepared them for the shock of this change. Everything tells them to buy now, the signs on the street and the new fancy shop windows and the television and the radio and the newspapers and the magazines. Everything. Buy, buy, and nowhere is anything teaching them the principle of self-discipline.

"They have never learned the first basic lesson of debt, that whatever they borrow they have to pay back. Under the Communists, debt was not allowed to a private citizen. Many people do not even know what the word *interest* means. So they are given this enormous freedom which they don't understand, and they buy everything immediately. The strain on these people, and their families, is tremendous."

She turned into a worn-out building with stone stairs beaten by countless feet into scrabbles of crumbling granite. She fished in her purse for yet another set of massive keys, led them downstairs into a dank and grimy cellar, and stopped before a solid-looking door.

Through Katya she said, "This is from a client. An honest man. Someone who is not part of any plot or secret action. He received these two pieces from a relative before the war."

A heavy skeleton key was inserted and twisted with both hands. She stopped with the door only half ajar and looked back at Jeffrey.

"There are questions everywhere. Questions from everyone, East and West. Too many evil men have hurt too many innocent people, so now there are questions about all hoards of private wealth."

Katya rushed to keep up with the woman's hurried speech. "This is an honest man whose family must have money now. There is a person in the West who claims their home. It is a historical right, granted to people who can show that they were forced out of their holdings by the Communists. Those who can prove this can have their holdings back. She doesn't have any quarrel with the law, just with the pain it is causing to innocent people.

"The person in the West is going to sell the house, and this family will lose the place they have lived in for more than thirty years unless they can come up with the money. There is an enormous housing shortage, and if they can't buy it they don't know where they will live."

The lawyer waited until Katya was finished, then said directly to Jeffrey, "I trust you. You trust me. This not bad man. Good man. Honest. Not many, but this one yes. Honest. You take?"

"I don't even know what it is yet," Jeffrey replied. "But if it is an antique and I think we can sell it, yes, I'll take it."

She nodded her satisfaction when Katya had translated, then opened the door and flipped on the light. Jeffrey stepped into the doorway and breathed a long sigh.

The room's single bare bulb shone down on two articles so fine that even the bare concrete walls with their covering of mold and dust could not alter their impact. Jeffrey stepped forward, feeling the thrill of discovery.

The first was an Italian work, probably Florentine, certainly from the seventeenth century or earlier. It was designed as a cabinet and rested on four graceful mahogany legs connected by a crisscrossing centerpiece. The cabinet itself was modeled after a single-story villa with a tiny roof terrace lined by an even smaller, intricately carved banister. The villa was flanked by four Grecian columns, and paneled with gracefully inlaid floral and fountain scenes. It was in immaculate condition.

The more valuable of the two items was at first glance the less impressive. Jeffrey had never seen one in person before, but he had inspected enough pictures to be almost positive what lay within the blank dark exterior.

From the outside, it was a simple hardwood cabinet, standing on short sturdy legs, rising up to about chest height. The exterior wood had been darkened by time and by its original finish to the point that it was impossible to detect either the grain or the type of wood. It was unadorned save for brass handles on each door, a keyhole designed for a ten-inch skeleton key, and a small wooden lockbox on the chest's top. But from the side Jeffrey could see the cleverly imbedded hinges and the three-inch thick solid wood from which the box was constructed; these two clues gave the cabinet away.

He stepped forward, swung open the doors, and felt a tingling up his spine. It was a royal family's jewelry chest. Date uncertain, but without doubt prior to seventeen hundred. Probably central European.

The interiors of the three-foot-high doors were a pair of solid ivory frames. Within these frames, birds had been designed from thin slices of semiprecious stone and set against a backdrop of onyx. The cabinet itself held ten drawers, five on each side of a larger central chamber. Each drawer was inlaid with a repeated pattern done in ivory and semiprecious stones. The central chamber door was framed by solid ivory pillars and faced with gemstone flowers in a vase of hammered silver.

The lawyer's roughly accented English brought him awake. "You can sell?"

Jeffrey eased himself from his crouch. He nodded. "Without a doubt."

The lawyer was genuinely relieved. "How much?"

"I can't say anything for certain without further evaluation."

When Katya had translated, the woman waved it aside impatiently. "Guess. This important for family."

He rubbed a hand across the side of his face. "This looks to be of what we would call museum quality. Both of them. We would sell it to a serious collector or to a house seeking to build up a selection of Renaissance works."

This time she did not even allow Katya to finish. "Words, words," she barked. "Family must know. How much?"

He took a breath. "At least fifty thousand pounds."

The lawyer made round eyes. She asked through Katya, "Fifty thousand pounds is one hundred and fifty thousand marks, is that right? Yes. I am not used to this new money yet. You will give us that for the two?"

"No. Fifty thousand pounds each. Mind you, they have to be evaluated. We must be absolutely certain they are genuine."

She listened to Katya's translation, then said directly, "But you think yes."

He feasted his eyes on the two works a moment longer, nodded. "I think yes."

"And if genuine, maybe worth more?"

"If the finishes are original, and if they are dated as I think they will be, then the right buyer could pay a lot more."

The cellar was very quiet. "How much more?"

Jeffrey shook his head. "I can't begin to say. Possibly . . . well, I wouldn't even want to guess what the possibility might be."

"Maybe twice, three times?"

He bent back over, traced a gentle hand across the safe's interior. "Possibly."

The lawyer spoke through Katya, who said, "There are other people who will need to sell family treasures in the days and weeks to come. This is not the only family with problems and things to sell. There are too many dishonest people seeking more than is their fair share. They will be happy to know I have found an honest man. Will you come back and do business here again?"

"Of course," Jeffrey replied. He allowed himself to be ushered from the room. "But you have to realize that there is a very big difference between the price paid for a good imitation and the value of an original antique. A world of difference. And I won't know for sure what these pieces are until I have completed a full evaluation."

"This is clear," she replied through Katya. "But I believe you will tell me the truth. You gave back money when you did not need to. You did not try to first tell me that the antiques were fake. The quality of honesty is very rare when such sums are involved. You must come back again. There will be other opportunities for business."

"I'd like that very much," he said, trying to keep his voice calm. "Thank you."

She flipped off the cellar lights, started up the stairwell, and continued to talk over her shoulder. Katya translated. "The next time you come the new autobahn to Schwerin will be open, and the power lines will loom like metal giants over the land. And with the coming of all that wealth and ease and comfort, something will be lost. I am not sorry to see communism go. It had to be. But with this blind rush to join to the West, I tell you that something truly will be lost."

═══

Jeffrey strode back toward Schwerin's old town as though he were walking on air. His first find. His first buy. He filled his lungs to bursting, feeling as though he were breathing champagne.

The family would receive an initial sum sufficient to cover the downpayment on their house—the safe's facades were worth that much alone. Once the pieces arrived in London and authentication was completed, another fifty percent of the minimum estimated value would be sent via the lawyer. Upon sale, the remainder minus commissions.

As they strolled back toward the center of town Katya said softly, "I am very proud of you."

"For what?"

"For the offer of help."

He shook his head. "It was Alexander's idea and Alexander's money."

"I think maybe you had a little to do with it."

"Well, with the arrangement, yes. A little."

She pointed to where a red-brick spire rose above the old city's rooftops. "I'd like to go in there and pray for the people before we leave. Do we have time?"

"If we hurry."

The church was erected around the year eleven hundred, a vast structure of red brick and stone and floored with colored tile. The forty-meter-high domed ceiling took a tour-guide's voice and bounced it back in rolling echoes; the guide paused with practiced cadence to allow the reverberated tones to silence between his phrases.

Jeffrey sat beside Katya as she knelt and prayed. He was content to spend his time looking about the chamber, happy to have the trip behind him, enormously pleased to be at peace with Katya.

The former Communist masters had stripped the churches of their finery and painted the ornate interiors a blank-faced white. All that was left were two wooden crosses, the altar panels, the empty bishop's chair, and a painting of Christ on the cross. All the stained-glass windows had been blown out during the war, replaced with simple translucent glass panels. Stripped of its multicolored lighting, the vast whitewashed chamber held all the warmth and hope of a tomb.

"I love these old churches," Katya said as they left. "It's as though I can feel in my heart the centuries of prayer."

Jeffrey pointed over his shoulder at the church entryway. "Did you see that kid there by the doors?"

"Which one?"

"He was standing at the announcement board when we went out. He was looking at that poster, the big one. It was a Bible verse, wasn't it?"

Katya nodded. "John 3:16. I saw it."

"He was just *standing* there. I'm pretty sure he was the same one I saw when we went in. I noticed him because of the expression on his face. A kid of fifteen, maybe sixteen years old, standing in front of a church reading and rereading a Bible verse."

Katya pulled Jeffrey to a stop, gave him a very tender look. "What was his expression?"

"Total confusion," Jeffrey replied. "Can you imagine? He had no idea what it meant. His face was all furrowed up as if he was trying to figure it out."

The light in her eyes reached out, caressed him, drew him to look both without and within.

"What does that mean, Katya? That he'd never even *heard* the concept of salvation before? Is that really the truth?"

"All but two of the city's churches have been closed for the past fifty years," Katya told him. "Two churches in a provincial capital of over one hundred thousand inhabitants."

He shook his head. "It's one thing to hear about it, another thing to see it."

"You couldn't belong to both a church and the Party," Katya went on. "You couldn't be seen in church, not even for a friend's wedding, and hold a government job. You couldn't go to church and apply for a government pension. To be a practicing Christian meant that at retirement age you received no social security, no payments of any kind.

"If you joined a church in spite of all this, your children were ostracized. Your home was threatened—remember, there was a terrible housing shortage. Some church members were simply tossed out on the street with nowhere to go. There was no social safety net for a believer. Your requests for anything—a new home, a passport, sometimes even a driver's license—were automatically turned down. You couldn't teach. You couldn't study at a university. You couldn't hold a management job or be an engineer or work at a sensitive position. You were always suspect. You were liable to be arrested at any time, charged with sedition and sentenced to long terms in prisons too horrible to describe. You were persecuted, Jeffrey. You and your family. You weren't wanted. The Communists did their best to grind the church and all believers into dust."

"This really happened," he said quietly.

"Just because it wasn't your family or your backyard doesn't make it any less real, Jeffrey. These are real people with real needs who have never even heard that Jesus Christ is the Son of God."

Their plane to Poland was delayed, a common occurrence according to Alexander. Jeffrey had ample time to see Katya off. When they arrived at her departure gate, she lifted her face for a kiss. "I've really enjoyed the trip, Jeffrey. It was very difficult at times, but I'm glad I came."

"Too short, though."

"Anything that is not for forever is too short," she replied.

"I wish you really meant that."

Katya enfolded him in a fierce embrace, mumbling into his chest, "I wish . . ."

"You wish what?"

"Sometimes I wish for too much," she said, releasing him and turning swiftly away. "Goodbye, Jeffrey. Have a safe trip. I will wait for your return."

When he returned to the Hamburg airport's first-class lounge, Alexander said, "You must forgive me this morning. I do not feel quite myself."

"You've had a pretty bad shock," Jeffrey replied.

"More than you perhaps will ever understand," he agreed. "It appears that some things one is not ever able to completely leave behind."

"I don't understand."

"No matter." Alexander cleared the air with a weary wave. "Let us change the subject, shall we?"

"Fine with me." Jeffrey allowed the smile to break loose. "I have some good news."

"Excellent. I cannot recall a time in recent years when good news would have been more welcome." Alexander made a visible effort to pull himself together. "I take it that this beaming visage of yours is not due solely to your departing lady friend."

Jeffrey shook his head. "I made a buy." He related the story of the two pieces.

Alexander listened in silence, then replied, "And on your first trip. Remarkable."

"I couldn't say for sure if they were genuine articles."

"Of course not. There is always the risk that the safe is decorated with stones of paste and tinsel. But you explained this and hinged payment upon authentication." He gave Jeffrey a respectful look. "I am surprised. There is very little these days that surprises me. And I am most pleased."

"Thank you."

"It is I who must offer the thanks. And I believe it is now time for me to divulge some matters of my own." Alexander sipped at a glass of water. "I am indeed grateful for the patience you have shown. It is most unusual for a man of your years to be willing to wait for a explanation about mystery trips to unknown lands."

"I figured you would tell me when it was time."

"Indeed. And that time has now arrived." Alexander inspected him solemnly. "I do not need to tell you how confidential these matters must remain."

"No," Jeffrey replied, his voice rock-steady. "You do not."

Alexander gave his head a single nod. "Very well." He looked around the almost-empty room, removed a silver tube from his pocket, unscrewed the cap, drew out a slender Davidoff cigar. "I hope you don't mind."

"You know I don't."

The lounge steward bustled over and lit the cigar with a long wooden match. Alexander nodded his thanks, waited for the man to depart, then said, "Approximately one third of our purchases come from the open market—auctions or public sales or through other dealers, usually in this latter instance from other countries. One third come from my own acquaintances and friends, built up over the years. And the final third, the source upon which we rely the most, is the East."

"The East?"

"Several places, but all channeled through one man. A relative of mine—ours, I should say. He escaped with me to London, then decided to return to Poland."

"Uncle Gregor?" Jeffrey made round eyes. "The priest?"

"He is not a priest, nor has he ever been. He is what is known as a lay brother, which means that while he does not reside in a monastery, he has made a formal commitment to live a life of service and poverty. Gregor is a most remarkable man, as you will soon discover. He lives according to rules which I have never fathomed. Yet I admire him tremendously, and rely on him completely. You should as well, Jeffrey. You may trust him with anything."

"Uncle Gregor deals in antiques?" This did not fit with what little the family had told of his long-lost relative. "I don't understand."

"I don't expect you to. Not yet. I will ask you to wait until we arrive in Cracow, and see for yourself how our arrangement operates. It would take too long to explain here, and even if I did, you would still not understand until you had seen it for yourself."

Jeffrey nodded. "So these long trips you make are to Poland?"

"Some of them, yes. I choose to cloak all of my trips under the same veil of secrecy, so that none draws more attention than any other. But yes, I do spend a considerable amount of time in Poland and some of the neighboring lands." Alexander smiled. "You have recently spoken with Gregor, by the way."

"When—" He made round eyes. "The blessing?"

"I beg your pardon?"

"The man I told you about, the one who knew my name and left the message that the shipment was ready." Jeffrey smiled at the memory. "He blessed me before he hung up."

"Yes, well, Gregor is known to do such things." Alexander drew on his cigar and emitted a long plume of smoke before continuing. "It is important for you to understand that while there, I wear two entirely different labels. Or have, so long as the Communist regime was in power. So much has changed in recent months that my new roles have not yet been defined. But my former status I must take time to explain now, if you would please be so kind as to bear with me."

Kantor paused to sip from his glass. "First of all, it is important for you to know that under the Communists it was illegal to export anything from Poland that was more than forty years old. To be precise, the law read that nothing made before 1947 could leave the country. But as with any totalitarian government—and believe me, young man, no matter what guise the Communists may have operated under, they were true totalitarians—the concentration of power within a few hands meant that *any* law could be circumvented if it suited the power-holders. The question was, how to make the power-holders see that my interests coincided with their own.

"By establishing this export law, Poland sought to preserve its historical heritage, or what was left after both the Nazis and the Soviets had ransacked the country from end to end. The problem was, only so many items of furniture or paintings or jewelry could be purchased and housed in a museum. And since there was no access to the outside markets, the prices for Polish antiques was set by the internal market. And this market, young man, was barely above starvation level.

"The summer before the Communist regime was toppled, a doctor in the capital city of Warsaw earned the equivalent of forty dollars a month. He or she survived by receiving gifts of food and services from clients who sought preferential treatment and medicines that were not out-of-date. That small example illustrates how close to collapse the occupying forces had brought my homeland. I could give you a thousand others, but you will see these for yourself soon enough. Forty years of Soviet oppression is not going to be wiped out in just a few months.

"As for antiques, the market barely existed at all. Pieces that caught the government's eye—which meant anyone from a museum director to a greedy official—were sometimes purchased. But just as likely the owner would be questioned as to how he or she came to own such an item of capitalist wealth, and then it would be requisitioned. End of story.

"The result was that few pieces ever made it to the open market, and when they did they were available at prices that to our eyes would scarcely be believed. As recently as three years ago, I walked through an antique store in Cracow and spotted items that were selling for less than *one-fiftieth* of the price they would bring in the West. A nineteenth-century Biedermeier cabinet for one hundred dollars. An eighteenth-century Florentine writing desk for about twice that.

"Again, you must remember, prices were so low because most people were so poor, and the nation repeatedly suffered from economic turmoil. Money was set aside for purchasing food when shop shelves were empty, not luxuries like antiques. And the fortunate few with extra money usually desired something new, something manufactured, something that appeared vaguely Western. There was simply no market for old furniture. None."

Alexander rolled his cigar around the ashtray until its tip was a brightly smoldering cone. "More than twenty years ago, I began advising the Polish government on items of national and cultural heritage. I will not bandy words with you, young man. I despise the Communists and their Soviet masters for what they have done to my homeland. But I am a Pole, and as you will soon discover, the Poles are some of the most patriotic folk on earth. They love their country, and it is only with great agony and despair that they will break with the land of their birth. I began this work as a means of maintaining some contact with Poland, and to help preserve a few of the remaining historically important antiques. Five years later Gregor developed his brilliant scheme. Not me, you see. Gregor.

"For over two decades now I have sought both inside and outside Poland to discover items that are closely linked to our history. Jewelry, paintings, ceramics, porcelain, amber, drawings, and furniture. Limited funds were placed at my disposal. I refused to either requisition pieces or identify my sources inside or outside of Poland. Inside the country I paid a fair price—what to the seller no doubt was a fortune. Outside Poland I bought on behalf of the Polish nation, if necessary using my own funds.

"In return for this, the Polish government began granting me export licenses for high quality pieces that I felt would fetch handsome prices in the West. I have been scrupulous in my dealings with the government. Absolutely scrupulous. I take out nothing that could even vaguely be described as a part of our heritage."

He puffed a few times on his cigar before continuing. "But there is so much that remains in our land from the centuries of invading armies and occupying forces. So very much. The history of our nation is not a happy one, and for a long and tragic time Poland even ceased to exist as an independent country. It is these items in which I deal, foreign-made goods if you will, and with which I have managed to create this little empire."

═══

It was long after dark by the time their plane touched down in Cracow, yet even so the transition was very harsh, very sudden. In the space of less than an hour, the Lufthansa plane had transported them from the efficient glitz of a new West German terminal to the dusty haphazard grayness of Socialism. The Cracow Airport was little more than a dilapidated warehouse with ugly appendages and gave no concern whatsoever to artistic appeal or passenger comfort.

Alexander was in his usual querulous bad humor upon their arrival. He passed through customs in utter silence, allowing Jeffrey to assist with his baggage. He then proceeded through the terminal and past the unshaven men offering taxis and hotels, and walked out into the night without saying a word.

A slender young man with jet-black hair stepped from the shadows, gave a formal half bow toward Alexander, and said something Jeffrey could not understand. Alexander replied with a brief word, then said to Jeffrey, "Our driver. His name is Tomek. Almost no English, I'm afraid."

Tomek met Jeffrey's gaze, solemnly shook his hand, motioned for them to remain where they were, and disappeared into the darkness. Beyond the airport's perimeter there were almost no lights.

"Things are certainly much simpler now since the Communists have been removed," Alexander murmured, staring out at nothing.

"What things?"

"Oh, logistics for one. Visas took a month to obtain without connections or bribes or both. Airport arrival formalities took two hours, departures up to five." He wiped a shaky hand across his forehead. "Waiting for taxis that never arrived. Being thrown out of hotels because a powerful Party official arrived unannounced with forty of his closest friends. Changing money illegally because the black market paid ten times the official rate. Waiting in line half a day to purchase a train ticket, only to find once boarding that your place had been sold to three other people as well. Standing in crowded train gangways choked with smoke, having your journey extended by hours because your train had been sidetracked to allow a freight train right-of-way. Shortages of everything and lines everywhere. Public drunkenness wherever you looked."

Car headlights appeared out of the gloom and stopped. Tomek led them over to a relatively new, boxy-looking car called a Polonez. Alexander allowed himself to be settled into the backseat, then leaned his head against the neckrest and closed his eyes with a sigh.

Once the luggage was stowed and Jeffrey was seated beside Alexander, he asked, "Are you all right?"

"I'm afraid not." Under the passing streetlights his skin held a sickly pallor. "This trip appears to have affected me more than usual."

The driver asked a question. Alexander answered curtly. To Jeffrey he said, "We must stop by my cousin's for a few moments."

"Shouldn't we be getting you to bed?"

"Perhaps, but Gregor is expecting us, and I was unable to reach him prior to my departure. It will be a short visit, I assure you."

Jeffrey could make out little of the city. Once the airport complex was left behind, the distance between streetlights lengthened until they became glowing islands in a sea of black.

After a long stretch of silent travel, Alexander stirred himself, lifted his head and said to Jeffrey, "One word of warning. Gregor's health is not the best, as you will soon see. He suffers from some ailment of the joints—my guess is severe arthritis. You must be careful not to overtire him."

"All right."

"The truth is, I don't know what it is exactly that ails my iron-willed cousin. He refuses to tell me, no doubt for fear that I would make a fuss. Quite rightly, I might add. I am fairly positive that his condition would be treatable in the West, but has not received proper attention here. He went in for an operation some ten years ago and came out with the most wretched limp."

"He won't leave to get medical care?"

"Gregor will not leave Poland for any reason whatsoever. You will find, if you work with him awhile, that my cousin can be the most exasperatingly stubborn old goat on earth." The car slowed and stopped at the curb. "Perhaps that is why I care for him as I do."

Gregor lived in a building that Jeffrey put down at first glance as an upscale slum. Even under the cloak of darkness, large bare patches of molding concrete lay exposed where the plaster had flaked off. Wires crawled up the building, held at intervals by twisted metal bands nailed into the wall.

Gregor buzzed them through the front entrance and was waiting on the second-floor landing when they arrived. "Welcome, my dear cousin, welcome."

"Hello, Gregor," Alexander replied, making no effort to mask his fatigue. "I hope you are well."

Gregor took Alexander's hand, grasped his other shoulder, and kissed him soundly on both cheeks. "You had your usual flight, I take it."

"Horrible," Alexander agreed, and turned toward where Jeffrey waited two steps behind him. "May I introduce you to Piotr's grandson. Jeffrey, this is Gregor Kantor."

"A pleasure I have waited a lifetime to realize," Gregor said, his English perfect yet heavily accented. He grasped Jeffrey's hand in a firm grip.

Gregor possessed the same regal features and strong gray eyes as his cousin. Yet his gaze held a gentler light, and his mouth a greater tendency to smile. "Come in, both of you."

"Thank you," Alexander replied, motioning Jeffrey forward. "I believe I shall remain standing."

Gregor lived in the smallest apartment Jeffrey had ever seen. But after a few days in Cracow—after seeing entire families eating and sleeping and living in one room, after seeing buildings with one single stinking toilet for an entire hall of overcrowded apartments, after visiting complexes with a thousand families housed per building and twenty buildings lined up in rows like giant concrete monoliths—Jeffrey changed his mind. At least Gregor had his own toilet and heat and a window that shut and a gas stove and electricity. But Jeffrey did not know about all these things his first night in Cracow. When he walked into what he thought was the apartment's front hall and then realized it was the entire place he thought, I'd go crazy in here.

Gregor read his expression and replied with a smile. "I would invite you to make yourself at home, but as you can see I don't have the room. All I can offer you is a chair and a cup of coffee."

Alexander refused to move beyond the entryway. "Your phone isn't working again."

"Yes, that is true." His gentle smile urged Jeffrey toward the room's only comfortable chair. "But I do have hot water. If I have to choose between the two, I believe I would rather have a nice bath and meet personally with whomever I can't call in a clean skin."

Alexander said to Jeffrey, "My cousin remains in this apartment in order to embarrass me."

"Nonsense. I stay here because it is central and meets my needs." He moved around so as to stand and look down on Jeffrey. With each of his right steps his body listed heavily, throwing his left hip out and arching his entire frame. He straightened, smiled down at Jeffrey, and said, "I have long since learned never to expect a civil word from Alexander after a flight."

Gregor was a frail replica of his cousin. He was as heavy as Alexander, and as tall, yet gave the impression of being scarcely contained within his frame. Jeffrey had a fleeting image of a strong breeze blowing him from his body, taking him to a place where those glowing eyes and warm look and gentle smile better belonged.

He remained standing over Jeffrey for a long moment. "He is the mirror image of his grandfather, don't you think?"

"My memory fails me at the moment."

"You must have noticed it. Did you have an opportunity to know your grandfather, Jeffrey?"

"Not so well. He died when I was still a kid."

"There. His voice even sounds like Piotr's."

"Perhaps."

"It is most certain. My dear boy, your grandfather was one of the finest men I have ever known, and I have known many people." He smiled down at him. "I am sure he would be most proud of you. Would you like a cup of coffee?"

"If it's no trouble."

"None at all. I was just preparing one for myself." He moved behind a ragged-edged curtain to what Jeffrey realized must be the kitchen alcove and pantry and, by the looks of things, a very cramped bathroom.

Alexander said, "You booked us into the Holiday Inn, I hope."

"Certainly not. I booked you into the Cracovia, which is just around the block, as you well know."

"It is also a testament to the Communist doctrine of minimizing taste and maximizing discomfort in their hotels."

"You weren't so choosy when they first opened it twenty years ago."

"At the time it was the only hotel approaching decency south of Warsaw. And they have not changed a thing since. Not even the sheets."

"Don't be absurd. How do you take your coffee, Jeffrey?"

"Black is fine, thanks."

"Such nice manners." Gregor limped back into the main room bearing a steaming glass with no handle. He carried it by wrapping his fingers around the upper edge, above the level of the coffee. Gingerly Jeffrey accepted it, holding it as Gregor had. He started to raise it to his mouth, then stopped when he saw a quarter-inch of coffee grounds floating on the surface.

Gregor, who had already turned to draw up a straight-backed chair, did not see Jeffrey lower the glass. "Next time upon your arrival I shall ask you to come visit me by yourself while my cousin keeps his ill temper downstairs in the car. He won't even allow me to meet him at the airport."

"I won't allow it because you make a scene when I refuse to submit to a ride in that deathtrap you call an automobile."

"There are a dozen better ways to spend money than paying Tomek to act as driver for the entire time of your stay."

"I have long since stopped trying to tell you what to do with your earnings. I suggest you do the same." Alexander pushed himself away from the doorjamb. "Come, Jeffrey. I am tired. We mustn't keep my cousin from his mole-like existence."

Gregor was not the least bit put out by their abrupt departure. "Yes, go on, my dear boy. We can become acquainted another time, when my cousin is not such a bother."

"Sorry about the coffee."

"Nonsense. I was just about to make a cup for myself."

He took Jeffrey's hand, leaned closer, and peered at him with bright gray eyes. "Alexander has told me quite a bit about you, and now that I meet you I see that he was not exaggerating. I am indeed glad that you have inherited more than just your grandfather's fine looks. I am even happier that my cousin has finally managed to find an assistant he can trust."

A voice called up from the front door. "Coming, Jeffrey?"

Gregor patted Jeffrey's shoulder. "Go on, dear boy. We shall have ample time to come to know each other. Of that I am sure."

The Hotel Cracovia took up an entire block. It faced the National Museum—the hotel's only redeeming feature, according to Alexander. In too soft an undertone to be heard by the sullenly inattentive staff, he described the hotel as typical of Communist hospitality. Jeffrey thought it was just plain tacky.

The lobby walls were one shade off blood red. The carpets were a mishmash of squares and floral patterns. The ceiling was water-stained and peeling. Light was supplied by military-like rows of hanging orange glass-and-brass globes, about the same size and aesthetic quality as a beer keg.

The guest rooms had beds nailed to one wall and a long table that served as both desk and television stand attached to the other.

The bathrooms were narrow enough, as Alexander put it before closing his door on the world, to do everything at once. The mirror was set at the perfect height for Jeffrey to inspect his navel.

As Jeffrey unpacked his single valise, he wondered about calling Katya. He placed a call through the hotel operator, who warned it might take as long as two days for a connection, then fell asleep waiting for the phone to ring.

Breakfast took place in a cheerless, institutional-style room. Alexander was already nibbling absently at a piece of bread. He waved Jeffrey to the seat across from him. "I hope you slept well."

"Okay, thanks. How about you?"

"I have found that as I grow older, sleep becomes a rare comfort at times," Alexander replied. "I spent most of the night chasing that most elusive prey, then found myself being chased in turn by ghosts I could not see, only hear."

Jeffrey inspected his boss, not pleased with what he saw. The man looked positively haggard. "Maybe you'd be better off spending the day in bed."

"Perhaps you are right. It shall certainly be no easier to find by the light of day what eluded me all last night. But at least I can rest." As the waiter approached their table, he asked, "What will you have?"

Once breakfast was ordered, Alexander said, "So. Tell me what you thought of my cousin Gregor."

"I don't think I've ever met anybody like him before."

"That is most certainly the case."

"He sure is enthusiastic."

Alexander smiled for the first time that morning. "My thoughts exactly. As a matter of fact, I once accused him of being overly enthusiastic about a life that had little to delight in. Do you know what my dear cousin said?"

"I can't imagine."

"He replied that the word enthusiastic came from two Greek words, *en* and *theos*. Together the words mean to be one with the

Divine. He then thanked me for the nicest compliment anyone had ever paid him."

"Which meant, mind your own business."

"In so many words. But my cousin did not stop there. He went on to say that I lived on the basis that comfort was essential to a good life. He, on the other hand, only needed something to be enthusiastic about. Something that would draw him closer to his Maker."

Jeffrey thought it over. "Did he find it?"

"Something to be enthusiastic about? That, my young friend, you must decide for yourself."

"I can't thank you enough for this opportunity," Jeffrey said. "All the opportunities, for that matter."

"The first opportunity—the job itself—I suppose was in part a gift, and for that you are most welcome," Alexander replied. "But you have earned all the others, and for this I too am grateful."

"Would you mind telling me why I was hired?"

"When so many local antique specialists would have given their best dozen years on this earth to become an associate in a Mount Street salon?" Alexander nodded. "Because before such a person arrived on my doorstep, their own self-interests would have already been cast in the fires of greed and ambition, and then honed to a killing edge."

"I think I see."

"They would have had ample time to learn the lessons followed by most people in this trade, concepts such as loyalty to no one but themselves. Or the belief that honesty is a commodity to be traded just like that slow-moving chair in the back room. Or that duty is a word that went out with sabers and cavalry charges."

"And with me you could start out fresh."

"At least so far as the antiques trade was concerned, yes. My primary wish was to obtain the services of an intelligent, honest, trainable assistant. So long as most of the actual purchasing fell into my hands, you would have ample time to study and to learn. Time that you have used well, I must say. I am most pleased with the manner in which you have filled your idle hours."

"I wouldn't call them idle."

"Just as I said. You came to know each piece in the shop so well that you fooled even the best of them. I have heard some rather dreadful comments about you from the vultures that frequent auctions, Jeffrey. There could be no greater praise than to have them see you as a threat sufficient to make them take notice." He examined Jeffrey from beneath his lofty eyebrows. "Most certainly you've been approached about how to line your own pockets while stabbing me and my shop in the back."

"I'd never do that."

"Of course you wouldn't. That is precisely my point. No doubt you've also received your share of offers in the meantime. Perhaps even a senior associate position in a major auction house?"

"A few," Jeffrey admitted.

"Don't take them. You're not ready yet. When you are, when you can buy as well as you now sell, there is a certain shop on Mount Street that awaits you."

"That's what I'm hoping," he confessed.

"I won't tell you not to get your hopes up, Jeffrey. I am too practical to waste precious time on such nonsense. And I will not describe this as a test, for if I were not already sure of the outcome I would not be inviting you along. No, I want you to simply keep in mind that this is first and foremost a learning experience."

"I understand."

Alexander leaned over the table. "You will need to come up to the room with me before you go. I want you to carry my money belt. It contains ten thousand dollars. You are to carry that much every time you go for a buy. Many people will demand a cash advance, and it is important that you be able to acquire something valuable without delay, to ensure that it is not sold to someone else before you can return. Before you go in for a buy, slip a couple of thousand into your pocket. If you need additional funds, go back out to the car. Don't let them know you are carrying more than what you have in your pocket. Remember, a thousand dollars is still a small fortune in Poland—more than many people earn in a year. And keep the money in your belt around to your back in case thieves search you."

"Things are that bad here?"

"Most of the people we deal with are repeat clients, and Gregor knows almost all of the others. But don't take chances. If they think you have money and are vulnerable, they may decide honesty is too expensive a virtue."

"I meant, things in general."

"Things in general, as you say, are disastrous. The police are increasingly ineffective, and thieves know this. Poland is becoming a lawless land. The last time I was here, I decided to take a walk around my Warsaw hotel. On the first corner were addicts moaning for their drug. On the next, Romanian refugees begging for pennies. On the next, two men beating each other's faces in. On the next was a police station with the men lounging out front. On the opposite corner was a church with its door locked and windows barred. At four o'clock in the afternoon."

He glanced at his watch. "Gregor will be expecting you in about a half an hour. He'll have been up since the crack of dawn, as always. You are sure you will be all right without me today?"

"I suppose so. I'd rather have you come, but you really don't look up to it."

"Which is exactly how I feel. This trip is not going as I had intended, but life seldom does." Alexander pushed himself from his chair with a visible effort. Jeffrey hurried over and steadied him with a hand on his shoulder. "Thank you. I shall rely on your young strength today. Give Gregor my regards, and tell him to teach you well."

———

"He is not ill, is he?" Gregor asked when Jeffrey explained Alexander's absence.

"Not really. Just exhausted." He related the happenings of the previous two days. "I have the feeling that it might have something to do with it."

"Ah." Gregor nodded his agreement. "I am so sorry to hear this. And on your very first trip as well."

"Why is he like this?"

"The reasons are for him to say, my dear boy. They are his memories, not mine. All I can say is that your experiences in Schwerin have brought his worst nightmares to life." Gregor began briskly preparing for departure. "That is enough on that, I should think. Shall we be off? We have much to do today.

"Despite what Alexander refers to as my apartment's minuscule proportions," Gregor said as they left the apartment, "it has several major advantages. It is a fifteen-minute walk to the old town, and the building has only five floors and thirty-seven apartments. That is nothing compared to the monstrosities that the Communists have erected. You will be visiting a few of them."

"I can hardly wait," Jeffrey said, casting a backward glance at the building. He took in the dull gray exterior, the flaking windowpanes, the crumbling front steps, the dusty strip of unadorned earth fronting the curb, and wondered what a disadvantaged place must look like.

"My building was erected in the fifties," Gregor went on, making his rolling way down the sidewalk. "At that time, buildings were still being made from brick and concrete rather than mortar blocks and steel. As a result this building is insulated, you see. My walls do not sweat in the cold. Nor do they freeze in the dead of winter, as happens in some of the newer buildings—the interior walls, I am speaking of. Sometimes I feel a little guilty not residing as most people do here, but as you can see my health is unfortunately not the best. One winter in such a place and I would be immobilized for life."

He stopped in front of a stubby car the color of old mustard. Jeffrey looked it over, tapped the plastic hood. It was a square cigar box on skinny tires, designed to grow old swiftly and fall apart. Gingerly he pushed down on his side; the car rocked like a boat in high seas. No shocks at all.

"Don't you think we would be better off having Alexander's driver take us around?"

"I wouldn't dream of such a thing," Gregor replied, climbing in and shutting his door. It bounced back open. He reached out with both hands and slammed it into submission. He inserted the key and ground the ignition. Jeffrey sighed in defeat, slid onto the narrow seat. The car sounded like a motorized sewing machine. "This is an East German car, a Trabant," Gregor said above the engine's whining putter. "In Poland they call them Hoennecker's Revenge. Hoennecker was the former ruler of East Germany."

"Back in the U.S., people put quarters in motel beds and don't get as good a ride as this," Jeffrey replied. He hung on to the door strap with both hands, tried to lift himself over the worst of the bumps. He turned his head as a bus coughed out a vast cloud of black smoke that engulfed their car. "Do they have a nickname for buses?"

Gregor nodded. "Skunks."

They left Cracow, turned onto a small secondary road, and began making their way through open farmland. The fields were verdant green, the sky a baked blue. Jeffrey rolled down his window and inhaled the fresh air.

They passed a smattering of run-down houses that gradually condensed and formed a small village. Jeffrey remarked, "It seems as if the main color of communism wasn't red. It was gray."

"The hardest lie to accept is one told time and time again," Gregor replied. "I would hear the Communists lie on the evening news, and some evenings I would just cry out for my country's pain."

Jeffrey eyed row after row of sagging sad-faced houses. "Why didn't they ever paint anything?"

"Ask a thousand people, my boy, and you'll receive a thousand reasons, all of them true. For the larger housing projects, there was no need to keep up appearances because all the property was state-owned. Resources went to new projects, not maintaining old ones. Buildings erected after the war with one bathroom for ten or eleven apartments—which was a vast improvement on no indoor plumbing at all—have remained exactly as they were built.

"Those families who wanted to improve their apartments had to fight against a system that controlled all supplies of *everything*. Paint and brushes, for example, had to be ordered through requisition, and could take *years* to obtain. What was received was used indoors on their apartment. No one but the state laid claim to the building as a whole, and the state's attention was always elsewhere. So the buildings were usually left to rot.

"Most village homes remained privately owned in Poland, but here again the supply problems remained catastrophic. Added to that was the lack of money, the people's sense of resignation over their plight, and a desire to blend in with their surroundings. A well-maintained private dwelling would attract the worst type of attention—thieves or tax inspectors."

Cobblestone streets and gray buildings gave way to a small central plaza. Two carts piled high with vegetables and pulled by bony horses with drooping necks stood in front of the only store whose sign Jeffrey could understand—Bar. They continued to the village's other side and halted in front of an old farmhouse.

Gregor stared through the front windshield at the house's dilapidated condition. "The Communists did not choose to give up power in Poland. They were *forced* to leave because they led the nation to economic ruin. Worse than that. They led the nation by an economic lie, and generations of Poles have paid the price for this lie."

From the front, the farmhouse was almost smothered by a veritable forest of dahlias. They began around ankle height up by the gate, and mounted steadily until arriving at the low-sloping roof.

As Jeffrey started to climb from the car, he was stopped by a hand on his shoulder. "Before we go in, I need to know how much Alexander has told you of the way we work."

"Just the bare bones." When they had returned upstairs after breakfast that morning, Alexander had outlined their purchase strategy. Gregor was responsible for both locating the items and making the initial check; he knew enough about antiques by now for him to be trusted to weed out any obvious fakes. Any purchases that had to be made immediately, in order to keep them from falling into other buyers' hands, he also took care of and stored for Alexander's arrival.

Purchases were concluded immediately on the basis of paying a fair price by Polish standards. Once the piece was sold, the full sales price less commissions—often a fortune by Polish standards—was passed on through Gregor. Gregor received half of the commission less expenses, plus an unidentified sum from the shop's total profit.

"Prices here are still excellent by Western standards, but nothing compared to what we found in the past. This is especially true with the smaller items."

"Because they can be smuggled easier," Jeffrey guessed.

"Exactly. The border guards are daily becoming more lax and open to bribery. People are taking their heirlooms out of closets and into the antique stores, and receiving prices that mount daily. The price that was unthinkable yesterday would not buy a bent spoon tomorrow.

"Nowadays people with something to sell are being approached by strangers from all over," Gregor continued. "The Italians are busy buying up everything they can get their hands on at rock-bottom prices. Meanwhile, they have lawyers who are lobbying the new parliament to change the export laws."

"We have new competition, then," Jeffrey said.

"Yes and no. Most of these strangers are sharks. They look to pay pennies for what they can sell for fortunes. The Polish people know this. Still, their families are hungry, their children are sick and needing medicine, many have lost their jobs. They hold and they hold and they hold, because this precious item is often the only real savings they have, the only security against trouble, the only hope for their old age. But in times as bad as these, sometimes it only takes one more small problem, one more calamity for them to give up and sell. When that happens, they may act out of panic and sell to whomever gets there first."

"Things are that bad right now?"

"Horrible. You will see that in your travels, I am sorry to say."

"So I should make an initial payment equal to what the Italians would pay as a total, is that right?"

Gregor gave him an approving look. "Alexander said that you were quick to catch on. Yes, that is exactly what I want you to do. And if it is something we can fit in the car, we carry it away with us. If not, I arrange to have a truck come by the same evening that we make our visit. These people are hungry, Jeffrey. They may decide to sell the item twice. It is best to remove such temptations as swiftly as possible."

"So where do we store it until it's time for shipment? A warehouse?"

Gregor shook his head. "Warehouses have become the favorite target of gangs. No, we have worked out a safer and a quieter place than a warehouse, Alexander and I. Someplace where we can keep whatever pieces I find and purchase before his arrival. Tomek works for me when Alexander is not here. He owns a truck that he and his son use to transport all the articles we purchase."

Gregor led the way around back to a swept yard made muddy by the morning's heavy dew. A host of tame ducks greeted their arrival with apprehensive glances and worried quacks. A truly ancient dog made do with a couple of wheezy barks, then watched in silence as they progressed through the ducks and chickens and mud.

An old woman pushed aside the draped cloth that served as her screen door, spoke what clearly was a greeting to Gregor, and led them inside. The house was built for people of her height; Jeffrey had to remain in a perpetual stoop. The ceiling beams were about five and a half feet high; the woman passed under them easily.

She was very heavy, standing almost as wide as she was tall. Her face had taken on the shape of a featureless circle and the color of unbaked dough. Her arms were thick and wobbled as she walked, her legs massive and encased in several layers of socks and flesh-tone support hose. She wore three sweaters and an apron over her faded housedress.

"I am so very sorry," she said through Gregor. "The house is too small, I am too poor; you must be used to so much nicer things than what I am able to offer."

"Everything is just fine," he said, wondering what on earth there might be of interest. The house was furnished with either rough-hewn pieces made from lumber scraps or just plain junk.

She ushered them into her minuscule sitting room, where Jeffrey found a table loaded with food—sliced ham, roast chicken, deviled eggs, fresh rolls, homemade pickles, vegetable salad, and two cakes. She said through Gregor, "Won't you have a little tea?"

Jeffrey whispered, "This is for us?"

"This is Polish hospitality," Gregor replied.

"We just had breakfast."

"It doesn't matter. We are her guests, and in Poland you offer your guests the very best of what you have."

The old woman stood with hands crossed in front of her stomach and watched them sit and begin loading their plates. She poured them tea and said through Gregor, "It's nothing, really. Just a second breakfast."

Gregor smiled. "The fact is, she has been preparing for several days for our arrival. She is not a wealthy person, as you can see. But whatever she has, she will devote to hospitality. It is the Polish way."

"Please tell her the food is great."

"Nothing would thrill her more than to see her American guest take seconds," Gregor said.

Jeffrey ate and examined the cramped surroundings. The walls were covered with a continual design that had been painted over the cracked limewash and decorated with religious prints—saints, crucifixes, photographs of icons. The floor was ragged carpet laid on ancient linoleum. Each room had a single bulb for illumination. The light filtering through handmade windowpanes was cloudy and vague. The entire house was neat as a pin and gave the impression of a snug little cave, saved from being claustrophobic only by its cleanliness and the woman's genuine smile.

When they could eat no more and refused her offer of yet another piece of cake or another glass of tea, reluctantly she allowed them to stand and follow her back into the narrow hall. She stopped at the entrance to the cottage's other room and said, "My husband was hit by a truck and killed last year. He was a victim of Poland's greatest killer—vodka. It was the driver who had been drinking, not my husband. He had never given in to the temptation, may the good Lord bless his soul. It was so strange to hear of his death from the official, when the house still smelled from his morning coffee and his shirts still hung from the line. Now I am alone, and my daughter has three babies and a husband who has been laid off. I have hoarded things I never needed for far too long."

Jeffrey followed Gregor's lead and stood patiently, nodding to her words, wondering why she continued to smile as she spoke, feeling the onset of a serious crick in his bent-over neck.

With a theatrical flourish she swept the curtain door aside and said through Gregor, "My daughter's room."

Jeffrey stepped through the doorway, looked around, and laughed out loud.

Gregor stepped up beside him. "She wants to know if anything is the matter."

"No, nothing. It was just a little unexpected, that's all."

Opposite the doorway stood a cabinet, so heavily carved as to make the exterior appear like a pile of unsorted sculptures—vases and grapes and bas-relief statues and hanging flowers and gods' faces and framed designs—all jumbled into something only a museum curator could love.

Gregor moved up beside him and said, "In the late seventeenth century, one quarter of the students at the major Italian universities were the children of Polish gentry. That particular generation transformed the country's tastes, as you can see. They drew it toward the ornate foppery of early Italian Renaissance style. This is a perfect example of the result."

"Horrible," Jeffrey decided.

"Perhaps. Alexander would certainly agree with you. But the last time we came upon such a piece, he said he knew of a dozen curators who would positively drool at the news."

Beyond the cabinet was a bed. It rested on a simple wooden frame, but around this was a second frame the likes of which Jeffrey had never seen. The floorposts were a foot square at the base, rising to carved Grecian urns that sprouted tall flowering plants. Each of the posts appeared to have been carved from one solid log, and supported an upper bedframe carved and gilded to appear like golden grapes hanging from a leafy vine. The carving on the headboard alternated between pastoral scenes and royal coats-of-arms.

"A young prince's bed," Gregor guessed, coming up beside him. "Remarkable."

"How did it get here?" Jeffrey ran a hand across the headboard, could not find any trace of a seam.

"That, my dear boy, is a story we shall most probably never know." Gregor turned back to where the lady waited in the doorway. "I'll tell her that you are interested in taking it, then, shall I?"

"This belongs in a museum," Jeffrey said, then corrected himself. "If it's real, that is."

"Oh, I imagine it is. Thankfully, most of the items I locate are authentic, especially ones of this size. Although the Communists had visions of making themselves the new royal class, with all sorts of special privileges, they had few resources for making replicas of anything. What was available usually went for massive statues of Lenin."

====

After leaving the farmhouse they drove slowly on past the village. The roads were narrow and in terrible condition. Jeffrey maintained his death's grip on the door strap and enjoyed his tour of the countryside.

The evidence of poverty was starkly vivid. No one he saw wore well-fitting clothes, much less anything new. The people themselves looked worn down to the point of absolute exhaustion. Even the children they passed had pinched, chiseled features and dark shadows under their eyes.

Almost all the farm work he saw was done by stoop labor. Women tilled fields with hand hoes, wearing headkerchiefs and high rubber boots. Men walked beside horse-drawn plows or wagons filled with produce or manure or wood.

There was very little car traffic on the roads. Trucks and buses wobbled along on uneven axles and belched deep clouds of smoke. People rode bicycles or walked along the road's edge.

It appeared that everyone he passed had some physical ailment—a pronounced limp, a disjointed shoulder, a bent spine, a missing limb, a scar. When they passed a group of people standing together or stopped for a traffic light, he watched intently but saw no smiles. All the faces looked closed to him, screwed down and clamped shut against a world that was always hostile, always a risk, never open or friendly or helpful or safe. All the voices drifting in through his open window sounded tired. Tragic. Resigned.

The village where their second meeting was scheduled was much like the first—a series of winding streets that led nowhere.

"I keep looking for a center of town," Jeffrey said.

"The war destroyed many towns' central structures," Gregor explained. "The Communists then came in and built endless rows of functional housing. This was vastly cheaper than restoring the grand old structures. The Communists were very big on functionalism. Beautification was not a word in their vocabulary."

He pulled up in front of a split-beamed log cabin, the spaces between the wood chinked with spattered concrete.

Jeffrey did not open his door. "They have an antique?"

"I have done business with them several times," Gregor replied. "Perhaps the pieces came from a friend or a relative or someone else who did not want to risk having his face seen."

Gregor opened his door and stood. When Jeffrey joined him, he said, "At the same time, it could very well have come from a midnight raid on the local manor. Flaming torches carried by a mob attacking in rage and panic against an official who had sold his soul to the Nazis, with the sound of the Soviet tanks rumbling in the distance. Quite a bit of that happened as well. If the booty was small, it might have been buried in the cowshed. If large, it may have spent the past forty years as one wall of the chicken coop.

"Even if the family was better off, the antique was always hidden," Gregor went on, making his limping way along the roadside. "Valuables may not have been dumped into a hole in the ground, but they were never on display. The room with the desk or the painting or the silver was never open to non-family. If the owners were fortunate enough to have a small garden plot, they might build the piece into the wall of their shed, or stack it behind all their tools. But the antiques were never there to decorate. They were held as the family's last resort, the item to sell when all was bleak and the crisis was life-threatening. Never for show."

Gregor walked with his swinging gait across the dusty street. "Never ask where the article came from, my boy. It's tempting, I know, especially when you want to establish provenance. But trust here is very fragile and very carefully given. Everyone fears questions. Questions may lead to suspicions, and suspicions to some sort of harm. Let them offer the information if they care to, but never ask." He looked up at Jeffrey. "They just might tell you."

As they approached the farmhouse gate, they were hailed from behind. They turned to see a short, slight man hustle across the gravel road on very bowed legs, his progress slowed by the water yoke suspended across his shoulders. The buckets hung from two metal chains and water sloshed on his pantlegs as he hastened to join them. With a practiced motion he swung open the gate, walked into the miniature yard, lowered the buckets to the ground, dropped the yoke, and motioned them inside. His neck and shoulders remained bent in the same posture they had while wearing the yoke.

He offered Jeffrey his hand, but could not manage to unfurl his fingers. Jeffrey fitted his hand inside the man's; it felt as if he were grasping an animal's horn.

The man's age fell somewhere between thirty and seventy, and he barely reached Jeffrey's rib cage. He and Gregor spoke a few words, enough for Jeffrey to see that the man had only two teeth in his mouth. Then he led them inside.

A narrow hall opened on one side into the cow stalls and on the other into the cottage's single room. The room's floor was hard-packed earth covered with layers of cardboard boxes opened and trampled flat. The ceiling was even lower than in the other farmhouse. Heat was supplied from a tiled wood-burning stove, along whose upper surface stood several pots left to simmer all day. The air was full of scents—cabbage and pork and potatoes and nearby animals and stale sweat.

In the center of the room an ancient woman half sat, half leaned on a tree-limb carved into a cane. Despite the day's heat she wore multiple layers of sweaters, a headkerchief, and bright yellow boots with the toes cut out. A pair of gray woolen socks peeked through the toe holes.

She eyed Jeffrey with a friendly glance and spoke a few words at Gregor.

"Babcha—that means grandmother, or old dear in Polish—says that if she had a couple of men as big as you to carry her, she'd be all over the village," Gregor translated.

Jeffrey grinned from his bent-over stance. "If I see anyone my size looking for work, I'll send him over."

The old woman cawed, showing a few lonely teeth, and said something that made Gregor laugh. "That was the first time she'd ever heard a language other than Polish. She asks if you'd talk some more."

"You mean, give a speech?"

The old woman laughed once more. "You've made her day," Gregor said.

The old woman waved her cane at the man, who rummaged in a rag pile by the stove and came up with a rotting burlap sack. He handed it over to Jeffrey and said something that Gregor translated as, "Their grandson is getting married and wants to buy a farm. Prices are very cheap now for anyone with cash. There is a real crisis in the farming industry because the government has retracted all subsidies, and market prices often do not cover their spiraling costs. A lot of farmers have gone under."

Jeffrey hefted the article and guessed its weight at more than ten pounds. He tried to match Gregor's casual tone. "Farmland wasn't . . . what do you call it when the state takes it over?"

"Collectivized. No, they started to, but the Poles in the government urged the Soviets not to insist. They feared a civil war. Land remained in the hands of the farmers who owned it already, with only the big estates being taken over by the government. Some of that land was also given out in small plots in an attempt to win the farmers over to their side."

Jeffrey nodded. He decided he had been polite long enough. Gingerly he unfolded the covering, stopped short when the article came into view. It was an eighteenth-century Meissen porcelain *brule-parfum,* an ornate container used to burn perfume—a sort of royal air-freshener. The central burner was square, each face decorated with delicate paintings of a young lady standing in her garden. The large base was of *ormolu,* or gilded bronze, as were the flower stems that wove a delicate pattern up each side of the burner. The flowers themselves were layer upon petalled layer of porcelain, some of the finest work Jeffrey had ever seen.

"This is a treasure," Gregor said softly.

Jeffrey nodded. Intertwined within the flowers were two cherubs, peeking out in timeless gaiety at a world of poverty and grime. "How on earth did it get here?"

"That is a tale we shall never know." Gregor drew himself upright and turned to the smiling old woman. "I shall tell her that we are interested, yes?"

=====

"Gregor was quite right not to ask where it came from," Alexander told him that evening. They walked beneath a sky turned into a crowning glory of brilliant hues by a slow motion summer sunset. "We are here to buy antiques, not tales."

Jeffrey allowed himself to be guided by the gentleman's silent directions, unsure if there was a destination, but glad to at least have Alexander up and about. "Don't you ever wonder?"

"Of course I do. And I am extremely grateful when someone trusts me enough to share a story or two."

His color was still not good, and his interest in the pieces was not as great as Jeffrey had expected. Alexander's attention remained caught by something only he could see, with only a small part of his mind given over to the matter at hand. "After a while you learn enough to make a few guesses. That first woman's house may once have been the servant's quarters to a manor that was bombed out of existence during the war. Perhaps the lord of the manor gave her husband those pieces when they went out of fashion, a gift to an able servant. But about that second item, one can only speculate."

Alexander indicated with a motion of his chin that they should cross the street and take a course that appeared to follow the first line of old buildings. The contrast between old and new Cracow could not have been greater, especially at this border area. New Cracow consisted mostly of unadorned and unpainted multistory structures of concrete; they had been streaked and darkened by decades of pollution and neglect. Old Cracow cried to every passerby of a distant royal past. Palatial residences crowded close to one another, a living museum of structures whose designs spanned more than nine hundred years.

"In December of 1981," Alexander said, "all of Warsaw talked about the possibility of starvation. All of Poland, for that matter." He led them onto a thin strip of green, beyond which rose remnants of an ancient city wall. "After months of protest marches and labor unrest, the Polish government had declared martial law. The Russians, everyone believed, were diverting food in order to discredit the Solidarity movement. The situation was growing more desperate by the day."

Alexander shook his head. "One day I went to the countryside near Lublin, and in a pub that night I heard one old farmer talking to another. He was using this loud voice that you would never have heard in Warsaw. He said, beating the table as he spoke, 'In 1943 there were three entire Nazi divisions in Lublin province. And there were the partisans. And all the refugees from the bombed cities. Besides that, because the Russians were approaching, Lublin was the only province supplying food to Warsaw! The only province, feeding three Panzer divisions and the partisans and its folk and a city of a million and a half.'

"At that point I noticed that the entire pub had grown silent. It was not just a listening silence, it was an agreement. This old man with one foot in the grave and nothing to lose was speaking for all of them. Even the chefs and dishwashers came out of the kitchen to listen and agree. I sat and watched, and I felt that here in this rotting little pub on the edge of a backward farming region, I had been brought face-to-face with the heart of Poland.

"So this man, who all the while totally ignored the effect his words were having on the people around him, continued to clump his fist on the table with the regularity of a heartbeat. He went on, 'So what does that tell you? That Poland is poor? That Poland cannot feed itself? No! It is the Russians who have done this to us, who have robbed and impoverished us! People don't need to fear starvation, and what's more they know it. They fear hunger because they're afraid to fear the real enemy. The people need to wake up and fear Russia! They need to open their eyes and see that here is a beast that will eat them whole! They need to recognize that the menace to the east does not care for them or their families or their land or their history, only for what they can take. They need to see it as a parasite that will suck all the blood from this great Polish nation, then cast the remains aside. There will be no tombstone for our nation, no marker in history, no more notice made than to any poor soul passing on in a Siberian labor camp. We will be gone, and that is that. Unless we wake up and know fear.'

"The man went on for over an hour to a completely silent group. Nobody said a word the entire time. When he stopped, he became just another trembling old gentleman in dirty farming clothes, and the pub became just another roadside hut selling simple food and watery beer and vodka. Mind you, in Warsaw the man would have quietly disappeared. That, my friend, is the power of a farmer in hard times. No one but a man supplying food could have spoken those words and lived to see another sunrise."

Through the trees up ahead, the dimming light illuminated a shadow-structure of towers and turrets all clustered tightly together. Jeffrey pointed. "What on earth is that?"

At first Alexander did not reply. They left the trees behind and stopped at the edge of a plaza that ringed the structure. His voice was none too steady when he finally said, "That is Florian's Gate."

In the foreground of Florian's Gate stood a sturdy circular barbican, a sort of mini-castle built as a first line of defense. It was constructed of brick and crowned by numerous peaked towers. The barbican fronted the gate itself, an older square tower connected to the medieval town wall. Both wall and gate were of stone, with upper reaches notched for bowmen and crowned by a tall wood-slat roof.

"In olden times each guild was assigned a gate," Alexander said, working to keep his voice steady as they walked around the barbican. "They had to both maintain the structure and arm it. St.

Florian was the patron saint of fire fighters. You'll find his statue in the tower's recesses. He's always shown suited in shining armor, pouring water from his helmet over a flame."

As they approached the tower's arched portal, Alexander took a firm grip on Jeffrey's arm. "If you would please allow, I will rely on your strength for just a moment."

Jeffrey slowed his pace to match Alexander's, feeling the fingers digging into his arm. They stopped fifty feet or so before the entrance; it was clear that Alexander was going no farther. Jeffrey searched the fading sunlight beyond the portal but found only crowds strolling down cobblestone ways.

"I haven't visited this part of Cracow in fifty years," Alexander said, still maintaining his clenched grip on Jeffrey's arm.

"Why not?"

"Centuries of history have passed through this gate," Alexander replied. "But for me it holds only one memory. It was here that I was arrested and dragged off as a sixteen-year-old boy."

"What for?"

"Reasons were not always given at that time. Events simply occurred. Survival was such a difficult matter that questions of any sort became luxuries one could not afford."

Jeffrey felt the chill of horror. "You were arrested by the Nazis?"

"I cannot imagine passing through that gate ever again," Alexander murmured. "Not ever. Even standing here, I am filled with dread and hopelessness." He pointed a shaking hand toward the portal's recesses. "Do you see the candles flickering there?"

"Yes."

"In the center of the tower gate is an altar. There is a brass frame imbedded in the stone, and in it is a sacred painting. Still today travelers stop and pray for a good journey, as they have done for almost a thousand years." He allowed his arm to fall back. "There were lilacs in the altar vase that day, and candles flickering where someone had come to pray earlier that morning. It was the last thing I saw before they loaded me in the truck and drove me away."

Alexander steered Jeffrey around and began walking away. "Where was mercy when I needed it? Why were my prayers not answered?"

Jeffrey fought against his rising sense of dread. "Where did they take you?"

"I have a favor to ask," Alexander said in reply.

Jeffrey turned to face him. "Anything."

His discomfort was plainly visible. "This is a most difficult matter, but I need your help, I'm afraid."

"All you have to do is ask, Alexander."

"Ah, but you do not know what it is that I wish to request."

"It doesn't matter," Jeffrey replied flatly.

Alexander inspected him, noting, "You are indeed a friend."

"I'd like to be."

"Very well." He took a shaky breath. "I am called to face my past. And because I know no other way to say it, I shall confess to being afraid to face it alone."

"You want me to go somewhere with you?"

"If you would."

"Sure. When do we leave?"

"Tomorrow at first light. I wish to have this done and behind me."

Jeffrey nodded. "I'll go over and leave a note for Gregor."

"Thank you, my young friend. Your strength will be most needed."

"May I ask where we're going?"

Alexander gave him a haunted, empty look. "Auschwitz."

The two-lane road to Oswiecim, as the town was called in Polish, had neither lane markers nor road-signs. They passed through village after small cluttered village, the stretches in between lined with chestnut and oak and silver-leafed birch. At times their branches reached up and over the road, weaving a green canopy through which golden sunlight flickered and streamed.

The slow-moving traffic held their speed to less than forty miles an hour for most of the way. Dark-fumed trucks thundered around horse-drawn carts, old men pushing wheelbarrows, sedately bouncing buses, and boxy East European cars. The only transport refusing to obey the unmarked speed limit were the newer Western cars, which powered around other vehicles and blind corners with aggressive madness.

Signals of newly planted capitalism sprouted alongside the way in the form of dilapidated buses converted into roadside cafes. Only the multitude of *Kapliczki*—shrines with a Christ or Madonna and child—bore fresh paint. Often someone was kneeling in prayer before them; always they were encircled by wreaths of newly planted flowers.

Alexander said nothing from the moment he seated himself in the car to the point when they arrived in Oswiecim, the village where the Auschwitz concentration camp memorial was located. He sat with shoulders hunched and face pointed slightly to the right, seeking to keep himself hidden from the driver beside him and from Jeffrey behind.

They passed the city-limits sign for Oswiecim. Kantor stirred and sighed the words, "It is indeed a heavy day."

Their way took them along two sides of a mile-long wall constructed from concrete blocks framed with steel girders and railroad sidings. It was topped by rusted steel pylons and coiled strands of barbed wire. Every fifty meters or so, a guard tower's peaked roof and blank windows stared down at them from beyond the wall.

They pulled into a vast parking lot where several dozen buses vied for space with taxis and private cars and minivans. Hundreds of people, most of them teenagers, milled about under the leafy shade trees.

Alexander seemed blind to all but his own internal world. He rose from the car with the slow trembling of an ancient man, blinked at the sky, murmured, "Why is there sun?"

Jeffrey moved up next to him. "I'm sorry, I didn't—"

"There should be no sun here. From this place the light should be forced to hide its face."

Jeffrey touched Alexander's arm. "Are you sure you want to do this?"

Alexander drew himself erect with an effort. "Come along, Jeffrey. My past is calling."

As they passed into the reception hall, a sign covering the entire left wall announced in seventeen languages that no child under the age of thirteen was allowed past this point. Alexander stood before it for a time before saying, "The Nazis were not so considerate."

The hall was lined with broad-framed photographs: multiple barbed-wire fences; a nighttime view of the infamous entrance gates; an Orthodox Jew in prayer robes and tefflin saying Kaddish; flowers strewn in great piles on and around the ovens used for cooking down the bodies; a snowy winter dawn casting gloomy light over the central prison square; a black-and-white sea of forks and spoons that at first glance appeared to be a pile of glinting bones.

Jeffrey halted before a poem posted at the door leading out to the camp. It read:

> Electric wires, high and double
> Won't let you see your daughter
> So don't believe the censored letter of mine
> Since truth is different,
> But don't cry, Mother
> And if you would like to seek your child

Look for the ashes in the fields of Birkenau
They'll be there, so look for the ashes
In the fields of Auschwitz,
In the woods of Birkenau,
Mama, look for the ashes, I'll be there!

Monika Domlke
Born 1920

As they walked into the green park bordering the camp, Alexander began, "In the morning of August 12, 1940, about a year after the German invasion, I walked down to Florian's Gate. The plaza there held a sort of unofficial market, a place where people gathered with things to buy or sell. I was looking for a pair of pants and a pair of shoes. Things were getting steadily worse, especially with respect to supplies. It was becoming harder and harder to find food and simple things like clothes. So that particular morning I went by myself on the streetcar to Florian's Gate.

"It was not a licensed market, so many sharp city people would wait there to take advantage of people coming in from the countryside, looking for wares they could not find in their villages. For example, a man would stand with one shoe held high up over his head until someone came by and asked how much for it. He would perhaps reply, two hundred zloty. They would bargain, and settle on maybe one hundred and fifty, the man would ask for the money, then hand over the one shoe. The country fellow would ask for the other shoe, and the man would say, ah, you want to buy *two*? Why didn't you say so? That will be another hundred and fifty zloty. A lot of small-time shysters like that operated around the gate. I suppose that was why the Nazis chose this place to make one of their sweeps."

They arrived at the looming metal gates. Jeffrey paused to look down the gravel path running between double rows of fencing and concrete pylons. He stood there a moment, willing himself to turn to steel, harden himself against whatever awaited him inside. Then they entered.

To his left were several red-brick barracks. To his right was the wood and brick camp kitchen. The camp itself was neat and orderly and incredibly silent given the number of people walking the paths. The loudest sound was that of wind rustling in the tall trees. Jeffrey walked the rock-lined path and felt grateful for Alexander's droning voice. Otherwise the silence might have smothered him.

"That particular morning, as the trams approached that side of town, they were being stopped by the German police—the *Schutzpolizei*, not the Gestapo. It was the first time this had happened in the city, the very first time. Eventually the Polish people came to call such sweeps by the name of *Lapanka,* the trap. But that morning it was too new, and there was no name. All we knew was that the tram was stopped and we were forced to get off."

The renovated prison blocks were red-brick two-story, utterly featureless constructions. Jeffrey followed Alexander's lead and stopped in front of one labeled *Block 4—Extermination Exhibit.* As he climbed the stairs with Alexander, he imagined the walls to be weeping blood.

"They started checking documents," Alexander continued, leading them down a bare whitewashed corridor. "I had documents, not real documents, saying that I was a gardener's helper. Documents saying one had work were most important. They looked at them and told me to step aside, along with several dozen other men. A few minutes later these covered trucks arrived and we were loaded up. We were not told anything, nothing at all. Not where we were going, or why we were selected, or how long we would be away. Nothing.

The first room showed wall-sized black-and-white photographs of the transport story, remarkably clear in their frozen portrayal of agony on one side and stiff military indifference on the other. Trains expelled masses of people; children stared with frozen fear at the camera, or were hustled through barbed-wire gates, or clung to their mothers' skirts, or wailed in timeless terror.

Alexander walked beside him, viewing everything, seeing nothing. "I cannot say I was particularly scared. Age certainly had something to do with it. I was sixteen at the time, you see, and at that age your own death is something quite difficult to imagine. It is very hard to look further than that day, or that week, to what might lie beyond, or what might be on other people's minds."

The next barracks greeted them with a sign that said in French, Russian, Polish and English: *This barracks houses all that remained of the victims' belongings and was found after the camp's liberation.* Jeffrey entered the first room, and found himself facing a wall of glass. Beyond it stretched forty feet of brushes. Shaving brushes. Hairbrushes. Shoebrushes. Toothbrushes.

"We were first taken to old Polish military barracks near the city," Alexander went on in his ceaseless drone. "On the way, I wrote a note to my mother on a scrap of paper, putting down her address and saying what had happened, that I was taken by the Germans and I didn't know where I was going or why, but that I would try to let her know. I threw three or four of them out from beneath the canvas covering on the truck, and the remarkable thing is that my mother received every one of them. I learned later that people picked them up, read the address I had scribbled, and took them to my mother. Every single one. When we left the barracks and were taken by trucks to the railroad station, I wrote several more, just dropping them outside the truck on the road. Again she got every single one."

In the next room was another glass wall with yet another pile, this one of metal bowls. Thousands and thousands and thousands of bowls.

Another room, another glass wall, another display—this one of crutches and prosthetic limbs and back braces. A wooden hand made for a child, with fingers perhaps two inches long, reached out to Jeffrey across the years.

"At the station they put sixty or seventy of us into a cattle car. At that time they weren't taking women to Auschwitz, only men. We had one container with water, and another for waste, with straw on the floor. It was a most unpleasant voyage. It was extremely crowded, and it stank horribly. There were Germans with machine-gun placements on the roofs of each car, and every time we came to a crossing where the train stopped, some people would try to escape. The Germans would machine-gun them, then go out and pick up their bodies and throw them back into the cattle cars with the rest of us."

Upstairs there were no rooms, just one long hall with glass walls to either side. Half of the entire floor was filled with shoes. Men's, women's, children's, babies' shoes—piled to the ceiling in a broken array of lost possessions and lost lives.

"We arrived at Auschwitz on August 15, 1940," Alexander continued. "They divided us up into rows of five and began marching us toward the camp. At that time there was only the one camp. Birkenau had not even been started yet. So we were marched across to the main camp, and through this big iron gate. Above the gate was written in big iron letters the words *Arbeit Macht Frei*—'Work makes you free.' So all of us thought we had been conscripted for a labor camp. It was still early enough that the truth about Auschwitz was not yet publicly known, you see. Perhaps there were rumors floating around, but they had not made their way down to the ears of a sixteen-year-old boy. Or to my fellows, for that matter. It did not even occur to us that we were being brought into an extermination camp."

The second floor's other half was given over to suitcases, turned upward to shout the names of those unable to claim them. Frank of Holland. Birmann of Hamburg. Ludwig of Baruch, Israel. Eva Pander of Recklinghausen. Gescheit of Berlin. Else Meier of Cologne. Helene Lewandowski of Poland.

"So they brought us into this central square. I suppose our transport held fifteen or sixteen hundred people. It took a very long time for them to process us. We had to go to one place where we had to leave all our clothing. Everything. Then to another place where they shaved us completely. Our heads, our bodies, everything. Then we were forced to bathe, and then given these Auschwitz pajamas. That is what I thought of them, those striped camp suits. We were left barefoot."

At the end of the chamber, diagonal to the suitcases, was a deep narrow display of baby clothing. Jeffrey simply had to turn away.

"Already some pretty terrible things were happening right there and then on the square. It appeared that the Germans wanted to see how people reacted to various situations. We had not eaten for twenty-four hours. So what they did was set out twenty or thirty large loaves of bread, heavy Polish bread, and then tell the people to come forward and take some. But every time people stepped forward, the Germans with their heavy boots and guns would beat them. The soldiers were laughing and joking as they did so, treating it as great sport. Still, because the people were so hungry, some would try to grab a handful, and they were beaten very badly."

Another downstairs room had two glass walls. One displayed Jewish prayer shawls hung from wooden frames whose outstretched fabric cried for attention. The second held a cobwebbed mass of eyeglasses, their thousands of lenses gathered in the case's forefront to peer silently into Jeffrey's aching heart.

"The water inside the train car had been used up in the first two hours, and afterward we had nothing more. While we were out there on the square, an elderly man was coughing very badly. Somehow he managed to get a soldier to bring him a full bucket of water, and for this he gave the German his gold pocket watch—this was before he had been stripped, of course. When we were stripped all valuables were taken from us. So the old man drank his fill, and then turned to us and said, anyone who wants can have some. But when we looked we saw that the old man, who had TB, had left the water scummy with coughed-up blood. Even so, many drank from that bucket—that is how thirsty they had become."

Upon their exit from the building, Jeffrey turned to read the name above the door. It said: *Block 5—Evidence of Crimes.*

"While the processing was taking place, the Germans brought forward a prisoner who had arrived earlier," Alexander continued as they walked toward the next barrack. "I suppose there were already thirteen or fourteen hundred prisoners there when we arrived. They had been there three or four months, from what I gathered later. Auschwitz had formerly been a Polish army camp, and when the Germans arrived they began gathering people from prisons around Cracow and sending them there. The soldiers brought out this prisoner with his harmonica, and from our group they brought out a Catholic priest and a Jewish rabbi. These men were tired, and hungry, and the rabbi with his long beard could barely stand up. They gave them a sheet of paper and told them to sing the words while the prisoner played the harmonica. The words were very obscene; these holy men stood there, forced to sing obscenities, while the guards listened and laughed."

Block 6 was titled *Prisoners' Life*. In the first hall, black-and-white etchings by former inmates loomed over display cases of passports and family photographs and personal documents. The pictures required no explanation—S.S. soldiers stripping newly arrived inmates of rings, Kapo guards pulling an inmate from line for a beating, new prisoners adding to a mountain of suitcases outside their barrack, prisoners being selected for experimentation.

"At the end of the processing they gave us each a number. My number was one-nine-one-four, *neunzehn-vierzehn*. We were told that if a German or a Kapo came up, we were to stand at attention and recite, *Politische Schutzhäftling, Pole, neunzehn-vierzehn, meldet hier zur Stelle.*"

Across from the etchings, against a backdrop of barbed wire, a wall display shouted in red letters a foot high the command: *A Jew is permitted one week to live, a priest two, anyone else a maximum of three months.*

Alexander examined the display with eyes blind to all but his memories. "There were already a hundred or so Jews here when we arrived. The Germans put them into what was called the *Straff* company. The penalty company. These people had it very, very bad. They were forced to haul this enormous roller around and around the square, while the Germans continually beat them. It was a horrible thing to watch. Horrible."

The barrack's central hallway was about seventy feet long and lined on both sides with three rows of photographs. Men were to the right, women the left. Beneath the pictures were written their number, their name, their date of birth, their former profession. Jeffrey made out the words for tour guide, teacher, sailor, waiter, lawyer, priest, religious brother, chemist. Beneath the profession was their date of arrival and their date of death.

Their eyes. Their eyes. Jeffrey felt their eyes searching him even when he walked the hall with his own gaze remaining on his feet.

"Every day we were gathered on the central square where they made us go through these extremely difficult, pointless physical exercises. We were already growing weak, and whenever anyone stumbled the Germans would immediately begin beating him. One

Kapo hit me over the head with his stick, here, I can still feel the place. The Kapos at that time were all German. We were told that they were criminal prisoners, and under them the men in charge of the barracks rooms were Polish criminals. I can still remember the man in charge of my barracks, a big man, very big, of perhaps forty-five years and completely bald. His number was four hundred. He carried this great stick with him always, and beat on us constantly."

At the back of the central hall stood a tall sculpture. It showed six women whose rags covered their heads and little else. They were nothing more than taut skin and staring eyes and jutting bones. The sculpture was entitled *Hunger.*

Alexander remained before the statue for quite a long while. "Our normal ration was a soup called *Avo* for lunch, a blackish mixture with perhaps a couple of rotten potatoes. Nothing for breakfast. At night there was so-called tea, water boiled with some unknown leaves, and hard, moldy bread. Bread was the common currency at Auschwitz, bread and cigarettes. The exchange rate was three or four cigarettes for a hunk of bread. People who really craved tobacco would exchange it, knowing full well that they couldn't last without food, and not really caring all that much. For some, the hunger for cigarettes was stronger than for food, especially as life lost its meaning. Then, when someone smoked a cigarette, they would inhale and then blow the smoke into the mouth of a friend. He would in turn blow it into the mouth of a third man."

One room was dedicated to children. Jeffrey refused to enter. Alexander stopped a few paces inside, turned back with a look of addled confusion, then shrugged his accord and led them down the hall, out of the building, and on to the next barrack. The sign above the door announced that it held a display of how prisoners lived.

"In our barracks room there were one hundred and seventy men," Alexander told him as they entered. "It was so tight that we were forced to sleep on our sides, and when one turned, all were forced to turn with him. No beds. We were sleeping on the floor, with only straw between us and the concrete floor. In the mornings we were kicked and beaten outside to the hand pump, where we were supposed to have our only wash of the day. One hundred and seventy men around a hand pump, with the Kapos beating us to make us hurry.

"One time I was late, maybe five minutes late coming out of the barracks. The Kapo marked my number, and about two weeks later a Gestapo soldier came up and called out five or six numbers, mine being one of them. We were penalized because we had been late coming out of the barracks. The punishment was something terrible. He stood there in the concrete corridor inside our barracks with a horsewhip and ordered us through truly horrible gymnastics for over two hours. Whenever we stumbled we were kicked and whipped until we were unconscious. One of the five men punished with me was killed, murdered, beaten to death right there before our eyes. I received one kick in the small of my back, on my kidneys, that I truly thought had killed me too."

Inside the barracks the central hall held two more walls of eyes. Jeffrey checked the professions in an attempt to escape the stares—seamstress, mayor, bureaucrat, blacksmith, activist. The wall opened for a doorway that framed a brick-sided barracks room as it was in 1944. Straw was laid beneath blanket rags. Three tiers of wooden beds rose like animal stalls in a room less than six feet high. The stalls were perhaps four feet wide. A sign by the doorway said that eight women slept in each of the four-foot-wide tiers. A thousand women to a barrack.

"After a time," Alexander said beside him, "they began marching us a mile or so every morning to the building site of Birkenau. This was the second stage of the Auschwitz death camp, and the larger one. I was ordered up on top of very steep roofs—I don't know what they had been before they were turned into Birkenau—and I cleaned them with a stiff wire brush. It was extremely steep, very dangerous work. One day a man working beside me fell to his death."

Block 10 was closed and the door barred. Beside the door a sign read: *In this block the German physician, Professor Clauberg M.D., conducted experiments dealing with the sterilization of women.* Three women knelt on the steps and prayed, candles lit before them.

"One morning while at work at Birkenau I happened upon some rotten potatoes. You must understand that by that time hunger was a ruling force in my life. It dominated my daily existence. Several of us there together swiftly gathered them up. It was approaching winter by that time, so we took these potatoes and put them on a fire there at the work site. While we were watching them, a German came up. All the others fled, but I was caught, and the German demanded to know who they were, these others who had been cooking potatoes instead of working. When I refused to tell him, he sent a Kapo to fetch him a special stick. It was very heavy, almost as thick as my forearm, and had nails hammered into it to give it extra weight. He ordered the Kapo to take my head between his legs, and then he began to beat me on my back and thighs. I was supposed to get twenty-five blows. On the eighth stroke he hit me on the kidneys, and I lost consciousness."

Beside Block 10, metal gates opened to a graveled courtyard. At its end was a bullet-ridden concrete wall, the Death Wall. Row after row of flowers and candles and wreaths and cards were set at its base.

"Every day, sometimes several times a day, they would tie a man's hands behind his back, and pull him upward on a tall post until his feet left the ground, suspended with his arms pulled back and up from behind. They were left hanging for two, sometimes three hours. The pain was indescribable. People who went through it told me afterward that they would rather die than endure it again."

The neighboring block contained a large room with a line of simple wooden tables. A sign described it as the camp court and said that almost all who were tried here were executed. Immediately.

Two opposing rooms were assigned for male and female prisoners to strip naked before being led outside to be shot. The sign above the men's chamber said that most had their hands bound with barbed wire.

"One day a pair of prisoners escaped, and we were forced to stand in the square until they were found. Eighteen hours we stood there, in the dead of winter. Any time anyone fell, he was beaten and kicked to the point of death. Eventually the guards found the fugitives, and they were punished with the Standing Cells."

In the cellar were the Standing Cells, arrived at through a barred crawl-space perhaps two feet square. Four prisoners were crammed into a space three feet wide, three feet long, and four feet high. Those placed there for trying to escape, according to the sign above the first cell, were left to starve to death.

"They had a crematorium already in operation. The prisoners knew about it, of course. Even I, as a sixteen-year-old boy, learned what was happening there beyond the wires. But many were already seeking a way to commit suicide. Many men threw themselves against the barbed-wire fence so the Germans would shoot and kill them. For many of the prisoners, death was preferable to an endless stay in this living hell."

Across from the Standing Cells was the first experimental gas chamber. Another chamber at the end of the cellar hall was the Death Cell, where prisoners were held before being placed inside the gas chamber. On one wall of this room, a prisoner awaiting death had carved the figure of Christ. Alexander stood there for a long time before turning and leading Jeffrey back upstairs.

At the turning that led away from Block 10, the walkways and window ledges were filled with modern-day casualties of Auschwitz; men and women, boys and girls, knelt and wept and prayed or just stared with blank-faced blindness at the passers-by whose legs would still carry them. The eyes of those crippled by what they had witnessed resembled those of the prisoners whose photographs hung within.

Alexander led him through the barracks dedicated to the Poles who died in Auschwitz and to the Polish war effort. He then turned down the path and led them out the gates to the main gas chamber and crematorium. They were located beyond the camp's perimeter fences in a smaller enclosure all their own. The entrance was a stone-walled path leading into the side of an earth-walled bunker.

The death chamber was a tomb of concrete, where 800 prisoners were gassed at a time. The next chamber held row after row of curved brick furnaces. Candles and flowers were strewn in the long metal trays used to pass in the bodies and bring out the ashes.

A guide standing beside Jeffrey told his group that the Nazis would notify the families of Poles who had been killed, saying that the relative had passed on of a heart attack, and that his or her remains could be collected upon making a payment. Whenever anyone appeared with the money, they would shovel up a boxful of ashes from whomever had just been incinerated.

Alexander led Jeffrey out into the bright sunlight and back to where their car and driver waited. The narrative continued as his softly droning voice kept them company on the journey back to Cracow.

"As soon as my mother learned of my arrest, she began seeking my release. My father was one of the commanders of the Polish forces fighting under General Anders, in the Polish Second Corps under British command, and my mother remained in Cracow all alone. Someone told her to go to the Gestapo headquarters, and time and again she went and pleaded with anyone who would listen to tell her news of her son. She was repeatedly thrown out on the street, just tossed out the door and down the stairs like refuse. But she kept returning.

"Then someone else told her that there was a German lawyer with connections. If she could get her hands on a thousand zloty, he would help her. So my mother sold her rings and went to this German; he took my name and promised he would do what he could. To this day, I don't know exactly who it was that in the end worked out my release. I don't know how many people my mother spoke to and pleaded with. But I do know that there was a commandant of the Polish police, a good friend of my father's from before the war. He had the responsibility of supervising Polish police in all of Poland under German military command. My mother went to him and pleaded for his help. But whoever helped her never admitted it, and so I have never been able to thank the one responsible for my release. But somehow, somehow, toward the end of January 1941, I was released from Auschwitz.

"That morning, as we gathered in the square, a German called out several numbers, mine being one of them. We were ordered to report to the *Schreibstube,* some kind of office. The head Gestapo, the chief Auschwitz commandant, made a little speech to us, which was translated by a Polish count who was also a prisoner there with us. It was a patriotic German speech, saying how lucky we were to live in these days and watch the rise of the German empire. Then we were ordered never to tell anyone anything of what we had witnessed inside the camp. If we ever did speak of it, we were told, we would be returned to Auschwitz immediately, and there would be no release for us except death. Then he ordered us to go, and to do well in the great new empire of Adolf Hitler.

"Five of us were released, and with typical German efficiency, they gave us back the very same clothes we had arrived in. Upon my capture in August I had been wearing a thin shirt, no jacket, white pants and sandals. Now it was mid-winter, with snow on the ground, and very, very cold. I was allowed nothing but these same summer clothes.

"Two Gestapo men took us to the Auschwitz train station and bought us our tickets. While we were waiting for the train to leave, a girl of perhaps eighteen or nineteen came up and took off her beret and said to me, 'Please take this so that your head won't grow cold.' We were still shaved, you know, and from our starved looks everyone could see we had just come from the camp.

"So the Gestapo put us in a third-class train compartment and stood there waiting for the train to leave. Then up came another attractive young lady. She spoke to the Gestapo in a very sweet voice, taking the button of one of their long leather coats and twisting it as she tried to persuade them. Finally he snapped, *aber schnell,* make it fast, and she rushed away. Five minutes later she came back with a huge package and shoved it through the train window to us, then turned and walked away. In this package were sausages and fresh bread and butter, everything.

"Eventually the train departed, and as we were sitting there and eating, a German officer came walking by our compartment. He opened the door and asked where we were coming from. He was a soldier, so we did as he ordered and told him that we had just left the Auschwitz camp. He stood there a moment, then asked if we would like to have a pack of cigarettes. He just handed them over, this German officer in uniform.

"We had to change trains soon after that, at the border between Germany and the General Government, or GG as it was known then. The German officer went into the waiting room and chased out the Germans—this was in Silesia, so the people there were mostly German. He came back and told us to go inside and lie down and rest. While we were lying there, he went inside and brought back big glasses of beer.

"By that time we had finished the food the lady had given us, and in the train restaurant there was a display of some really appetizing sausages. We were still extremely hungry. We searched our pockets and came up with forty-eight pfennigs between us. The price of a sausage was four marks and something. But we were moving into the GG area, where the zloty was the official currency, so I took the money and went to ask if we could get maybe a little slice with it while we could still spend it. An old lady was tending the counter. I laid down my small coppers and asked if I could please have a little something for this money. She stood there and looked at me, and looked at me. Finally she said, 'Yes, sir, right away.' And she gave me four kilos of sausage. Mind you, this was during wartime rationing. That was how bad my appearance was after leaving Auschwitz."

The car pulled up in front of their hotel. Jeffrey got out, rushed around, and helped his friend get out. Alexander stood very slowly, raised his eyes to the heavens, and blinked several times.

"Can I help you to your room?"

Alexander lowered his gaze to the pavement at his feet. "No thank you, my boy. It is time to face the fact that I am alone. It cannot be put off any longer."

With that he turned and climbed the stairs and disappeared through the doors.

CHAPTER 14

Jeffrey was already awake when Alexander called him shortly after six the next morning. "I am sorry, Jeffrey. My attack of memories has become most severe. I fear staying here in Poland just now would only make matters worse."

"I understand."

"Yes, I thought you would. I am catching a flight in two hours and leaving you here in charge. I shall return to London and assist your young lady in running our shop. Please call when you can. Until later, then. Goodbye."

═══

When Jeffrey climbed to the second floor landing, Gregor was waiting for him with a bulky sweater wrapped around his shoulders, his eyes full of concern. "My dear boy, are you all right?"

Jeffrey rubbed a tired hand down his face. "I didn't sleep so well last night. I think I've inherited Alexander's voices."

"Yes, we all have the night whispers from time to time. It is the price of being human."

Jeffrey nodded. "It was some day."

"I am sure it was. Alexander stopped by this morning and explained his departure. I told him that it was no doubt the best thing to do, and that we would get along fine here together." Gregor turned and limped heavily into his apartment. His movements were much stiffer than usual. "Where are my manners? Come in, Jeffrey. Come in."

"Are you feeling all right?"

He waved a dismissive hand. "It is simply another attack. I have long since learned to accept the complaints of this cantankerous body. I will be fine in a day or so. Sit down here and tell me everything."

Jeffrey did as he was told. Gregor stood above him, silent and still, save for occasionally pulling the sweater closer around his chest, consumed by the act of listening.

"Poor Alexander," Gregor sighed, once Jeffrey was finished. "If only he would not insist on carrying that burden alone."

Jeffrey nodded. "I keep wishing I had known what to say."

"In cases such as this, it is sometimes best to say nothing at all. To listen from the heart, without judgment, without impatience, is sometimes the greatest gift one can give." He turned toward the alcove and winced at the sudden movement. "Would you like a glass of coffee before we go?"

"Okay, thanks. Are you sure you're all right?"

"As I said, I have these attacks from time to time. The nicest thing about them is that they pass. I don't suppose you would object to using Alexander's car and driver this morning? I don't believe I would be able to drive."

"That would be great."

"I thought you would approve. Tomek has promised to come by as soon as he sees Alexander off. It shouldn't be too much longer."

Gregor moved into his alcove. "In times like this, I often find that words of my own can do nothing at all. What Alexander needs more than my words in his ear is the Holy Spirit speaking to his heart. Perhaps sympathetic listening will help him to quieten enough to hear that stiller voice speaking deep within. I can hope, at least. And pray."

Jeffrey thought back over the day. "It was incredible how caught up Alexander was in remembering," he said. "All his life he's tried to put the Auschwitz experience behind him, but when he was walking around with me, it was the most real thing in his entire existence."

Gregor pushed the curtain aside. "These experiences were so great, so powerful, that at times other aspects of life dim to unimportance. For some poor souls, the experience leaves the rest of life caught in shadows. All life carries the grayness caused by that which they can not overcome."

Jeffrey shook his head. "I don't see how anybody could ever leave something like that behind."

"Perhaps you can't," Gregor agreed. "I resent these people who rest in the comfort of their faith and say with smug glibness that if only a person in pain would believe a bit more strongly, or pray a little more, the Lord would heal their every wound. I know too many devout believers who remain crippled by their pasts to ever agree with such nonsense. No, all I can say for certain is that the Lord has promised us a peace that surpasses all understanding. Even in the midst of our suffering, this peace is promised us. Peace for now, salvation forever."

Jeffrey felt the rising up of his own old shadows. "How can you have peace in the middle of suffering?"

Gregor set a glass of coffee down at Jeffrey's elbow. "Better you should ask how a man might have peace at all in this world, my boy. Now you let that sit until the grounds have settled to the bottom of the glass."

"I don't think I understand."

"About how to find peace? Of course not. Such understanding can only come through experience, not an exercise of the mind." Gregor pulled over a straight-backed chair, settled himself, went on. "There was another survivor of Auschwitz, a man by the name of Father Bloknicki. Before the Nazi invasion, Bloknicki was an atheist, a philosophy professor. Like a lot of Polish intelligentsia, he was declared a threat to the new German state and shipped off to a concentration camp. Once in Auschwitz, Bloknicki looked around himself and realized that intelligence or education made no difference whatsoever as to the presence or lack of evil in a man. He spoke German, and he discovered that many of the officers and even some of the enlisted men were intelligent, well-educated people. And yet here they were, making it their life's work to foster evil.

"Bloknicki decided that there had to be an underlying concept of morality. There had to be something *behind* life, something that granted man a choice and gave him both strength and purpose. There had to be a God. Then and there, in the horrors of a factory of death, he gave his life to Christ.

"By a clerical error—or miracle, whichever you prefer—Bloknicki was released long before the end of the war. He did the only thing a man of God knew to do in the Poland of that time—he became a priest. He first started working with alcoholics, and was imprisoned once again, this time by the Communists, because of his success in both curing and converting the addicted men.

"While in prison this second time, he received a vision from God as to how to work with young people. He was to involve lay people, utilize the Scriptures, and foster an atmosphere of communal prayer and Bible study. He began as soon as he was released, and enlisted the help and the support of many other local priests. Then he came into contact with several Protestant mission groups and asked them to help as well. This was a most unusual request. The government, some of the Protestant mission boards in the West, and the Polish church hierarchy began to oppose him. But still he went on.

"By the seventies, this little group of believers had become what is now known as the Oasis, the largest mission organization operating in all Poland. They would arrange to come into a medium-sized village for a fifteen-day revival and prayer retreat, and literally take over every square inch of available space. They would usually have with them thirty or forty thousand students. They slept in primitive farmhouses or makeshift tents, and held their classes in barns. By the time martial law was declared in the eighties, over a million young people had taken part in these revivals."

Gregor sipped at his coffee. "Even in the darkest of hours, people have a choice. They can turn toward self, or they can turn toward God. They can turn toward hate, or they can turn toward forgiveness and love."

Jeffrey shook his head. "I just don't understand how you can have such confidence in your faith after all you and your family have been through. Where is the assurance for Alexander when he comes out of the concentration camp and finds his sister imprisoned and beaten to death? Where is God when your country has been occupied and your people imprisoned and tortured and murdered?"

Jeffrey ran half-clenched fingers through his hair. "I don't see how you can praise God and then turn around and see the misery and the poverty and the pain that surrounds you everywhere."

Gregor's kind, tired, patient eyes shone with an otherworldly light. "Has there been such pain in your own life, Jeffrey?"

"Not like this. What has happened here is a lot worse than anything I've ever gone through. But it doesn't make what I've known any less real for me."

"No, of course it doesn't. That was not what I asked."

"I know. It's just that I feel a little silly talking about my own problems when I'm surrounded by things I couldn't even imagine before coming to Poland."

"Pain is pain," Gregor replied simply.

"It seems to me you're trying to avoid my question by talking about something inside my life."

"The world is such a big place," Gregor replied in his own mild way. "Greater men than I have spent lifetimes discussing your questions. I'm afraid my little mind is only, able to deal with such things one person at a time. I only asked you, my young friend, because I hoped to help you find an answer for your own life, if such an answer is indeed needed. I will leave it to you to find answers for the rest of the world."

Defeated by the man's calm honesty, Jeffrey stretched back in his chair and replied, "Then the answer is yes."

"I see. And did you turn to God and ask Him to end the pain?"

Jeffrey nodded glumly.

"And He did not reply."

"Not a word," he replied bitterly.

"You and Alexander have more in common than you realize," Gregor said.

The door buzzer sounded. Gregor cast aside his blanket, reached for a well-patched sweater hanging by the door, slipped it on, and pocketed a small book from his shelf. "That will be our driver. We have an appointment in less than an hour. We can discuss this as we drive."

═══

Gregor said nothing more until he had made his way to the car, walking like a boat passing through heavy seas. The effort of motion required all of his attention. Tomek helped him settle in the backseat, nodded a solemn greeting to Jeffrey, started the car and headed them out of town.

Once they were surrounded by dusty shades of summer greens Gregor said, "Before I begin, Jeffrey, I must warn you of one very grave danger. Only you can say whether or not the warning applies, of course. I only ask that you search your heart very carefully before setting it aside.

"Sometimes in our selfish attempts to keep God out, we develop questions to which we believe there are no answers. Then we set them up as barriers between ourselves and God, and we never seek an answer. If a response is offered us, we either cast it aside with embittered anger over someone daring to challenge our defenses, or we immediately throw up another unanswerable question. The truth, you see, is that no answer is desired.

"Doubt can be a most valuable instrument of growth, if it is seen as a challenge. If it is a fuel used to search for *more* answers and a *deeper* understanding, then you who are poor and hungry in spirit shall inherit both profound answers and the kingdom of heaven. Believe me, my boy, if your search for answers is truly open-hearted, the Lord will reward you richly. But beware the blindness you are causing yourself if your questions are nothing more than defenses to keep Him out."

Jeffrey pondered the question. "I guess that's partly true. But I really did need God and He really wasn't there. Maybe all I'm trying to do is keep from getting burned a second time."

Gregor gave him an approving glance. "Your honesty is most admirable and most rare, Jeffrey. Very well. Let us look at the fact of your own suffering. And make no mistake, I do not question your pain. This matter of relativity is mere nonsense. Whatever it was that caused you pain was clearly something profound, and it carried a lasting effect. You have suffered. That is enough.

"For just a moment, I would like to ask that you remember whatever it was that caused you pain. Go back in your mind to that moment when you decided that God was not listening, and you turned away from Him."

"I remember," Jeffrey replied grimly.

"I know this is difficult for you, my young friend. I truly do. But try to see if one fact was not true for you right then. When you were in the midst of your suffering, did you not become more aware of how other people were living in pain? Did you find that barriers within yourself were crumbling?"

Jeffrey felt wracked by memories and by remembered pains and by a truth he had never recognized before. "Yes."

"Yes. You felt it. The barriers fall as all lies must fall, if we are to remain honest with ourselves. The veil is ripped away, and you find yourself able to walk the valley that others know. This is a basic truth that we seek to flee from all our lives, my dear young friend, that no one can minister to a suffering soul except one who has passed through these flames and retained an open heart.

"Emotional, spiritual, physical pain—it doesn't matter. Pain of any kind reduces the highest of us, even the great King David himself, to the lowest level of loneliness. We flee from it. We rage against it. We battle it with every weapon we have.

"You yourself know the desperation of searching for an end to your misery. And if the heart is awake, as yours surely is, you wish there could be a cure for *every* sufferer. You wish you could touch them, and cure them *all*.

"But you cannot. You can't even keep your own puny self from knowing this horror called pain. You can't even lock the door to your own life and tell this nightmare called suffering to stay out. It breaks down the door and *forces* itself upon you.

"So what do we do? Well, it is certainly possible to blame God. 'You didn't listen to me,' we say to Him. 'You forced me to endure this horrible pain! You crippled me, or at least allowed it to happen.' This is the way it begins, you see. And the next step is of course very clear. We then turn our backs on God. We seek to punish Him as He has appeared to punish us. And once that is done, we continue our walk into darkness by *hating* God. By *cursing* God.

"What we do not ever want to see is that sometimes there is no earthly cure, no earthly solution. The stronger we are, the more we wish to see every problem in our life as temporary. To realize that something must simply be accepted and borne is to acknowledge that our own strength is not sufficient, that the world is not always under our control. This realization is such a hard task. So very, very hard."

Gregor reached into the pocket of his voluminous sweater and emerged with a tiny pocket New Testament. "I brought my English version along." He handed it to Jeffrey. "Would you please be so kind as to read from Second Corinthians, chapter twelve, verses seven through ten?"

It took quite some time for Jeffrey to find the passage. He squinted and braced the book with both hands against the car's jouncing journey, and read:

> To keep me from becoming conceited because of these surpassingly great revelations, there was given me a thorn in my flesh, a messenger of Satan, to torment me. Three times I pleaded with the Lord to take it away from me. But he said to me, 'My grace is sufficient for you, for my power is made perfect in weakness.' Therefore I will boast all the more gladly about my weaknesses, so that Christ's power may rest on me. That is why, for Christ's sake, I delight in weaknesses, in insults, in hardships, in persecutions, in difficulties. For when I am weak, then I am strong.

Gregor nodded. "Even the great St. Paul has a painful thorn thrust deep into his side, and the agony has crippled him. He has *great* suffering. Three times the man who spoke with God begged Him to grant a cure. God refused to give a complete healing. Do you hear what I am saying, my young friend? God said that He *knew* of Paul's suffering, yet refused to end it. He said *no*, I will *not* heal you. Not because you are a sinner and should be punished. Not because you have been found guilty. No. God recognizes Paul as a true disciple of Christ. So why does the divine Healer not heal? How can this be?

"It happens, my dear young friend, because God has something *even better* in store. Yet what can be better than a cure? What? The answer is, *the presence of God.* He gave Paul the grace to *bear* this suffering, and in so doing, to bear witness to His glory.

"In times of suffering, if we resist the temptation to blame God and curse God and hate God, He will strengthen us, deepen our faith, and *see us through.* It is not what we may want, it is not the end of our pain coming at the time and in the way of our choosing. But He in His own perfect way will *use* our imperfections and our weaknesses to the glory of His name. And in so doing, He will enrich us beyond all measure.

"He will deepen our life, our wisdom, and our faith, through the act of suffering. He can and will use the sufferer to reach those who might otherwise never know the glory that awaits them were they to only open their hearts to His call. He will help us to stretch out our hand, and give light to those who are entering into their own dark night."

The building had one entrance and two elevators for five hundred apartments set on nineteen floors. It was one of several dozen identical concrete monoliths grouped together on the outskirts of Cracow. The entrance doors, cracked wire-mesh glass and rusting frames, flapped noisily on their hinges.

The entrance hall was unpainted concrete—floors, walls, low-slung ceiling. Bent and scarred postboxes wept rust down the damp side wall. Meager light filtered through two fly-blown overhead globes. Mildew painted gray and green streaks in the corners. The air stank of refuse.

"We see fewer small items nowadays," Gregor said, all business now that they were approaching a sale. "But as I said the other day, most buyers are out to spend as little as possible and will happily lie to the seller if it means paying a few dollars less. Others follow the person home and steal whatever is there. We, Alexander and I, are still approached by those who have done business with us in the past or heard of us from people who have, especially those with something truly valuable to sell."

"Like today?"

Gregor tugged sharply at the elevator door and motioned Jeffrey to enter. "That, my dear boy, we shall soon see."

The elevator complained like a cranky old man as it clanged past each floor. It stopped on the seventh; Gregor pushed the door open with his shoulder. In the concrete-lined hallway squalling babies competed with echoing televisions and punk-rock music. Refuse littered the passage.

Gregor paused outside a battered door and said to Jeffrey, "As I have said before, it is best not to ask too many questions."

His knock was answered by a balding man in unkempt clothes who greeted Gregor with a gap-toothed grin, a handshake, a clap on the shoulders, and words with the permanently slurred, coarsened quality of a vodka-and-cigarette fanatic. Gregor replied, turned and introduced Jeffrey. The man gave him a long, hard-eyed inspection before nodding a greeting.

He led them into the cluttered apartment of a dedicated bachelor. Empty vodka bottles and dirty plates littered every flat surface. Newspapers were scattered across the threadbare sofa and much of the floor.

A younger man, slighter and darker than their host, rose at their entry and stared at them with feverish eyes. Their host waved a hand toward the younger man and said something to Gregor, who translated. "This man is from the Ukraine, a section of the former Soviet Union which borders Poland. I have done business with our host several times before. He is Ukrainian himself, and keeps contact through his family with smugglers crossing the border. He will translate for us."

The host bustled off to the kitchen alcove. Jeffrey seated himself at Gregor's nod and gave the Ukrainian visitor a frank examination. He had black red-rimmed eyes, and skin the color of old leather. He was very slight, standing no more than five-three and weighing perhaps a hundred pounds. Despite the man's twenty-odd years, his full beard was going gray.

When their host had returned and handed around tulip-shaped glasses of heavily sweetened tea, Gregor began a three-way discussion with the pair. He would ask a question to the host, who would then translate to the Ukrainian, who replied with a hoarse whispery voice. This was then translated back to Polish for Gregor.

Eventually Gregor turned to Jeffrey and said, "I asked him what the wait at the Polish border was like before passing through customs. He said this trip it was twelve days. It gets a little worse each time—I already knew this from the news reports. There are so many Soviets on the brink of starvation, you see. Anyone with something to sell is desperate to make it to Poland or Czechoslovakia. Polish currency is now freely convertible—you can change it for dollars or marks or whatever. The ruble is not. The Soviets have no faith in their monetary system, and are fearing the possibility of a total collapse. They are very keen to lay their hands on hard currency.

"This man also said that only the very small items are getting through these days. For months now the Polish border guards are trying to stop the smuggling of alcohol and cheap wares, and each car is searched carefully. You cannot bribe your way through, because the guards would then know you have something valuable and just confiscate it.

"Many people use the waiting time at the Soviet-Polish border as an indication of the state of the Soviet economy. They say it is a much more honest evaluation than anything the government puts out."

"He must have something very valuable to make a trip like that," Jeffrey ventured.

The Ukrainian waited through the laborious translation process and sipped at his glass of tea with fingers that trembled from fatigue. "He hopes so," Gregor eventually replied. "He says the worst part of waiting at the border was the fear of bandits. He hasn't slept very much for twelve days. He dared not travel with another man, because two men seen together was an automatic signal both to the border guards and the thieves that there was something of great value somewhere in the car.

"The Russian mafia has taken over the border area, according to this young man. He actually used the word mafia. They charge five dollars for a liter of water—one tenth of the average Russian's monthly wage. Anyone who pays too quickly or buys too much has his car broken into at night. Keep in mind, there are no camping parks or hotels. They eat and sleep and live in their cars throughout the twelve-day wait. When the thieves pick their prey, he is beaten, maybe killed, and the car driven off somewhere to be searched at leisure."

"What about the police or the border guards?" Jeffrey asked.

The man paused from his tea to give Jeffrey a look of bitter humor. "He says the line is over thirty miles long," Gregor replied. "At night the guards never go farther from their hut than the circle cast by their lights, no matter how bad the screams. Every day or so there is another body to be brought out, identified, and buried."

"Then why do people do it?"

"To trade," Gregor replied, not bothering to translate.

"Seems like an awful risk," Jeffrey said.

"That depends on how hungry you are, wouldn't you say?"

Without preamble the small man stood, unbuckled his belt, and dropped his baggy trousers to the floor. With a grimace of pain he peeled black tape from either thigh and brought out two small packets wrapped in grimy rags. He fastened his trousers, sat back, motioned toward Jeffrey, and demanded something in a tense voice.

"He wants to know if you will offer him an honest price."

"Honesty is the only thing I have to offer," Jeffrey replied. "Ask him if he has any idea what he wants for the items."

The smuggler gave a grin that split his dirty face and exposed teeth the color of aged teak. He said one word. "Valuta."

"It's a term you hear all through the Eastern Bloc," Gregor explained. "It means Western cash. Transferable currency."

The older man spoke. Gregor nodded and said to Jeffrey, "He says to tell you that valuta means cash that you can buy something with. Money with a purpose."

The smuggler began speaking, the older man nodding and translating. Gregor passed it on. "You stand in line for everything today in Russia. A fistful of rubles won't buy you bread. His sister has a sick baby, and last month waited three days in line for condensed milk. Each night the people in line would mark their place on one another's palms, agree to a certain time to be back the next morning, and return and check carefully to make sure no one had broken into place. It's been like that since early last winter. Sugar, milk, bread, meat, paper, soap—everything is either hard to find or just not available."

"So how do they survive?"

When the translations were made, the man took his rag-covered bundle, set it firmly into Jeffrey's hands, looked him hard in the eyes, and said hoarsely, "Valuta."

Jeffrey unfolded the rags from the smaller of the two parcels. It was a tiny case, no larger than his palm, of aged cedarwood. He had seen enough of these, and of the seal embossed on the top, to know that it was an original case from the House of Fabergé, court jewelers to the Czars of Russia. At least, that was what it appeared to be. He willed his hands to remain steady, and opened the box.

Inside rested a crystal *flacon à sels*. He recognized it immediately from the pictures he had studied. Almost every book on Fabergé contained an example, as it had been a favorite Christmas gift of the Empress Alexandra. It was designed as a container for either smelling salts or special healing salts brought in from some distant land, but as with many Faberge items, it was probably rarely used. Such an item, even when originally acquired, was seen as a work of art to be enjoyed as such, rather than something that required a function.

The crystal jar was slender as a lady's finger and octagonally shaped, the tiny dividing ridges chased with gold laurel bands. The cap was hand-fashioned from red gold in the form of an Eastern crown, and topped with a cabochon sapphire. It rested on a silk lining stamped with the Imperial Russian Eagle and the words *Fabergé, London, Paris, St. Petersburg* in Cyrillic, the Russian alphabet. Jeffrey had seen the words often enough in his reference books to identify them immediately.

The object within the second bundle was equally impressive: a slender gold box, perhaps twice the size of a pack of cigarettes. On its underside was scripted *Jean Fremin, Paris, 1759*. Jeffrey did not recognize the jeweler's name, but traditionally only artists with better-known houses signed their work. The sides were decorated with carefully etched desert scenes done with royal blue enamel, or *basse taille*. Jeffrey opened the lid to find that the inner lining contained a miniature painting done on ceramic. It showed a young woman seated in her drawing room. The colors, preserved by second-firing the ceramic once the portrait was completed, were as vivid as the day they were painted. The miniature was held in place by an intricately scrolled bezel of gold.

Another round of translation ended with Gregor asking, "How much do you think they are worth?"

He was accustomed enough to the question now not to cringe. "Please tell them that I cannot give a true figure until they have been evaluated by experts. Which I am not." He waited until this had been translated, and saw the small man nod his understanding. He went on. "But if they are real, which I think they are, they will be worth quite a bit."

The tension was palpable as Gregor translated and returned with, "How much is that?"

"At least ten thousand dollars. Minimum. Per item."

Gregor took out a pen and a piece of paper. As he wrote down the figures, he said to Jeffrey, "My insistence on this little act almost cost us the first deal with the gentleman seated to my right. He had clearly intended to use his mastery of Ukrainian as a means of exacting a larger commission. But I stood my ground, and he has come to see that my insistence on honesty has earned us more new business, and therefore more profits, than he would ever have gained from one large killing."

He picked up the paper, held it over one piece and then the other, and said each time the single word, "Dollar."

The Ukrainian's eyes grew round, then he nodded and spoke sharply. The translation was, "It is agreed."

"Make sure he understands that we won't know anything about their real worth until the evaluation is completed."

The translation came back, "He wants two thousand dollars now for both pieces. He needs that to buy essential things for his family. The rest he will receive later by means that we have already worked out. And two hundred dollars more for our friend here."

"All right." Jeffrey brought out the money. The man watched him count, scooped up the money, shook hands swiftly all around, and headed for the door.

"Wait," Jeffrey called out. "Ask him what it's like over there."

The small man turned from the door long enough to give him a haunted look. Through Gregor he replied, "Hell."

══

Gregor was visibly in pain by the time they returned to the car. "All this movement has aggravated my condition. I fear that

I must take a few days off and rest. I am indeed sorry for having let you down."

"You haven't let anyone down."

"Perhaps, perhaps not." Gregor spoke to the driver, who nodded and started off. "Would you please allow me to make one stop on the way home? It is personal business, some medicines I must drop off, and which must be done today."

"Sure."

"Thank you." He gave instructions to Tomek, then continued, "The problem we face with my being ill, you see, is that I have arranged our buys to a rather precise timetable. Many of these people face extremely dire needs. For us to postpone our visits raises the risk that they will seek other buyers, even if they know they may well be cheated." Gregor shifted in his seat, searching for a more comfortable position. "I shall endeavor to heal as fast as possible."

Their way took them out beyond the rows of high-rise concrete tenements that ringed the city, into the verdant green countryside. The roads became increasingly narrow and potholed. They turned into a small grouping of nondescript houses, stopping before what appeared to be a Victorian manor. Its pale yellow paint had long surrendered to the march of winds and rains and winters, its fenced-in yard equally neglected.

"Where are we?"

"This is what I do with my income from the antiques," Gregor replied. "That is, here is one such project. Would you like to come along?"

"Sure."

"Splendid. It won't take long."

A set of new swings and slides on one side of the entrance gate stood in glaring opposition to the house's general state of disrepair. To the other side of the path leading toward the front door was a massive pile of coal.

Gregor noted the coal spill as they walked toward the entrance. "Ah, it arrived. Excellent. Only nine months late. Just in time for next winter, I suppose."

"What is this place?" Jeffrey asked.

"A state-run home for young orphans," Gregor said, pushing open the door and shouting into the dark interior. "I work with the very young and the very old, you see. I seek out the ones who are least able to work for themselves."

A slatternly woman in a filthy apron and gray-grimed dress waddled out on dilapidated slippers, dried her hand, and offered it stiffly to Gregor. He bowed over it as though greeting royalty, turned and pointed to Jeffrey. The woman gave him an indifferent nod and pointed back down the murky hallway.

"She is now alone, at least as far as the state is concerned. Her two assistants were let go, as the state no longer had money to pay them. She is responsible for cleaning, cooking, and tending to the needs of sixty-one children."

"That's impossible."

"I have hired two young village girls to come in and help her. But all the state orphanages are suffering from funding cut-backs, and I can only do so much." He turned and walked down the hall. "Come. Let me show you something."

They entered what had once been a formal sitting parlor, and was now a sort of holding pen for young children. There was not a stick of furniture in the room. Some of the children held ragged toys, others blankets, but they were not doing anything. Five- and six-year-old children just sat and rocked constantly, hugging themselves and humming a single note. Their blank faces yearned for what they had never known.

Gregor stepped through the doorway, and immediately they *surged* toward him, gluing themselves to him, reaching for any part possible to touch, to hold, to hug. Their little voices keened a wordless cry.

"They have food and clothing, these children," Gregor explained over the clamor. "But they have no love. If you are feeling brave, I dare you to smile."

Jeffrey did. Gregor bent over, shook a child loose from his sleeve, and turned the boy around. He pointed toward Jeffrey and said something. Immediately several children turned and searched his face, then *flung* themselves on him.

"Alcoholic parents, unwed mothers, families who cannot afford another child," Gregor said above the loud keening. "Most are not the victims of disaster, but of neglect—which of course is a disaster all its own, as far as these children are concerned."

Uplifted faces searched Jeffrey's face with a yearning that threatened to pull his heart from his chest. He stroked a little face, found his wrist held with a ferocity born of lonely panic.

"The children here are neglected," Gregor said. "They are intellectually and emotionally starved. Their parents are either dead or too tired, too worried, too beaten down, or too drunk to give them the love and the attention they need. We—myself and the people with whom I work—try to set up visiting schedules using people with a good heart and a strong faith. We have book-lending trucks for the older children. We arrange for doctors to make regular visits. We set up groups small enough to give each child some personal attention, and take them out to show them a bit of the outside world. We try to awaken hope, to stimulate thought. It is so much more important than giving them a piece of candy or another bit of clothing."

As they were leaving the house, with a dozen-dozen little faces pressed to the windows, Gregor told him, "It is far worse in the handicapped children's homes. I would not dare to take you there on your first visit. Under the Communists, these little people were simply written off. They spend their time lying in bed for lack of wheelchairs and people to push them. They need everything, my dear boy. Everything from toys to baths to hands who will bathe them with love."

———

Jeffrey was immensely relieved that the first call to come through that evening was the one to Alexander. He shouted over the static, "How are you feeling?"

"Not well, I'm afraid. It seems that I am powerless to silence voices I have no desire to hear. It makes me wonder if perhaps there is not some message which I should heed. Much as I detest the notion, it is not one that I am able to shake."

Jeffrey resisted the urge to tell of his conversation with Gregor. Now was not the time. "Gregor has been taken ill."

"Ah," Alexander sighed. "This trip has proven to be a veritable deluge for you, Jeffrey. Perhaps you should return home and wait for a more opportune moment to make your debut."

"I'm doing okay, really. I've found some good pieces, and Gregor says there are some other things that we'll lose if we don't move swiftly."

"Gregor tends to know best about such things." Alexander's voice gathered a bit of strength. "I take it you have a plan."

"I really need an interpreter, someone I can trust. I was wondering if I might ask Katya to join me."

Alexander was silent a moment. "I have had a most delightful time coming to know your young lady. The more we talk, the more I am reassured with your choice." There was another pause, then he said, "I find myself unable to face the prospect of returning to Poland at this moment. I must therefore agree with your idea. You will impress upon her the need for secrecy."

"As hard as I can."

"Very well. Do as you see fit. I would be grateful if you would try to call from time to time. I realize that it is sometimes harder to find a telephone line to the outside world than it is to find the crown jewels of Russia, but nonetheless I would like to hear from you when it is possible. Your calls do me more good than I shall ever be able to convey."

"I'll try every night," Jeffrey replied. "Take care of yourself."

"I shall do my utmost, although I must say that my efforts seem of little avail just now. Perhaps you might ask my cousin to remember me in his prayers."

"I'll tell him," Jeffrey replied. "But I imagine it's going to be superfluous. I don't think he's ever stopped."

———

The call to Katya took another four hours. After apologizing his way around an extremely irate roommate who answered the phone, he said, "I need you."

"Where are you?" The voice sounded totally asleep.

"Don't you want to know who this is first? Katya, wake up. This is the real world calling."

"Jeffrey?"

"Katya, come on. I can't give you time for coffee. It took three bribes and two shouting matches to get through to you once."

"Aren't you supposed to be in Poland?" She worked the words out around a yawn.

"Where do you think I'm calling from? Of course, the way these phones operate I might as well be on the dark side of the moon. Katya, are you awake yet?"

"Sort of."

"I need you. My world is unraveling here. I can't even talk to my driver."

"You have a driver?"

"It's part of my inheritance from Alexander."

"He's dead?"

"Come on, wake up, Katya. No. You spent this afternoon with him in the shop."

"Oh yeah," she said around an enormous yawn. "I remember now."

"I've had to take over for him."

"He wouldn't tell me why you had to stay there all alone." Katya yawned again. "Can't this wait until morning?"

"No!"

"There's no need to shout, Jeffrey."

"Take a deep breath, Katya. You have *got* to wake up." There was a long pause. "Katya?"

"I'm here, Jeffrey." Her voice sounded more focused.

"I need you. Can you come tomorrow?"

"You want me to fly to Poland? Really?"

"Desperately really. Can you meet me here in Cracow?"

"I've never been to Cracow."

"I sure hope you're awake. Can you come?"

"Yes, I'm awake." There was another pause, then, "Yes, all right. I'll come. If you really need me."

The pleasure he felt at her words bordered on pain. He had not even wanted to admit how much he had been missing her. "I do. In more ways than one."

"What is that supposed to mean?"

"Let's leave the discussions for your arrival. You need to call Alexander at Claridge's first thing tomorrow morning. He will make your travel arrangements and fax me your arrival details. And, Katya, it's very important that you don't discuss this with anyone besides your mother."

"You've explained the need for secrecy. I haven't forgotten." Her voice took on the tone of a little girl's. "It will be nice to see you again, Jeffrey. Especially in Cracow."

Greeting Jeffrey with a fierce hug upon her arrival, Katya allowed him to take her first by the hotel and then into the center of town. She made no attempt to hide her excitement. "I've always wanted to come here."

"Gregor suggested we walk to the central square and have lunch there," Jeffrey said. "Then we meet with him, and afterward get back to work."

Following the hotel receptionist's directions, Jeffrey led her the seven blocks to where entry into the city's old town was announced by a return to cobblestone streets. Katya walked slowly, her eyes bright with discovery, her gaze touching everything.

She pulled him over to one side. "Look at this old state-run store. That's how drab everything looked the last time I was in Poland. You can't believe how startling it is to come back and find so many new signs of capitalism springing up. Let's go inside, so you can see for yourself how it used to be."

The lamp store fully retained it's stodgy socialist style. Wares were displayed on unpainted plywood shelves. "This is everything the shop has," Katya whispered. "There isn't any back room for extra stock, and there's no need to ask the shopkeeper anything. She's here just to take your money. And don't expect her to thank you or ask you to come again."

The glass globes were dusty, the wares outdated, the bulbs packed in little gray cardboard boxes stamped with smeared Russian Cyrillic. The shop was empty save for a bored young woman camped behind her magazine, the air dusty and undisturbed by change. Katya picked up a hand-blown ceiling light and read the tag. "This translates into thirty-seven cents. They set the price before the government changed, and they never bothered to alter it. They'll just sit here and wait for the government to get around to selling the shop and putting them out of business. It's called Communist initiative."

Next door was a new store, its window set in a shiny copper frame on a marble base. Its wares suggested the shop was still so new that the owners were not yet sure what would sell—women's high-heeled shoes competed for space with Japanese watches, cordless telephones, electronic pocket games, pressure bandages, and bras.

No one on the street smiled. People stared at shop windows, darted their eyes everywhere, or stared at nothing. Everyone they passed seemed to give him one swift glance, recognize in an instant that he was foreign and Western, then turn determinedly away.

An old woman in a filthy woolen shawl came by, begging with a tear in her eye and a crack in her voice. She shuffled from one passerby to the next, never raising her steps from the stones, her feet encased in men's work shoes that slapped softly against her feet. Jeffrey gave her the equivalent of twenty cents, and was rewarded with a sign of the cross made by hands knotted with arthritis.

When they entered Cracow's vast central square, Katya pointed to the tall age-blackened church with its two spires of totally different designs. "It's called the *Mariacki*, and it's over a thousand years old. Part of it, anyway. There's a living legend attached to it, as there is to a lot of this city. Most of the stories are based on fact. So much has happened here that they don't need to make anything up."

"I thought you told me you hadn't ever been here before."

"When did I say that?"

"On the phone last night."

"I don't remember."

"I'm surprised you remembered which city to go to, you were so asleep."

"I was awake by then. It's true, though. This is my first visit to Cracow."

"So how do you know about all this?"

"I read, Jeffrey. They have books about Poland. It's not the middle of darkest Africa or anything."

"So tell me the living legend."

"Legend isn't right. Legend has to be fiction. Living history is better." She pointed at the left-hand spire. "Every hour a trumpeter comes out and plays the *Hejnal,* which is an old Hungarian word for revelry. He plays it to the four corners of the globe. The trumpet call always cuts off in the middle of a note. It symbolizes the time the Tartars invaded Cracow—I'm not sure when, I think around six hundred years ago. A Tartar arrow stopped the trumpet call when it pierced his throat."

"That's a pretty grisly story to repeat every hour for six hundred years."

"A study of Polish history is a study of war." She looked up at him. "There's a lot of sadness, but a lot of beauty, too."

Like you, he thought. "I'm really glad you came," he said.

She allowed her gaze to linger a moment longer before pointing to the square's central structure. "Let's go in there."

As they walked toward the massive edifice, she said, "This is called the *Sukiennice,* or Cloth Hall. It was built in the fourteenth century to house the cloth, thread, cotton, wool, silk, and dye merchants who clothed the upper half of Central Europe. At that time, Cracow was the capital of the second largest kingdom in the world after the Holy Roman Empire, and cloth was a very important industry."

Wrought-iron lamps hung down the hall's narrow hundred and fifty-foot length. The merchants' stalls were converted into shops selling crystal and amber and tourist trinkets and silver and hand-knit lace. The vaulted ceiling was lined with the old royal shields from the Polish-Lithuanian Empire, which at its height had stretched from the icy wastelands crowning Europe through modern-day Czechoslovakia, Hungary, Bulgaria, Austria, Romania, the Ukraine, and parts of Turkey.

"There isn't the danger I used to feel here in Poland," Katya said as they crossed from the Cloth Hall to a large cafe at the edge of the square. "There is still sadness, though. Too much of it."

"You'll be meeting Gregor later," Jeffrey replied. "That's one thing the two of you will certainly agree on."

The Café Kawiarnia Sukiennice was a series of bright white and red chambers. The ceilings were domed, the rooms small and interconnected, the windows decorated with wrought-iron, the atmosphere splendidly foreign.

"Look around these rooms," she said. "Every face is a character, an individual. When I go out in London, I feel as if everybody has spent hours polishing off all their individuality. They wear stylish clothes, they fix their hair just so. Then they sit somewhere and pretend that everything in their life is perfect.

"Here they can't, Jeffrey. It's a luxury they can't afford. They come as they are, they sit here because they want to be with a friend or talk with family or just have an ice cream. They don't seem to have on the false facade. They sit without the lies which wealth creates. You look around here and you see a roomful of extremes. Every face is a story. I *love* that. I am sorry for the hardship that created it, but that does not make me love the result any less."

———

As they waited for Gregor to buzz them into his apartment building, Jeffrey warned her, "As far as Gregor is concerned, you are something of a risk. I imagine he's going to test you a little."

"Of course he will," Katya replied, and pushed on the door as the latch sounded.

By the time they made their way up the two flights of stairs, Gregor had returned to his bed. He sat propped up by a half dozen pillows, wrapped within a voluminous shawl. Still he greeted them with a genuine smile. "You must excuse me for not rising any more than absolutely necessary. When my joints become inflamed, there is no better healing salve than rest."

"Can we do anything to help you?" Katya asked.

"Thank you, my dear. That is most kind. But I have a very sweet old woman who would mother me to death if I let her." He shook Katya's hand, inspecting her frankly. "My cousin was most impressed with you. I can see why. Sit down, my dear. Take the comfortable chair there."

He turned his attention to Jeffrey. "You had your walk around central Cracow? What did you think?"

"I feel as if I've been sent back to school," Jeffrey replied, bringing over one of the straight-backed chairs. "I never realized how little I knew. I think before I came to Poland, my clearest impression of the East was of people standing in line."

"It was quite a true image," Gregor replied. "Before, when people saw other people standing in line, they automatically assumed it was for something worth buying. If they had time, they got in line too."

"It was a favorite way of passing a few idle hours," Katya agreed. "If you got to the head of the line and it was not something you needed, you'd buy it anyway. There was always someone you knew who could use it."

Gregor gave Katya a thoughtful look. "You built up obligations—in a good way, of course. The word is *Rewanz*, a positive revenge."

"Reciprocation," Katya offered. "Returning a favor."

"Exactly. You balanced obligations. You helped out neighbors because you knew they in turn would help you out."

Jeffrey asked, "So what happened if someone always took and never gave in return?"

"That very seldom happened," Katya replied. "Too much was at stake."

"No one would ever remind you," Gregor agreed. "You were simply expected to remember."

"You were always conscious of when it was your turn to give a gift or extend an invitation," Katya explained. "There was a sense of honor and duty involved in not allowing the relationship to get out of balance."

There was a moment of silence, with Gregor smiling and nodding. "So, so. Tell me, my dear. When were you last in Poland? This is most certainly not your first visit."

"No. It was two years ago, just before the first cracks in the Communist power-structure appeared."

"Things have changed," Gregor said mildly.

"I've noticed."

"Yes, we passed through our period of euphoria, and now we're in a period of worry. Already we are forgetting what we gained, and are spending all our time wanting for more."

"Many of the people I've seen on the street look shell-shocked," Jeffrey said.

"Indeed they do," Gregor agreed. "They have come to realize that with the opportunities of change comes the darkness of uncertainty. That was one thing which the Communist regime stifled, you see. Change. Security for the worker was achieved by imposing iron-bound laws backed by fear."

"I have never seen so many people on shopping streets," Katya said. "Everybody stops and looks at all the windows, standing there for hours."

"The shortages are gone," Gregor said. "Nowadays the only thing that is hard to come by is money. Unemployment is rising daily as more and more obsolete factories are losing their government subsidies and are being forced out of business. The government is in virtual bankruptcy, services are being cut back, and with the West in recession there is little help coming. People are worried over how to make ends meet, and afraid of being hungry."

"Not just for food, from the looks of things," Katya said.

"Exactly. They are hungry for things they have seen in television and magazines and never had the chance to try or taste or wear or drive or own. Their hunger for experimenting in all these new Western wares is immense. Overwhelming is a better word. They are overwhelmed by desire for things they now find in stores, which before were nothing more than wispy visions of a world they weren't sure really existed at all."

"I remember," Katya said. To Jeffrey she explained, "Russia was always sending propaganda throughout Poland about what a great life communism was giving them. Poles *knew* this was a lie. But when they saw pictures from the West—on television or in a magazine or from a cousin in Chicago—they not only believed that the wealth was there, but also that it was easy to have. *Everybody* in the West was rich, in their eyes. There was this misguided notion that dollars were lying along the American streets just waiting to be picked up. And this has been the great disenchantment. All these fabulous goods are now on display here in Poland, but almost no one can afford them. Simply to be joined with the West does not guarantee immediate wealth."

"The people are exhausted," Gregor went on. "They are stretched to the last possible limit, and this is causing an incredible isolation. Isolation of people, isolation of families, isolation of regions. Dialogue is gone. When I go to a council of regional Protestant and Catholic churches, theological differences are a luxury that no one can afford. The topics are how to feed the children. How to obtain medicine for the sick. How to stop the spread of pornography among the young. How to combat alcoholism."

"The Communist system guaranteed a certain stability," Katya said. "Despite oppression and foreign domination and persecution and fear, it nevertheless offered the common folk security. There was bread. There was heat. There was a roof over everyone's head. These were valuable things to people who had been totally devastated by war after war after war."

"But the cost." Sorrowfully Gregor shook his head. "My goodness, the cost. Look into the eyes of a nation taught not to strive, to hope. There you will find the cost."

There was a moment's silence; then Katya stood and said, "Perhaps you two would like to have a moment alone together. It was very nice meeting you, Gregor."

He extended a hand and a very warm smile. "My dear, the pleasure has truly been my own."

"I'll see you downstairs, Jeffrey."

As her footsteps echoed down the stairway, Gregor said, "That is a remarkable young woman you have found for yourself. Or perhaps that God has found for you. I wondered at Alexander's decision to allow a stranger to work with you, but now I see that he was correct."

"It means a lot to hear you say that."

"Yes, I can also see a bit of the Mongol horde in Katya. It is true for many of Eastern Europe's most beautiful women—the mysterious slant to their eyes, and cheekbones shaped by icy Steppe winds."

Jeffrey couldn't help but smile. "I thought you weren't supposed to notice such things."

"Who on earth told you such nonsense? Not my cousin, I hope."

"No one did."

"My dear young friend, faith does not make one a eunuch. It simply points out the borders of correct thought and action. There is a very great difference between appreciating beauty and *desiring* it."

"I suppose I've never thought of it like that," Jeffrey confessed.

"Human society says so long as the person is not violated, there is no harm in lust. But God says you must draw the line at appreciating, before it hardens into sinful thought." Gregor smiled. "Such beauty is always a joy to appreciate."

Jeffrey felt the familiar ache. "And what if I can't appreciate her without wanting her?"

Gregor turned an understanding gaze on Jeffrey and replied gently, "Then temper your desire with God's love. And want her first as your wife."

Jeffrey looked toward the open door. "For the first time in my life I can think about taking that step without diving for cover. I just wish I knew how she felt about it."

"You are most fortunate, my boy. The girl loves you dearly."

"Alexander said the same thing. I wish I knew how you two could be so certain. She sure doesn't show it."

"In her own way, she makes it perfectly clear, I assure you. She does not tell you what you wish to hear because you are not yet ready to receive it."

"I'm ready all right."

"No, no, listen to what I am saying. The girl loves *you*. Not the man you want to become, and certainly not the man you want the world to see. She loves *you*." He reached to the side table for pen and paper. "The question is whether you are able to make peace with the true Jeffrey Sinclair. She has, you may rest assured of that. She has seen you as you are and she loves you. That should help you quite a bit."

Gregor scribbled busily. "Give this to Tomek." He held out the paper. "He will take you to meet a gentleman in a village less than an hour from here."

Jeffrey accepted the slip. "Do you think I could come by and talk with you some more?"

"Nothing on this earth could give me more pleasure," Gregor replied. "Perhaps you can stop by alone in the mornings before you begin work."

"That would be great. Thanks."

"My dear boy, it is I who thank you." Gregor adjusted his shawl. "And now you should be going. It is best to return before nightfall. Vodka remains the greatest hazard on Poland's roads, and you have more difficulty recognizing who is caught in its clutches after dark."

As they left the main road and made their way through small townships, Jeffrey said, "I wonder what life is like in these villages."

"For most young people with intelligence and ambition, it is an imprisonment for the crime of daring to hope and to dream." Katya shook her head. "It is because of the pressures *against* success that the Communists have so beaten down this people."

"You and Gregor agree on that point."

"I imagine there are a lot of things where Gregor and I agree."

Outlying villages gave way to a concrete forest of high-rise tenements, and they to an unending stream of three-story apartments. The street became hemmed in by gray sameness—without pause, without individuality. Buildings appeared to lean inwards, pressing down on the sidewalks and the streets and the people with a draining force. Here there is no hope of change, they seemed to say. No hope of improvement. No way to escape.

"Even in the poorest villages there was at one time a castle and a cloister," Katya told him. "Wars have done away with one or both in many places. In the villages where the Communists rebuilt, they did not feel a need to spend money on a heart, a town center. The streets have an aimless feel, none of them leading anywhere."

The car stopped a block away from what appeared to be the town's only park—a dusty, unkempt stretch of grass with a few twisted trees. Beyond the park loomed a factory, its trio of smokestacks defiantly dwarfing the park's stunted growth. Jeffrey and Katya left the car and entered a first-floor flat, where a man identified himself as the former factory manager.

"I'm out of a job," he had Katya translate once they were seated on a rock-hard sofa. "I didn't move fast enough."

Jeffrey nodded as though he understood, and practiced patience. The man was overweight as only a once-skinny man could be. A pronounced swayback gave his overhanging belly an even greater bulge. His eyes and hair were grayish brown, his voice equally drab. Katya kept her face blank and nodded in time to his words. She waited until he was finished, then turned back to Jeffrey. "I do not like this place, can we please hurry?"

"What did he say?"

"Nothing of importance." She rushed through the words, blurring them together. "He probably speaks a little of our language. I'm talking just to fill the air. Can you ask me to ask for the furniture?"

Jeffrey nodded solemnly, as though receiving information of great importance. He replied, "May I please see the items for sale?"

The man nodded and led the way down the hall to a door that he unlocked and ushered them inside. The room held a set four Biedermeier pieces, one of the few intact sets Jeffrey had ever seen. They were all of ash, another rarity, the grain so fine as to outshine the paintings on the walls above them.

Biedermeier furniture dominated the style houses of central Europe from 1815 to around 1850. Its strict lines and lack of gaudy exterior decoration was intended as an absolute rejection of the overblown carvings and intricate mosaics of earlier periods.

Closest to Jeffrey was an upright secretary-cabinet, the fold-down face flanked by black side pillars. Its straight unyielding lines were made more delicate by the ash's grain. Beside it stood a waist-high chest of drawers, and beside that a sofa table on a center-column and platform base. The real prize sat against the back wall—a settee fully nine feet in length. Rising from the silk upholstery was a long back piece carved from one single massive tree. The circular arms were also entire tree trunks, but scrolled with a waved pattern that gave even their massive breadth a delicate air.

Jeffrey worked to keep his voice calm. "Anything else?"

The man deflated instantly. In broken English he said, "Is not okay?"

"It's excellent. Really first rate."

The room lit up again. "And the price?"

"Equally high. Are there any more pieces for sale?"

With unrestrained eagerness Jeffrey was led to the bedroom, where a suite of garishly modern quasi-Western furniture sidled up to one piece that dominated the room.

"Polish," the man announced proudly.

"It certainly might be," Jeffrey replied, stooping for a closer look.

"No might. Is. Is. Have picture in book."

Polish Biedermeier was called Simmler, after the major factory in Warsaw at the time. It was very rare, as few pieces had survived in this war-torn land. The chest of drawers was of nut burl, and the tree that had sacrificed its roots for the facade must have been massive—the top and each drawer was covered by one solid strip of veneer. Jeffrey felt a keen sense of pleasure; if authentic, it would be a nice piece for Alexander to present to the new regime.

When they were back in the car and under way, Jeffrey asked, "What did that factory manager say that so upset you back there?"

"It wasn't what he said," Katya replied. "He's probably like a lot of others, but it was sort of like having a snake crawl out of the grass when you're not expecting it."

"What do you mean, like the others?"

"Oh," Katya sighed. "He probably started off a staunch Communist, not just a Party member for the sake of his card but a real activist. That was more or less required for somebody in a position like his. But like a lot of them in the late eighties he saw the writing on the wall and started working strong for Solidarity. He was too shrewd to go down with the Communist clunker, too flexible, too awake.

"Then came the time for the government to sell all the state-owned companies. As long as the Communists were in power, all companies were state owned. All of them, Jeffrey, from the local newspaper vendor to the biggest car factory. Private companies were against the law. So now the new government was to sell these companies. How? By auction. When? At a time to be announced. To whom? Whoever bid the most money."

"Here comes the catch," Jeffrey guessed.

"But of course. The problem was, how was the auction to be announced? Well, if the company director was shrewd and kept his old ties, it might have been with one group of placards that were conveniently misplaced, and one well-timed telephone call."

"So what do you think happened here?"

"Who knows? Maybe a foreign company decided it was a perfect entry into the new capitalistic Poland, and all the attention kept everybody honest. Or he was caught trying a fast one. Or maybe, just maybe, the people in this region responsible for the auctions were intent on being honest. That happened, too—not everywhere, but more often than you might think."

As they passed beyond the high-rise apartment houses and re-entered the countryside, Katya pointed to a small chapel where a crowd was gathering. "Could we please stop for afternoon Mass? It would be lovely to hear one in Polish again."

Sheep grazed in a pasture beside the priory, and blossoming fruit trees gave the enclosure a sweetly perfumed air. Under the shade of a dozen ancient trees stood over two hundred people with hands folded in front of them, facing toward the unseen priest.

"There is no room left inside," Katya whispered as they approached the crowd. "It is the same all over Poland."

Katya stood and listened, and Jeffrey contended himself by watching those around him. The children played quietly or stood and faced the church with their elders. The attitude was prayerful, respectful, peaceful. The contrast to the hopelessness he had felt in the street could not have been greater.

Once they were again under way, Katya asked him, "Why isn't Alexander here with you? He wouldn't tell me anything."

"We went to Auschwitz two days ago," Jeffrey replied simply.

"Alexander went back to London because of seeing Auschwitz? I don't understand."

"It's a little hard to explain."

The driver said something. Katya turned forward and replied briefly.

"What did he say?"

"He said that yes, Alexander looked very pale when you returned from Auschwitz. What happened there, Jeffrey?"

He turned to the driver. "I didn't know you spoke English."

"Not speak," the man replied, his accent most guttural. "Understand few words."

The driver began speaking in Polish. Reluctantly Katya turned her gaze from Jeffrey and listened in silence. When the driver finished, she sat there for a moment, then without turning back she told him, "He says his school was taken to visit Auschwitz when he was sixteen. What he remembers most was that there was one enormous boy, much larger than anyone else in his class, who used to bully everyone horribly. He says the boy was very cruel and liked to hurt people, especially the smaller children. He would take money from them, and if they didn't have money he would beat them up. At Auschwitz their class was first taken into a big hall where they saw a documentary made by the Russians when they liberated the camp. What he remembers most is that the only one who lost control during the film was the bully. He started weeping so hard the whole hall could hear, and then toward the end when they showed some victims of the medical experiments, he fainted."

Katya was silent for a moment, then said, "I think that's horrible."

Jeffrey shrugged. "There are bullies all over the world."

"I wasn't speaking of the boy. I can't believe they brought schoolchildren to see such horrors."

Jeffrey watched the canopy of verdant tree limbs sweep over their car like a translucent tunnel. Eventually he said, "When I arrived there, that's exactly what I thought, too. I couldn't believe there were so many buses in the parking lot—there must have been twenty or thirty of them, mostly Polish but some German and Czech and English. And kids everywhere. Well, not really young kids. Teenagers. Some probably in college, but I guess most were in their last couple of years of high school. And I thought the same thing. How can they allow their own children to come and see such a nightmare. Why keep it alive?

"Afterward, though, when I walked out, I understood. I don't know if I agree with it, but I do understand, I think. There was one of those barracks, one of the camp halls, that had been set up as a Polish museum. And it wasn't to the people lost in the camp—well, not most of it anyway. It showed life under the Nazi occupation.

Alexander translated some of it for me; it was all in Polish. Besides the millions of Jews who were slaughtered, four million Polish Christians died during the occupation. Four million, Katya.

"That was about one-eighth of the entire population. And that was just the number *killed*. There was no estimate for those injured. I guess there wasn't any listing. Let's make it conservative and say another quarter of the population. And then on top of that, how many carried emotional scars?

"There was one document talking about the critical situation for children. By the winter of 1943, they were being restricted to a diet of two hundred calories a day. I stood there trying to remember what our daily intake is—something around three thousand, I think. Then beside the document they had a photograph of two little kids, ten or eleven years old. They were dressed pretty nice, ragged but clean-looking, the boy in a little suit with short pants and the girl in a dress with a petticoat. They looked like puppets, Katya. Just painted sticks inside clothes five sizes too big. They had little shoes on with newspapers for socks. Their legs were so thin I could have made a circle with my thumb and forefinger around their *thighs* and still have room left over. Their faces were so shrunken I could see the edges of their skulls jutting out from around their eyes. And their eyes . . . I can't get them out of my mind. I have nightmares about their eyes."

The driver turned onto a four-lane highway and speeded up. The road was almost empty. He glanced at his watch and said something. Katya did not reply. Her eyes were fixed on Jeffrey's face, her attention unwavering. The driver glanced into his rearview mirror, and lapsed into patient silence.

"When I walked out of the camp," Jeffrey went on, "I looked at all these kids visiting the camp in a totally different way. When I went in, I was watching them and half-wondering which one might have had a relative or the relative of a friend who had been here. When I came out, I wondered if any of them came from a family that *didn't* suffer during the war.

"Auschwitz isn't a monument just to a concentration camp. I didn't understand that before I went. It is a monument to a tragedy that covered the whole country. Auschwitz wasn't some isolated island of destruction and death, it was just the eye of the storm. And the storm almost destroyed them.

"Maybe Poland is wrong to show their children this factory of death. There's always the chance that the kids will go away feeling only hate. But maybe they want their children to be able to come back and understand, this is why Auntie Martha walks funny. And why Greorge's father's back is all crooked. And why Grandpa cries whenever he gets drunk and talks about the war. Not because of Auschwitz, but because of what Auschwitz *represents*."

Katya's violet eyes enveloped him. "You've changed, Jeffrey."

He didn't deny it. "These past couple of days, I have been seeing this whole place differently. Before, I couldn't help looking down on them—the Poles, I mean. They're so *sad*. And it's really crazy how much they drink, Katya. After seeing Auschwitz, though, I've been kicking myself for ever feeling superior. This was just one more horror in centuries of occupation and oppression."

"You have learned a lot this trip," she said quietly.

"Back in the camp I was constantly bracing myself. Every time I entered one of those barracks, I felt I had to get ready to face something more horrible than what I'd heard about those places. But it wasn't like that. I didn't see anything new. I just came out feeling different."

"That it was more real for you," Katya suggested.

Jeffrey shook his head. "No, it's always been real. But afterward I saw it in a different way. More personal, not for me, but for the people who had died there. They stopped being this incredible number, four million, five million, and started being individuals. The faces on the walls, the glasses, the names on the suitcases. Each belonged to a person. They shouted out, *I was somebody. Me.*"

He looked out the window. "After it was over I just walked out and returned to the world. I felt such an incredible shock. On one side of the fence is a place of death, and on the other a world of life. I felt as if there should have been a more gradual transition, a no-man's-land, or at least a warning—beware, beyond this point life starts again."

He was silent for a long while, staring out at the summer scenery, seeing the shadows of other days crowding up around them. Katya waited patiently, her eyes resting upon him with an unblinking steadiness. "Going there brought all the sadness I've found here in Poland into perspective. For the very first time, I'm beginning to understand why so many people walk around wrapped in tragedy. Why so many of the children already look so old."

"It wasn't just the Nazis," Katya said quietly. "You must understand this to understand Poland. Stalin ranks with Hitler as the greatest murderers of modern times. They scarred Poland so deeply that the wounds may never heal. There are no records of how many Poles he shot or sent to Siberia. None. Records were simply not allowed."

"I tell you," Jeffrey said. "These have to be the strongest people on earth, not to be crying all the time."

Rain transformed this world. So long as there was sunshine, it was possible to believe that at least one direction was open to escape. With the rain the sky closed down, a gray ceiling to a wet gray world. The sense of imprisonment was complete.

Jeffrey hurried through the blustery summer rain to Gregor's apartment, climbed the stairs, found him propped up in bed and looking very worried. "What's the matter?"

"There has been a most unfortunate change of plans. Have you ever heard of a place called Wieliczka?"

"No, I don't think so."

"No matter. Poland's most famous salt mine is located in that village. We store our purchased antiques there."

"In a salt mine?"

"It has served us well for over twenty years. Cool salt air is ideal for preserving fine wood." He plucked fitfully at his shawl. "The mine is a labyrinth longer than Poland is wide. During the last war whole airplanes were constructed in its depths. We have handled a number of articles for people of that region, and like miners all over the world, they are experts at keeping secrets."

"They want more money," Jeffrey guessed.

"It seems that they too have been hit by the economic crisis," Gregor agreed. "It is not just that they want more money. I am now concerned at just how long they will remain trustworthy."

"How much do I pay them?"

"They want another five thousand dollars. I would suggest you agree. Otherwise there is the risk that the articles may not stay sold." Gregor reached to his side table, and handed over three sheets of paper covered with a cramped scrawl. "I have prepared an inventory of those items I purchased before your arrival. You should use this as an opportunity to make sure none of the pieces have grown legs."

Gregor leaned back and seemed to melt into his pillows. "Have a successful trip, my boy. I shall be with you in my prayers."

———

The salt mines' central building was painted a bright pastel, its wrought-iron gate and ornate veranda giving the place a very cheerful look. Children swarmed and laughed and did nothing to hide their excitement. The adults around them, both those with the children's groups and other visitors to the mines, watched their antics with genuine fondness.

Katya returned from calling for their contact. She saw the direction of Jeffrey's gaze as she sat down beside him. "The Polish people truly love their children," she said. "Oh, there are some exceptions, mostly brought on by too much stress and hardship and alcohol. But for the most part children here are really loved. The majority of parents have forced themselves to develop an incredible amount of endurance and patience for the sake of their children." She brushed at a wayward strand of silky black hair and went on, "They remain patient with an impossible life, all for their children. They endure suffering so that their children may have a home and food and learn hope. They imagine a better world for their little ones, and now, God willing, they may see it."

"There is so much to learn here," Jeffrey said.

Katya pointed to a marble plaque alongside the entrance. "It's a line of poetry from a Polish writer. It says, 'You praise what is foreign, and remain blind to the riches at your feet.'"

Jeffrey returned his gaze to the children. "This really is a land of contrasts. Night and day. I've never been in a place where there is so much to hate, but so much to love as well. So much beauty."

"A land of night and day," Katya said, and smiled at him. "I like that very much."

A young man in miners' coverall and torch-lit hat made his way through the children. He gave them a perfunctory greeting, asked about Gregor, shrugged at Katya's reply. He was a short, solidly built man who spoke in quick bursts, which she hurried to translate.

"He says his name is Casimir," Katya said. "We are here for a private tour if anyone asks, and we are going to take the standard route as far as we can."

Casimir pushed his way through the heavy fire door and led them down a sloping narrow tunnel. They came to a square mine shaft lined with wooden stairs. Jeffrey took time to look over the banister and saw a group of teenagers descending far below them; beneath that was nothing save the stairs tunneling into darkness.

"There are 320 kilometers of tunnels," Katya continued to translate. "We'll go down 300 meters today, which is 890 stairs. He says not to worry; we'll take the miners' elevator back to return to the surface.

"This is the oldest working salt mine in the world, and has been in operation for over eight hundred years. The earliest commercial sale document they have is dated 1281, but it speaks of a mine that's been in existence for at least one hundred years before that."

It took them almost fifteen minutes to reach what Casimir said was the first of three stages of descent. Jeffrey flexed his knotted leg muscles and reached over to touch what looked like logs frosted with ancient ice. It was salt.

Cramped halls made for people far shorter than he opened unexpectedly into massive domed caverns. Their guide took evident pride in the mine, and showed no hurry in reaching their goal. They passed cavern after cavern filled with statues, all carved from salt by the miners in their free time.

One cavern showed a salt peasant kneeling before a salt queen and her warriors beneath a hoary salt icicle ceiling. "In 1251," Casimir said through Katya, "Queen Kinga's father gave her a salt mine in Hungary as a wedding present. She threw her engagement ring into the salt pit to commemorate her ownership. The legend is that a miner here in this very mine, some thousand kilometers away, found the ring. He went to her court, offered the ring, and told her that it was a sign from God for her heart and her wealth to remain in Poland. She went on to become one of Poland's greatest rulers."

In the next cavern, another set of salt men knelt and crawled in narrow passages with salt torches held above their heads. "Ever since a fire in 1740," Casimir told them, "the highest paid miners were the ones who crawled the new passages with torches held to the ceiling. Methane was given off in the mining of salt, and they tried to ignite the little gas bubbles before they gathered. These miners did not usually live long."

They passed down a second long set of stairs to the mine's next level, where the air took on a crisp feeling. It tingled in the throat and left the lungs feeling scrubbed.

They entered the largest of the mine's forty-four underground chapels, where saints, altar, chandelier, walls, chalice and cross were carved from salt. "Construction was started in 1600," he told them. "And it was used by the miners for weddings, baptisms, funerals, masses, and daily prayers until the Austrians conquered Poland about two hundred years ago. Their governors decided that the Poles prayed too much, and closed all the chapels down."

The hall was over two hundred feet long. Light came from six fifteen-foot-high salt-crystal chandeliers. He walked in awed silence across a floor shaped like geometrical flagstone, which was also carved from salt. The walls were decorated with salt crystal bas-reliefs from the Gospels—the stable birth, the flight to Egypt, Christ carrying the cross, the Last Supper, Thomas doubting the resurrected Christ.

The passage from the second to the third levels was through a cavern so vast it was hard to catch its height. It twisted around in a rough-edged spiral, crowned with a roof like a thatched cottage—only here the thatch was made from entire trees, and each of the supporting columns from two dozen logs lashed together with iron bands.

At the cavern's base, Casimir stopped and waited in silence. Jeffrey understood why this place had been chosen; its size gave them the possibility to look both ahead and behind to spot any nearby groups, and the distant walls were perfect reflectors for footsteps and voices. They stood there for about three minutes before Casimir placed a finger to his lips and led them on.

A hundred meters beyond the cavern, Casimir turned off the main corridor into what appeared to be a dead end. He reached inside a box set above the wall's support logs, and switched on a light; instead of a simple indentation in the tunnel, they faced a metal gate. Beyond it a narrow corridor stretched down at least a quarter mile.

Walking the corridor's length was the only moment during the entire passage that Jeffrey felt the weight of stone and salt and earth bearing down above his head. From ahead of him Casimir spoke in a low voice, and Katya translated, "Down here they developed chambers where the entire collections of both the Vavel Castle Museum and the National Museum can be kept in an emergency. Otherwise they aren't used—except by us."

He stopped before a door recessed in the side wall, like hundreds of others they had passed, marked in no way at all.

The overhead bulb came on to display a chamber stuffed with antiques. Jeffrey fumbled for Gregor's list, began checking off items, resisted the urge to hunker and gawk. A set of Louis Phillippe furniture. An early German secretary so inlaid with burl veneer it was hard to tell the original wood. An English commode of mahogany in impeccable condition. A bureau cabinet, possibly of fruitwood, definitely central European, the ornate carving around its edges creating a frame for the grain's natural artistry. A *fin de siècle* glass-fronted cabinet, its sides carved into a bouquet of blooming lilies.

Jeffrey maneuvered his way among the room's treasures through the narrow U-shaped passage. When he returned to the entrance he was sweating. "All there," he reported.

"Of course it is," the man replied through Katya, his eyes turning hard. "For now."

"What's that supposed to mean?"

"Prices of everything are going up faster than anyone can believe," Katya translated. "Storage space especially."

"We were told that you wanted another payment," Jeffrey replied, forcing his voice to remain steady. "I've been authorized to pay you."

The miner's eyes held a greedy light. He spoke again, and Katya said, "There's a lot of wealth here. Somebody is getting very rich from all this."

"You're getting your share."

"That's good to hear." Casimir nodded in the direction of the room. "We have to work day and night to make sure nobody gets in and steals away these riches."

—

"The furniture has to be moved soon," Alexander told him by phone that evening.

"Gregor agrees with you. He said that if we can't get the export documents and move it out of Poland, he has another place where we can take the items. It's an old folks' home he works with who'll give us part of their cellar."

"Such a move would be expensive," Alexander said. "And risky."

"Gregor wants to know how long you think it will be before the furniture leaves Poland."

"That is hard to say," Alexander replied. "I needed to make new contacts this trip."

"Is there anything I can do?"

"It would be far better to obtain the proper export documents and ship the furniture immediately." Alexander paused. "I am indeed sorry to burden you with all this your first trip, Jeffrey."

"It happens. To tell the truth, I'm really enjoying myself."

"Indeed. Experience is most certainly the best teacher."

"What exactly would you want me to do?"

"There is an expression in Polish that says, 'He walks after things.' It refers to a man who can get things done, especially when dealing with the government. That is what you require. Someone who will walk your export documents through a different labyrinth, this one inside a government ministry."

"So how do I go about finding someone like that?"

Alexander paused and said finally, "Perhaps this should wait until I am feeling better and can come down to help you, Jeffrey."

"Maybe so, but at least let me try."

"Very well. You are looking for someone whose interests coincide with yours. Perhaps it will be someone with whom I dealt in the old government—Gregor knows most of them. This is doubtful, as past services rendered to a disgraced regime will not carry much weight now. No, it will most likely be someone from within the art world who knew of my earlier efforts, who now has a position in the government."

"Any ideas who that might be?"

"Again, Gregor may be able to tell you. It is part of his responsibility to keep track of such things while I am not around. But because you will be working with someone new to our operation, you are going to need some gift, some important favor or service to offer them. He or she will want to make sure that we still have either assistance or articles of value to bring to the table."

"That's not a lot to go on."

"No, but keep your eyes and ears open. Something may turn up. If you can find that hook, obtaining the export documents should not be too difficult. Many of the new administrators have a very real contempt for the laws instituted by the Communists, and rumor has it that regulations governing the export of antiques are soon to be changed in any case."

"So I'm to find both a person who can actually write the documents, and find something that I can offer them, like maybe an antique of Polish importance."

"That would be the best, of course. But such items do not grow on trees. Have you come across anything you might use?"

"A Polish Biedermeier chest of drawers. Not enough on its own to warrant this kind of special treatment."

"No. Well, a service of some kind, something you can offer that no one else can do, this too would be an excellent gift."

"Sounds impossible."

"Yes, it may well be. In that case, we shall simply have to hope that our friends in the salt mine do not decide to sell the merchandise twice."

"And that you get well soon," Jeffrey added.

"Thank you, yes, it would be very nice if we were to be able to seek this new door together. I have often thought in the past that it would be so much nicer to work with another."

"You have Gregor."

"Ah, but Gregor is often ill, as you can see for yourself. Not to mention the fact that his somewhat peculiar attitudes makes him unsuitable for the rough and tumble of business."

"What would you use as leverage if you were here?"

"That, my friend, is what we must apply ourselves to identifying," Alexander replied. "And with great diligence."

Friend, Alexander had said. "Gregor has somebody he wants me to go see tomorrow. It's a long shot, something he hasn't felt was all that important until this came up."

"He gave you no details?"

"He said he didn't have any to give me, except that the man spoke English, and that I needed to go alone."

"Strange that he would not have mentioned it before."

"It's a long shot at best, like I said." Jeffrey took a breath. "And the meeting has to take place at Florian's Gate."

"Ah. Well." The life drained from Alexander's voice. "It is certainly one that you must handle yourself, then. Call me when you return. And watch your back."

awn painted the promise of a beautiful day in heaven-wide hues of gold and blue when Jeffrey left the hotel the next morning. He walked the brief distance to Gregor's apartment and found him moving painfully about his little alcove fixing tea.

Jeffrey took him by the elbow and guided him back to bed. "Let me do that for you."

Gregor did not complain. "I am most grateful, my dear boy. Just be careful that the stove does not singe your fingers as it has mine."

The kitchen was nothing more than a walk-through closet with a cramped little bathroom at the back. On one side wall, a tiny refrigerator clanked and shivered beneath a dripping faucet and battered sink. Set into the wall overhead was a draining rack for all the utensils and plates Gregor owned—none of which matched. On the opposite wall, twin gas pressure tanks supported a plywood board, upon which rested a portable cooker. A safe distance above this were more shelves, containing a bare minimum of canned and boxed food.

Jeffrey filled a pot with water, lit the stove with a kitchen match, set the pot in place, and went back to the main room. "Do you mind if I ask why you returned to Poland after having escaped?"

"Because I was called," Gregor replied simply.

"That's it?"

"That is more than enough, and all I can offer to someone who has never known the experience. But the *how* of my return is perhaps more interesting. Would you like to hear of it?"

"Sure."

"Very well. On March 5, 1946, Sir Winston Churchill gave an address in America, and we heard it on the air the next day. You are too young to remember, but in these times the radio was our lifeline, our source of joy and entertainment and news. That particular talk became famous later, but it was new then. I still recall the words. He said, 'From Stettin in the Baltic to Trieste in the Adriatic, an Iron Curtain has descended across the Continent.'"

"I know the expression," Jeffrey said. "I suppose everybody does these days."

"An iron curtain. I can't tell you what an impact those words had on me. I felt the iron curtain had come down inside me, and my life's work was waiting on the other side. It was a very wounded time for me. Zosha, my wife, had died—just before Christmas of that first year in London. Her health had never been good, and she had not really recovered from the strain of our escape from Poland. On rare occasions when my anguish would subside, I would catch hold of this feeling, a very clear sensation that I was being called back home.

"By that time, there was a tremendous amount of suspicion and numerous rumors—and a growing body of hard factual evidence as well—about Stalin's death grip upon Poland. We heard ever more horrific stories of mass arrests and executions. Polish patriots, officers, and intellectuals were being denounced as fascists and shot. Stalin's true nature was being shown by wave after wave of oppression and terror. I knew exactly what I was going to find upon my return. It was impossible for a Pole to meet a Pole anywhere—on the street, in a shop, at the club—without hearing of another atrocity. Street-sweeps were being instituted again, just as in the time of the Nazi occupation. The secret police were again arriving in the middle of the night to steal away whole families and relocate them to Siberia. Yes. I knew what awaited me. But I also knew I was called, and that I was going to go.

"There was one main problem, however. No, that is incorrect. There were two. The first was, how on earth was I going to escape back into Poland. The Polish border police mirrored Stalin's growing paranoia and hatred of everything tainted by the West. All arriving Poles were viewed as spies. After all, why would anyone who had managed to escape wish to return, unless it was to overthrow Stalin's puppet government?

"My second problem, and my greatest worry, was Alexander. I realize that in this day and age you will find this difficult to understand, but I did not want to go against his wishes. I loved and admired him very much. I wanted to go back, yes. I *knew* I was going to return. But I also wanted to do so with Alexander's blessings.

"I began by dropping hints, making it as clear as possible to a man who had no faith in God that I felt this same God was calling me back. But I did not tell him directly that I was going, so he did not have a reason to ask me to stay, do you see? I simply let him know of my desire, and I waited. And I prayed."

Jeffrey caught a whiff of steam from the boiling pot. He moved into the alcove, dropped a pinch of tea leaves into two glasses, filled them with water, picked them up gingerly around the rims, and returned.

"Ah, excellent. Thank you so much, my dear boy. This first cup of tea has become a ritual that holds my mornings together." Gregor blew on the tea and sipped it.

"I don't see how you can drink it like that. The water's still almost boiling."

"Practice, my boy. A practice best done on winter mornings when you have passed a night without heat, and when you awaken to an apartment so cold you are not sure that your pipes are still running." He sipped again. "That night in London, I switched off the radio and went down to the *Ognisko*. Do you know it?"

"Sure. The Polish Club in South Kensington. Alexander takes me there whenever he's in town."

"It was quite a place back then, not a club in the sense of being exclusive. Anyone could enter. It was a place where the Poles of London would gather and feel that they *belonged*. It always made me feel better just to go in there, to hear the Polish voices, smell the stuffed cabbage cooking. I am sure many others felt the same. The atmosphere was always lively in the evenings, filled with serious flirtations and mock conspiracies—and laced with good vodka and cheap cigarettes.

"I went upstairs to a room devoted to the most serious of pursuits—bridge. The stakes were by our standards very high. A game had just broken up, and in the corner of the room I saw Alexander talking with Piotr."

Jeffrey straightened up with a jolt. "Piotr my grandfather?"

"Indeed. I don't know how much you know about what your grandfather did during the war—"

"Nothing at all," Jeffrey replied. "I've never even heard anybody mention it before."

"I thought not." There was a mischievous twinkle to Gregor's eyes. "You didn't think he had been a jeweler all his life, did you?"

"I guess I never thought of it."

"The steady hands and the trained eye that made him a good jeweler in America made him a master at the forgery of documents."

"My grandfather?"

"I assure you, my dear boy, I am not exaggerating. A true master forger. He had been very active in the Polish Underground Army. He was an artist of sorts. He had a name for creating the best false documents anyone had ever seen."

Jeffrey leaned back. "Incredible."

"Indeed. War has a tendency to bring out the strangest traits in men, the best and the worst. In your grandfather's case, I am happy to say, it was the best. In any case, he and Alexander were talking to a man in uniform that everyone addressed as *Prosze Pana Kapitana,* or Mister Captain Sir. I suppose he had a name, but to me and the others he was an aristocrat and a war hero, someone who bolstered our own feelings of patriotism by simply allowing us to recognize him in this honorable way.

"London was really the center for maintaining the struggle for Poland during and after the war. The Polish government-in-exile was headquartered there. Almost everywhere you went in Polish circles, there was some bit of intrigue, some preparation for rescue or revolution. The Captain-Sir was talking to Alexander and Piotr about a man who had worked undercover for them just outside of Warsaw. The man knew a tremendous amount about Red Army activities and intentions. The Soviets had almost consolidated both their position and their new political power. To be sure, they often made promises to hold elections, but by the end of 1945, it was clear to almost everyone that any elections which were held would be rigged. Moscow-trained Communists held key posts in the ministries of Justice and the Interior. They completely controlled the police, the courts, the press, and the new government propaganda machine. It was simply a matter of time before they would eliminate the remaining nationalists in the government structure, and consolidate their power.

"It was time, the Captain-Sir declared, for their undercover man to get out. His situation was becoming too dangerous, and they needed his information back in London. Your grandfather was very concerned, because this man was a friend. The Red Army and the Polish government were cracking down quite severely. No Poles were being allowed out—of course, this had been the situation since the Russians had invaded, but it was growing continually worse. Stalin's paranoia was mounting. He had secret police planted everywhere."

Gregor cradled his cooling glass with both hands, his gaze bright with remembering. "The captain and Piotr were discussing a plan to make their man a set of American documents. You see, there were quite a few Americans going in and out of Poland on these inspection-evaluation missions for reconstruction and foreign aid. What concerned them, and what they were trying to work out, was how to get the documents safely into Poland and in his hands.

"I positively jumped forward, as though struck by a lightning bolt. 'Send me,' I said.

"'Impossible,' Piotr replied. 'There's a slim chance you could get through, but it's very unlikely. The situation is becoming impossibly tough at the borders. They could ransack everything you have, find an American passport among your things in someone else's name, and then what?'

"The captain agreed. 'They would have you drawn and quartered, and our missions both in England and in Poland could collapse.'

"'Then send me with one set of travel documents,' I replied. They did not understand. 'I will enter on the American passport, then turn it over to your man for him to exit with. We will simply need to have someone on the other side insert his picture where mine had been before. Or place his under mine, so that I can peel mine off. There must be a way to do that.'

"The captain thought it could work. The document would be stamped upon entering Poland, and there would be no problem exiting a few days later.

" 'Impossible,' Piotr repeated. 'Gregor gets in, delivers the documents, and then what? He'd be trapped there.'

"Alexander spoke for the first time, and told them, 'That has been my cousin's plan all along.' He looked at me with an expression of sadness and defeat, because he knew I had found the one way of returning to Poland to which he would never object. Then and there, it was decided that I would be the courier."

Gregor smiled at Jeffrey. "As you know, Piotr by then had a very good connection in the American Embassy."

"My grandmother?"

He nodded. "She was already his wife by that time, your grandmother. She was so much in love, terribly infatuated with Piotr. When he asked for her help, she could not refuse. Her first sense of loyalty was to him and his causes.

"She dug out an American passport from the vaults, one of hundreds that had been returned to the embassy over the years— perhaps stolen, perhaps lost, who knows. It did not matter. She found one for a Mr. Paul W. Mason. Older than I, not as old as the man waiting near Warsaw. A few travel stamps—Mexico, Canada, Italy, some of the places that I had once dreamed of visiting and now never would.

"Your grandmother prepared a lovely letter of introduction on embassy stationery, and once I had used the letter to obtain a Polish visa, she arranged for a Mr. Paul W. Mason to travel to Warsaw with an American engineering delegation. She booked his return for four days later with a different group.

"Then Piotr worked his magic. He substituted my picture on the passport and forged the embassy seal that covered the photograph's right side. He then took a photograph of the man in Warsaw and embossed it with the same quadrant of seal. I hid this photograph in my package of playing cards, glued between the joker and the ace of hearts. Once I was safely in the country, I lifted my photograph off with a razor and glued his into place. The documents were passed on to our man, and he returned to London in my place.

"When I arrived in Cracow, I informed the authorities that we had fled the Nazis and wound up in a small Carpathian village, someplace so remote that they would not bother to check. There my wife fell ill, I explained, and after her death I returned."

Jeffrey asked, "And all this time, you could never tell anyone here you ever went to the West?"

"The world of an oppressed people is a world of secrecy, my boy," Gregor replied. "There were many things no one told anyone, not even their family. It was not discussed, it was not questioned, it was simply done. For myself, I was forced to pretend that the West had never existed for me."

"Did you ever regret coming back?"

"I have only one regret. And that is, when I die I will not be buried next to my beloved Zosha, whom I laid to rest in London. I must leave it to the Lord above to bring us together somehow." Gregor glanced at his watch. "Goodness, look at the time. You must be on your way, my boy. This is one appointment for which you cannot be late."

━━

Florian's Gate was one of the few remaining portals from the fortified medieval city walls. Beyond it ran a street open only to pedestrian traffic and lined with small shops making the transition from dingy government-run outlets to colorful Western-style boutiques.

Just to the right through the archway was a long stone wall where dozens of artists hung their works in hopes of obtaining a few foreign dollars or marks or francs—anything that would help them to buy further art supplies and feed the hungry mouths at home. Most of the art was very bad—amateurish landscapes, gaudy nudes, predictable still-lifes. A few were good, two or three truly exceptional.

Jeffrey strolled along the makeshift outdoor gallery until he came upon a man fitting the description Gregor had given him. The man was of small stature, with a long thick silver moustache and hands with fingers like stubby cigar ends. He wore a pale gray oversized shirt as an artist's smock over navy-blue pants and shoes so scuffed the color had long since disappeared. He was working intently on what appeared to be a Monet landscape, a scene from the artist's garden at Giverny.

"Mr. Henryk?" When the old man turned toward him, Jeffrey continued. "Gregor tells me you speak English. Your work is good. Very good."

The old man turned and bowed his head slightly. "Parlez-vous francais?"

"Some," Jeffrey replied in English. "A few words. From school, one long vacation a few years back, and now I have some business there."

The man switched to English. "I love France. I *adore* France."

"You've lived there?"

"Ah, no. The closest I've ever come to France is copying a Frenchman's brushstrokes," the old man replied. "But it has always been my dream to go to Paris, to see the art. Yes, that has been the lifelong dream of this artist."

"If it's so important, why not go? You have your freedom now. You can take the train."

Henryk faced Jeffrey straight on. "These eyes are still good," he said. "These hands are still steady. But these legs, no; I could not manage on my own. For me the end of communism came ten years too late."

"Perhaps you can find someone to take you."

"My wife, yes, she would go. But her dream of Paris is a dream of luxury. Fine hotels. Famous shops. Wonderful food. Things that would require much money. And once seeing these things, my wife would not wish to ever return to the hardship of life in Poland."

The man went back to his painting. "Yes, I should like to see Paris before I die." He dabbed at his easel and said casually, "I should also like to tell my secret."

"And what secret is that?"

"If I tell you my story, will you make it possible for my wife and me to live in Paris?"

Jeffrey laughed. "That depends on how good your story is."

"I have reason to believe," Henryk said, "that a painting by Peter Paul Rubens hanging in the Vavel Castle Gallery is a forgery."

"And what makes you say that?"

The old man turned slowly around. "Because I painted it."

Jeffrey worked at keeping a straight face. "Maybe we should go somewhere and talk."

"An excellent idea." Swiftly the man packed up his brushes and paints and folded his easel. He walked over and set them down before another artist, exchanged a few words, and returned to Jeffrey. "I am at your disposal."

At the man's guidance they walked the half block to the Jama Michalika. Once they were seated, the man said, "This is a cafe by day and a cabaret by night. It gained a most positive reputation under the Communists by being closed down many times. They staged very strong political satire. How do you describe the way you clean metals?" he asked, making a dipping motion with his hand.

"An acid bath?" Jeffrey guessed.

"Exactly. They gave the Communists an acid bath. The Communists did not approve."

The room was decorated with dark hues; it had a warm and snug feeling despite its size, an atmosphere of intimacy despite the lofty stained-glass ceiling. The lighting was indirect, the framed drawings along the walls mostly savage caricatures, the numerous showcases full of Punch-and-Judy puppets depicting Communist politicians.

When the waitress appeared, Jeffrey asked, "Coffee?"

"No, a small glass of champagne, if you don't mind. I want to get into the mood for Paris."

When the waitress left, Henryk continued. "Oh, Paris. You can't imagine what magic that name holds for me. When I was a little boy, my father gave me an album filled with prints from the great French masters. I loved that book. I would spend hours studying each page. That book is why I wanted to become an artist. I too wanted to create something so beautiful, so moving. And to go to Paris . . . well, the dream started then."

"About the Rubens," Jeffrey pressed.

"Ah yes. In the late nineteen-thirties, as a young graduate of the Academy of Fine Arts, I was hired by the curator of the Vavel Castle Museum. It was my job to inventory paintings, clean the frames, do occasional touch-up work. I was very good at that, you see. Very good. So I began to undertake more and more complex restorations for them. There is a real art to that. You can't imagine. You have to be so careful about texture and color and lines and tension and brushstrokes. Your brush must move like the brush of the master."

The waitress returned, set down the two glasses of champagne, and departed. The old man raised his glass, inspected the golden bubbles for a moment, and said, "To Paris."

"To a good story," Jeffrey replied.

Henryk sipped, then set down his glass and went on. "I had a very good boss, a fine man whose heart and soul were broken by the war. A man who dreamed of leaving Poland, much as he loved his country. He asked for my help. He knew he could trust me, and I knew in turn that he would take care of me, that my job would be secure, that I could stay with my art, and not be forced into the factories like so many of my generation.

"You cannot imagine the displacement during and after the war. Displacement of everything. People, families, governments, and art. There was a tremendous stockpile of paintings just outside Warsaw in an old warehouse. The Nazis started the collection in their raids throughout much of Europe, and the Soviets inherited the collection when they marched into Warsaw in 1945. What was there in that warehouse, I cannot even begin to imagine. All of the great names. Treasure troves of jewelry. Tons of silver, literally tons. Crystal. Furniture. Eventually the Soviets loaded a convoy of lorries and hauled most of the treasures to Moscow.

"One of the *aparatchiks* came up with the clever propaganda idea of rewarding Stalin's new Polish allies with a few pieces of art from our own warehouse. Plans were made to disperse a portion of the collection to Poland, to Czechoslovakia, and to Hungary. And so one morning, May 19, 1950, a truck pulled into the castle courtyard and started unloading crate after wooden crate of these masterpieces.

"You can imagine how we felt as we opened up these crates, unwrapped bales of tapestries, opened treasure chests, examined the cabinets and chests—so many that we could not even store them in the museum's unused chambers. The mind boggles at what the Soviets must have taken with them back to Russia.

"A few days later, the curator came into my workshop. It was a funny place for an atelier really, deep in the basements with just a little light through a grimy window set at street level. But I was left completely undisturbed, and I had room to work. Such space and freedom was an unknown gift for my generation. I counted myself blessed and rarely spoke about where I worked or what I did. That day, the curator said he had a special assignment for me. And a favor to ask.

"He brought with him a flat wooden crate, about the size of this table. He set it in front of me, and with the tip of a screwdriver slowly loosened the edges and lifted the top. In one sweeping motion he drew out the Rubens. The Portrait of Isabel of Bourbon, painted in 1628. It was absolutely stunning. There was a tiny brass name plaque on the frame in the center, as if a Rubens really needed to be labeled. The curator asked, 'Can you do this kind of work?'

" 'Well, sir,' I said. 'A Rubens. It would be an honor, a challenge. But it does not look in such bad shape to me.'

"The curator was sweating very heavily. 'It is perfectly all right,' he said to me. 'It does not need to be repaired. It needs to be traded for my freedom.'

"And so I began my work. First I had to find an old canvas, which I did by painting over a meaningless portrait that had sat in our cellars for several centuries. Millimeter by millimeter of painstaking effort, and four months later I was ready to bake and oil and smoke and in this way age our new work by the old master. Or so the world would think.

"We placed my work in the original frame, tagged with the little brass plaque that said Rubens, and hung it with great ceremony. The delay was explained by the need for substantial restoration work.

"Things were quite fluid and confused after the war. Our curator had thought it would be a matter of months before he could slip away to the West in some delegation, and there find a buyer for the original. Questions would not have been asked in the West. Even from within our Soviet-made cell we knew that there was such a place as a Swiss bank vault, where buyers could be brought to view a work, with absolute secrecy as to the seller's identity. The forgery in Cracow would immediately be denounced, and the experts would cluck and say they suspected it all along, and would quietly blame the Soviets' artistic judgment for having thought it a true Rubens in the first place.

"But the curator was not permitted to leave. He knew too much about art, about what art the Soviets had stolen and what had been confiscated during the war and never returned. He was also a little too outspoken for the regime's own good. And so they denied his application for a passport, and posted him to the art history museum in Kielce."

"I've never heard of it," Jeffrey said.

"Hardly anyone ever has. It is a small provincial town—for a man such as him, it was a Polish Siberia. He died soon after, never having exchanged the Rubens for his freedom. A few days after his death, I received a visit from my new curator, who warned me that a factory job at the Lenin Steelworks awaited anyone in our section who ever tried to escape."

Jeffrey had trouble getting out the words. "Where is the Rubens now?"

The old man shrugged. "I imagine the curator hid it."

"Where?"

Henryk reached into his pocket and pulled out a coin. "If I wanted to hide this coin, I could put it here, under the sugar bowl. But there is always the risk that someone will come by and move the bowl and find my coin."

He reached back into his pocket, pulled out a handful of change, and placed the single coin in along with the others. "But if I place my coin here, no one would pay it any attention. I would be the only one to know that it had any special value."

"It's still in the museum," Jeffrey breathed. "He put it in a crate with false markings and stored it somewhere in a cellar."

"It would not be questioned," the old man said.

"And you've found it," Jeffrey pressed.

Henryk looked Jeffrey square in the eye. "I would so very much like to see Paris before I die."

On the way to their first appointment the following day, they stopped at a crossroads where Jeffrey found himself staring at a soot-darkened entrance to an apartment house. A middle-aged man had pried open vast double doors and set down a chair. He had no teeth, so his chin almost met the tip of his nose. One shoulder looked sawn off, leaving a sharp slope that began at his neck and ended with his rib cage. He eyed the passersby with a narrowed squint, showing no reaction, following them in one direction, then taking hold of another with his rheumy eyes and following them back as far as he could see.

When the light changed and they drove on, Jeffrey found he could not leave behind the image of that man's slanted frame, nor the lines that had turned his face old far before his time. "I don't understand how there can be so many people with such awful health problems. It's like a trip back to the Dark Ages."

Katya's voice took on the tone of the patient teacher. "Will you do something for me?"

"Sure. Anything."

"Think of the times in your life when you had to have surgery."

"Okay. Do you want me to tell you?"

"If you like."

"I had my tonsils and adenoids out when I was a kid. I broke my leg and it had to be set by surgery when I was fourteen. Let's see, I had problems with my wisdom teeth and they finally decided to put me under to take them out. I think that's all. Oh, and I tore a tendon in my shoulder playing touch football in college and they had to sew it back."

"Okay," Katya said. "Now imagine that each one of these is a major calamity, a life-or-death risk."

"A torn tendon?"

"What if there's no doctor? Worse yet, what if the doctor says your shoulder's not worth worrying about, go home and rest for a week. Or a month. Or six months. Then you can either apply for a pension or go back to work—it's your choice, but whatever you do you're going to have to live with the pain and weakness of a badly healed tendon for the rest of your life."

Katya shook her head. "In a place like this, the smallest splinter in a child's hand can break a mother's health with worry."

The *Komenda Wojewodzka,* or Cracow regional police head-quarters, was on the main road running from town to the Nova Huta steelworks. From the gate it appeared to be a single ten-story high-rise. The driver pulled up in front of the main gates, spoke at length to Katya.

"He says that there are three identical buildings erected behind each other, so that from the street they won't seem so imposing," she told Jeffrey. "And the rumor is that they go almost as far underground as they rise up."

"I'm afraid to ask what's down there."

"Prison cells and interrogation rooms," she said, staring out the window at the buildings. "Come on, let's go before I lose my nerve."

Their documents were carefully searched by the guard before calling the name Gregor had printed on a card. They waited under the guard's undisguised suspicion before a small officer with sad eyes and nervous gestures came up, shook hands, and ushered them through.

"This gentleman is responsible for the children's section," Katya explained as they walked past the trio of the high-rises, and came to a vast paved lot filled with armed personnel carriers, riot buses with wire screens for windows, water cannons, bales of barbed wire, and mountains of crowd-control barriers.

"Tell him I hope he won't be offended, but this is the strangest place I've ever been to look at antiques."

The man laughed, and the atmosphere lightened considerably. "He says that they heard of Gregor through the state orphanages where they sometimes take kids."

"I thought it was supposed to be a secret."

"It is," the officer reassured him through Katya. "Not all of them know how Gregor gets his money, and those who do wouldn't dare endanger this income. For many of the village orphanages, Gregor's money is the difference between providing homes to needy children and catastrophe. They told me because they trust me. They know my first concern is for the children."

At the far corner of the back lot stood a yellow cottage. Beside it was a small fenced-in lawn with a rusty slide and swing. He ushered them through the door and into the front office, its desk spilling papers, the air smelling of cheap disinfectant. They sat at the small conference table and accepted his offer of tea. He left and returned swiftly bearing the customary steaming glasses.

The police officer did not mince words. "It is impossible for an outsider to comprehend how crime is increasing," Katya translated. "The criminal mind senses the growing lack of authority and *leaps* at the opportunity."

"A lot of people have talked about this power vacuum," Jeffrey said.

"It is on everybody's mind," the officer agreed. "The new government is trying to rebuild a democratic process and at the same time dismantle the Communist power structure. You cannot imagine the problems this is causing. All laws passed under the Communists are now being questioned, which means that nobody is really sure what the laws will be tomorrow.

"The police situation is even worse. I was originally placed in the children's division, which other policemen call the nursery and say it's not real police work, because I refused to join the Communist party. Now they have to replace most of the officers, all at the same time, with untrained people. Why? Because only party members could rise through the ranks.

"To make matters worse, there is a tremendous budget crisis. The government is basically broke. Our own police budget has been cut thirty percent in two months, while in this same two-month period, prices have almost doubled. And so with an exploding crime problem, our hands are being chained. This week, for example, the Cracow police did not have enough money to buy petrol for their cars. All but the emergency police had to do their beats on foot.

No Cracow police car has radio. At the same time, the criminals are driving around in stolen Mercedes with car radios and telephones, and more and more of them are getting away."

"What about the kids?" Jeffrey asked.

The officer blew out his cheeks. "Families are being hit hard by rising prices and unemployment. The pressures are breaking some of them apart. We see a lot of young children being either kicked out or running away. The mafia groups are using young children for a lot of their thefts because sentences are lighter and the children will basically work for food and a place to sleep."

"That's what you call them? Mafia?" Jeffrey interrupted.

The officer smiled and replied through Katya, "Too much American TV. Organized gangs are mafia. Police officers are called Smurfs. Detectives like me are Kojaks."

The smile disappeared. "At the same time that the government has a money crunch, housing and living costs have skyrocketed. This has hit orphanages, hospitals, foster homes, everything that relies on state money. Last month, orphanages in the Cracow area had to cut down on the amount of food each child could have."

He leaned across the table, his eyes boring into Jeffrey. "One thing I want you to understand. There are police, good men, who have gone on the take. I can't blame them anymore. They have families to take care of, and they've seen their salaries cut by thirty, sometimes even fifty percent. But I want you to know that every cent I will get from this is going to our children. They have cut my budget to almost nothing. I don't have enough to buy clothes for the ones in rags, or feed them."

"I believe you," Jeffrey said solemnly.

The detective led them back through a pair of locked doors, down a hall opening into bunk rooms and a kitchen-lounge. Jeffrey looked through wire-mesh windows and saw a number of children dressed in a variety of oversized, patched clothing. They looked extremely young.

As they walked, the officer continued. "There's a Russian mafia operating in Poland these days. They steal cars mostly—Mercedes, Volkswagens, BMWs, Audis are the favorites. We know some of the tactics now; any racket this big is bound to give some clues away over the months."

He said something further to Katya, who nodded her agreement and then said to Jeffrey, "Every week there is an entire page of the local newspaper where they list in small print the car types, years, and license numbers of those stolen in the past seven days."

"A big business," Jeffrey replied.

"Very big, very organized," the policeman agreed through Katya. "They have two normal ways of taking the cars across the border to Russia—that is, two we know of. Sometimes they pack the car in a wooden crate, put it in a big truck, and fill the remainder of the truck with potatoes. The border patrol can't empty every potato truck—there are dozens every day this time of year.

"The second way is to make copies of the customs seals used to close containers that have been checked and made ready for shipment. Then the day the ship leaves Gdansk for Russia, they load twenty or thirty last-minute containers, each with anywhere from one to three cars."

Jeffrey asked, "Can't you get help from the Russian police?"

The man shrugged. "Interpol doesn't operate in Russia, and even if they did they wouldn't bother with such a small matter as a car. Not now. Not when the rates of crimes involving bodily harm and death are rising like rockets. The thieves know they are relatively safe, and it is making them bolder. They have border guards between Germany and Poland who are now operating on the mafia payroll. When a nice car comes driving through, the guards ask the driver where he is going and where he plans to stay, and then they sell the information. The car is tracked until a good time and place arises for it to be stolen. Nowadays, however, the thieves swiftly become impatient. We're getting reports that they follow the car to a filling station or cafe, kill the driver and the family and anyone else in the car, rob the bodies, and drive away."

He opened another pair of steel-rimmed doors and led them through the unkempt playground toward a metal shed. "Every week we are uncovering new scams. Last week, we learned that a group was repackaging used motor oil in false brand-name cans. This week it is a major Swedish company selling frozen fish. The market has been slow because not so many people can afford their prices. So when the expiration date was reached, they repackaged the fish into boxes and bags with new expiration dates and shipped it out as fresh caught."

He unlocked the shed door. "My men busted a ring of children used to steal household items. This was never a problem before—probably because so few houses had anything worth stealing. We were led to a warehouse full of radios, televisions, everything. We also found this."

The officer swung open the door, reached to an upper ledge and switched on a flashlight. The yellow beam hit upon a drinking horn. Jeffrey took the light, stooped over, and entered the shed.

The horn itself came from a truly giant bull; it was well over two feet long if the curve were straightened. The horn was not chased in silver, it was *sealed* in the metal, inside and out. Three royal emblems were stamped around the horn's mouth. A miniature knight knelt beneath the horn upon a rocky ground of solid silver, and with his back and both hands offered the horn cup to his master. From the knight's dress and the ornate hand-carved battle scenes along the horn's silvered sides, Jeffrey guessed it to be from the early sixteenth century. Gingerly he hefted the piece, guessed its weight at thirty pounds, most of it silver.

From behind him the police officer said through Katya, "I have fought with myself over this for five days. I cannot answer the questions of right and wrong. I can see no further than the needs we have. I must feed these children. I must clothe them. I must give the sick ones medicine. I must heat the building at night. Some are criminals, yes, but they still are children, not animals. The government cannot help me, so I must do it myself. No one anywhere in Poland has declared such a piece missing, I have checked. So you must sell it. But not for me. For my children."

═══

The outer walls of the Vavel Castle were built of massive red brick, and crowned a hill of summer greens. Beneath the castle's lofty visage flowed the calm waters of the River Vistula. A broad paved walk wound its gradual way up the rise to the first castle gates. Jeffrey and Katya joined the throngs of strollers and walked past the statue of St. George, who according to tradition did battle on that very site to make the world safe from dragons.

Pavement gave way to brick cobblestones as they drew nearer to the first ramparts. The central church's six domes were gold-plated, the acres of gardens bearing ancient gnarled trees, the inner towers imposing.

The palace proper was reached through yet another set of ramparts. The innermost keep was a paved yard of perhaps two acres, and surrounded on all four sides by buildings five stories high. The palace was in dreadful condition, with very little paint and even less of the original murals remaining. Limestone stucco had been washed away by decades of wind and rain to reveal the raw stone, and in places the stone itself was crumbling. Yet despite the rust-covered ironwork and crudely reinforced pillars and a quiltwork of patches over the worst cracks, the palace remained enormously impressive—redolent of history, age, and tragedy.

The castle museum had one room given over to paintings by the workshop of Rubens. It was dark and lofty, floored in geometric marble, windowed with tiny hexagons of glass still bearing the center mark of handwork.

"There's not much light," Katya said.

Jeffrey nodded. "Harder to detect a forgery. If it's good."

The walls had probably once been gaudy with gold and silver gilt arranged in a series of intricate designs; now the gilt had faded to match the dull background hues. The ceiling paintings had long been lost to water stains and mold. Only the paintings hung from the walls kept a fragile hold to the breath of artistic life, and most of them were in dire need of restoration.

Katya signaled to him from across the room. Jeffrey joined her and recognized the Rubens from the guidebook he had purchased downstairs. It was the smallest painting in the room, an oval portrait barely three feet high. It depicted an attractive young woman whose delicate face was almost overwhelmed by the stiff circular collar of her dress.

The painting was a series of frames. An ornate gilded square framed an equally extravagant passe-partout, also gilded. This gave way to a dark background and dark clothing that framed a pale face, which in turn framed a pair of brilliant dark eyes. It was a masterful interpretation of a somewhat lackluster lady.

Katya whispered, "What do you think?"

"That I wish I knew more of what to look for," he replied. "If this is an original and we take it any further, we're going to look like proper fools."

"It's very dark," she said, moving up closer. "I can see little flecks of dust and stuff."

"If somebody was going to copy a major piece, this would be a perfect one to choose and a perfect place to hang the fake," he agreed quietly. "Come on, we won't learn any more here."

═══

"I may have found us a way out," he reported to Alexander that evening. "Emphasis on the word may."

Jeffrey related the meeting and his visit to the museum. "There's no way I can tell whether or not the painting is real, though. None at all."

"But your Mr. Henryk does not expect to be paid until the original has been found?"

"He's not my anything, and no, he doesn't want a cent up front."

Alexander's voice took on a touch of its old strength. "Then there is at least a slight chance that he is telling the truth."

"So what do we do?"

"What we are most certainly *not* going to do is call in an independent expert. The fewer who know of this, the better chance we have of gaining our own goals."

"If this guy is for real."

"As I said, for the moment let us assume that there is at least a chance. At the same time, you must be very honest about your own lack of knowledge when you speak of it."

"Speak with whom?"

"Yes, that is indeed the question." Alexander was silent for a moment. "Several years ago I helped the central Warsaw museum gather together a collection of paintings. It was not supported at all by the Communist regime, because we sought pictures of the royal city of Warsaw. We searched after quality pieces that depicted an era of our almost-lost heritage. There is now an entire wall in the Warsaw museum of some two dozen paintings hung tightly together, forming a collage of what our capital was like some three hundred years ago. One may look briefly and see a city of palaces and gardens and light, or linger and walk its streets, greet its people, enter royal residences and stand awed by their riches."

"It sounds beautiful," Jeffrey said, relieved to hear the renewed life in his friend's voice.

"It was a most satisfying work. History has not been kind to Warsaw. The second World War reduced much of it to rubble. The pleasure we knew from bringing this collection together was immense. It was a silent call to all our people to look, to study, and to imagine."

"How it once was?"

"No," Alexander replied. "How they might make it yet again."

"So you think maybe one of those people you worked with is still around?"

"There is a very good chance," Alexander agreed. "I was brought into contact with a number of museum officials and painting experts who had no love for the Communists. You leave this with me, Jeffrey. With any luck, a few of them might have resurfaced in the Ministry of Culture."

Jeffrey arrived at Gregor's apartment the next morning to find him up and about. "You look a lot better."

"Yes, thank you, my boy. My body has decided once again to be agreeable." Gregor smiled warmly. "Life takes on a very special joy on such days. I feel more grateful than I know how to put into words. I was just boiling water for tea; would you care for a glass?"

"Sure. Thanks."

"I see no reason to interrupt the excellent work you and your young lady are accomplishing," he said, moving behind his alcove. "There are a thousand other things for me to see to, and so if you agree we shall continue to meet in the mornings, and then go our separate ways."

"If you like. It's been really nice working with Katya."

"I am sure it has." Gregor reappeared and deposited a steaming glass on the narrow table. "Sit down, my boy. Make yourself as comfortable as my little dwelling will allow."

"I spoke with Alexander again this morning," Jeffrey announced, pulling out a chair. "He may have found us a contact inside the Ministry of Culture."

"Excellent. I had no doubt that Alexander would locate a connection for us. He is positively brilliant when it comes to solving such puzzles. Did he say how he was feeling?"

"I asked, but all he would say was that he felt he should return to Cracow. It sure would help me a lot."

"Whether or not Alexander returns," Gregor said, "I don't think you should count on his direct assistance just now."

"Why not?"

"Sooner or later he is going to have to face his past. If this is the case, there will be little room left in Alexander's world for anything else. Call on him in emergencies, but otherwise try to give him the space and the solitude he requires." Gregor brought over his own glass and eased himself down. "If only I can remember to pace myself for the next day or so, I shall hopefully not suffer another attack until the first frost. That is not always easy, however. I tend to be much harder on my own weaknesses than on anyone else's."

"I don't know, you were pretty tough on mine," Jeffrey confessed.

"Ah. You have been thinking about our little discussions, then."

"A lot. Especially at night. I don't seem to be able to sleep. I think too much."

"The difficulty, my dear boy, is that you are trying to understand my actions from a perception based within this world. Why, you may as well try to understand Polish simply because you have learned English. The languages are so totally different that even the *sounds* you think you recognize represent different letters.

"No, there must be a return to your life's most basic building blocks. You have to start right at the foundation." His eyes sparked with joy. "Which means you must begin by tearing down."

"You don't make it sound very appealing."

"Of course I don't. And it never will be, so long as you look at it from an earthly perspective." He blew the steam from his tea and took a noisy sip. "The world says there is no greater tribute you can grant yourself than to say, I can make it on my own. *My* perspective says there is no greater deception.

"The power within our own will and our own body and our own confined little world is comfortable, and it is tempting. It gives us a wonderful sensation of self-importance. Thus most of us will try to live outside of God until our own strength is not enough. Yet the way of the cross is the way of inadequacy. We need what we do not have, and therefore we seek what is beyond both us and this world.

"Here, let us try this. Would you take a question away and think on it for a day or so, then come back and let us talk again?"

"I guess so."

"Excellent. I will give it to you in two parts. The first question is, what would happen to your life and your world if you were somehow able to erase from your mind, your heart, and your memory—from your very existence, in fact—the motivation, 'What is in it for me?' "

Jeffrey snorted. "That's impossible."

"We are not talking possibilities here, my boy. We are talking *challenges*. So. Will you do it?"

"You want me to go out and ask myself, how would it be if I never considered what I might gain from a particular course of action, is that it?"

"Precisely."

He shrugged acceptance. "And what's the second question?"

"The second, is, who deserves to be served in selfless devotion and total love?"

Jeffrey waited. "That's it?"

"That's it? That's it? What do you expect from an old man, the keys to the universe?"

"I guess you were right about it being a different language."

"Indeed I was. Will you think on these questions?"

He nodded. "I can't say I feel very optimistic about ever solving them."

This did not trouble Gregor in the least. "The asking is what is most important, my boy. Who knows, you may even find the answer there waiting for you."

Jeffrey shrugged on his jacket. "We're supposed to be at our first buy in less than an hour. It's time I was going."

"Yes, I suppose it is. Here, let me offer you one little clue to help you in your search. You will find it possible to not just find the answers but also understand the questions only if you are willing to turn your back on this world. A single life does not have room for both worlds, my dear boy. You will eventually learn to hate one and love the other." Gregor's gaze left traces of light as he searched Jeffrey's face. "Now, which world will you choose?"

The actress sat enthroned upon the splendor of a brocade sofa, surrounded by the lore of days gone by. Her apartment was a high-ceilinged collection of rooms in one of the beautiful old town buildings. The floors were of inlaid parquet, the silk wallpaper bore an oriental design. High arched windows were covered with plush velvet drapes.

"When martial law was imposed on Poland in the eighties," she said through Katya, her voice a throaty purr, "the militia filled the streets, breaking heads with their batons and making the world cry with their tear gas. In the *Stary Teatr*, we would make the nation weep with joy, and strive to fill hearts with the same hope the police wanted to beat to death. It was a sad time, yes. But for an actress with work, it was a grand time."

The passing years had honored the actress. Her formerly beautiful features bore the marks of age and too many parts played for too many people, on and off the stage. Yet her eyes were as clear as dark green emeralds, and her voice caressed and sang words that lost nothing by being in a language Jeffrey could not understand. Her hair was piled in an auburn wealth that filtered down in teasing wisps around her ears.

"When the shops were empty," she went on through Katya, "when the lines were growing daily longer, we fed their spirits. Our lives had purpose then. We were the voice of a people who were afraid to speak for themselves. We reminded them of who they were. The theater was filled every night, with people standing along the back and down the sides. We worked to keep our people alive, playing the classic Polish pieces, stories of patriotism and pride and endurance with success at the end. When we performed the plays of Mickiewicz, the audience would stand and *shout* the lines back at us, crying from their hearts the words which were forbidden to them in the outside world, but tolerated here as part of the play. We granted them a determination to survive the enemies of the night and the morrow."

The animation left her face with the departure of her memories. "Now the world is changed, and people struggle to put the past behind them. And the crowds do not come anymore. The theater has been saved by the new government, but there are few positions open to an actress who has committed the crime of growing old."

.She waved a languid hand toward a glass-fronted display case. "These are gifts from people whose faces I cannot remember. Take what you can sell. I will use the money to spend a few more days reliving the time when my life had meaning, when I knew how to give the people what they needed."

=====

They left the actress's apartment and continued on to a stretch of green which Katya called *planty*, lined on one side by the medieval town wall. Katya pointed out graffiti from student demonstrations against the Communist regime which translated as, Don't kill us unarmed children.

They sat on a park bench, the afternoon sunlight making playful golden streamers through the breeze-tousled trees. A trio of beautiful young girls walked by arm-in-arm, giggling over some private gossip. Jeffrey turned his face upward, closed his eyes, and thought back over the past several days.

He had begun to see things in the people's faces that had not been visible before, things he had missed in his concentration on their sadness and their injuries. He was finding a strength, a silent power of endurance, bearing weights no one else knew about. He saw the wisdom of pain in their faces, and determination tested by fires he dared not even imagine.

Another transformation was tied to this first one, a change as startling as it was revealing. As he learned to understand and love these people, he came to know and accept Katya's reserve. Her own stillness mirrored the strength he found in so many of these people, the ones who had not given in to the bottle or the hopelessness or the fury. She had her own sorrows, her own battles to conquer, and in growing through them she had equipped herself with a faith and a strength that remained unshakable. Jeffrey marveled at the power that this slight young woman held in her heart.

He opened his eyes to find Katya staring at an old woman on the next bench. The woman was watching a group of children playing with bright-eyed eagerness. The old woman's gaze was the only part of her with life—her body looked little more than a shell.

When the last child had left and the *planty* was empty, the crone edged her way up from the bench by degrees. When erect she was just over four feet tall and dressed entirely in black—kerchief, sweater, blouse, skirt, stockings, lace-up shoes. She listed to one side and leaned heavily on her black cane as she walked. She moved one foot forward eight inches or so, then the other sort of fell forward to meet the rest of her body, another tiny step, and on she went.

"Look at her," Katya said. "She was born when her country didn't even exist, except in people's hearts. When she was a teenager, Poland gained independence for the first time in over a hundred and fifty years. Her children were still in school when Hitler invaded and wiped out one-fifth of the country. She survived, but she probably saw her own relatives killed right before her eyes. Almost everyone did."

Jeffrey slid his hand into hers. She looked down at it uncomprehendingly, then turned back to the slow-moving crone and continued with her story. "When Hitler was finally defeated, Stalin and his hordes took the Nazis' place. No doubt she struggled to keep what remained of her family strong and together through forty nightmarish years of Communist occupation. Her children and grandchildren are now either grown or dead, and today Poland is independent again. If she has any thoughts on it at all, I bet it is for those children she was watching. What flicker of hope she still has, she has willed to the children of this nation."

═══

That afternoon Katya accompanied Jeffrey to the Ministry of Culture. It was located down Ulica Grodzka, a street leading from the main market square. The building probably dated from the early eighteen hundreds, which meant that sometime at the beginning of that century either a new structure had been erected on the site or an older one restored—there had been a structure on that spot for over twelve hundred years.

The building was again newly renovated, painted a pastel peach on the outside, with large wood-framed windows and a massive oak door taken from an earlier medieval structure. Inside, it still smelled of fresh paint. There was no receptionist to direct newcomers, no plaques or directions on the walls, no signs by the doors. Jeffrey hesitated a moment in the utterly bare foyer, then started down the central hallway, calling out if anyone was there.

A voice called down from the galleried landing above. "Ah, Mr. Sinclair! Please come up! Welcome! Welcome!"

Jeffrey followed Katya up the winding staircase and met the man's outstretched hand at the top. He was in his late forties and wore a Western-cut double-breasted suit and silk tie, rather than the standard gray Communist garb. Beneath the well-trimmed gray hair was a rounded pasty-colored face and gold-rimmed glasses over alert brown eyes. More than anything else, the eager friendliness marked him as a member of the new regime.

"I'm sorry, we are still housecleaning," he said, leading them down the hall and stopping before his office. "Come in, please." He waited until they had entered, closed the door, and stuck out his hand once more. "I am Dr. Pavel Rokovski."

"Jeffrey Sinclair," he replied, growing accustomed to the traditional formality. "This is my associate, Katya Nichols. She speaks Polish, if you require it."

"*Bardzo mi milo,*" Dr. Rokovski said, taking her outstretched hand and bowing down as though to kiss it. He stopped when her hand was about ten inches from his face, and rose back in a formal, practiced motion. Katya stood with graceful inattention.

"*Prosze, prosze.* Please, sit down. I speak some English. It is good to practice. Maybe some coffee?"

"Coffee would be fine, thanks."

"I also have some very good cognac," he said, returning to his door. He hurried across the hall, said something in the tone of one used to giving orders, hurried back, closed the door behind him.

"I think it's a little early in the day for cognac," Jeffrey said. "But you feel free to go ahead."

"No, I wait too." He seated himself behind his desk. "I am so very pleased to meet you, Mr. Sinclair. Mr. Kantor's advice has been very helpful in the past. When he called me last night to say you wanted an appointment, I was very happy to rearrange my schedule. I understand you have some information."

"Yes, sir. I have to say, though, I don't know how reliable it is." He hesitated, went on, "And it's important that you understand that I have to keep our sources absolutely confidential."

Dr. Rokovski waved his hand toward himself, urging Jeffrey on. "Of course, of course."

"Research on antiques, as you know, is the reason for my visit here." Jeffrey leaned forward. "And of course you know that we have several applications pending here in your ministry for export permits."

Dr. Rokovski was giving nothing away. "Mr. Kantor would certainly have something very interesting to discuss if he were to call me at night and say it is urgent for us to meet."

"We think it is, yes."

"Well, then. In that case we would certainly owe you and Mr. Kantor a favor."

The coffee arrived; Dr. Rokovski leaped from his seat, took the tray from his assistant, and with formal bows poured and served the coffee. He then returned to his seat and said, "Among trusted allies of the new Polish government, such export documents are just formalities. I'll see that your applications are expedited."

"You realize that we intend to export nothing that might be even remotely considered as a part of the Polish heritage."

Dr. Rokovski nodded. "We have the greatest respect for Mr. Kantor's honorable name."

"Thank you." Jeffrey took a breath. "About this other matter, as they say in America, I have some bad news and some good news. The bad news, Dr. Rokovski, is that we believe one of the Old Master paintings exhibited at your Vavel Castle Museum is a forgery."

Dr. Rokovski turned even paler than before. "This is always possible. May I ask which one?"

"The Rubens portrait."

"The one of Isabel of Bourbon?"

"I'm afraid so."

Rokovski bent toward his desk, picked up a paper clip and began unbending it. After a moment he looked up and said in a resigned voice, "And the good news?"

"The good news," Jeffrey replied, "is that we also have reason to believe that the original is in Cracow. Probably in one of the museum's underground vaults."

Rokovski leaned back. "A Rubens lost in our own vaults? But everything is carefully inventoried."

"Yes, but if a certain painting was packaged and mislabeled, it might go unnoticed for a very long time."

"I see," he murmured. "May I ask how long?"

Jeffrey hesitated. "A few decades."

"So long." The head slowly nodded. "And who else knows?"

"The three of us, and of course Mr. Kantor."

"No one else?"

"You need not concern yourself with it going any further," Jeffrey replied firmly.

"And do you think you could identify this mislabeled carton in the museum vaults?"

"I would need to do a little more research, but yes, I think I could."

Rokovski glanced at his calendar. "Tomorrow I am scheduled to be in Warsaw. Could you complete this research by the day after tomorrow?"

"I think so, yes."

"Then meet me here at three o'clock that afternoon. We will go together to the museum." Dr. Rokovski rose to his feet. "And of course you understand, in a matter of this delicacy, everything must remain between us."

Their morning appointment was only a few blocks from the hotel—a priests' residence attached to a church-run children's hospital. As they strolled through the morning sunlight, Katya talked about the Catholic church in Poland. "To be Catholic does not necessarily mean to be religious in Poland. From 1772 to 1918, Poland was partitioned between Russia, Prussia, and the Austro-Hungarian empire. For a good deal of this time, Poland ceased to exist as a country. Patriotism to the Polish nation was a crime punishable by death. You could not call yourself a Pole without being arrested. Your language was outlawed and could not be spoken in public. You could not be seen to own a book on Polish heritage or literature. The Austro-Hungarian empire swore to erase Poland's memory off the face of the earth."

"But you could be Catholic," Jeffrey guessed.

"A *Polish* Catholic," Katya emphasized. "The Catholic church became the only legal haven for Poles. The only place where people could defy the occupying forces and be Polish. All the hymns were Polish. All the prayers were in Polish. All the confessions were in Polish. Christian instruction was given to the children in Polish, so that when the language was outlawed in the schools, they were still able to learn."

"Which meant every family would send their children to church," Jeffrey said. "Whether or not they were religious. Smart."

"*Every* family," Katya agreed. "It was the only way for their children to remain their children."

"And then history repeated itself under communism," Jeffrey said.

"In a way it did. Under Communist rule, church activities were restricted to the church buildings themselves. The church was too powerful to outlaw entirely, which was of course what the Communists wanted to do, and did accomplish in other Eastern Bloc nations. Here, they had to be satisfied with cutting off all outside charitable and evangelical efforts.

"Their ruling allowed churches to be seen as totally separate. They became totally isolated from the regime and its oppression. They became havens, islands of safety and peace to which the people could turn and find a renewal of hope."

"Just like before," Jeffrey said.

"All the nuns were thrown out of hospitals and schools, so that there was no threat of evangelism in state-controlled operations. The church used these experienced women to set up religious schools and local church clinics. Because this could take place only inside the churches, children at the age of five or six were introduced to the church and religion, even by families who otherwise would not be seen within these walls."

"What about other denominations here in Poland?" Jeffrey asked.

"Today, there are less then forty thousand Baptists in Poland, out of a population of just under forty million," Katya replied. "The other Protestant denominations are somewhat smaller. At the same time, we are seeing an interesting phenomenon, something unique in all the world, as far as I can tell. Many of the people who have either lost their faith as Catholics or never had any faith at all are finding it in Protestant-run Bible studies. But they do not leave the Catholic church. The Catholic church is history, culture, and heritage. For many, to leave the church would mean to break with an important part of their past, and they do not wish to make such a break."

"They are forcing an internal revival," Jeffrey guessed.

"Exactly. Even in some of the small villages you can find spiritual renewal. Home churches and evening Bible studies are springing up all over the country. Not only that, but they are maintaining their very close ties with the Protestant churches. These new believers have no time for those who wish to quarrel across established lines of doctrine. They have found faith, and it is too precious to allow somebody else's arguments to stand in their way."

"A strong Polish nationalism is emerging," the priest told them through Katya. "It is wedding itself to the Polish church. A number of priests are becoming involved in what is called 'black power.' It means church involvement in politics, named so because of the color of priestly robes. It does not usually signify running for office. More often it is a priest who takes an active interest in local or national politics, backing certain candidates, weaving politics into his sermons."

He was an intelligent-looking man in his mid-forties, his face seamed by years of hard work and worry. In the background could be heard faint cries and shrills of laughter as children thundered down unseen halls. Here in this room, however, all was at peace. They sat in a small entrance chamber, the only furniture being a simple crucifix on the wall, five straight-backed chairs, a small center table, and a large item in one corner—the piece they had come to acquire.

"Although I do not agree with those who are so politically oriented," the priest continued, "I can understand their concern. Many parish priests work with under-educated people who are totally confused by these new earthshaking transitions. In the last election, *seventy-eight* political parties fielded candidates. How is a sixty-year-old man who has never been allowed to vote for anyone but the appointed Communist official going to understand what to do? Naturally, he will turn to his local priest, as he has done on numerous occasions in the past when faced with problems and an uncaring, too-distant government."

Jeffrey forced himself to concentrate on what the priest was saying, although his eyes were continually being pulled back toward the article in the far corner. The priest had waved at it as they entered, said a parishioner had given it after a miraculous cure of his son, and they were going to use the proceeds to equip a modern surgical clinic. After that he had dismissed it as of no consequence, and Jeffrey had been forced to sit on his hands and wait for a chance to examine it.

It was a medieval chest, most probably intended for a palace chapel. It was perhaps four feet high, three feet deep, and seven feet long. Its curved roof and sides were carved with a variety of royal shields. The front was embossed with a painting of ladies-in-waiting serving men-at-arms. All but the painting had been covered with a layer of fine gold flake, then lacquered for protection.

"There is another group within the Polish church, however," the priest went on, intruding into Jeffrey's thoughts. "And this group is growing in strength every day. Their first concern is the Kingdom of God, and this is what they are called. They are a charismatic renewal group, who see a very real need to return to the basic elements of faith in Christ.

"This group is pushing hard for contact with Protestant mission groups," the priest continued. "Their concern is not church membership, but faith renewal. They fear that what communism has not done, secularism and capitalism may achieve. Now that our enemy of the past forty years is defeated, another more silent and pervasive enemy may gradually erode church attendance. These priests and their followers believe that there must be a vocal declaration made of the importance of salvation, a concentration on this very first point above all else.

"There is a problem, however. If the evangelical arm manages to dominate, and if political involvement is limited, a vacuum may appear. This is a very real fear within the church just now. Democracy requires pressure to operate, as you in the West well know. Here in Poland, you must remember, there is *no other organized moral voice*. There are no groups to push the government to remember the sick, the infirm, the needy—you have a word for this in the West, I believe."

"Lobbyists," Jeffrey offered.

"Exactly. There is no one here to apply this pressure in the name of God and service except the church. Two months before the last election, for example, in the midst of massive price rises on everything from bread to milk to bus tickets, the government decided they had to cut social security payments—the same payments that had not risen since the Communists were defeated. Retired people who were unable to fight for themselves had seen their purchasing power reduced by over half when the new regime deregulated prices.

And now what was to happen but a second reduction of over thirty percent. There was only one voice organized to fight against this measure. The Polish Catholic Church."

The priest stripped off his glasses and began polishing them with a pocket handkerchief. "The evangelists point to another area where the church has tried to apply pressure, and failed miserably. I refer to abortion. Because this is very important to many of us, we have studied what is happening in your country, and we have made a very important discovery. In America, opposition has come from a groundswell of individuals, all joined together to combat it. In Poland, it was very different. Here the church tried to *order* the government to outlaw this. The result was disastrous.

"People who might otherwise have been behind such a measure have not only opposed the proposal to ban abortions, but also opposed the church. Why? Because it represents to them the same dictatorial demands as they knew under the Communists. They had no voice in this decision; it was ordered from above. The result has been, as I said, a very real calamity. The evangelists are saying that so long as the church tries to involve itself in politics, the danger of this schism deepening will continue.

"The fact is, church attendance is falling. The question is, how many of those who have stopped coming have lost a living faith, rejecting this new group that is attempting to become another authority over their lives, and how many came to church simply to escape the storm of life under Communist rule?"

That afternoon Jeffrey returned from a second meeting with Mr. Henryk to find Katya in her room surrounded by government forms, handwritten lists, and a Polish-English dictionary. He sat down on the floor beside her and began helping her with the tedious business of making a complete inventory for the export forms.

Once the forms were completed, they went downstairs for dinner, then returned and gathered up the papers, content to sit together and enjoy the feeling of a shared intimacy.

"This is the way I always thought a confessional would feel," he told her. "Quiet and intimate and protected. As though I could say anything I wanted and it would be all right."

"We all need a place where secrets can be revealed," she replied, setting aside her papers.

"We're not talking about the same thing, though, are we."

Katya shook her head. "I carry my place with me. Wherever I go, wherever I am, whatever happens."

"I used to feel that way."

"I know."

He leaned back. "That reminds me of something I haven't thought of in years. Back then, the greatest part of being religious for me was this feeling I had. I had a friend, somebody I could talk with about anything. I would talk with God and tell Him *everything* and He would always be there and everything would always be okay. He was my perfect friend."

She gazed at him with eyes more open than he had ever seen. "You really miss Him, don't you?"

Katya was too close to him for there to be any room for a lie. "I don't know if I really believe God exists. I miss the feeling, though. I see what I used to have there in your eyes, and I miss that."

She watched him, her eyes two gray-violet pools where he could lose himself for all his days. Jeffrey whispered, "I really love you, Katya."

She did not flinch, she did not draw back, she did not belittle his confession with indifference. Instead, she cradled his hand in both of hers, bent down, and kissed it with the soft caress of butterfly wings.

Katya stroked his hand and murmured, "I've been so afraid."

"Of what?"

She kept her eyes on his hand. "Of falling in love. Afraid because it had already happened, afraid because . . ."

There was no longer enough room in Jeffrey's chest for his heart. "Because why?"

She turned to him in mute appeal, a yearning gaze that beckoned and pleaded for he knew not what. Slowly, very slowly she shook her head.

"Why won't you tell me, Katya?"

Her gaze did not waver as she asked, "What pushed you away from faith, Jeffrey?"

At that moment, in an instant of realization, he knew that the entire journey had been leading up to this question. Not just the evening. The thread leading to this had been woven into their relationship from the very first moment of their meeting. Some hidden part of him had been waiting for this, waiting and knowing that when the question came, he would tell her.

"When I was driving with Gregor the other day," Jeffrey began, "I was listening to him talk about faith and suffering, and at the same time I was going back over what happened to me. It was like being able to see it through his eyes and his perspective, which was totally different from how I felt about it at the time."

"How long ago was it? I mean, whatever happened to you."

"Hang on a minute, I'll tell you, I promise. But I want to tell you about this first." He related what Gregor had told him, then said, "As I was listening to him, I kept seeing things about myself I've never really understood before. Back when the problems all started, I'd get really mad and scream at God in my head, saying, you let my brother go through this and you let him hurt and you let him degrade himself, so to heck with you. But I was *really* thinking, you said I was special because I believed and I got baptized, but since you came into my life, it's been worse than it ever has before. That was why I left God behind, Katya—because He didn't do anything but make things worse for *me,* not for my brother or my parents or anybody else. I cared about them only after I'd finished caring about myself. He'd let *me* down. I didn't want to have anything more to do with Him."

The drawing away that he half expected didn't come. Katya's gaze remained open, her look filled with love. She said, "Tell me about your brother, Jeffrey."

"My brother. Yeah. The brother I don't have." The pressure in his chest built to an enormous bubble that *demanded* to be released.

"What was his name?"

"Is. What *is* his name. Charles. Chuckie was the kid; I don't know what he wants to be called anymore. My parents call him Charles. I guess they figure he's outgrown Chuckie. Either that, or they want to keep some kind of barrier between who Chuckie was and who this Charles is that he's become."

Katya's only movement was a soft caressing of his hand, one finger gently stroking out a reminder that he was not alone, that someone was there and listening and caring.

"Chuckie was a great kid. He was two years younger and I always felt like he was the kid for both of us. My mother used to say that I was born old, and that's the way I've felt. She has this picture of me, it was always the first thing she'd unpack whenever we arrived in a new home. My dad is sitting in his living-room chair, his slippers are on and he's got the paper spread all around him with the front section spread open and just low enough so you can see him frowning as he reads. And there I am, about four years old, sitting in this tiny little chair. I've got my bunny slippers on and I've got my legs crossed like Dad and I've got the funny papers spread all over me and I'm wearing an identical frown."

"It sounds adorable," Katya said.

"I guess so. Mom sure thinks it is. But that's the way I was. Chuckie, though, was always into everything. There was never anything steady or 'normal' about Chuckie. If he was happy you could hear him shouting and singing and laughing a block away. It was the same if he was sad. He *hated* being sad. When he was down he'd become just as mad as he could, and let the whole world know it.

"Chuckie didn't get on well with all the relocations my dad's company put us through. When he was still little, he'd get sick—real sick. His favorite was bronchial pneumonia, but he pretty much covered the range from appendicitis to the bubonic plague. A lot of my first memories of a new place were of Mom dragging us around to different hospitals and doctors' offices—I was still too little to be left at home. And Chuckie was not exactly what you'd call an ideal patient. He didn't like the move, he didn't like the new home, he didn't like being sick, and he wanted the whole world to be angry with him. It was tough.

"Right after his fourteenth birthday we moved again. All I can remember about that first couple of weeks was unconsciously waiting for Chuckie to get sick, and then somehow not being happy when it didn't happen. Instead of getting sick, Chuckie sort of went away.

"The move was to Phoenix. I had just turned sixteen, and my dad gave me this clunker of an Olds, so what I really thought about was getting out and stretching my wings. So while Chuckie started fading into the shadows, I was busy being a teenager."

"You were a Christian then, isn't that right?"

"Yeah. I got baptized on my fifteenth birthday. I know, I know, a Christian's not supposed to be so selfish about himself, right?"

"That's not at all what I was thinking. Just because you're a Christian doesn't mean you're all of a sudden going to be made perfect. It just means you're called to work toward certain standards. Meeting these standards is a goal you'll be working for all your life."

"I like the way you say that."

"Why?"

"I don't know. You make it sound, well, approachable, as if I'm not being asked for the impossible."

She squeezed his hand. "Go on with the story."

"Mom was busy unpacking and getting us settled, and I was busy with this new school and new freedom, and Dad was busy with his new job. Nobody really seemed to notice that Chuckie had disappeared. His body was there, but he wasn't. He just left.

"We moved again at the end of the school year, and about that time we finally started noticing things—well, we finally started *talking* about things that we'd all been noticing for quite a while. Money was missing. Silver, too. And other things, little things like Dad's gold cufflinks that he wore only when he and Mom went out on special nights, and one of Mom's necklaces, and my new camera, and some other stuff.

"And the liquor was going down a lot faster than ever before, or so my Mom thought. They'd never really been big drinkers, but it was always there, and the bottles never seemed to be full anymore.

"First it was Dad who talked to Chuckie. Then Mom. Then Dad and Mom. Then me. Then all of us. It didn't do any good, though. Nothing at all. You can't imagine how sincere that kid was when he denied it. His pupils would be dilated to the size of bullet holes, and he'd be so sincere denying he was on anything that I'd go away believing him. Denial is the name of the game with somebody like that. They deny it to you, to themselves, to everybody who tries to get underneath the shell and make them face up to what they're doing. You don't know what lying is until you've tried to talk to an addict about his habit."

"Chuckie was on drugs?"

"Drugs, booze, anything he could buy or steal to stick down his throat or up his nose. It was like a metamorphosis in reverse. When we moved to Phoenix I had a colorful little butterfly for a kid brother. When we left there and moved to Philadelphia I had a worm.

"Philadelphia was the wrong place to take a kid with a drug problem. I guess we should have figured that out before, but Mom, Dad, and I never really complained about where the company was going to send us next. We knew without ever talking about it that this was just one of the prices we had to pay. And no matter how bad it was, we knew that it wasn't ever going to be for too long. But Philly was bad. Really bad. The only good thing I remember about Philadelphia was that as the problems with Chuckie got worse, my parents and I kept growing closer and closer together.

"Chuckie started selling drugs in Philly—or at least he got *caught* the first time there. I don't know if he'd already started in Phoenix or not. Philadelphia was something from another world, though, with guys out of your worst nightmare hanging around the school fence, dripping with gold jewelry and selling everything. I mean everything. And Chuckie was into it all."

"It must have been awful for you," Katya said, her voice carrying a shared pain.

"You can't imagine. We'd get called down to the police station in the middle of the night, and I'd go down with Dad because Mom was having hysterics and I didn't want him to have to go alone. When my baby brother would come out, sometimes he was still drugged up. Sometimes he'd been sick all over himself, or had somebody else in the tank get sick on him. It seemed like we were in court almost every week.

"Finally the judge gave Dad an ultimatum. Either Chuckie went into a state-run rehabilitation program for under-age drug offenders, or he was going to reform school. I know it sounds strange, but that's really the first time that any of us admitted that the problem was out of control. Things like that happened to other people, not us. But this time it was us, and it wasn't just out of our control, it was out of our hands. Dad signed the papers and Chuckie went to a hospital for drugged-out teenage criminals.

"It just gets worse and worse," Katya murmured.

"That's the way it is with an addict. Alcoholic, druggie—they're all addicted, and the problems are the same. You wouldn't believe the letters we got from him in the beginning—how they were beating him and treating him horribly. Those letters just tore my mother up. The people we spoke to on the phone didn't help any; they all had the same deadpan delivery that made them sound like they'd do anything for a buck. Most of them were recovered addicts, and they knew all about the tricks the kids used to try and get out, or try and stay high.

"When we picked him up six weeks later, they warned us that Chuckie displayed all the symptoms of a recividist."

"Denial," Katya said.

"Right. They say that the biggest step to help a recovering addict is for the addict to admit that he or she has a problem. Chuckie never admitted once in all this time that he was taking *anything*. Not drinking, smoking, snorting, anything. Not even after we started finding his stash and pipes and empty bottles and roaches all over the house. Never. It was all a big conspiracy. And the people at the center were right. As soon as Chuckie got out, he started up again. Nothing at all had changed, except once he was back he stopped trying to hide it at all."

Jeffrey's mind went back to the uncounted days and nights—the sounds of his dad yelling and his mom crying and Chuckie cursing. At last his parents stopped trying to confront Chuckie at all, and the boy would come home late at night in a drug-induced stupor, crash around the house, and finally fall into bed, unchallenged.

In January there was yet another visit to the court, after his brother—still too young to have a license—tried to drive the family car through a concrete bridge support. The dust settled just in time for one more move, the last his parents would ever make. By then they were involved in Al-Anon support groups and classes on co-dependency, learning how to deal with their son's addiction, struggling to keep their marriage and their home intact.

There was none of the usual joking and half-worried excitement about this move. There was no time for that, no place, no energy. The three of them went through the accustomed motions with grim determination. Chuckie came and went like a wraith, occasionally sobering up long enough to realize that their world no longer revolved around him.

The day after they arrived in Jacksonville, Florida, they laid down the law to Charles—all three of them, together. They formed a united front and gave him the ultimatum in no uncertain terms. He was moving out.

Charles was told that an apartment had been rented for him near the university. A bedroom was going to be made up for him in their new house, but he could stay there only if he allowed himself to be tested for drugs and alcohol every day for two months. The only way he would be welcome in their home was if he was sober.

Charles whined and begged and pleaded and cried and finally stomped his feet and screamed curses and punched a hole in the dining room wall. He spent only one night in their home; he came in around dawn, falling down drunk. Jeffrey and his father poured him into the new family car, drove him over to his new furnished studio, and dumped him fully clothed on the bed. They pinned a note to his shirt—since he was too drunk or stoned to understand what anyone was telling him—saying that if he was kicked out of this apartment, for any reason whatsoever, he was on his own. Charles missed seeing his father and his brother drive back home, both of them dry-eyed and grim-faced, neither having any more tears to shed.

"I left God behind in Philadelphia," Jeffrey went on. "I can still remember the exact moment. I was packing up Mom's porcelain figurines—she would buy herself one new figurine each time we moved. She loved them, she really did. She'd spend hours taking them out of this display case we had in the living room and dusting them off and just looking at them. It was her concession for having to move, and it gave her something nice to look forward to. She'd spend days and days going around all the shops in the new town, coming home with little pictures she'd take with her Polaroid. And the higher up the ladder Dad went, the nicer the figurines became. It was the one thing she always made us pack ourselves, and we always drove to our new home with them stowed somewhere safe in our car.

"So there I was, packing up the figurines, and I had this mental image of deciding it was time to stick God back somewhere in a box too—one that I never intended to open again. Nothing I'd heard in Sunday school or church ever got me prepared for what we were going through, and nobody was able to help me. The Bible sure didn't."

Katya did not contradict him as he expected. Instead she asked, "What happened to Charles?"

Jeffrey took a deep breath and steeled himself. "Charles wasn't exactly what you'd call pleased to all of a sudden lose his family. Only I doubt that he thought of us as family by then—more like a haven and a source of money and somebody to beat on emotionally."

Katya nodded.

"Anyway, we'd get calls from the landlord or the police to ask if we knew that Charles had been here and done this or that. My parents absolutely refused to get involved. Every once in a while Charles would call and scream over the phone about abandonment and heartlessness, but they really stuck to their guns. Al-Anon had taught them how to detach from Charles' problems. After about nine months or so, just as I was getting ready to go off to college, I started seeing smiles around the house again, hearing laughter. You can't imagine how nice it is to hear laughter until you've lived in a house without it for a year or so."

"I can imagine it," Katya said softly.

He looked at her. "Yeah, maybe you can."

"What is that supposed to mean?"

"Ever since I've gotten here, I've been coming to grips with what lies behind that silent strength of yours."

This time it was different. This time the defense mechanism did not automatically freeze him out. There was no indifference, no denial, no drawing away. She simply said, "Finish your story."

"Okay. So Chuckie, I mean Charles, began going to greater and greater extremes. He got kicked out of his apartment, but by then he had a girl who took him in. Charles was growing up into this really good-looking kid. And there was something else about him, something other than his looks that drew the girls like a magnet."

"Certain women are attracted by guys with those kinds of problems," Katya said. "They usually have a tough external shell, and this type of girl wants to work her way inside. It's almost a motherly sort of reaction."

"You've met guys like this yourself."

"Every girl has. She can be attracted by the toughness, and maybe pride herself on her ability to understand this man that the rest of the world can't. Women in such situations put up with an enormous amount of abuse—physical or emotional—infidelity, unreliability, whatever. And still she works very hard to keep pleasing this man. She's never confident of her hold on him, except for this idea that she alone understands the soft, inner, hidden man."

"That's beautiful," Jeffrey said.

"It's tragic," Katya corrected.

"No, I mean the way you expressed it. Your insight."

She did not deny it. "Sometimes I feel as though I can see things and understand things that the rest of the world just keeps on trying to shut out. Maybe it's part of the gift of learning compassion, coming to understand more through trying to care more."

He turned and looked away.

"Did I say something wrong?"

"No," he sighed. "It just really hit home."

She waited a moment, and when he did not go on, she said, "Finish your story. Please."

"About two months after I started classes," Jeffrey continued, his voice a monotone, "I got a call from Mom. All the time she'd spent and the work she'd done to rebuild her life had been destroyed. She was crying so hard she couldn't talk, and finally had to give the phone over to Dad. He sounded worse than she did, really hollow. At two o'clock in the morning, Charles had gotten drunk at some party and climbed a tree. And he'd slipped out and fallen on his back and broken his spine."

"Oh, Jeffrey."

"He was paralyzed from the waist down," he went on, rushing now, pushing it out. "I listened to Dad tell me, and I wasn't thinking about Charles or Chuckie or whoever he was. I was thinking about my folks. And me. If they weren't strong enough to do the obvious, I was. I just cut him out. Right there. Cut him out completely. I didn't have a brother anymore. My folks were just too weak to do it. So I was going to do it for them. I told my dad I wasn't coming to the hospital, not then, not ever. And I didn't want them to mention his name around me ever again. As far as I was concerned, my brother was gone. Dead. Out of my life forever."

"What did your parents say?"

"That's a funny thing. Dad didn't object, and Mom never mentioned it. Not ever."

"And you never saw your brother again?"

"Once. I went to see him once more."

It was after his grandmother asked him, just before his departure for England. His brother was back in the hospital for surgery. All those years of sitting in a wheelchair had given him bedsores, and they'd become infected.

That was the worst part of going to see him, having to do it in the hospital. It was almost as though his grandmother's request had rolled back time, pushed him back nine years to the hospital visit he'd refused to make.

Charles was parked in a special air-bed, an incredible contraption with a pump built into its base. It pushed air continually up through a load of silicon sand into a bottom sheet of fine-mesh nylon; it let the air out in a continual cool blast that ballooned the sheet's slackness up and around Charles's limp body.

The years had softened Charles's features, but not as much as Jeffrey had expected. There was a slight blurring to the strong lines, but part of this was caused by the Demerol that Charles had control over. He had an electric pump connected to his IV, and every fifteen seconds or so Charles would push the button and give himself a dose. Jeffrey couldn't help but grin when he finally figured out why Charles kept such a grip on the button; at first Jeffrey thought it was for calling the slowest nurse in history. Charles would wait until a bleep announced that his next dose was up and charged. Knowing Charles, he'd have told the doctors he was in terminal pain. Giving that guy control over his own drug supply was the silliest thing Jeffrey had ever heard of.

That set the tone for their meeting, at least on Jeffrey's side. Charles acted as though he had seen his brother the day before—sort of bored and casual and not really concerned one way or the other. Jeffrey was standing there, trying to come up with something to say, when he caught sight of himself in the mirror across from Charles's bed.

His button-down Oxford shirt was crumpled from a day of running around, his top button undone and his tie at half-mast. His shoulders were hunched up as though he were getting ready to charge the line, and there were worry-frowns creasing his forehead.

Then his mother had appeared in the door, all bright and brown from her daily tennis and solid in her happiness. That amazed Jeffrey more than anything, how both his mom and his dad had somehow recovered from all the stuff life had thrown at them, and kept hold of both their happiness and their love for each other.

His brother took his cue like a consummate actor and folded inside the bed's balloon-sheets like he'd been hit with a sudden attack of real live pain. Jeffrey stepped back, watched his mother straighten her shoulders and take a breath and do the bravest thing he'd ever seen her do, which was meet her son with a smile. It was a forced smile, and the brightness had a brittle, lacquered quality to it. But it was still a smile, and the determination that she showed in not allowing Charles to drag her down into the pit again left Jeffrey speechless.

He left the hospital that day absolutely certain that his mom and his dad had found a strength that he didn't have, and hoped he'd never need. Not ever. For him the best way of dealing with his brother was by continuing to deny he even had one.

Katya drew him back with, "Do your parents believe in God, Jeffrey?"

"Not before all the mess with Chuckie started. Church was a place to go and make some social contacts, you know, help us get settled in. That's how I got into faith in the first place. I was just looking for a nice group of kids. Sometimes it was easier to find people to talk to a new kid at church than at school. But then I met this Sunday-school teacher who was really on fire.

"When I started reading the Bible and going to weeknight services and talking about getting baptized, my folks treated it like just another phase I was going through. They trusted me, and even though they didn't understand what I was doing, they figured it was okay since it made me so happy.

"The co-dependency group my parents started with in Jacksonville was connected to a church. The Al-Anon support group, too. And the more time they spent with the people in those groups, the more their conversation got sprinkled with these spiritual terms. Their new spirituality came at the same time when I was putting the lid on my box, so I made it clear that I didn't want to hear anything about faith. They still referred to it every once in a while, just letting me know it was there if I want to talk about it. But I'd just ignore it or change the subject, and that was it."

He watched her for a moment, savoring this feeling of closeness and friendship. This is what a true love ought to be, he decided. A best friend. He asked, "What are you thinking?"

"You probably won't like it," she replied.

"But it's something I ought to hear, right?"

"I can't decide that for you, Jeffrey."

"I trust you," he said. "Tell me."

"Somewhere along the way," she said quietly, "people have come up with the impression that if they believe in Jesus Christ, they won't have to suffer."

Her words did not need volume to have impact. Jeffrey shifted in his chair.

"Then when something hits them," Katya went on, "they question themselves and they question their faith: What have I done to deserve this? Has God found doubts in me, reasons to condemn me for my lack of faith, flaws in my beliefs that I have tried to hide even from myself?

"Then comes rage: I held up my part of the bargain, and look what you've done to me. But the Bible doesn't promise total protection, Jeffrey. Not even to the righteous man does it promise that. Look at Jesus Christ. Look at the apostle Paul. Look at Job. The Bible says that Job was an honorable, righteous man. A man who avoided evil. A man who honored God. And yet God allowed him to suffer terribly. There is no clearer message to me in all the Bible than this, Jeffrey. We see that even the most righteous man on earth is open to the pain of life."

Her eyes were wide open, her gaze seeking out the deepest wells of his heart. "Listen to me, Jeffrey. If we are faithful to Jesus Christ only when our lives are in the sunshine, then we do not truly love Him, no more than a true love on earth exists only when times are good and the couple live in harmony with each other. Genuine faith, and genuine love, does not always guarantee total protection from the risks and turmoils of life.

"Genuine faith consists of loving God *no matter* what the circumstances. We accept that our life is in His hands, *no matter* what the chaos of this world might bring, *no matter* what troubles confront us at the moment, *no matter* how we might hurt. We have placed our life in His hands and we *keep* it there."

She sat and watched him in silence, as though sensing that he had been stripped bare and needed time to put himself back together. When his eyes turned outward once more, and he truly saw her, she asked quietly, "Will you pray with me, Jeffrey?"

"Not now, okay? I want to think about this some first. Maybe later, but not now."

She did not try to hide her disappointment. "I will wait for that day as I have waited for nothing else in my life."

"When you talk like this you sound a thousand years old."

"Love is eternal, Jeffrey. Whoever loves in His name knows the gift of love's eternal wisdom. There is no other way."

Jeffrey was coming to love these walks alone in early-morning Cracow. His days began with a quick breakfast, a telephone call to Katya's room to outline the day, and then off to Gregor's. On pretty days he stretched the walk by a dozen or so blocks, walking and watching and thinking.

This morning, however, a mist hung heavy over the city, muting sounds and closing off vision to ten paces ahead. People appeared first as gray-black shadows, firming into living shapes at the last moment, then disappearing just as swiftly. Jeffrey examined the faces and thought of all that had filled his past weeks.

Gregor greeted him with the casual air of a dear friend. Jeffrey pulled up a chair close to his. "I've been thinking about what you said."

"That is the best news I could possibly hear this morning," Gregor replied. "Except for the news of Christ's return."

"I was just wondering," Jeffrey said, "how you came to be religious."

"I don't know that I am what you would call religious," Gregor told him. "Being religious is in my view an external action, something I would do for the outside world. I find myself too busy to pay such things any mind."

He settled deeper into his pillows. "As for coming to faith, that happened in the darkness of the Nazi occupation. In those days, every Polish family had a Bible. And in almost every family, the Bible always remained on the shelf. I started reading the Bible during the war, not out of faith, but out of the need for distraction.

"I stayed in Cracow during the war. Our own house, quite a beautiful place, was taken over by the Nazis for use as a local office. We took what we could carry and moved to our cleaning lady's flat nearby."

"What happened to the cleaning lady?"

"She was there with us. She had two sons who were missing. Many young men simply disappeared during those dark times. We were all the family she knew, and when we lost everything, she simply took us in. She was embarrassed to have us stay there— after all, she had been the one who had scrubbed our floors. She treated us like privileged guests for more than three years. That was an eternally long period to a young teenager full of life and energy.

"I was fifteen when the Germans invaded, and it was danger- ous to go out with the curfews and the uncertainty. Because all the schools had been closed by the Nazis, I finished high school by tak- ing private lessons in a small group that met at the local seamstress' house. I felt a constant restlessness then, a frustration over not being old enough to fight, and not being well enough to rebel against my parents' wishes and fight anyway. Even then I had this problem with my joints. I would have liked to die fighting for my country, especially after Alexander was taken. It was very hard to stay home and hide and do nothing to bring Alexander back.

"Our cleaning lady, Pani Basha, was not an educated woman. In her house were only three books—the first and last volumes of Sienkiewicz's Trilogy, which is a sort of novelized summary of Polish heritage, and a leather-bound Bible. I turned to that book not out of faith, certainly not seeking guidance. What on earth could a book written two thousand years ago teach a young boy who was bored and distracted and worried and hungry and afraid? No, I turned to it out of restlessness.

"I read it like a novel, beginning with Genesis and finishing with Revelation. Then I read it more slowly. Then I began reading books out of sequence, and gradually I found myself absorbing dif- ferent messages. The sheer *complexity* of the book astounded me. No matter how much I studied it, nor how often I read and reread a passage, there was always something which I had missed before. Another lesson. A deeper meaning that I only then was beginning to understand.

"When you have troubles, especially troubles which are so big that you know before you begin that you cannot conquer them, you feel as though you are the only one. No moment could be darker than the present moment. But I found the Bible to be full of war and destruction and hunger and suffering. And as I burrowed deeper and deeper into its pages, I also found that there were answers—not just to their pain and their distress and their distant troubles, but to *mine*.

"These men cried out to God, 'Father, do not forsake me.' And so, in my own small way, as a restless teenager caught up in a crisis not of my making and certainly out of my control, I too cried out. And God listened."

Gregor pointed toward his empty glass. "Do you think you might make me another tea?"

"Sure," Jeffrey said, rising to his feet.

"You are a good and honest man," Gregor said. "Alexander is fortunate to have you as an assistant, and a friend, if I may add."

"He is my friend," Jeffrey replied, hiding his embarrassment behind the alcove curtain. "Besides Katya, maybe my best friend."

"How wonderful for him. This makes what I am about to say all the more easy. I would like to lay my own responsibility upon you, if you will allow it." Gregor waited until Jeffrey reappeared. "You may call it a duty of our own partnership, if you will."

Jeffrey returned and set down the steaming glass. "Fire away."

"I want you to promise me that each and every day you will pray for Alexander's salvation."

Jeffrey hesitated. "After all these years, I would have thought you'd have given up by now."

"One never gives up. One never loses hope. One continues to petition the Maker of all miracles, and one hopes for those who have not yet learned how to hope for themselves."

"After all that he's been through, I'm not surprised that he doesn't believe."

"That is indeed true," Gregor replied. "There are many people such as our Alexander, who have felt the need to cast away all semblance of faith in order to survive their ordeals. They have managed to survive where all but a handful were crushed and killed—or worse—because of simple strength of will. There is no denying the power and the self-confidence that they have earned. Yet I have also seen such people reach a crossroads where they come to recognize a need for power greater than what they themselves hold."

Gregor's eyes held a luminous quality. "There is always hope, my dear boy. Always. So long as there is life and the presence of the Lord in your heart, there is always hope. I am called to remain here with my arms outstretched, just as Christ did throughout His life and on unto death, and hope. And pray. Yes, that most of all."

Jeffrey found his eyes drawn to the simple crucifix hanging from the wall. "I've never thought of it in that way before."

"There are an infinite number of lessons to be drawn from the cross, my boy. Just as there are an infinite number of paths that lead man toward salvation." Gregor himself turned to face the crucifix. "All human hope lies at the foot of the cross. In the two thousand years since it first rose in a dark and gloomy sky, it has lost none of its luster, none of its power, none of its divine promise."

Jeffrey turned back to Gregor. "All right. I'll do it."

"Think carefully on this, my dear boy. This is a vital decision. You are accepting a duty that you will carry with you for as long as you or Alexander lives."

He nodded his understanding. "It's okay. I accept."

"Excellent." Gregor positively beamed. "I feel most reassured by your help."

Jeffrey rose to his feet. "I've got to meet our painter Mr. Henryk again. He's supposed to get me some information Rokovski needs. When Katya gets here, tell her I should be back in an hour. We'll need to go straight on to our next buy."

"I will do so, my dear boy. And know that you go forth with my prayers accompanying you."

It was a moderate palace, as palaces went. The cream-and-white exterior gave it a fairy-tale lightness, accented by vast sweeps of windows. Dual exterior staircases with curving balustrades led around the ground-floor ballroom to a porticoed and pillared entrance on the second floor. The grounds were unkempt and barely a step away from forest, save for one sweep of still-green lawn directly in front of the palace.

Katya and Jeffrey entered through gates so rusted and decrepit that no amount of effort could close them. Jeffrey tried to focus his mind on the business at hand, but found it next to impossible. The information he had received from Mr. Henryk was nowhere near as complete as he had hoped.

"Gregor told me a little about this place while you were meeting with your mystery man," Katya told him. "He said it once belonged to an adviser to the king. After the Soviets installed the Communist regime it became an institute."

The closer they came to the palace, the more cracked and faded became the building's exterior. "An institute? For some disease, you mean?"

Katya shook her head. "Bunnies."

"What, raising rabbits for labs?"

"No, just to study." She smiled at him. "The National Communist Institute for Bunny Research."

"In a palace?"

"Don't expect Communism to make sense, Jeffrey. It will drive you to madness trying to apply logic to an illogical system. Just accept it. The former palace of a royal adviser is now a bunny farm."

"That's incredible."

"There were a lot of incredibles under Communism." Katya was no longer smiling. "The count who lived here was exiled to Siberia, and his children fled to Paris with the family jewels sewn into their clothes."

"But they could come back and reclaim the place now, isn't that right?"

"Gregor said they wouldn't because the government wants them to pay a maintenance fee for the past forty years, and they can't afford it. So I imagine it's like most other unclaimed properties. There's no for-sale sign out, but it's available for the right price. With the situation Poland is facing economically, they'd sell just about anything if the price was right."

The director appeared at the front door, a stocky woman in her early fifties, her hair chopped short and left in unnoticed disarray. She was dressed in clunky shoes and the inevitable white lab coat of authority. Behind stern square glasses, her eyes were intelligent, direct, impatient.

"This palace was built in the second half of the nineteenth century in the Italian style," she explained through Katya. Jeffrey listened and looked around as she led them into the upstairs foyer. Its mirrored ceiling, supported by interlaced girders, supported one of the largest chandeliers he had ever seen—perhaps eighteen feet high. The floors were inlaid with an intricately repeated Rococo pattern.

"It's all new," she told them. "Everything. The chandelier was brought in three years ago, before the Communists held a major function here. It is supposed to be a replica of the original.

"After the Nazis were driven from Poland and the Soviets took control," she went on, "the palace was repeatedly sacked by soldiers, the new Communist government, and by locals. Everything was taken. The floor and the marble fireplaces were chopped up and carried off. Afterward the government gave it to the institute because no one else wanted it. The palace was nothing more than a hollow shell. A bomb could not have done more damage."

"There must be a lot of money in bunnies," Jeffrey said, working to keep a straight face.

"I am not going to translate that, and you behave," Katya said sharply.

"Little by little we have repaired things," the woman continued. "We found good tenants to take over a series of rooms, and charged them a deposit large enough to make the initial repairs to that section. We arranged with the woodworking department of the local university to send up their best students. An office for the government agency responsible for lumber is here, and they made sure we could find enough wood. We fought our way through red tape for several grants from the government's historical society."

She led them through vast double doors into a formal parlor with a twenty-foot-high vaulted ceiling and rosewood floor. "Nine months ago we began work on the palace's final wing, and discovered a section of the cellar that the looters had missed. It was not surprising, really. In our own initial survey we missed it also. The door was more or less buried underneath a layer of soot, and was directly behind the old palace furnace. We found it only because we finally had enough money to repair the heating system."

Before Jeffrey stood a set of eight matching *caquetoire,* sixteenth-century Renaissance chairs. Originally of French design, they were also known as 'gossip chairs,' and had seats broad enough to accommodate a matron's multi-layered skirts. The legs were delicately turned, the armrests and connecting rails carved with *lunettes*—repetitive motifs in a semicircular pattern. The chairs' back panels were carved with *Romayne* work—oval-shaped portraits, probably of the original count who had ordered the chairs—depicting a stern-faced patriarch dressed in a Roman helmet.

"These are fantastic," Jeffrey said, kneeling before one after the other. "A major find."

"Yes, that is what we were supposed to think," the director agreed.

Jeffrey looked up. "What does she mean by that?"

"When we found them, we were naturally ecstatic," the woman explained through Katya. "But we wondered. Were they considered too old-fashioned and just stored away in a back room and simply forgotten? It was logical. But even someone such as I who knows nothing of antiques could see that they were of value. So why were they placed in a room with a door blocked and hidden?"

She walked to the side doors, opened them, and said, "So we brought them out and began digging. And we found this."

Slowly Jeffrey rose and walked over. The doors opened into a small parlor, now set up as a conference room. The central table was intended to seat around twenty people, but all the chairs were gathered to one side. The long table was covered with green felt, and on its surface was displayed a complete formal dinner service.

"I imagine it was the most valuable item in the house besides the jewels," the woman said. "But far too heavy for anyone to escape with. It was packed in four great chests."

The plates, the serving dishes, and the silverware were all gilded. Gilding was accomplished by mixing a very fine gold dust with another substance that would make it adhere to a surface. Originally honey was used, then a century later an amalgam of mercury was substituted. While the mercury resulted in a finer and more consistent pattern, it was also highly poisonous, causing first sterility and later death. Apprentices to the gilders were encouraged to have children while still quite young.

The dishes were unadorned save for an embossed family shield. Jeffrey picked up one plate, turned it over, read, "Stuttgart, 1718." He set it down very gingerly.

"There are dishes for thirty and silverware for twenty-four," Katya translated. "They must have ordered replacements in case of breakage."

The director stepped around the table and faced Jeffrey. "This has become more than simply an institute. We house a conference center, offices, research labs, almost a dozen companies. We have turned one set of the old farm buildings into a distribution center, and want to do the same to the other seven barns. We, the companies who are housed here, are now the largest employer in the region, and people have come to count on us. But the government has no money, the historical society has been shut down, and the work yet to be done on this building is enormous. We need a new roof. I will not bother you with the figures for roofing an entire palace, but believe me, it is very high. The electrical system is antiquated and a fire hazard. We have two telephone lines and need fifty. The garden—you have seen our garden? It is turning into a jungle.

"The village school had a wall cave in two weeks ago, and now they are using the old palace greenhouses. They have no heat or running water, concrete floors, and lighting by an extension cord strung over from the main house. When we talk to the government we are rewarded with a lot of hand-waving and replies that there is no money, no money for anything."

She plucked a straight-backed chair from the tangle by the back wall, turned it around, and sat down facing Jeffrey. "So. You know our need. And now, young sir, we shall discuss price."

━━

That afternoon the three of them—Jeffrey, Katya, and Dr. Rokovski—arrived at the Vavel Castle's central courtyard to be met by the museum curator, a nervous portly man in his late fifties who fussed about Dr. Rokovski like a mother hen.

"Ah, and these must be your guests from America." The curator's accent was far heavier than Dr. Rokovski's. His nervous eyes barely seemed to focus on them as he went through the formalities of bows and handshakes. "I understand you are experts in the conservation and storage of works of art."

Jeffrey showed momentary confusion before catching Dr. Rokovski's frowning nod from behind the curator. "Ah, yes."

"Mr. Sinclair is doing a preliminary survey to see if his company might be able to assist us in updating our methods," Dr. Rokovski covered smoothly. "This is his associate and translator, Miss Katya Nichols."

"Fine, fine. Well, shall I escort you down?"

"Oh, that will be quite all right, Mr. Stanislaus. I know how busy you are. And I do know my way quite well around here."

That was clearly not what the curator wanted to hear. "I am sure it's not like in the West. We have so much to learn here, and so much to do. My small staff has been so busy, working day and night just in the viewing halls. The special collections here in the West Wing, the permanent exhibitions . . . well, you can imagine, so much has been left undone in the cellars. We haven't even cleaned properly."

"We all certainly understand that you have tremendous responsibilities," Dr. Rokovski replied, and avoided further protestations by blocking the curator and ushering Jeffrey and Katya inside.

They passed under a stone archway, walked down a narrow corridor with a high vaulted ceiling and lamps set where torches once had burned, and finally stopped before a vast oak-beamed door lashed with rusting iron bands broader than Jeffrey's hand. Dr. Rokovski spoke to an alert guard and was given a ring containing a half dozen massive keys. He inserted a skeleton key almost a foot long and weighing over a pound, and used both hands to grind it around.

"This is the entrance to the vaults," he said, using his shoulder to push the door aside. "We combine modern alarm technology and video cameras with the best of ancient security."

They entered a small antechamber and descended down a wide spiral staircase of worn stone. He fumbled in the stairwell's murky half light. Fluorescent lights hanging unevenly along the ceiling blinked on. A series of ancient armored doors stood sentry down a long hallway. Each had a small square window with iron grids set at eye level.

"We call them the museum vaults now," Rokovski said. "But as you can see their earlier purpose was quite different. I shudder to think what might have happened here centuries ago."

The dungeon's air was damp and close, and smelled of nothing more sinister than cheap antiseptic cleanser and old varnish. A wall apparatus kept constant record of the temperature and humidity. Jeffrey reached into his pocket and pulled out a slip of paper. It contained the information from the latest meeting with the old painter, Mr. Henryk. He handed the paper to Rokovski. "I think this is the chamber we are looking for."

Rokovski examined the paper and noted the hotel's imprint across the top. "This is your writing?"

"It is."

He turned and walked down the hallway, checking stenciled markings against the page as he went. They passed thirty doors, fifteen to each side, before the corridor opened up into what was clearly an unused workroom.

Dusty easels were stacked in two corners. Jars blackened with dust and old cleanser held scores of paint-smeared brushes. Floor-to-ceiling shelves built of warping plywood and covered with dust were filled to overflowing with chemicals and paints and rags and palettes and instruments whose use Jeffrey could only guess at. Set high in the wall to their right was one solitary pressed-glass window, giving meager light from the outside world. Jeffrey stood and looked up at it and wondered at the man who had called this place a haven.

In the far end of the workshop was a pair of doors. Between them stood the sort of old wooden card files that Jeffrey remembered from his high school library. Cards were crammed in so tightly that several of the drawers could not even be closed. There were further cards scattered across the floor, all covered with illegible scrawl.

Rokovski sighed and waved at the cards. "Our museum archives. It is shameful, *nie?*"

"Looks as if you could use the consultant I'm supposed to be," Jeffrey agreed.

Rokovski checked the page a final time, then fumbled with his keys and inserted a slightly smaller one into the left-hand door. The door groaned open. Rokovski reached inside and switched on the single bare overhead light bulb.

The entire room appeared to be carved from a single stone. The air was cool and stuffy. Stacked against all four walls were broad, flat wooden crates covered with dust and cobwebs.

Rokovski held up the sheet of paper. "This is all you have?"

Jeffrey nodded. "It is probably in this room."

"But all these crates are simply numbered. There's no description on them, just on the archive card." The art director let out a groan. "This is impossible."

"No it's not," Katya said. "You two start opening the crates, and I will start checking the numbers against the archives."

Rokovski stared at her. "You don't even know what you are looking for."

"Something odd," Jeffrey replied. "Something that doesn't fit inside a museum vault."

"What if it is simply listed as a painting by another artist, one that does not exist?" Rokovski ran frantic fingers through his hair, gazed around the room. "Only an expert would know that the painting title is false."

"I don't think someone trying to hide the painting would have done that," Jeffrey replied. "There's too much chance that it would have been discovered." To Katya he said, "Look for something that doesn't fit."

"I understand," she replied. "Do you have a pen and paper?"

Rokovski fumbled in his jacket and handed them over. "I don't have time to spend days looking for a painting that might not exist at all."

"It exists," Jeffrey replied grimly.

"You had best hope so," Rokovski replied, stripping off his jacket and taking it back into the workshop. "You have the most at stake."

Jeffrey watched him disappear, then turned in silent appeal to Katya. She smiled her encouragement. "Something odd. Don't worry, Jeffrey. I understand."

—

Crate after crate was dragged out into the workshop, pried open, inspected, sealed shut again, and returned to the growing stack just inside the storage room door. Soon all three of them were sneezing and coughing from the dust that grew thicker with each disturbed crate.

Most of the crates were filled with bad portraits of arrogant-looking people, the kind of art even a close relative would prefer not to display. There were one or two passable scenes of war-time chivalry, and many paintings that were simply damaged beyond repair. Rokovski managed a few halfhearted jokes over the first few uncrated unknowns, but by the time sweat worked its way down both their faces, all attempts at humor had vanished.

While they worked their way down one wall, Katya started on the other side, listed a dozen numbers, then began painstakingly checking the files. Jeffrey struggled not to despair; they had managed to inspect only nineteen crates in the first hour, and the room held at least four or five hundred. The only consolation was that Katya appeared to be making three times the progress they did, although Rokovski greeted her each time their paths crossed with another derisive snort. It was clear he expected to have to go back and duplicate her efforts. Jeffrey was not sure the man was wrong.

Katya reentered the storage room chanting a number under her breath. Something in her tone made both the men look up from their labors. She fingered dozens of crates, examining the stencils. "Here. Check this one next."

"What for?" Jeffrey asked.

"How nice," interrupted Rokovski, fatigue giving rise to sarcasm. "Did you find that under 'R' for Rubens?"

"No," she replied, her poise untouched. "This number corresponds to a card labeled *Projekty Studenckie, Akademia Sztuk Pieknych.*"

"Student projects from the Academy of Fine Arts," Rokovski translated. "What on earth is that doing here?"

"It seems to me," Katya said, "that student work has no place in a museum vault. And anyone checking the inventory would open this crate last."

The crate was dragged out with renewed haste. Rokovski jammed the screwdriver under one corner, slipped, cursed and slammed it back into place with a vengeance. The wood creaked and complained and finally gave. Together he and Jeffrey pulled off the lid.

The first painting they lifted out was a mediocre pastoral scene. Next came two standard still-lifes, and under that a snowy landscape with a frozen river. Jeffrey reached for the next painting, the next to the last one, and as he pulled it out his heart lurched.

"There's something here," he said.

"It's too heavy by far," Rokovski agreed.

The painting was of dead hunting trophies. They turned it over, laid it flat, and saw that set into its back was a second, smaller, older frame.

"Bingo," Jeffrey said.

The student painting was just large enough to allow the smaller frame to fit snugly inside. They discovered as they tried to remove it that small thin nails had been hammered through the outer frame to seal it in place, to ensure that it would not be easily inspected. Because there were no nailheads, they used the screwdriver to probe between the frames, damaging the outer frame if necessary, and breaking the nails with a sharp upward twist. When all six were broken and the inner frame free, Jeffrey found his hands were shaking.

He turned to Rokovski and said, "You do it."

"With pleasure." He reached down with trembling hands, gently separated the inner frame, and lifted out the painting.

It was the Rubens.

They knelt around it in silence for a long, long while. Finally Rokovski stood, moved to the workshop table, cleared off a space, and gingerly set the painting down. He walked around it, inspecting it from various angles.

"I must say that when you told me about this," Rokovski said quietly, "I came back by the museum and looked carefully at the painting on exhibit. I inspected it as best I could without drawing attention to myself."

"So did we," Jeffrey replied.

"I could find nothing that left me thinking that here was a forgery. Nothing. But I am not an expert at classical painting, and I thought that perhaps I was wrong. Perhaps, you understand, just perhaps. And now that I stand here before this original, I see that indeed I was."

"It is a masterpiece," Katya agreed quietly.

Some of the other exposed paintings that littered the cramped little room were quality pieces, but there was something more to this one, something that drew the eye despite the room's poor lighting and the painting's relatively small size. The pale face framed a pair of dark eyes whose depths contained an unfathomable spark, a mysterious light that *demanded* attention.

It was indeed a master work.

———

That evening, while waiting to go to the airport and meet Alexander's plane, Jeffrey told Katya of his talk with Gregor. She listened to his account with the same absorption that she had shown him the evening before. At the conclusion she told him, "You're going to have to reach some decisions of your own before you can pray for Alexander, Jeffrey."

He nodded. "I've been thinking about that."

"What are you going to do?"

"I've got to get my own relationship with God back in order," he replied.

She reached across and took his hand. "It's the way I have always dreamed of our relationship beginning."

He stared at her. "This is what you've been waiting for?"

"I couldn't say it, Jeffrey. I couldn't ask. It couldn't be something you decided on because of me. It had to be something you did for yourself, for Him." She drank him with her eyes. "It's been the hardest thing I have ever waited for in all my life."

"All this time, all . . ." Slowly he shook his head. "This is incredible."

"My father became a Christian because it was the only way that Mama would marry him," Katya said. "Mama once told me she thinks making him give that promise was the greatest sin she ever committed. It kept him from ever finding Christ on his own, and in the end it drove him away from both of us, because he was living a lie, one she forced on him."

"So you waited," Jeffrey breathed, dumbfounded. "And hoped."

"And prayed," she added. "Prayed harder than I have ever prayed for anything in my entire life."

"But why the distance, Katya? Why the coldness? Was that because of your father, too?"

"No," she replied quietly. "Well, yes, I suppose in a way it all comes back to that first great hurt. But my first year at university, I met an older man. I gave too much too fast, Jeffrey. I didn't take time to see who it was that I was spending time with. I let myself be taken in by a lie, by a mask he wore because it suited him. I can look back now and understand that all he really wanted was to have me. When I refused, and explained that my faith didn't allow it, he tried every way he could to force me away from God."

She dropped her eyes to the hand she held in hers, her voice as gentle as the finger stroking his palm. "I was so busy trying to convince myself that deep down he really cared for me that I couldn't see the truth. And because of that I stayed around longer and let him hurt me more. I did not understand how a man could lie so, could care so little for me as a person that he would keep tearing at what was most important in my life, trying to destroy my faith just so he could sleep with me. Then one day I finally realized that he didn't care for me at all, just for my body, just for satisfying some hunger of his. It made me feel like dirt.

"After that, my life revolved around my studies and taking care of Mama. " She looked up, gave him the slightest hint of a smile. "And then this dashing young man came up to my table at the university, and he was neither a student, nor a believer. All the same problems, all the same mistakes, all over again."

She reached across and traced a feathery line down the side of his face. "And I could feel myself falling head over heels for him," she whispered, "like I had never fallen for anyone in my entire life. And I was so scared, Jeffrey. So very scared."

"There's no need to be frightened, Katya."

"I'm beginning to believe you," she said, and leaned forward to kiss him.

Alexander was his normal silent self on the ride into Cracow from the airport that evening. Jeffrey played the patient companion and said little of his own activities, other than the fact that perhaps the solution to their export document problem had been discovered. Alexander replied to the news with a single nod of his head and the request that they go straight to Gregor's apartment instead of the hotel.

Gregor limped out to the landing, greeted his cousin with the traditional pair of kisses and the words, "You have been on my heart night and day, dear cousin. Night and day."

"I am grateful." Alexander seemed unsure of why he was there. "Is it too late for us to speak?"

"Of course not. I have just put on water for tea. Come in, come in."

Gregor led him to the apartment's only comfortable chair. "Pull it up close to the bed, cousin. I have perhaps done a bit too much today, and my bones are eager for a rest."

"Perhaps I should return tomorrow, then."

"Nonsense. I can rest while we are talking." He turned to the alcove and asked over his shoulder, "Will you take tea with us, Jeffrey?"

He looked uncomfortably at Alexander. "Maybe it would be better if I left."

"There is no need as far as I am concerned," Alexander replied. "You have walked with me this far; you may as well be in for the kill."

"No one is to be killed," Gregor replied, returning from the alcove bearing two steaming glasses. Silently he nodded Jeffrey toward a straight-backed chair in the room's far corner. "Although there would be no greater gift you could give me or your Maker than a decision to die to the things of this world."

Alexander sipped at his tea. "Even if I did consider the act as a serious possibility, I would find it positively mortifying to see the look of satisfaction on some priest's face. Imagine his pleasure at bringing a long-time offender like me to his knees."

It was one of the few times Jeffrey ever heard Gregor take a sharp tone. "If he takes pleasure for himself, then he is no priest, no matter what his earthly garb."

"Perhaps not, dear cousin. But your standards are sadly not held by all."

"They are not mine and they are not standards," Gregor replied hotly. He eased himself into a seated position on his bed and stretched his legs out with a sigh. "They are instructions, the first of which is true humility. You kneel to no mortal force when you cast your sins on the Savior. You bow your head to no mortal power."

Alexander smiled. "Do I detect an open wound?"

"There are some human failings I find harder to forgive than others," Gregor replied. "I do not ever want to think that a prideful Pharisee in priestly robes stood between you and eternal life."

"Eternal life," Alexander murmured. "There were times when I truly thought that I would live forever. Or at least that my days should never end."

"God willing, you shall have eternal life. He stands and knocks at the door to your heart. Will you not let Him enter?"

Alexander reached over and patted Gregor's shoulder. "You will be the death of me."

"The life, dear cousin. The life of you."

"An interesting concept. Quite an amusing change from the memories crowding up around me."

"Memories far easier to bear if you bore them not alone," Gregor replied.

"Yes," Alexander murmured, turning his gaze toward his steaming tea. "The burdens have become quite heavy."

"Do you wish to speak of them?"

Alexander hesitated and said to his glass, "It is so hard sometimes to understand how we feel. Our emotions are so very abstract.
So we give them form, a name or place, and through this name an
identity. For me, all fear, all dread, all hatred, is located at Florian's
Gate. These feelings, this place, I have avoided all my life."

"Many of us have such a place," Gregor said quietly, "although
it is not always something with a form as concrete as yours. To
walk through this portal would be to confront these fears, to press
through them, and to leave forgiveness in their wake."

"I could not," Alexander replied. "You are asking the impossible."

"Only because you insist on taking that walk alone," Gregor
said. "You treat your fears and your hatreds as your most precious
possessions. You allow them to define who you are, where you go,
what you think. Imagine, my oldest and dearest friend, how life
might be if love were there in their place."

Alexander gave no sign that he had even heard. He was silent
for a very long time, the loudest sound in the room being the tick-
ing of Gregor's bedside clock. Then he said, "I survived my time of
suffering because I was *determined* to live. It was *my* strength. *My*
will. And yet, as I find myself coming to face the same door which
I escaped from so long ago, I wonder, my dear cousin. The past
reaches up to surround me, and at times I feel that I have escaped
from nothing at all. And the strength of my will does not appear to
be powerful enough this time to save me."

Gregor shifted his head, looked upward, and said to the ceiling,
"It is possible to hurt so much, suffer so terribly, that life loses all
meaning. This you know, my friend. You have seen it for yourself,
and known its appeal. Death becomes not necessarily something
welcome, but rather something *acceptable*. It can be a mental pain
that pushes you to this brink, or emotional, or physical, sometimes even spiritual. Those who disbelieve the extent of another's
suffering simply because the wounds are not visible are not only
insensitive, they are dangerous. They literally push a sufferer toward
death's door."

"That is one accusation I would never make of you," Alexander
said quietly. "Your sensitivity is most painfully accurate."

"One basic element of suffering," Gregor went on, "is the way it makes time slow down. A sufferer finds it increasingly difficult to see beyond this moment of pain. He or she finds it almost impossible to believe that the suffering will ever end. It becomes the all in all of life. Pain is the start, the now, the finish."

"Indeed," Alexander murmured, his shoulders bowed, his head lowered almost to his hands.

"A sufferer comes to dread the night," Gregor told the roof above his head. "Once it arrives, it never seems to end. The darkness can become suffocating in its power to isolate, to smother hope, to increase aloneness. The person thinks, 'How long before I get up? The night drags on, and I toss till dawn.' Those are the words of Job, my old friend. He knew, and he said it well.

"Yet in the midst of this intense suffering, God's people have recourses that others do not have. In the thirty-sixth chapter of Job, the sufferer says to me and to all who know pain, 'But those who suffer, he delivers in their suffering; he speaks to them in their affliction.' Do you see, my dear Alexander? God comes to us in the midst of our pain. He promises to *be* there, to live through it with us. His presence is very real and very personal in such times."

He turned to Jeffrey. "Would you be so kind as to take the Bible from the shelf there and read from the first chapter of Second Corinthians?"

"Sure."

"Thank you so much. Begin with the second half of verse eight, would you, and read through verse ten."

Jeffrey fumbled with the unfamiliar pages, eventually found the spot, read:

"We were under great pressure, far beyond our ability to endure, so that we despaired even of life. Indeed, in our hearts we felt the sentence of death. But this happened that we might not rely on ourselves but on God, who raises the dead. He has delivered us from such a deadly peril, and he will deliver us. On him we have set our hope that he will continue to deliver us."

"In life or in death," Gregor said, "we are in God's strong hands."

N ova Huta was considered a Communist masterpiece," Katya told him the next morning as they drove toward their final appointment. "It was Poland's first planned city, built to staff the largest steel plant in the world, the Lenin Steel Works."

The driver turned off the main thoroughfare onto streets that were clearly not meant for cars. They were little more than broad sidewalks, about twelve feet wide. Graveled sections had been added at irregular points where cars could be pulled off and parked. Kerchiefed old women crammed together on a small front stoop and watched the car pass with grim suspicion.

"At the turn of the century, Cracow was once considered one of the jewels of Europe. Beginning in the year 900, it was the capital of one of the largest European kingdoms. It housed the third oldest university in the world. It had been Eastern Europe's center of intellectual thought and scientific exploration for over five centuries. But the Communists feared Cracow as a breeding ground for dissension, and worked to destroy its preeminent position. They decided the best way to do this was to change it from a center of intellectual growth into a worker's city."

The three-story houses looked like dark gray barracks. They stood in endless rows beneath tall birch trees, stretching out in every direction as far as Jeffrey could see. Their uniformity was jarringly oppressive, at direct odds to the summertime green.

"So the Communists chose a forest preserve outside of Cracow for the new factory, and razed it to the ground. Homes for the tens of thousands of steelworkers were built, and slowly the factory itself took form. They constructed the furnaces to burn soft coal, since that was what Poland had the most of, even though it is the most polluting fuel on earth, and extremely inefficient."

They pulled up in front of a building indistinguishable from its neighbors except for a faded number painted above the front door. The driver stopped the car.

"The result was that soon after the plant opened, it started raining black dust all over Cracow," Katya continued. "That is why these buildings are this color, Jeffrey. They were originally white. The dust is so thick in wintertime that people have to brush it off their car windows before they can drive. Nowadays rain here is so acidic that it is killing all the trees in Cracow and eating away at buildings that have survived almost a thousand years."

They walked up the cracked sidewalk, pushed their way through the front door, and followed Gregor's instructions to the second floor. The woman who opened the door was not extremely old— Jeffrey would have guessed no more than sixty. But unseen winds and burdens of a hard life had aged her. Her walk was labored, her hands palsied, her eyes weak and watery behind thick lenses. She led them into her sitting room, walking on legs that seemed to battle against her, forcing to throw her body around with each step. But the pain did not slow her down; she fought against her body with stubborn determination.

She seated them on her sofa, asked if they would take tea, and disappeared into the kitchen alcove. Her voice drifted out.

"She asked what we think of Nova Huta," Katya said.

Jeffrey hesitated, decided on the truth. "It's not as bad as the high-rises. But I'd imagine all these black buildings look like something out of a nightmare in the wintertime."

Katya turned and translated to the hidden woman. They were rewarded with a brief chuckle. "She says you are correct," Katya told him.

The woman reappeared, wiping her hands on the little apron tied to her waist. "After the war," the woman told them through Katya, "when you finished your studies the central government gave you a paper called a Work Directive. This paper told you where you would work, what you would do, and which place you would live."

The woman pulled a straight-backed chair from the narrow dining table, turned it around, and eased herself down. With a deliberate motion she wiped one edge of her mouth with an unsteady hand. "You were expected to work and live in this place for the rest of your life.

"Nova Huta was a new development then. It was one of the few places where new housing was going up. New housing meant electricity and indoor plumbing, a toilet for every family, and heat. My husband and I were sent here.

"There were problems. There are always problems. My husband managed a tobacco factory which was next door to the steelworks. We both came from good Warsaw families. All of the other people around here were steelworkers. They wore overalls and helmets and had steel smut on their faces all the time. When we arrived, we were the only people in the entire area with a university education. I cannot tell you how alone it made us feel.

"But you learn not to think about happiness, or wishing you had a different job or a better place to live, or neighbors who could be your friends. You just get on. You survive. You protect yourself. You find something to live for. A purpose. A profession. Something. For me, it was my family and my God."

The teakettle began whistling; with visible effort she pushed herself from her chair and clumped into her little kitchen alcove. She continued to talk, her reedy voice holding an emotionless quality. "In the late forties," Katya translated, "many, many families in Poland began receiving Work Directives, notices that they were to be transported to Siberia. They had twenty-four hours to put their lives in order. They could take twenty kilos of luggage. My stepfather was a mining engineer, and one morning he received a directive to report to a mine in a village that no one could find on the map. He and my mother and my grandmother were sent. My name was not on the list, we learned later, because my birth records had been lost. Otherwise I would have been shipped off as well. My mother took me to my godmother's house, where I lived and waited for my parents to return.

"Fifteen years later, when Poland and Russia signed one of their Friendship Treaties, Poland asked them to re-instate the transportees, or at least those who had survived. My mother came home first.

My stepfather had been sent to work in some other place and she had not seen him for seven years. He came home a month later and died three days after his arrival."

She returned and served them steaming glasses from a cheap tin serving tray. Through Katya she continued. "My grandmother had become sick on the trip to Siberia. They were traveling in cattle cars with no heat and little food. At one point the guards grew tired of her moans, opened the doors, and threw her from the train."

The woman went back to the kitchen. As she rummaged away from view she said, "Before she left for Siberia, my grandmother gave me her valuables. I was the only grandchild. Although I was quite young I knew that she was going and would never come back, so I didn't want to take them. I was hoping that if I refused she would have to either stay or return and give them to me later. But she insisted, and because I loved her I finally agreed. The jewelry I sell bit by bit, all except her wedding ring, which I wear as my own. That I will wear to my grave in memory of her and of my husband."

She returned with a crumpled plastic ice cream carton that she handed to Jeffrey. It still held the cold of the freezer. He hefted it, and felt the solid weight shift around.

The woman peered at him through thick lenses. "My son-in-law lost his job when his factory closed down, and my daughter is pregnant again." The edges of her mouth pulled up in a vague smile. "I am soon to take a trip to a place much farther away than Siberia. It would have been nice to leave these remaining pieces to my own granddaughter, but the money is needed. Perhaps she will remember me some other way."

———

"I am so glad you could join me," Dr. Rokovski gushed as Katya and Jeffrey entered the restaurant.

"What a charming place," Katya said, admiring the beamed ceiling. "Isn't it, Jeffrey?"

"Mmmm." He shook Rokovski's hand and allowed himself to be ushered to a small quiet table upstairs in the Restaurant

Wierzynek, one of Cracow's finest, located in a corner of the main market square. Jeffrey sat down, barely holding on to his impatience. It was not a good day for a three-hour dinner. Alexander had not appeared all day. When Jeffrey rang his room that afternoon he had received no reply. In a panic he had rushed over to Gregor's, fearing the worst, to find his friend limping about the tiny apartment, absolutely certain in his faith that Alexander was both all right and exactly where he should be—alone.

To top it off, the export documents had not been approved. Only Katya's insistence kept him from simply asking Rokovski for the crucial papers. He had held to his side of the bargain. There was work to be done. Too much for the time available. And now this.

"It is one of my favorites," Rokovski said. "I'm enough of a patriot to believe that history can add a special aroma to the best of food, and believe me, this restaurant holds claim to both."

"I love it," Katya said, clearly determined to retain her buoyant mood.

"I'm sure this has been quite a day for all of us," Rokovski said.

"And busy," Jeffrey added, jerking back when Katya kicked him under the table.

"No doubt. And I am indeed grateful that you would take the time to join me here. Some things, I am sure you will understand, are better discussed in the privacy of a public place." Rokovski showed pleasure at his own remark. "I am happy to report that the painting is now safely locked away in my own office cabinets."

"We are certainly glad to have been of some small assistance, aren't we, Jeffrey," Katya said.

After recrating the Rubens with the students' paintings, Rokovski scrawled a note on the archive card stating that the referenced paintings were being assigned to the ministry. Once they were back upstairs, he instructed the curator to have the crate delivered to his office. He wanted to use these relatively unimportant paintings, he explained, to test a new chemical conservation process proposed by the American group.

"Now then," Rokovski said. "If you would allow me to order for you."

Jeffrey waited through an endless discussion between Rokovski, a smiling Katya, and a theatrical waiter. Rokovski eventually turned back to him and said, "This restaurant used to be the private residence of Nicolaus Wierzynek, a very powerful member of the regional government. In 1364 Cracow was the site of the Great Conference of Monarchs, and Nicolaus was allowed to host the senior visitors for several dinners. Just think, my young friend, here in this very room sat the King of Denmark, the Holy Roman Emperor, the Prince of Austria, and the Polish King Casimir the Great. The food was so lavish and the service so faultless that it was decided then and there to make the place an eating establishment upon his death. And so it has been for over six hundred years, making it one of the oldest restaurants in all the world."

"How fascinating," Katya replied. "A bit of living history."

Jeffrey tucked his legs far under his seat and said, "Dr. Rokovski, we are now booked to leave Cracow for London the day after tomorrow."

"We will certainly be sorry to see you depart," Rokovski said.

"Yes. Thank you. The thing is, when I went by the ministry this afternoon, they said that my export license was still being held by your office."

"Ah," Rokovski smiled. "The license."

"Yes, sir. I was wondering if maybe I could come by and pick it up first thing tomorrow morning."

"Yes, of course. But I was wondering if I might impose upon you one further time."

Jeffrey felt his stomach sink a notch. "Impose?"

"Yes. Could you perhaps take along a little excess baggage?"

"How much is a little?"

"It would be quite a small parcel, actually. Perhaps the size of this table?" His eyes retained their smile. "Quite flat. Not heavy."

Jeffrey cast a glance at Katya, astonished to see that she was watching Rokovski with round eyes. "You mean the size of a painting?"

"Precisely." Rokovski leaned across the table. "Not officially, you understand. I want you to smuggle it."

"You want—"

"For the ministry," Rokovski went on, his voice pitched low. "We cannot possibly be seen selling a Rubens masterpiece. We would be announcing to the world that we are paupers. It would be taken as a willingness to exchange the priceless for mere money. But we are, you see, truly bankrupt. Our coffers at the ministry are empty. Our roofs leak. Our finest works are deteriorating so badly that some I fear can never be restored. And so much more needs to be done. You saw the condition of the museum vaults, our inventory, our security, the primitive level of our efforts."

His voice was quietly intense. "And then there is my big dream. No art in Poland has suffered so much in the past fifty years as that of our churches. I have blueprints for the renovation of an unused portion of Vavel Castle, which would house some of the finest religious paintings and statuaries in all of Europe. Of course, we could barely afford even the blueprints, to say nothing of the enormous restoration required by some of these pieces. I will not horrify you with stories of how they have been abused these past five decades."

They waited while the waiter arranged their plates; then Jeffrey asked, "So how am I supposed to smuggle this out?"

"Your export documents will include a letter from my office thanking you for the most kind offer to display some of our students' artwork in your fine establishment." Rokovski positively beamed. "The painting in question has already been placed back inside its home of the past forty years."

Jeffrey thought it over, decided it was workable. "How would you like us to send you the money after selling the painting?"

"You will not send it to me at all. A foundation has already been established for donations to the new museum wing for religious art. I would simply expect to find one morning that a large anonymous donation has been made to our foundation."

Jeffrey looked around the restaurant as he ran the idea through his mind. "I don't see any problem with that."

Rokovski visibly relaxed. "I must tell you, Mr. Sinclair, I was most worried about taking up such a crucial and sensitive matter with someone I had only just met. But Mr. Kantor spoke very highly of you, and I am beginning to see why."

"I think this is something that Mr. Kantor would agree with fully," Jeffrey replied. "It's a pleasure to act on his behalf."

"As it is for us to work with you. I need not tell you that a successful resolution of this matter will pave the way for our future assistance wherever and whenever you might require it. I think you will find us to be very good friends, Mr. Sinclair. Very good friends indeed."

Jeffrey and Katya entered the hotel lobby on their final morning in Cracow to find Alexander seated near the front entrance, puffing contentedly on a cigar, looking positively peaceful. He rose to his feet, gave Katya a small bow. "Good morning, my dear. Jeffrey."

"Good morning, Mr. Kantor," Katya replied. "How are you feeling?"

"Better. I must say that I do indeed feel better."

"You look it," Jeffrey declared.

"Yes, I am happy to say that I rose with the dawn, ate a breakfast fit for a king, and have since been seated here thoroughly enjoying both the morning and this fine cigar."

"We have been praying for you," Katya said quietly.

Alexander looked at her for a long moment. "I cannot tell you how happy I am that my young friend and assistant has found you, my dear."

Katya slipped a soft hand into Jeffrey's. "Thank you."

"It is I who am grateful. To both of you." He looked at Jeffrey. "I understand from Gregor that you are due for a final meeting with Rokovski."

"In twenty minutes."

"Might I come along?"

"Of course."

"Excellent." He turned to Katya. "Gregor asked me to convey an invitation to accompany him to one of his orphanages. He thought you might like to have a chance to see his little charges."

"That would be wonderful. I imagine you two could use some time alone as well." She raised herself up on tiptoes and kissed Jeffrey. "Until later, then."

"Have an excellent morning, my dear," Alexander replied, bowing at her departure. He watched her leave through the front doors. "A most remarkable woman. Am I correct in detecting a change in the atmosphere between you?"

"This trip has been important in a lot of ways," Jeffrey replied.

"Indeed it has." Alexander gazed at him fondly. "I am very proud of you, Jeffrey. You have handled yourself tremendously well."

"Thanks. I've really enjoyed myself."

"One often overlooked element of success is the ability to enjoy your work."

Jeffrey shook his head. "I can't get over how much better you look."

"Thank you. Yes, I have indeed suffered through a very dark night. But I am allowing myself to hope that dawn has finally arrived." He leaned over, put out his cigar, and said, "Perhaps we should be going, and you can fill me in along the way."

====

Rokovski was absolutely delighted to see Alexander enter his office with Jeffrey. "Mr. Kantor! How excellent to see you. I do hope that your health is better."

Alexander accepted the proffered hand, replied, "*Nie mozna narzekac*. I cannot complain. Thank you for asking."

"And Mr. Sinclair." Rokovski rewarded him with a genuine smile. "Would you gentlemen care for tea?"

"Well," Rokovski said once they were seated and served, "as they say in the spy novels, my friend, mission accomplished."

"Indeed," Kantor replied. "I have been most pleasantly surprised by the way events have unfolded."

"You have received copies of all the necessary export documents, Mr. Sinclair?"

"Everything is perfect," Jeffrey effused. "They were waiting for me at the ministry yesterday morning. Thank you again for your help."

"On the contrary, I am immensely grateful to know that we have begun what shall no doubt be a long and mutually beneficial relationship." Rokovski glanced at his watch. "I was informed that your shipment left on time yesterday, once the export documents were processed. It should be crossing the border at Frankfurt an der Oder just about now. No news is good news, so I'm sure all is well."

"Thanks to you," Alexander said. "We are very pleased to know that we have friends such as yourself upon whom we can rely."

"It is I who am pleased, Mr. Kantor. I cannot tell you how much this means, not only to me and to Cracow, but to all of Poland."

"It is always an honor to do something for Poland," Alexander replied. "There is one further point that my young associate thinks should be mentioned before we conclude our business."

"Of course," Rokovski replied, giving Jeffrey a sincere smile.

"We will naturally handle this sale of the painting in the most confidential of manners. My associate has an excellent working relationship with a major dealer. She has expressed a keen interest in acquiring items which are not intended for either public auction or display."

"An American," Jeffrey added. "Very professional, and very discreet."

Rokovski nodded approval. "Exactly what we require."

"But it is necessary to warn you," Alexander continued, "that with the same Rubens allegedly hanging in the museum of Vavel Castle, there is always the risk that at some time in the future an expert might be sent to inspect your painting. If he or she concludes that yours is indeed a forgery, it would be impossible to insure that the news will not leak out."

"Well, my friend," Rokovski replied, turning expansive, "I'm afraid it won't be me the expert will be visiting."

"I don't believe I understand," Alexander said.

"I told your young colleague about my big dream. I had a second big dream, which will come as no surprise to you. And that is the accumulation of as many Polish works of art and antiques as possible to restore our heritage. I'm sure you are familiar that museums regularly exchange paintings to complete one special collection or another. For many months I have been negotiating with the state museum of Moscow for the return of a series of paintings by Matejko. These paintings, I might add, each occupy one entire wall of the exhibition rooms."

"Brilliant," Kantor murmured. "Absolutely brilliant."

"They disappeared from Poland just after the Red Army arrived in 1945. The Cracow museum authorities were given some lame excuse about their being transported to Moscow for safekeeping. I have been struggling to find something from our collection that they might be willing to take in trade, but was getting nowhere. Shortly after Mr. Sinclair met with me, it occurred that a Rubens might pique their curiosity."

"My friend," Kantor said, "you have made your country proud."

"Needless to say," Rokovski went on, smiling broadly, "they were absolutely delighted. Being the gentleman that I am, I insisted that they send their top Old Master expert to authenticate it. I mentioned to them on the phone that over the years there had been some rumblings about the painting's authenticity, and I would not want them to be disappointed."

"Of course not."

"The expert arrived here yesterday, and his initial report is most positive. It appears that Moscow is anxious to take advantage of our offer before we wake up and realize how one-sided it is. We have just this morning heard that the six Matejkos are already being crated for shipment. They will be unveiled at a special exhibition commemorating the Vavel Castle's thousandth anniversary."

Alexander returned his smile. "It is a pity that your coup will have to remain in secret. You deserve a hero's reward."

"I shall receive my reward every time I stand before the Matejkos, and as I watch my new museum wing for religious art take shape." Rokovski stood with his guests, walked around his desk, took Alexander's hand in both of his. "My friend, Poland shall never perish."

"As long as we are alive," Alexander replied solemnly.

They stood together for a moment before the director released Alexander's hand and reached for Jeffrey's. "Mr. Sinclair, I shall look forward to many further opportunities to work with you."

"Nothing could give me more pleasure," Jeffrey replied.

Rokovski ushered them downstairs, bowed them through the main portals, shut the door behind them. Once they were back on the street, Jeffrey stood and blinked in the sunlight. "I can't believe it's over."

"A job well done." Alexander's eyes were moist. He looked straight across the market square, a slight smile on his features.

"What's next?"

"There is a small church not far from here," Alexander replied. "My mother used to go there when I was young. I believe I might like to stop by for a moment."

"Sure. I love these old churches. Which one is it?"

Alexander motioned out over the square, out beyond the colorful market stalls and the throngs of people and the flower sellers, out across the expanse of history. "Just on the other side of Florian's Gate," he said.

ACKNOWLEDGMENTS

While *Florian's Gate* is indeed a work of fiction, I have tried very hard to remain true to the actual situation I found in the newly liberated lands of Eastern Europe. The learning process that unfolded during my trips, as well as during the preparatory work done before traveling, was both challenging and rewarding. I found myself being forced to rethink much of the perspective I have inherited from my Western culture, and as a result I feel that I have been granted a unique opportunity to grow and develop both as an individual and as a Christian.

My research trips to Poland were made infinitely richer through the kind hospitality of Isabella's family. Their warm and giving nature come truly from the heart, and they shared with us the very best of both what they had and who they were. I am truly thankful to be a part of such a wonderful family.

Many powerful lessons came to me through these visits with my wife's family. Despite the pain that was recalled along with the memories, they shared a number of the events which they either witnessed or experienced themselves during the past five decades. What touched me most deeply, however, was not the experiences themselves, but rather the way in which they were described.

Virtually all the events woven into the Polish section of this book come from their experiences, and where possible are kept exactly as they were related to me. I say this so that there can be no question as to the reality of their suffering. And yet, throughout my visits with them, they never overcame their natural humility to the point of really believing that what they had to say was of any special significance, or could be of interest to others.

Isabella believes that there are two major reasons for this: First, *everyone* in Poland suffered horribly as a result of both the war and Stalin's subsequent domination of Eastern Europe. Because they have spent their lives surrounded by other families who experienced the same or even worse traumas, they cannot understand how great an impact their stories might have on someone from the West.

The second reason is that they see themselves as simple people— they are not famous, they have not conquered their difficulties, they have not made a great name for themselves. They have simply endured, and their life stories are nothing more in their eyes than struggling to live and to survive despite all that is placed upon their minds and hearts and shoulders. They shared their experiences with me in acknowledgement of my becoming part of the family. But they never could understand why I insisted on taking notes. They never could see why their stories moved me as they did.

My wife's assistance is found on every page of this book. None of her family in Poland speaks English, so all of their stories and observations were painstakingly translated by her. She taught me constantly from the wealth of knowledge which she has gained through her travels and studies; Isabella attended the University of Cracow for a year, and has returned numerous times since then, including one visit just as martial law was imposed. It has been a very rewarding experience to work with her on this book. I feel that I have begun to understand a fragment of the beauty and the strength which is contained within the Polish spirit.

My wife's father, Olgierd Kaliszczak, was prisoner number 1914 in the Auschwitz concentration camp. All that is described here in this book—from being picked up during a random street search to being released because of his mother's untiring efforts—comes from his memories, and is written using his words. The only change I made was that Olgierd was actually arrested at a market square in Warsaw instead of Cracow. It was the first time that he had ever spoken of his experiences in such detail, and it was a tremendously difficult endeavor. I am extremely grateful to him, both for the painful act of remembering, and for granting me the gift of this sharing. I would also like to offer my heartfelt thanks to his wife, Danka, who gave me my first lessons in Polish hospitality at their home in Virginia. The key, I have learned from her and others, is to give the very best of what one has, and to give from the heart.

Janusz Zurawski is former director of one of Poland's largest construction engineering groups. He and his wife Haluta opened their hearts and home to us, and aided me greatly in gaining historical insight into the Polish character. Dr. Teresa Aleksandrowicz virtually took responsibility for us during our second visit to Warsaw.

Marian and Dusia Tarka shared numerous experiences that were truly difficult to relive, including the incident of the Siberian conscription—the woman who returned is a very dear friend of theirs. Their son, Slawek, was kind enough to spend several hours discussing the current crisis within the Polish police.

Olek Tarka and his wife Halinka were of immense help and support. From Olek I received much of the general economic perspective. Halinka personally took me around several villages near Cracow so that I might visit the homes and cottages which were described here.

=====

Andrzej Koprowski, S.J., is the former head of media for the Polish Catholic Church, and currently directs programs on both national radio and television. Grzegorz Schmidt, S.J., is a rector of the Catholic University of Warsaw and editor of the Catholic magazine *Przeglad Powszechny*. Both of these gentlemen were kind enough to assist me in developing a perspective for the church's overall efforts.

Amid the incredible chaos of shifting from communism to capitalism (until recently, virtually no private commercial establishments were allowed), I found a number of people who were truly passionate about their fledgling antique trades, and who were delighted to speak about their experiences with a total stranger. Marck Lengiewicz is president of the Rempex Auction House. Barbara Zdrenka is owner of Warsaw's Antykwariat Dziel Sztuki Dawnej, a fine establishment with a remarkable collection of truly beautiful small items. Monika Kuhne is manager of the Noble House in

Warsaw, a very up-market shop with some breathtaking pieces. The staff of Cracow's Connoisseur Antyki were all most patient with my endless questions.

Adam Konopacki is one of the few Polish art and antiques consultants who has, in a short span of time, established a name as a trustworthy evaluator. He was extremely helpful in giving me an overview of the Polish antiques trade, the characters involved, their backgrounds, and how the 'industry' is developing.

Waclaw Wlodarczyk is miner number 142 in the Wieliczka Salt Mines. When he learned the reason for our wanting to visit the mines, he took it as a personal challenge and led us down into the older unused areas—an exciting and somewhat frightening experience. Some of these areas had clearly not been refurbished for decades, and the wood under our feet and around our heads bore that strange hoary frost and weak parchment feel. I am very grateful for an experience that I will not soon forget.

John Hess is director of Youth With A Mission's efforts in Cracow. It was from him that I learned of Father Bloknicki and his Poland-wide mission project described in this book.

Rev. Konstanty Wiazowski is president of the Polish Baptist Union, and Rev. I. Barna is general secretary. They were most kind in assisting me with my research; when our work took longer than expected, they invited Isabella and me to take part in a wedding celebration that evening. It was an exceptional time for both of us, and we are truly grateful for their congregation's open-hearted welcome.

=====

The story of stealing antiques in East Germany by putting the owners into prison and sometimes torturing them into signing the sales documents is true. The trial is currently underway for over a dozen defendants. The scandal has now reached the top echelons of the former government.

Renate Trotz was co-founder of the Schwerin New Forum, the nationwide democratic group whose peaceful protests ushered in the fall of East German President Hoennecker and the rise of democracy. She is also an attorney, and in this capacity was most helpful in gaining background information on the unfolding scandal.

Thilo Schelling and his assistant Kathrin Dobrowolski are responsible for working with West German and international companies who are starting up operations in the former East German state of Mecklenburg. He gave up a secure senior position in Dusseldorf in order to be a part of the rebuilding of new Germany. He provided a most enthusiastic and realistic overview, which helped tremendously in coming to understand the enormous problems—and opportunities—that face the new German states. His assistant deserves a special note of thanks for her open-hearted discussion of what it meant to live through the transition as a young woman professional. I am very grateful to both of them for their time and heartfelt assistance.

Help also came from the new Mecklenburg government's Secretary of State, Wolfgang Pfletshinger, and Minister of Commerce Lehman. Despite the enormous demands placed upon their time and energies, they stopped long enough to offer their perspectives with candor.

Rainer Rausch is a lawyer from Munich who has given up his practice, his home, and his former life in order to work with the evangelical church in Mecklenburg. He works both in attempting to regain assets stripped by the former Communist regime and in assisting people who have been persecuted because of their role within the church. He kindly assisted with gaining a clear perspective and with making introductions for me within the region.

Dr. Seyfarth is the head of Mecklenburg's only evangelical seminary, situated in Schwerin. He is a very deep-thinking, profound, and inspiring gentleman who grasps the problems facing his region with the gentle humility of one who truly loves Christ. I am indeed grateful for the insights that have gone into the making of this book, and for the lessons I gained personally from him.

Irene Heinze is the historian at the Castle-Museum of Güstrow in Mecklenburg. She spent an entire afternoon walking Isabella and me through their collection, explaining in detail the history and the significance of both the palace and the pieces housed there.

Several times a year, my wife and I try to schedule a four-day silent retreat at a Carmelite monastery near Oxford. During one of these visits we met a Polish gentleman, Brother Jerzy, who became the basis for the character of Gregor. He has remained a good friend and true example of Christ's love at work.

———

My stepbrother, Lee Bunn, is a recovering alcoholic. His story formed the basis for the character of Jeffrey's brother, and I am immensely grateful that Lee feels confident enough about his own past and recovery to allow me to use his experiences as a part of this book. Lee became a part of our family several years after my departure for Europe at the age of twenty-one, and we have never spent as much time together as I would like. The segment about being moved from place to place is fiction; the story of his fall from the tree is sadly true. I am proud and happy to say, however, that Lee is now a member of A. A., and has not only come to grips with his own debilitation but truly grown in stature and strength through his walk with the Lord. His mother, my father's second wife, has taught me a tremendous amount about strength through faith; it was Patricia who introduced me to the concept of co-dependency, and to the healing power of faith in such tragic circumstances. Her example has proven to be a valuable beacon to others experiencing such pain.

Seven weeks before I began work on this book, the pastor of my church in Düsseldorf, Bill DeLay, entered the hospital for what we thought was appendicitis, but what turned out to be a tumor. He hovered at death's door for four days, then two weeks into his hospitalization had a relapse and again almost died. His four-month sojourn ended with a return to full health, but during his recovery Bill suffered tremendous agony. The result of this experience was a five-part sermon series on the theme of suffering. Much of that has been incorporated into this book. Bill and his wife Cathy have continued to offer great assistance with both the scriptural messages required for my book, and the biblical wisdom necessary for my own continued growth. I am very grateful for their love and prayerful support.

My mother, Becky Bunn, is the former owner of an antiques gallery and has managed several others. I am indeed grateful for the experiences and wisdom she has shared with me, and for the appreciation I have gained through her for fine woodwork. She now leads her own church's Stephen Ministries Outreach Program; I have gained great insight in how to work with people in pain through our talks. Thanks again, Mom. Your words stay with me through the years.

＝

Amelia Fitzalan-Howard is client services manager at Christie's in London. She was kind enough to spend several hours touring both the house's public showrooms and the underground treasure rooms. Edward Lennox-Boyd is manager of the furniture department, and explained the finer points of several pieces they had recently auctioned. These included the chest of drawers described during the Christie's scene near the beginning of the book; in this case I used the lowest initial estimate, because I feared the actual sales price would have seemed too unbelievable—the piece finally went for one and a half million pounds, over 2.75 million dollars.

Dr. Fabian Stein, director of Ermitage, Ltd., along with his partner, Alexander von Solodkov, runs one of the world's leading shops for Fabergé jewelry. He spent several days walking a total novice—me—through the artistic endeavors of one of the world's foremost jewelers.

Nancy Matthews, publicity director of the Franco-British Chamber of Commerce, received her initial training in antiques from the world-renowned Sotheby's School. Her assistance in making numerous contacts within the London antiques trade was invaluable.

Bryan Rolliston is co-owner of the Antique House on Kensington Church Street, and in the midst of a hectic day at the Grosvenor House Antiques Fair he took time to answer in exhaustive detail my questions about his pieces and the market in general.

Norman Adams owns the Adams store on Hans Road in the Kensington district of London, and is a passionate specialist in eighteenth-century English furniture. I am indeed grateful that he would share a bit of his knowledge and love of fine antiques with me.

The Grosvenor House Antiques Fair, under the patronage of Her Majesty Queen Elizabeth the Queen Mother, was for me something of a mind-boggling experience. I am extremely grateful to the staff of their very capable press office for treating a green newcomer with such tact and polite patience.

Please feel free to contact me via my Web site: www.davisbunn.com.

THE PRICELESS COLLECTION

Book Two

THE AMBER ROOM

THIS BOOK IS DEDICATED TO MY FATHER
THOMAS D. BUNN
WITH LOVE AND THANKS FOR THE DIVINE
GRACE THAT HAS MADE US FRIENDS.

"My son, if you accept my words and store up my
commands within you,
Turning your ear to wisdom and applying your heart to
understanding,
And if you call out for insight and cry aloud for
understanding,
And if you look for it as for silver and search for it as for
hidden treasure,
Then you will understand the fear of the
Lord and find the knowledge of God."

PROVERBS 2:1–5

"Until a man has found God and been found by
God, he begins at no beginning, he works to no end.
He may have his friendships, his partial loyalties,
his scraps of honor. But all these things fall into
place, and life falls into place, only with God."

H. G. WELLS

AUTHOR'S NOTE

As with *Florian's Gate*, antiques described in these pages, including the medieval chalice, do indeed exist. Prices quoted are based on actual sales or market estimates at the time of the original writing.

Information on reliquaries was garnered from a number of sources, and fashioned to suit this story.

As to the Amber Room, all information given in these pages leading up to the end of World War II—including its label as the Eighth Wonder of the World—is true; the Nazis did indeed loot this treasure from the Czar's Summer Palace outside St. Petersburg in 1941, and reassemble it in the Konijsberg Museum. The treasure subsequently vanished during the chaotic days toward the end of the war.

It is also true that on his first diplomatic visit to Germany, Russian President Boris Yeltsin stunned his Bonn hosts by declaring that his investigators had located documents showing exactly where the Amber Room was buried. The German government agreed to purchase this information with an additional gift of four hundred million marks, about three hundred million dollars, in emergency aid. The information, however, proved to be virtually worthless. The reasons for this will be revealed in this story.

The search continues . . .

Jeffrey Allen Sinclair worked hard at maintaining his calm. This bank vault was the closest he had ever come to being entombed.

"You oughtta give me some room for maneuvering, kid." The buyer was a silver-maned gentleman whom Betty had introduced only as Marv. His accent was New Jersey, his manner brash. "One point one mil plus change is kinda steep."

The Swiss bank's central underground vault was tucked discreetly behind the safety-deposit chambers, and reminded Jeffrey of a fur-lined cave. Plush maroon carpet, toned to match the thousands and thousands of burnished metal boxes, covered every available surface—floors, walls, ceilings, private inspection booths, even the wheeled tables used for carting security boxes back and forth. This padding sucked sound from the air, leaving a brooding oppressiveness, a sensation that human passage here was barely tolerated.

The Rubens portrait of Isabel of Bourboun was a splash of life in the deadened chamber. Recessed lighting fell with vivid clarity on the painting, leaving the three seated viewers and the rest of the room in shadows. That and the painting's obvious mastery of execution lent the portrait a singular power.

"That was the agreement," Jeffrey said, feeling as though the walls were eating his words. "We've done our part. We've had an expert authenticate and appraise the painting, and we've sought no competing bids. In return, as we told Betty—" with a nod in her direction, "we expect no negotiation on the established price."

The painting had been entrusted to him by Dr. Pavel Rokovski in Cracow, to be smuggled out of Poland. Jeffrey was instructed to sell it as quietly as possible to someone who would respect the Polish government's need to keep the sale very private.

"Buy it, Marv," Betty urged. An antiques dealer who had done business with Jeffrey on a number of occasions, she projected a polished self-assurance unaffected by their surroundings. "If you don't, I will."

"Yeah, yeah, okay." Marv sighed, reached into his coat pocket, and drew out a single-page banker's draft. "Can't shoot a guy for trying."

Jeffrey accepted the draft, counted the zeros, read the words, resisted the urge to kiss the document. "Maybe you two could decide on the transport arrangements."

Betty inspected the tall young man seated beside her with evident approval. Since Jeffrey had begun working at Alexander Kantor's antique shop in London eighteen months before, she had taken great pleasure watching him grow in the trade. She replied, "That's already taken care of."

"Yeah, the lady said you were for real; she did all the detail work before we got here." Marv shifted in his leather-lined seat. "Got something I wanna ask you, kid."

"Jeffrey," Betty corrected. "The young man's name is Jeffrey. He's just done you a great favor, Marv. The least you could do is try to remember his name."

"Taking over a mil offa me is a favor?"

"Giving you the right to buy a Rubens at any price is a favor, and you know it."

"Okay, Jeffrey, then."

Betty rose to her feet. "Well, Jeffrey, I owe you one."

"Seems to me it's mutual."

She shook her head. "You took me at my word."

"I trust you, Betty."

"I'm sure someone else has paid me such a nice compliment, but I can't remember when. Can I buy you lunch?"

He glanced at his watch. "I don't think there's time. I've got a plane back to London at two. Alexander's expecting me."

"I'll walk you out, then, if that's okay."

"It'd be great."

"You've already taken care of the export documents?"

He nodded. "They're with the bank manager. He'll get a confirmation on this check and hand them over."

"That's it, then." She turned toward the automatic door. "You ready, Marv?"

"We're right behind you," Marv replied. He waited for the door to sigh shut behind her, then said, "You're okay, kid."

"Thank you, sir."

"No muss, no fuss, just like the lady said. I like that." He was a well-groomed man in his fifties, with the look of a silver-maned wolf. Not a fox—a fox was too sleek an image, too polished. But a winter wolf, yes. Jeffrey could easily picture Marv emerging from snow-covered woods to howl at the moon. "The lady tells me secrecy's top on your list with this one, am I right?"

"It would help us a lot if the painting effectively disappeared, yes."

"Say no more, kid. And don't you worry. Where this painting's gonna go, it might as well stay buried down here in this vault." He gave the portrait another long look, nodded once. "Okay, that's enough. Let's get outta here. This place is giving me the heebie-jeebies. Tomb of Crazy Eddie the Carpet King."

On their way past the long rows of gleaming metal drawers, Marv asked, "You got anything else like this hanging around?"

"This is the first painting of world-class standing I've ever handled," Jeffrey confessed.

"Who said anything about paintings?" He stopped their forward progress by jabbing two fingers into Jeffrey's chest. "Look, you're a good kid. You're smart, you got class, you keep your ear to the ground, am I right?"

"I try."

"Sure you do. Okay, here's the thing. My wife, she likes paintings. Personally, I don't have all that many that keep me interested. This one, yeah, maybe I'm gonna put it in my study—don't worry, kid, that's one place nobody but nobody ever goes. But like I said, my wife's the one who's nuts over paintings."

The man touched the knot of his tie with a manicured hand. "What I'm after, personally speaking, is unique. You with me? One of a kind. Stuff a museum'd take one look at and start picking their jawbones up off the floor. Something like the Wright brothers' first airplane."

"I think that one's in the Smithsonian."

"Yeah, I wrote 'em a while back. Offered to do my patriotic duty, help bail the government out, take the sucker off their hands. Didn't even get a reply. They got some nerve."

"You're looking for the kind of item that nobody else has," Jeffrey interpreted.

"See, I said you were a bright kid. Not just anything, though. No miniature Disney castle made outta silver-plated tongue depressors, you with me? It's gotta be unique, and it's gotta be class."

"How about historic?"

"Yeah, sure, history's okay. But mystery is better. Like the long-lost treasures of the great Queen Smelda. The solid gold throne of the ancient fire-worshiping king of Kazookistan. Stuff like that."

"Last I heard, solid gold thrones don't come cheap."

"Listen, kid. You bring me unique and class and mystery all tied up in one little bundle, the sky ain't high enough for how far I'd go."

———

The Union Bank of Switzerland straddled the Parade-platz, Zurich's central square, and was connected to the main train station by the mile-long Bahnhofstrasse. This central pedestrian boulevard was lined with the most expensive shops in all Switzerland. Jeffrey took great draughts of the biting winter air as he rejoined Betty on the sidewalk and enjoyed playing the wide-eyed tourist. Fresh snowfall muffled sounds and gave the ancient facades a fairy-tale air. Streetcars clanged and rumbled, roasting chestnuts perfumed the air, and passersby conversed in guttural Swiss German. It was a good time to be alive.

As they walked, Jeffrey told Betty of his conversation with Marv after she had left the vault. She was not surprised. "Marv was born about six hundred years too late. He imagines himself sitting in his mountain fastness, surrounded by suits of shining armor and all the treasures from his crusading days."

"More like a prince of thieves," Jeffrey offered.

Betty shrugged and said, "As it is, Marv has had to make do with thirty dry-cleaning businesses and half the garbage-collection companies in New Jersey. He sees himself buying respectability with his art." She shook her head. "On second thought, he's probably better off living in current times. He can twist the secret knob in his mansion and walk down the stairs that nobody but a builder, fifty or sixty stonemasons, and half of Princeton know about. Then he can sit in front of his latest acquisition and dream about a time when he'd have ridden off into the sunset in pursuit of stolen treasures and damsels in distress, and forget the fact that he'd probably have gotten himself killed. Romantics tend not to survive in romantic times."

"I didn't know you were a cynic."

"Cynic? Me?" Betty laughed. "I just don't like losing clients with more money than sense. They're too rare to sacrifice to the call of the wild."

"Personally, I think the times we're living in are about as romantic as they can get."

Betty arched an eyebrow. "You don't mean to tell me you're in love."

"Afraid so."

"Utterly charming, Jeffrey. Who is she?"

"You'll meet her the next time you're in London."

"Not the beauty you've hired as your assistant."

He swung around. "How did you hear about that?"

"My dear Jeffrey, the price of success is that everything you do becomes the stuff of rumors. Is she as beautiful as they say?"

"I think so."

"Marvelous. Tell me her name."

"Katya." Speaking the word was enough to bring a flush of warmth to his cheeks.

"How absolutely delicious. A hint of mystery even in her name. You must tell me all about her very soon."

"When are you coming back to London?"

"That depends on you. Do you have anything to show me?"

"We just got in a new shipment last month. No Jacobean pieces, but some excellent early Chippendale. I was going to give it over to another dealer. You know we don't often keep the English stuff. I could hold it for you, though."

"Don't ever let an English dealer hear you call Chippendale 'stuff.' They'll hand you your head. But I must say you are tempting me."

"There is one other item. I have a friend—well, a dealer in London—who comes as close as any dealer I know to being a friend. Except you, that is."

"You are very kind, sir."

"Andrew has a piece I really think you'd like. It looks like an early Jacobean sideboard. American."

That stopped her. "You're certain?"

"Reasonably. I think it was originally done as a church altar."

"Then hold it for me." She resumed their stroll. "If you're right, Jeffrey, you may have yet another excellent find to your credit."

"And if I'm not?"

"Then there is no harm done, none whatsoever. Jacobean from either side of the ocean is still a highly sought-after commodity."

"How high should I go?"

She shook her head. "I believe this is an admirable opportunity to raise our level of trust another notch or two."

"You want me to bid on it for you?"

"I want you to secure it for me," she replied firmly. "All I ask is that you use your best judgment."

Jeffrey was visibly rocked back on his heels. "Thanks, Betty. A lot."

"You are most welcome, my dear. I believe we are marking the beginning of a long and beautiful friendship. I do not count many as true friends. I'm pleased to include you among them."

They walked on in companionable silence until Jeffrey asked, "Was there any special reason why Marv hit on me about the big-ticket items?"

Betty smiled at him. "You'll be pleased to know that your uncle Alexander's mystique is now being attached to your name."

"You're kidding."

"Where did you go for almost a month this past summer?"

"I can't answer that."

"Of course you can't," Betty answered smugly. A puff of ice-laden wind funneled through the closely packed buildings and painted frost on their cheeks. She pulled her fur-lined collar tighter. "It certainly is bitter out here, don't you think?"

"You're changing the subject."

"Marv is what you might call perpetually hungry. He is far from dull, despite the impression he might give. You don't rise to the top of the New Jersey garbage heap without being remarkably agile and intelligent in a rather base way." Betty pointed toward an art gallery's front window. "Do you have time for me to pop in here for a moment?"

"Of course."

The shop's interior was stifling after the icy air. They shed coats and mufflers, stamped warmth back into their feet, denied the attentive saleswoman's offer of assistance, strolled around the spacious rooms.

"They occasionally come up with some real prizes here," Betty explained. "I like to stop in whenever I can."

"Marv treated my discovery of another new find as a real possibility," Jeffrey persisted.

"Lower your voice," Betty said softly. "There have been rumors. All of a sudden, everywhere I go I'm hearing tales right out of my children's storybooks. Nazi spoils popping to the surface. Bankrupt Eastern European countries selling off things the world hasn't heard of for centuries."

"What kind of things?"

Betty turned a sparkling gaze his way. "Treasures, Jeffrey. Mysteries in gold and silver. Hoards of legendary kings and queens."

She patted his sleeve. "You will remember your friend if you ever stumble across one, won't you?"

The place held that certain smell of an all-night tavern, one distilled to an ever-stronger proof the closer the hour crawled toward dawn. The establishment had no name—bars such as these in former East Germany seldom did. It was a single vast chamber in a run-down district of Schwerin, and possessed all the charm of a subway.

Everybody smoked. Many patrons stayed with the cardboard-tipped Russian cigarettes said to be packed with sawdust and droppings. Others bit down on acrid-smelling cigarillos fashioned by wrapping shreds of Black Sea tobacco around straw as crooked as the fate that drew the patrons here. They spoke from throats filed down with metal rasps. Laid over the fumes like plaster off a trowel was the smell of unwashed bodies packed too closely together for too long.

The only Western import was Jägermeister, a foul, seventy-proof brew of roots and herbs meant to soothe an overstuffed belly. Here it was sucked from tiny one-shot bottles wrapped in coarse paper, taken between drafts of good East German beer. Jägermeister was the perfect companion for boilermakers, since it both numbed the belly and zapped the head with lightning-bolt accuracy.

The crowd kept itself carefully segregated. Hotel porters, security, police, and prostitutes all gathered up by the counter, where the coffee machine blew clouds of steam like a patient locomotive. The professional drunks huddled together at the two tables flanking the door; they were blasted by icy wind and snow flurries every time someone entered or left. The tavern's far side was held by the taxi and truck drivers, either off duty or on break or unable to sleep beyond the routine of catching naps between rides. They kept their backs turned to the rest of the world and talked in the tones of those most comfortable with secrets.

The one they called Ferret sat as usual in his own world, at a table on the edges of the first group. His overly large head was buried in a sheaf of papers. His eyes were so poor he read with his nose almost touching the page. Those who knew him said it was because he rarely saw the light of day.

He had the body of a worm and the mind of a camera—whatever the eye scanned the memory never lost. In days gone by he had used this mind to protect his body, shielding himself behind the strength of others who used his abilities for gaining and holding power. Now the power holders were disgraced, either in hiding or in prison. It was only a matter of days before the investigators started working one rank further down and came upon Ferret.

The majority of the Communist overlords had held on to power so long they had not believed the cowed East Germans would dare take it back. Ferret had watched the first mob gather before the Stasi headquarters in Leipzig and had known differently. He had listened to the mob sing freedom songs and spent the long night hours stuffing files with any possible importance into boxes and bags and wastebaskets. Hauling them down to the loading platform and stuffing them into the city maintenance van had been the most strenuous exercise Ferret had done in his entire life.

He had driven the entire next day, stopping only when darkness and exhaustion forced him to pull off the narrow, rutted excuse for a road. Every passing car had jerked him awake, foggy-brained and panic-stricken, but his hunch had paid off. The police had been too overwhelmed with concern over their own future to worry about a dilapidated van and a few missing files.

The second day of driving had brought him to Schwerin, the capital of the former East German state known as Mecklenburg-Vorpommern. Ferret had used a set of false identification documents, prepared years before for a contingency just such as this, to check into a lakeside resort with a walled-in parking area. The following day he had bribed his way into a filthy cellar storage room turned into an illegal studio apartment—no ventilation, no windows, a one-ring cooker plugged into the overhead light socket, bathroom one floor up via an outside stairway. With the eleven-year apartment waiting list, this was the only room available anywhere. It was his only because he had Western marks to slip the landlady.

In the old days, Ferret's official title had been that of Prokurist for the Local Workers' Council in Leipzig. It was as high a position as the Ferret could manage and still maintain his inconspicuousness, but Prokurist was pretty high indeed. It made him the man with power to sign—that is, the power to approve checks, authorize contracts, organize budgets. Ferret had kept his position by making no decisions at all, only furthering the decisions of those who knew the value of a Ferret and fawned over him with the dedication of a love-addled Romeo.

What the title did not give away was that the Ferret was also the Stasi's local mole.

It had been a perfect match—the secret police whom everyone feared, hated, and refused to speak of, and a man who preferred invisibility to any power or position. Ferret had fed Stasi the information it used as fuel. The Stasi had shielded Ferret with its might.

Until the night Ferret saw his carefully constructed world begin its demise in the flickering flames of a hundred thousand candles.

=====

"Had the belly pains again this morning, I did." Kurt, the man seated at Ferret's right, was a former Stasi spy, and Ferret's contact in the secret police. He and numerous other mid-level henchmen remained safe from the West German prosecutors simply because there were so many of them. Those who were being picked up tended to be the targets of strong grudges and those who could be found. Kurt was not immune to grudge holders, but a set of false documents and a different name was keeping him safe. For the moment.

"Spent three hours sitting in line at the clinic," Kurt complained. "Probably caught the plague or something. You should have seen the lot in there. Pathetic."

The third person at their table was not impressed. Erika, the name she had recently assumed, was the former assistant chief jailer at the notorious Dresden women's prison. Like Ferret and Kurt, she was now just another bit of flotsam washed up on the new tide of democracy.

Erika pinched the Russian cigarette's filter, pressing the cardboard tube into a tighter hole to restrict the bitter smoke. She motioned toward Ferret, speaking as if the little man were not there. "Take a look at those old papers. What's he working on?"

"Our freedom." Kurt had obeyed the Ferret's frantic midnight call and left town with a second van loaded to the gills with stolen Stasi files. "How did it go last night?"

"You see the creep at the end of the bar—no, don't turn around. The blue suit with ice for eyes. He'll be over in about three seconds for his touch."

"The cops saw you?"

"Not me." She punched her cigarette into ashes. "Your buyers didn't have a clue."

"They're not mine." Kurt swung one arm over the back of his chair, risked a casual glance toward the bar, waved at somebody who wasn't there. "The one with the rug on his head?"

"He's been my contact," Erika replied. "Until yesterday it all ran smoothly. But he's got a lever now, and he's going to use it."

The police who frequented the tavern were those who valued the universal language and pocketed a percentage of every deal cut on the tavern's far side. For them a regular visit to its crowded depths was necessary—they had to keep a careful eye on their golden-egg-laying taxi-driving geese.

The routine was well known. Truckers brought the black-market wares in from all over the globe, but mostly from the faltering East. Taxi drivers found the local buyers. In the tumultuous days since the nation of East Germany foundered off the maps and into history, cities like Schwerin had taken on the smell and feel of the Wild West. This left a lot of room for policemen unsure of future paychecks to increase their pocket change.

Contact with the undercurrent of gray goods was far from difficult, especially since most of the newer taxi drivers were former

comrades in one guise or another. These days, each new face behind
the wheel of a cab brought a new story. One entire table in the taxi
drivers' corner this evening was made up of former army colonels,
another of air force pilots. Communist Party henchmen formed
a good solid block, most of them from the innumerable middle
levels—the paper pushers and wheel greasers and slogan shouters
who had neither the clout nor the foreknowledge to protect themselves when their house of cards came crashing down.

Another contingent of new nighttime taxi drivers, as well as
street sweepers and bricklayers and every other job where identification papers were not too carefully inspected, were former Stasi mid-
level spies. Stasi was the popular nickname given to the MFS, the
Ministerium für Staats Sicherheit—the Ministry for State Security.
The East German secret police had provided a model for numerous
smaller nations around the world, wherever money was tight and
security was deemed of far greater importance than human rights.

And now it was gone.

The police who huddled by the counter and kept a money-
lender's eye on the nighttime traffic had seen what happened to
the Stasi—four hundred thousand jobs gone in the blink of an eye.
They knew the prevailing opinion about cops; since the Wall's collapse they were universally known as Honecker's Henchmen. They
saw the West German police flash by in their Mercedes patrol cars,
with their sneering contempt for Ossie cops—Ossie was slang for
a citizen of former East Germany, Wessie for those from the West.
They had heard about the Bonn government's refusal to upgrade
either their salaries or their equipment. Ossie coppers who were
willing to stop living on false hopes and face up to Western reality
knew it was only a matter of time.

The straight-edged fools in police uniforms who had crossed over
to Bonn's side could say what they wanted—nobody could do away
with forty-six years of Communist laws overnight and understand
what the West Germans wanted to put in its place. Not the police,
not the lawyers, and not the people. The uncertainty of life under a
new system nobody comprehended or, if truth be known, really cared
that much for, was enormous. The chance for gain was even greater.

Kurt swiveled back around and murmured, "Here he comes."

The cop's joviality only touched the bottom half of his face. He pulled over a chair and sat down. "Any reason for sitting next to the window?"

"It keeps away the flies," Kurt replied. "Most of them, anyway."

"It's so cold over here it burns. Ferret here must have a frozen back." He twisted his head around. "What's that you're working on, Ferret?" The Ferret raised his head, squinted in confusion through bottle-bottom glasses, murmured, "Oh, hello, Inspector." The head dropped back to an inch or so from the page.

"Not inspector anymore," the man replied. "Just policeman now. And how long at this job is anyone's guess."

"Tough," Erika replied.

The dead smile returned. "You probably heard, they brought in your colleagues from the Zoo this morning." The Zoo was the tag neighbors had given the central prison in East Berlin, named for the sounds that rose from its confines, particularly at night.

"I heard."

"Yes, thought you had. Well, in times like this it certainly is nice to have friends who can cover for you, yes?" He leaned forward. "Since when did you work with the Viets, Kurt?"

"I don't know what you're talking about."

"No, of course not. And you don't have any connections to the vodka trade out of Poland, either, I'm sure."

"I wish I did."

"Yes, I suppose so. Did I mention that they've raised the bounty on nailing Eastern bootleggers? Five thousand marks it is now, with vodka top of the list. Five thousand marks. Almost enough to make a man go legal."

Unification had brought a flood of West German marks into the defunct East German economy. Traders from the poorer Eastern lands flocked over the border by thousands of ill-defined paths, bringing anything they could buy cheaply and sell for more— Chinese T-shirts available in Cracow for fifty cents, Pakistani sweaters, prime Polish vodka that went for two dollars a liter in Poland and five times that in Germany.

The worst of the illegal traders were the Vietnamese, invited over to study or work or simply visit as friends of the former Communist regime, and now refusing to go home. The new Wessie bureaucrats were denying them residency visas; they lived with the constant threat of deportation and a growing hatred of the new authorities. Their tightly knit community slid daily toward overt violence and blatantly illegal activities.

The policeman rose to his feet and nodded to the little group. "I'll be on my rounds tomorrow if you need to see me."

Kurt watched him move away. "How much does he want?"

"Half," Erika replied.

"Too much."

"He saw the buyers unload the van, Kurt. Chaing told me. Stood and watched them."

"That's impossible."

"Not if they did it behind the all-night gas station."

Kurt scoffed. "Nobody's that stupid."

"Your traders are."

"I told you, they're not my anything."

"They're going to be our noose if we don't pay the man."

Ferret chose that moment to raise his head. "I don't think we will," he said. "Pay him, I mean."

Kurt turned his way. "Why not?"

"We'll need that money."

"You've found it?"

The bulbous head dropped once more. "Perhaps."

"Perhaps isn't good enough."

"More than perhaps." Ferret lifted his gaze. "My freedom is resting on this as well, you know."

"What are you two going on about," Erika demanded.

"Ferret's been hunting for something," Kurt replied, his eyes remaining on the strange-looking little man with the large head. "Something big."

Erika twisted her head to examine Ferret's folder and saw handwriting on a yellowed sheet. "How old is that?"

"Old," Ferret replied, placing a possessive hand to shield the page.

"Forty-seven years, to be exact," Kurt told her. "Ferret and I have been talking. We need a third."

"A third for what?"

His eyes still on Ferret, Kurt asked, "Do you have any contacts left in the Dresden archives?"

Erika showed the world her best poker face. "I might. What's in it for me?"

"Freedom," Kurt replied. "Papers. Money. Lots of money."

"So what is it you're looking for?"

"Can you keep a secret?"

Erika snorted. "I should. I've had a lifetime of practice."

"A treasure, then," Kurt replied. "One called the Amber Room."

Erika thought it over. "What do I have to do?"

The Ferret raised his watery eyes and said quietly, "We are looking for a certain man."

Jeffrey stepped further back into the Cafe Royale's entrance hall as the front doors admitted several well-dressed patrons and a blast of freezing wind. "Meeting Dr. Rokovski the day after my return from Zurich is a little too much coincidence for me," he murmured to Alexander, his uncle and boss.

Located just half a block off Piccadilly Circus, the Cafe Royale had been a hub of the London social whirl for over a century. It was one of the few public haunts of Victorian England that had managed to remain financially afloat since World War II. The bars and restaurants displayed typically Victorian proportions—an almost endless series of overdone rooms set on seven floors.

"You know full well that I absolutely must speak with Pavel now," Alexander replied. "I need his blessing on this gala business. I should have already requested it, if truth be known, but it was something I wished to do in person."

"It'd be a lot nicer if we could have this meeting after the check is cleared and the Rubens deal over and done with."

"Don't be so nervous," Alexander replied. "Rokovski is not in London on our account, of that I am sure. He is here for a conference and is meeting us because I invited him."

"I still don't like it. What if he's upset because the sale took so long to go through?"

Alexander shook his head, his own calm unruffled. "The gentleman is a professional, and a professional will understand that in a sale requiring absolute discretion, patience is of the utmost importance."

"You're sure?"

"See for yourself." Alexander pointed through the glass portals to the street, where a taxi was depositing the Dr. Pavel Rokovski, director of the Polish Ministry of Culture's Cracow division and Alexander's primary contact for his export of Polish antiques. "Does that look like the face of a worried man?"

"Alexander. And Mr. Sinclair," Dr. Rokovski effused, striding forward with an outstretched hand. "How wonderful to see you again."

"Please call me Jeffrey."

"Of course, thank you. I am so sorry to be late. I decided to take the tube because I was warned that traffic is terrible here in London. I found the right line, but I am afraid that I took it in the wrong direction. The next thing I knew, I was in—what do you call it?—Hendon Central." He seemed very comfortable in English.

"That's quite all right," replied Alexander. "It was nice to have a moment to catch our breaths at the end of the day." He gestured them forward. "Come, gentlemen. Our table awaits."

They were led to their place in the front bar, where paintings in elaborate gilt frames fought for space on richly brocaded walls. Rokovski settled into a French settee upholstered in red velvet, took in the ornate high ceiling, heavy drapes, and rich carpeting. "Some of our castle's royal chambers are not as fine as this."

"I quite enjoy the ambience," Alexander agreed. "And its location makes the cafe an excellent rendezvous point."

"I'm sorry that my schedule is so tight," Rokovski said, "but the conference planners do have us on a treadmill."

"I quite understand," Alexander replied.

"I would love to stay and explore London by night," Rokovski continued, "but instead I must be back at the South Bank Center for a reception by seven. You know I am here to make contacts for a variety of traveling exhibits we hope to lure to Cracow in the coming months."

"It is wonderful that you would take time for us at all," Alexander said. "I am delighted that we could meet even briefly, as I have some very good news for you. We can now confirm that the Rubens has been sold. The price, even in this difficult market, was at the high end of our preliminary estimate."

"Splendid, splendid," Rokovski said, his eyes dancing from one to the other. "Would it be indelicate to ask the figure?"

Alexander nodded to his assistant. Jeffrey kept his voice discreetly low. "One point one five."

Rokovski showed momentary confusion. "One point one five what?"

"Million," Jeffrey said. "Dollars."

"So much," Rokovski breathed.

"The transfer will go through tomorrow, less our commissions and the payment for the initial information," Alexander said. "In accordance with our arrangements."

"This is wonderful. Just wonderful. It will mean so much for the preservation and expansion of our religious art collection."

"This service has brought me great satisfaction," Alexander assured him. "I am indeed grateful for the opportunity to be a part of this transaction."

"When may I use these funds?"

"Immediately," Alexander replied. "That is, as soon as the bank has finished with its paperwork."

"Excellent." Rokovski showed great relief. "You see, in anticipation of the sale's being a success, I have already committed our museum to urgent repair and restoration work for which we do not have the money. I can't thank either of you enough. I am only sorry that others cannot know of your extraordinary contribution to this effort."

Alexander nodded his formal thanks. "Speaking of contributions, Pavel, it has occurred to me that your project to house the nation's collection of religious art requires both more funding and wider public support. I have therefore taken it upon myself to lay the groundwork for a fund-raising gala to promote your efforts."

Rokovski was baffled. "What means this, gala?"

"It is a quite well-known event in Western circles," Alexander replied. "Various charities organize deluxe receptions or dinner parties, charge an outrageous amount per plate, and invite hundreds of people."

"And these people will come?"

"Given the proper mixture of exclusivity and good cause," Alexander replied, "not only will they come, but they will pay for the privilege. I expect to sell these tickets for two hundred pounds."

Rokovski gaped. "Per person?"

"You're quite right," Alexander smiled. "Two hundred fifty would be much more appropriate for such a worthy cause."

"You see, Dr. Rokovski," Jeffrey explained, "not only do you raise money for your cause through selling tickets, but you also attract the attention of celebrities and the media."

"Call me Pavel, please."

"Thank you. This leads to further private donations and sometimes even bequests."

"I see," Rokovski nodded. "So this must be a very special party for all such special people."

"I intend to hold it at the Ritz," Alexander replied. "I have booked the grand ballroom, and I expect no fewer than six hundred would-be patrons of Polish art."

"Incredible," Rokovski breathed. "And what are you going to showcase?"

It was Alexander's turn to show confusion. "What do you mean?"

"Is that not the correct word? Most conferences I have attended have some type of centerpiece to excite the participants' imagination. An example you can show the people of what you are trying to do. Some photograph or brochures, perhaps even the real thing."

"The real thing?" Alexander leaned forward. "Bring an example of Polish artwork over for the event? That would be extraordinary."

"I have an idea," Rokovski said. "There is a collection of exceptional religious artifacts within the Marian Church. We should find you something small yet beautiful, an article that would represent the wonder of Polish religion and heritage. Something easily transportable—perhaps a medieval chalice. I know the curate, Mr. Karlovich, quite well."

"This is a splendid proposition," Alexander said. "This would help the project immensely."

"Of course, I will arrange all the necessary export documents," Rokovski said, writing in a small pocket notebook. "I suggest we extend to you three pieces. First, the article from the Marian Church—but I do not have direct control over the church, you understand. Approval must be given by the curate."

"I understand, and am indeed grateful."

"As for pieces within the national collections, well, of course, those are within my jurisdiction." He thought for a moment, nodded to himself. "Might I suggest a small oil painting of the Madonna and Child? And there is a splendid miniature altar in the Czartoryski Collection. An exceptional piece, I promise you."

"The three together would comprise an extraordinary exhibit," Alexander enthused. "Such treasures would go far to convince the guests to become true patrons of artwork from Poland."

Rokovski glanced at his watch, rose to his feet. "Then I will call you from Cracow the day after tomorrow. We can ship the altar and the painting, there is no difficulty at that point. I must warn you, however, that Curate Karlovich would insist on a personal envoy to transport whatever article he loans you to London and back."

"I had planned to travel to Poland on other business next week," Alexander replied. "I will see to this matter, and please give Mr. Karlovich my personal assurances."

London's East End was a completely different world, run by a different sort of people and held in place by different laws. Jeffrey loved the feeling of passing through alien gates and was delighted to see Katya enjoying it as well.

He motioned toward a bakery whose front window displayed only opaque frost and several dozen icicles. "Sorry about the cold."

"It's too early to worry about little things like that." She snuggled happily against him on the taxi seat. "Some people haven't even gone to bed yet."

"Some people do this every day."

"Not me." She prodded his shoulder into a more comfortable shape. "I should have brought my pillow."

He reached into his satchel, poured coffee from the thermos, held it toward her. "Maybe this will help."

She tasted the cup and choked. "What is this?"

"Coffee. What did you think?"

"It goes down like tar." She looked at him with eyes cleared from the slightest hint of sleepiness. "I'm glad you're better at antiquing than you are at making coffee."

"It woke you up in a hurry."

"This is too exciting to worry about things like sleep," she said. "My first antiques market. How much can I spend?"

He showed genuine alarm. "Nothing."

She chuckled. "Got you."

He sank back in the taxi seat. "Be still, my heart."

"What are we going for, if not to buy?"

"Sometimes we find bargains or smaller pieces for the shop," Jeffrey explained. "But less often in the London markets than in those out in the country. Usually, I just like to come and look and learn. Today, though, I've got to see Andrew about a piece I want to take from his shop. He's been away for a week, and his assistant said he'd be back in time for today's market."

They crossed over Tower Bridge, with its soaring ramparts and trademark red brick keeps. Their taxi passed block after block of small businesses and corner cafes and derelict warehouses before letting them off in front of a tumbledown building marked by piles of refuse and crowds of people. Jeffrey paid the driver and steered Katya around the gossips and sharp-eyed thieves and runners and sniffers. Runners owned items but could not afford their own shop, he explained as they walked, while sniffers looked for price discrepancies.

Jeffrey stopped her by a burly young man squatting beside several boxes of goods, their covers thrown to the side.

"Go in a High Street shop with ten quid," the street hawker called to the jostling, friendly throng. "They'll throw you out on your ear. 'Ave a look at this then. Atomizer spray, 'ave a gander at the brochure, sixteen quid for the large size. And the perfume, twenty-two fifty for the blokes with more wallet than sense. Goes on the top like that. Bath soap and men's cologne, all top o' the line, right? And what am I gonna do for you, then?" Smack went the broad-bladed hand on one box. "Not seventy quid as they'd take you for on the High Street." Smack! "Not sixty." Smack! "Not even fifty nor forty nor even thirty." Smack! "Ten pounds is all I'm askin'."

He hefted the half-dozen gaudy boxes between two grimy hands.

"Ten quid for the lot. Who's got a lady or two waitin'? Not to mention a posh cologne for yourselves, gents. Ten quid, price of your cab ride home after she thanks you proper. And you ladies, how's about a gift for yourselves, then? All right, who's willing to part with a tenner?"

Satisfied with the show, the crowd moved forward with money outstretched as the hawker hastily stuffed his wares into shopping bags. Jeffrey took Katya's arm and led her inside.

Bermondsey Market was a rabbit warren of plywood booths and rickety stalls with whitewashed pegboard walls, crammed in what once had been a warehouse for the river traffic. The gathering began each Friday morning at four o'clock and ran until noon. Rents were outrageous, considering the surroundings.

The first buyers to arrive were always the professionals, in and out with time left over for a hot cuppa before heading back to wind up their shop shutters. By nine o'clock the pointed banter of the dealers had been replaced by a babel of languages. Well-heeled aficionados from a dozen countries paraded in furs and jewelry, looking for a buy on the cheap. Their dollars and francs and liras and yen and marks kept the stallholders well fed.

Across the street was the outdoor spillover market, crowded with shopkeepers on the waiting list for a stall in the building. On cold days like this they cursed and suffered and lowered prices to draw customers out into the winter weather.

The market's interior was warmer only by degree. Jeffrey could still see his breath as they strolled around the stalls closest to the wide-open entrance. Stallholders either wore layers of sweaters under voluminous greatcoats or stood around in sweatshirts and jeans and pretended not to feel the cold. Many wore old woolen mittens with the fingers cut off for more dexterity when goods and money changed hands.

Jeffrey strolled and nodded at familiar faces and inspected wares and listened to the swirl of talk, Katya by his side. Hearing a familiar voice, he turned to find Andrew leaning across a glass-topped jewelry case, talking to a young shopkeeper with a street-hardened face. Andrew wore a camel-hair overcoat and cashmere scarf against the chill, but the stylish clothes did not erase the marks of tougher times from his face and bearing. He had been the first to admit Jeffrey into the inner circle of London's antique dealers, a gift of confidence that Jeffrey had never forgotten.

"You don't mind if things come to market by different routes, then," the stallholder asked Andrew.

"No, of course not," Andrew said, his casual tone belying the gleam in his eyes. "Long as it hasn't grown wings and flown out somebody's window with half the local force tailing it, I'm quite pleased with a good piece, however it arrives."

"This is the fellow I came to see," Jeffrey murmured to Katya and motioning toward Andrew. "Why don't you have a look around, then come find us out by the tea wagon when you're done."

"All right." She gave him an eager smile and wandered off.

Jeffrey inched closer to the pair.

"How's it going in Albania, then?" the young man was demanding of Andrew, motioning with his head toward the unseen stalls across the street.

"Cold," Andrew replied. "Let's have a look at the emerald. Is that Indian?"

"Victorian, more like. Done up to suit somebody arriving home after playing tourist out with the natives." He slipped the gold floral design with an emerald heart into Andrew's hand. "Anybody buying anything?"

"What, outside?" Andrew slipped a jeweler's loop out of his pocket and screwed it in. "Too cold to tell. I put this eyepiece in to have a look at a bit of merchandise, and it froze to my skin."

"Scares people off, the cold. I was out there for eight years, next to that old duffer propped up in the corner behind you. Used to give me nightmares, hearing the weather report for a day like this."

"Shows how soft you are."

"Easy for you to say, isn't it? What with the posh West End shop and six little helpers all in a row. Open at ten, close at four, with a two-hour lunch in between. Stretch out in back for a quiet nap after tea."

Jeffrey sidled up. "Sounds like a good life to me."

Andrew turned and showed genuine pleasure. "Hello, lad. Out for a gander, are you?" He handed back the piece to the stallholder, adding, "Let me know about that other little item, will you?"

"Right you are."

"Come on over here, lad," Andrew said, drawing Jeffrey out of the stream of buyers. "Now, what can I do for you?"

"I passed by your shop the other day. Your salesclerk said you were up north at an auction," Jeffrey said. "I might have a buyer for that piece in your window."

"Oh, I couldn't bear to part with that one," Andrew replied automatically. "Was actually thinking of taking it home."

The piece in question was the seventeenth-century oak sideboard Jeffrey had described to Betty. "Do you think it was made in America?"

Andrew's gaze turned shrewd. "You had more than just a gander at it, didn't you?"

"I thought it might be, from its size," Jeffrey replied. "My buyer is from the States. I think she'd go for it. In a big way," he added.

"Really?" Andrew brushed at his sleeve in a calculated display of disinterest. "Pity they couldn't clean this place once a year or so, wouldn't you say?"

"She'd probably be willing to offer upward of thirty thousand for it."

"Dollars or pounds?"

"Pounds."

Andrew shook his head. "I'm so taken with it myself, lad. Tragic, it is. Really don't think I could part with the item."

Jeffrey refused to be driven higher. "But you have to eat."

Andrew sighed his agreement. "I suppose you'll want it carted round to your place, then."

"You don't think I'd send her around to you, do you? Leave me out in the cold?"

"No harm in hoping, is there?" The business done, Andrew permitted himself a grin. "Come on, then. I'll let you buy me a cup of tea. Strongest thing we can get around here, this time of day."

They walked out the back entrance and over to a trailer-stall that sold steaming cups of tea. Andrew accepted a cup and stepped into the relative warmth of an unused loading dock. "You remember our friend Sydney Greenfield?"

"Purveyor to the would-bes and has-beens—sure." Jeffrey permitted himself a smile. "Sydney's all right."

"In a manner of speaking." Andrew nodded. "Saw him the other day. Passing strange it was. Sydney was fitted out in a whole new wardrobe, Saville Row by the looks of it. I asked him what was the occasion. Know what he said?"

"I couldn't imagine."

"No, nor I. Stood right there and told me he'd come into a bit of the folding stuff."

"More than a bit, by the sounds of things."

"All right for some, I told him. Was it legal?"

"What a question."

"Swore up and down it was legit. New clients, he said." Andrew sipped, sighed a sweetened steam, sipped again. "Mate of mine, next shop down but one, said he saw Sydney down Portobello way last week."

Portobello Road was another of the famous weekly London markets. In recent years it had become much more of a tourist event, and therefore much pricier, than the other two. Portobello was on Saturday, Covent Garden on Monday, and Bermondsey on Friday. All others were pretenders to the first ranking.

"Shocked him no end, it did," Andrew continued. "Sydney's been going through some hard times, you know, owed money to half the dealers down there. So happened he was paying them off."

"And he said this new business of his was legit?"

Andrew shrugged. "There he was, my mate said, yapping away with everyone, peeling notes off this roll he couldn't hardly get out of his pocket, it was so big. My mate strolled over and got the big grin, the back slap, like Sydney hadn't been playing a ghost for the past couple of months. Anyway, my mate asked him, where's my five hundred quid. In my pocket, Sydney said, and it's yours on one condition. It's mine anyway, my mate told him. Wait, Sydney said, you'll like this. Spread the word about, I've got a truckload of goods to unload."

"Sydney?"

"Not what you'd call top-quality stuff, Sydney told him." Andrew's face settled into bleak lines. "Heard some tales toward the end of last summer, from a bloke I use sometimes for ornamental work. Told me Sydney came in with a crate of odds and ends, asked him to see what he could do with it. This bloke did a load of patching, came up with a sort of Sheraton-Empire-Chippendale-Florentine bit of old rubbish."

"Is that legal?"

"Long as the seller declares the item for what it is, lad, there's no harm in working puzzles. This bloke's just as hard hit by the recession as the rest of us. Anyway, Sydney started coming in every few days with another patchwork job, been at it ever since. Now he's out about town with money to burn."

"Something smells funny," Jeffrey said slowly.

"Yes, well, it's been hard times for the likes of our Sydney." Andrew tossed his cup into a nearby rubbish bin. "Problem is, I'm afraid he's stepped over the invisible line on this latest caper. Gone from a bit of malarkey to something out and out crooked."

"You sound worried."

"I am. I've always had a soft spot for old Greenfield."

"Me too."

"Yes, thought you did. But it's a short road he's traveling, if he's turned to dealing in the false bits. I don't like the idea of one of our own going down in flames."

Katya chose that moment to look out the back door. She walked toward them, carrying a slender package wrapped in brown paper and bound with twine. Andrew rose from his worried stoop and touched the knot of his tie. "Hello, what's this, then?"

Jeffrey waved her over. "Sorry this has taken so long."

"That's all right." She raised her package. "I found a present for Gregor." She then turned and smiled a greeting to Andrew. "Hello. I'm Katya Nichols."

"You most certainly are." He bowed over her hand, straightened, and said to Jeffrey, "Mount Street's bringing in a different sort of clientele these days, is it?"

"Andrew's a dealer in Kensington," Jeffrey explained to her.

"The dealer in Kensington," Andrew murmured, letting her hand go with reluctance.

"Katya works in my shop."

"If that's all you could think to do with this one, lad, then my estimation of you has just plummeted." Andrew turned back to Katya. "Salaries are much higher over Kensington way, my dear. Shorter hours, much nicer working conditions, better lot of goods, five-hour lunch breaks highly recommended."

She treated him to the sort of smile that did not need to de-scend from her eyes. "And what is your specialty?"

"Any odds and ends the lad here leaves for the rest of us to handle."

"Andrew loves to give me a hard time," Jeffrey explained.

"Hand on my heart," Andrew insisted, "I've never put the lad down. Had enough of that when I did my apprenticeship as an electrician's helper."

"You never were," Jeffrey said.

"Straight up. Put paid to that as soon as I could, too, and never looked back. Gave me all sorts of trouble, that did. Proved a total ruddy disaster."

"So why did you do it?"

Andrew shrugged easily. "The old man said if it was good enough for him and all that. My first day on the job, walked into this house where they had a dog the size of my car. Gave me a bit of a whuff, it did. I played like the space shuttle, shwooosh. Took me thirty seconds to get my feet back on solid ground."

"A bit of a whuff," Jeffrey repeated, smiling at Katya.

"Second assignment," Andrew went on, "we had this lady offer to take me and my mate upstairs. I was married by then, knew my dear would have me guts for garters if I was to go and try that. I thanked her kindly, said there were some pleasures I was meant to forgo in this life." Andrew shuddered at the memory. "Decided then and there I wasn't made for hard labor. Too dangerous."

Jeffrey asked Katya, "Would you like a cup of tea?"

"Love one, thank you."

"How about you, Andrew? One more?"

"Chip off the old concrete, you are."

As he made for the wagon, Jeffrey heard Katya say behind him, "So then you moved into antiques?"

"Well, no, there was a bit more to it than that. What happened was, a couple weeks later I bought the wife a birthday present from a neighbor, a lovely little bit of gold and such. Cost me upward of a hundred quid, it did. That night I started worrying that maybe I'd been took, so I stopped by a mate of mine who worked in this jewelry store. Told me it was early Victorian, offered me nine-fifty on the spot."

Jeffrey returned, handed out the cups, and asked, "What did you end up giving your wife?"

"A brand-new kitchen, can you imagine? 'Course, that was after I spent all I made from that sale and all we had left from the dole going around the neighbors, buying up whatever they had they didn't need. Got took a few times, of course, but did right well in the end."

"So you stayed with jewelry?" Katya asked.

"Bits and pieces, now and then," Andrew replied easily. "I've kept my passion, Victorian mostly. That's what brings me around here."

"You mean you collect for yourself?"

"Oh my, yes. Fact is, lot of dealers start off as collectors. Once they're good and hooked, they find themselves with too many lovelies and strapped for cash. Then along comes something new which they absolutely must have, and they sell a piece they've grown tired of. If they're careful and don't get taken, they find themselves shocked to the very core at how much they make. It hits them then, doesn't it? How maybe here's a way of making pleasure pay off."

"Don't let Andrew fool you," Jeffrey said. "Very few manage not to get taken in this business. He also happens to be a very successful dealer of French Empire furniture and accessories, among other things."

"Why the interest in Victorian jewelry?" Katya asked.

"It was a fussy period, the Victorian era," Andrew replied, with the enthusiasm of a true collector. "It was preceeded by the Georgian, and a very severe style that was indeed. All straight lines and hard angles, nothing for the feminine or the foppish. Soon as the Victorians came, jewelry and furniture and houses all went in for a great load of foppery."

"I heard the railroads had something to do with this change," Jeffrey said.

"Well, perhaps not so much on the style itself, but certainly on its rapid spread. Before, you see, most people had a ten-mile radius which was their entire world, cradle to grave, as it were. All their lifelong, that was as far as their purses and their work would allow them to travel. The railways changed all that. Everyone, right down to a simple carpenter or jeweler or purchaser of a new home, could travel right into London-town and see the sights and learn about the latest fashion. Suddenly they could get ornaments from anywhere in the kingdom."

"Or designs," Katya offered.

"Exactly. Queen Victoria was a marvelous one for jewelry. She wore tons of it herself, yellow gold in the day and white gold at night. After her beloved Prince Albert died, she went in for funeral jewelry in a big way as well. That's done in dark stones, you see, often with strands of hair either enameled or set in lockets, lots of inscriptions, in loving memory of the old so-and-so, what have you. Rings and brooches and great pendants dangling down."

Jeffrey glanced at his watch. "We need to be getting back. I'm opening the shop today."

"Where's your man Kantor, then?"

"You know better than to ask that."

"Right you are, lad. And about that other little item, you didn't hear it from me."

Jeffrey smiled. "What other item?"

———

Jeffrey saw Katya off to her class with a kiss before placing the call to Poland. Conditions were improving; it took less than a half hour to obtain a line to Cracow, and once made the connection was fine.

"Is that you, Jeffrey?" Gregor's heartfelt pleasure could be sensed even over the telephone. Gregor, Alexander's cousin, was a deeply religious gentleman who had escaped from Poland during the war, only to heed what he felt was the Lord's call to return and serve the poor. He also served as Alexander's primary contact in Cracow. He financed numerous charitable efforts through locating long-stored antiques to be sold in the West. "How are you, my dear boy?"

"I'm fine," Jeffrey replied. "It's great to speak with you again."

"I, too, have missed your questing voice. When do you plan to visit with me again?"

"I'm not sure. Alexander should be arriving tomorrow to see about something from the Marian Church for—"

"I know all about the article and the gala. Alexander spoke with me the other evening. I am glad to say that my dear cousin has wisely decided to forgo the exertions of further purchasing trips after this one."

This was news. "He hasn't said anything to me about it."

"He has so much on his mind just now, I doubt seriously if he can remember his own name. But never mind. This will most likely be the last antiques shipment he will arrange for himself. And why not, when he has a perfectly able assistant to see to such matters."

"Then I guess I'll be seeing you sooner than I thought."

"As soon as possible after the gala," Gregor replied. "And nothing could bring me greater pleasure, I assure you. As a matter of fact, I thought that was why you were calling."

"No. I have some news." Jeffrey found it necessary to take several breaths before the band across his chest eased. "I wanted you to know that I'm thinking about asking Katya to marry me."

"My dear Jeffrey," Gregor effused. "How marvelous for you both. Are you asking for my advice?"

"I suppose I am."

"Do it!" Gregor shouted the words over the line. "There. Have I done my duty well?"

"You're sure this is the right thing?"

Gregor laughed. "Ah, my boy, you make me feel young again."

"I guess that means yes."

"Indeed it does. When will you ask her?"

"In about three weeks, after she's completed her exams. That is, I'll do it unless my nerve gives out between now and then."

"I shall pray that it does not. As I shall for your peace of mind, and hers, and for your joyful life together."

"Thanks, Gregor. Thanks a lot. It helps just to know I'm not going into this alone."

"My dear young friend, we are never alone."

"I know that." Jeffrey hesitated, then continued, "At least, sometimes I know it."

"Yet there are other times, moments when you feel most alone," Gregor finished for him. "You wonder who the Father truly is and where He is to be found."

"That's it exactly," Jeffrey agreed, and felt immense relief to have his doubts and fears pushed from the confining space of his heart. "Now that I've started looking, the fear that I won't find God is enormous."

"Do you read the Bible?"

"Every day."

"Do you pray?"

"I try," Jeffrey replied. "I feel as if I'm talking to the wall."

"Have you discussed this with Katya?"

He nodded, to a man a thousand miles away. "She tells me to be patient and keep looking."

"Wise advice from a wise woman."

"She says it's a problem a lot more common to new Christians than the quick-fix preachers would have me believe."

"That's what she called them? 'Quick-fix preachers?'" Gregor laughed delightedly. "You shall make a worthy couple for His work."

"I don't see how I can do much if I can't find Him."

"He will find you, my dear young friend. Never fear. If you search in earnest, then He would withhold His gift of the Spirit only for a purpose. It will all be clear to you soon enough."

"You're not just saying that to make me feel better?"

"My dear Jeffrey." Gregor sounded genuinely shocked. "I would never dream of doing such a thing. When you find your doubts rising, try to remember that the Lord Jesus did not tell His disciples to go out and look for the Spirit."

"He said wait and He will come," Jeffrey finished. "I read about that the other night."

"Perhaps it would also help you to speak to others whose faith you admire. Ask them how they came to find the Father, what special moment stands out in their memory. Learn from their experiences."

"All right. Thanks."

"I thank you. It is always a delight to teach someone who truly seeks to learn. Now, when do you think you will be in Cracow next?"

"A couple of months, I suppose. Right after Alexander's gala."

"Excellent. Anything of utmost urgency my dear cousin can see to while he is here. We will speak more upon your arrival. In the meantime, seek out those who hold fast to faith. Ask them to share the moment of their illumination."

The moment of illumination. Jeffrey liked that phrase. "I will."

"Splendid. And take care of our dear Alexander."

"I'll try. This gala is either driving him crazy or making him happier than he's been in years," Jeffrey said. "It depends on when you catch him."

"The gala, yes. Well, either it is a worthy activity or a harmless pastime."

"You don't mean according to whether or not it makes money?"

"Of course not. Listen to me, Jeffrey. A man can rebuild an entire nation, but if his eyes and ears and heart and mind are tuned to the clamor of his fellowman, his works are empty of eternal blessing."

"So what happens if you can't find God? Do you just stop working?"

"Not at all. You must do three things while you work. First, you must earnestly seek the Lord and never, ever believe that worthy action is a substitute for a daily walk in faith. Second, you must always dedicate your efforts to the Lord and seek His acclaim only. And third—can you guess what the third action is?"

"Love."

"The most crucial element of all," Gregor agreed. "Without love, your greatest effort is but dust blowing in the wind."

"It's really wonderful talking with you like this again," Jeffrey told him.

"Make Christ your teacher, search for a knowledge of divine love," Gregor replied. "And give your darling soon-to-be fiancée my heartfelt best wishes."

Erika found her former colleague, Birgit Teilmacher, fairly comfortable in her position as file keeper in the Dresden archives' new location—an abandoned underground bunker system left over from World War II. Birgit had served as secretary to the director of the women's prison, and anyone who held such a job was both Party member and Stasi informant. But no one had time to investigate secretaries—not yet, anyway. Birgit's punishment for the moment was simply to be relocated and forgotten.

Erika entered the concrete-walled room. "How does it feel, spending eight hours a day underground?"

If Birgit felt any surprise at the unannounced visit, she masked it well. "I wish it were only eight. They've got me doing the work of five people down here." She inspected the other woman's solid girth. "You haven't been sticking to your diet."

Erika shrugged off her knee-length black-leather coat. "It doesn't pay for people in my new profession to be too petite. Gives the jokers ideas."

"Set it down over there." Birgit motioned to a corner filing cabinet. "You really should get another coat. That one makes you look as feminine as a tree trunk."

"It so happens I'm attached to that coat," Erika replied. "It's the only thing I have left from my old life."

"You should have chosen something else." Birgit hefted a vast sheaf of papers. "I'm kept busy these days making records of change. Know what these are? Statistics on abortions. These are the latest hospital records. Abortions are up by over five hundred percent since the Wall came down."

"People get to choose between a new child and a new car," Erika replied. "The new car wasn't available before." She took a seat and asked, "How are you?"

"Enduring." Birgit's features took on a thoroughly bleak cast. "What choice do any of us have these days?"

The Ossies were coming to resent the Wessies their economic invasion in ever-stronger terms. Companies that had been the life-blood of small Ossie communities were being bought up for pennies, with the new owners showing nothing but horror over the factories' condition. The best machines were stripped and often taken back to Western factories, or so the rumors went and the pulp newspapers accused—accusations most people were only too happy to believe. Ossie management and workers had been fired wholesale, with the remaining few required to retrain under Wessie technicians. Wessie workers, brought in at breath-taking salaries to work the best jobs, showed with every word and gesture their scorn for the East—people, land, factories, the lot.

Other companies, now controlled by the West-dominated be-hemoth called the Treuhand, had been declared wasteful or polluting or decrepit or junk and were closed down overnight. A land that had never known even half a percent of unemployment now had forty-three percent of its work force on welfare—at a time when rents had risen by six hundred percent and food prices had jumped almost twentyfold.

On the other side of the vanished border, the West German government leaders faced a nightmarish dilemma. They knew beyond the slightest doubt that unless the situation in the East stabilized before the next election, they would be ousted. Their only answer was to spend as much as possible as fast as possible, and haul the new eastern states up by their bootstraps. Yet in the first two years alone, unification had cost the German people five hundred billion marks—over three hundred billion dollars. Infla-tion had been capped only by introducing a temporary income-tax hike and by raising interest rates to twice the highest level they had been since World War II. A nation of Wessies listened and wondered at the black hole called former East Germany that was bleeding their wealth.

But the Ossies themselves felt they were seeing only the tiniest trickle of all this wealth. Their wage levels, when they could find jobs, remained frozen at forty percent of Wessie workers on the same jobs—and Ossie prices were now at Wessie levels. The Porsche 928s and Mercedes 600s they were seeing with increasing frequency on their newly repaired roads bore Wessie license plates and were driven by their new Wessie bosses.

The Ossie tabloid press took great glee in throwing out infuriating little snippets about who was really growing rich on all this supposed rebuilding. They greeted the Ossies each morning with the news that there was now a five-year waiting list for the hundred thousand dollar BMW 850i. That the West was seeing a boom for new luxury housing like nothing in the country's history. That Cartier jewelers sold more gold and diamonds and emeralds in the former West Germany than in the rest of the world combined.

While this went on, they stood helpless in the face of public shame. Every day, another lake in former East Germany was declared dead from overpollution. Each night, commentators monitored reports on another twenty thousand, thirty thousand, two hundred thousand Ossie employees who had been fired from jobs found to be totally profitless, totally without value to the new German federation. The Ossies sat in their little rooms and felt themselves growing smaller, their lives ever more meaningless. They watched, helpless and failing, as their entire way of life was slowly strangled away.

The Ossies knew what was happening. Years of Communism did not make them dumb, only bitterly suspicious. To their eyes, everything pointed toward the fact that the Ossies were being doled out crumbs, like beggars at a rich man's table.

And daily their resentment grew.

"It was one of the things we learned best, wasn't it," Erika replied. "How to endure."

Birgit did not deny it. "They arrested everyone who worked at the Berlin prison. Everyone. Right down to the—" she hesitated, then settled on "—guards."

"I heard," Erika said, probing softly. "It worries you, does it?"

Birgit shrugged. "So what is this new profession of yours?"

"Driving a taxi."

"Where?"

"Best not to say," Erika replied.

"Under a different name, I suppose."

Erika nodded. "And here you are," she said, "down in a hole."

The Dresden archives used to be kept partly in the Stasi's city headquarters, partly in the Communist Party building, and partly at City Hall. Nowadays, however, the Stasi building was a cultural center, the Communist Party building housed the new regional Ministry of Economics, and the City Hall's archives were being scrutinized by imported Wessie investigators.

This investigation was no easy task. The one product the Communist regime had produced in greatest amounts was paper, and nothing had ever been thrown away. Wessie investigators for one region, when asked to give an approximate date for completing their inquest, laughed and took the reporters on a tour of the two hundred rooms filled with uninspected files. They then told the reporters that more than half the people who should be charged with criminal offenses would escape trial by dying of old age.

There was also a rising tide of Ossie resentment over how many were being hurt, and how badly. The public was now permitted to inspect their own Stasi files, and surprises were frequent and harsh. One woman discovered that her husband of twenty-six years had been a Stasi informer since their engagement. The governor of the state of Thuringen was deposed on accusations of having informed for Stasi, although more than two-thirds of the populace thought he had done an excellent job. A new Ossie member of the German parliament was found to have informed for the Stasi after graduating from college over twenty years ago; the shame of this discovery caused him to commit suicide.

Initial studies suggested that over a third of the Ossie population had informed for Stasi at one time or another. Out of a population of eighteen million, almost six million had at one time or another fed the Stasi's endless appetite for information. Did this mean they all would be threatened with exposure and punishment? Would all families and friendships and working relationships be seared by the light of this new day?

"How can we be treated like criminals?" Birgit was not a large woman, but her wiry form crackled with an energy that made the room seem too small to contain her. "I did what I was told. I followed orders. I pledged my life to the Party. Is this what I deserve?"

"Let us hope you never have to ask those questions of a Wessie judge," Erika said.

Birgit deflated. "I have nightmares."

"Don't we all."

"Not of the past. Of the future."

"What is there for us to fear of the past?" Erika leaned across the desk. "I am working on a way out."

Birgit inspected her former colleague. "You mean money."

Erika nodded. "A lot of it."

"Enough for me?"

"Perhaps."

Birgit inspected the paper-clouded desk, the rough walls with their plastering of clammy concrete, and asked quietly, "What must I do?"

"Are we safe here?"

Birgit gave a humorless laugh. "These walls are half a meter thick. There are seven meters of earth between us and the road overhead. Why would the Wessies bore holes just to bug the archives? They haven't even bothered to give me new ventilation."

Erika said, "I need help locating a certain man. He changed his name after the war, of that we are fairly sure. He was born and raised here in Dresden. Where he moved afterward, I don't know."

"That's all?"

"I have his name. An old picture. His rank in the army during the war."

Birgit grimaced. "Gestapo?"

"No. Transport corps."

"Ah, of course. For movement of treasure. That's it, isn't it?"

Erika remained silent.

"Of course," Birgit repeated. She raised her eyes to the bare bulb overhead. "I could try and find fingerprints, match old records. Everyone had to have prints taken for the new identity cards issued back in the late forties. He was born here?"

"Yes. And lived here until enlisting. The records would still be here?"

"Here or Berlin. You'd be surprised how many survived the bombings. Leave that with me. I still have a few friends."

"How long will it take?"

"As long as I need," Birgit replied. "How much do you pay?"

"Four thousand marks now, more later."

"How much more, how much later?"

"A lot more, hopefully not long from now. We are all feeling the pressure these days."

"It would be nice to receive more now."

"It would be nicer still if we had it."

Birgit examined her. "Can I trust you?"

"You know who I am, you know—" Erika hesitated, then finished with, "you know."

"Let me see your new identification," Birgit demanded.

Erika thought about it, then reached into her shoulder bag and handed over the green Wessie identity card. Birgit examined it carefully, compared it with the professional taxi license Erika also supplied, and made note of Erika's new name and address. "First-class product."

"It ought to be. It cost enough."

"But it will work only so long as you don't try to leave the country."

Erika nodded. This was well known. Stasi had issued over thirty thousand false West German passports during the last year before the Wall fell, as well as about the same number of American passports, and it had proven immensely difficult to determine who owned them. In the early weeks of transition, many files had been lost to a sudden spate of fires. Other paper piles had been fed to the compost heaps of newly avid gardeners, and honey had been discovered coating hard disks in several central computers.

The Wessies were aware of the traffic in false papers, as many Ossies sought to grow new faces and leave behind old lives. The Wessies instituted a policy of checking ID papers at all border crossings. Before, this had been done on a random basis only. Nowadays, even the border guards on trains were equipped with hand-held computer links into which every name and ID number was punched.

"We will need to cross only one time," Erika replied. "I hear the Dutch border is full of holes."

"You think you will make enough from this to disappear forever?"

"Forever is not my concern," Erika said. "A year or two of comfort is as far as I care to look just now."

"Four thousand marks," Birgit said thoughtfully. "Think of what comfort four thousand Wessie marks would have brought under the old regime."

"Under the old regime," Erika replied, "I would not have been asking."

"No, I suppose not." Birgit toyed with her pen. "What if he's dead?"

"Then," Erika replied, "we spend our remaining days dreading every knock at the door, every ring of the phone, every unmarked letter in the post."

Birgit nodded, expecting nothing else. "I will see what I can do."

The day of Alexander's return from Cracow, Jeffrey received a call from Frau Reining, an East German attorney based in Schwerin. She had first contacted them the previous summer, while defending families who had been victimized by the former Communist regime. Since then, she had become a valuable ally in their hunt for rare antiques. The line rained a constant barrage of static as Jeffrey yelled a hello.

"Fräulein Nichols, she is there?"

"In fifteen days," he shouted. Frau Reining spoke a truly awful English. They normally relied on Katya and her fluent German for translation. "She prepares for her exams. You call her apartment?"

"Ach, nein, I wait four, five hours for this line. We try this with no Katya, yes?"

"We try," Jeffrey agreed.

"Have three Stück for you. You understand Stück?"

"I think so. Big schtukes or little?"

"Big. Wood. Old."

"Right. Antique furniture."

"Very beautiful. You buy, yes?"

"I'll have to check them out first."

"What?"

"Yes," Jeffrey surrendered loudly. "I buy."

"Good. Also have other seller. In Erfurt. South. He needs honest man."

"Thank you," he yelled.

"Find one honest man, no need to look for other. You understand? This man, he too is honest. I know."

"I believe you." He cleared his throat, shouted, "You want me to come to Schwerin?"

"Not here. Erfurt. You know?"

"No, but I'm sure I can find it on a map."

"What?"

"I find."

"Fräulein Nichols, she know it. Capital of Thuringen." Through the static he heard the sound of a match being lit, of smoke being drawn. "Man is Herr Diehl. Spell Dieter-Igloo-Europa-Heinrich-Ludwig. Siegfried Diehl. Godly man. You understand?"

"I think so," he replied.

"He suffered much. The Communists make him pay much. Too much. More than . . . how do you say tenth for church?"

"Tithe."

"Yes. Communists no stop at tenth. Or half. They take all. Job. Pension. School for children. Home. He pay much for religion. Good man. You see."

Jeffrey scribbled, hoped the spelling was close enough for Katya to figure out. "All is ready for me now?"

"Yes. You go with Fräulein Nichols. Siegfried, he has no English." She coughed, shouted over the static, "When you go?"

"We have a lot going on right now. I'll have to speak with Mr. Kantor, but I—"

"What?"

"Four or five weeks, maybe."

"Not sooner?"

"I don't think so."

"So. I tell Siegfried."

"You're sending your antiques to," he hesitated, not wanting to name the town, "Siegfried's shop?"

"Pliss?"

"Your schtukes." Jeffrey was growing hoarse.

"Ah. Yes. With Siegfried. You go, look for shop on bridge."

His hand hovered over the page. "He works near a bridge?"

"Not near. On. On bridge. Shop on bridge. Called Glock, means bell in German. Look for Bell Shop on bridge."

That evening Jeffrey made his way on foot to the Grosvenor
Apartments, a red-brick Victorian structure overlooking Hyde Park.
The floors had been converted into luxury apartments that rented
by the week or month. Three weeks before departing for Poland,
Alexander had let out his Geneva apartment and made this building
his permanent residence. It was Jeffrey's first visit to Alexander's new
home. The old man had insisted on being allowed to, as he put it,
let the dust settle before inviting in guests.

Alexander answered the door. "My dear young friend, my
nephew, come in. Come in."

"Thanks. Welcome back." Jeffrey took a step and pointed to
the delicate French commode decorating the entrance hall. "I know
that piece."

"Don't go around pricing the furniture, that's a good boy."

"I was wondering what happened to it. I thought I had a buyer
lined up, then I come in one morning and, poof, it's gone. You took
it to Switzerland, didn't you? And now it's back here."

"Yes, well, that's one of the benefits of ownership, isn't it?"

"And the sofa there. Isn't that part of our Biedermeier set? Yes.
I see the secretary in your living room."

"My dear young man, I'll thank you to turn off the calculator
in your eyes and drop the urge to call a moving van. Now come in."

Jeffrey silently took note of the two late medieval tapestries
adorning the walls where the foyer opened into the living area. He
had a client who was still asking about those.

Two long steps separated the white marble foyer from the living area's split-beam floor. The furniture was sparse, each piece set
on silk Persian carpets and spaced to be viewed individually, like
fine jewelry displayed on beds of multicolored velvet. Tall windows
at the room's far end overlooked Park Lane and the park beyond.
Noise from the constant traffic speeding by seven floors below was
reduced to a steady hum.

"This is beautiful," Jeffrey declared.

"I'm so glad you like it. Sit down. Can I offer you anything? A coffee, perhaps?"

"Coffee's fine, thanks." Jeffrey selected an eighteenth-century Dutch high-backed chair upholstered in white silk. "I'm sorry you wouldn't let me meet you at the airport."

"The older I become, the more I am inclined to suffer through my little foibles in private," Alexander replied. "And how is your dear lady?"

"All right, as far as I know. I talk to her every evening, but we won't be seeing each other for another two weeks."

"Yes, she has exams, doesn't she? How are they progressing?"

"All right, she thinks. She sounds very tired, though."

"I'm sure she must be."

Jeffrey cleared his throat, decided to have it out while his nerves were still intact. "I'm thinking about asking her to marry me."

"My dear boy!" Alexander's face lit up with genuine pleasure. "What absolutely splendid news."

"If she'll have me."

"Of that I have no doubt. I am most pleased with this excellent decision on your part, as well as with all that is behind it."

"A queasy stomach," Jeffrey offered. "Clammy hands. Unsteady legs."

"Divine inspiration, true love," Alexander countered. "A joining for life. I wish you every success."

"Thanks, Alexander."

"Now, then." Alexander lowered himself into a chair. "As a pre-wedding gift, you must allow me to bestow upon you an engagement ring."

Jeffrey sat absolutely still. "It's too much," he finally said.

"Nonsense. I have the perfect item in mind. It was one of my very first purchases after the war, and I have held on to it for sentimental reasons."

Faced with the old gentleman's delight, Jeffrey swallowed his protests. "You did the same thing when my grandparents became engaged."

Alexander's strong eyes glimmered. "How kind of you to remember."

"My grandmother told me about it when she heard I was coming to work for you." Jeffrey faced the old man squarely. "That was one of the best things that's ever happened to me, Alexander."

"You do me much kindness." It was the old gentleman's turn to pause and taste from his cup. "Such a mood should not be dampened by the mundane. I propose we leave our business affairs until later."

"Fine with me."

"Excellent. I do have something rather fascinating that you might care to hear about this evening."

"The pieces for the gala," Jeffrey guessed.

"Exactly. The altar and painting from Rokovski are indeed splendid. The chalice from the Marian Church, however, is something truly unique."

"Chalice is another word for the cup used in the Communion, isn't that right?"

"Ah, that is your Protestant upbringing." Alexander topped up his and Jeffrey's cups from a sterling silver coffeepot. "The development of the chalice is a story steeped in two thousand years of mystery and intrigue."

"Great," Jeffrey said, his enthusiasm undisguised. "I love the stories in this business almost as much as I do the pieces themselves."

"Do you indeed?" Alexander nodded approval. "I am indeed happy to know that you share my love of mystery."

"Sometimes it wakes me up at night," Jeffrey confessed. "I'll lie there and see pages of the books go through my head. I think of these incredibly beautiful pieces, and feel as if I'm reaching across the centuries to talk with the makers, learn their secrets, share with them the pleasures of creation."

"It is a passion that has never failed to ignite the fires in me," Alexander agreed. "I have wondered if this is what fuels for some the desire of acquisition. For myself, it has never been necessary to hold on to any particular item. To find is more than enough. To watch it pass through my hands, and for a brief moment to be a part of its history, that is adequate. I suppose my earlier experiences have left me too aware of the brevity of life and the transient nature of all possessions. But of that we shall not speak tonight." He smiled at Jeffrey. "Tonight we shall revel in the mysteries."

"Sounds good to me."

"Excellent. Then tell me of your favorite piece, my boy. Make it live for me."

"Favorite. . . ." Jeffrey settled into his chair, leaned his head on the back rest. "That's a hard one."

"Do not speak of the mundane. Reach back into the shrouded mists of time and describe what has so held you enthralled."

"There's a piece in the shop's basement right now that I'm holding for Betty," Jeffrey said. "Ever since it arrived, I haven't been able to get it out of my mind."

Alexander stripped the foil off a long Davidoff, snipped the end, struck a long match. "Some of my vices have proven more difficult to leave behind than others. I do hope you won't mind."

"You know I enjoy the scent," Jeffrey replied. "As to somebody else's vices, if I ever reach perfection myself, maybe I'll feel I've got room to criticize."

"Thank you." When the cigar was well lit, Alexander leaned back in his chair, set his feet on the stool, and retreated behind his fragrant cloud. "Carry on, Jeffrey."

"The piece was made in America," he began. "I'm almost positive of that. But it's an exact replica of an altar table I found in a book on the Cambridge churches, only smaller. The Cambridge altar was made in the days of King Henry VII, when the Church of England was formed by a king who wanted a son and heir so badly he was willing to break with Catholic Rome and force an entire country to accept a new doctrine."

"Excellent," Alexander murmured. His only feature which showed clearly through the fumes were his eyes, colored like the smoke and lit bright as the cigar's burning tip.

"The way I imagine it," Jeffrey went on, "there was a man who lived then. A truly gifted man, who could take the hardest of oaks and feel the veins and trace the patterns buried within the wood. He was a man of faith who tried to follow the Word, and he was troubled by the goings-on in the house of God."

Alexander leaned forward. "His name?"

Jeffrey thought a moment, decided, "Matthew."

Alexander settled back. "Go on."

"Matthew was an artist of wide repute. In fact, he became so well known for the quality of work that even the great bishop in Cambridge heard his name. He was called in to make this new altar table in commemoration of some great earthly event.

"Matthew knew that the church was notorious for declaring artists' work to be donations and paying poorly and slowly. He was also aware that to refuse someone as powerful as the bishop was to court death. But more importantly, Matthew wanted to contribute his work to such a great and holy place as the Cambridge Cathedral. Matthew accepted the task. And he put his very best effort into this work.

"He sat there day after day, praying and meditating on the structure that would house his piece, the building with which his work would need to wed. He sketched the church's medieval stained-glass windows. Then he sketched the cathedral's great cross, which was made around the year eleven hundred. And as he worked, he listened to the talk that swirled around him.

"He heard the church officials whisper gossip, tales and politics and subterfuge and things of this earth, which he felt had no place in the worship of his Lord. In time he began work on the actual cabinet, but he was a very troubled man.

"He carved the front panels as a series of reminders, calling all who served from the table to remember the One they served. He harkened back to the earlier days, when faith was the reason for their gathering, not the words of earthly kings. He carved the cross. He carved the apostles as they appeared in stained-glass windows made when the church was young. And when the piece was done, he stayed to see Mass celebrated upon his creation, and then he left the cathedral, never to return."

"My dear Jeffrey," Alexander said quietly. "You surprise me."

"Mathew had a son," Jeffrey went on as if Alexander had not spoken, "who took his father's name and trade. In time he passed both on to his own son, along with the story of the Cambridge altar. The grandson grew in stature and talent to match that of his grandfather, and shared with him his dislike for the church's earth-bound concerns. As he grew older, his dislike for the church's tainted ways grew so strong that Matthew decided to leave his home and everything he had known behind and take his family to America. But before he left, he traveled back to the Cambridge Cathedral and made careful sketchings of his grandfather's altar.

"Throughout that long voyage, the storms raged and threatened to consign him and his wife and his children to the bitter depths. He suffered during that trip. There is no question of that in my mind. He suffered badly. The food was terrible, the cold almost unbearable, the wet and the stink their constant companions. He and his family were not oceangoing folk, and at times their seasickness made them wish one of those huge waves would swamp their little vessel and put an end to their trials.

"Matthew and his family arrived in the Virginia colony just as a new church was being built. One much smaller and simpler than the Cambridge Cathedral, but filled with the Spirit that had called to his grandfather's heart. Matthew had no money, only his tools and talent and the desire that burned in his breast. His contribution to the new church was yet another altar table, one miniaturized to fit the smaller surroundings. But the panels were exactly the same, Alexander. Exactly the same cross, the same cup, the same apostles.

"And when Matthew looked upon his finished work, he knew peace in his heart. He knew then that his decision and the voyage and the new beginnings were right. Here he and his family had found a home where their lives could be dedicated to worshiping God, not to men's unending struggle for power."

Jeffrey leaned back, went on, "There's one more thing. The legs of this piece were carved with a symbol of the man's own struggle. An interlocked series of fish traced down each leg, but set on the inside face, where few were likely to see them. The secret sign of the fish, first used by the Christians of the Roman labyrinths."

The room was silent save for Alexander's occasional puffs. Then, "I congratulate you, Jeffrey. You have made it live for me."

The old gentleman stood. "Come. I have made reservations for us at the Connaught. Over dinner I will share with you a mystery of my own."

A biting wind kept them company during the walk from Alexander's apartment to the Connaught. Yet it was a clear night, and the air tasted dry and clean. Jeffrey delighted in the city and the companionship. Alexander walked alongside him, puffing contentedly on his cigar, eyeing the buildings and the passing people with a lively interest.

As they turned the corner onto South Audley Street, Jeffrey asked, "How is Gregor?"

"All right, I suppose." Alexander fanned his smoke with an irritated motion.

"What's the matter?"

"My dear cousin does not approve of my activities."

"You mean, the gala?"

"I'm sure I don't know," Alexander replied peevishly. "I have not asked, and he has not said. All I can tell you is that he continues to challenge me with what he leaves unsaid."

Jeffrey could not help but smile. "I know what you mean."

"Do you? How reassuring. I thought it was perhaps the voice of my conscience that was nagging at me."

"Maybe that's why Gregor gets under your skin," Jeffrey offered. "Because he says what you're already thinking on a deeper level."

"Whatever the reason, he is positively the most unsettling man I have ever met." Alexander tossed his cigar aside. "He is typically very blunt about matters dealing with the state of my soul. This new reticence of his has been most disturbing."

"Disturbing." Jeffrey nodded agreement. "That's exactly what he does to me."

"Does he indeed?"

"Every time we speak. He's always saying what I least expect to hear. And what unsettles me most."

"And still you turn to him?"

Jeffrey sought a way to express what he felt. "Somehow just being around him gives me the confidence to take the next step."

Alexander stopped on the Connaught doorstep and stared at Jeffrey a moment. "It is reassuring to hear that I do not face these unanswered questions alone."

"There's a world of difference between knowing what I need to do and doing it," Jeffrey replied.

"There is indeed," Alexander agreed. "Nonetheless, it pleases me immensely to know that I face this quest with a companion." He opened the door, motioned Jeffrey through. "Come. Let us dine."

The Connaught occupied a corner of Carlos Place, which stood a mere jot and tittle away from the clamor of Berkley Square. Its view was of nothing more appealing than a pair of city streets and a matchbook-sized patch of green flanked by waiting taxis. The hotel's interior was all ancient wood and rich decorum. The public area was a dozen rooms laid out as a series of tastefully decorated formal parlors. Guests of the hotel and restaurant, many of whom continued to frequent the establishment for decades, walked across creaking floorboards and spoke in quiet, cultured tones. Ties and jackets for gentlemen, and appropriately refined dress for ladies, were required at all times.

The restaurant reminded Jeffrey of the leather-and-wood-lined study of a very wealthy man; the original oils adorning the walls were worth millions. The bill of fare was unabashedly English and leaned heavily toward succulent roasts, platters of steamed vegetables, ruby-toned clarets, and thick treacley desserts.

Once they had ordered and were again alone, Alexander confessed, "I have known a growing pressure within me to come to terms with these new demands of faith—and yet, so often, I feel that I am groping in the dark."

"I find faith mysterious too," Jeffrey admitted.

"Well, then," Alexander replied, "perhaps we shall have the pleasure on other cold nights of comparing our walks in the mists of misunderstanding. But for now, I need to speak of other matters."

Alexander lowered his voice. "Recently, I have recognized that my strength and days are precious commodities, and health a gift that must be harbored. I therefore intend, as time goes on, to leave an increasing amount of the purchasing and travel to your capable hands. I shall reserve my time and strength for those pursuits that have not received the attention they should during earlier years. That is, if you do not object."

"I'm deeply honored," Jeffrey replied.

"On the contrary, it is I who am grateful to the Lord with whom I am just beginning to have a nodding acquaintance for gracing my latter years with such a friend as you." He took a brisker tone. "I shall remain increasingly in London, minding the shop while you are away. Thus the reason for this flat. As you accept these new responsibilities, I should hope that you would take advantage of my experience."

"And wisdom," Jeffrey finished for him. "Of course I will."

"Excellent." Alexander leaned back as the waiter set down his plate. "Now, let us turn our attention to something more in tune to this splendid repast."

"The chalice," Jeffrey reminded him. He nodded his thanks to the waiter and took a first whiff of fragrant steam as the silver dome over his plate was lifted.

"Precisely. The chalice has a most interesting history," Alexander said. "It is one of the few elements of Christianity that has fascinated me over the years."

Jeffrey could not help but smile. "We're talking about an antique. Of course you liked it."

Alexander did not deny it. "Part of the joy of collecting is the wealth of legends that spring up around the items. The older the piece, the more enchanting the stories. Imagine, if you will, that some magnificent object has stood in one corner or another, protected by nothing more than its owner's greed or love of art—"

"Or both," Jeffrey offered.

"I will thank you not to interrupt the flow of history," Alexander said crossly. "Now look what you've done. I've forgotten what it was I wanted to speak about."

"Greed?"

"Ah, yes. History. Thank you. This object has stood surrounded by intrigue and wars and power struggles, heard secrets spoken from lips whose commands sent hundreds of thousands into mindless battle, observed the endless march of time."

"If it only had eyes," Jeffrey murmured.

"You have the romance of a horse's nether regions," Alexander snapped.

"Sorry," Jeffrey said, hiding his grin behind his glass. "Just slipped out."

"It must be something they put in American baby formula. Saps away the ability to wax lyrical about anything but the color green on its money."

"This was interesting, it really was," Jeffrey soothed. "You were going to say something about the chalice?"

"Are you sure you can stay awake for another few moments? Keep your mind off your bank balance?"

"I try not to think on that too much. Red ink scares me."

"The legend of the chalice is as old as Christianity itself. It began with Joseph of Arimathea, the wealthy Jew who was granted care of Christ's body after the crucifixion. The story goes that Joseph was also given the cup that Christ had used at the Last Supper, the one which held the wine that Jesus declared was His blood, and from which the apostles all drank. As Joseph washed the Lord's body, some blood flowed from His wounds, and Joseph caught this blood in that vessel.

"When the Jewish authorities discovered that Christ's body had disappeared from the tomb, they frantically began a search for a scapegoat. This makes perfect sense, you see—that's why I think there might be a grain of truth to the legend. An essential element of their desire to kill Jesus was to end the turmoil caused by His claim to be the Messiah. Now, if His body had disappeared, then His followers could easily either proclaim that He had not died, or that He had risen.

"At that point, therefore, the authorities were not looking for answers; they had no time for such niceties. They were looking for someone upon whom blame for this misdeed could be publicly laid. And Joseph was the perfect scapegoat. He was rich, he had been identified as a follower of Jesus, and he was as well known in some circles as are the rich of today. In other words, he was not some nobody just pulled off the street—perhaps that is why the Lord's body was entrusted to him in the first place.

"Whatever the reasons, Joseph was seized by the authorities, accused of stealing the body, thrown into prison, and denied food. After several days of this harsh treatment, according to the legend, Joseph received a visitation from the risen Christ, who was said to have entrusted the cup to him, along with instructions to share the secret of the communion with all believers.

"Joseph remained in the cell for forty years, fed by a dove that came every night and dropped bread into the cup. When he was finally released, in A.D. 70, he immediately left Jerusalem on a trip that was filled to the brim with adventures. He made his footsore way to England and finally settled in Avalon, the Celtic name for the heavenly other-world, located in what today is known as Glastonbury.

"Joseph then received another vision, which instructed him to establish a church on that site and spend his remaining days sharing communion with all who came seeking truth. And it is there, my young friend, that the shroud of time falls over the legend until it is revived in the days of King Arthur."

"The Grail," Jeffrey said. "You're telling me about the Holy Grail, aren't you?"

"Precisely. In very early medieval times, the idea of the Grail fell into disfavor with the church. Alchemists, as magicians of that day were known, began to say that the Grail was not a cup at all, but rather a hollowed-out piece of stone called *lapis exillas*, or *lapis lapsus ex caelis*, which translates as 'the stone fallen from heaven.' This stone was said to have remarkable properties, healing anyone who touched it and stopping the aging process for anyone who kept hold of it. Great wizards were said to remain unbounded by time through tying a portion of this grail stone around their necks. So long as it remained upon their persons, the only sign they would show of passing years was the whitening of their hair. Their bodies would remain locked to the age they had been when first touching the stone.

"Naturally, the church was less than pleased by the rise of such heretical nonsense, especially when it was supposedly connected to the person of Christ. So they split the concept of the Grail, and all the legends attached to it, from the concept of a chalice, or the cup used in taking Communion."

Alexander folded his napkin and set it beside his empty plate. "And now, if you would be so good as to come with me, I have something back in the apartment that I wish to show you."

Jeffrey rose to his feet. "You left the Polish pieces in your apartment?"

"Just the chalice, and just until tomorrow," Alexander replied, and led him from the room. "The other pair will arrive closer to the gala event. Security in my building is quite good, I assure you. But in any event, I will settle the chalice into one of our shop's display cases. That is, after it has been photographed by a professional. I have decided to use it as the centerpiece for my invitations."

The wind had abated by the time they left the restaurant. After the chamber's overly warm confines, the dry, crisp air was invigorating. They strolled at a comfortable pace along quiet city streets, the streetlights' golden glow splashing against centuries-old facades and creating an aura of different evenings and other eras.

"The curate at the Marian Church was decidedly one of the strangest characters I have dealt with in years," Alexander told him as they walked.

"How so?"

"He had quite the most remarkable eyes I have ever seen. Almost fanatical in their brilliance."

"You didn't call him weird just because of the way he looked at you."

"I did not say weird at all, and no, it was not just his eyes. There was an aura of strangeness about the man. Something I can't quite put my finger on. As though he dwells in worlds that no other mortal could fathom."

Jeffrey smiled. "I hear another story in the making."

"Indeed. My entire encounter with the gentleman was quite remarkable."

=====

The Marian Church's rectory was a centuries-old stone cottage, connected to the cathedral and to Cracow's main plaza by a broad cobblestone way. Alexander used his umbrella handle to rap sharply on the stout oaken door, which was swiftly opened by the curate himself.

Curate Karlovich was a wild, Rasputin-like figure. A man of astonishing intensity, he was tall and slender, with thick black hair as disheveled as the beard that cascaded in unruly curls down his front. He was dressed completely in black—black sweater, black trousers, black thick-soled shoes. On his left hand he wore an enormous gold ring, which he tapped on whatever surface was nearest in accent to his words. There was a disturbing aura about the man, evident from the first moment of their contact.

"Mr. Kantor! Greetings, greetings!" He leaned forward with outstretched hand. "Dr. Rokovski told me I should expect you this morning. Indeed, I cannot tell you how very opportune your visit is."

"Thank you. I imagine Dr. Rokovski explained—"

"Yes, of course! I am sure a man of your discernment will very much appreciate what I am about to show you. Please follow me." The curate turned and hurried through an arched wooden door, down an ancient stone-lined hallway, and into the Marian Church. He led Alexander to the center of the nave, genuflected slightly, and waved Alexander toward a massive pillar in the left corner.

An elaborately carved staircase encircled the front half of the pillar, leading up to one of the church's three medieval podiums. Karlovich unlocked a small door that had been hollowed from the back of the same pillar, the wood bowed so as to fit the pillar's gradual curve. He switched on a dim light and pointed Alexander down a set of very steep, very narrow stairs. Alexander lowered his head and made his way gingerly downward. Above and behind him, Karlovich slammed the door with a resounding boom, locked it, and hastened down to the cellar landing.

"Please come this way," Karlovich announced. He moved swiftly along a cave-like passage carved from the solid stone upon which the church stood.

"How old is this tunnel?" Alexander asked, struggling with the too-small confines, the coffin-still air, the meager lighting, and the strangeness of it all.

"A thousand years, perhaps two. Perhaps even more. Its age is a mystery as complete as the reason behind it first being carved." The ancient stone bounced and jumbled around the words that were spoken in electric haste. "I suppose it goes without saying that this place is closed to the public. In fact, very few of our church officials have access here. We cannot be too careful with these treasures."

"I quite agree," Alexander replied, walking with one shoulder twisted slightly back in order not to rub against the passageways' narrow confines.

"I have worked on my own here for nearly twenty years," Karlovich said. "Sometimes I think I am alone in my appreciation of these things—their beauty and their intrinsic value."

"Dr. Rokovski has told me your collection is most impressive." He was immensely relieved when the tunnel widened and ended against a gate of iron bars.

"Yes, Rokovski would understand. But most people, they think the job of a church curate is to keep the candlesticks counted and the pews dust free." His keys jangled as he fitted one into the gate's lock and twisted. "Here we are."

Alexander peered beyond the elaborate wrought-iron gate and made out a crude but spacious semicircular gallery. "This place has quite an eerie feeling to it."

"Indeed. Some centuries ago, this chamber served as a crypt." The gate shuddered its protest as Karlovich shouldered it aside. "There may still be a few bones around here, for all I know."

Karlovich pointed toward a sarcophagus no more than five feet long, its time-worn stone top carved with the image of a medieval knight. "Come have a seat on my little bench."

Reluctantly Alexander did as he was instructed, saying a silent apology to whoever's remains rested within.

The curate approached a series of crude wooden panels that covered the three opposing walls. They were made of ancient oak planking, banded together with long iron bars whose ends made up hinges on one side and locks on the other. It required a pair of skeleton keys, each almost a foot long, to unlock the central double panel, and all of Karlovich's strength to move the two massive doors aside.

Alexander squinted through the dust raised by Karlovich's effort and saw an expanse of rusting wire-mesh screens. Karlovich reached into the upper recesses and flicked an unseen switch. At once the cages' interiors were illuminated.

Alexander leapt forward at the sight.

Karlovich was clearly pleased with the reaction. "I did not think you would be disappointed with my little display."

"Disappointed?" Alexander said, his voice catching. "This is such treasure as dreams are made of."

The hollow enclosure held hundreds of gold and silver items. Each was worthy to be a centerpiece for a major museum's religious art collection, yet here they were crammed together like cheap souvenirs in an Arab bazaar. Alexander saw crosses and carvings and statues and reliquaries and icons and chalices. Most were heavy with jewels—pearls and coral and amber, emeralds the size of grapes, giant rubies carved in the crudely uneven facets of very ancient times. Many were adorned with intricate patterns of semiprecious stones.

"You are looking for one special item, yes?" Karlovich unlocked one of the smaller wire-screen doors. "Something very special for your fund-raising efforts in London."

"That is correct," Alexander replied. His breath came in short bursts, as though a giant hand had clamped itself around his chest.

"Something that would capture the imagination, symbolize the sacred, and impress upon these potential benefactors the importance of collecting and preserving such works. A chalice, perhaps." Karlovich reached into the recesses. "We are not just talking about art. We are speaking about our religion and our tradition."

"I find these chalices incredibly striking," Alexander agreed, striving to keep his voice level, to keep the pleading from his tone. "Perhaps not as fragile as the other pieces."

"Then a chalice it shall be." Karlovich pulled out a heavily carved chalice of solid gold, almost eighteen inches high. "Might I present you with a personal favorite. This dates from the end of the fifteenth century, when Cracow was the royal capital of the great Polish-Lithuanian empire and this church was the seat of worship for the patriarchs and kings of the age."

"A splendid choice," Alexander said, fighting the urge to reach forward, hold the chalice in his own hands, examine it more closely.

"It is, of course, made of hammered gold. The filigree at the base here is exquisite, wouldn't you agree? We believe it was made here in the vicinity of Cracow. At one time there were rumors that it originated in an Italian city-state, but nothing has substantiated that so far as I know. Fifteenth century, that much is certain. The shape and size is very typical for that era."

Rising from the octagonal base was a slender pillar whose lines gracefully joined with a wreathlike central carving. Above this, an inverted crown was fashioned into the base of the cup itself. The rim held a smooth, highly polished finish.

Karlovich held the chalice up before his dark, gleaming eyes and stared at it as though hypnotized. "A chalice," he murmured. "Yes. The Holy Grail. The circle of the sun, of wholeness, of completion. The mystical symbol of man's search for continuity and perfection. Yes, it is all here in a chalice. Here the wine is placed for the mystery of Communion, that we might drink and share in the eternal promise and thus come full circle."

Reverently he handed the chalice to Alexander. "Guard it well."

still don't see why you put so much stock in what that little mole with the big head says," Erika said.

"Not mole," Kurt replied. "Ferret. He's the most ferocious man I've ever met."

Erika laughed at that. "You want to sell me for an idiot."

"It's the truth, I tell you. He gets his teeth into something and he never lets go. Never. He'd take on an elephant, know it'll probably kill him in the end, and still never let up."

"Sounds suicidal."

"You don't understand," Kurt said with unaccustomed patience. "There's method to his madness. Ferret's built himself a reputation, see. Nobody took him on. *Nobody*. Maybe they didn't like him or want to work with him, but even then they left him alone. The Ferret stayed safe and dry no matter which way the winds blew."

"Until now."

"Yes, well, these aren't winds, are they? More like an eruption."

They were driving the Schwerin-to-Berlin autobahn in a nondescript rental truck. Their progress was slowed to a crawl by the snowy slush and by the two emblems of East joining West— perpetual roadwork and traffic.

"Ferret and I," Kurt went on, "we've been together fourteen years. I've never seen a mind like his, not even in the snakes at the top. He wants to stay out of the light, though. He's fanatic about that. That's why I know I can trust him. He pushes me to the front, so I keep him hidden."

"What about me?"

"We thought you'd fit in, or we wouldn't be driving out here together."

"Speaking of which, I don't see why you need me tonight."

"Let's just say helping out with matters like this is part of the deal."

"An obligation."

Kurt shook his head. "Think of it as a favor."

"A favor is something I can turn down."

"Not if you're smart."

He was doing it again, hinting at something without ever saying anything outright. She kept her voice casual. "So, what does Ferret have his teeth into now?"

Kurt took his time replying. "He's been going through those old records ever since I met him. I thought he was crazy, just a weird little guy spending all night reading garbage files from just after the war. Called it his hobby. Said he was putting together puzzles."

"Booty," she guessed. "He's after the Nazi booty. I heard it was all myth."

"Some of it was. Most of the real goods went with the ones who survived and fled to South America. The Odessa, that's no fable. Ferret traced a dozen or so of these puzzles, followed them all the way to Argentina or Paraguay. A couple of times he found something he'd been searching for in auction catalogs, maybe traced the seller back to a Gomez Schumann in Montevideo. Crazy how all those old Nazis gave their children Spanish first names."

"The treasure," Erika reminded him.

"Soon as one piece was identified," Kurt went on, "Ferret called the puzzle finished and moved on. He used his title to send off for other such records and start a new search. He spent all his free time searching. His flat was a kitchen, a fold-up table, a mattress, and three rooms of papers."

"Why not just blackmail the Nazis living in South America?"

"No future in that. They have a reputation for nailing anybody who gets too close. Stuck to their old ways. No, Ferret's been after something *clean*. Something with a future."

"After all these years." Erika shook her head. "You really think there's something left?"

"Something big." Kurt had on his grim, bloodless smile. "Big enough to relocate us permanently."

Erika examined his face. Sweeping lines of rain-flecked light streaked Kurt's face from shadow to parchment yellow and back again. "You don't know what it is, do you?"

"I know enough."

"The Amber Room, that's all," she pressed. "I heard him the same as you. I looked it up—know what I found? Amber is petrified tree sap. That's what you're looking for? A room made from old resin?"

Kurt shook his head. "We're looking for freedom and the money to enjoy it with."

"How can you sound so sure about something that's nothing more than rumor? If it's real, why haven't the Russians found it already?"

"Palm trees," Kurt mumured. "I've always wanted to live where I could catch my own fish and drink rum all day."

Erika leaned back in her seat, stared out at the slush-lined autobahn. "I don't believe this."

"Sleeping on the beach," Kurt continued. "Watch the stars through swaying palms. Hear strange bird calls."

"I've gotten hooked up with a pair of clowns."

"Turn the color of old leather and grow a beard. Be a legend to the tourists," Kurt said. "Watch sunsets and strolling girls in small bikinis."

"Who is in charge of this circus, you or Ferret?"

"Drinks with bunches of fruit stuck in the top. You remember the so-called fruit we used to get? Oranges from Cuba the size of olives and stuffed with seeds. I was ten years old before I saw my first banana."

"Where are we going anyway? Can you tell me that much?"

Kurt signaled his exit, took the snow-covered ramp slow and easy. "It doesn't matter," he replied. "Just look ferocious and keep the boys honest. You're probably real good at that."

It was amazing, Kurt thought as he watched the guy stomp and slip over frozen muddy ground toward him. Put a red star on his cap brim and he could be coming straight from the other side.

"I ain't no spy," the guy growled in English. He had the slightly seedy look of quartermaster sergeants the world over. His American uniform was crumpled, his boots loose-laced and grimy. An enormous beer gut was held in place by a strained webbing belt. A two-day growth of beard peppered his face. Teeth the color of old ivory chomped on the shreds of an ancient stogie. A bluish web of spidery veins spread out across flabby cheeks from a dedicated drinker's nose. Knuckles were scarred by the same fights that had chipped segments from his trio of heavy rings.

But what kept Kurt from worrying about his own health, standing in a frozen empty clearing in a stretch of forest halfway to Berlin, was the avarice gleaming in the quartermaster's eyes.

"Ain't got nothing against unloading butts before us Yanks pull out." The cigar was unplugged long enough for the quartermaster to spit a long brown stream onto the iron-hard earth. "But I ain't no spy."

Kurt knew the man was talking about the enormous trade in black market American cigarettes that was going on before the bases closed.

The clearing was turned a whitish silver by headlights from two trucks. Behind the lights, ghostly half figures moved in stealthy haste, slipping and cursing on the icy earth and sending long plumes of frozen breath into the starry sky.

Kurt stood with all the patience he could muster. The quartermaster's accent was so thick that he could barely make out the man's words as English. And he knew from experience that the man wouldn't understand anything Kurt tried to say in return. Kurt's English was rudimentary at best, learned from books and not from practice. In his former life, there had been few opportunities to converse with native English speakers. He just stood and waited for the quartermaster to finish his grumbling protests so they could get down to business.

The collapse of the Berlin Wall was beginning to show effects in areas further and further afield, like ripples spreading out from a stone dropped in a pond. Something big enough to uncover the rotting muck at the bottom of the pond.

The Soviet empire, with its iron girdle of vassal states, no longer posed a threat to the free world. The Americans, therefore, were pulling out of Berlin in a very big way. Orders came down the line two or three times a week, whittling away at what once had been the greatest concentration of American military anywhere outside the States. Some garrisons had been stripped to the bone. Others had been shut down entirely.

The entire spy apparatus, listening stations and all, was being torn down and packed up and shipped a thousand miles to the east, sometimes much farther. Stations were being planned for formerly unheard-of sites, borderlands in Poland and Czechoslovakia, even inside Russia, and pointed toward China. Old hands read orders containing their new postings and shook their heads in amazement as their universe was redefined—then got busy with their packing.

Some items, however, were not to be removed in the mass exodus. It was decided, for instance, that it would be easier to restock a minor item like cigarettes at the new locations than to move the supplies already in Berlin. But this relatively minor decision was more complex than it seemed. American soldiers were per capita the largest group of smokers in the United States. Added to that was the fact that there were somewhere around half a million American soldiers, diplomats, agents, and dependants in and around Berlin, and *all* of them bought their butts at the PX's vastly reduced prices

Given these facts, a minor logistics decision took on somewhat larger implications.

Like how to liquidate two *warehouses* full of cigarettes. Just in Berlin.

Suddenly the official German channels became swamped with offers of cheap smokes. Supermarket chains found faxes waiting for them each morning, the quoted prices dropping at a panic rate the closer it came to pulling-out day. Yet no matter how low the offers dropped, these legal channels could absorb only so many cigarettes.

So when supply officers arrived in the mornings to learn that a hundred thousand packs or so had disappeared into the frozen night, the hunt for thieves was perfunctory. After all, the whole shebang was due for closure in less than three months.

Overnight, therefore, a new product began appearing on the black markets of Poland and the Ukraine—even as far away as Moscow, Budapest, and, if rumor was to be believed, Istanbul. Enterprising traders offered cigarettes that had actually been made in the United States with top-quality American tobacco—and at prices which were equal to or slightly less than the local imitation.

For it wasn't just the Berlin-based warriors who were being shipped Stateside; the same post-Cold War demilitarization was taking place all over Europe, with the same loose trail of cheap tobacco flooding the markets. Polish border guards were eating well these days, their meager income supplemented with bribes from dealers like Kurt.

But that wasn't why the quartermaster continued his foot-stomping inspection of the frozen ground at his feet.

"I read the file three times," he grumbled. "Can't figure out what you guys want this junk for. I mean, the guy's been dead for forty-seven years! He some friend of yours?"

Kurt made do with a nod, knowing a question had been asked but not at all sure what the man had said. Kurt had decided the quartermaster's blustering was all show. The man was going to hand over the documents; he was just easing his conscience. So Kurt waited, stifling his need to shiver. He could feel the freezing air grab hold of his face and pull the skin taut.

He himself did not know what was so important about these records of an interrogation in a World War II American prisoner-of-war camp of a German soldier who had died of dysentery four months later. All Kurt knew, in fact, was what Ferret had told him—the man's name, his date of birth, date of capture, and date of eternal release. That much was included in the official record Ferret had plucked from his ever-present pile of yellowed documents. It was a copy of the death certificate that should be on top of the file Kurt was bargaining for. It was Kurt's only way of authenticating what was to be passed over.

A shout rose from the darkness behind the trucks. The quartermaster signaled to his men. He stomped across the frozen earth, reached into his inside pocket, and drew out a thin manila envelope. "Let's see the money."

Kurt pulled out two envelopes and hefted one in each hand. "Cigarettes," he said, raising the right. Then, raising the left, he specified, "Cash."

Erika emerged from the shadows long enough to wave one impatient hand. Kurt handed over the right-hand packet.

With a final oath, the quartermaster gave in to greed and passed over the envelope. Kurt backed off before the money could be grabbed, opened the envelope, drew out the slip of paper from his pocket, and compared it to the top paper in the file. They were the same. He flipped through the aged papers. Three additional pages. Not much for almost the entire profit they would gain from this shipment.

"Read it on your own time, buddy," the quartermaster said and gestured impatiently for the money.

Reluctantly Kurt handed it over, and wondered at the cost for what seemed so little gain. The man slit the packet with a practiced motion, counted swiftly. Another shout came from the trucks. "Inna minute," the quartermaster called back. He finished counting and stuffed the packet in his coat. "Don't ever ask me for stuff like that again."

Kurt nodded. "Next week, more cigarettes?"

"Maybe," the quartermaster growled. "I'll be in touch." He turned and stomped away.

Jeffrey and Katya celebrated the end of her exams by traveling to her mother's home in Coventry. It was a strangely silent train trip. Jeffrey found it impossible to do as he wished—to caress the dark, wayward hairs spilling across her forehead, or kiss the line of her neck, or confess that her weeks of absence had truly wounded him. Too much was trapped inside him to come out just then. Even to say he had missed her remained an elusive goal. He made do with brief glimpses into those violet-gray depths, an occasional squeeze of her hand, and fleeting conversation about anything but that which filled his heart to bursting.

"I received a letter from my brother yesterday," he finally told her. "The first ever."

"I'm glad," she answered, her voice little more than a sigh, a velvet breeze that wafted gently by him. "It's time you two made peace."

He nodded agreement. "He wrote like there hasn't been any break at all, like it was yesterday the last time we were together. He's going to AA every night, and he's been sober for two hundred days. That's the way he said it, counting it one day at a time. He says he rewarded himself with three chocolate sodas and this letter. And he's started writing poetry."

"Your grandmother must be very happy," Katya said.

With that expression of quiet understanding, the dam controlling his emotions and his thoughts threatened to yield. But he could not do it, not then, not without saying it all. And he was determined not to rush, not to push himself upon her when she was still so tired from her studies. So he settled back and said nothing more the rest of the trip.

Once inside the Coventry train station, he gave Katya's gloved fingers a quick squeeze. "I'll be right back."

When he came running back a few minutes later she asked impatiently, "Where did you go?"

"I remembered something important."

"What are you trying to hide behind your back?"

"A bag of switches."

"No, they're not. They're flowers. Did you get those for Mama?"

"Don't tell me she's allergic or something. Breaks out in hives at the sight of a bloom."

A look from the heart and to the heart passed for a fleeting instant across her features, the first since her return. She raised up on tiptoe and kissed him soundly. Dropping down, she grabbed his hand, swung him around, and said, "Time to go."

"You're blushing."

"I said it was time to go, Jeffrey. Mama's waiting. Look, there's a taxi."

Magda's place was just as he had last seen it—cluttered and hot and overly close. The old woman opened the door, grimaced her greeting, accepted Katya's kiss. Then she hobbled back to her seat on feet swathed in stretch bandages and covered by lumpy support hose. Her dress skewed to starboard, her head was a mop of disorderly gray. Once seated, she said, "Good evening, Jeffrey."

He suddenly felt very shy. "I wanted you to have these."

She showed genuine surprise. "You brought flowers? For me?"

He made do with a nod.

She accepted the bundle, peeled back the paper, looked a long moment. "Orchids in the middle of winter. And carnations. Did Katya tell you they were my favorites?"

"No, I didn't," Katya replied, her eyes resting on Jeffrey. "They're beautiful."

"Yes, aren't they?" She lifted them up to her daughter. "Be a dear and put these in water, won't you?"

Though the woman's English was accented, her years in the Baltimore area when Katya was growing up were evident in her facility with the language.

When Katya had disappeared into the kitchen, Jeffrey eased himself into the chair nearest Magda and ventured, "I owe you an apology."

"I don't recall being offended, young man."

"It wasn't for anything I said."

She inspected his face. "My daughter was correct. You are indeed an honest man." A bony hand covered with age spots reached across and patted his arm. "The flowers are a splendid peace offering. Thank you."

His heart hammering in his throat, Jeffrey forced himself to say, "I need to ask you something, Mrs. Nichols. Well, two things, if I may."

"Mrs. Nichols, is it?" She raised her gaze as Katya entered the doorway. "Please leave us alone for a moment longer, daughter."

"What's the matter?"

"Go see to Ling. He's probably getting lonely out in the back room. The poor thing sings all the time nowadays, and there is no one to listen except me." Since being deposited in Mrs. Nichols' care last summer, the little bird had become a permanent member of the household. "We won't be long, will we, Jeffrey?"

He shook his head, not willing to look in Katya's direction, and waited till Magda said, "Very well, young man. I am listening."

He swallowed. "I love your daughter very much, Mrs. Nichols. I want to ask your permission to marry her."

"I see." The piercing gaze did not waver. "And how does my daughter feel about this?"

"I think she agrees. I hope she does."

"You're not sure?"

"I've learned to take nothing for granted with your daughter, Mrs. Nichols." He swallowed again. "And I decided that I wanted to ask for your permission first."

"So. You do me much honor." The sharp gray eyes crinkled slightly. "Wise and honest and honorable besides. Very well, young man. You have my blessing. You may return to calling me Magda now."

He permitted himself a shaky breath. "Thank you." The words seemed totally inadequate. "I'll try—"

"Yes, yes." She silenced him impatiently. "I know you will, Jeffrey. Do not embarrass yourself. It is not necessary. Polish women are good nurturers, and my daughter has enough Polish blood in her to make a good wife." She looked at him a moment. "Katya is most fortunate to have found a man such as you. I hope she realizes it."

"You're very kind."

"Not at all, young man. I simply seek to answer honesty with honesty," she replied. "Now, you said two things. What was the other thing you wished to speak about?"

"May I ask you how you came to faith?"

"What a remarkable question." The piercing gaze returned. "What an exceptional husband you shall make. Young man, I would have to go back many years and many miles to answer that question."

"I'd really like to know."

"Yes, I see that is true. Very well, I shall tell you." Magda grimaced and shifted one leg. "Would you please be so kind as to place another cushion under my feet?"

"Sure." He selected a pillow from the pile by the settee, then helped her raise her feet and set the additional cushion in place.

"Thank you so much. Do you know, my very first memory is of pain in those feet." She stared down at them. "I have not thought of that in years."

Jeffrey settled back in his chair, immensely glad to have his first question behind him, but too full of the strain to feel any elation—yet. He inspected the sagging, wrinkled features and decided he had seldom seen a more unattractive face, nor one with more determined strength.

"It was around the time of my third birthday. I know because of what my mother told me years later. It is the only memory I retain of my earliest years. Yet it is so clear that all I have to do is close my eyes and I can still see it, hear it, and feel the cold. We were walking, you see. Or rather, my father was walking. He carried me on his back. He and my mother had lined his knapsack with blankets and placed me inside it. Once I was strapped into place, they began their trek.

"There were seven families on this journey, mostly German Volk who had been hired by distant landowners to come and work on their vast estates. My mother was Polish, from a small village near what then was the German border. I remember that she made the most beautiful lace I have ever seen. My father was a skilled tanner and leather worker. They had worked for a landowner in what today is Hungary, on an estate so big it contained eleven whole villages. But the First World War wiped out much of landowning families' wealth, and the Depression finished them off entirely. Whole regions were starving, cities throughout Europe were filled with bread riots, Communists battled Fascists for power, and peace was nothing but an empty word.

"In 1935 my father and mother, along with six other families related by blood or marriage, decided that if they stayed where they were, they would perish. My mother had a sister who was married to a Polish farmer, a landowner with many serfs, who said in a letter that he would offer us roof and bread and a warm hearth. My father was not pleased with leaving behind a home he had built with his own hands, but a starving man cannot afford the luxury of argument.

"They set off in late October, a week after the letter from Poland arrived. If you have never tried to gather seven men and seven women, along with their children and their grandparents and even a cousin and great-uncle or two, and point them toward an unknown destination, with no money and very little food, you will not understand the arguments and indecisions and hesitations that filled their lives. They were leaving behind the only life they knew, risking everything for a future that was utterly unknown. Still they went, because as they looked around them they were impressed with the fact that to stay meant to die.

"That week of indecision almost cost them their lives. An early snowfall blanketed Europe, and rumors swept their village of signs and portents pointing toward the century's worst winter. It was this same snowfall that silenced the arguments and finally pushed them to move, for there was no fuel in my father's village. The train of wagons bearing coal for their stoves had never arrived.

"The morning my family set off for Poland, others began the trek to Budapest, where later that month more than six hundred thousand people rioted for bread and heat. It was a very bad winter, young man. There were riots in cities and hamlets from Berlin to Paris, from Königsberg to Constantinople. We heard rumors of war in Spain—and speculations that the war would spread. Women gave birth to babies and cried when tiny mouths first sought the breast, for they didn't know if a world would exist where the little ones might live and grow strong.

"But all of these things were told to me much later, long after we arrived in Poland, and after my father had learned of the madness that swept the land of his forefathers. My father hated the Fascists with a loathing that frightened me as a child. He was a gentle, caring man, with great strong arms and a warm lap and a barrel of a chest. The only time I ever recall hearing him curse was when he would speak of the Fascist regime. No doubt he would have viewed Stalin and the Communist lies with the same contempt, but by the time the Communists arrived in Poland my father was already dead, killed by a Nazi bullet in the Warsaw Uprising, fighting for a country he had come to call his own.

"My father sought out the good people in Poland, and what he found in them he loved. The Poles are a great people, Jeffrey. They truly are. Their sense of honor and duty and love of God is very great, great enough to sustain them through a century and a half of military occupation, followed by two world wars, the Nazi demons with their death camps, and fifty years of the Communists. Ask yourself this, young man. If two hundred years of such hardships had befallen the United States of America, would your people—those who survived—still be capable of calling themselves a nation?"

"I don't know," he replied softly.

"Well, on to my story. The estate where my parents settled lay in Upper Silesia, and that region was soon to be the flash point kindling the German invasion. You see, Poland had ceased to exist as an independent nation in the eighteenth century. It remained parceled out between the Austro-Hungarian, Russian and Prussian empires for one hundred and fifty years. At the end of World War I, when the Austrian kings were vanquished and the empire was destroyed, the boundaries of Europe were redrawn. Upon this new map Poland once again existed, and it included a portion of what once had been the Prussian empire. There were many, many Germans still living there, some of them landed and titled gentry. So the Fascists claimed this land as their own, a part of the Fatherland usurped by foreigners. But it was nothing but an excuse, you see. The Fascists intended to rule the world, and Poland was simply a good place to start.

"My father hated lies of all kind. To him, truth was the bond that held the world in place. It was the gift that one man of honor offered to another without expecting anything in return. For him, the Fascists were transforming Germany into a land built upon lies, cemented into place with hatred. It was evil spawned and evil bred, and if truth had no place there, neither did he.

"I grew up knowing only Polish friends, speaking Polish except in our home, where I spoke German. My father was very proud of my ability with the difficult Polish language. He never did learn the language very well, but he made friends even in those suspicious times by the fervor of his hatred for the Fascists. Everyone in the area could see his horror when Germany invaded. He joined the local underground, and he spent the war years helping to hide and transport Jews seeking to escape the Nazi massacre. Because he was German, you see, there was less suspicion cast his way by the local military authorities.

"My childhood memories are all of faces appearing in the darkest night. Frightened faces. Exhausted faces. Faces who looked as though they never expected to see the light of day ever again. They were hidden in a secret cave my father dug beneath our coal cellar. Sometimes they stayed in that dark, airless hole for as long as a week, until the next stage of their passage was prepared. They came and they went, and I would scarcely ever hear them or see them unless I helped my mother take them food. I knew without anyone telling me that I should never speak of the ghost people living in our cellar. Even at nine and ten years of age, I knew that to speak of them would be the death of us all. And I burned with pride for the bravery of my dear papa and mama.

"It was in those days that I learned to pray, sending off these silent families into the darkness of an evil-laden night. Hard times and hatred allowed bad people to take over our homeland, my father often said to me. These new rulers were intent on killing all who challenged their ideas of racial purity or political loyalties. We had only one recourse, he told me every night as he opened the worn Bible and sought out a passage. We had only one refuge, in faith. Over and over he said to me, we must climb the stairway of prayer and enter into the most Holy Place."

The kitchen door creaked open and Katya's face emerged. "Mama?"

"What is it, daughter?"

"Do I have to stay in here all afternoon?"

"We won't be much longer," Magda replied, her eyes remaining on Jeffrey.

"Can't I join you?"

"Your young man and I are just getting better acquainted," Magda replied. "Give us just a few more minutes, daughter. I am almost done." She waited until the door had closed, then asked, "Have I bored you, young man?"

Jeffrey leaned back in his chair, feeling as though he had been holding his breath. "Not at all. I have a thousand questions, though."

"You must save them for another time. We cannot keep my daughter cooped up all night." The eyes crinkled once more. "You are an excellent listener."

"There's a lot to learn."

"I see you mean that. Very well, I shall await your questions with pleasure. For the moment, let me simply tell you what I intended to, which was my very earliest memory. It was of our trek to Poland. We moved mostly at night, you see. The woods were often safer than the roads, for the roads were ruled by thieves. In the woods there were only wolves, and the animals were said to be much kinder to those they caught than the thieves.

"My mother used to talk of that walk, of how she trod endlessly behind my father as he broke a path and flattened the snow. Many times she wanted to stop and go to sleep, she said. It was only looking at my tiny face that kept her upright and marching onward.

"Mama used to say that I only thought I remembered what I did. She said I heard her speak of it so often that the memory became my own. But that is not true, young man. I can still see the icy nighttime landscape with the great shadow-trees and their dark branches cutting jagged edges through the sky overhead. Many nights there was a bright moon, our only light, and it transformed the forest into another world, one I have often returned to in my deepest dreams.

"Only my head rose from the knapsack's confines. I remember clearly the way blankets were wrapped securely around my arms and legs. It would be so very hard at first, when we set off each day at dusk, not to squirm and complain at being trapped. But then, ever so slowly, the icy fingers of cold would begin to claw their way into my papa's leather satchel and wrap a steely grip around my little hands, and it would grow steadily easier to remain still and drift in and out of wakefulness. I knew what the cold was trying to do, you see. I had seen in my dreams how death sent the beasts of winter in to snatch me away from my body. After a few hours of traveling, I would be rocked to sleep on my papa's strong back, and then I would see the beast of cold there nibbling at my fingers and my feet, trying to cut the cords and let death draw me up and away.

"Then I would start awake, and there would be my mother's face, drawn and exhausted and worried, and I knew, as little as I was, that I had to be strong for her. When we were bedded down for the day in some kind farmer's barn or an empty house or if necessary in a riverbank cavern, I often heard my mother ask why I remained so quiet. Not even a whimper of sound, my mother would say, how is that possible for a girl of her age? And my father would look at me, and somehow I knew he understood, because instead of answering he would bend over and caress my forehead and tell me over and over that I had to be strong, and that when I could not, I had to ask

God to be strong for me. That was my first lesson of faith, young man. I have carried it with me all of my days, and it has served me well. When I found that my strength was not enough, I turned and let God be strong for me. And He has never let me down. Never.

"The trip took twenty days. We lost six of the people who started off with us, two to thieves, one to a wolf, the rest to the beasts of hunger and cold. I lost both of my little toes, and no matter how my parents and the doctor might blame it on frostbite, I knew."

Magda nodded her head slowly, holding Jeffrey transfixed with glistening eyes. "Oh yes, young man, I knew. I had slept and dreamed and watched the beasts of winter gnaw them off."

———

On the train ride back to London, Jeffrey remained silent and reserved. A half hour into the journey, Katya asked him, "What are you thinking?"

"Something your mother said."

"Are you going to tell me what you talked about?"

"Later I will. Right now, it's still a little raw."

"Yes, I see it in your eyes. Mama's stories have a tendency to do that sometimes." She reached for his hand. "Just tell me what you were thinking of, then."

"I was just wondering how it was possible for Poland to keep such a strong sense of identity over such a long period. Two hundred years, Katya. I know you told me about how the church became an anchor for the people, their language, and their heritage. But it seems to me that it wouldn't be enough. There must have been a *lot* of strangers who moved in, people who after a while started calling themselves Poles. And what about all the Poles who went overseas?" He turned and looked out the window. "I tell you the truth, when I think about the dreadful things your people endured, it feels as if somebody is stabbing at my heart."

She bent over, kissed his open palm, raised it and set it upon her cheek, totally unmindful of the stares gathering from other parts of the train compartment. "Thank you for caring, Jeffrey."

"The more I learn about all of this, the more I am amazed at who the Poles are."

"You're as much a Pole as I am, Jeffrey. One grandparent, the same as me."

"Just in blood. I don't speak the language. I don't understand the culture, I've never even traveled there before last year. When she was young, my mother reached this stage where all she really wanted was to fit in with her friends. She wouldn't even admit that her father had been born outside the United States. The whole idea of being half Polish embarrassed her." He shook his head. "I wish there were some way I could go back and meet my mother when she was growing up, and tell her that she *must* hold on to her heritage, to learn the language and keep contact with the family. If not for her, then for her unborn son."

"I heard a story once," Katya said. "A group of cows had gathered in a barn, and a flock of sheep were grazing on a nearby meadow. It came time for one of the sheep to lamb, so she went into the barn for shelter. By the time the lamb was born, a heavy snowstorm had started falling. Several of the other sheep, those with young offspring and a few of the weaker ones, also moved into the warm, safe barn."

She gazed at him. "Now tell me, Jeffrey. Does the lamb become a cow simply because it is born and spent its first days in the warm, safe barn, or is blood more important?"

"Your stories are as harsh as your land. Where did you hear them?"

"When we were still living in Baltimore, my father got into financial trouble. I was very little, but my mother went to work in a ceramics factory," Katya explained. "Mama was in her late thirties when I was born. They had tried and tried for years to have children, and they couldn't. Then they gave up, and a couple of years later I came along. Before I was born, Mama had started painting designs on pottery that a friend was casting. She had always painted, and she enjoyed applying her skills to ceramics.

"Mama left me with a neighbor, an old Polish woman I called Chacha Linka. *Babcha* is the word for grandmother or old woman, and Halinka was her name. Chacha Linka was as close to pronouncing it as I could come. She never learned much English, and she only spoke to me in Polish. I don't remember ever actually learning the language, but Chacha Linka talked to me in Polish all the time, so I must have picked it up. I can still remember coming home one day and saying something to my daddy and being so amazed that he couldn't understand me. It just didn't make any sense. How could I know something my daddy didn't?"

She turned to the window for a long moment, seeing out beyond the industry-scarred landscape to the world of remembering. "Chacha Linka had more stories than anybody I have ever known. A lot of them were about the Bolsheviki. That's what she called the Russians until the day she died. Bolsheviki. Even though the revolution had been over for seventy years, she still called them that."

"Sounds like a name out of some old black-and-white movie."

"Not for her. *Bolshoi* means large or big, like the Bolshoi Ballet—the Grand Ballet. Bolsheviki meant members of the Great Party, although the Communists weren't really so numerous. Lenin used that name to make it sound as if they represented all the people. It was propaganda appeal, making it appear bigger than it really was."

"All that doesn't sound like the makings of a kiddie's fairy tale."

"Some of the stories scared me," she agreed. "Some of them were awful. Really gave me nightmares. But some of them were beautiful."

"There's so much I don't know," Jeffrey said quietly. "So much to learn. It's like a treasure trove. You make me feel so *enriched*."

She turned back from the window to give him a look of pure gratitude. "There's something I've wanted to speak with you about for a very long time. I wonder if maybe now is the time."

"We won't know unless you try."

"Do you know what it means to tithe?"

"Sure, I know the word. Ten percent of what you make."

"Ten percent that is dedicated to the Lord's work." She hesitated, and in that heartbeat's span was transformed into a shy little girl. "I was wondering if you would like to tithe with me."

The way she said it brought a burning to the back of his eyes. "It sounds fine, Katya."

"You don't have to if you don't want to."

"No, I'd like that. Really."

"I just thought . . ." Again she paused and searched, her cheeks touched with a rosebud of blooming red. "I thought it might be a nice part of joining our lives together."

He reached across for her hand. It was on his tongue to ask her, but he checked the words at the very last moment. Not then. Not there.

"I was thinking maybe we could find something, a project or a need the next time we're in Poland together, and dedicate our work on it to our Father." Violet-gray eyes peeked out from beneath the protection of long, dark lashes. "Do you like the idea?"

It was hard not to say what was on his mind, hard to hold to his original plan, hard to only bring out the simple words, "I like it very much, Katya."

She looked at him with eyes that were never spent. Katya held his hand with both of hers and blessed him with her gaze for the remainder of the trip back to London.

The further from the main highway Kurt traveled, the more treacherous the road became. Four lanes dwindled to two, then the asphalt gave way to brick. Ice and snow packed between the stones created tiny, unseen deathtraps. Wrecks littered the roads, usually where slow-motion Ossie plastic cars met Wessie speed machines too intent on showing off to pay attention to the road and the weather. Kurt's neck throbbed from the tension of trying to keep a fixed appointment time under impossible conditions.

Kurt slowed for a truck entering a factory gateway, corrected a momentary skid, slowed even more. Near the Arnstadt city limits the road became flanked by the Karl Marx Industrial Estate, the high nameplates over each entrance now crudely whitewashed out. Chemical works gave way to cement factories, then to steel mills and a power station. On the other side of the street, high-rise workers' barracks marched in endless rows. Not a tree could be seen in the more than seven miles of factories and tenements.

He passed through the utterly charmless town and started climbing hills along a bone-jarring road. The radio kept him company with a mixture of American sixties' pop, Wessie rock, and a clear-speaking, carefully neutered Wessie announcer. Every trace of the old regime had been wiped from radio and television. No one listened to the Ossie musical groups anymore. No one talked about them. No one even admitted that the music had ever existed.

Kurt had eyes the color of dried mud. His face was as scarred and battered as a building site, marked by early bouts with various poxes. He tended toward gray in everything he wore—gray suits, ties, striped shirts, socks, dark gray shoes. It left him looking like a lump of angry mold.

Kurt considered himself an out-of-work spy, which he was, but not with the dangerously glamorous past as he would have liked. His spy trips abroad, the ones he referred to in mysterious half tones when chatting up bar girls, had been as overseer to trade missions visiting industrial fairs; they had been boring as only a trade fair could be for someone who had not the first clue about the subject on display. The other East German delegates had immediately pegged Kurt for a stooge, and shunned him throughout the trip. His only company had been other Stasi stooges, most of whom spent their time either shopping or drinking or touring the local porno houses. Kurt had found their company worse than being alone.

The fact that Kurt treated every trip abroad as an all-important mission earned him kudos from the home office and a reputation among traveling technicians as the ultimate pain. His presence on a technical trade mission meant that each morning at breakfast, every mission member had to submit a report on the previous day's activities—what they had learned, whom they had visited, what technology they had managed to pry loose from suspicious Western salesmen. But the Stasi bureaucrats liked Kurt's thoroughness. While his efforts never granted him his sought-after position as either an embassy staffer or a Western-based agent, they allowed him to travel at least twice a year to the West. In a country as tightly controlled as East Germany, this freedom was nothing to sneeze at.

But for Kurt it was not enough. He had always wanted to be an international spook, always seen himself as made for a dangerous life. He took whatever self-defense courses were offered. He wore a full-length black-leather overcoat long after warm weather transformed it into a mobile sauna. While shaving he practiced heavy-lidded expressions, and imagined himself squeezing information from a suspect with his gaze alone. He refused to marry, avoided any long-term connection that might close the book on overseas assignments. He slaved nights over correspondence language courses, though he had no aptitude for foreign tongues, and proudly slaughtered both Russian and French and Spanish—for some reason, English had always baffled him. Every report he submitted featured a tone of overblown intrigue.

Yet Kurt was never allowed to make the transition to full-time international spy. The hierarchies were distinct and separated by light years; international spies were normally chosen while still in university. In later life, the transition was possible only with that most treasured of possessions—a Party patron. Someone so high and so mighty that rules could be completely ignored, stomped upon, transgressed, and leave the receiver unbruised by having done the impossible.

Kurt had no such connections. He was too harsh in attitude, too abrupt in speech, too lacking in the ability to fawn and grovel. Kurt rose within the national hierarchy by sheer brute ability. His dream for a last-minute transfer remained unquenched. His bitterness knew no bounds.

———

Kurt's contact was standing where he had promised, beneath a glaring sign sporting a death's head, a crude picture of an explosion, and the ominous words in German, "Deadly Danger of Bombs and Mines. Do Not Enter." Kurt pulled into the narrow gravel pathway and stopped. The man was barrel-chested and short and powerfully muscled. He was dressed in the lightweight clothes of one who has learned not to feel the cold—denim overalls and unbuttoned jacket and a battered construction helmet. He thrust out one grimy hand, and said in greeting, "The money?"

"It's here," Kurt replied, climbing from the car.

"Let's have it, then." When Kurt handed it over the contact counted carefully with stubby, blue-cold fingers. He pocketed the bills and said, "There's only ten minutes of light left. Let's go."

Kurt cast a nervous glance back at the sign. "I don't see why we can't talk this over in the car." When the man did not stop, Kurt swore under his breath and started up the gravel slope.

"Talk all day and it still wouldn't be clear," the man said, pausing by a second sign that proclaimed, in bold red letters, *Lebensgefahr,* Life-Threatening Danger. The man went on, "Yeltsin made his little speech and walked off with almost half a billion marks. Those fools in Bonn should have come up here and checked it out before handing over the money."

"Checked out what?" When newly elected Russian Premier Boris Yeltsin made his first official visit to Germany, he stated at the opening press conference that he knew where the Amber Room was buried. The news captured the headlines of every newspaper and magazine in Germany, and many in the rest of Europe. Yeltsin said that his researchers, in their investigation of newly uncovered postwar files, had unearthed clear evidence of where the Nazis had stored the most precious of their plundered treasures.

Yeltsin promised that he would disclose this site in return for additional emergency aid to his ailing nation. The Bonn government took his proclamation in stride, determined to allow nothing to upset relations so long as Soviet troops remained stationed on German soil. They replied that, in celebration of Yeltsin's visit, they had already decided to give an additional four hundred million marks in emergency aid.

Yeltsin's lackeys then identified the site as the caves bored into the Jonastal, the Jonas Valley, outside Arnstadt. The caverns had been dug during World War II by prisoners brought from the neighboring Buchenwald concentration camp.

After the first flurry of activity and official investigations, there had been nothing from Bonn except stony silence.

Kurt's eyes cast another glance at the sign's warning. "Shouldn't we find a safer place to talk?"

The man snorted. "We've had droves of fat Bonn politicians come parading up here for months. Not to mention trucks and bulldozers and backhoes and even sonar equipment. I doubt if you'll find anything they haven't."

"So why the signs?"

"The same reason all the Wessie fat-bellies left empty-handed." He pointed to veined white cliffs rising above frozen pines. "Yeltsin said the treasures were buried in a cave. And then one of the researchers in Moscow admitted that it wasn't the Amber Room that was mentioned in these records they found, but other treasures the

Nazis hauled off from that same area around St. Petersburg. Hah. We *know* that. Everybody within fifty kilometers knows that."

Kurt showed exaggerated patience, hoped the man would come to the point before his feet froze to the ground. "So why isn't everybody out digging?"

"Because we like living more than we like golden caskets." In one sweeping motion he took in the tall pines rising up between them and the steepest cliffs, and the bone-colored stone looming up beyond them. "Look. The SS brought Buchenwald prisoners up here, had them dig caves. Not cave. Caves. Hundreds of them. Thousands, maybe. Nobody knows, see? Not how many, not even where. Some were used to store bombs from the munitions factory in Arnah. Why? Because bombers can come and find a building and bomb it. Harder to target a seven-kilometer-wide cliff face.

"Some caves for bombs, and some for treasures. At least, that's what the legends say. My father used to talk about the truck convoys that came through Arnstadt after the night curfew forced everybody indoors. Truck after truck after truck without lights, grinding through our city, all headed for the Jonas Valley. Official propaganda said all the trucks were full of bombs, and there was less danger of air raids hitting the trucks at night. But there were stories. Still are. Too many to be just smoke, for my mind."

He stabbed the air with an angry gesture. "But which caves were for bombs? And which for treasures?"

The faint breeze stopped. In that moment of utter stillness, snowflakes drifted down from a leaden sky. Kurt searched the cliff side. "So why don't I see any cave openings?"

"Because when they pulled out, the SS set off dynamite charges along the crest of the cliffs," the man replied. "See all those hills of rubble behind the pines? Man-made avalanches, the lot. Covered over all the cave openings."

Kurt nodded. "So you don't know where to dig."

"Not so fast. See how white the cliffs are? Chalk. Softest stone there is. The Nazis' dynamite shifted the *mountains*, not just the openings. The caves are rubble."

The man lifted his white construction helmet, wiped at the stress that knotted his brow. "While the Wessies were all crowding around down here, making speeches for the press and getting in the way, we pounded steel rods fifteen meters long into the cliff face at likely looking places. Three men getting paid five times normal wage and sweating bullets, holding the rods in place, while two men with hammers took turns banging the rods in five centimeters at a time, and all the while waiting for a bomb to turn the rod into a giant's spear.

"They found three caves. In two and a half weeks. Three caves from how many, a thousand? All empty as far back as they could go, which wasn't far." He shook his head. "We cleared out the openings with shovels and a backhoe, a bottle of schnapps between each team before they started and another two when they stopped. They sent in bomb demolition experts with maybe fifty kilos of lead clothing and equipment per man. The experts got in about ten meters, and the rock overhead shifted a little—they shift all the time, these cliffs. They're permanently destabilized by the dynamite. There was this little rumble and a little puff of dust out the cave mouth, then screams and six men in lead blankets came running out so fast they didn't hardly touch earth."

Kurt was truly sorry he had missed that. "What happens now?"

"They stop, what else? You can't bulldoze a cliff filled with half a million tons of forty-five-year-old unexploded bombs in caves that could shift any minute."

"Buried forever, then."

"Until we develop something that can see through solid rock, that's my guess."

"If it's here at all."

"Oh, something's here. They didn't go to all that trouble just to hide some bombs." The man shook his head. "Raise a tombstone to the Nazi treasures, let the SS have the last laugh; that's my answer. There's already been enough blood spilled over whatever's buried there."

——

Kurt drove back into the worn-down drabness of Arnstadt and called Ferret from the safety of one of the new telephone boxes the

Wessies were planting in every city square. "It's impossible to tell," he reported.

"No matter," the little man replied in his flat, childlike lisp. "What did you find?"

Kurt relayed the events of the afternoon. "The chalk cliffs stretch for maybe seven, eight kilometers. It's an impossible task. It'd take years to sift through a tenth of the area."

"But as yet they have found nothing?"

"Three empty caves." Kurt admitted to his own doubt. "How can you be sure that this Amber Room of yours is not buried there?"

"I'm sure," came the quiet reply.

"Then why must I travel to Weimar?"

"To be even more certain. As long as they have not found the first treasure, we can proceed with the knowledge that *our* treasure is elsewhere."

Our treasure. Kurt felt the thrill of sudden wealth. "So where is elsewhere?"

"That we shall soon talk over upon your return," Ferret replied. "And remember what we discussed before you departed Schwerin."

"I haven't forgotten."

"The first order their workers will receive," Ferret went on, "once something has been found, is to deny everything. So don't listen to their words. Watch their eyes. Their eyes won't lie."

Jeffrey made his way down Mount Street from the printer's, barely able to see above the boxes stacked in his arms. He kicked at the shop door until Alexander emerged from the back to usher him in.

"Thank you, thank you. Another trip, and I do believe my back would have sought refuge in traction," Alexander said as he lifted the top box.

"Don't even joke like that." Jeffrey put down the rest of the load and looked around the shop. Engraved invitations in matching envelopes were stacked like ivory mountains on two Empire side tables. "Those are ready to go?"

"Nine hundred," Alexander replied with tired satisfaction. "Your four are all that remain."

"I bet you'll be glad to see the last of this."

"On the contrary, I've quite enjoyed the effort." Alexander gave a weary smile. "Several times I've caught myself wondering why this aspect of godly service was not granted more attention."

"That service is fun?"

Alexander shook his head. "No, that it is fulfilling." He bent over one of Jeffrey's boxes, slit the tape with a practiced motion, and held one of the cards up to the light. "Marvelous," he declared. "Simply marvelous quality, wouldn't you say?"

The invitation was a large folded card of textured ivory with gilt edging. On the cover was a splendid color photograph of the chalice. Alexander opened the invitation and read in dramatic tones, "Patrons of the Religious Heritage of Poland request the honour of your presence at a gala banquet on Saturday, the twenty-fifth of February, in the Main Ballroom of the Ritz Hotel, Piccadilly,

London W1." He tapped on the smaller type with the edge of his pen. "Black tie, R.S.V.P., et cetera, et cetera."

He separated the reply card, read off, "Kindly reserve—" he lifted his head to explain the blank for number of places, "for the gala banquet hosted by the Patrons of the Religious Heritage of Poland. Enclosed is our cheque at two hundred and fifty pounds per reservation."

He replaced the card. "I think our response will be very good indeed. Just today I received word that some royalty expect to attend."

"That's great."

"Minor royalty, mind you. But their presence will certainly add a nice touch to the program, don't you think?"

Jeffrey followed him into the back office, where every seat but one was covered in a deluge of papers and forms. "The Brits sure love their royals."

The sound of the doorbell brought a moan from Alexander. He raised his head from the pile of documents, printouts, address lists, and menu forms, and threw his assistant a harried look. "For the next three weeks, until this gala is behind us, you shall have to deal with all but the emergencies. Except for your trip to East Germany, of course, which I am beginning to regret."

Jeffrey looked to the corner mirror that afforded a view of the shop's front door. "It's Sydney Greenfield."

"Not an emergency by any stretch of the imagination," Alexander replied, dropping his head back to his work. "He's all yours."

Sydney Greenfield owned no shop of his own, yet managed to eke an income from offering the goods of others to buyers in and around London. Jeffrey had not seen him since hearing news of his changed fortunes. As he walked toward the entrance, he observed that Sydney had replaced his usual shiny broadcloth for an elegant outfit whose hand-tailored lines did their best to mask his girth. Sydney entered with his usual panache, yet looked oddly unbalanced without his sidekick, a little parrot of a man known to the world simply as Ty.

Jeffrey shook hands and led Sydney to a pair of eighteenth-century walnut armchairs. Once his guest was seated and had been offered coffee, Jeffrey asked, "Where's Ty?"

"Down with a case of the throat, poor man." Greenfield sipped from the delicate porcelain with his little finger cocked at a ridiculous angle. He waved a careless hand toward the back of the shop. "Might have a buyer for that little item there in the corner. That is, if the price is right."

The piece in question was a French side cabinet made in Paris around 1855, the interior lined in fragrant cedar and the exterior in highly polished ebony. What made this cabinet so extraordinary was the high-quality *boulle*, the brass and tortoise shell inlay, that adorned the facade. The pair of front doors were bound with shining hinges and corners and keyholes, their central panels decorated with shimmering maidens playing lyres. The top and central pillar featured trios of angels fashioned of such gentle hues as to vanish and reappear with the passage of light.

"That's a rather pricey item," Jeffrey warned.

"I'm sure it is, lad," Greenfield replied easily. "But if the article was going into the home of an old and trusted associate, I imagine you might be willing to lop off a nought or two."

Jeffrey lifted his eyebrows. "Andrew told me you were on to something big."

"Oh, yes." Greenfield showed vast pleasure. "It's amazing how many people are out there with more money than taste."

"Well . . . he was wondering if you'd actually crossed the line."

"Andrew's a fine man, one of the few I'd take such a question from without getting my hair up. I haven't, lad, and that's the truth. On my honor, I haven't." He drained his cup, held it aloft for a refill. "No need to, as a matter of fact."

"People will buy your creations knowing they're rubbish?" Jeffrey went for the tea pot.

"Pay good money for them in the process," he replied. "You see, lad, I've spent donkey's years dealing with people who've scrabbled all their lives for the filthy lucre, as it were. Never had time to learn taste, they didn't. So here they are, finally striding along the top of the muck heap, and some bloke comes by and offers them a pretty bauble for their living room at sixty thousand quid. They go right through the ruddy roof, they do."

"I'm with you," Jeffrey said.

" 'Course you are. Always knew you for a sharp lad. So up I pop with a pretty little dresser or chaise longue or what have you, maybe not quite so pretty but not bad all the same."

"And the price is half the other."

"Not even, lad. Not even. Both are old, though, you see. Both have that scent of class to them."

"After a fashion."

Greenfield waved at the words as though swatting flies. "Details, lad. Mere details, in their eyes at least, and that's where it counts. Dealers in the genuine articles and people in the know aren't likely to be invited into homes of such as these, you see. So they look from one item to the other, and most times decide they'd just as soon have what I'm selling and pocket the extra."

Jeffrey thought it over and decided, "Smart. Very smart idea."

"I agree," Alexander called from his alcove.

"Thank you both. I take that as high praise, indeed, coming from professionals such as your good selves." Greenfield set down his cup, glanced around the shop, went on, "Mind you, if I'd been given the choice, I'd much rather spend my days surrounded by such beauties."

Alexander emerged to walk over and shake Sydney's hand. "You are always welcome here. Always."

"You're a real gentleman, you are, Mr. Kantor. And I've said the same to anyone who listens."

Alexander accepted the compliment with a solemn nod. "We don't always have a choice as to which cards life deals us, though, do we?"

"No, Mr. Kantor, we don't. And more's the pity."

"Of course, if you are as successful as it sounds, you might have an opportunity to fill your own life with the genuine articles."

"Just what I'm hoping to do," Greenfield replied, eyeing the cabinet.

Alexander smiled briefly. "You yourself are certainly one of those able to appreciate works of art for what they are."

"Kind of you to say so, Mr. Kantor. I try to be."

"Well, if anything in this shop ever takes your fancy, I believe we could make you a special offer of twenty percent off our price." Frosty gray eyes twinkled. "Don't you think that would be appropriate, Jeffrey?"

"A special dealer's discount," Jeffrey agreed.

Greenfield looked from one to the other and said gravely, "I'm touched, gentlemen. I truly am."

"Now, you'll have to excuse me. I am literally over my head in preparations for this gala."

"Of course, of course." Greenfield stood and shook the proffered hand, hesitated, then pointed toward the glass-sided Art Deco display case where the chalice stood in solitary splendor. "I hope you gentlemen won't mind me saying this, but it seems passing strange that you'd leave that article on display in your shop like this."

"What makes you say that? Our security is exemplary." Alexander had already turned and retreated to his alcove. "Besides, everything here is heavily insured," he said over his shoulder.

"Maybe so, but this isn't your own goods, now, is it?" Greenfield walked over to the cabinet. "It's one thing to run a risk with something that's here to be sold. Holding a priceless item you're supposed to return is another kettle of fish, far as I see it."

"We've never had any trouble before," Jeffrey said.

"But these ads and the invitations you've done with the chalice in all its glory," Greenfield objected, shaking his head. "You're announcing to all the world you've got this medieval artifact here in your shop. Sounds dodgy to me."

Jeffrey turned to where Alexander stood by the alcove's entrance. "Maybe we should arrange for a night security guard."

"No good, lad," Greenfield said. "You'd just be erasing all doubt that the chalice is here. What I'd suggest is, lay it low in a vault. Myself, I use Barclay's up by Charing Cross. Best security in the business, by my vote. They know how to deal with works such as these."

"Coutts is our bank," Jeffrey said doubtfully.

"We're not talking about banking business, now, are we? This is security. Offer it to the biggest museums, they do. Make a professional job of it. They'll rent you guards, armored security display cases for the event, cart it over in an armored car, bring it back, no muss, no fuss."

"Another problem." Alexander wiped a weary brow. "Just when I need it least."

"Handling it that way would be a load off our mind," Jeffrey pointed out.

"What you've got here is priceless, irreplaceable," Greenfield said, bending down for a closer look. "An incredible risk. If you allow, I'll have them come by to collect this beauty and put it in storage until your gala evening. Armored car would take it both ways, set you up with a portable alarm system, display case, guards for the evening. Just say the word."

"Maybe we ought to move it," Jeffrey agreed.

"See to it, then," Alexander complied.

"That's the spirit," Greenfield straightened. "Be a pleasure to help out gentlemen like yourselves, take part in a worthy deed. I'll just go have a word with the men in charge and get back to you."

Once Jeffrey had ushered Greenfield out of the shop, he returned to Alexander. "Did you mean what you said, about regretting this East Germany trip?"

Alexander did not raise his head from the sheaf of papers. "You must admit, it does come at a rather inopportune time."

"Do you want me to put it off?"

"No, of course not. I simply wish for the impossible, to have you go and at the same time have you stay and help."

"I suppose I could call and put them off."

"No, you cannot," Alexander replied firmly. "Business like this simply cannot be postponed. You are building what may prove to be lifelong business relationships."

"I'll be back as soon as I can."

"Take whatever time is required," Alexander said. "I'll muddle on along here quite adequately, I assure you."

"Is there anything I can do to help out now?"

"There is, as a matter of fact." Alexander hefted a ream of faxed pages. "I've received these menu suggestions from the Ritz, but I have so much going on I can't seem to decide on anything. Could you and Katya possibly meet with the banqueting manager and take care of it for me?"

"Any chance we could ask for samples?"

But Alexander was already buried once more in his work. "Just no heavy sauces, that's all I ask. I would rather our guests go home inspired than bloated."

Jeffrey reached for his coat. "No problem."

"Oh, and chocolate. We must have some chocolate for dessert. I've already been forewarned that one of our honored honorables throws quite a tiff unless indulged with a chocolate finale."

══

Jeffrey walked over to where Katya waited in the Ritz Hotel's marbled foyer, watching the bustling scene with bright eyes. He told her, "Even the bellhops in this place sound as if they've graduated from Cambridge."

"I've spotted two film stars in the past five minutes." She gave herself an excited little hug. "I almost forgot there was a world out there beyond my exam papers, and now look at me."

"Yes, look at you," Jeffrey agreed. "Come on. The banqueting manager's been held up, so he's arranged that we're to have tea as his guests."

The Ritz Tea Salon was in the middle of the hotel, up three stairs and through an entrance adorned with floral trellises. The chamber itself was done as a fairy queen's garden. Little marble-topped tables dotted a pink and gold salon adorned with gilded cupids and hanging flower arrangements. Waitresses whisked about in starched crinoline and petticoats.

Tea was served in delicate porcelain and poured through a silver strainer. Tiny sandwiches and scones and muffins arrived on a three-story circular silver palaver. Clotted cream and strawberry jam in little silver bowls completed the repast.

Katya watched with wide eyes as Jeffrey poured her tea. Leaning over, she said in an awestruck whisper, "I feel as if I'm inside a box of valentine chocolates."

Jeffrey whipped open the banqueting menus, said, "Okay, now to business. I think we should go for steak and baked potato. No, on second thought, how about a real treat—barbecued baby back ribs and coleslaw. I'm sure this crowd hasn't ever seen anything like that before."

Katya gave him a horrified look. "You can't be serious."

" 'Course I am. Get them some bibs, sure, and we'll need something great for starters." He pretended to read down the page. "Here it is. A paper plate piled high with boiled shrimp. Tartar sauce for dipping."

She reached across and plucked the menus from his hands. Katya studied the pages, a frown of concentration puckering her features. Then she brightened. "Oh, look at this. Lobster mousse on a bed of spinach and wrapped in strips of smoked salmon. Doesn't that sound wonderful as a starter?"

"Personally, I'd rather have the shrimp," he replied, loving her and her enthusiasm.

"Then for the main course, yes, stuffed pheasant in a sorrel and peppercorn sauce with a frou-frou of vegetables." She smiled. "When I was a little girl, I used to think that if I ate a peppercorn I'd grow a mole."

"What?"

She returned to the menu. "It made perfect sense to me."

"A frou-frou of anything doesn't sound very appetizing to my ears. I think we'd be a lot better off going with corn on the cob."

Katya ignored him and turned the page. "And what to drink?"

"We'll just stick some wash buckets full of ice and bottles in the middle of the tables," Jeffrey replied. "Let everybody grab whatever they like."

She lifted her head to reply, then focused on someone behind him. "We've got company."

Jeffrey swiveled in his chair and caught sight of the Count di Garibaldi, a real-estate magnate who was both a friend of Alexander's and a long-time client. The old gentleman was bent over the hand of a ravishing young woman less than a third his age. She wore a clinging bit of nothing and a king's ransom worth of jewelry, and had two giant Afghan hounds in tow.

Katya made innocent eyes. "She must be his niece."

"One of many," Jeffrey agreed, rising to his feet. When the Count had finished following the young lady's swaying departure with frank admiration, Jeffrey waved him over.

"Jeffrey, Katya." The Count approached them with a regal air and a genuine smile. "This is indeed a great pleasure."

"How are you, sir?"

"Quite splendid, thank you. And how is Alexander? Not waning, I hope."

Jeffrey smiled. "Practicing his dance steps the last time I saw. He wants to have his jig down properly for the occasion."

"He's teaching you his odd brand of humor, I see." The Count glanced at his watch. "I'm a bit early for an engagement. May I join you for a glass of sherry?"

"It would be our honor."

"I received something quite remarkable in the mail this morning," Count di Garibaldi said, pulling Alexander's invitation from his coat pocket. "Of course I would be delighted to attend and offer whatever support you might require."

"Alexander will be very happy to hear that. Thank you."

"And this chalice. Lovely, just lovely. But do you know, what strikes me is how Italian in appearance it seems. Yet you say this is Polish?"

"It came from a Polish collection," Jeffrey replied. "And Alexander was told it was probably made in the Cracow region."

"Interesting. Most interesting." The Count slipped on a pair of reading spectacles, pointed at the picture. "You see this filigree work at the base, that appears very Florentine to my eye. In fact, the whole thing appears somewhat familiar, as though I had seen it before. I don't suppose that is possible."

"Extremely doubtful," Jeffrey said. "The whole collection's been locked in a crypt for ages."

The Count was clearly not convinced. "I don't need to tell you that I am quite well connected in Rome, and I feel that I have . . . Well, no, I suppose I am mistaken if you say this is definitely a Polish piece."

"It is definitely from a Polish collection," Katya said.

"That is the whole point of this event," Jeffrey added. "To show the beauty of Polish religious artifacts and to create a fund for their preservation."

"Well." The Count folded his glasses and placed them with the invitation back in his pocket. "I am so looking forward to seeing you on the evening. I am quite sure it will not only be a great success, but a splendid fete for all present."

Dinner that night was a most intimate affair, prepared in Jeffrey's minuscule kitchen, a place so narrow that passing each other gave them excuses for gentle contact and sweet caresses. They ate, and tasted nothing but the sight of each other. They drank, and knew little beyond the flavor of their love. They shared silences that transcended all need for words, and they spoke simply to enjoy the sound of each other's voice.

After dinner, Jeffrey led Katya the brief distance to Park Lane, then through the underpass and into Hyde Park's dark confines. It was a cold, clear night. From their unlit path winding through ancient trees, the stars appeared to rest just overhead, silently flickering friends set there to keep them company.

"I'm really excited about our trip to Erfurt," she said, snuggling deeper inside her coat, her arm hooked through his. "It's an unexpected gift, a reward for these past months."

Jeffrey nodded, not able to think of such things just then. He stopped her by the lake's edge, checked in all directions to make sure no one was near.

Then he looked at her. In the silvery light, her eyes were expanding, growing, drawing him in.

She pointed to where the lake ended. "That was where we found Ling."

He nodded. His heart had swelled to the point that it blocked his words.

"I've always thought it was a gift from God, finding that little bird." She gazed unblinkingly up at him. "Keeping us together. Showing me that love can overcome all odds, all fears, all reason."

She did not drop her gaze as she slipped one hand into his. "I've never thanked you for that lesson, have I?"

There's no need, he thought, but could not speak. He remained immobile, mute. Now that he was here, the words would not come.

Katya retrieved her hand, slipped off her glove, ran her fingers down the side of his face. "The answer is yes, Jeffrey."

"I haven't asked you yet," he said, his voice a bare whisper.

"This is my gift of thanks," she said. Frozen smoky veils billowed around her face in time to her soft-spoken words. "I love you, Jeffrey Allen Sinclair."

"Will you marry me?" Did the words come from him? He seemed to stand at a distance, his heart hammering a frantic pace, and felt like he was watching a stranger speak for him. "I love you, and I want you to be my wife. Will you marry me, Katya Nichols?"

She wrapped her arms around him, said to his chest, "I have loved you since the very first moment I saw you."

"Is that a yes?"

"Yes for now, yes for tomorrow, yes for all the tomorrows God grants us."

She looked up at him with eyes as luminous as two earthbound stars. "You may kiss the bride."

The bar was on a small side street two blocks from Schwerin's official Soviet Officers' Club. As surrounding old-town structures emerged from construction scaffolding all bright and shiny and renovated, the officers' club had sunk to ever-greater depths of obscurity. The front facade, the only portion of the club that had ever been painted, was now gray and grimy and flaking. The remaining exterior was crumbling brick and black-veined plaster. The double entrance doors no longer closed entirely and had to be chained shut at night. To either side were shattered marquees featuring brawny men and women on smudged, fly-blown posters.

The back-street bar where Kurt stood and drank and waited was little more than a hovel, its planked flooring scuffed and seldom swept. Huddled in the dimly lit depths were hard-drinking men and women who felt far more at home in such remnants of the old regime than in the shiny renovations in this unfamiliar and frightening Germany. Here gathered those who were shunned by the new democracy, and who in turn eluded the attention of new masters they neither knew nor welcomed. As the city's face-lift crept farther and farther, they retreated in grumbling hostile throngs and watched helplessly as the noose of new laws and alien changes settled around their necks. Kurt waited in the smoky bar and sipped his beer and sighed at the irony of it all.

Kurt's position at the bar's back corner offered him an excellent view of all who entered and left, including the Russian who stepped into the gloomy depths. Kurt remained hunkered over his drink, watching from the corner of his eye.

Iron discipline kept the Russian's advancing age in check. The body was ramrod straight, the gaze as direct and unbending as his spine. His uniform was neat and pressed in rigid lines, and his officer's cap bore the gold stars of senior rank. Kurt straightened slightly. Immediately the colonel's gaze swung his way. Kurt waited to breathe until the piercing eyes continued their careful sweep of the room.

The colonel walked to the bar, set his cap to one side, spoke quietly to the bartender. Russians were not an uncommon sight in this bar—either aides waiting out their superiors' stay in the officers' club or officers seeking less public places to do their drinking. Yet this man was very different from the others lost in the convenient shadows. He did not unbend even when drinking his beer. His hair was gray and short-cropped, his face lined but without any telltale sagging. Kurt moved closer, wondering what it must have cost such a man to come here.

The officer did not raise his eyes from his glass as Kurt sidled up beside him and asked in very poor Russian, "Buy you a drink?"

"My glass is full," the officer replied, his German heavily accented but exact.

"You are allowed only one beer?" Kurt pressed on in Russian.

The officer turned and held him with eyes the color and temperature of a Siberian winter sky. "I'll not stand here and listen to you desecrate my mother tongue."

Kurt switched to a venomously soft German. "I have money and I'm buying. But that doesn't interest a man of principle like you. Of course not. No doubt you come here to mingle with the locals. Show off your medals." He turned and stomped off to his corner table.

Reluctantly the officer picked up his cap and beer and followed Kurt. He stood over the table and announced, "We speak in German."

"We can speak in Swahili for all I care," Kurt muttered to his stein.

The officer remained standing. "I will not be insulted with offers to buy my coat or my boots."

"I wouldn't have to kill time in this dive waiting for an officer, if that was all I was after," Kurt snapped. "A hundred of your soldiers are standing on the street corners selling everything from their belts to their guns to their commandant's medals. I could dress and arm a platoon in five minutes out there."

It was true. Stricter punishment had removed weapons from display at the roadside stands, but all could still be had for a price. In recent weeks, enterprising Wessie journalists had exposed the depths of the crisis by purchasing one hundred automatic weapons, a case of grenades, fifty land mines, twenty kilos of plastic explosive, a rocket launcher, and a late-model tank. All from broke, hungry Russian soldiers hanging around Ossie city squares. All for pennies on the dollar. They even filmed a negotiation to buy three jet fighters from disillusioned pilots.

Kurt reminded himself of his purpose and offered a truce. "Why do we quarrel? It wasn't so long ago that we were almost allies."

"True, true," the colonel subsided. "Perhaps because I am so angry with my own fate, I strike where there is no need."

"I know the sentiment," Kurt admitted, "all too well."

"Problems are mounting," the colonel said, "here and at home." With a deft motion he raised and drained his glass and set it on the table. "Perhaps I will have that drink after all."

Kurt was on his feet at once and headed for the bar. He returned swiftly, carrying a pair of vodka shots and glasses of beer. Russian boilermakers for them both. He motioned with the beers for the colonel to be seated. "Join me."

The iron-hard man fought briefly with himself, nodded agreement. "My men are hungry," the colonel replied, and sank heavily into a chair. "Our salaries have remained the same, while the ruble has been devalued to *one-fifteenth* of its former worth. Our shipments of supplies from Russia have almost stopped. There is no food. No coal. No money."

"Yes, well," Kurt said with feigned nonchalance. "That's why we are here, I suppose."

"We serve a nation that no longer exists and has no barracks to return us to," the officer persisted. Muted earth tones of browns and deep reds colored his uniform, from heavy wool greatcoat to carefully tended boots. The only bright splashes were the gold stars of rank on his shoulders and cap. "We have a dozen new masters, and no masters at all. Every night there are screams and fights among men who have lost their esprit de corps."

"With that I cannot help," Kurt said. "With the food, perhaps. But not the fact that you are now a federation at war with itself."

"I was a good officer," the soldier continued. "My men were good men. We had a duty and we did it well."

"You were an oppressor," Kurt flashed, his control momentarily snapping. "You were never wanted here. Never."

The frosty eyes narrowed. "Our task was not to be loved."

Kurt backed down. "Yes. Well." He raised his vodka. "To the past."

"Much safer than the future," the colonel agreed, and tossed back his glass. He breathed fumes, blinked hard, and asked, "You heard of the Kazakh riots?"

"Yes." Seventeen thousand soldiers at the Biakanur Space Center in Kazakhstan had rioted, leaving three dead and countless wounded, many fatally. Earlier, their officers had bartered their services as common laborers to the space center authorities in exchange for food and cigarettes. The center no longer had money to pay employees, and the soldiers were slowly starving. It had been a good agreement, except for the tragic fact that the soldiers had never been paid. The center itself had not received their own promised provisions, and had been left with less than enough to feed themselves. The troops had responded by burning down all they had built and several other buildings besides.

Kurt sipped his beer. "Now perhaps we can get down to business." The flat tones of a defeated soldier returned. "To business." He raised his glass once more.

"I need information," Kurt said. "Nothing sensitive or harmful to your precious nation." He grinned coldly, corrected himself. "Nations."

The officer let it pass. "What kind of information?"

"About a German soldier. He was captured by Red Army soldiers as they invaded Poland—"

"The correct term is liberated," the officer noted, his tone dour.

Kurt waved it aside. "He was questioned and sent to a POW camp, and he died in Siberia in 1946. We wish to know what he said during his interrogation."

"Forty-seven years is a long time to carry a grudge," the colonel ventured.

"He was a doctor," Kurt persisted. "No SS horror. Nothing involved with state security. You break no code."

The colonel bridled. "I break every code just by being here."

"Uncertain times," Kurt soothed. "They call for special measures. Would you not rather search this out for me than sell your guns?"

The colonel subsided. "This will cost you."

"Of course it will."

"Even before I know if it is possible, I will have to make payments of my own."

Kurt frowned. "It would be far better to promise payment upon delivery."

The officer snorted. "We have had our fill of promises. We have warehouses full of promises instead of food."

"There is that," Kurt admitted.

"I will be paid for the search, and more for the find," the colonel declared.

Kurt's hand slid into his pocket, emerged with an envelope. "The doctor's name and our first payment then."

The colonel slipped the envelope beneath the table's edge, counted, pursed his lips. "The first of many payments, if they are all of a size."

"No snippet of information can be too minor," Kurt told him. "We seek all possible details."

Hard eyes bore down. "It would help to know what you are seeking."

Kurt forced himself not to flinch. "Details," he repeated. "We are collectors of the minutiae, and we will pay the most for the most complete report."

Because of the snow and ice and threat of more, Jeffrey and Katya flew from London to Frankfurt-am-Main, then took a train to Erfurt. Berlin would have been a marginally closer airport to Erfurt, but all the flights were booked solid by the movers and shakers seeking to influence or lean on or sell to or feed off the new-old capital's massive restructuring.

The sky hovering above the German landscape was leaden gray, the clouds so close as to rest upon the undulating hills marking the old border country. There was little snow, but the mid-afternoon frost appeared permanent, unchanging, an eternal part of this heavy-laden landscape. Trees were bowed and motionless, their limbs burdened and hoary white. Even the grass beside their slow-moving train was frozen at icy attention.

They had their compartment to themselves, which was good. They needed the time alone to balance their love and their decision with the demands of business. They spoke of many things and left the most remarkable unsaid. The entire world seemed new, yet unchanged. Their conversation was casual, yet eternally serious, since now it was part of a lifetime they had agreed to spend together.

Jeffrey sat alongside Katya and watched her and spoke with her, and all the while he marveled at the fact that she was to be his wife. His *wife*. He could not help but smile. The word alone boggled the mind.

"Why are you smiling?"

He shook his head, unable to voice his thoughts just then. Instead he said, "Would you mind if I asked you how you came to faith?"

Katya looked at him a long moment, then asked in return, "Is that what you and Mama talked about?"

"Partly," he said, and felt an ease between them, a fluidity that could not be contained. His *wife*.

She sat beside him, very prim and proper in a dark-gray suit of softest wool. From time to time, however, one stockinged toe would emerge from her pumps to caress his ankle. There was a casualness to her motion that spoke of rightful intimacy. "It was probably very sad."

"It was."

"I don't want to hear about it right now, okay? But please tell me some other time."

"Whenever you like."

"My faith." She brought up one of his hands to give it a closer inspection. "I don't feel as if it's mine at all. It is a gift from the Father that I hold in trust."

"That's beautiful," he said softly.

"Mama was always strong in her faith, and I was raised to simply accept it as a part of life. As young as I was, I could see how much it meant to her in those tough times after my father left."

"You don't have to talk about this if you don't want to."

"It's all right. For me, growth in faith has always meant realizing that there's a lot I don't know, and probably even more that I don't have right to know. This keeps me from ever being too dogmatic about things, remembering times in the past when I thought I had it all perfect, only to discover later that it wasn't nearly as correct or complete as I imagined."

He moved back far enough to be able to see her face. "You sound so wise when you talk like this, Katya." He searched for some way to explain how he felt. "It humbles me."

She rewarded him with a brief kiss before returning to her story. "A few years after my father was gone, we moved to England. As I grew older I kept looking for a healing faith in all the wrong places. I was sure I was going to find it in a church or in a person. Somebody who was going to sit me down and draw out this path and tell me where to put my feet and say, go from A to B to C and then you're home. But faith doesn't work like that.

"I think what I really wanted was somebody who would be my new daddy. Somebody who would be there when I needed him, who wouldn't leave me. It took a long time before I finally accepted that I really wasn't getting to know God at all, just another man—a preacher or a deacon or somebody in the church. They were substitutes, and sooner or later I was going to have to start looking myself. Studying the Bible by myself. Praying by myself. Making contact directly with Christ, by myself. Making the relationship a *personal* one.

"When you grow up in the church, you know all the right answers. But that doesn't mean Christ is in your life. There are a lot of people who call themselves Christians and who hide from God when He manifests himself. In Genesis, it is not God who runs from people, but people who flee from God. Some things never change."

Katya bent over his fingers, sliding a feather-light caress around each in turn. "This lesson wasn't fully learned until I went for a semester as an exchange student to Warsaw. I went primarily to improve my Polish, but I also studied what they called History of Political and Legal Doctrines."

"Sounds most riveting," he said, eyebrows raised.

She settled his hand in her lap. "It wasn't so bad, really. And it gave me some incredible lessons in keeping my temper."

"I'm all for that."

"The class was taught by a staunch Party member. I mean a real flag waver. I was the only Westerner in the class, and he kept saying these things as though hoping I was going to explode. I never did, though. There wasn't anything to be gained by giving him the pleasure of seeing me lose it."

"What was the class about?"

"It was an exhaustive coverage of obscure Soviet bureaucratic Communist thinkers. Not Polish. Soviet."

"And the Polish students didn't complain?"

"Not in class. Not in hearing-range of the professor. If a Pole made it as far as university, he had already learned to keep his mouth shut around Party members, especially when it came to complaining about the Soviets." Katya's eyes were frosty. "The Soviet theory of history is linear. That is, all events represent a class struggle and lead inevitably to socialism. This phrase is repeated ad infinitum—the *inevitability* of socialism. So all the studies concentrated on events that supported this perspective. Everything else was virtually ignored.

"History studies revolved around uprisings, strikes, workers' actions, and the cruelest possible examples of capitalist exploitation of workers. The thrust, the key, was always the ownership of production. Their basic principle was that until workers owned *all* land and *all* resources and *all* factories and *all* stores—through the central government, of course—these uprisings would continue. It was *inevitable.* Events so obscure they did not even deserve mention in a Western encyclopedia or textbook were treated as turning points on the path to Communism."

He made a face. "How could you put up with that stuff?"

"It was hard," she admitted. "But these are the lies that shaped Poland for over forty years. I kept reminding myself of that, and I studied the Bible harder than I ever had in my life. There, at least, I knew I could remember what truth really was. And when I finally returned home I knew that one reward of the journey, something I would treasure for all my days, was this coming to know a personal relationship with my Savior. Beyond the confines of any church or doctrine or earthly activity. He was my Lord, and He was my friend."

======

At the last stop before crossing the former border, the gray-suited West German train conductors gave way to a pudgy man with one wandering eye and a rail-thin girl with spiked blond hair. They wore uniforms of electric blue, replete with broad leather belts and shiny brass medals. They barked a demand for tickets, inspected them minutely. Katya asked them a polite question, received a smirk and several short words in reply.

"The conductors are much more imposing here," she whispered when they departed. "Less discreet than the West German officials."

"I noticed," Jeffrey replied. "What did you ask them?"

"When we would arrive at the old border crossing. They said to watch for the tank barriers."

Rolling hills gave way to a broad, flat expanse, a plateau that afforded a clear view in every direction of a frozen, silent winter scape. Soon enough the fields began growing a tragic crop of watchtowers and giant lights and crossed railings dug into metal-lined trenches. Although the barbed wire had been removed, the former dead man's zone remained marked by row after row after row of ten-foot-high concrete pillars. They stretched out to both horizons, endless lines like slender tombstones.

"Before the Wall fell, borders like this were a lot noisier," Katya told him, her voice subdued. "The dogs had vicious-sounding barks, especially at night. And the guards were always shouting, never just speaking."

Standing in the middle of the field was a single abandoned building, a vast multistoried structure washed to unpainted grayness by passing seasons.

"It must have been a prewar factory," Katya guessed. "It was in the fire zone; see the stands where they had the spotlights and the machine-gun placements?"

"I see," Jeffrey replied quietly.

"Look at the building; you can see how all the windows and doors on the first two floors are bricked up. It was probably too close to the Western border to let even the guards use; they might have tried to escape."

Their train swung around a bend, and the roadway border appeared. Tall stone and mortar guardhouses loomed over a point just prior to where the road diminished from four well-paved and brightly marked lanes to a narrow, rutted passage. The towers showed bare walls toward the east; all windows and gun emplacements and entrenched vigilance faced the other way.

Once beyond the border, barbed wire sprouted and grew everywhere. Everything was fenced—roads, train tracks, nearby houses, footpaths. The train slowed for another bend, and slowed, and slowed, and remained slow. The track became increasingly bumpy, the surroundings ever more grim.

"It's like another world," Jeffrey said.

"We've passed through a fifty-year time warp," Katya replied. "The price of Communism. One of them, anyway."

The houses were immediately older. Instead of Western double-paned windows, there were warped squares of hand-drawn glass set in flaking wooden panels. Shutters and doors and walls shed paint like old snow, if they were painted at all. Bricks stood exposed through shattered plaster, timbers bared ancient cracks. Bowed walls were supported by tree trunks stripped and replanted at an angle. Weeds grew waist high through cracked pavement. Cars turned tiny and plastic and sputtered smoky spumes.

At the first station after the border, the train ejected a steady stream of people. Most carried boxes and bales and bags and pushed strollers that contained not babies, but more boxes and bags. The people looked very tired. Exhausted.

"Shoppers," Katya explained. "There is still greater variety in the West, and the people trust the stores there more than they do the ones here."

Signs of renovation and new construction dotted the landscape like flecks of bright new paint on an old scarred canvas. Flashing lights and yellow construction trucks signaled road works almost every time a highway came into view. New, unfinished factories rose alongside structures built more from rust than steel. But despite the evident signs of change, the predominant color remained gray, the main impression one of deep fatigue. Bone tiredness of both the people and the land. That, and cold.

They arrived in Erfurt two hours late. Night had fallen hard on the city, engulfing it in almost total darkness. Occasional streetlights poured tiny islands of light into a sea of black. Here and there, apartment windows glowed in yellow solitude against the night. But the dominant feeling was of darkness.

Their hotel, the Erfurter Hof, was located just across a cement and asphalt square from the main train station. The centuries-old building had been redecorated in a bland Communist style, all hard edges and overly bright colors and charmless prints of big-muscled men and women in determined parade. Jeffrey and Katya were joined at the check-in counter by a large group of weary business folk in rumpled suits and dresses, all off the same train from the West as themselves.

Jeffrey collected their keys, joined the elevator's silent throng, and walked Katya down to her room. He saw his own weariness mirrored in her face. "I don't understand how I could grow so tired just sitting down all day."

"Travel does that," she agreed. She offered her face up for a kiss. "I hope you sleep as well as I intend to."

His room was high-ceilinged and furnished with lightwood beds and chairs and low tables screwed into the floor. Jeffrey drew his drapes against the train station's constant rumble and gave in to his utter fatigue.

Erika paused on the Schwerin office building stairs to catch her breath and go over Ferret's instructions. It still rankled, this working at the beck and call of a half-finished man. He sat downstairs in her car, waiting for her to walk up and talk and go down and report. Then she had to smile. At least he had let her drive.

A ride with Ferret in the driver's seat was the most harrowing experience of a passenger's lifetime. Fear was an ever-present companion from the moment Ferret nodded his acceptance of the address and leveled his nose as close to the windshield as the steering wheel permitted. Ferret's vision was so poor he could scarcely make out other cars, especially at night, which was the only time he drove. He tended to stick to quieter byways and hope he would not meet anyone at crossroads. Traffic lights were seldom seen until the last possible moment. This meant he had the choice of standing on the brakes or shooting the intersection at blinding speeds. Either way, his passengers lost years.

Erika sighed, a sound she was making more and more these days, and walked down the hall. At least this work required a few of the talents she had developed over the years. And though she did not understand what they were doing, it afforded her a small hope of moving on, of escaping this place where life as she knew it had disappeared.

For most Ossies, the nation of East Germany had been a prison, a landlocked cell without doors or hope of release. The slightest glimpse toward the outside world had been both forbidden and frightfully dangerous. If a child had happened to mention at school that his family watched Wessie programs intentionally beamed over the Wall, the entire family—children included—had faced arrest, interrogation, and loss of job and hearth and home.

Ossies had responded by turning inward, especially in the smaller communities. Villages had become islands, struggling to provide barriers against a world that was beyond their control or understanding. Automatic suspicion of newcomers had kept Stasi infiltration to a minimum. Choosing brides and husbands from local stock had preserved local solidarity, even if communities were so small as to require inbreeding. Anything had been deemed better than letting in the dangers of the unknown, the outside, the secret, the hidden.

But for the keepers like Erika, the former system had provided security, sufficient wealth, and the thrill of life-and-death power over the masses. For them, the Wall's collapse had been the unthinkable brought to life, the subsequent investigations and trials beyond belief. Across the former country, worried conversations began and ended with the argument voiced by every defendant brought into court: We served our country as we were trained and ordered to serve. How can another country come in and fire us and put us on trial and accuse us under a different country's laws? How is this possible? Show us where we broke the laws of our own country! Show us!

Erika watched the unfolding drama from the relative safety of a new identity in a strange town and wished only to be away. Questions of guilt left her tired. As far as she was concerned, the difference between Stasi tactics and those of the West—such as the headline-grabbing 1982 alliance between Pope John Paul II and President Reagan to keep Solidarity alive after Poland declared martial law—was that the West had won the undeclared war. Safety did not rest in reason. These days, safety was possible only for those who could come up with enough cash to buy a new life.

Erika rapped sharply on the door, then pushed it open at the sound of a woman's voice from within. She entered a cramped office overflowing with books and ledgers, looked down on a middle-aged woman whose dark hair spilled over her face as she continued to peruse legal documents. Without looking up, the woman raised a nicotine-stained finger toward the chair across from her desk. Erika remained standing, waiting with patience born of a lifetime's experience.

The silence extended through another minute, then the woman slammed the tome shut and reached with a practiced gesture for her cigarette pack. It was only then that she raised her eyes and focused on Erika. With that first glance, her motions ceased.

Erika felt the faintest thrill of pleasure and a fleeting memory of a former world, when it had rarely been necessary even to show her badge to get total and unswerving attention. Badges had been superfluous for one accustomed to holding Stasi power. People had looked and seen and understood. Their freedom had depended upon diligent attention and absolute obedience.

Then the woman forced herself to relax, a conscious effort that cost her dearly. The shaking fingers that plucked out the cigarette told of her difficulty in casting aside the lessons of a lifetime. She lit the cigarette, dragged deeply, said with the smoke, "Yes?"

Erika felt the bitter disappointment of one robbed of her rightful place, and it grated into her voice. "Frau Reining?"

The woman nodded. "You are the woman who called for an appointment, Frau." She leaned forward, glanced at her calendar, said with evident skepticism, "Frau Schmidt?"

"Yes." Erika swallowed her bitterness. To stoop to such nonsense. Yet she knew how to follow orders, that much she still carried with her. She spoke as Ferret had instructed. "I represent a seller of an antique who wishes to contact a Western dealer. One who knows his business and can be trusted to offer a fair price."

"I see." Frau Reining took in almost a quarter of her cigarette in one drag. "And why come to me?"

"You are involved with several court cases involving compensation for stolen antiques. We had hoped you were in touch with people within the Western markets. Trusted people," she continued by rote from Ferret's own words, "who respect our need for confidentiality."

"We?" Frau Reining asked. "You are agent for the seller?"

"We will be pleased to pay a fee for this introduction," Erika evaded. "In hopes that it will help us avoid a costly mistake."

The woman showed no reaction to the offer, just as Ferret had predicted. And as he had said she would, Frau Reining asked, "It is a German piece?"

"No," Erika answered, more sure of her footing now that Ferret's strange-sounding predictions were proving accurate. An honest woman, Ferret had described Frau Reining. A freak of nature. One who couldn't be bought. Erika stifled a vague wish that things were still as they once had been, when she could have tested this ridiculous claim.

Erika had known a great many women to change their tune when faced with fear. Not just a little fear. A real fear. Of real pain. Pain promised by blood-spattered walls and a room filled with the stink of others' agony. Such women would enter a prison interrogation cell, see hopelessness painted on all the walls, and know there was only one hope, one escape—through utter submission. Through giving in to terror and doing exactly as they were told. At such times, fear stripped away strength and exposed principles for what they were—mere luxuries.

Once she had led a prisoner, a Christian caught handing out Scripture tracts, into the cellar punishment chamber. The woman had taken one look around, and as her legs gave way she had spoken words Erika would never forget. She had raised her eyes to the gray-spackled ceiling and cried, *Oh, dear Father, protect me from the eater of souls!* Erika had no idea what those words meant, but she liked the ring of them.

All she said to Frau Reining now was, "The article we wish to sell resides in Poland." Which was another mystery to Erika, but here again Ferret had seemed both certain of his facts and unwilling to discuss them further.

"Poland." Reining showed surprise. "There has been a very unscrupulous history of antique dealing under the old regime. I have learned to be very cautious."

"Poland," Erika repeated, and continued as instructed. "It has been there since the war."

"I see." Frau Reining ground out her cigarette. "Normally I would not become involved in such a matter. But as the article is not in this country, I see no reason why I should not help you."

Erika reacted with stony silence, her thoughts and desires hidden behind a practiced mask.

Frau Reining reached for her notepad. "I will give you an address. It so happens that my contact is at this moment in Erfurt."

"We would prefer that *you* represent us," Erika replied as Ferret had instructed.

"Represent you how?"

"We wish to arrange a meeting on neutral ground. In Dresden. This week would be excellent." This moved up Ferret's time plan slightly, but the contact was nearby, and the little man had said to set up a meeting quickly. Within a week or so if possible, Ferret had told her, though why she did not know. They still had nothing to sell.

Erika handed over Ferret's typed instructions. "Please pass this on to your contact and confirm that you've done so by calling the number below."

Frau Reining was clearly unsure of herself. "I suppose I could—"

Erika slipped an envelope out of her pocket, set it on the desk. "This is a retainer. Let us know when further funds are required." With that she turned and walked from the room, glad to be done with this freakish woman and her foolish, unchallenged principles.

Jeffrey awoke while it was still dark to find that the room's heat had been cut off. The air was so cold that it poured through the hotel's windows as if they were open. The bathroom tiles burned his feet, and he could see his breath. He put clothes on over his pajamas as well as a second layer of socks, stripped covers from the second bed, and piled everything on top of his own. Eventually he returned to sleep.

Breakfast was served in a plain, high-ceilinged hall so large the businessmen and their rattling papers were reduced to tiny, harrumphing dolls. Katya arrived looking incredibly fresh, and she was followed to his table by every eye in the room.

He rose and said in greeting, "You look beautiful."

She kissed him twice. "One of those was for last night, in case I forgot."

He fought off a rising blush brought on by curious gazes. "You didn't, but thanks just the same."

She ordered breakfast from the waitress, then said, "I called the antiques dealer, Herr Diehl. He is eagerly awaiting our arrival. He sounds like a very nice man."

Jeffrey nodded. "Was your room cold last night?"

"Freezing. And my bath water was brown."

"Mine, too."

"Rusty pipes," she said. "Probably there since before the war."

"In a first-class hotel."

"They haven't changed the radiators, either."

"I slept in both my sweaters last night."

"Good." She smiled. "You're learning to adjust to life in the glorious East."

Their way from the hotel to the Krämer Bridge took them down ancient cobblestone streets now used as pedestrian passages. Gradually the city was awakening from its long sleep, with a charm and heritage that even the depths of winter could not disguise. Some of the houses were minuscule, built for the smaller peoples of six and seven hundred years ago. Most buildings remained scarred from the old regime's determined neglect, yet everywhere there were signs of change—flashing store lights, cheerful window displays, enthusiastic street hawkers, new construction, fresh paint.

If Katya had not announced their arrival at the bridge, Jeffrey would not have known it. The line of old houses simply opened for yet another cobblestone way with ancient dwellings standing cheek-to-jowl along both sides. There was no sign of a river, no indication that they were stepping up and over a waterway. But a stone plaque attached to the first bridge-house stated that this was indeed the Krämer Bridge, built of wood in the twelfth century, then of stone two hundred years later. Closely packed houses lining the bridge showed chest-high doors, tiny waist-level windows, and bowed walls.

The *Haus der Glocke*, the Bell House, was a closet-sized shop halfway along the bridge. A cheerful little bell above the door announced their entry. They stood in the minuscule patch of free floor space and looked around. Gradually the shop's clutter took on a certain cramped order. Along the walls stood a glass-fronted display case for pocket watches, a glass-topped table for old ivory and meerschaum pipes, and another for rolling pins etched with household scenes from the last century. One corner cupboard held pewter, another antique jewelry. Higher up, decorative household items battled for shelf space with old silver serving pieces. Two wall cabinets displayed clocks, and a third showed off miniature oils in ornate cases. Hand-wound gramophones on ornately carved legs elbowed against antique dolls and horsehair footstools.

Katya looked around and declared, "This is a happy shop."

"Full of memories of better times," Jeffrey agreed. "Two of the clocks in that cabinet are museum-quality pieces, as well."

A slender man with thin strands of snow-white hair appeared from what Jeffrey had dismissed as a broom closet and now realized was the shop's office. "Herr Sinclair?" the man asked.

"That's me. Herr Diehl?" Jeffrey shook hands. The slender fingers held a surprising strength. Katya exchanged a handshake and introductions with their host and translated for Jeffrey. "He is delighted that we have found our way to his little shop."

"Ask him if we are allowed to carry off those two clocks on the top shelf over there."

The spark of a dealer's heart showed in Herr Diehl's eyes as Katya translated. She told Jeffrey, "He is very glad to hear that Frau Reining was correct as to your eye for quality as well."

"As well as what?"

"Honesty is a most valuable commodity in such uncertain times," Herr Diehl replied through Katya.

"It's a good way to begin business," Jeffrey agreed. "On both sides."

Herr Diehl motioned for them to follow him. They skirted a narrow mirror-backed cabinet crowded with porcelain figurines and discovered a claustrophobic stairway that etched a passage along the house's back wall.

The stairs creaked and groaned under the dealer's weight. They were so narrow that Jeffrey found it necessary to turn sideways. The stairs emptied into a single cramped chamber floored with bare, ancient planking and a thick coat of dust. Lighting came from one bare bulb and a single tiny window. Yet the poor surroundings could not detract from the glory of the pieces awaiting inspection.

"I judged these to be of collector's quality," Herr Diehl said through Katya. "Articles that would require a larger showcase than what I could manage here in Erfurt."

"You judged correctly," Jeffrey agreed solemnly and approached the first piece, a secretary-cabinet constructed of solid walnut, with other light woods inlaid in a series of delicate floral patterns framed by mosaic swirls.

Lines tended to blur between lands and eras in Central European antiques. Wars and revolutions had redrawn national boundaries and allegiances, often with dizzying speed. With each change, woodworkers and silversmiths and ironmongers and jewelers had adapted anew to the tastes of those who could afford to buy. In the space of a century, therefore, the style of locally produced pieces had changed from Florentine to Russian, from Austro-Hungarian to Prussian, from French to Persian. This particular piece was German, probably from the eighteenth century, but executed in Italian Rococo style.

The second article was most likely eighteenth-century Austrian in design, as the Austro-Hungarian Empire dominated much of central Europe at that time. The inlay was subtly crafted to suggest a patriotic figure within swirls of clouds. Done during an era of occupation, when overt patriotism to anything but the empire was punishable by death, it was a most ingenious piece.

There were three pieces from the Baroque period, the name given to the Renaissance in countries north of the Alps. One was a remarkable chest hand carved in the shape of a vase, narrow legs rising and expanding to a pair of drawers that both broadened and curved outward in gentle waves. The piece was made from wild cherry wood, the original fittings of dark bronze fashioned like draping sprigs of ivy. Another chest of drawers, also constructed of cherry, displayed the traditional Baroque curved front. Beside it was a late-Baroque commode with typically extravagant Rococo inlay in the form of Grecian urns. This piece, too, was solid cherry.

A great deal of cherry had been used in central European furniture around that time. Four hundred years ago, several royal decrees had ordered all roads to be lined with cherry trees. As the neighboring cities expanded and required larger roads, however, these trees had gradually been chopped down and fashioned into furniture. Cultivated trees like these were known for their smooth, long grain, as contrasted with the cramped, gnarled grain for wild cherry.

The final item was a woman's bureau, signed and dated 1809, and again carved from solid cherry. It was a piece made to stand alone, to draw the eye of everyone who entered the chamber. The finish was Empire at its best, simple and silken, accenting a wood so fine as to hold a jewel-like shimmer.

Jeffrey straightened from his perusal, released a breath he felt he had been holding on to for hours. "Magnificent," he declared.

The dealer showed a trace of anxiety and asked through Katya, "You would like to take them?"

"Every article you have here will be a valuable addition to our shop," Jeffrey replied flatly.

The man released a sigh of his own. "Then my own assessment was correct."

"I will need a second opinion on a couple of the more valuable items, and all of them will require a closer inspection before appraising," Jeffrey said. "But my first assessment is that you have brought together an excellent group."

"That is good news. Excellent news. You will make many people very happy." Herr Diehl appeared at a momentary loss. "You can perhaps accept more furniture?"

"Of this quality?" Jeffrey permitted himself a smile. "As much as you can deliver. No problem." Katya quickly translated.

The dealer puffed out age-dappled cheeks, said, "You cannot imagine the difference between this discussion and those I have had with other Western dealers."

"Maybe I can."

"Yes, perhaps so." Through Katya he went on, "I have spent hours trying to fathom what on earth they were talking about as they inspected the undersides of drawers and ran their hands over nail heads and questioned provenance. Is that what you call it, provenance? The history of the owners."

"Provenance, yes," Jeffrey nodded, and added, "All of that we will need to do as well, but not now. Yet even if the provenance proves questionable and it turns out we are looking at articles pieced together over several different eras, which I doubt, their quality is still enough to warrant a high price."

"Not according to your competitors."

"They were offering you a flat sum?"

Herr Diehl nodded. "And making it sound as if they were doing me an enormous favor."

Jeffrey gave silent thanks for his competitors' greed. "I'll have to check a bit further before I can say anything for sure, Herr Diehl. But my first guess is that you've got well over two hundred thousand dollars in furniture up here. After commissions."

"So much," he murmured.

"I try to keep my first estimates conservative." Jeffrey weighed his alternatives, decided now was not the time to hold back. He pointed toward the Empire secretary and the cabinet with the dreamlike patriotic inlay. "There is a good chance those two pieces alone will fetch over that figure."

"If you can speak with such decisive authority, Herr Sinclair," the dealer replied, "then so can I." He extended his hand once more. "I shall look forward to doing business with you for years to come."

"Likewise," Jeffrey replied. Then he motioned what looked like two large doors on the front outside wall of the room over the street. "I assume you bring the pieces up from the street through this large opening."

The man chuckled after Katya's translation. "Yes, yes, as you have seen, the stairway is far too cramped for these pieces of furniture. We use ropes and many strong backs. And the ones you want will come out of the room the same way."

Herr Diehl then became the formal host. "My shop is unfortunately too cramped for us all to sit and talk comfortably. May I invite you to a nearby cafe?"

Jeffrey and Katya allowed themselves to be led back down the narrow stairs. Herr Diehl ushered them outside, locked up his shop, and started toward the bridge's far end. As they walked Katya said to Jeffrey, "He speaks a beautiful German. I wish you could understand it."

"Your translation sounds almost courtly." He motioned toward the ancient structures lining the bridge. "It fits the surroundings."

Herr Diehl beamed as Katya translated. "For a number of years, there was little with which I could occupy my mind, as the only work permitted me was hand labor. So I read. I read the Bible. I read everything I could find about antiques. It was an excellent way of immersing myself in times where troubles such as mine did not exist. I also read classical German literature, Goethe especially. There was a man who made heavy Germanic tones sound light and graceful as an aria."

"Frau Reining mentioned that it had been hard for you as a believer under the Communists," Jeffrey said.

"All Christians in this country had their own experience," Herr Diehl replied. "There were some imprisonments, yes, but in truth they were a minority. On the other hand, if you accepted Christ into your life, you *knew* what your lot would be. There was no question. You would lose your public name. You would never be granted a position that held any power of decision or authority over others. Promotions would be permanently blocked. You would wait weeks, months, years, for the simplest of government documents, even a driver's license. You would never be considered for new housing, no matter how many children you might have or how great was your need. Your family would suffer as a result of your action, from the eldest to the youngest, without exception. Your children would never be permitted to receive a higher education. Yet all this became, in a sense, normal for us. There was no question but that this would happen, you see. It came as no surprise. This was the way of life in our country for so long. You entered into such a decision with your eyes open.

"Under the Communists," Herr Diehl went on, "there were enough Christians in the cities for us to find comfort. The situation in the villages was far worse. A few women attended services, those who were too old or too insignificant for the Stasi to trouble over. Priests and ministers were barely tolerated by the local citizens, and they often went weeks without a friendly word from anyone outside the handful of believers. If asked, I suppose most villagers would have said that, yes, it was probably good to have a pastor around, for funerals and such. But not for them and not for now; they had to worry too much and work too hard just to survive in this life. There were frequent suicides among ministers, which the state made sure received nationwide publicity as a way to declare all who believed in God, even the preachers, to be mentally unstable.

"In the cities, with their larger populations of believers, the situation was different. The state gave us no choice but to get along, to form ourselves into a unified body. Minor disagreements over personality or style of worship fell into insignificance when faced with the issue of our very survival."

They arrived at the bridge's far end, which was anchored by a miniature church of ancient brick, so small as to appear a replica made for little children. "This is the Aegidien Church, erected in 1125 as a sanctuary for travelers and resident merchants alike." Herr Diehl led them to a cafe set slightly below the level of the bridge proper. "This was originally a small monastery, a standing invitation to the weary and the hungry and the fearful to turn from the world of money and peril and woes."

The door was narrow and little over four feet high, the stone walls almost three feet thick. Inside, the ceilings were arched and colonnaded, the floor stones sanded down by eight hundred years of use. Lighting came from ancient bronze torch holders adapted to electricity.

They selected a tiny alcove whose picture window overlooked the pedestrians. Herr Diehl ordered sandwiches and tea for them all. The waiter returned swiftly with a tiny saucer piled with a reddish dust. Katya and Herr Diehl shared a smile at the sight.

"What is it?" Jeffrey asked.

"Paprika and salt," Katya replied. "It's for our sandwiches."

"Why is that humorous?"

"It's something from the old regime. Pepper was rare, especially in government-controlled restaurants where they couldn't charge for it. Pepper had to be imported. Paprika could be grown here, so it was often served as a substitute. I think it tastes awful."

Herr Diehl spoke, and Katya translated, "These are lingering signs of what once was everywhere. We are able to smile at them now because the shadow is gradually drawing away."

Jeffrey asked Katya, "Do you think it would be all right to ask how he became a Christian? I don't want to offend him or anything, so please don't—"

Katya swiftly turned and spoke in a language made graceful by her lilting voice. Herr Diehl seemed genuinely pleased by the question and replied at length.

"Some stories are easier to end than to begin," he said. "I know that the ending arrives when I have opened the eyes of my heart and known the presence of the Lord. The beginning is somewhat more difficult, as it resides in the confusion that was everyone's life at the end of the war."

Jeffrey shook his head. "I love the way he talks."

"You should hear it in the original," Katya said.

"The crippling of my beloved Berlin began about two years before the Russians arrived," Herr Diehl told them. "I was two years old, and the year was 1943. Our home at that time was a large apartment building with an inner courtyard in the city center. Still today I remember the British and American bombing raids so well, so vividly. Still I can see the planes overhead, great, booming sheets of hundreds and hundreds of metal birds.

"Every night they came. It was all automatic after a few months of the bombing, our reactions. The sirens would start. I would rub the sleep from my eyes, and wait for my mother to come and take me from my crib. I had a little wooden toy car, green and gold, and I made it my responsibility to carry the car downstairs. My mother and my father had their packed suitcases and their little carry-sack of provisions. I had my little toy car.

"In the cellar we were twenty, maybe twenty-five. We heard the planes, we heard the piping sounds the bombs made as they fell, we heard the explosions come close, then closer, then shake us violently, then move away. We heard the tak-tak-tak of the antiaircraft guns. Then it grew quieter, and then the sirens called that it was over, and we went back upstairs to sleep. Sometimes it was already light when we came up, and we would go outside, and it was a different world! The windows were gone. The building next door had vanished. The street had great, gaping holes. Fires. Running, shouting people. Great engines with different sirens trying to race around the holes and the rubble in the streets.

"A neighbor would come to stand beside us and say that we had no electricity and no gas and no water. It was not so frightening for me, though. Either my father or my mother was always beside me, holding my little hand.

"The end of the war came at different times to the German people," Herr Diehl explained. "Like waves from several different storms crashing upon our little island. The American troops moved fastest across our defeated nation, and we in Berlin kept hoping they would arrive first and rescue us from the dreaded Soviets. But they stopped just outside the city and waited for the Soviets to catch up.

"Refugees from the East brought horrible stories of what we could expect from the Soviets. I will speak about these refugees again in just a moment. Their true plight did not become clear until after the war ended, as the stream of homeless people struggling westward became a flood. At the time of the Soviets' approach to Berlin, they remained few enough for their faces to be seen as individuals, for their voices to be heard.

"I was four years old in 1945. I was what they called an autumn child; my father was fifty-five and my mother forty-nine. To say the least, my parents had not been expecting me. When the Soviets arrived, we were living in South Berlin, a section perhaps a half-hour tram ride from the center city. Our home in the heart of Berlin had been totally destroyed in the bombing raids. It was our great fortune that the day our house was bombed, my mother and I were with my father in South Berlin where he worked on a company project. Everyone else in our apartment house died when the bomb took the front walls and the cellar away. Completely away. I will never forget going back and seeing our apartment. The back of the house stood, the front was gone. No rubble, no stone, nothing! Our home was dust. And yet the back rooms were still so complete I could see the pictures hanging in what had been my parents' bedroom. It made such an impression on my young mind, how the house had been split as if with a giant's knife.

"So we moved to this less-destroyed section, into a house owned by the company where my father worked, just as word came that the

Russians were advancing. Our first night in this strange new home, we began to hear their guns booming in the distance. It sounded like thunder, and the light they made on the horizon looked like the first faint colors of a false dawn.

"As a child, I thought the Russians were evil ghosts. I had never seen a foreigner, you see. Then one day my father, who had been too old to be a soldier, was gathered up and taken away with all the other old men who still had two arms and two legs. He was given bits and pieces of several uniforms. I remember the right sleeve had been sewn from a different jacket and was four or five inches shorter than the left, and there was a dark stain over the jacket's middle and a hole that had been sewn up in jagged haste. He was given only one weapon, a hand grenade.

"Four weeks later, he came back, dug a hole in the garden, stripped off his uniform, and buried it. Thirty minutes after that, the first Soviet soldier walked in. He stepped up to my father, who by then was dressed in his best suit and trying not to appear nervous, and asked what time it was. My father opened his pocket watch and answered, almost one o'clock. The soldier said, good, and took the watch. That was my first experience with a foreigner.

"South Berlin was a very dirty place. Filthy. Before the war, it had been the center for Eastern Germany's coal-processing and steel works. My father had been born there and had sworn never to return. He had been forced by circumstances to live there again, had been conscripted and sent off to fight in a losing war, then returned only to greet the Russians and hear that they were to make our house the Soviet army's district headquarters. We then had to live in the tiny, damp cellar while Soviet army boots clumped and thudded over our heads. But we did not complain overmuch, at least not very loudly. At least we had a roof.

"There was a park and a garden across the street. This became very important for us, because we raised vegetables there. It kept us alive, that park—us and our neighbors. We swiftly learned that our chances of survival were better if we could learn to live as an extended family.

"The Soviets were very bad, and most of the stories you hear of their atrocities are true. They took the last of our possessions—our clothes, furniture, carpets, jewelry, anything that had survived the war. But for me they often showed a different side, as many were kind to children, and sometimes they fed me from their kitchen. Even at that early age, I knew I was incredibly fortunate. I still had my mother and my father. There were few such complete families then. Very, very few.

"We lived through those first two years with great difficulty. Those words do not describe the times, but no words would, so I will not try. My father had been an electrical engineer who worked for the coal and electrical combine. Before the war, all big German companies had their headquarters in Berlin. But now Berlin was no more. Destroyed. Leveled so completely that soldiers coming home from the fronts or the POW camps could not even find the *streets* where they had lived, much less their houses or their families.

"My father found work with a little coal company during the days, and at night he pedaled his bike to nearby villages and rewired the damaged electrical systems in cottages and farmhouses. He was paid in milk and vegetables and sometimes meat. He slept when he could. My mother sewed.

"Because my father worked for a coal company, we had heat. Others did not. Old people simply froze and died. The two winters after the war were *extremely* cold. The cities were hell, simply hell. People risked their lives to steal coal. There was no wood at all.

"Coal shipped by trains was sprayed with chalk over the top. When it arrived officials would look down on the train cars; a dark spot meant that some of the top coal had been stolen. The suppliers would then be penalized or sometimes jailed. So the suppliers hired very tough men to walk back and forth on these exceedingly cold trains and beat off people who raced up at crossings and tried to steal enough coal to keep their families from freezing.

"My father knew this for a fact, because sometimes he had to travel for the coal company and talk to the officials at the other end. There was no gasoline, of course, unless you were with the occupying forces. It took days and days for him to obtain the permits to travel by train, and then he was forced to sit on the coal wagons, atop little runner stations. In the open. He would sit like that for hours, wrapped in blankets my mother gave him. Once he traveled with the really privileged, inside an unheated boxcar. He never spoke of what he saw when he rode on the coal cars. Yet I could see how haunted his eyes looked when he returned from his travels, and hear how his sleep was disturbed by nightmares.

"There was no infrastructure in those early days. No cars. No trams. No streets sometimes. No resources. No food. The land was empty and barren and blown up and scarred, a landscape from hell. And the government was horrible in the East of Germany. Simply beyond description.

"The Soviets sent back German Communists who had escaped from the Nazis by fleeing to Russia and fighting with the Red Army. They came back to take over the new Communist government. And they *hated* the German people. They were merciless. The old people, the weak ones, the young, they suffered. And then they died.

"To make matters worse—much worse—there were refugees. *Millions* of refugees. Germans from the former Eastern provinces— now part of Lithuania and Poland and Czechoslovakia and the Soviet Union, lands that had been part of Germany for centuries—all who could, fled to what was left of Germany. But when they arrived, starving and battered and stripped of everything of value, they found nothing left for them. No homes, no shelter, no food, no medicine, no heat, no sympathy. They came, they starved. They, too, died.

"Some months into that second year, I contracted typhoid. That was both very good and very bad. The bad side was how sick I became—very high fever, so high I almost died. This sickness stalked the city, with panic walking on one side and death on the other. At night I thought I was hearing ghosts, as screams and wails drifted through our little cellar windows, but later my mother told me they were real, the cries of mothers powerless to hold their children to this battered earth.

"Within a few days, the authorities gathered all the sick children who were still alive and placed them in a cinema. All the hospitals had been destroyed by the bombing raids, and this cinema was one of the few large halls that remained. It was something straight from my worst nightmares. There was very little medicine. There were not enough doctors or nurses, so most of the time I was left alone with my pain. The air was fetid, full of the smells of sick and dying children, too full of smells to breathe. The lighting was a dim, yellow glow, and there were frequent blackouts when the power failed.

"Every night children died all around me, their cries and choking gasps reaching out, threading their way through my fever to clutch at my life and pull it from my body and carry me off with them. And I was alone. More alone than ever in my life, before or since. We were not allowed visitors. I had not seen my parents since I was placed on the stretcher and carted away. I lay there in the putrid gloom and felt myself being consumed by the flames of my fever. And I cried, and I called out to a God I knew only through a child's prayers."

Katya choked back a shaky breath and reached for her glass. Both Jeffrey and Herr Diehl were immediately solicitous. Quietly she calmed the gentleman, then said to Jeffrey, "I'm all right. Really."

"We can stop now if you want."

"No, we cannot," she said with a shake of her head. "I have to hear the end. If I stopped now I don't know if I could ever go to sleep again. Just hold my hand, would you?"

He grasped it with both of his, tried to rub away the coldness in her fingers.

"As I lay there in my fear and my fever and my pain," Herr Diehl continued, "I felt something come upon me. I had not prayed for a healing, because I did not know what prayer was, beyond the words we spoke on Sundays and before meals and the little rhymes that sent me to sleep. I had simply called, and my call had been heard. That much I knew then, even in the midst of my fever-dreams. There was never any question that I had been heard, or that my call had been answered. A peace descended upon me, a love and a comfort that left me quiet and able to rest through that night and all the nights to come. It was only later that I could place words to the feeling. I had formed a solemn friendship, you see. The rest of my life, I have simply tried to hold up my side of the friendship that was forged on that dark and glorious night.

"That doesn't mean my life has been made easy, or even good. A good life does not exist for a Christian in a Communist land, especially one who feels led to tell his brothers the Good News. But never again did I face my trials alone." He paused and gave them both a gentle smile. "There was just one time when I did not share the miracles of my faith, at least not immediately. The day I returned home from the cinema-hospital, the Soviets moved out. My mother told me it was because they were frightened of infection.

"She was so happy to have both her son and her home back," Herr Diehl explained. "I could see no reason to argue with her."

Kurt's car crawled toward Weimar along roads made treacherous by rain-dampened cinders. As he drove he was struck by the realization that this was the first winter he could ever remember not seeing bent-over old ladies carrying coal buckets up from black piles dumped in front yards, alleys, and street comers. Perhaps there was something to this progress after all.

Though home to Goethe and Schiller and Thomas Mann, and former capital of the German Republic, Weimar had suffered badly during the Communist years. Now with the new influx of capitalism, the city was gradually becoming two. Within the ring-road that encircled the central city, the old town saw renovation progress at a hectic pace. Outside the loop, however, life ground on as slowly as ever. People struggled to survive, and Wessie promises to lift their lives had little meaning.

Since the region produced soft coal, the Communists had ordered all buildings—offices, apartments, hotels, hospitals, museums, factories—to employ that cheapest, most easily available source of heat. The city, hemmed in on three sides by high hills, therefore spent long winter months under a fog of soft-coal soot. Roads became slush-covered, buildings eroded as though dipped in acid baths, paint disappeared in a matter of months, cars were lost under thick black coatings. All the wealth and glory of Weimar had fallen victim to Communist homogenization, gradually fading beneath an ever-thickening layer of ashes and bureaucracy.

Approaching the ring-road at a snail's pace, Kurt decided he could make faster progress on foot and pulled into a parking space between two plastic Trabants. He opened his door and felt his shoes grind through a centimeter of cinders.

He followed his contact's instructions to what fifty years before had been known as the Gau Forum. It had been renamed Karl Marx Platz at war's end, and was now one of many nameless streets and squares awaiting new signs.

In the early thirties, the Nazis had taken a minor plaza at the outskirts of the city center and had transformed it into a gathering point for the new power brokers. The expanded eleven-acre square had become the Gau Forum, where Nazi parades drew hundreds of thousands of fanatics, reinforcing Nazi visions of fulfilling the Weimar Republic's lofty ambitions.

Buildings had been erected in stern Fascist style, with two long three-story arms extending down either side of the plaza from a central Nazi Party headquarters. Two balconies had been set at opposite midpoints; from these Hitler had often stood and incited the roaring mobs.

The Communists had converted the two arms into engineering and agricultural colleges and transformed the central building beyond all recognition. A modernistic glass-and-steel facade masked the original stone, and a fifteen-story office building loomed at its back. The clash of Fascist colonnaded stonework with Communist glass and steel, all surrounding a square of sooty-brown grass and stunted trees, gave the place a thoroughly grotesque appearance.

Kurt entered the main building's glass-walled annex to find himself in a sort of everyman's restaurant-cafe. Communist taste was stamped indelibly on everything—the orange globe lights, the fake-marble floors, the plastic ceilings, the cavernous size. Three or four hundred metal-limbed tables stretched out into the distance. The long side walls sported murals sixty feet long and forty wide, depicting strong-limbed Communist workers marching into a dull-red future filled with nightmarish Picasso-esque ovoids and triangular three-headed sphinxes. The place was virtually empty.

Kurt walked to the window table where his contact sat peering into the depths of his coffee. Kurt asked, "Why meet here?"

The young man raised his head and inspected Kurt with glittering eyes. "Brings back memories, does it?"

"I didn't like such places before. I certainly don't now."

"You should." The man's eyes were blue, yet shaded so dark as to seem opaque. His hands were scarred black with oil and soot. "You built them. You and your kind."

"I didn't come for an argument. I need information."

"Have some coffee first. Go on, it won't break you. Costs only fifty pfennigs. One of the few bargains left these days."

The single cafeteria line served brown a sludge that appeared to have been cooking since before the Wall came down. Seven bored attendants sat around talking in loud voices bouncing off distant walls. Kurt stood and waited long enough to know bitterness over a life and a world made into myth overnight. Finally one of them slouched to her feet and took his order.

While Kurt waited, he glanced back toward the table where his contact waited, hunched over his own cup. Kurt shook his head. One part of his former life that Kurt did not miss at all was having to deal daily with such oddities.

The prostitutes, for example. His duties had included shaking down whores who pandered to the low-class hotels. Not the big internationals—no, those hustlers were specially trained and monitored by the international section, the glamour boys, the department Kurt would have given his right arm to be a part of. No, his lot had been the third-rate inns catering to low-rent tourists from other Warsaw Pact lands. The prostitutes had known he wasn't high up the power structure—otherwise he wouldn't have wasted time on them. They had treated him like dirt.

And the gays. All the fair-haired boys trapped and suffocating in little villages where their lives had been made pure hell by the local Party roughs. They'd sell their souls for a ticket to a big city, where they could get lost within a crowd of their own kind. They made Kurt promises of eternal devotion for work and resident cards, then forgot his name once they had developed their own contacts—especially the pretty ones, who would sidle up close to someone with *real* power and then could thumb their noses at the likes of Kurt.

And circus acrobats, like the young man waiting for him here, all of them with madness and mayhem in their eyes.

And there were the Christians. Kurt's last promotion had come in return for finding a Protestant minister and turning him. That is, he had found the man's flaw and widened the crack into a crevice. Kurt had learned the Stasi lesson well—to teach a man fear, to find out what he seeks to hide from the rest of the world, and then threaten to expose it. All men had at least one such secret, most men more. No matter how big or trivial or horrible the secret, the key lay not in its size but in its capacity to inspire terror through having someone—spouse or family or business or village or congregation or whomever—find out. A well-functioning Communist regime made it their business to find out these secrets and then to exploit them mercilessly.

Kurt had been good at that. Very good. As the Protestant minister had discovered to his misery. The minister's failings would have been considered minor by anyone not bearing the weight of others' misfortunes, or "souls," to use a word that Kurt had never understood. But neither superstition nor concern for the unseen had stopped Kurt from using what he had learned, confronting the man with his usage of church funds to supplant his own meager stipend and demanding that he help the Stasi cause by supplying the names of all new converts to this strange escape called religion.

The Protestant minister had dreaded Kurt and his power. The minister had lived in fear of him until the fear had become too much to bear and driven him to take his own life. Toward the departed minister Kurt had felt neither remorse nor sorrow, nor really even thought of him at all. By then Kurt's promotion had been official. Also by that time the minister's information had borne fruit; there were others within the church that had secrets to hide or families to protect and were willing to pay for their own protection with yet more information.

Kurt paid for his coffee and carried it back to where the out-of-work acrobat waited. He sat down and asked, "Do you have what I need?"

"Let's see the money."

Kurt slipped the cash from his pocket and slid it across. The man lowered his cup, fanned the bills, and counted slowly. He held the bundle up and asked, "Where's the rest?"

"Half now, half when we're done," Kurt said. "Think maybe you could drop your hands a little?"

"Who's to see?" The man pocketed the bills. "Besides, it's not illegal anymore, is it? More's the pity, far as you're concerned. Before, you'd have just popped me into a hole somewhere and waited for me to cook long enough to produce for you, right?"

He was big and blond, very much of both. His flaxen hair hung down below his shoulder blades. Like a bushy foxtail, it was, when tied back as now. It sprung out from the rope knotted behind his head, the same rope tied up and around his forehead, then twisted and fastened at the nape of his neck. It was the man's trademark— the way he wore his hair in a loop of old rope, that and his strength. When released his hair fanned out like a rampant lion's mane. On him it looked natural.

He was dressed in the only clothes Kurt had ever seen him wear—tattered pullover, shapeless khaki pants, bulky pea jacket, filthy sneakers. But no amount of dirty sacking could disguise the rock-solid bulk beneath. The young man was huge. Even his hands were oversized mallets. And he had strength to match his size.

The young man had been recruited fresh from training as an acrobat and promised a place with one of the major international touring circuses if he would both inform on his comrades and act as a courier for Stasi secrets. He had agreed and done a decent job, after a fashion.

Kurt had been the young man's contact, his "keeper" in Stasi jargon. Kurt had always thought the term especially apt with this man, with his lion's mane and his animal strength. He had remained surly and hard to handle throughout, giving Kurt the impression of facing a barely tamed big cat without benefit of chair or whip. When Kurt had mentioned to his superiors the young man's offer to break Kurt across one knee, they had smirked and shrugged. What do you expect from a performer? they asked him.

Before the Wall came down, circuses had been one of East Germany's most famous exports. They had been small affairs by Western standards—one ring, a tent one truck could haul, three dozen animals at most, perhaps twice that number of performers and trainers.

Everybody had worked to pitch and dismantle the tents. The boss had also been the bookkeeper, lions' feed had been cooked next to the acrobats' stew. They had toured the back roads and villages from Leningrad to Budapest, sometimes as far away as Peru and Mongolia and Cuba and North Africa. People in entertainment-starved Communist villages had sometimes waited in line for days for tickets.

Places in top schools for acrobats and performers had been more sought after than seats at the Berlin Medical Academy. Would-be dancers and stage performers and acrobats and mimes and many actors had seen the circus as their one hope for artistic expression, let alone foreign travel. The result had been a level of circus talent far surpassing anything seen in the West.

Now, with the state subsidies withdrawn from circuses and their schools, and with television and movies pouring in from the once-forbidden West, all the circuses were closing. And the dancers and performers and acrobats and mimes went hungry.

"Even half is a lot of money for a little information," Kurt said.

Huge shoulders gave a shrug. "Buy and sell, buy and sell. The law of the capitalist world, right? Besides, I need it for a ticket to Australia. Word is they're hiring acrobats." Blue-black eyes glittered. "And what I've got is not a little information."

"Tell me."

"Amazing what people will tell a day laborer," the young man replied, refusing to be hurried. "That's what I'm doing, by the way. Shoveling dirt in some forsaken hole, worrying night and day about losing my acrobat's touch. Trying to fight off the bottle's call, though it's hard when I can't see a way to hope."

Kurt had debated long and hard before contacting this man. He was temperamental, hard to handle, often abusive. But he was the only contact Kurt still had who was in Weimar and available. "Tell me," he repeated.

"Got me a job on the digging crew, I did. Learned me a lot."

"You might as well get started," Kurt said. "I'm not paying you any more than I promised."

"Always a tight one, you were. Tight with money and tight in your mind. Like you wore a steel band wrapped around your head, always tightening it up and trying to squeeze the stuffing out. I always thought a good whap on the chin would do a lot to loosen you up."

Kurt kept the queasy fear from his face. "There's still half your money left to earn."

The young man leaned back and smirked knowingly. "What's got you so interested in this?"

Kurt replied with silence.

"You're after Nazi treasure, aren't you?" When Kurt did not reply, he went on, "Well, you won't find it here."

Kurt searched the man's eyes for the first hint of gold fever as Ferret had instructed, found only the same barely controlled power. "Tell me what you found."

"Empty rooms. Dust. Tunnels with walls two meters thick."

"Artwork? Strange-shaped packing boxes?"

"Bones," the young man replied. "You know the SS used concentration camp prisoners to build the cellars."

"Yes."

The young man pointed at the floor. "Twenty meters below us is the Asbach River. When the Nazis started building their parade ground, they hollowed out a deep channel, filled it with concrete, and diverted the river. Then they put another layer of concrete on top and built a long cellar separated into little chambers by thick concrete walls. On top of that, another cellar. On top of that, a third. Then the plaza was set back in place. That's why trees don't grow big here, see. They're trying to dig roots into concrete reinforced with iron rods."

"Must be frustrating," Kurt probed. "All this work and nothing to show for it."

"The Wessies want to pay me to poke holes in Nazi walls, it's fine with me. Same with the others. The money's good, and jobs aren't easy to come by." The dark eyes glittered. "Lots of fools with money around these days."

Kurt let it pass. "How far down have you worked?"

"We break into the second level next week."

"Six months of digging and you're still on the first level?"

Muscles bunched as the man leaned across the table. "You think we just open a door and prance in?"

"Of course not."

"Listen, mate. It's like drilling into lines of coffins with walls thick as I am tall. Bones. Water to your waist. Rats, big ones. And every time the drill hits air on the other side, we're all standing there wondering if this is the one that makes those cursed rooms our own coffins." Huge hands bunched into killing fists. "Word is, the Nazis stored bombs down there, gas canisters and shells to keep out fools like me. You know what a bomb would do, going off inside a concrete coffin?"

Kurt nodded. He did, as a matter of fact. When he was still a child, one of his teachers had taken great delight in passing on a story that had made headlines throughout East Germany. After conquering France, the Nazis had lined the entire Atlantic coast with massive concrete gun emplacements. These bunkers had proven to be far more difficult to dislodge than the German soldiers. The story had been told of a village on the southern coast of France that had finally come up with a means of ridding their beaches of these bunkers.

It seemed that the villagers had already tried and failed at drilling through the six feet of concrete poured around a webbing of inch-thick steel rods. Picking them up and hauling them off had proved equally impossible, as the bunkers weighed upwards of five hundred tons each.

So the village had decided to load the bunker with all the remaining unexploded bombs left in a nearby Nazi munitions depot.

They had chosen a bunker fairly removed from the little town, filled it to the brim with bombs and grenades and mines, cleared out all the curious onlookers, and set the whole thing alight.

The bunker had done its best to fly away, but its upward progress had been hampered by the fact that there were two openings at ninety-degree angles from each other—the narrow entrance, and the even narrower cannon-slit. So after rising a mere thirty feet off the earth, which admittedly was not bad for a bunker weighing almost one million pounds, it had turned into the world's largest whirligig. Before returning to earth with a resounding boom, it had stripped every tree within twenty miles of foliage, blown out all the village windows, and overturned the local train station. The bunker itself had been unharmed. Kurt's teacher, along with many other men across the war-torn nation, had taken great pride in this proof of quality German workmanship.

"So you don't think anything's down where you've been working?" Kurt asked.

"What difference does it make what I think? But the boys with the charts and the maps and the ties, they're starting to talk like no treasures came any closer to here than Ulm."

The young man toyed with his coffee cup. "Story goes, when the Americans occupied Weimar in 1945, back before the partition was worked out, they looked around here a little but didn't find anything. Then the Russians came in, and when they started rebuilding this place, they found bombs and gas canisters. Thousands and thousands stored in a field where they built that office block out back. There's one old man working with me who remembers it, said the Nazis stored munitions here because Weimar didn't have any industry and wasn't being bombed. Rumor was, though, the Nazis buried treasure *under* the bombs. But the Russians dug around and didn't find anything. Then the Americans found the treasures in Ulm, and everybody figured that was where it had all been stored."

Kurt knew the Ulm story. Every German his age did—how the Americans had needed over a hundred trucks to clear out the paintings and artwork and valuables stored in the Ulm depot, then spent years trying to track down the lawful owners. Finally what wasn't claimed had been parceled out among the victors and stuffed into museums around the world. The spoils of war.

Kurt decided he had enough. "I'll be back in a month or so," he lied, passing over the rest of the cash.

"Anytime, at least for as long as it takes for me to earn my one-way ticket." Dark eyes followed him as he rose to his feet. "Just don't come empty-handed. Information costs a lot these days, like everything else. We're all busy learning the capitalist tricks, even you and your old mates, right? Buy whatever you want, because everything has its price. New laws for a new world." He counted the second set of bills, and stuffed them in with the rest. He was still sitting there when Kurt glanced over his shoulder on his way out.

Katya joined Jeffrey at the breakfast table with an announcement. "Frau Reining just called."

"Where's my kiss?"

She greeted the approaching waiter, ordered breakfast, said, "She wants us to go to Dresden."

"I asked you a question." He was only half kidding. "I can't get my motor started just with coffee anymore."

She leaned across the table, smacked him soundly. "You'll need to be awake for this one."

"I'm all ears."

She smiled mischievously. "Your mouth says one thing and your eyes another."

He kept his voice flat for the benefit of the waiter pouring her coffee. "Take your pick."

"I'd better not."

"What's that supposed to mean?"

She waited until they were once again alone, then opened her heart and confessed as much with her eyes as with her words. "I dreamed about you last night."

"Katya, I—"

"Don't say it." Pleading now. "I need your help, Jeffrey. I have to have it. I'm not strong enough by myself."

He nodded. The heat burned a dull ache in his belly.

She reached across the table for his hand. "I feel as if I'm walking along the edge of a cliff. Just the slightest push and I'll fall over."

A thousand arguments crowded for place in his mind. He struggled, fought, won he knew not how, and remained silent. He raised his eyes to find her gaze resting on him, gently pleading, openly yearning, full of the same conflict he battled against. "I love you, Katya."

"Thank you," she said quietly.

He hid behind his coffee, waited while the urge to kiss her again subsided.

"Did I tell you Frau Reining called?" Her voice was as unsteady as his own inner balance.

"I can't hold on to patience for very long," he replied.

"I know," she sighed. Softer, "I can't either."

"What are we going to do?"

When she didn't answer he ventured another glance and found her looking shy. "Did you want a big wedding?"

"No." Emphatic.

"Me neither."

She hesitated, then said, "I don't know if the girl is supposed to be talking about these things, but—"

"But why have a long engagement," he finished for her, and knew a surging thrill.

"I've always dreamed of being a June bride," she said softly. "If that's all right with you."

"Perfect," he managed, though from where he sat June seemed several lifetimes away.

Joy shone from her eyes. And something more. "I think I've just lost my appetite. Do you think there's time for a smooch out of sight before our appointment with Herr Diehl?"

He was already on his feet and reaching for her hand. Without really caring he asked, "So what's in Dresden?"

Katya almost skipped alongside him. "Nothing that can't wait till after a real kiss."

═══

They found a sheltered alcove and enjoyed the intimacy of the kiss. Their mutual desire to see their new relationship grow into permanence filled them with both peace and anticipation as they finally went to find their new friend.

With another hour before their train departed for Dresden, Herr Diehl guided them from his shop, eager to play the tour guide.

"In old Erfurt," he told them as they strolled along the bridge's cobblestone length, "the houses had names, not numbers. Before, my own shop was the city's bell house, as the name says in German. It was the only place licensed by the city to sell bells. The blacksmiths would bid for the privilege of making anything from cowbells to carriage bells to the great bells used in churches—but not by price. Prices were fixed by each guild, including the iron-mongers' guild. So they could compete only on terms and quality."

"All houses were named after the people's professions?" Jeffrey asked.

"Not necessarily." He motioned toward a nearby shop, a book-store, which had a hand-beaten copper sign of a stork hanging outside. "According to the old records, this was named the *Haus zum Storchen,* the Stork's House, because the family who lived here had forty-three children. They were weavers and embroiderers of fine linen, a very lucrative profession. It required a special training, one that was highly sought after because of its special combination of artwork and craft-training. No doubt the shrewd weaver decided the best way to keep his trained employees from leaving was to draw them from his own family.

"There were sixty-two merchant houses along this bridge, all licensed by the king to do business with the international traders, and all carefully controlled. Then, as now, from no place could a passerby see the water. The houses formed continuous four-story walls along both sides. They sold and traded in the products of distant lands—pepper, sugar, saffron, soap, paper, silk, brass, bronze, gold, silver, jewels, ornaments, rare objects, illustrated manuscripts.

"For over five hundred years," Herr Diehl continued, "this bridge was a key destination along the Paris-Kiev trade route. It is hard for us to comprehend how vital these overland routes once were. There was no alternative, you see, none at all. The seas were pirate-infested and governed by unruly gods of wind and storm, and dragons were believed to lurk just beneath the surface. No right-minded medieval businessman would dare place his life or the livelihood of his descendants in such a precarious position. So he and his caravans traveled overland. If he was poor, he joined a group of other traders, praying they were trustworthy, and carried his wares on his back. With time and success and good fortune came first servants and donkeys, then horses, then wagons and armed guards."

The dealer nodded his head in time to his words. "Yes, these land routes dominated international trade until Christians once again chose that most dreadful path—arguing over how to worship the Lord of love with swords in their hands."

"The Reformation wars," Jeffrey said.

"What a name," Herr Diehl replied. "How in God's holy name could you ever reform faith with a sword?"

Jeffrey shook his head. "I can't fathom it."

"The Catholics and the Protestants between them unleashed a tide of blood over the land," Herr Diehl went on, "and suddenly waterborne dragons seemed vastly more appealing than land-based madness. Many merchants began taking their wares to distant buyers by sea, and most of the land routes slowly shriveled and died.

"But before the flow of history was rerouted with a bloody and heretical sword, these very same land routes reigned supreme." Herr Diehl's voice lifted as he swept his hand to encompass all the shops along the bridge. "Imagine what the merchants of that day and age must have seen. Each voyage from Paris to Kiev, a distance of over two thousand miles, could take as long as one year. There would be rumors of wars and new borders and greedy tax officials up ahead, many of them formed from thin air by local merchants who sought to separate the travelers from their goods at panic-stricken prices. The shopkeepers who manned this bridge were the gatherers of news and gossip, and they spiced it with their own self-interest before serving it to footsore travelers."

Cathedral Hill dominated what once had been medieval Erfurt's central market. Herr Diehl led them across an ancient street and into the vast open market square. "After Martin Luther's proclamation sparked the rise of Protestantism," he continued, "Erfurt was one of very few cities that stubbornly refused to declare itself for one faith or another. The people and the ruling princes were so adamantly unified that they fought off the scalding rhetoric of both churches and clung to sanity."

The frigid air had a metallic edge that burned the nostrils. Katya's voice as she translated was muffled by the scarf she kept wrapped around the bottom half of her face.

"The prince and people demanded that both churches, Catholic and Protestant, be allowed to coexist," Herr Diehl explained. "It balanced their power, you see, and kept either from dominating the government and private life. The ruling family, the government, and the royal court were all good Catholics. The tradesmen, farmers, guilds, and merchants were Protestants. As a result, during the unbounded horrors of religious conflict, all Christians were safe here. And Erfurt remained a successful center of international commerce long after the land routes began to decline and other merchant cities were either put to the torch or starved into legend-filled graveyards, inhabited by walking ghosts."

The vast plaza was lined with ramshackle stalls selling everything from hand-knit shawls to imported oranges. The throngs of buyers were surprisingly quiet, silenced by the effort of walking and standing and shopping in the icy air. Jeffrey and Katya followed Herr Diehl beyond the market to where a broad stairway rose up almost three hundred feet. At the summit, a pair of colossal churches stood side by side.

"The first church is the one on the left," Herr Diehl told them as they climbed. "It was erected in 1154 as a monastery and remained true to the faith, so the story goes, through kingdoms and centuries. During the Reformation, the monks ridiculed the Pope's political ambitions and refused to back his demands for a war against their Protestant brethren. In reply, the Pope commanded that a second church be built, close enough and big enough to dominate the original."

One church alone would have been majestic. But the two together looked ridiculous. Both were vast structures whose spires reached heavenward several hundred feet. Vast swatches of stained-glass windows arched between flanking buttresses of stone and dark-stained mortar. Nearby four-story buildings were easily dwarfed by the twin churches.

"And so stands a warning to the church of today," Herr Diehl went on, his tone somber. "A witness to what can happen when doctrine becomes more important than the straightforward laws of love given us by the simple Carpenter. Whenever one of us opens our mouth to condemn the way another worships, we set another brick in the wall of such a monstrosity. We offer our beloved Savior up to the nonbelievers as a point of ridicule. If we as the saved cannot agree to disagree in peace and love and brotherhood, what do we show the nonbelievers but the same discord and disharmony from which they seek to escape?"

When they arrived at the top, Herr Diehl opened his arms to encompass the two churches and their outlying buildings. The stone path between the central structures was as broad as a two-lane highway, yet the churches' sheer mass narrowed and constricted the way to a choking tightness. There was no divine relief offered here, no hope or lightness, only an overbearing weight and looming threat.

"The Stasi closed both churches and the monastery," Herr Diehl went on. "They took over all but the worship halls and made this compound the central headquarters for the region's security operations. They required no sign to remind the people of their presence. From this height they were seen by everyone who took to the streets of Erfurt."

He faced them and said solemnly, "I tell you this with the sincerity of a man who has sought to live the life of a true believer. It was a just punishment for the church's maneuverings in the ways of this world, and for the misery their worldly ambitions caused the men of their day."

When Jeffrey and Katya said their goodbyes, Jeffrey said, "We cannot express our appreciation for this visit with you, a new Christian friend. Thank you for your insightful explanations of the history of this fascinating city. We hope to return for more than simply doing business with you, Herr Diehl."

———

The journey by train from Erfurt to Dresden lasted four hours and took them from the carefully tended farmlands of Thuringen through the industrial might of Leipzig and on into the old royal enclave of Saxony. Their entry into Dresden was marked by more of the same—tall, dilapidated apartment buildings, bleak forests of smokestacks, aged factories, and everything dressed a dreary gray.

They stayed in the Ship-Hotel Florentine. It was only after a dozen or so telephone calls, Katya told him, that she had been able to find them rooms at all. Like all the other major cities of the former East Germany, Dresden had become a boom-town. The few decent hotels were so packed with industrialists that enterprising Wessie hoteliers had floated tourist ships down the Elba River to Dresden, where they were birthed and used as floating hotels.

Jeffrey deposited his bags in his quarters, then returned to meet Katya by the ship's ramp. "I'm paying two hundred dollars a night for a room the size of a packing crate."

"Every room is full," Katya reminded him.

He was not through. "My bed is exactly eighteen inches wide. And my bathroom is smaller than an airplane toilet."

"I heard the receptionist tell someone on the phone that they're taking reservations six months in advance." She smiled up at him. "We have two hours until our meeting. Would you rather spend it complaining or taking a look at the city?"

They walked down the riverside pathway with traffic thundering alongside. Beyond the road towered Dresden's medieval city walls, granting them an astonishing view into what Dresden once had been—a royal city, a seat of power and palaces and parliaments. With each breath, Jeffrey felt himself overcome by the scents and sounds of living history mingling with the diesel fumes and construction dust.

Only a small portion of the city remained intact after the Allied bombing during World War II. The surviving buildings now lay beneath blankets of grime and neglect, the tall roof statues stained so black they appeared carved from coal. Yet they still bore witness to a city that once had been a treasure trove of art and architecture, of power and wealth.

They entered the wall through lofty gates built to admit mounted cavalry with lances raised in royal salute. Behind rose the skeletal remains of the Frauen Church, over seven hundred years old when destroyed in the war. They walked on, passing one of the five inner-city palaces that remained out of almost two hundred royal residences. Beyond them rose the royal opera house, erected from stones still blackened by the firebombs that had consumed it in 1944. The first act of the new city council had been to rebuild it as a beacon of reassurance to a cowed and battered populace. Jeffrey and Katya joined the quiet throng of German tourists who braved the cold to read the council's proclamation. It promised a future of hope, a city with renewed purpose, and opportunities for growth and improvement in their own lives. Jeffrey searched the faces around him as he listened to Katya translate the words and saw how deeply these grim-faced individuals wished to believe.

Everywhere were the signs and sounds of renovation—jack-hammers and rumbling trucks and tall cranes, warning signs and dust clouds and great crews of men scrambling over war-torn surfaces. More ruins gave way to a palace that Jeffrey took for the grandest of all the old buildings until he caught sight of the one rising behind it. Beyond that loomed yet another. Each was more astounding than the one previous.

They escaped the snow within a street-side cafe. Jeffrey listened as Katya gave their order to a waitress who looked to be poured into her dress. He watched her walk away, wondering how she managed to breathe. He turned back to find Katya watching him. "Was I staring?"

"You know you were." Katya forgave him with a smile. "The shoes and dress are all pre-unification. See the dyed cork heels and fake-leather straps? Very Communist chic."

"She's kept the dress because she can't afford a new one?"

Katya shook her head. "Denial. It's a universal feminine trait. As long as she can get the zipper up, she's still a size eight."

When their lunch arrived, Katya nodded toward a young man seated at the next table. She told Jeffrey, "Buy him an ice cream, please."

The young man was small and slender to the point of evident hunger. Dark eyes peered out of definite slants in leathery skin. The face was all hollows and sharp angles. "What for?"

"Buy him an ice cream, Jeffrey. If you won't, I will."

"You'll have to, anyway," Jeffrey said with a shrug. "I don't speak the lingo."

Katya motioned to the waitress and spoke to her at length. The waitress gave them both an odd look, then moved away.

"He's a Russian soldier," Katya explained.

"How do you know?"

"Lots of things. The plastic belt. The quietness. He doesn't even move his eyes. When the waitress went to his table, he pointed to the menu to order, and when the waitress brought him a coffee he looked crushed. He couldn't read the menu and didn't know how to ask for something to eat. It's probably his only leave. And his only money. I read that the soldiers in some barracks are selling their boots for food. The officers are so ashamed they're keeping the enlisted men locked inside the compounds for weeks at a time."

The waitress brought over a large metal boat of ice cream; the young man's eyes turned into enormous pools. Katya leaned across the gap between their tables and explained with her hands that it was a gift. The young man bowed almost to the seat and smiled openhearted thanks.

"Watch," Katya whispered. "Watch how he eats."

The man became totally locked into his ice cream. It *consumed* his attention. He ate each little mound in turn, taking tiny slivers with his spoon, making it last and last and last. Each time he felt their eyes he turned and gave them another genuine smile.

"That look makes me want to cry," Katya said.

"My little Samaritan," Jeffrey said quietly.

"I feel so sorry for him," she said, turning away. "He is hated here. He lives in a hell called an enlisted men's barracks, and when he leaves here, what will he go back to? What hope does he have?"

When they left the cafe, snow flurries opened to reveal frantic scurrying clouds, then closed into curtains swept sideways by the wind. They followed the example of others and stayed up against the nearest building as they walked.

The Semper Gallery, their meeting point, proved to be the last bastion of old Dresden. Beyond it was all garish modernism and broken pavement and traffic. Buildings were glass and concrete and steel—and tasteless. The contrast to the Semper palace could not have been more stark.

They crossed a wooden bridge over a moat, then passed under a multistory arch formed as a gilded crown and colonnaded pedestal. Inside were acres of carefully sculpted gardens, all now brown where it wasn't covered with snow, empty and waiting for spring. Scaffolding covered two thirds of the surrounding ornate palace, over a thousand feet to a side. The sound of construction followed them everywhere.

Katya pointed through the falling white veil to where two black-leather-coated individuals watched them. "Frau Reining said they would be wearing red scarfs."

It was only when they were a few paces away that Jeffrey realized the second person was a woman. Her face was all angles and hard lines, her expression stubborn and suspicious.

Her pockmarked companion spoke with a voice roughened by a metal rasp. Katya translated, "He wants to know if you are the one."

"The one what?"

"Let me tell him yes, all right? I don't feel comfortable with this pair."

The uneasiness he felt from their gaze hardened into genuine dislike at the thought of Katya's fear. "Tell them the question is out of a third-rate spy movie, and it's too cold out here for games."

Katya hesitated, then spoke in a soft voice. The man stiffened, then turned and stomped off. The woman watched him go, then turned back to Jeffrey with a smirk and spoke a few words.

"I don't understand," Katya said.

"What did she say?"

"End of drama."

"This is ridiculous. Tell her we're leaving."

Before Katya could speak the woman held up her hand, pointed to where the pockmarked man reappeared through the colonnaded atrium. With him scuttled a little figure bundled within a shapeless greatcoat. On closer inspection, Jeffrey decided the man looked like the offspring of a giant mole.

When he spoke, the man had the gentle lisp of an ageless Pan. "I hear that you are an honorable businessman, Mr. Sinclair," the little man said in greeting. The act of translating those few words had been enough to give Katya's voice a colorless tone.

Jeffrey bridled. "No one has said the same about you."

Katya glanced his way. "How do you know that he can't speak English?"

"I don't know, and I don't care. I don't even know what we are doing here." He looked down at her. "Can we please get out of this snow?"

"Don't you want to know what he's got to sell?"

"Look at these people, Katya. Tell me how you think they came up with something of value."

Katya hesitated, then turned back to the trio and spoke in her lilting German. The strange-shaped man replied in sibilant tones. Katya translated, "This place is a most appropriate spot for our meeting, as the palace resembles greatly the former home of what I have to sell."

The pockmarked man's dull stare rankled almost more than Jeffrey could stand. He turned sideways and asked, "Is this guy all there?"

"I don't know, but his German is very precise, very educated."

"They all give me the creeps."

Katya nodded, waited for his move as snow dusted her hair with a faint, damp frosting.

"Tell him he has one minute to get this over with."

The little man showed no irritation. "What we are selling is currently being sought by three different governments, all of whom believe it is in their territory—Lithuania, Russia, and our own German government. We know they all are racing down false trails. We know this for a fact, Mr. Sinclair."

"What is it?"

"We are not selling the article," the little man continued in tones as gray as his skin, "but rather the article's location."

Jeffrey took in the bottle-bottom glasses pinched onto the smidgen of nose, the peach-fuzz hair, the sloping forehead, and decided this was the strangest human he'd ever seen. "You want me to buy direction to an antique?"

"We will supply you with a sample of the merchandise, which will leave no doubt in your mind whatsoever," the other replied. "Payment will be required only after you have received the sample. We seek nothing in advance."

That slowed Jeffrey down. "You don't?"

"We are most serious in this endeavor, I assure you, Herr Sinclair. We have unearthed a hoard of world renown. And for this we wish to receive a mere two million dollars."

Jeffrey laughed out loud. "Come on, Katya. Let's go back to the ship."

The man's lisping voice stopped him. "Naturally, we are leaving ample room for you to add your own percentage."

"Tell the man it's been swell," Jeffrey replied. "But I deal in antiques, not fairy tales."

The unlined, snub-nosed face remained expressionless as he spoke. Katya translated, "He wants to know if you have ever heard of the Amber Room."

CHAPTER 19

What did they look like, these three?" Alexander asked.

"The little man looked like a . . . well, to be frank, like a skinless frog," Jeffrey replied. "Flanked by his and her linebackers."

Katya laughed. "They did not."

"That guy with the pox," Jeffrey persisted. "If he was any more clueless, you'd need to water him twice a week."

They were seated in Alexander's spacious living room, the night's chill kept at bay by a carefully tended fire. Their return trip from East Germany the day before had been long and tiring but uneventful, their arrival most welcomed by Alexander. The gala was weighing heavily upon him. Together they had put in a full day's work on final details, then Katya had pushed aside the old gentleman's objections and insisted that he allow her to prepare dinner.

"The man wasn't dull," Katya replied. "He was careful."

"Who would we be that he needed to go back, get the little guy, sneak him out to see us?" Jeffrey stated flatly.

"Habits of a lifetime die hard," Alexander observed.

"And he didn't have the pox," Katya said.

"Whatever. They—"

"You didn't like them," Alexander concluded with a wry smile.

"I didn't like any of it. This isn't antiques."

"But they wanted nothing up front," Alexander reminded him.

Jeffrey shook his head. "I don't understand what they're trying to pull, but whatever it is, it smells."

"As soon as that man opened his mouth, you were angry," Katya said, her head cocked and smiling now. "If you had been a dog, you'd have broken your chain and gone for his face."

"I wish I had," he said, liking the image more than he should have. Chase the guy down a few blocks, come trotting back with a mouthful of trousers. "I can't believe we went all the way to Dresden to meet those clowns."

"Yes, well, despite your impressions, there may be something to this," Alexander said. He looked between the two of them, staring at him in shock. "In my experience, it is the offbeat character who takes the wild risk. He has nothing to lose, you see. All the normal channels for gain and ambition are closed to him. He walks along gray paths, neither legal nor criminal, skirting the edges, looking for those chances that others have missed."

Jeffrey thought that over. "But how could a trio like that come up with something hidden in Poland?"

Alexander's gaze snapped to full alert. "That is what they said? Why did you not tell me?"

"I thought I had."

"It wasn't them," Katya said. "Frau Reining said it when she called to set up the meeting."

"And what did she make of those people?"

"She only met the woman," Katya said with evident amusement. "But she would have sympathized with Jeffrey."

"Why does that make you smile?" Jeffrey asked.

"It's so unlike you," Katya replied. "The suave and debonair man of the world with his hackles up and his teeth bared."

"I didn't know you thought I was suave."

She nodded. "Sometimes I can hardly believe you can be so polished and not let it go to your head. You—"

"Yes, well," Alexander interrupted, "this exchange is all quite fascinating, but I am still not clear on how Frau Reining entered into this picture."

The touch of Katya's gaze lingered upon Jeffrey long after her eyes had turned away. She described Frau Reining's contact with the woman and finished with, "Frau Reining is positive the woman is Stasi."

"Former Stasi," Alexander corrected, not looking disturbed by the news. "That might explain how they gained access to secret information. Did she say anything more?"

"I don't think she was very interested in knowing anything else," Katya replied.

"Yes, I can imagine it must have been an uncomfortable reminder of a world she thought lost and gone forever," Alexander agreed. "My dear, do you know of the Amber Room?"

"I've heard of it," Katya replied. "It always sounded like something from Ali Baba and the Forty Thieves."

"In this case," Alexander said, "I assure you, the legend is real."

"I have to see to something in the kitchen." Katya stood. "This is a story I want to hear from beginning to end. You have to promise to talk about something boring until I get back."

Alexander watched her leave. "I don't suppose your making moon eyes at each other has affected business overmuch," he commented, his gaze on the door through which she had disappeared.

"I don't make moon eyes," Jeffrey argued.

"My dear young man, lunar landings could be made upon the glances you cast at each other." Alexander sipped at his coffee. "But no matter. You are entitled to them."

Jeffrey sighed and shook his head. "Silly—"

"Yes, but much of love to an outsider is seen as silliness. Just as faith in the unseen must be to a nonbeliever."

Jeffrey looked at him. "You're still having questions?"

"Doubts, my boy. Let us call them by their correct name. Doubts."

"Me too," he confessed.

"Not that God exists, nor that I am now seeking Him." Alexander set down his cup. "Only whether I shall be able to find Him."

"I know what you mean," Jeffrey responded, breathing out another long sigh. "Did you talk to Gregor about all this?"

"I tried." Alexander showed irritation. "He would not discuss it except to say, 'you are on a path, my friend.' His manner reminded me of a proud parent praising a baby's first steps."

"And he's usually so . . ." Jeffrey searched for the words, "direct in what he says."

"Scathingly so," Alexander agreed. "But not in this instance. All he would say further is that I should listen to the Master's words."

Jeffrey compared this with his own recent telephone conversation with the Polish Christian and came up only confused. "Are you reading the Bible?"

"Every morning."

"Do you pray?"

"I do indeed, and with unceasing difficulty. I feel as though I am waiting for the arrival of something that I remain unable even to name." He shook his head. "I have had several discussions on this point with the bishop—he's agreed to attend our little event, by the way. The poor man is mystified by my unconstructive searchings and assures me that all is quite in order. But whenever I permit myself the least little bit of self-satisfaction, I find the image of Gregor's most sardonic smile dancing in my mind. And I realize that I must continue with my quest for the unseen."

"A quest for the unseen," Katya said, reentering the parlor. "What a beautiful way to put it."

"Please excuse an old man's ramblings, my dear."

"No discussion about a soul's honest yearnings could ever be described as ramblings," Katya replied, seating herself. "And if you will excuse me for saying it, I agree with our friend Gregor. To acknowledge your heart's unquenchable desires is a great step."

"And what must I do now?"

"Wait," she said with quiet firmness. "Wait on the Lord. You are called simply to prepare the vessel. It is the Father's task to fill it."

Alexander eyed her with evident fondness. "You do an old man's heart a great deal of good, my dear."

"And a young man's," Jeffrey added.

"Thank you." She clasped her hands before her and raised her shoulders like an excited little girl. "Can we please come back to your story? The Amber Room?"

"But of course." Alexander settled back in his chair. "It was at the very dawn of the Russian empire that our story begins. Peter the Great, the first emperor of all Russia, ascended to the throne in 1682. He was determined to lift his country from the Dark Ages that had dominated since the Mongol hordes swept out of Siberia and laid waste Russia's heartland four hundred years earlier.

"Europe was the key, Peter knew. He intended to bind his great land to the heart of Christendom. To do this, he established a new capital alongside the Baltic Sea, the warmest waters within his empire and the closest to Europe. He reclaimed vast stretches of land from swamp and inhospitable tribes, named the new city Saint Petersburg, and declared his intention to make it the Paris of the East.

"As a wedding present to his new wife, Catherine Alexejevna, he gave her the estate of Saari, which lay twenty-six kilometers from Saint Petersburg—a most important distance, as you will soon learn. The succeeding emperors and empresses added to the initial buildings, until the estate had grown from its original palace of sixteen rooms to one that stretched over almost as many acres. Palaces of other royal family members sprang up nearby, along with those of princes and noblemen whose power and wealth bought them the right to summer with the ruler of all Russia. This vast village of palaces and riches became known as *Zarskoje Selo*, and its centerpiece was the Catherine Palace.

"We must now turn our attention to one of Peter's neighbors, the largest of the German principalities and by far the most aggressive in matters political and military. Frederick William I, ruler of the Prussian empire, was concerned about this newly unified behemoth to his East, but he was plagued even more by wars and rumors of wars from his northern neighbor, Sweden. Less than a century before, you see, tribes of ferocious blond giants had swept across a land weakened by the Protestant-Catholic wars and laid waste to almost half of Europe. Frederick William wanted to maintain good relations with Russia so that his strength and attention could be directed toward the clearest and most present danger—the one to the North.

"It was then, in 1717, that Frederick William decided to give Emperor Peter the Great the Amber Room.

"*Das Bernstein Zimmer*, as it was then known, had been designed by German and Danish craftsmen for Frederick William's own palace, the Charlottenberg in Berlin.

"Most amber came from the Baltic shores—what now is shared by Germany, Poland, Lithuania, and Russia, and back then was dominated by the Prussian and Polish kings. But the amount of amber which this room required surpasses modern understanding. Nowadays we sell amber by the milligram. Records from 1944 tell us that the amber used in the Amber Room weighed in at *twenty tons.*

"Nowadays, amber is considered by most people as simply another semiprecious jewel. But it is not really a stone at all, rather the fossilized sap of pine trees. And just as there are a number of different types of pines, there are great differences in the colors and shades of ambers.

"The amber was fashioned as wood might be for inlay upon fine furniture. Where various tones of cherry or olive or satinwood might be used to design a floral arrangement and background, the amber was sorted by color shades. But where wood would be kept to razor-thin slices, the amber was carved at thicknesses of an inch or more. The carvings were then fitted together to form panels rising from floor to ceiling, depicting a vast variety of scenes—Grecian urns, cherubim by the hundreds, romantic landscapes, prancing stallions, royal emblems. Hundreds of thousands of amber pieces carved and polished and fitted precisely together, to cover the entire room.

"The gift of the Amber Room to Peter the Great marked the signing of a treaty of unending friendship between the two powers, and was intended to go in the Winter Palace in Saint Petersburg. But it was soon moved to the Catherine Palace at *Zarskoje Selo,* where it adorned one of the royal chambers.

"And such a chamber it must have been," Alexander went on, shaking his head. "Only one color photograph remains, taken toward the end of World War II. That picture shows a vast hall, perhaps sixty feet long and forty wide, with ceilings rising up twenty-five feet. Between each of the amber panels were wide mirrors with solid silver backing and solid gold frames. The three chandeliers were of solid silver, as were the hundred or so candelabras set into the walls. There was also a central table with vast silver and gold candelabras.

"Hundreds and hundreds of candles dancing and flickering on panel after jeweled panel." He smiled at the thought. "Those fortunate enough to view it gave it the name, Eighth Wonder of the World."

The darkness was not defeated but retreated grudgingly before the cloud-shrouded morning. Night had left its shadows everywhere, on dank and sooty sidewalks, around corners of crumbling buildings, in the tired faces of early risers—silent reminders of the darkness's inevitable return. The cities of former East Germany were never far from the night.

The dwindling crowd within the Schwerin tavern had come to its lowest ebb. Conversations were muted and sentences seldom finished, words carelessly tossed out by people reluctant to make the effort. Eyes were dulled and distant from a night of little hope and the prospect of a bed with less warmth.

Erika chose that time to set her hands upon the table and stretch them out wide, as though clenching the grain itself. Her nails were broad and flat, her hands very strong. She announced quietly, "My friend has found the man."

Kurt gave her an awful look. "You've been sitting here for almost an hour, and you just now decide to speak?"

"I've been trying to decide whether to tell you at all," she snapped back.

"What's that supposed to mean?"

Ferret raised his eyes from the aged yellow pages before him. "It means, Kurt, that she no longer is content to do our bidding. Doesn't it, my dear?"

"I've a right to know," she said stubbornly.

"Of course you do." The hissing voice carried no sense of warmth and even less inflection. "You are a most valued member of our team, a full partner with every right to know all about our little quest."

"And how much it's worth," Erika replied. "Don't forget that bit."

"Of course I won't. The question is, where do I begin?"

"Begin by asking her if she can trust her contact to give us the right information," Kurt spat out. "We don't need just any address from an old Berlin telephone directory."

"I didn't say I had an address," Erika replied, her eyes on Ferret. "I said I had the *man*."

Ferret peered back at her through spectacles so thick they made his eyes appear to swim. "You are sure of this?"

Erika nodded. "You didn't tell me he had been posted in Königsberg, did you?"

"No," lisped the little man. "I did not."

"'Colonel in charge of Division Transport,' wasn't that right?"

"As I said," Ferret replied, "you have every right to know."

"Start with how much," Erika demanded. "I like to get the big things out of the way."

"As I said to our Western contacts, how would you feel about half a million?" Ferret asked. "Dollars."

Even Kurt showed surprise. "You really think they'll pay what you asked?"

"I should think two million dollars is not too much to ask for the location of the Eighth Wonder of the World," Ferret replied. "Would you?"

Erika recovered sufficiently to ask, "Who gets the fourth share?"

"I would imagine the man who remains yet unknown," Ferret replied. "He shall probably wish to have a share. If not, well, that would only mean more for us."

"Not to mention papers for our way out of here," Kurt said.

"And my friend in Dresden," Erika added. "She's holding out the most important bits until we work out the next payment."

"There are many incidentals attached to our quest and our escape," Ferret agreed. "But these we may leave for later. What matters now"—he turned to Kurt, "is that our lady partner has a wish to know."

"And a right," Erika added.

"Of course, my dear. Well, the story begins in 1717, when the world was shaped far differently from what we know today, and was even more unstable than these dark and uncertain times.

"As you know," Ferret went on, "Kaliningrad, as it is today known, was the capital of East Prussia before the war. Königsberg it was called then, a place full of palaces and wealth the likes of which we can only dream about today. Now it is Lithuania's main port, and little is left of its once glorious past."

His two listeners sat in utter stillness. Deadpan faces had long since lost the ability to react, but there was no masking the feverish glitter in their eyes. They remained blind to the cafe, the early morning, and all the new faces morning faces strange to their habitual nighttime crowd.

"During the war years Königsberg was ruled by a man called Erich Koch," Ferret went on. "His title was *Gauleiter*, which back then meant both Nazi Party leader and chief of the regional government. In effect, he had the power of life and death over all who lived there, and he ruled with an iron hand. On June 22, 1941, when the Nazis rolled the Blitzkrieg into Russia, Koch was also given the position of Kommissar over all Ukraine."

"A license to steal," Kurt offered.

"All completely legal," Ferret agreed. "As Gauleiter and Kommissar, he also carried the title of *Künst-Schutz Offizier*. In that capacity, as officer in charge of the security of treasures, he was entitled to 'relocate' all appropriated treasures to Nazi Germany.

"He robbed the treasure houses of Minsk, Pinsk, and Kiev," Ferret went on. His lisping voice did not require strength to hold his listeners fast. "But he had to hurry. There were many treasure troves, and only so many trucks and trusted soldiers could be spared. The Nazis surrounded Leningrad and began the famous siege, then continued on to their destiny and death on the icy Steppes before the Moscow gates. Koch, in the meantime, arrived at *Zarskoje Selo*, which held the treasure troves within the Catherine Palace and lay just far enough outside Leningrad to be within the Nazis' grasp."

"The Catherine Palace," Erika said. "All this is true?"

"Most well documented, I assure you, if you only know where to look," Ferret replied. "There are no complete records, however, on how much the Nazis transported back to Königsberg. The wealth in the Catherine Palace and the other royal summer residences was so great that it simply overwhelmed the Nazi record keepers. We do know that the transport required seventy trucks. Think of it. Seventy trucks brought together in the midst of the greatest siege in modern warfare, and simultaneous with the push across two thousand miles of enemy territory to Moscow."

"They must have found something special," Kurt said.

"So many things, so special, that they left behind *twenty thousand* treasures. We know this because that which remains now makes up the permanent collection of the Catherine Palace Museum, one of the greatest such exhibitions in all the world."

The morning sun poked through an opening in the clouds and glinted against the condensation-streaked window. Erika leaned far back in her chair so her face could remain in accustomed shadows.

"And these are the leftovers," Kurt said, shaking his head. "Amazing."

"Amazing is the right word," Ferret agreed, his voice barely above a whisper. "Amazing that among the treasures selected by the Nazis was an entire royal chamber with amber walls. Koch lost no time in stripping these jewels from their frames and wrapping the segments in cigarette paper. They must have been well aware of what they held, for the records pertaining to this one room are the most complete of the entire shipment. Upon each strip of paper was recorded the segment's place in the wall puzzle—quite a daunting task, I would imagine, what with the pressure to complete this work and continue on behind the army's march to Moscow. Day and night, as guns boomed in the distance, the amber was rolled in wadding and packed into iron chests. Twenty tons of amber in all."

The Ferret spoke with scarce movements of his thin, bloodless lips, his lumpy body curved over the ever-present file, his pale, soft hands resting motionless upon the yellowed pages as though drawing sustenance from their ancient script. "Once the trucks arrived in Königsberg, unskilled workers and soldiers reassembled the pieces in a chamber of the central castle. Some amber was destroyed, one entire panel went missing and was never restored. Even so, this chamber became the single most popular museum exhibit in all Nazi Germany. And for good reason."

"For as long as it lasted," Kurt offered.

"It remained there for almost three years," Ferret replied. "Until July of 1944. One month after it was taken down and relocated, the expected waves of bombers arrived. The British carpet-bombed Königsberg for three days and nights, destroying almost half the city and leaving behind fires that burned for another five days before they were finally extinguished."

Erika shifted uneasily. "I've had enough of the history lesson."

"It is distasteful, I agree," Ferret said, "but an important part of our story."

"I don't see how," Erika said. "All that is better dead and buried."

"You asked for the scoop," Kurt snapped. "Button up and let him get on with it."

Erika flared. "I don't take that from anyone."

"Please, please," Ferret hissed out. "Let us act as partners, yes? We have a long road yet ahead."

Kurt held her fast with his gaze, then said to Ferret, "Get on with it."

Instead, Ferret stripped off his glasses, revealing surprisingly small eyes. They were a weak-looking, washed-out blue in color, and very red-rimmed. He pressed two childlike fingers to the bridge of his nose. "I really must insist on a truce here," he murmured. "We are seeking to unearth the hidden, do the impossible, escape with both freedom and the money with which to enjoy it. Such bickering must stop."

Erika leaned back in her chair, grumbling, "My old man used to get drunk and talk about the war and the bombings. On and on he went. Then he'd start beating on anyone he could grab. Almost every night. It gave me the creeps then, and it does now."

"My dad died in the war," Kurt said, subsiding. "I remember the bombings, though. Horrible, they were. Worse than horrible."

Erika looked at him, the makings of a cease-fire in her eyes. "You were a war child, too?"

He nodded. "Born in thirty-nine."

"You've five years on me, then. My old man, he said I was born in a bomb shelter and got covered with dust the minute I came out." Her tone now was conversational. "I never knew my mother."

"Me neither. I was a Young Patriot of the Great and Glorious Communist State," he said wryly, referring to the title given war orphans in the fifties.

Erika looked amused. "Fired with the true Communist spirit from the cradle."

"When young," he admitted. "Now I live for myself."

"The only logical course," Erika agreed.

"I knew all the right slogans, and I could shout with the best of them," Kurt went on. "But in truth I learned long ago to care for the State about as much as the State cared for me."

"I too lived the great lie," Erika said quietly.

They shared a look of understanding before Kurt repeated to Ferret, calm now, "Get on with the telling."

"With pleasure." Ferret refitted his spectacles. "The chamber was dismantled, as I said, in June of 1944. It was first placed inside the castle cellars, but after the British bombing leveled the castle, it was thought safer to locate it elsewhere. A temporary home was found in a local brewery, where it was walled into a disused storage room. The officials asked a local count if he would allow them to store it in his cellar, but he refused on the grounds that the cellar was too damp. So it was decided to transport the Amber Room along with other valuables in what proved to be the last recorded transfer of treasures before the fall of the Nazi empire."

Erika shook her head. "You sound so sure."

"I am."

"How can this be?"

"I have been searching," he replied, "for the pieces of a puzzle. Those who made this search before, the bureaucrats who were ordered to do so by their communist bosses, sought with logic. When logic failed them, rather than admit defeat, they declared that there was in fact no puzzle at all—that the treasure had been destroyed in the bombing. But this I know to be false. I have found what they were too lazy to seek out. Doors in the West have been opened to me that remained ever closed to them and their endless demands for secrecy."

Erika asked, "So what do you have instead of logic to solve these puzzles?"

"He lives with them," Kurt replied, the gleam strong in his eyes. "Don't ask me to explain it, because I can't. But I've been with him for almost fifteen years, and I know it for fact. Accept it."

"You must remember," Ferret said, "that many of the puzzles are indeed false, the treasures forever lost. More than many. Almost all. I have spent years and years walking upon paths which in truth no longer existed."

"But not this time," Erika said, hope in her voice.

Ferret shook his head. "No. This time I am sure."

Erika thought it over, nodded her acceptance. "So a final transfer of the Amber Room was made."

"It left Königsberg in December of 1944," Ferret agreed. "The last available eighteen working trucks were loaded and placed upon flatbed railroad cars. There was very little gasoline left, you see. Certainly none to be had once they left territory controlled by their *Gauleiter*, no matter who signed and stamped their passes. In those last chaotic days, all remaining supplies were hoarded by the lucky and shared with none."

"A lot of treasure was left behind, I wager," Kurt said.

"More than was taken," Ferret agreed. "Room was made only for the priceless."

"Like the chamber," Erika offered.

"Just so. The twenty tons of amber were stored this time in seventy-two steel chests, each so massive it took four men to shift. These cases took up three of the eighteen trucks. The train pulled out under cover of night, barely before the nemesis arrived."

"The Russians," Kurt said.

Erika smiled without humor. "You mean to say our saviors, don't you?"

"The invasion began on January 26, 1945," Ferret continued. "Königsberg fell on April 9. Between those two dates, the city was pounded into the dust. When the Russians finally entered the city, not a single building remained intact. Not one. The seven-hundred-year-old capital of the Prussian empire was totally obliterated."

With nervous gestures Erika fished a Russian cigarette from a crumpled pack. She spent a moment composing herself and pressing the paper-tube filter into various shapes. She finally lit it, drew hard, sighed with the smoke. "Cursed memories."

Kurt had the decency to look away. "But the chamber was already gone."

"Not according to the Soviets and their official story," Ferret replied, "I am happy to say. After searching for almost twenty years, they claimed that it was destroyed in the bombing and that the rest of the story was myth. But the Soviets have now fallen, and the new Russian government claimed that new evidence points a finger at cliffs filled with Nazi bombs."

"But you claim otherwise."

"I do not just claim," Ferret replied. "I know. I have had access to information which the Russians did not."

Kurt's eyebrows crept up. "The American quartermaster sergeant?"

"A mere conduit. But the records he gave us were invaluable."

"And the soldier who died in Siberia? The one whose records were supplied by the Russian colonel?"

"That is a bit of the puzzle overlooked by the logical plodders. They sought to do a job; their reward was security and nothing more. Finding or not finding the hidden treasures had no effect on their salary. Not a formula for stimulating independent thought."

"What about my trips south?"

"Doing away with possible loose ends," Ferret replied. "We had to be sure, you see. The caves at Jonastal and the underground bunkers in Weimar were intended as the collection point for all such treasures. The Königsberg shipment was supposed to have traveled there, just as Yeltsin said."

"*Supposed* to be there."

Ferret nodded. "No trace was found, no evidence that the trucks arrived."

Kurt waited, asked the expected question. "So where is the Amber Room?"

Ferret turned to Erika, who had managed to reinstall her stone-like visage. "You have the man's address?"

"My friend does. As of last year. He is old, and he may have died, but as of last year he still lived there."

"Let us hope that this essential thread remains within our grasp," Ferret replied. "I suggest we travel as soon as it is dark."

"Twenty tons of amber," Kurt said. "How much is that worth?"

Ferret blinked. "Nothing and everything."

"What is that supposed to mean?" This from Erica.

"It does not matter how much it is worth," Ferret said, "if we are not alive and free to enjoy the wealth."

"Let me see if I understand," Erika said. "We're going crazy looking for a treasure that isn't there—"

"Oh, believe me, it is there."

"—so that even if we do find it, we can't sell it," Erika finished. "That makes as much sense as one of Honecker's old speeches."

"Let him talk," Kurt said, but mildly. Erika shot him a glance, saw no rancor, subsided.

"As I said to our American contact, we do not sell what we cannot recover," Ferret explained. "We do not struggle to take what we could never escape with. There is no war to mask our efforts, no crisis to blind people to the unearthing and transporting of seventy-two heavy chests. No. We sell what is weightless, what can be packed in the smallest coffer and carried without being a burden to anyone."

"Information," Kurt said, nodding. "Smart."

"We will sell a treasure map," Ferret continued, "and leave the struggles over unearthing and the battles over ownership to the nations."

"While we make like the wind." Kurt smiled, exposing yellowed teeth. "We're in the pirate business. I like it."

"We will not be greedy," Ferret said. "We want the wealth of the fortunate, the ones able to enjoy the spoils. We will ask only so much that it is easier to pay than to give chase."

"Five hundred thousand apiece sounds like a fortunate number," Kurt agreed. "When do we leave?"

B ut twenty tons of amber," Jeffrey protested. "Seventy-two gigantic steel chests. How could anybody make something that big just disappear?"

It was two weeks since their return from Dresden, the day of the gala event. Despite the blitz of last-minute details, every free moment, every lapse in their work, every pause for coffee or food was spiced with reflection over the undiscovered.

"The war essentially turned much of Europe into the world's largest flea market," Alexander explained. "Priceless items were sold by the pound, and treasures were passed around like tourist mementos."

"That's hard to imagine." Jeffrey continued with his careful checking and organizing of the calligraphic place cards for the tables, grateful for the conversation to break the tedium of preparation.

"I understand. But this does not make it any less true. In Nazi-occupied territories, well-placed generals arrived for inspections with scores of empty lorries. Their hosts, the heads of the local military governments, offered roomfuls of treasures in order to remain in the general staff's good favor."

"Treasures," Jeffrey repeated, thinking of his friend Betty.

"I realize it must sound strange to you, having never lived through such horrors yourself. But you cannot imagine how much was flooding the German-controlled markets, especially toward the end of the war. There was literally a sea of goods swept up by the German armies, mind-boggling amounts from cities and palaces stretching from Paris to the gates of Moscow. An entire world of treasures, carted off by the conquering armies. And then defeat, and rout. Retreats planned in haste and executed in blind panic. With wave after wave of Allied bombers destroying roads and rails and airports. With few trucks that still ran and petrol scarcer than emeralds."

"So it wasn't just that records might have been lost," Jeffrey said. "Quite possibly, there were no records to begin with."

Alexander tossed his pen aside. "My dear Jeffrey, an entire castle could have disappeared into the morass of those final days without it going noticed or recorded.

"Mind you," he went on, "this was not always the case. There were of course specialists on the German staff whose only job was to catalogue and ship the booty. Yet even at the best of times, when Germany was winning and the legendary German efficiency was in firm control, these people were worked to the point of exhaustion. In many documented cases, they only managed to view the tip of the iceberg. Most of these professionals were assigned to headquarters staff, used by the senior officers to catalogue what they themselves intended to hoard."

"Which left everyone else below them without expert assistance."

"Precisely. Officers in the field were laws unto themselves when it came to such matters, so long as a certain flow of goods continued to arrive at headquarters. This meant that much of the loot they happened upon was diverted to their own warehouses or parceled out to their men as rewards. And almost all of these items were catalogued by enlisted men, many of whom did not have a clue as to what they were handling. For example, I have seen records in which a Matisse, three Renoirs, and two Van Goghs were listed as 'six gilt frames with pictures.' "

Jeffrey strapped together the final dozen cards for the last table and announced, "That's done."

"Splendid. I am so grateful for your assistance, Jeffrey. It would have been an impossible task to take on alone."

"It's been enjoyable. Really."

"Yes, knowing that you share my appreciation for both our profession and such events has been a reward in itself." Alexander glanced at his watch. "What time did you want to be off?"

"In a few minutes." The excitement that had been tugging at him threatened to spill over. He pushed it away with another question. "What do you think the room actually looked like?"

"Magnificent, without a doubt. I would imagine it to be as richly textured as a sunrise," Alexander mused. "That was undoubtedly the designer's intention, you know—to create an inlaid chamber fit for a king."

"An amber chamber," Jeffrey said for the countless time that week. "Incredible. Almost like walking inside a jewel."

"Oh, far more grand, I should imagine," Alexander replied. "Remember, the amber was of a hundred different hues, from the deepest topaz-brown to a fine white-gold champagne. Whatever the amber's shade, light transforms it into something that appears both molten and eternally still, a prism of softest hues. Imagine the color of sunlight through dark ale, or honey, or a fine white wine—this has always been amber's most appealing quality to me, its ability to take whatever light is cast upon it and transform it into something divine."

"But a *room* of it," Jeffrey said, awed by the thought.

"Yes, imagine." Alexander leaned back in his chair and said to the ceiling, "Hundreds of thousands of facets matched in both tone and texture, then carved like bits of a vast, room-sized puzzle. The result was a set of three-dimensional walls that appeared to flicker and flow."

"And all the light unsteady and shifting," Jeffrey continued, captivated by the thought. "Imagine what a cloud passing before the sun would have done to the walls."

"Exactly. The light of that era would have been splendid for amber. Vast floor to ceiling windows, all those chandeliers and candelabras, and tall mirrors reflecting the candlelight; the walls would take on a life of their own, flickering at hints of mysteries within their unfrozen depths. Yes, I would imagine that a chamber of amber would be the most mystical of earthly experiences. Especially at night, as its residents pondered vast affairs of state or read from ancient texts, or sought answers in the depths of walls whose very form appeared to flow with the power of thought."

Alexander rose to his feet, began gathering up the neatly stacked and bound place cards. "A famous Russian poet, a guest of the czar, was once invited to sit in the Amber Room. Upon his return to the more mundane realms, he wrote that when the sun shone in the room or the candles played over the walls at night, the room appeared to be *alive*. Every stone, every ornament, every single minute element of this timeless work combined to create a symphony of silent beauty."

Alexander closed his briefcase, snapped the locks, asked, "You will be meeting me at the prearranged time?"

"With Katya," Jeffrey said, rising as well.

"I do wish you would tell me what all the mystery is about. This is definitely not a night for further surprises."

"Everything we've been able to think of has been done," Jeffrey replied. "I went by at lunchtime, and the display cases and guards are all in."

"That was not what I was speaking of, and you know it. You have something up your sleeve for this evening, I've been catching wind of it now for several—"

"I've got to be going," Jeffrey interrupted, heading for the door. "See you at the Ritz."

======

Claridge's had no bar. Instead, hotel guests gathered in a parlor the size of a manor house's formal living room, furnished accordingly with overstuffed settees, graceful Chippendale high-backed chairs, Empire coffee tables, original oil paintings, crystal chandeliers, and the largest handmade rug Jeffrey had ever seen. Service was provided by footmen in brass-buttoned uniforms festooned with braid and buckles and ornamental finery. In the far corner, a quartet strung theater tunes together with light Strauss waltzes and Brahms melodies. The parlor's atmosphere was subdued yet striking, and reeked of wealth.

Jeffrey escaped the blustery winter damp by waiting in the hotel's white-marble front lobby. He had time to check his dinner jacket for unnoticed stains, his starched shirtfront for wayward studs, and his silk bowtie for recent skews before he spotted Katya alighting from a taxi. The long velvet box in his pocket bounced against his side as he hurried for the door.

He paid Katya's driver and ushered her back inside. She wore a dark gray overcoat with black velvet piping at arms and sides that ended at the cuffs in a curlicue of intricate handwork. Cloth buttons fitted within miniature matching designs formed double-breasted rows down the front. The velvet collar was high and stiff and rose to meet her shimmering black hair.

Jeffrey brushed at raindrops sparkling on her locks. "You look like a Russian fairy princess."

She replied with a curtsy and said, "Thank you, my dashing prince."

He took her arm and ushered her into the hotel proper. "I'm sorry not to have come for you, but I just did not have time—"

"That's fine, Jeffrey, as I told you before." She slid her arm through his and moved toward the cloakroom. "But why Claridge's?" she asked as she began unbuttoning her coat.

"I promised . . . No, wait, you'll see." He helped her with the coat and handed it to the cloakroom attendant. Underneath Katya wore an off-the-shoulder gown of emerald green silk, slit along one side to reveal sheer stockings and matching high-heeled slippers. Her only jewelry was a tiny gold cross nestled in the base of her neck. His heart was squeezed tight by the sight of her. "Katya, I can't believe how beautiful you are."

She rewarded him with a smile that caught his breath. "When you look at me like that, I feel as if I need a fan to hide behind," she said.

"Come, my love." He led her down the central hall, past the porter's desk, through the high portico, and into the formal parlor, conscious all the while that every eye in the hotel was upon them. Well, upon her.

A liveried footman bowed a formal greeting and led them to their table where he held Katya's chair. Her eyes were round as she whispered to Jeffrey, "What is all this?"

"Wait." He seated himself beside her and waited for the footman to depart. "I am doing this for all those who have helped to bring us together, Katya. May we honor them all our days with our love for each other."

"The way you say that makes me shiver." She looked at him for a long moment. "You sound so . . . well, so formal."

"I've thought about this moment for a long time," Jeffrey replied. "It's not so much formal as important."

"What is it?"

"I'm not doing this for me," he said. "Well, I am, but it's for others too. Especially the reason why I'm doing it here. I promised someone."

"Jeffrey Allen Sinclair," she said sharply. "You cannot make me cry tonight."

"I have something for you," he persisted. "It just arrived yesterday, and I know she'd want you to wear it tonight."

"Who is that?"

"My grandmother. When she became engaged to Piotr, my grandfather, Alexander gave her this and then took them here for dinner. She wants you to have this as her engagement present, and she asked if I would give it to you here, her favorite hotel in all the world. She asked me to tell you that she is very sorry not to be here, but her health won't allow it, so she hopes we will be traveling over to America very soon. She says that from what I've told her, she is sure you are a gift from above." He had to stop and swallow hard. "She also hopes we will be as happy as she was with Piotr, and that we will remember her and the love she holds—"

"Oh, Jeffrey. Please—"

"The love she holds for us both," he finished. He brought the long slender black box from his pocket. "This is for you, Katya."

"I can't."

"Please. I want you to have it. We both do."

Gingerly she accepted the box, pressed the little catch, swung open the top, gave a trembling sigh. "Oh, Jeffrey."

There were sixteen emeralds in all. Eight formed the necklace's first row, five the second, and a single gem twice as large as the others hung below in solitary splendor. Each was framed within a casing of yellow gold, and suspended upon a netting of intertwined red and white gold rope. The final two jewels were set as matching earrings and hung from little perches on the box's silk-lined top.

She reached over, asked, "May I have your handkerchief, please?"

"Here."

"Thank you." She dabbed at her eyes. "Am I a mess?"

"You are the most beautiful woman I have ever laid eyes on," he answered truthfully. "Would you like me to help you put it on?"

"All right." She swiveled in her seat to present him with her back.

He lifted the necklace, threaded it around her neck, fastened it, pressed her skin with his lips. "Turn around."

"How does it look?"

"Stop patting it for a second so I can see."

"Is this really for me?"

He nodded. "Do you want to try on the earrings, too?"

"Tell me how it looks, Jeffrey. Please."

"As though it were made for you. Truly." And it did. The jewels' shimmering green accented her skin's creamy whiteness and her eyes' sparkling depths. The gown looked like it was made for the jewelry.

She leaned forward to kiss him. "I don't think I can find the right words to thank you just now, Jeffrey."

"You don't have to say anything."

"Yes, I do, and I will. But not just now." She rose to her feet, taking the box with her. "Now if you'll excuse me for a moment, I must go see this for myself."

U nlike many great hotels, the Ritz carried the splendor of its lobby and public rooms into the main ballroom. A pair of liveried waiters flanked the double entranceway. Within these portals, the first guests milled about in the formal anteroom, itself much larger than many great-rooms. Beyond the polished-wood floors with their Persian carpets and valuable antiques stood yet another set of crested double doors, these leading into the ballroom proper.

Each of the ballroom tables was set for twelve and crowned with a vast floral centerpiece. Massive gilt chandeliers, nine in all, cast soft brilliance over the immaculate setting. In the hall's very center stood the display cases, of gray steel and security glass, holding the trio of precious Polish artifacts.

Alexander stood just inside the first set of doors, giving last-minute instructions to the obsequious maître d'. The old gentleman was resplendent in well-fit finery; the only mark of color to his severe, black-and-white evening wear was a small gold medal on watered silk that hung from his lapel. Jeffrey had never seen such a medal before, had no idea what it meant.

The old gentleman's eyes lit up at the sight of Katya. Alexander waved the maitre d' away and focused his entire attention on the young woman, pausing a very long moment before bowing and kissing the offered hand while Jeffrey looked on.

"My dear," he murmured. "You look absolutely exquisite."

Katya touched her free hand to her neck. "I believe I have you to thank for these."

"Tonight the past has come alive for me once more," Alexander replied quietly.

"I only wish Piotr and his wife were here for me to thank as well," Katya said.

Alexander looked at Jeffrey. "In one respect, they are. A part of them."

"A magnificent part," Katya said, looking up with pride at her husband-to-be.

Alexander nodded. "May I say how delighted and happy I am for you both."

"Thank you," she said, joy shining in her eyes.

"I suppose Jeffrey has told you of my engagement present," Alexander said.

"Not yet," Jeffrey replied.

"Then I shall. My dear, my first purchase as an antiques dealer was a ring. I have kept it long enough. I have asked Jeffrey if I might be permitted to offer it as an engagement ring, a mark of the affection I hold for you both."

Katya reached for Jeffrey's hand. "Please, I'm going to cry again."

"Very well." He clapped his hands. "Enough! I too shall be no good at all tonight if we continue thusly. My dear, please be so kind as to go reassure the Count. He is over by the display case trying to convince himself that he has seen the chalice before. In Rome of all places."

"Of course," Katya agreed, and departed with a regal curtsy for Alexander and a brief hand-squeeze for Jeffrey.

They watched her elegant passage. "A magnificent young woman," Alexander said. "And a worthy mate for you, my friend."

"I only hope I can be the same for her."

"You will, you will. Of that I have no doubt." Alexander's manner became brisk. "I have reluctantly decided that you two will be at separate tables tonight."

"All right." Such was to be expected.

"You are both too valuable to these guests to squander on a single grouping. I shall place Katya as hostess to a table of old Polish nobility. They will treat her like the queen she is."

"She'll like that," he said. But he missed her already.

"Your table will be a mixed lot. More males than females—there are several like that. Can't be helped, I'm afraid. But there is one gentleman in particular whom I have placed beside you, a photographer."

"He must be doing well to be able to afford this evening's gala."

"Oh, he's here as the guest of one of our wealthier patrons-to-be. His name is Viktor Bogdanski. I'll introduce you when he arrives." Alexander patted Jeffrey's arm in parting and turned to greet new arrivals.

Jeffrey mingled as the room filled with wealth and power. Ignoring the uncomfortable sense that these people lived in a world in which he did not belong, he greeted clients he had met in the shop, made polite conversation as he drifted from circle to circle, kissed the air above innumerable age-scarred and bejeweled hands. Alexander was constantly beckoning him toward new faces, making sure that all present understood who he was.

Katya came over from time to time, to smile and share a few words before being pulled away once more. The Count had appointed himself responsible for ensuring that everyone met her. Yet no matter where Jeffrey was or with whom he spoke, he remained acutely aware of her presence. The brief glances they shared across the elegantly crowded room sparkled with an intimacy they knew was on display for all to see, and yet which they could not help but show.

Eventually Alexander led him to a small, neat man with a sharply trimmed beard that stood quietly in a corner, nodding and smiling slightly when attention turned his way. Jeffrey's first impression was of a man utterly content with his own solitude.

"Jeffrey, I would like to you to meet Viktor Bogdanski. Viktor, this is the friend I have spoken with you about."

Viktor offered his hand. "Alexander seldom speaks as highly of anyone as he has of you."

"I seldom have reason to," Alexander replied. "Now, I shall leave you two to discover why I wanted you to meet."

Jeffrey watched the old gentleman glide back into the beautifully dressed crowd. "This is the most comfortable spot I've found all night."

"I share your sentiment wholeheartedly."

"And so, tell me, why are you here?"

"Ah." The man sipped at his drink. "I happen to believe in what is behind this charade. Events like this are a necessary nuisance. They are as close to real need as many of these beautiful people would ever care to come."

Jeffrey spoke of a concern he had carried since the project's onset. "Do you think perhaps the money should be going to something more, well . . . ?"

"Urgent?" The man shrugged. "I try not to judge the actions of others. I am also an artist of sorts, and I consider that there is more to the rebuilding of a nation than just filling bellies and healing physical wounds. Preserving a sense of national heritage is a most worthy endeavor." He smiled around his beard. "That is, I would think so if I were to judge such goings-on. Which I won't."

Jeffrey motioned at the sparkling throng. "The trickle-down theory at work."

"Exactly." Viktor examined him frankly. "Alexander tells me that you are new to the faithful fold."

"Newly returned," Jeffrey admitted. "Or attempting to make my way back."

Viktor nodded approval. "It is good to know which way to turn when the wind blows."

"I am not all that sure I've got it clearly worked out," Jeffrey admitted.

"Toward the unseen sun," the photographer said emphatically. "You must remember where it was when you last saw it, and reach for it in hopes of its reappearing soon."

Jeffrey thought over the man's words as Alexander called the gathering to silence, welcomed them, repeated the night's mission, and invited them to find their assigned seats according to both the seating chart beside the doors and the place cards by each seat.

As they moved slowly toward the double doors, Katya came up and slipped her hand into his arm. "Would the handsomest gentleman in the room be so kind as to escort me to my table?"

He looked down at her and said quietly, "I'm so proud of you."

Her violet-gray eyes shone at him. "I wish I could kiss you."

"Alexander told me to cool down the way we were looking at each other," he told her. "He said there were some hearts in this room too old for such obvious passion."

"The Count put it differently," she replied as they entered the grand ballroom. "He said the sparks we were generating might set some of these varnished hairdos alight."

They arrived at her table. Jeffrey made the obligatory circle, exchanging stiff-backed bows with aged Polish aristocracy, kissing the hands of dowagers. He held the back of Katya's seat, accepted a smile that touched him at levels he had not known existed, then walked to his own table.

The first courses were set in place. The glasses were hand-cut lead crystal, the plates rimmed with gold leaf, the waiters swift and silently efficient. Jeffrey returned toasts and exchanged polite conversation with the others, wishing he felt more comfortable with such social chatter.

Viktor eventually pried himself free from the matron to his left, and turned to Jeffrey. "I detect a yearning for a fare of greater substance."

"You are right there."

"Very well, I agree." He gave a sort of seated bow. "You begin with a question, and let us see where it takes us."

Jeffrey thought of Gregor and asked, "How did you come to faith?"

That brought a chuckle. "You do not act in half measures. I like that."

"If you'd rather—"

"Not at all." Viktor waved it aside. "It is a most worthy question. What matters the surroundings to such as that?" He thought a moment. "I shall have to take us back to some rather dark days in my nation's heritage in order to answer you, however. It all took place during the early days of martial law in Poland."

Jeffrey nodded. "That's fine, but only if you care to do so."

Viktor's dark eyes turned inward. "I suppose there are many bad things that happen during a state of siege, but among the worst is to be a photographer for the losing side. What my eyes saw, my camera captured. Thus was the moment preserved on my film and in my mind and heart for all my days. The bitterest truth and the harshest image.

"My life was my pictures, and my pictures sought to give life and reality to what otherwise could not be imagined. I sought to show the outside world the chains my country was seeking to cast off, the price my people had been forced to pay in carrying their weight for so very long.

"The date was December 11, 1981. I can't say that it was a typical evening. There was more excitement than usual, a tension throughout Poland that you could almost touch. I had captured some great material over the past several days. Massive demonstrations of workers. Students clambering on the shoulders of their fellows to look over the militia's riot gear and talk to them, shout at them, plead with them to wake up and remember who they were. A series of footprints in fresh snow forming the word *zwyciezymy*, which means 'We shall overcome.' Sympathy strikes by trainees in the fire department, who of course were seen as a great threat by the authorities, since firemen were officially part of the power structure.

"The clever activists among us, the ones who treated politics as a chess game, were speculating that a state of emergency would be declared. I would listen to such talk, but I seldom took part. My task, my life in those days, was simply to be the eyes for those who sought to see but who, because of distance or barriers, could not. And yet I did listen, and much of what I heard made sense. The situation economically and politically was getting out of hand. There was no food on the shelves; everything had been diverted by the central authorities in an attempt to browbeat the people, force them by fear and by hunger into submission. The queues were unimaginable, even for bread."

The room swirled about them in wafts of rich food and expensive perfume. Jewels glinted and flickered in the chandeliers' glow. Rich fabrics, starched shirtfronts, and polished cuff links caught light and sent it spinning with each gesture and every word. As Jeffrey sat listening to Viktor, he felt a new dimension growing from the night. There was the world that he saw, and the world of Viktor's memories, and both held portents he could scarcely comprehend.

"We expected the decree might come in mid-December, when the *Sejm*, our Parliament, was to meet," Viktor continued. "Under the Polish constitution, only the Sejm has the power to decree a state of emergency. That evening, I was working on my photographs at the Solidarity press office in Warsaw, preparing a portfolio that friends would attempt to smuggle out of the country. It was a very good collection of images. As I was sorting them, our halls were suddenly filled with the militia's navy-blue uniforms. They said they had warrants for our arrest. We were accused of anti-government activities.

"It is strange what you think at a moment like that. I was only worried about my camera. I looked over my shoulder as they led me from the room in handcuffs. They were going through my files of stills and slides and negatives. One of them picked up my camera, opened the back and stripped out the film, then with a casual motion swung it against the wall and smashed it. I felt as though I had lost a limb, and part of my life spilled to the ground with the little pieces of glass and metal."

Jeffrey felt a chasm growing between him and the room's glittering display as the man continued with his soft-spoken story. "Midnight Saturday they declared martial law. Sunday morning there were no phones, no radio, no papers—no one knew what had happened. All of this I learned later, from friends who had either gone underground and escaped the first sweep or were not listed by the police and remained free. My own story was quite different. But before I tell you what happened to me, first I shall speak of what my nation experienced.

"Later that day, Jaruzelski appeared in uniform on television. Jaruzelski at that time was Secretary of the Polish Communist Party and head of the armed forces—the first time one person had ever held those two posts. He announced that martial law had been declared. But it is important to note that the words in Polish for martial law are the same as for a state of war or a state of siege. You can imagine the reactions. Some said it was just the next stage of the argument between Solidarity and the government. Others relived that time of terror when the Soviets had invaded."

Jeffrey glanced up and was astonished to find the entire table watching and listening. He inspected the circle of faces and sensed an unwavering quality to their attentiveness, a solemn sharing of what the photographer was saying. They listened with an intensity born of shared concern, a somber gathering that knew already of what the man spoke and yet listened with the patience of ones willing to allow the moment to live yet again. Jeffrey searched their faces, found a common bond and a collective strength rising from their love of the Polish nation.

"Monday came to those not arrested," the photographer went on. "For those of us in prison, the names of passing days meant little. People who were free went back to work and found that everything was much the same, yet altogether different. Everybody worked under much tighter control. Only one telephone line functioned in each factory, no matter how large the company. A stooge for the regime was placed in charge of the outgoing line. Every other hour, someone at Party headquarters would call to ensure that all was quiet.

"There was a curfew from ten in the evening to six the next morning. You were forbidden to leave town. You were forbidden to buy petrol. Train services were cut back, and a special Party permit was required to buy a ticket. Tanks were stationed on many street corners. Soldiers were everywhere. The military scrambled the army units. The central authorities did not want sons standing across the barricades from their sisters and mothers. So units were sent to distant cities—Cracow to Gdansk, Gdansk to Warsaw, Warsaw to Wroclaw, and so on.

"It was a very cold December, and on every street the soldiers kept bonfires burning in order to stay warm. Our cities remained shrouded in smoke from these fires throughout the cold winter weeks.

"Our cities lived a very oppressive life. People had no way of knowing what was happening. The papers said only what the government told them to say, which was the lie of convenience.

Everyone on television wore uniforms. You could see how nervous the announcers were, how *terrified*. The authorities forced these reporters to dress up in military uniforms and read the Party line.

"The despondency was made very bitter because it arrived on the crest of hopes that Solidarity had ignited. Over all this loomed the constant fear that our friends to the east would arrive—that is how Soviet propaganda always described itself, 'Poland's friend to the east.'

"That first Monday, everyone went into the stores and bought out everything they could find—all the flour, all the sugar, all the cans and boxes of preserved food. After that, no further shipments of food arrived. The shelves remained empty. Grocery stores kept open because they were told to do so, and yet they had nothing to sell except perhaps a few bottles of vinegar. Sales clerks just stood behind the counters. Then in the spring, when the first vegetables arrived, even the vinegar disappeared. People used it to pickle vegetables at home.

"Suddenly there were ration cards for everything—meat, alcohol, cigarettes, butter, cooking oil, flour, even cards for shoes and undergarments and little chocolates for the children. But the fact that you had a coupon did not mean you could buy the article. Usually the stores had nothing to sell. It simply meant you had the right to enter a store to ask.

"Rumors started then. People stood in line ten, twelve, fourteen hours just because of a word from a friend of a friend of a friend that this store *might* get a shipment of shoes or socks or sugar or bread.

"Basically, martial law was the latest brutal reminder of how Poland was manipulated by Russia. People lived under a constant cloud of depression, waiting, waiting, fearing the worst. They knew, whether or not it was spoken. International attention kept us from being annexed, but we were totally under the power of our friends to the east.

"I have talked to all my friends about this time, trying to fill in the gaps, seeking to close the void that my arrest caused in my life. I could not take pictures of that vital time, so I borrowed the images of friends. I remember only darkness and silence and cold.

Over my absence of light and memories of bitter fear, I have set the recollections and photographs and experiences of others."

Waiters appeared in unison to sweep away the plates and set dessert in their place. The photographer's gaze was very bright, but he spoke in quiet tones; the people on the other side of the circular table had to lean forward to catch his words. Their table remained an island of focused silence in the swirl of evening splendor.

"My own glimpses of the fall of Poland's night came through a tear in the canvas side of the army truck which carried us off that Saturday evening. We were not taken to the local prison. I heard a guard say as we were processed that the prison was already full. We were taken to an army barracks. I was led off alone and locked inside a cellar storage room. There was nothing in that room. No window, no heat, no water, no mattress, nothing. For light I had a single bulb strung from the ceiling. Hours later, two soldiers, an officer and an enlisted man, came in. They put down a blanket, a pail of water, and a slop bucket. I asked the officer how long I was to stay there. 'Until I have orders to release you,' he said. 'How long will that be?' He did not answer, only shut the door and locked me in.

"There was no way of telling the passage of time. There was no day or night, only the bulb dangling from the ceiling. After a time, my fears began to take control of me. Food did not come regularly, or so it seemed, and I grew terrified that they would forget me, that I would be left to starve. Then there was the fear that the bulb would burn out and I would be left in the dark. I spent several days fighting off sleep, terrified that I would wake up in the darkness and never see the light again.

"Weeks passed. I know that now. At the time it was an eternity, marked only by occasional meals handed to me by guards ordered not to speak, and by my growing fears. Then came a point when I realized I was going insane. That became my greatest fear of all, of losing my mind and my memories and my ability to give the world meaning through photographs. I decided I would kill myself in order to keep that from happening. But I did not know how. I was given no utensils with my food, I had no weapons or any other sharp article, and there was nothing in the seamless concrete walls from which I could suspend my blanket and hang myself. I spent hours and hours and hours searching for a way out of this man-made hell and finally fell asleep.

"I dreamed of a time as a very small child, so long ago that I was still in my crib. I recalled something I had not thought of for years and years. My mother used to come in as I was going to sleep, sit down beside my little bed, and say a rosary. I would fall asleep to the sound of the clicking beads and her murmured prayers.

"I awoke with a start, crawled to my knees, and prayed to a God I did not know. I asked for rescue. As I prayed, I had an image of something falling from myself, as though I were shedding an old skin. I did not know the Bible then, and I could not describe what was happening. All I could say was that I returned to sleep with a calmer spirit.

"And then I had a second dream. It was not of the past, but of a scene I could not recognize. I was looking out over beautiful green hills lit by very bright sunshine. In the valley below me was a small village of triangular-shaped thatched roofs—it was a very peculiar design. I was certain I had never seen anything like that place or those houses ever before. But it was not the scene itself which had an impact on me. I awoke with a sense of overwhelming peace, a feeling so strong that there was no room left in me for despair or doubt or even fear. I sat in my bare concrete cell and knew that I was going to be all right. I could not say how, or even if, I was going to be released. But the power of that peace was enough to make me know beyond doubt that I was not alone, that I was going to be all right."

A waiter appeared to collect the untouched dessert plates. The bejeweled matron seated beside Jeffrey waved the waiter away with a sharp motion. No one else at the table moved. All attention remained fastened upon the photographer.

"A short while later, an amnesty was declared. I was released, along with many others. It was night when I came out of the bar-racks. A friend was there to meet me, and he and his wife drove me immediately from the barracks to a place where I could rest and recover, a family cottage in the Tartar Mountains, down on our southern border. By the time we arrived I was too tired to pay any attention to the surroundings. I went straight up to bed.

"The next morning I awoke, walked to the window, pushed open the shutters, and cried aloud. There before me was the exact same scene I had dreamed of in prison—the green slopes, the tiny village with the thatched cottages, the bright morning sunshine. And the feeling. It was there as well. The peace and the love and the assurance that I was not alone, would never be alone, that I was loved for all eternity."

The man who answered the door at the Dresden address which Birgit had supplied to Erika was not an aging Nazi colonel; he was a middle-aged Wessie who looked at the trio on his doorstep with ill-concealed disdain. His family was now the sole occupants of the building, reclaiming the home that had been stripped from their grandparents when the Communists took power.

Even Ferret showed true emotion at that point, demanding in shrill anger to be told where the old man had gone. But the Wessie had never been taught to fear the authorities and replied with bored hostility. He had no idea where the occupants of the seven cramped apartments the Communists had made of their home were now. Then he rudely ordered the trio away with threats and closed the door upon their fury.

The following two weeks were spent in helpless panic as Erika returned to her friend and Birgit returned to her records. They could do little then but wait—wait and worry and fret over the unknowns. What if the old man had moved away to another city? What if he had spent several frigid nights in the open, then taken his secret to an unmarked grave? Such questions left them tired and eaten with worry and snapping at each other. To be so close, so close, and then to—no, better not to say.

Then Birgit came through again.

The old man had done as any good Ossie would do, trained as they were from birth to follow any instructions from authority without argument or question; he had given his corrected address when accepting his monthly pension check.

There was an entirely different flavor to this second journey. They drove in grimly determined silence through a night turned treacherous by fresh snowfall. Not a word was spoken between Schwerin and Dresden. Not a word.

The address belonged to a two-room hovel, a place that could be called a residence only because of the housing shortage and the lack of governmental control. It was a plywood shack set at the back end of garden plots stretching between an autobahn exit ramp and the railroad lines leading into Dresden. As in many European cities, sections of otherwise unusable property had been parceled out to the very poor, granting them a tiny postage stamp of earth where flowers and vegetables might be grown.

The shack stood at the garden's far corner, easily shaken by the man-made thunder of passing cars and trains. Smoke from a wood-burning stove poured from the tin pipe poking out of the roof. A pair of wires slumped down from a solitary pole, signaling that the shanty at least had electricity and perhaps the luxury of a phone. There was no indoor plumbing; a hand pump sprouted a long icicle in testament to recent use.

The three sat in the car a very long moment, frozen into immobility by two weeks of worry. Finally Ferret spoke. "I will handle this myself and do the talking." He waited; there was no dissent. "Very well. Let us begin."

═══

The frail old man opened his front door and took an involuntary step back. The man and woman facing him were both of a size, as the saying went, solid and beefy and cloaked in knee-length leather trench coats. The starchy diet of the East had weighted them with undue pounds, yet their menace remained intact. The old man clutched his chest at their faces and the sweep of memories that accompanied the sight. He had seen many such faces through the years.

Then a third figure stepped forward, smaller and slighter than the pair, but no less menacing. "We have questions, Herr Makel," the little man said, his sibilant whisper matched perfectly to a face unmarked by age or emotion.

"I—I know no one by that name."

"We have not driven through nine hours of traffic and snow to stand in the night and talk drivel, Herr Horst Makel. We know who you are, and we are here for information."

"May I see your identification?"

"Of course not," the little man snapped. "And you will stop wasting my time with idiotic questions."

The old man drew himself up as tall as years and arthritis would allow. "We are living in a democracy nowadays. The old days are gone."

"The new days have a lot of hunters out looking for Nazi criminals," the stranger replied.

"I have committed no crimes," the old man cried out.

"Of course not. It was simply convenient to spend forty-seven years living under a false name, working as a tool-and-dye maker. *Nicht wahr, Herr Oberst?*" The little man waited through a very tense moment, then stated flatly, "We are coming in, Herr Colonel."

He shouldered past the sputtering old man and entered the threadbare cottage. The silent pair walked in behind him and camped solidly by the door. That left the old man the choice of either arguing with a pair as pliant as two large trees or following the strange, unfinished man into the parlor.

"I don't understand what this is all about, but—"

"Czestochowa," Ferret replied. He pronounced the name correctly, so that it sounded like *Chenstohova*. He then waited and watched as the old man deflated. "It has to do with Czestochowa, Herr Colonel."

"This is insanity," the old man replied, fainter now.

"It must have been agony to know all that wealth was just across the border, yet there was no way for you to get at it." Ferret selected the most comfortable of the chairs for himself and settled down with a sigh. "Was there, Herr Colonel? Always the risk that if you applied for a passport and someone checked the fingerprints, they would come up with things better left buried."

"I don't know what you're talking about."

"No, of course not. You don't happen to have a glass of schnapps, do you? It's been a long drive."

"I want you out of my house immediately."

"No, I suppose not." Ferret stretched out his short legs. "Well, to business. We've taken it quite far enough to have you turned over to the authorities. No doubt they'd be kinder to a former Nazi than the Ossies and their Russian comrades, especially once they caught the first whiff of riches. With the Wessies, torture has been outlawed, or so they say. Still, no doubt Spandau Prison would seem rather unpleasant if one were doomed to spend the rest of one's days there. I imagine that would be the fate for one with your record, no matter which authorities were in charge."

"Authorities," the old man spat his contempt.

"Our feelings exactly. Interlopers from the West out to buy us heart and soul. Everything for a price, especially loyalty. But we are not of them, and we come with a proposition."

"I have nothing to say."

"Not so fast, Herr Colonel. The night is young. Let me tell you what we have, and you might wish to sing a different song."

The old man groped for a chair, said nothing.

"You were commander of the Königsberg Transport Division at the end of the war." Ferret raised one gloved hand. "Don't deny it, Herr Colonel. We have proof. I assure you, I did not drive this distance on such a night to bandy hunches about. So. You were given a certain cargo to transport the last week before the Russians overran your position. An unlisted cargo, one so large it required three trucks. The trucks were carried by train as far as the rails remained intact, in order to save precious petrol, then you continued on by road, or what roads existed after the bombings.

"Strange, is it not, that a transport commander is ordered away from his post on the eve of a crucial battle and given three trucks and strings of petrol canisters, items which by that time were almost impossible to come by. Strange also that such a valuable cargo was granted no guards whatsoever, not even relief drivers. Stranger still is the fact that passes were issued, granting you passage through the entire Third Reich. It indicates, does it not, that this unlisted cargo was destined for somewhere so secret that only a handful of people ever knew of its existence."

"Less than a handful," murmured the old man.

Ferret nodded his satisfaction. "A *most* secret place. So secret that your three trucks did not travel with the rest of the convoy, once they were off-loaded from the train. Perhaps not even you were informed of the destination, only the SS officer who accompanied you." Ferret leaned forward. "The one you shot."

The old man blanched. "I killed no one."

"Or had shot. It does not matter. What is important is that the driver who ran off into the woods, the one you shot and thought dead, was of that rarest of breeds, a patriot who survived. He described the scene to the authorities, Herr Colonel. Fortunately or unfortunately, as the case may be, it was to *American* authorities that he finally confessed. Interrogators in a prison camp, a lieutenant and two over-worked sergeants, who paid no attention to the report of another dead SS officer. The driver died soon after, thus no one who might have pieced the puzzle together ever had the chance to question him."

The old man remained silent, his rheumy eyes turned inward on a scene he had replayed through ten thousand sleepless nights.

"The SS officer's demise took place at a crucial juncture in the road," Ferret continued. "As you well know. The right-hand fork took you south of Berlin, around Dresden, and on into the heart of the dying Third Reich. Or perhaps I ought to say, it *should* have taken you westward. Because you chose the left-hand fork, did you not? The one which led you south, around the remains of Warsaw, past Cracow, to the Czech border and then Austria and Switzerland and—"

Ferret leaned forward and gave his dead-eyed smile. "But there is no need to dwell on what did not happen, is there? Because it was in Czestochowa that one of the overloaded trucks finally broke down, burdened as it was by half the payload from the third truck. The truck for which you had no driver after the patriot fled into the night. Payload so valuable that you refused to leave it behind. By then you had opened one of the crates, had you not? You knew that your secret cargo was simply too precious to leave stranded in a driverless truck."

"Not a night goes by that I do not see it in my dreams," the old man murmured.

"It must have been a hellish night," Ferret went on. His eyes held an intense gleam in the room's meager light. "The Russians were less than thirty kilometers away, weren't they, Herr Colonel? The line was collapsing; the road was choked with German soldiers streaming back from the front—those who could still walk, that is. And then what should happen but that you meet an officer more concerned for his wounded men than for your papers with all their fancy stamps and empty words. How cruel fate was, Herr Colonel, to curse you with two heroes within the same night."

"Fate," the old man grumbled. "There is no more wicked a word."

"The officer was not only patriotic," Ferret continued. "He was conscientious. He took your papers, as he promised, and handed them over to the authorities, along with the report of how he forced you at gunpoint to off-load your cargo and give him the truck for his wounded.

"The petrol he siphoned from the broken truck, along with the remaining canisters, was almost sufficient to see him across to the Americans as well. He was not only patriotic, this officer, but smart. He knew that there was less chance of a summary execution from the Americans than from the Russians. But in the end he failed. Despite the siphoned petrol, the truck died before he could reach the Americans' front line. He was held there by the love of his men, and he waited with the empty truck for the Russian tanks to catch up with him. You will no doubt be pleased to know that he ended his days in a Siberian labor camp. His men did not survive that long."

"Pleased," the old man muttered. "I'll be pleased to see him in hell."

"That can be arranged, Herr Colonel," Ferret replied quietly. "But we had hoped you would prefer to take your share of the wealth and disappear, as we intend to. We can even offer you a passport, and a ticket to anywhere in the world. America, even."

"Never."

"France, then. Or Australia. South America. Iceland, as far as I am concerned." The little eyes hardened to agate. "What concerns us, Herr Colonel, is that you help us."

Ferret rose to stand over the old man and demanded, "Now tell us, Herr Colonel. Where did you bury the Amber Room?"

Jeffrey responded to Alexander's urgent fax by arriving at Heathrow Airport two hours before his Cracow flight was scheduled to land. The plane was delayed as usual, which meant that Jeffrey was fit to be tied by the time the customs doors opened to admit an Alexander burdened by more than his usual post-flight fatigue.

Jeffrey rushed forward, took hold of Alexander's overnight bag, and demanded, "What's the matter?"

"Not just yet, please. Allow me at least a moment to recover my wits."

"Sorry." He directed them toward the car-park. "I decided to hire a car and drive you back myself. From the sounds of your fax, you had something to say that was for my ears only."

"A correct observation." Alexander showed confusion when Jeffrey stopped in front of a small stand selling freshly squeezed fruit juices at outrageous prices. "What is this?"

"Something Katya suggested. She said it would give you the stimulus you required and be much better for you than a quart of coffee."

"How kind of her to think of me. Very well, Jeffrey. Purchase the libation and let us leave this madhouse behind."

Jeffrey remained silent as he threaded the car through the parking deck's maze, paid the fee, and entered the aggressive stream of rush-hour traffic pressing forward at a snail's pace. For once, the slow speed bothered him not a whit. He was still far from comfortable driving a car on the left hand of the road, with the steering wheel on the right.

Once they were on the motorway and packed snugly between other cars and trucks on every side, Jeffrey asked, "How are you feeling now?"

"Much better, thank you. I do believe Katya was correct."

"Will you tell me what happened?"

"Yes, I suppose there is no reason to delay the news any further." Alexander settled back in his seat. "I arrived in Cracow yesterday afternoon and went directly to the Marian Church. As you well know, I wanted to be rid of the responsibility for the chalice as quickly as possible, and I returned it in person because I had accepted it personally from Karlovich. The curate was there waiting for me, I handed it over, thanked him as gracefully as I knew how, and departed. As far as I could tell, nothing was the matter.

"I proceeded directly to Gregor's—he has almost completed preparations for your buying trip, by the way. We took care of a few minor items, and then I went to my hotel, had dinner, and went to bed. There was no good reason for my staying the night, except that the idea of two international flights in one day positively curdled my blood."

Alexander sighed. "The next morning, Rokovski arrived in an absolute panic."

===

Rokovski called Alexander's Cracow hotel room in a state of hysteria. He bluntly refused to allow Alexander to come down and meet with him in the lobby. Instead, he rushed up to Alexander's room, banged on the door, and came in absolutely beside himself— his tie loosened, his hair disheveled, his face creased with worry. He walked blindly past Alexander's outstretched hand and threw himself into the plastic-veneer chair by the window.

"I don't even know where to begin," Rokovski announced.

"What is it, old man? What's wrong?"

"I have some dreadful news. Dreadful. Karlovich called me first thing this morning, insisting that I come over at once. That man is not easy to deal with, I don't need to tell you." Rokovski mopped his brow with a crumpled handkerchief. "I went to his office immediately this morning, and told him that he seemed most distressed on the telephone.

" 'Distressed! Distressed, indeed!' he said, pulling on his beard and pacing the floor. He said, 'I am more than distressed. I am shocked. Horrified.' "

"What about?" Alexander demanded.

Rokovski held up his hand. "Wait, my friend. Wait. I want to lay it out for you just as it was presented to me. Hopefully our two heads will then be able to make some sense of this matter." Rokovski kneaded his forehead. "I asked him, 'What is it, the chalice? I know Mr. Kantor planned to return it yesterday. Has there been some damage?'

"Karlovich fell into his chair at my question. 'Damage?' he said. 'No. Damage can be repaired. But such damage as this is permanent.' "

"I am growing more alarmed by the moment," Alexander said, leaning forward in his chair.

"As was I. I demanded that he tell me what he was talking about. Karlovich fastened me with those great, glittering eyes of his and said, 'The chalice that has been returned to me is not the chalice I was good enough to lend.' "

"Impossible," Alexander exploded, leaping up.

"That was exactly my reaction, but Karlovich was most insistent."

"How can that be? Did you see it?"

"Yes, of course. It was there in his safe. He pulled it out, still in the leather carrying case, set it on his desk, and motioned for me to take it." Rokovski pantomimed his movements. "I looked at it very carefully, placed it back down, and said, 'I don't know what you're talking about. This is exquisite. To think that this could be a forgery is, well—' "

"Positively absurd," Alexander finished for him.

"You will understand that I did not wish to say it outright, but that is what I was thinking."

"How could anyone have duplicated it in the short time that it was in our possession?" Alexander scoffed.

"My thoughts exactly. As you know, I have quite some experience in these matters, and this is what I told him. But the curate raised his hand and declared to me, 'As God is my witness, this is not the chalice from the Marian Church collection.' Then he said something equally remarkable."

"Go on," Alexander said impatiently.

"'As I was putting the chalice away,' the curate told me, 'it struck me that something was amiss. I recalled the pattern of the signets around the central structure, and that two of the signets bore a different symbol. Yet with this chalice, there is the same letter in each of the faces. I wasn't sure, of course, but I was dreadfully worried. So I went through my records and found this.'

"My dear Alexander, you should have seen the mess about his desk. Stacks and stacks of books and drawings and portfolios with half-unrolled papers all over the floor behind his desk. A pile of dusty leather-bound tomes almost as high as his table. And on top was a very old portfolio. He opened it to a page, undoubtedly ancient, of museum quality itself."

"Get on with it, man," Alexander snapped.

"Yes, of course." Rokovski mopped his brow once more. "The page had detailed drawings of the chalice with explanations in Latin along the top and down both sides."

"You are certain it was a drawing for *the* chalice?"

"No, of course not. How could I be? And yet Karlovich was so sure, so completely certain. He pointed to that broad center section and said, 'You see, on this wreathlike portion surrounding the stem, there are two different emblems, just as I recalled, directly opposite each other. The other signets are all identical to those found on this chalice here. And yet what I did *not* know was that this central section contained a secret. One I discovered only when examining the description written here.'

"He stabbed at the writing on the left side of the page, and said, 'Our chalice had a secret compartment. By pressing these two opposing signets, one carved with alpha, the other with omega, the cup portion of the chalice detaches to reveal a small, hollow compartment inside the stem. If you will examine this particular chalice, you will find no such compartment.' "

Alexander mulled it over. "And you searched."

"Quite thoroughly, I assure you. No such symbols were carved anywhere on this chalice, and I could find no compartment. And while I searched, Karlovich kept stabbing at the bottom left corner of this diagram and talking. He said, 'But the gravity of the matter does not hinge on the lack of the secret compartment. You cannot imagine how I shuddered with amazement and horror as I examined this small inset at the base of the drawing. This shows the contents, which now are also missing.' "

"And those contents are?" Alexander demanded.

"Mind you," Rokovski cautioned. "It is a legend only. There is no evidence save for an ancient drawing, one that no one has inspected in decades. Even centuries, perhaps."

"And save for Karlovich's insistence that the chalice I returned is not the one I received from him." Alexander shook his head. "To think that such a thing could happen."

"I, too, can scarcely believe this was taking place. While I sat in the man's office and examined what looked for all the world to be an ancient and valuable chalice, this gentleman began pacing back and forth amidst the scattered documents, bemoaning the loss. 'Of course I knew nothing about the compartment. Or that the chalice was also a reliquary. I would not have dreamed to allow such a sacred treasure to leave Polish soil. And now, alas, I make this dreadful discovery.' "

"The man sounds like a bad actor," Alexander retorted. "He actually called this supposedly missing chalice a reliquary? As if the compartment held some religious artifact?"

"He did."

"And did he also perhaps mention what that artifact was?"

Rokovski gave him a stricken look. " 'A small fragment,' he told me. 'One about the size of your thumb. A thorn, to be precise. From the final crown worn by the Son of God.' "

Alexander was on his feet. "You expect me to believe that such a relic could lie forgotten for centuries in a Polish crypt?"

"I expect nothing. I am simply telling you what was reported to me." Rokovski looked up in appeal. "Did you offend him in any way?"

Alexander thought it over. "No. Certainly not intentionally. Nor do I recall anything which might have indicated by look or word that he was offended."

Rokovski threw up his hands. "Then I don't know what to say."

"My dear Dr. Rokovski, I assure you—"

"Your reputation is one bound with an honor that goes back decades, Alexander. I do not know what the answer is here, but your honor is not in question."

"Yet the chalice is."

"According to Karlovich, yes."

"There must be some mistake."

"Perhaps. But I can assure you that the chalice you returned was not the chalice in his drawings."

"They differed only in this secret compartment and the signets?"

"And the contents," Rokovski added. "If the drawings are indeed of the chalice that he gave to you. If he was correct about your chalice's having those differing emblems."

"But why would the man go to such trouble?" Alexander ran frantic fingers through his hair. "I admit to being at a complete and utter loss."

"As am I." Rokovski hesitated, then said, "Alexander, I hate to ask you this, but did anyone other than yourself have access to the chalice?"

"Only about eight hundred guests at my gala." He shook his head. "No, forgive me. It was a feeble jest. Security there was impeccable. I had the chalice at my shop, which is most carefully secured and guarded, and then as an extra precaution it was removed to a vault at a leading bank."

"Well," Rokovski sighed. "I certainly am not going to make formal enquiries at this point. Whatever search we make must be done as discreetly as possible."

"So you do believe that the original chalice is missing?"

"What choice do I have? Why would this man lie to me?"

Alexander settled back into his chair. To that question he had no reply.

——

Alexander told Jeffrey he had gone directly to the Marian Church and found Karlovich awaiting his arrival, the chalice still on his desk. Alexander seated himself and examined the artifact, determined not to allow the curate's all-pervasive energy to force him into a hasty conclusion. After quite some time, he set the chalice back on the desk and declared, "This is absolutely extraordinary handiwork. I am virtually certain that this chalice is genuine gold and silver, and that the work dates back several centuries. Possibly more."

"Whether that is true or not," Karlovich replied coldly, "I as a simple curate cannot say. But what I can tell you is that this is *not* my chalice."

"Who else might know of this secret compartment of which you spoke to Rokovski?"

"I don't know. I would have thought no one in all Poland. No one alive, in any case. The cellar has been closed to the public and to most priests since before the war. Secrecy over our collection was the only insurance we had against its being stolen by either the Nazis or the Russians. In fact, this collection has been kept in virtual secrecy since the Austro-Hungarian invasion two hundred years ago. Even the existence of the crypt itself was a fact known only to a handful of people."

Alexander sat and listened intently to this dark-bearded, powerful man with the eyes of a zealot. The curate clearly felt he was telling the truth. "What do you intend to do?"

"What can I do? I certainly could not make a formal enquiry without losing my job for allowing the reliquary to travel outside Poland, not to mention perhaps causing an international outrage. And of course we must not scare the thief into some rash act. Clearly this was done with the intention of not being detected."

"I assure you that I am a man of honor, and that I shall do whatever it takes to right this situation. What do you wish me to do?"

"Find me my chalice," Karlovich replied. "But do not worry about your good name, Mr. Kantor. I am most willing to keep this entire matter very quiet. I understand the importance of your reputation, and I would not want to taint it with any hint of impropriety."

"You are most kind," Alexander murmured.

"And of course, your success in retrieving the chalice would depend upon secrecy."

"Rest assured I shall do everything in my power to unravel this mystery. Yet what if the chalice is not recovered?"

Karlovich spread out his arms. "Then perhaps you would consider arranging to have a suitable sum of compensation paid. Such money would of course be devoted to the most noble of church purposes."

"I understand," Alexander said quietly, wishing that were so.

"I have no idea when others might discover that the chalice you returned is not in truth the reliquary. I can only hope that my purpose in life has been accomplished by then, and that I have been called to my eternal home."

Alexander rose in confused defeat. "Please be so kind as to give me a few weeks. I shall come back to you, either in person or through Dr. Rokovski. I know the market in religious antiques quite well, and I shall try to draw out this piece by posing as a buyer. Failing that, I am of course most willing to offer some financial compensation, however meager it may be in comparison to your loss."

CHAPTER 25

The next morning dawned clear and still bitterly cold. Jeffrey and Katya joined Alexander in the tiny alcove of the shop for coffee and commiseration, their conversation marked by numerous pauses and deep sighs.

Alexander stood up and went for a despondent walk about the shop. They heard him murmur from near the front window, "How on earth did this happen?"

"It's not your fault," Jeffrey said for the hundredth time already that day.

Alexander chose not to hear him. "Forty years in the antiques trade, and here at the crown of my career I am confronted with accusations against which I have no defense."

"And when you were doing it for charity," Jeffrey noted. "It wasn't even business."

Katya reached in her carry bag, brought out a yellow legal pad, and announced, "It seems to me that what we need most right now is clear thinking."

Alexander's tone was querulous. "How am I to defeat an accusation for which I have no evidence and one I cannot make public?"

"It's not just the chalice," Jeffrey agreed. "If this gets out, all our Polish sources are going to shrivel up like a dried prune."

"Not if," Alexander said, returning to the alcove and dropping into his seat. "When."

"The way to defeat this problem is to solve it," Katya replied crisply. "We must outline all the possibilities. Everyone is a suspect."

"This is absurd," Alexander declared, but could manage no heat.

"We have to trace the line of possession of the chalice," she insisted. "We must examine every opportunity and motive for theft."

Jeffrey recalled her finding the Rubens in a crowded basement vault and felt a slight lift to his spirit. "What are you suggesting?"

"First, we have Karlovich," Katya said. "From the sound of it, he's not a totally stable character."

Alexander snorted. "You simply cannot go about accusing the curate of Cracow's central cathedral of being a thief."

"He accused you, didn't he?" Katya scribbled busily. "Then there's the three of us."

Alexander raised his hand at that. "Let us just say here and now that we trust one another, shall we? I don't care to see my world upset any more than it already is."

Katya nodded agreement. "So it was in your flat for one night—"

"Where no one entered," Alexander replied. "Not even the porter. Security in my building is meticulous."

"Then we have those people with access to the shop," Katya went on.

"There's the three of us," Jeffrey mused. "Plus the cleaning lady—no, she was off the week the chalice was here before it was moved to the bank. I remember because I had to vacuum and dust. Then there were our customers."

Alexander showed the first hint of renewed interest. "Did you ever allow a customer to be alone in the shop?"

"Not for an instant," Jeffrey replied emphatically. "Not ever."

"No, nor I. And I must say, I found myself especially vigilant with the chalice here, although I suppose we have several other items that approach it in value."

"What about when you were traveling back from Cracow?" Jeffrey asked. "Did you put it down at any time? Ever out of your sight?"

"Not in any place, not at any time," Alexander replied. "I shall not take you through the rather gruesome details, but suffice it to say that I suffered several indignities rather than part with the case for even a moment."

"We need to see if our security firm has any videotapes left from the days it was here," Katya said, writing quickly. "Although they usually erase them once a week, I believe they told me."

Jeffrey looked at her. "You talked to the security firm?"

She did not raise her eyes from the pad. "This is my job now, Jeffrey. Security is a part of it. Okay, could someone else have gotten into the shop?"

"In off-hours?" Jeffrey shook his head. "All Mayfair would have heard the alarms."

"No alarm system is foolproof, of course," Alexander responded, "but ours is very dependable. If someone did break in, it would have to be a very skilled thief. A professional. And no such professional would swap one valuable for another. And allow me to assure you, the chalice I returned to Cracow is unmistakably precious."

"He also wouldn't have left the shop's other valuables intact," Jeffrey agreed. "The same goes for entry into Alexander's flat. Some of his antiques are first-rate."

"Right." She continued writing and said, "Then there was the photographer who shot the pictures for our invitation."

"I remained by the chalice throughout the session," Alexander replied. "I have also checked the photographs most carefully. All I can say is that the two signets facing the camera were identical. Five are not in view; of them I can say nothing at all."

Katya made swift notes. "That brings us to the transportation to and from the bank vault. Then you have the display. Then the return of the chalice to the church, and that afternoon until the discovery of the switch."

"Barclay's Bank is above question," Alexander replied. "Their reputation is certainly more valuable than the threat of scandal over a single item."

"A king's ransom of valuables is stored in their Charing Cross vaults," Jeffrey agreed. "Why go to the trouble of switching just one item?"

"I indeed concur," Alexander said. "And as for attracting the attention of international thieves, how did they come to hit on us so swiftly?" Jeffrey shook his head. "We had the chalice only for how long? Four weeks?"

"We did publicize it widely in magazines and publications," Katya pointed out. "Not to mention the three thousand invitations to the gala."

Jeffrey felt a sinking feeling. "What about Greenfield?"

"What are you saying?"

"I think we've got to include him. It was his idea to put the chalice in the bank's vaults."

"I certainly cannot confront the man directly," Alexander objected. "And, unfortunately, the bank won't tell us any details unless I give them ample reason, which would of course raise the threat of scandal. The question is how to speak with him without making this nightmare any more public."

"But could he have made a switch?" Jeffrey felt an inward cringe. The thought of a friend stealing from them sickened him.

"In the bank?" Alexander pursed his lips. "If there was an accomplice in the bank, perhaps. What might be more likely is in the arrangements regarding the display case."

"We were so busy with the gala details," Katya agreed.

"I can't think of any moment the three items were left alone, from the time the bank security people brought in the three treasures to when they were actually sealed in the cases." Alexander seemed to dim slightly. "But we were all so busy. It is possible, I suppose."

"I hate this," Jeffrey declared. "Greenfield is a friend."

"He is a somewhat distorted character, but I agree, he is indeed a good man at heart. I cannot imagine—" Alexander shook his head, sighed, "But I suppose we must."

"And the security people who guarded the display case in the ballroom," Katya added. "We'll need to speak with them as well."

Alexander regarded her gravely. "Painful as this exercise is proving to be, my dear, you have instilled in me a morsel of hope. For that I must thank you."

"The atmosphere has lightened in here incredibly," Jeffrey agreed.

"It's really nice," Katya confessed, "feeling a part of all this. Even in the middle of such a bad time, I truly feel fortunate."

"As do we," Alexander said gravely.

"Hang on," Jeffrey said, straightening in his chair. "Did whoever took the chalice know about the secret compartment?"

Alexander nodded. "I quite agree. We must also consider the possiblity that it was not an antique, nor silver and gold, which lured the thief. This may be the key. The replica of the chalice, or whatever it is that I looked at, is impeccable. To make a forgery like this would take a tremendous amount of preparation."

"And time," Katya agreed.

"And effort," Alexander continued. "I examined the chalice in the curate's office quite carefully, I assure you. If it was a forgery at all, the work was remarkable, the materials first-rate. I would have staked my reputation that I was looking at a product of fifteenth-century craftsmanship."

"So the thief was possibly after the fragment," Jeffrey agreed. "But who would have known about it?"

"We also have to ask ourselves who would be willing to go through all this trouble for the relic," Katya urged.

"Even Karlovich didn't know about the secret compartment until two days ago," Alexander protested.

"So he *said*," Katya replied.

"I can't see why he would allow such an item out of the country if he knew about the relic," Jeffrey said.

"There were too many other items in the collection to choose from," Alexander agreed.

"Unless he had a reason," Katya said.

"Let's not allow ourselves to become carried away," Alexander said. "Karlovich is a bit off-balance, there's no question about that. But we can't go around blaming him. The fact is, we are responsible. What we have to come to grips with, assuming we all trust one another, is that we let the chalice out of our protection and our control—either when we sent it to the bank vaults or at some other moment along the way."

"So what do we do now?" Jeffrey asked. "The police aren't of any use to us."

"Quite the contrary," Alexander agreed. "But perhaps, just perhaps, greed will work on our behalf."

"What do you mean?"

"Suppose that we pose as buyers of ancient religious artifacts and let the thief or his accomplice come to us."

"You're going to pay to get it back?"

"I am certainly prepared to do so," Alexander replied.

"But why would anyone who stole something from you try to sell it back to you?"

"Not us in person, of course. We shall have to utilize the services of a front. We shall make other arrangements. Much more discreet." Alexander leaned forward. "Now here is my plan."

CHAPTER 26

K urt settled the second of Erika's suitcases in the trunk of her car, paused, and looked down at the compartment's contents. There were four cases made of battered cardboard and vinyl, two for Erika and two for Ferret. Little enough to show for their lives. Kurt shut the lid with a solid thunk and felt a curtain come down inside himself.

His attention fastened on a newly erected billboard that towered above the road and the colonel's shabby cottage. It proclaimed in giant letters and bright colors the wonders of a certain washing powder. He smiled without humor, compared the capitalist slogan with those of his Communist days. The colors and words were different, but the intent was more or less the same as far as he could see—to convince the unbeliever that something was true. Were they lies? Kurt kicked at the icy ground, remembered a lesson from his early training—the easiest lie to sell was the one wrapped in a covering of truth.

"We're Building the Germany of Our Dreams." That one had been a favorite during his teen years. For a time it had been plastered almost everywhere. The propagandists had slapped it across acres of buildings. They had competed over who could erect the largest billboard, all in red and white and fiercely, angrily proud. Then had come "There Is One Germany and We Are All Working for Her Development." As prophetic a statement as he had ever heard, although perhaps not in the form the propagandists had intended. The year before the Wall fell it had been, "Our Ambition Is a Strong and Unified Socialist Germany." Take out the word socialist, and the ambition had come true.

Ferret scuttled out from the cottage, nodded to the colonel leaning against the doorpost, and said something Kurt could not hear. The colonel made no response. Ferret turned with a minute shrug and hurried down the muddy path. A battered overstuffed briefcase was clasped up close to his chest like a child with a favorite toy.

Ferret approached the car, stopped, and peered up at Kurt through the over-thick lenses. "You know the plan," Ferret said. It was not a question.

"We have gone over it a dozen times," Kurt replied. "More."

"At this stage, I prefer repetition to mistakes." Bundled within his oversized coat, Ferret looked more than ever like a bespectacled mole. "You will stay here—"

"And await your word," Kurt interrupted, boredom fighting for place with irritation. "You will call if the amber is found."

"When," Ferret corrected. "When the amber is found, and when the agreement is made. Until that moment, you will not allow the colonel out of your sight."

"Then I shall contact the Schwerin lawyer as we discussed, and then travel to Poland." Kurt cast a sideways glance back to where the old man hunched in the house's shallow doorway, out of the bitter dawn breeze. The colonel's shanty stooped and swayed beneath its burdens of neglect and age.

Kurt watched the Ferret bundle himself into the passenger's seat. He shut the door, nodded a farewell. Then he turned to where Erika waited by the driver's side, the little plastic taxi sign now permanently removed. He said, "The final departure."

"I never thought this day would come," she replied. "After Birgit found the man, I still could not believe it was real. Even now I wonder."

"That was her name?" Kurt asked. "Birgit?"

Erika gave a momentary start, then saw his smile. "You made a joke."

"A poor one."

"It does not matter what you know now. We shall not return."

"No," Kurt agreed. "Any regrets?"

She looked out over the icy landscape, admitted, "Some."

"I was not necessarily speaking of the departure," Kurt said.

"Nor I." Erika's gaze returned to him. "Some nights I wonder if anything will ever come of all this."

"Nights are the time for me to wonder how it will be to live the life of an alien."

It was Erika's turn to smile. "We have been aliens since the Wall's collapse. It is our fate. The place we choose to reside no longer matters."

He reached around her, opened the door, and said, "I also find myself wondering about our new residence."

"Where do you think we shall go?"

Kurt pointed with his chin toward the waiting Ferret. "He likes Argentina. They've fifty years of experience in burying German records."

"Nazi records, you mean."

He did not deny it. "Ferret and I, we had contact with them once. Trying to get hold of old documents in another treasure hunt."

"They did not help, did they?"

Kurt shook his head. "We kept the contact, though. The man let us know he could be used for buying other papers."

"He said that?"

"Passports, drivers' licenses, even birth certificates if the price was right." Kurt lifted his eyes to tree boughs slumped beneath their loads of snow and ice. "At the time, of course, we saw no need for such things—"

"And never thought you would," Erika finished, a wry bite to her words.

"And I suppose you had perfect vision when it came to such events."

Her good humor remained. "Naturally. That is why I'm here."

He subsided. "I suppose Buenos Aires would be an acceptable place to have been born."

"Now that our own homeland is no longer," Erika agreed, climbing in and starting the car. She reached for the door. "You know, I think I might just learn to like being rich."

Kurt watched the vehicle until it was out of sight.

Andrew, Jeffrey's friend and fellow antiques dealer, opened the door for a heavily laden Jeffrey and Katya, then led them through his shop to the back office area. "This the lot?"

"Nineteen books on the crucial subjects," Jeffrey said, setting down his load next to the oversized art books he had brought by the week before. "Katya's box has some prints and imitation artifacts."

"To add a bit of atmosphere," Katya said.

Andrew gave her a look of mock injury. "Atmosphere? And what does my little world have now?"

"A beautiful feel," Katya replied. "Truly."

"You know the way to a man's heart," Andrew said. "Pity about the choice you've made. Choice of men, that is."

"I think I did rather well," Katya replied with a smug smile.

Jeffrey was too frantic to share in their banter. "You understand these books are on loan?"

"Not part of the fee, I take it."

"Not on your life. A couple I had to borrow, several I haven't been able to peruse yet myself. And some of these have been out of print for over a century."

"All right, lad," Andrew replied easily. "Speaking of fee, we haven't gotten around to discussing that."

"Alexander said to tell you that he is doubly in your debt," Katya said. "First for trying to assist us, and second for doing so confidentially."

Andrew thought it over. "Coming from the old gent, I'd say that's not bad, not bad at all."

"You can add my gratitude to his," Jeffrey said. "For what it's worth."

"Ah, well, seeing as how I disagree with the run-of-the-mill lot and their comments, I'd treat that almost as highly as the other. Maybe even a notch above his, seeing as how you're the up and comer."

"Thanks, Andrew. I won't forget this."

" 'Course you won't. I'm not aiming on letting you, now, am I?" Andrew reached into an overstuffed drawer, came up with a set of clippings, passed them around. "Here's the copy and bills for the first set of ads. Cost you a packet, especially the daily rags. The Times wanted eight hundred quid per day."

"We've got to move ahead as though there were big money behind it."

"Right you are, then. Here, have a gander at how the lucre's being spent."

The ad was a standard four-by-eight inches, framed in double black lines. The text took up less than half the space and simply read: "Major international collector seeks to acquire pre-seventeenth-century religious art and artifacts of the first order. Sellers of second-quality items need not apply. Paintings, manuscripts, altars, reliquaries, ornamental works, and other items will be considered. Utmost discretion and confidentiality guaranteed. Payment may be affected worldwide. Interested parties should contact . . ." and below was given Andrew's name and shop address.

"Perfect," Jeffrey declared. "Can I keep this one?"

" 'Course you may, lad. You paid for it."

"I'm leaving on a buying trip next week. I don't suppose—"

"You'll be hearing from me the instant I pick up the first bit of news, lad. The very instant, don't you worry. As to timing, that's out of our hands, now, isn't it."

Jeffrey nodded glumly. "Alexander's really taking this hard."

"Only on account of the weight you two put on reputations and the like." He caught the look in Jeffrey's eye and added, "Just kidding, lad. Of course he is."

"You don't speak any other languages, I guess."

"No, but I understand Yank fairly well. And Sydney Greenfield works in Kentish, which I can get around in."

"I don't believe it's Greenfield we're looking for."

"You've said that half a dozen times already. And I've told you I agree with the lady here—we've got to look everywhere. All the same, I do believe you're right. This doesn't look like something our man would be up to. Did I ever tell you he was decorated in the Korean War?"

"Sydney Greenfield?"

"Goes against the grain, doesn't it. But there you are. Ruddy great gong it was, too. Pinned on his chest by the head honcho himself. Said it was for bravery and valor beyond the call of duty, or some such."

"Are you sure we're talking about the same guy?"

"Hard to believe, I admit. Had a rough time getting the man to speak of it at all. I heard rumors about it for years and finally cornered him at the local. Wouldn't let him go until I had the scoop."

"What did he say?"

"Told me he didn't remember what he'd actually done," Andrew replied. "Scared blind, he was. Honest. One minute he was there on the sand, the next he was two miles inland, sitting by a bombed-out farmhouse having a quiet smoke with the boys. Still, they gave him the VC when it was all over. Told me he stood there and let them pin it on his chest, didn't have a clue what all the fuss was about. That's the way to go to war, I told him. Just skip over the nasty bits."

"I've always liked Sydney," Katya said. "Did Jeffrey tell you he was completely honest about his dealings in the repaired furniture?"

"Yes, he did. Glad to hear it too, I was." He clapped Jeffrey on the back. "Don't look so glum, lad. From the sounds of it, nobody's actually said Alexander stole the piece, am I right?"

"The implication is enough."

Andrew nodded. "Yes, and that's why I'd take your word of a debt over a lot of other people's checks. You're a strange one for this trade, though, you and your boss both."

"Thanks, Andrew." Jeffrey tightened his scarf. "Now, remember, the most important thing at this point is to retrieve the chalice."

"Or reliquary," Katya added.

"Or whatever it is, right. But we'd be interested in looking at anything of really top quality that comes in, especially if its origin is central European."

"For this cause your boss has gotten himself involved in?"

"If the chalice is recovered," Katya explained, "we'll have substantial funds available both from the gala itself and promised by new patrons specifically for expanding the Polish religious heritage collection."

"If it's not," Jeffrey added, "then paying for such pieces out of the firm's pocket should buy us some breathing space. And time."

"Hopefully we'll be hearing from the thieves or their fences before long," Andrew said. "As to this other matter, in such a case as I come up with a few class articles, I imagine I'd be splitting the commissions with you."

Jeffrey shook his head. "They'd all be yours."

"That's a good sight more than fair." Andrew ushered them back to the front. "Any time you feel a touch of the nerves setting in, feel free to give me a call. But best you not be seen around here for a time, in case they're having the premises watched. And don't you worry, lad. You'll be hearing from me the instant I catch wind of anything."

The waiting was hard, as waiting always is. The word alone meant that control and action and power had slipped from his hands. Kurt had never been good at waiting, and the seven days hung heavy on his hands.

The old colonel moved about his own home like a silent wraith. Kurt wondered about that whenever the old man slipped in and out of view. The colonel carried with him a thoroughly defeated air. He had been so since their arrival, as though telling his secret had robbed him of his final reason to live. He sat now, the strength and ramrod straightness with which he had confronted them upon their arrival a thing of the distant past. He awaited his fate with a helpless air, stooped and old and tired and sad.

The phone call came on the seventh evening at the prearranged time. Even though he had awaited it anxiously, the bell caused Kurt to actually leap from the earth.

"You found it, then." Kurt felt his voice was disembodied, spoken by another—one whose knees had not gone weak at the news and whose heart was not hammering like thunder.

"Did I not just say that?" Erika permitted herself a chuckle. "Though I had to stand and gaze for quite a while before believing it myself."

"How did it look?"

"Rats," she said. "Big ones. And bones. Our colonel left no tongues alive to tell tales."

"I meant the—"

"Don't say it," Erika warned.

"I was simply going to ask about the merchandise."

"Unimpressive. Covered in mud. And other things."

"But you're certain?"

"Ferret is positive. I have come to trust in our little man's judgment. That surprises me almost as much as our find."

He repeated, "How did it look?"

This time she answered him. "Fistfuls of dark glass, carved with weird designs, covered with the filth of ages. Ferret only let me clean a few, he says each piece was wrapped in tissue paper—"

"Covered with the place-code for putting it back together," Kurt finished for her. His heart was beating so hard it was difficult to get the words out. "I remember him saying it."

"Yes, well, for that reason he did not let me clean but a few. And those . . ."

"Well?" Kurt urged.

"I do not wish to sound absurd."

He bit off the remark that came first to his tongue, said, "Tell me."

"Great jewels," she replied. "Glass vessels full of molten gold when held to the light. All the shades of a bronze rainbow. Like nothing I have ever seen in my life."

"An amber rainbow," Kurt said. He thought he heard the old colonel stir behind him, give off a ghostly sigh of defeat. But his attention remained fastened upon what he himself would never see.

"I told you it was absurd."

"You did well," Kurt replied. "After all, the only glimpse I shall ever have is through your eyes."

"Perhaps not. I am hoping to convince Ferret that we should keep a few mementos."

"With one for me, I hope."

"How not?" She spoke in muffled tones to someone in the room, came back with, "Ferret says now is not the time for idle chatter. He says to contact the lawyer and set up the meeting. Not by phone. It is possible that there are still listening ears."

"Tomorrow," Kurt said, the excitement making his voice rise. "I will travel back to Schwerin at first light. There is too much ice on the roads just now to risk driving at night."

"Tomorrow is fine."

"She will give those antique dealers the when and where as we discussed." Kurt continued talking now simply to hold on to the contact. "At the city whose name I cannot pronounce."

"Czestochowa," Erika replied. "You will wait until we have confirmed it all went smoothly."

"And then travel to Poland."

"Where we shall not meet."

"As was agreed," he said. "It is safer, and yet I worry."

"By the time you arrive, we will have gone on to Switzerland to await the transfer of funds." Again the muffled talk, then, "Ferret says that you can trust us."

"I have no choice."

"No." She paused. "But in any case you can. You have my word."

"It is enough." And to his surprise, it almost was.

"Ferret says, do you remember where to go upon your arrival?"

"For the hundredth time, yes."

"We shall call you once the money has been received and pass on the remaining details." A smile came to her voice. "Palm trees."

"What?"

"Your dream. Beaches of white sand. Does Argentina have beaches?"

"And coconuts," Kurt replied, and suddenly wanted to laugh out loud. "And all the rest."

"You will hear from us," Erika said.

Kurt hung up the phone and turned back to where the colonel sat in his lone and ragged chair. Kurt looked closer, realized that the old hands were motionless. Kurt moved forward, saw how the jaw had fallen slack. The old colonel's eyes stared sightlessly at the feeble fire. Kurt bent to place one ear next to the frail chest, wondered idly if he should not list the cause of death as a broken heart.

Regular as clockwork, you are," Andrew said when he realized it was Jeffrey calling. "Still off on your travels this week?"

"Tomorrow," Jeffrey replied.

"Won't do me any good to ask where, will it?"

"Not a bit."

"No, didn't think so." Andrew gave a sigh. "Have to tell you, lad. I'm having the time of my life reading about all these lovelies. Something I didn't know the first thing about before."

"A whole new world."

"That's it exactly. Not to mention the three buys I've made so far. Good bit of brass, they were."

"Alexander says to tell you they're all really first-rate."

"Yes, I thought so myself." His tone sobered. "Nothing on the chalice, I'm afraid."

Jeffrey did not try to hide his disappointment. "I can't stop hoping."

"No, nor I. I did come across something rather interesting, though. Found a description and a sketch of what looks like the chalice in question."

"The one we brought from Cracow or the one we took back?"

"The only one I've seen, whichever one that is. I assume the one you're looking for—I ruddy well hope so, seeing as how that's the one I've got my eyes peeled for. And from what you've said, on the surface there isn't much difference between the two."

"Sorry. Stupid question."

"Yes, it was. No matter. Case of nerves does that to a body. Anyway, it says here—hang on, let me see if I can lay my hands on it." The phone was dropped, then Jeffrey heard the sounds of rummaging. Andrew lifted the phone again. "Yes, here it is. Found it in one of the old tomes you brought by, dated 1820. From the looks of it, the book hasn't been opened in over a century. Says that in 1475 a chalice was designed by this goldsmith called Bertolucci for the Holy See. What a name, the Holy See. Sounds like some great marble bath with a dozen gilded cupids spouting scented water. Anyway, one chalice was made in silver and gold with a secret compartment as a reliquary, while two others were produced at the same time *without* this compartment, so that the reliquary could be secured in the Vatican vaults while a similar chalice was used during Mass and other religious ceremonies."

Jeffrey felt a peal of hope pick up the pace of heart. "Very interesting."

"Yes, isn't it just?"

"I don't know what it means, though."

"No, nor I. Perhaps you ought to run this lot by the old gent, see what he can make of it. Tell him it appears to me that the 'thick plottens,' or whatever it is they say in the spy flicks."

"I'll do that."

"Pass on my regards while you're at it."

"I will, thanks."

"Don't mention it. This favor I'm doing, turns out it's loads of fun. Not to mention the odd commission."

"You're a great help, Andrew."

"Not yet, I'm not. But there's always hope."

———

Jeffrey hung up, turned back to where Katya and Alexander waited. "Andrew's found something."

"So it sounded," Alexander said.

"One of the older volumes describes what appears to be our chalice, and provides a small sketch. Interestingly enough, three chalices were made, only one of which had the secret compartment for the relic. Apparently they were made in Rome. For the Vatican."

"Rome," Alexander said. "Our dear friend the Count will be most pleased to hear that he has been vindicated after all."

Jeffrey nodded. "He was so sure he had seen it before."

"The man has a most incredible memory. People take him for a fool all too often, but behind that clownish exterior rests a brilliant mind, one that has lofted him up from obscurity to immense wealth."

"And his interest in antiques is borderline fanatic," Jeffrey added.

"What was it he said," Katya asked, "something about having seen the same chalice in Italy?"

"I don't have to remind you," Jeffrey mimicked with eyebrows raised, "of the exclusive circles I travel in while visiting Rome."

"Let's take this one step at a time," Katya suggested. "We've learned that there is definitely a chalice with a secret compartment and two other chalices very similar to it."

"And the chalices were made in Rome for the Vatican," Alexander added. "Or at least so this book has declared."

"We need to follow up on this," Jeffrey agreed.

"Indeed. Do these chalices exist, and is one of them still in the Vatican collection? That's what we need to know next," Alexander said.

"I know my way around the university libraries," Katya offered. "I could check to see if this reliquary is catalogued anywhere in the official Vatican collections."

"Splendid," Alexander declared. "Jeffrey, when we arrive in Cracow tomorrow, while you begin your work on the next shipment, I shall make my report to Rokovski."

"Not Karlovich?"

Alexander shook his head. "The less I see of that man, the better. There is something about him which I find, well, disagreeable." He looked at Katya. "My dear, I shall need you to assist Mrs. Grayson from time to time in the shop."

"And to spend every possible moment in the library stacks," Katya added for him.

"Precisely. I shall return the day after tomorrow. Unless your research requires more time, the following day you shall travel out to assist Jeffrey."

"I'll start first thing tomorrow morning," she assured him.

"Excellent." Alexander patted his knees with evident satisfaction. "This is most reassuring. I was positive that the crafting of the piece I returned was so exquisite as to make it impossible for it to be a modern imitation."

"And now there are three," Katya said.

"Perhaps." Alexander nodded. "If so, it explains the situation, at least in part."

Jeffrey asked, "But why would anyone have switched them?"

"That," Alexander agreed, "is a question we must diligently pursue."

=====

Jeffrey rented a car upon their arrival at the Cracow airport. The driver Alexander had used in the past was now working daily for Gregor, either transporting purchased antiques or aiding with one of the numerous children's projects. Alexander acted as navigator on their drive into the night-darkened town, guiding him through streets whose names had been rendered out-of-date by the demise of Communism.

"Good evening, Alexander," Gregor said in greeting when they arrived at his minuscule apartment. "Welcome back."

"Hello, Cousin," Alexander replied wearily, returning the formal double kiss. "You are looking well."

"Thank you, I am feeling marvelously fit for a winter's eve." Gregor turned to Jeffrey and smiled warmly. "My dear young friend, what a joy it is to see you again. Come in, come in."

Once they were seated in the tiny parlor and the formalities of offering tea were completed, Gregor turned his attention to Alexander. "Tell me how you have been, Cousin."

Alexander made a visible effort to push aside the flight fatigue. "We continue to receive an excellent response from the gala, I am happy to say. A number of new patrons have joined our cause."

"That was not what I was asking, but I am glad for you nonetheless."

Alexander looked at him sharply. "Why do I detect a note of disapproval in your voice?"

"I do not seek to judge," Gregor replied.

"Criticize, then. It is there clear as day."

Gregor sipped at his tea before replying quietly, "We are told in Proverbs not to boast about the day. The Hebrew word is *hellal,* which means praise when applied to God, but boast when applied to man. Do you see? When we place ourselves in the spotlight, we assume a strength we do not have. We are indulging in self-worship, or self-praise. We have robbed the Master of what He gave to us only on loan, and claimed it for ourselves."

"I do not think I seek to praise myself," Alexander protested, his voice lacking its customary strength. "And neither does the bishop. I have spent considerable time with him recently. He is a most admirable man, and he speaks of God in terms which are much easier for me to follow than those of others whom I do not care to name."

"My dear cousin," Gregor replied. "I seriously doubt that the Lord will deem to speak to your heart through the bishop."

Alexander looked genuinely peeved. "Why on earth not? Besides you and Jeffrey here, the bishop is the person with whom I feel most comfortable discussing this whole affair."

"Precisely for that reason do I think He will select another."

Alexander showed alarm. "You don't suggest I contact one of those glossy television pundits, do you?"

"I think you should do away entirely with the thought of finding God through those who have achieved worldly fame."

"And, pray tell, why should I? I am simply seeking to meet people in keeping with my own nature."

"It is not your nature that we are discussing here."

Alexander swatted at the words. "I will have none of your vague hints and mysterious wanderings."

"All right, then. What if God has something else in mind?"

"Why should He? The bishop speaks a language I can understand."

"What if God chooses to use a different voice?" Gregor persisted. "The cry of a lonely child, for instance. Will you hear that in a bishop's chamber? Or what if He speaks through a woman of the streets? What if He calls to you from the bitter cold of an old man's empty hearth, or the shameful solitude of a prison cell?"

Alexander shifted uncomfortably. "Why is it that your questions tear at me, Gregor?"

"Perhaps because God may choose to speak through me just now, though that is only something you and He can tell. In any case, I hope it is not just me behind these words."

Alexander gave his cousin a hard look. "I suppose the next thing you'll be saying is that I should tell others about this mystery called faith."

Gregor gave him an easy smile. "Where would you be today if someone had not told you about Christ?"

Alexander remained silent for quite some time. Finally he stood, turned toward the door, and said over his shoulder, "I shall think upon what you say."

"Search for your answers within God's Word," Gregor said. "And in prayer. Remember it is His voice you should be listening for. His word to you is something only you will hear, and only within the depths of a hungry heart."

Jeffrey waited to speak until he could hear Alexander's measured tread upon the lower floor's landing. "I feel so uncomfortable sitting here while he talks with you like that."

"Don't let it trouble you," Gregor replied. "He needs you just now, you see, especially when meeting with me. He is afraid of facing the Lord alone. He needs a friend. Someone he can trust. Someone who will share the quest with him."

"I like to think I'm his friend," Jeffrey said.

"Of that you need never doubt," Gregor assured him. "Alexander himself speaks of you in those terms, and he is not one to bandy such a word lightly about."

"I wish I could help him more."

"Always remember that the very nicest compliment you could pay my cousin is to declare him a patriot," Gregor replied. "He is struggling with the utterly alien concept of a faith that calls for him to trust in the unseen, and he is trying to place it into terms that he can fathom. So, he is seeking to reach God through actions tied to his patriotism and his desire to rebuild the artistic heart of his homeland."

"I don't think I'll ever understand you," Jeffrey declared. "You praise Alexander for making the same mistakes as I do, or at least that's how it seems. Then you turn around and tell me to reach for the stars."

"I urge you to reach higher than my beloved cousin," Gregor replied calmly, "because that is the call I hear within my heart. I look at Alexander and see a man doing all that he can to come to grips with his newfound faith."

Jeffrey asked dispiritedly, "And what do you see when you look at me?"

"Once a mason showed Michelangelo a block of marble and said, it's of no value; there's a flaw right the way through it. Michelangelo replied, it's of value to me. You see, there's an angel imprisoned in it, and I am called to set the angel free." Gregor's eyes shone with a burnished light. "When I look at you, my friend, I see a man striving to grow wings."

———

Once at their hotel, Jeffrey bade Alexander a good-night, only to call his room an hour later. "Sorry to bother you, but I've received an urgent fax from Katya."

"Wait a moment." There was the sound of Alexander sitting up and turning on the light. "All right. I'm ready."

"I'm not sure I understand what she's saying," Jeffrey began tentatively.

"Then let us apply two heads to the problem," Alexander replied.

" 'My research has turned up important information pertaining to the chalice,' Jeffrey read. " 'Nothing conclusive, but it is perhaps another piece in the puzzle.' " He paused, not sure of Alexander's reaction to the remaining portion.

"Is that all?"

"No," he said slowly. "There's a little more."

"Well, read it, Jeffrey, read it. It is far too late for dramatics."

"'I have received a call from our lawyer colleague in regard to the room decorations which we recently discussed. It appears that events are developing at a rather rapid pace. Because of what she said, I have moved my departure up to tomorrow morning. Perhaps you would prefer to postpone your own meeting until after we have had a chance to speak.' "

"She was right to be discreet," Alexander said, fully awake now. "Is this about—"

"It must be. There is nothing else that might justify such a move on her part. Thank you for this little gift, Jeffrey. I shall certainly repose with a lighter heart, thinking that perhaps I might have some good news to pass on to Rokovski tomorrow."

"She said it was not conclusive," Jeffrey reminded him.

"I was not speaking of the chalice," Alexander replied. "Good-night."

Winter's fierce grip held the morning in a blanket of frigid stillness. Jeffrey walked alone through the darkness of a late-arriving dawn. He took a longer way despite the cold that bit hard through his clothes, savoring the solitude and the alien feeling of this medieval city.

The warmth of Gregor's building came as a welcome relief, as did the old gentleman's smile. "Look at the frost on your scarf. How long have you been out there?"

"Long enough to need a glass of tea," Jeffrey replied. "I hope I'm not too early."

"My dear young friend, I have been up for hours."

"Me, too."

That brought him back from the kitchen alcove. "You did not sleep well?"

"I never do, my first couple of nights here or in Eastern Germany," Jeffrey replied. "There's so much hitting me."

"A new world," Gregor agreed. "And a world of new challenges." He returned behind the curtain, asked, "What do you do with your time, then, during those sleepless hours?"

"Read," Jeffrey replied. "Think. Pray. Or try to."

"Your perspective on faith remains unchanged?"

"Far as I can tell."

Gregor limped back into view bearing two steaming glasses. "Here, my boy. That should put the warmth back into your bones."

"Thanks." Jeffrey accepted the bell-shaped glass and held it carefully around the upper edge. As with most such vessels used to serve tea and coffee in Poland, the glass had no handle. Curving thumb and forefinger around the rim, above the level of the steaming drink, was the only way he could keep from burning himself.

"Tell me, Jeffrey," Gregor eased himself down. "Do you still doubt the existence of God?"

"No, I don't guess so. Not anymore."

"And yet you have failed to find whatever it is that you search after. How can you therefore hold on to this newfound assurance that God is truly there for you?"

"There's too much going on that I can't just explain away." Jeffrey took a gingerly sip from his glass, sighed a steamy breath. "I look back over these past five or six months, and I see changes I could never have made myself. A relationship more peaceful and filled with love than anything I've ever had in my life. A job that absorbs me and brings me satisfaction. A sense of purpose. An honesty with things really deep inside myself, facing up to things I've always run away from before."

Jeffrey lifted his glass, sipped carefully once more. "Things are changing. I can't stop and say that this minute, this hour, I feel God's presence. But if I look back over the past weeks and months, I can feel something there. It's as though an invisible hand is guiding me toward something. What, I don't know. But I do think I can see God at work in what is happening."

Gregor shook his head. "My boy, if only you could hear your own words. They are such a declaration of the path you have chosen."

"You make it sound simple."

"No, I make it sound straightforward. There is a very great difference. As the blessed Mother Theresa once said, it is not how God calls you that is important, but rather how you reply."

"But now that I've recognized this need in me, I'm *afraid*. I'm afraid of making a mistake, of doubting too much, and maybe of doubting too little as well."

"Afraid not to find and afraid to find," Gregor murmured. "Both prospects can be terrifying."

"Everywhere around me I see signs of how this religion has redesigned my life."

"Not religion. Call it by its true name."

"Faith, then," he conceded.

Gregor nodded. "Religion is external, faith is internal. And it is not the external that calls for change, but the internal."

"But change for what? Where am I going? I'm looking for something, and I can't find it. I don't even know what to call what it is I'm after."

"What do you truly want?" Gregor demanded. "An explosion? Do you seek a thunderbolt? What if God chooses to come to you in a whisper, or a soft call to a listening heart spoken with the first breath of a new dawn breeze? What then? If your ears are tuned only to the great and brilliant, will you miss the beauty of a tiny songbird, a whisper of divine joy meant only for your own questing heart?"

Jeffrey remained hunched over his glass. He sipped, waited, sipped again, taking the words in deep. "All my life I've worried about finding something that mattered enough to really care about having it and keeping it. Now that I've found it, or at least I think maybe I have, I don't know where to look."

"If you don't know where to look, don't keep searching," Gregor replied. "It is that simple. Wait and let it come to you. Learn the strength of patient expectation. Learn the joy of knowing you are a cup for God to fill, a vessel intended to bear His divine fruits of life and love to a thirsty world. Be patient and know He will find you."

Gregor paused for a silent moment before adding, "And He will, my boy. He will."

—

Jeffrey returned to the hotel so he and Alexander might go out together to meet Katya's plane. She greeted Jeffrey with a tight hug and the older gentleman with, "I hope you're not upset that I changed my plans without asking."

"My dear young lady," Alexander replied, "anything that might even possibly inject a hint of good news into my meeting with Dr. Rokovski deserves to be shared without delay. This is why I insisted on imposing upon your reunion here."

"You're not imposing," Jeffrey and Katya said together.

"Thank you both. So let us return to our vehicle and hear what you have to say."

Once beyond the airport grounds, Katya said, "I suppose you want to hear about the chalice first."

"You are correct."

"I don't have anything certain," she began, "and Andrew reports nothing new on his front."

"Then let us hear what you do have, so that we may draw our own conclusions," Alexander said, pointing. "Left here, Jeffrey."

"The university library has a fairly extensive historical arts collection."

"More than extensive," Jeffrey added, skirting around a pothole of unknown depths, pulling back sharply to avoid losing his door to a barreling truck. "Vast is a better word. I've gotten lost in their arts section half a dozen times. More."

"I searched their records of the Vatican collections and found a picture of the chalice," Katya reported. "It is claimed to be a reliquary."

"In the Vatican," Alexander said. "How fascinating."

"I thought so, too. So I called the cultural affairs department of the Vatican embassy in London and told them I was a student doing research."

"All true," Alexander murmured. "And all brilliant, I should add."

"Thank you. I said I was just wondering if such an item had ever been loaned out, or might be. The man was positively shocked. Certainly not a reliquary, he replied. It would never leave the vaults beneath the Vatican. No reliquary has ever been released. Never. It has been centuries since any outsider has viewed a fragment from the crown of thorns. All such reliquaries are most carefully guarded, very seldom shown, and *never* allowed outside the Vatican."

Save for Alexander's directions, silence reigned through the remainder of their drive back to the hotel. Jeffrey pulled into the parking lot, turned off the motor, declared, "This doesn't add up."

"I quite agree," Alexander said, opening his door. "Come, we shall be much more comfortable pondering the impossible inside."

They selected Alexander's room as a gathering point once Katya had checked in. When the old gentleman opened his door to permit them entry, Jeffrey immediately started with, "The curate must have made a mistake."

"Come in, both of you." Alexander stood aside. "Please forgive the lack of space. My dear, take that comfortable chair in the corner. Would either of you care for tea?"

"No, thank you."

"The drawing he showed you was for the Vatican's reliquary," Jeffrey persisted. "Not the chalice he gave you."

"That is certainly a possibility," Alexander replied, settling onto the second straight-backed chair. "However, I am not convinced."

"The curate was very certain," Katya said.

"Precisely. The man was absolutely positive that the chalice he gave me was not the one he received in return."

Jeffrey shook his head. "You're saying the Vatican only *thinks* it has the reliquary?"

Alexander leaned back and mused to the ceiling, "If they were to discover its absence, they certainly would be keen to have it back."

"Wait, wait," Jeffrey protested. "How did it get to Poland in the first place?"

"As to that," Alexander said, still speaking to the ceiling. "I have no answer. And to many other questions besides."

"I discovered something else," Katya announced.

"My dear, your researches have been indeed phenomenal."

"Just by chance," Katya went on, flushed by the praise. "Eleven years ago, Pope John Paul made an announcement that, in celebration of the beginning of the third millennium, the Vatican's reliquaries will all be placed on display."

Alexander sat up straight. "What?"

"The exhibit is scheduled to begin in the year 2000," Katya went on. "And to last for three years."

"If the reliquary had indeed found its way to Poland," Alexander said, "this would put extreme pressure on the Vatican curators to see it returned." He was on his feet. "You must excuse me. Rokovski needs to hear about these findings."

"And Gregor has business for us to attend to," Jeffrey added.

Alexander looked down on Katya. "My dear, you have done excellent work. I thank you. From the depths of a despairing heart, I thank you for the work you have accomplished."

She raised a timid hand. "There is one thing more."

"The other item in your fax," Jeffrey remembered.

She nodded. "The German attorney, Frau Reining, called. The people Jeffrey and I met in Dresden are ready to deliver the sample."

Alexander slowly sank back into his chair. "When?"

"The day after tomorrow."

He pondered the news, then shook his head. "Tempted as I am to remain, this you must do yourselves. We do not have evidence that these findings about the chalice are anything more than simple conjecture, and Andrew should not be left without an immediate contact. I shall therefore report this possible development to Rokovski and urge him personally to accompany you to—where did you say this meeting was to take place?"

"Czestochowa," Katya replied. "At a hotel near the Cathedral of the Black Madonna."

CHAPTER 31

Winter appeared to vanish with the dawn. The sun rose in a pristine sky and banished the bitter cold as though it had never existed.

"A glorious morning," Gregor, arms outstretched, said in greeting. "Let us hope it is truly the arrival of spring."

"Katya said that I should wish you a happy Name's Day," Jeffrey said. "She is only giving us a couple of minutes alone. She is impatient to see you herself."

Gregor ushered Jeffrey inside. "There is a saying that when it is pretty on Saint Gregor's morn, winter has been banished to the depths of the sea, and spring has truly begun."

"When you talk about things like the saints, it makes me feel as if I'm coming from a totally different world." Jeffrey accepted his glass of tea with a nod of thanks. "Does it bother you that I'm a Baptist?"

"My dear boy, the only thing that concerns me is whether or not Christ will know you when the day of reckoning arrives." He sat and straightened his back in the slow way of one who is aware of possible pains. "We shall someday stand before the throne to be judged for our reward. I am speaking about believers here. From my own studies of the Scriptures, I understand that there shall be a second judgment for non-believers. A truly terrible thing. Too terrible to even contemplate. No, I speak here of the judgment of believers. When we stand before His throne, I do not think the majestic Lord will ask us to which denomination we belonged. I believe He will ask us how well we have loved."

"I don't feel I know Him at all," Jeffrey confessed.

"You will," Gregor replied with utter certainty. "For the moment, take heart in the fact that He knows you. His knowledge is perfect. Just come to live by that and you'll do fine."

Jeffrey gave a dispirited shrug. "I guess I need to have a better handle on religion."

"As I said yesterday, the *last* thing you need is religion," Gregor replied emphatically. "Religion won't ease your restlessness. Christ entering your life, my dear young friend, *that* is the answer. Not the laws, not this or that sect, not any certain form of worship. The answer is found in knowing Jesus Christ. The solution is being filled with the Holy Spirit. The Lord has said, 'I will let my goodness, my graciousness, my presence pass before you.' And He will, Jeffrey. Open yourself, and He will do as He promised."

"So, how should I worship?"

Gregor smiled. "My favorite definition of worship is to turn toward and kiss."

"Turn toward what?"

"Yes. That is the endless question of those whose thirst remains unquenched. You must open yourself and let *Him* show you where to turn. Seek Him with the eyes of your heart, not with the eyes and mind of material man."

Jeffrey allowed a fragment of his frustration to surface. "That sounds more like poetry than an answer I can use."

Gregor gazed at him fondly. "Those same words could have been said by your grandfather," he replied. "In a different tongue, but with the same honest spirit. He would be very proud of you, my boy."

"For searching in vain?"

"No. For searching in *honesty*." He shifted painfully. "Could you please be so kind as to set one of those cushions behind my back? Ah. Much better. Thank you. Now then, pay attention to me, Jeffrey. When Peter stood on the mountainside and witnessed the Lord's divine majesty unveiled during the Transfiguration, what did he do? He did as most of us would have done. He wanted to jump up and set up tents and build stone monuments and move around and *do*. And the Lord said to him, Stop. Be still. Relax. Don't strive.

Receive. My young friend, I share with you this same message. Take the single solitary step of being open, and let the Lord work the miracle before you."

"You're saying that I shouldn't be so ambitious," Jeffrey said.

Gregor looked dismayed. "Is it so easy to misunderstand me? The Good Book is full of calls for us to be ambitious. The key is what we are to be ambitious *for*—ourselves, or Him. I cannot imagine that the Lord would endow so many of us with this focused power and then have us call it sinful. That is in my mind utter nonsense."

"That's a relief," Jeffrey said. "I could see changing my ambition to suit His need a lot faster than I could see getting rid of it completely."

"It is an unfortunate human trait to call qualities that we ourselves do not have a sin in someone else. We wish to be comfortable with where we are and who we are, and therefore we do not see that someone else may be driven to *greater* heights, to *greater* service, through a quality that is bestowed by our Maker.

"Paul himself calls us to make service our ambition. The word used when First Thessalonians was written was *philotemesti*. It means to hasten to do a thing, to do it quickly, to exert yourself to the fullest while doing it. It says that we must consider the focus of our ambition to be a vital action, and we must therefore expend whatever energy is required to do this thing."

"It sounds, well, thrilling."

"Of course it does." His eyes shone with a light that humbled Jeffrey. "Take the one essential step, my boy, and then wait. He in His own good time will come, will enter you, will fill you. Not because you've been good. No. Not because you deserve it. You're too honest to suppose that. Rather, because He is the God of unfailing love, and He has been waiting for you to turn and invite Him in."

"But I've asked Him," Jeffrey said plaintively. "At least I've tried. But when I say it, I can't even do that right."

"You can do it perfectly," Gregor replied. "With God's help. He has built up an expectation within you. A longing. A thirst. He wants your life to be aggravated and restless with longing for what only He can give."

"That's it," Jeffrey said, immensely relieved to be understood. "Like an itch I can't scratch, though your description is much better than mine."

"In the second chapter of Acts," Gregor told him, "a group of people witnessed the effects of the Holy Spirit for the very first time. Before their very eyes, the invisible was made visible. And they questioned it. They asked, is this truly of God? For remember, my young friend, these people considered themselves to be believers. At the same time, those who were honest with themselves must have found God to be extremely distant, a power on high rather than an integral part of their inner lives. Certainly they lacked this personal contact with a living Savior, and the Spirit that was His gift to believers.

"I find myself looking back across the incredible distance of these two thousand years and living the experience with them. I see myself being forced to choose—do I remain with the acceptable and the visible and the traditional, or do I reach into the invisible and recognize the hunger that gnaws at my heart? I stand with these baffled witnesses, ignited by the yearning within me to search the unseen realm. Yet I am anchored by the calls of this world, afraid of choosing, knowing that I must choose, realizing that not to choose is in itself a choice.

"Yes," the old man continued, "I can very easily see myself standing with this crowd, terrified by the changes demanded by my empty existence, seeking some way to ignore the call and remain with what is comfortable, what is defined by the elders and the leaders and the people in power.

"But I cannot. I am called by the voice of my heart to turn toward the unseen and accept the Holy Spirit. I am called to dance with the joy that such madness brings."

====

The buzzer rang, startling them both. Jeffrey stood and released the downstairs catch, then waited while Katya climbed the stairs. She arrived slightly breathless and very excited. "Hello, Gregor."

"My dear young lady, what a joy it is to see you again. Come in, come in. How was your trip?"

Katya accepted his invitation for tea and watched him stir about the cramped apartment with his listing gait. Once the water was boiled and tea served and Gregor seated, Katya lifted her package. "I brought something for you."

"My dear child, how thoughtful."

"It's nothing, really." She watched him unwrap the package with shy eyes. "Just something I saw that made me think of you."

"There could be no greater gift than your thoughts and prayers." He lifted up the frame. "Marvelous. I am deeply touched."

He turned the antique frame around. The yellowed parchment was decorated top and bottom with brilliantly hand-colored pictures depicting two of Christ's parables—the shepherd returning the lost sheep to the fold and the man finding a pearl beyond value. The center contained a hand-lettered verse. Jeffrey read the delicately scrolled words, "Teach me, Lord, in the ways of the wise."

"Jeffrey took me to my very first antiques fair a few weeks ago," Katya said. "I found this, and I thought of you."

Gregor pointed to the empty wall at the end of his bed. "I shall hang it there, where it will be the first thing I shall see upon rising each morning. Thank you, my dear."

"Those are two of my favorite parables," Jeffrey said.

"Do you know what a parable is? A heavenly truth clothed in an earthly body. It is a way to make the unknowable clear, the unseen perfectly visible." He smiled at Katya. "I am deeply touched by your thoughtfulness."

"Has Jeffrey told you that we are traveling to Czestochowa tomorrow?"

"Is that so?" Gregor was clearly delighted. "May I impose and accompany you? I have long wanted to make another pilgrimage to the Cathedral of Jasna Gora."

"It wouldn't be an imposition," Jeffrey replied. "But I thought pilgrimages went out with the Middle Ages. Something you only find nowadays in books that make fun of the old practices."

"Our modern world is too swift to criticize what it does not understand and to condemn what it finds the least bit uncomfortable," Gregor replied. "A pilgrimage is nothing more than a prayer with feet."

"I think it would be wonderful to have you along," Jeffrey said simply.

"I've heard about this place all my life and never been there," Katya said. "My mother has a copy of the picture in the church, the Black Madonna, on her bedroom wall."

Gregor asked, "What time is your meeting there scheduled?"

"Lunchtime."

"Do you think it might be possible to arrive in time for the eleven o'clock Mass?"

"Certainly. I'll just call Rokovski and ask if we can meet him there." Jeffrey stood and signaled to Katya with his eyes. "We must be going."

"Indeed you do. Business is waiting." Gregor pushed himself erect and saw them to the door. "You know where the Russian market is?"

"I have found it on a map," Katya replied.

"Splendid. Until tomorrow, then."

==

A continuing thaw left Nova Huta's Russian market swimming in a sea of mud. Visitors paid it no notice, except to walk on tiptoe through the deepest puddles. When Jeffrey and Katya arrived, the sun was shouldering aside clouds and casting an unfamiliar light upon throngs who jostled good-naturedly among the acres of stalls and peddlers. They joined the crowds strolling, gawking, pointing, laughing. They listened to people arguing prices in a mishmash of Polish and Russian and Ukrainian.

The slender young man whom Jeffrey had last seen in a Cracow apartment with two valuables strapped to his thighs spotted them first. He shouted them over with the under-handed come-hither gesture of the East. Beside him stood a young-old girl in her twenties dressed in layer upon layer of sweat shirts, her unkempt dark hair tied back with a length of ragged cloth. Her face was as hard and unflinching as her eyes. Before the pair of them were piles of wrenches and crowbars and hammers and hacksaws and nails and screws and manual drills.

The Ukrainian nudged his companion and spoke to her in a Russian singsong. She spoke in turn to Jeffrey and Katya in Polish, her mouth barely moving in the rock-hard face.

"He says their profit from the last trip was enough to go into business," Katya translated to Jeffrey. "At least, I think that's what he said. This girl's Polish is dreadful. I can barely understand her."

"Buy-sell," the man shouted happily in an English so heavily accented as to be barely understandable. "Valuta."

"Valuta," Jeffrey agreed, liking him. "Tell him I'm glad things have worked out so well."

Their conversation attracted attention from nearby stall-holders and patrons. The gawkers and gossipers began to gather and watch and listen and point and talk words that needed no translation. Look, an Englishman speaking with another woman—listen to her Polish. And how do they know this pair from the other side?

The young man waved his hand proudly over his wares, said through the dual translators, "Even after bribes to the border guards on both sides, a good day brings enough to keep both our families alive for a month."

By now the crowd hemmed them in on all sides. The woman spoke a warning; the young man grinned and jerked his head for them to follow. He clapped the next stallholder's shoulder in passing, said something that was answered with a grunt and a shift of position by the man's thick-set wife.

Jeffrey and Katya followed the pair by stalls selling everything from tatty sweaters to sheets to pocket watches to aspirin to Russian fur-lined gloves and hats. Most of the sellers were women, hard-faced and very large and looking older than their years. The stalls were rudimentary in the extreme, waist-high blocks of poured concrete with wavy plastic roofs supported by rotting timbers. The entire market lot was surrounded on all sides by multistory Communist-built apartment bunkers.

They crossed a mud-swamped parking lot and stopped beside a thoroughly trashed and battered Soviet Lada. The young man opened the trunk, tossed out sacking and roof-ropes, and pulled out a single remaining wooden crate.

"On the black market the dollar sells for two hundred and ten rubles and it's going up every day," he said through the laborious translation process. "Prices shoot up fifty, maybe a hundred percent each week. Pensioners get enough money each month to feed themselves for three days. There is trouble brewing."

"So why don't you get out?" Jeffrey asked as he watched him gingerly unwrap multiple layers of padding.

"Family," he answered briefly. "Parents and uncles too old to move. And where would I go, what would I do? Here at least people come to me and say, sell this, help me, bring me valuta so I can feed my family another month."

The box held three individually wrapped parcels. The young man tossed back the final layer of matting in one to expose a pair of delicate porcelain "Easter eggs," so named because they were often given by royalty as gifts at the end of Lent. These were painted with tiny yet beautifully accurate pictures of the Sansouci Palace of Potsdam. Jeffrey squinted more closely, made out people no higher than a pinhead moving across a graceful bridge. He knew from his reading that they had been painted with a magnifying glass and a brush made from a single horsehair. Each egg represented a month's work by a skilled artisan. They bore the stamp of Meissen, dated 1710. Museum quality.

Next emerged a case the size of a small paperback book. The outside covers were of engraved silver, framing a solid block of ivory. Gingerly he accepted the case from the grimy hands and opened it to find a *Diptyque*; on each block of ivory, two carvings, one above the other, depicted scenes from the life of Christ. Cases such as this one had once adorned the private chapels of late medieval royalty. From the formation of the carved figures and the surrounding decorative motif, Jeffrey guessed that the piece dated from the fourteenth century. Possibly earlier.

Reluctantly Jeffrey handed back the item and accepted the third. His initial disappointment faded when he realized that he was not holding a painting as he first imagined, nor an icon, but rather a seventeenth-century *Adoration*. The frame took the form of an altar, with Doric columns of ebony and silver holding up an ornate frieze and a cross inlaid with polished semiprecious stones. The centerpiece was a painting on what appeared to be a sheet of lapis lazuli. The stone's deep blue had been used to depict a starlit sky from which a finely painted cloud of angels sang hosannas over Mary and the Christ-child.

Jeffrey looked up. "These will feed a family for a lot longer than a month."

The young man answered his unasked question with grave words. Katya's tone matched his as she translated, "In 1917, when the Communists began taking control of the countryside, some of the villages heard what was happening in the cities, churches looted and desecrated or burned to the ground. Priests handed the church heirlooms to devout families, as they knew that most of their brothers in the cities were vanishing without a trace. The villagers were sworn to guard these treasures and to return them to the church once the Communist threat had passed. But now the villages are starving, and the sick are dying untreated. The priests are giving dispensations to sell off what treasures survived."

Jeffrey looked back at the treasure in his hands. "Your village will eat well for a long time to come if this is authentic."

"I am an honest man," the man said strongly. "A good man. I take a little and give most back. This is not for me."

"I believe you," Jeffrey replied. And he did. But he explained, "There are a lot of replicas coming out of Russia just now. All this will have to be carefully authenticated."

The young man nodded. "But the last shipment, they were real?"

"Yes."

"Then take my word." He waved an arm covered to the elbow with grime and grease. "Genuine and old."

Jeffrey cast another lingering glance over the items, nodded agreement. He thought so too.

"You can buy icons? Good ones, old. Silver frames. Some gold."

"I don't know," he said doubtfully. "There's a wall of icons now in one London antique store."

The young man was not surprised by the news. "But if I bring you ones as special as these?"

"Then I can buy them. I don't know the price, but I will buy any of this quality." He traced the pattern of the blue-veined sky. "Definitely."

"For a lot of people and villages, the only thing of value they have left is the icon. Stored away since the Revolution. Now they either sell or starve."

Jeffrey inspected the young man. "Things are that bad?"

"Come and see," the man replied, his animated face turning as flat as his companion's. "Some things you have to witness to understand."

"Maybe I will."

"You come see me first here, I'll take you to the *real* Ukraine. And more things to buy. Real treasures."

"Maybe this summer," Jeffrey said, the idea of a new adventure sounding appealing.

The woman lost her patience, snapped at her companion and started to move away. The Ukrainian smiled, held her shoulder, and gestured with evident pride at her spirit. He soothed her with a few words, then turned back to Jeffrey and said something more which was translated as, "Five thousand dollars now. It is a lot, but I must have it now. The rest you give to your priest, along with word on when you can come with me across the border."

Jeffrey felt the thrill of stepping out into the unknown. "Gregor is not a priest."

The young man shrugged. "The honorable man, then. In a world like this, which is harder to find?"

CHAPTER 32

The Baroque era in Poland," Katya said from the back seat as Jeffrey drove out of Cracow the next morning, Gregor beside him in the front, "was a golden age in more ways than one. During that period, the nation entered into years of relative stability and vast political power. So long as far-flung powers did not ignite the flames of war, as sometimes happened—"

"Too often," Gregor murmured. "For century upon century, war was seen as a valid arm of everyday politics."

"This stability brought unbridled economic growth to Poland," Katya continued. "And with this growth came phenomenal wealth to the ruling classes. Poland's location made it a bridge between empires—the Ottomans to the south, the Swedes and the Prussians to the north, the Muscovites in the east, and the tottering Holy Roman Empire to the west. For much of this period, the Polish-Lithuanian Empire was the only one of these powers that was not at war."

"A bridge of culture, and a bridge of trade," Gregor agreed. "For seven months a year, ice closed off all the northern seas, so that the only way to arrive to the new empire of Muscovy was overland. The only safe overland passage, with decent roads and stable government and security against brigands, was through Poland."

"And every time a cargo came through the empire, a bit was left behind in the form of taxes and payments and trades," Katya finished. "Since there were fewer wars to drain the coffers of either government or commerce, the gentry grew rich."

"Incredibly so," Gregor said. "Sadly, the wars that swept through this land afterward left little evidence of what Poland possessed. But believe me, my dear boy, Poland once set the definition of what it meant to be wealthy."

"A will dated 1640 tells of one woman's estate," Katya explained. "She left five thousand diamonds and emeralds to her daughters. And she was not a princess nor a queen, Jeffrey, simply the wife of a wealthy landowner. Another landowner of this same period left his children a cloak woven of solid gold thread, embossed with eight hundred rubies. Yet another deeded to just one of her children over eight thousand pearls."

The hills lining the new four-lane highway to Czestochowa were speckled white with old snow. The lower reaches nestled beneath a gently falling mist, the sky descending to wrap distant hills in ghostly veils. Ancient castles and hill-top monasteries emerged from the haze-like painted apparitions before melting from view. Jeffrey decided he had never seen a more beautiful winter landscape.

"When the pillage of this great land began," Gregor said, "the stories that circulated spoke of wealth beyond the greediest of imaginations. Warlords swept in like packs of wolves following the scent of a fresh kill. One country estate contained so much art that the Swedes required one hundred and fifty wagons to cart it away. Another castle, which fell to the Austrian army, listed over seven thousand paintings in its archives."

Tree-lined rivers appeared from time to time, impressionist glimpses that flowed into the white-shrouded distance. Carefully tended farms gave way to forests of silver birches, tall and graceful and otherworldly in the floating mists.

"But during the period of stability," Katya went on, "this outward display of wealth was carried over into how Poles worshiped. By this time, the Polish Catholic church was referred to simply as 'our church.' Rome was scarcely granted the time of day. The Vatican was so embroiled in trying to keep the Holy Roman Empire from scattering to the winds that little more than passing complaint was made. At least the name Catholic was kept."

"Keep in mind as well," Gregor added, "that the tide of Protestantism swept much of Europe at the onset of this era. While wars scarred the face of many countries, Poland opened its arms to all sects, including many that even the Protestant church considered too heretical."

"I love it when you two do this," Jeffrey said.

Gregor showed genuine surprise. "Do what?"

"Trade off on each other. Tell a story together."

Gregor looked at Katya in surprise. "Were we doing that?"

"I don't know," Katya replied, looking mystified.

"Yes, you were, and it's great," Jeffrey assured them. "Please continue."

"Very well," Gregor agreed. "Where was I?"

"Heretics."

"Ah, yes. Thank you. Calvinists formed a very large colony here under the protection of the king. Lutherans dominated several regions, converting even the ruling princes. Aryans, who were condemned by every other church body in Europe, populated several cities. There was even a point when a majority of the Sejm, Poland's parliament, was Protestant. In the almost two centuries that religious terror and oppression swept through the rest of Europe, only seven people were sentenced in Poland for religious crimes, and five of them were Catholics convicted of burning down a Protestant church. When a Papal envoy arrived to complain, the Polish king was heard to say, 'Permit me to rule over the goats as well as the sheep.' At a time when other countries, Protestant and Catholic alike, were torturing people before burning them at the stake just for reading the wrong book, upholding the cause of human rights like this was extraordinary."

Katya took up the story. "Many historians feel that it was precisely because of this liberal attitude that Poland eventually returned to the religion of its heritage. In any case, by the middle of the eighteenth century, Catholicism was again the predominant form of worship, and churches in wealthier regions reaped the benefits of their princes' and patrons' riches."

"Regions such as Czestochowa," Gregor added.

Katya nodded. "One patron decided such an important painting of the Madonna and Child needed to be clothed in robes of more than just paint and so gave a cloak of woven gold and encrusted diamonds. Another donated a cloak of gold and emeralds. Another of silver and rubies. Yet another had an embossed metal plate designed and covered with a sheet of hammered gold, then set in the wall to slide over and protect the painting when it was not being viewed."

"So what is so important about this painting?" Jeffrey asked.

Katya leaned forward to glance at Gregor, who smiled and nodded. "After you, my dear."

"It's hard to separate fact from legend," Katya began. "All that can be said for sure is the original painting is at least one thousand five hundred years old."

"What?"

"That is the minimum," Gregor confirmed. "But being an incurable romantic, I prefer the legend."

"So do I," Katya agreed.

"Which is?" Jeffrey pressed.

"That it was painted by Luke on the tabletop from the holy family's home in Bethlehem," Katya replied.

"Luke, as in the writer of the Gospel?"

"There is much to argue that the story might be true," Gregor said. "Legends and early historians both agree that it is so. There is also another image of Mary and the Christ-child in Florence, Italy, which authorities insist was also painted by Luke. The two paintings are remarkably similar."

"This one was reportedly taken from Jerusalem by the Roman Emperor Constantine around the year 300," Katya continued. "Constantine stopped Rome's persecutions of Christians when he himself was converted. He is said to have placed this painting in his own chapel, where it remained for over six hundred years. By that time, the eastern Holy Roman Empire was collapsing. Constantinople was warring with enemies on every side, including some of its own provinces. Allies were desperately needed. In return for an oath of fealty, the painting was given to Prince Lev of Rus, as the lands to the north were then known. Prince Lev moved it to his own palace at Belz, where it remained until 1382, when his descendant Prince Vladislaus decided to relocate it to a new monastery he was starting in Czestochowa."

"All of this is carefully documented, I assure you," Gregor added. "From the gift of the painting to Prince Lev in the year 900 to today, the deeds of authentication still exist. The only question is whether it was truly painted by Saint Luke."

"In 1430 the monastery was attacked by bandits," Katya went on. "The painting was shattered by sword blows. The king ordered it restored no matter what the cost, but painters were unable to make their colors hold fast to the old picture."

"We know now the reason. Very early painters made their primitive colors hold true by fusing them onto the wood with a wax coating," Gregor explained. "But at the time it was an international calamity. There are records within the monastery of letters from all over the civilized world, asking for reports on the progress of repairs."

"So the painters put a new coating on the repaired table-top," Katya said, "and then painted the picture again. They kept to the original as exactly as possible, except for one thing. On Mary's face they painted in a long jagged scar, to show for as long as the painting existed that it once had been desecrated."

=====

Czestochowa proved to be, in effect, two cities in one. The outlying town was the same collection of dreary buildings flanking pitted and crumbling streets they had seen everywhere in Eastern Europe. The inner city, however, the hill of Jasna Gora, was something else entirely.

The hill was separated from the rest of the city by a broad expanse of gradually rising green, bordered by a series of glass-fronted restaurants and gift shops. Beyond their covered ways, a number of enterprising capitalists had set up suitcase-stands; several dozen competing boom-boxes blared out a cacophony of religious music, while other sellers kept watch over postcards and picture books fluttering in the breeze.

The hilltop was buttressed with red-brick fortress walls; these descended far below the footbridge that crossed from the paved walkway to the first of three vast ornamental gates. The hill took a swooping dip down into a grass-covered canal before joining the fortress at the base of what once had been a very deep moat. Small, barred windows rimmed the brick facade above the ancient, mossy waterline.

Beyond the first wall came a second and beyond that a third, each marked by guard towers and high stone gates crowned with royal seals. And past the third gate rose a village from another era, lined with narrow cobblestone streets which wound amidst ancient buildings and stone fountains with time-sanded facades. Windows wore hand-drawn panes that flowed downward with the patience of centuries.

At one end of a cobblestone plaza rose the church, where a steady stream of people made their way through high arched portals. Jeffrey stood far enough inside to be protected from the wind while Katya and Gregor bought books from nuns at a glass-fronted stall. He watched the faces that passed. Over and over he found himself inspecting hardened features and their eyes that showed a surprisingly gentle light.

The painting was not in the main church at all, but in a side chapel that could be called small only when compared to the central hall. It was reached through a series of three other chapels, each of which could easily have held a thousand people. A multitude of naves and alcoves and doors led to still more chapels and prayer rooms. All these ancient halls had been renovated several centuries ago in lavish Baroque style. Distant ceilings bore ornate and gilded frescoes surrounding religious paintings, with these in turn encircled by cherubim heralding the King's return on long, silvered trumpets.

After this parade of wealth and glitter, the painting's chapel was surprisingly plain. There were no marble-pillared side chapels bearing massive paintings, nor giant gilded angels, nor rising ranks of candles, nor elaborate chandeliers. Mosaic floorings, tapestries, and ceiling pictures had no place here. The floor was hard granite worn smooth and grooved by six centuries of pilgrims' feet. Jeffrey passed through the ancient oak door, looked around the small entrance portico, and wondered what all the fuss was about. Then he turned the corner, entered the chapel proper, and saw the nave.

The front section was protected by floor-to-ceiling iron bars, connected by a gilded, hand-wrought pattern of leaves and vines. Great double doors were swung open, and chairs were set in cramped rows up to the banister and communion table.

The altar reached up almost to the distant ceiling, a massive structure covered with intricately detailed scenes. The apostles gathered to either side, life-sized bas-reliefs whose hands held scrolls and books and lifted them up to the angels on high. And in the center was the painting of the Black Madonna.

She was not black at all, but rather had an olive-skinned complexion that could have been called dark only by light-skinned medieval folk who never in their lives had seen a southerner. Her face had the stiffness and lack of expression Jeffrey had seen in very early religious mosaics. Her eyes were slender as tears and slanted upward. The Christ-child in her arms was a miniature rendition of the mother who held him. Whatever the actual date of the painting, one thing was utterly clear in that first glimpse; it was very, very old.

The painting was gilded like an icon and hung above the chapel's central cross and altar. Penitents made circles around the front chamber on their knees, murmuring prayers along with those who sat in the front rows. Gregor had found his own place to sit, and Jeffrey followed Katya to the last row of seats and sat down beside her. An older woman moved forward; Jeffrey stood and offered his seat. He then backed up against one of the central pillars, not at all sorry for the chance to look around.

Perhaps six hundred people were standing and kneeling and sitting in the chapel, and this was a midweek morning of no special importance. Jeffrey bowed his head and said the Lord's Prayer. As he spoke, he had the fleeting impression of all their softly murmured voices melting together to form one great prayer sent lofting upward, all joined as though spoken from one great heart.

Hearts. He opened his eyes, looked around the chamber, and saw that the old stone walls were not quite so plain as he had first thought.

Tiny silver hearts were hammered into the walls, hundreds of thousands of silent witnesses presented by believers who wished to testify that prayers had been answered. Jeffrey looked out across the chamber and found himself bound to the six hundred years of believers who had come and worshiped within these same walls. How many had known the questions he faced? How many had yearned for more understanding, more wisdom, more knowledge of the Lord? How many had come and stood and thirsted?

Mass began. Katya was too caught up in her own prayers and the priest's scripture readings and message to come back to him and translate. Jeffrey did not mind. It was enough to stand and listen to words he did not understand, surrounded by people he did not know, and yet somehow be filled with the feeling, the knowledge, that he was not alone.

Here in these foreign surroundings was a flavor of something he could not explain. Jeffrey stood by the ancient pillar in an alien church in an alien nation and was filled with an absolute certainty that he was in the presence of something greater than himself. He stood and inspected his heart and yearned for a greater knowledge of his Savior.

His mind touched on concepts that he only half understood. His heart knew the longings of one not yet fulfilled, yet in some strange way the act of honest searching brought him joy. He was aware of a contentment that came not despite his lack of wisdom but rather because he hungered for more. He watched the others with eyes that searched inward, and he realized that always before he had seen his hunger as a fault, a failing, when in truth it was a gift. It forced him to continue walking, keep searching, keep struggling to throw off his burden of isolation from his Lord.

His eyes were drawn back to the walls and their silent, shining testimonies, and he somehow felt a kinship with the centuries of thankful messages. One alcove was given over to crutches—tiny ones for children, ivory-tipped canes for the elderly, crutches of every size and make and description—rising up the trio of high walls and covering every inch of space. Two other alcoves were full of crosses and rosaries and medallions bearing prayers of thanks in a multitude of languages.

But the majority of space was for the hearts. None larger than his hand, some as small as a fingernail, they covered half a dozen alcoves, each with three walls ninety feet wide. A silver sea of thankful hearts.

A s the three emerged from the church into the damp chill, Gregor patted Jeffrey's arm. "Thank you for allowing me to be a part of this. And thank you both for the Mass."

"I hope it wasn't too tedious for you," Katya said, "since you did not understand the priest." She took hold of Jeffrey's other hand.

"I enjoyed it," Jeffrey replied. "I learned a lot."

Katya smiled up at him. "And what did you learn from a sermon given in Polish?"

"I don't know if I can put it into words."

Gregor nodded his understanding. "The most valuable of lessons are seldom those that can be restricted by man's limited tongue. Especially at first."

They descended the hill and walked to the city's one large hotel, a glass and steel structure designed in the best of Communist 'sixties style. While they shed their coats and scarfs and gloves at the cloakroom, Jeffrey glanced into the restaurant its windowed door. "These places all look the same, don't they?"

Katya did not need to turn around. "All such hotels were built around the same time. All the menus were printed by the central supply office for all restaurants. All the chairs and tables and plates and glasses for all Polish restaurants were manufactured by the same factories."

"All most boring and functional only."

"Stimulation of individual tastes ranked low on the list of Communist priorities," Gregor said, opening the restaurant door and ushering them inside.

A swift glance assured him that Rokovski had not yet arrived. Jeffrey followed the others to a table by the window, inspected the plastic-bound menu, listened as Katya passed his order to an attentive waiter, then turned and gave in to the pleasure of people-watching.

Food arrived at the next table over, and all conversation halted as if a switch had been thrown. The intensity with which the people ate was something he rarely observed in the West.

Katya saw what had caught his attention. "You never see people picking politely at their food here," she told him quietly. "If they do, they are foreigners. A Pole has been hungry too often to play at eating. If food is put in front of him, he *eats*."

A newcomer waddled in and took the table across from them. The man wore his triple chins with a nervous air. He was too small to be called overweight, yet every inch of his little frame was padded to the point of absurdity. He was all bone, fat, and skin, from the looks of it, with no muscle at all. His flesh shivered with every step. Everything about the man was gray—gray suit, gray and white striped shirt buttoned to a neck that folded over and swallowed his collar, gray shoes, gray eyes, gray pallor to his skin. His lips were buried in a tight little grimace that brought his chin almost into contact with his pudgy nose.

Jeffrey leaned toward Katya, asked, "How do people allow themselves to get that way?"

She responded like a mother teaching a child something that he could not have yet learned, but should know. "Maybe because he's lazy. Or maybe because he hasn't had any choice. You don't find many sports centers in Poland. These are not an exercising people. Either you are a professional athlete or you maybe play a little soccer on vacations, or you do nothing. Maybe it's because life requires so much hard work of them. Maybe food was so difficult to find when they were young that it would have been foolish to use up more calories than necessary. Or maybe they have never been taught to think that, after a certain stage in life, personal appearance is still important."

Jeffrey nodded gravely—maybe a bit meekly also.

He spotted Rokovski entering the restaurant and rose, along with Gregor and Katya, to greet him.

"My dear Jeffrey," Rokovski walked over with hand outstretched. "How wonderful to see you. I hope you haven't been waiting long."

"Not at all. You remember my fiancée, Katya Nichols."

"But of course." He bowed over her hand and continued, "Alexander informed me of your betrothal during his last trip. May I add my own congratulations and best wishes."

"Thank you. And this is Alexander's cousin, Gregor Kantor. Dr. Pavel Rokovski."

"It is indeed an honor to meet Alexander's illustrious cousin," Rokovski said formally.

Jeffrey showed surprise. "You know of him?"

"There are not so many who have forsaken the chance for both wealth and position to aid the needy that they would go unnoticed," Rokovski replied, holding fast to Gregor's hand, "or would their name remain unspoken in the highest of circles."

"You do me great honor," Gregor murmured.

"On the contrary," Rokovski said, "it is you who does honor to both your name and our nation."

As they resumed their places the waiter appeared. Jeffrey asked, "Would you join us for lunch?"

"Thank you, perhaps a bite of something." He waved away the menu, spoke briefly to the waiter, then turned back to the table. "You have heard from them?"

"Nothing."

"So we are to wait, then." He did not seem troubled. "A small price to pay for the return of such a treasure."

"I'm afraid we don't know that for sure," Jeffrey warned.

"Our dear Alexander took the greatest of pains to explain the situation," Rokovski assured him. "Several times now, in fact. I am well aware of the unknown factors, but I must say I agree with him that there is at least a shred of hope. To make such an offer of evidence without payment in return suggests that they are indeed serious."

"You haven't met them," Jeffrey muttered.

"I beg your pardon?"

"Jeffrey is not overly impressed with them," Katya explained.

"Ah, yes, Alexander mentioned that as well. I find it good to have reservations when entering into such affairs," Rokovski replied easily. "Although my enthusiasm runs away with me from time to time, I must confess. So it is good to know that someone else will remain my anchor, should that be the case here."

Over lunch the dreaded subject arose. "I don't suppose you have any word of the chalice?"

Jeffrey shook his head miserably. "Nothing at all."

Katya's brow furrowed. "That's not exactly true," she objected.

"Yes," Rokovski agreed. "Alexander discussed with me your remarkable findings. I found them to be of the greatest interest, although I could not successfully fit the pieces together."

"We're missing some crucial element," Jeffrey said.

"My sentiments exactly. For that reason, I have placed two of my best researchers on the matter. Already they have come up with what might be yet another fragment."

"Which is?"

"As you may know," Rokovski said, "there was a point in our history when Poland and her church stood calmly and watched as much of Europe went up in the flames of religious conflict."

"The Reformation Wars," Jeffrey said. "We were talking about that just this morning."

"Indeed. Well, Poland's church became very independent-minded during this period. Rome was unable to complain very loudly, for at least the wealth and power of Poland remained Catholic, even if they did refuse to join the battle against the Protestants." Rokovski shook his head. "My country has committed a number of very foolish acts in her long past. Yet here stands one of the shrewdest moves in all European history, one country who retained its senses through two hundred years of religious insanity. I wish words could express how proud I am of the rulers who forged this dangerous path.

"In any case, the Polish kings found it much wiser to appoint their own bishops than to risk having Rome bring in someone who would ignite the fires of battle. They sent messengers to Rome informing the Pope of their decisions. This policy was a matter of great distress to Rome.

"In the midst of all this turmoil, with diplomatic missions and Papal letters going back and forth, an emissary arrived from Rome. He stated that the Pope wished to have a particular cardinal appointed, someone he could trust. A man who would be a voice for Rome in the midst of the Polish empire's growing might. The emissary arrived bearing gifts, gestures of goodwill, and so forth. One of these gifts—bribes, if you like—was a golden chalice."

Jeffrey leaned forward. "*The* chalice?"

Rokovski shrugged. "That we have yet to confirm. But the dates do correspond."

He pushed his plate aside and leaned both elbows upon the table. "I must tell you something else, something that should not go beyond this table. I do not trust our curate, Karlovich. I have been forced to spend quite a bit of time with him as this investigation has progressed, and I have grown more and more concerned over the man."

"In what way?"

"Nothing specific. He simply gives me the sense of being overly enthusiastic. In a number of questionable directions, I might add. There is a very fine line between passion and fanaticism, and one great danger of fanatic belief is the certainty of having infallible judgment."

Further conversation was halted when Katya took in a quick breath and pointed. "They're here."

All turned to see a large blond woman in a black leather trench coat enter the restaurant.

"Perhaps I should wait outside," Gregor said, not rising with the others.

"Nonsense," Rokovski replied, not taking his eyes from the woman approaching their table. "We shall simply consider you as Alexander's honored emissary. Which you are."

She stopped before them, gave each of them a blank stare. Her eyes met Rokovski's, where they remained. She set a pair of battered plastic suitcases down at her feet and said a few words in German that Katya translated as, "You have five days."

"That should be adequate," Rokovski replied. "How——?"

She interupted briefly, drew an envelope from her pocket, and placed it on the table. Katya translated, "Two million dollars are to be deposited in an account in Zurich, Switzerland. Details are listed here."

"We will need some form of guarantee," Rokovski said. "Some promise that we will actually receive the remainder of the treasure after payment is made."

The woman had clearly been expecting the question. Immediately after Katya finished her translation, she responded with, "One of our number will check into this hotel in five days. He will deposit with you his passport. He will remain for twenty-four hours after you have received the location details. In return, you will deposit with him a guarantee of safe conduct to Switzerland on the evening of the sixth day." Eyes turned hard as agate. "No tricks."

"No tricks," Rokovski repeated. "It is agreed."

═══

"Rokovski is over the moon," Jeffrey reported to Alexander that evening by telephone.

"He thinks it is genuine, then."

"He won't say anything, but you should have seen his eyes when he opened the cases."

"What did they contain?"

"Amber," Jeffrey replied. "Pieces about the size of my hand—opened—mostly."

"Splendid," Alexander said, his enthusiasm growing.

"All different shades. White as powder to golden to a dark tea shade. Carved with designs on one side and left flat on the other. They looked sort of like puzzle pieces." Jeffrey paused. "I wish you could have been there."

"My dear boy, thank you for saying so. But I am quite content to live the experience through you."

"There were bits of yellowed paper stuck everywhere on the amber."

"The wrapping," Alexander said definitely. "There were always rumors that the Nazis had placed the amber in tissue paper that contained markings for how the walls were to be fitted back together again."

"That's what Rokovski thinks too. He's having the paper tested now. He says that will be the clearest assurance that the pieces are genuinely from the Amber Room."

"Although he already believes it to be so," Alexander finished for him. "As do I."

"He says some of the whitest amber isn't even available anymore."

"Bone amber," Alexander said. "Extremely rare."

"There are pieces six or seven inches wide of the stuff," Jeffrey said, remembering the light in Rokovski's eyes when he picked up the first piece, carved in the shape of a blooming rose.

"The Amber Room. I can scarcely believe that it might indeed be within our very grasp."

"Don't get your hopes up too soon, may I caution, Uncle."

"My dear Jeffrey," Alexander replied, "I shall indulge myself as I please on this account. It makes up for the distress over this other matter. Almost."

Tell me," Gregor said the next morning, once Jeffrey had been settled in the apartment's most comfortable chair and tea had been served. "Have you spoken with others about how they came to know the presence of the Almighty?"

"Some," Jeffrey admitted. "I was just thinking about that this morning. I read that part in the Bible, you know, where Jesus says that you have to die and be born again. It seems as if they were all brought to a point that made them look to something more than their own human strength."

Gregor gave him a look that illuminated the reaches of his heart. "My boy, I shall make a prediction. A time will come when you shall make a wonderful teacher for our Lord."

He had to laugh. "You've got the wrong man."

"If only you could hear the growing wisdom in your own voice or recognize the hunger in your breast for being the gift that it is." Gregor smiled at Jeffrey's discomfort. "Enough of that. Being broken, as this experience is also known, is another name for facing a need greater than yourself. I find it most wonderful that our Lord promised that we as believers would never ever face such an overwhelming defeat again. The trials we encounter, once the turning has been made, shall never break us. I find that truly beautiful. Once the path has been found, we are given a shield for all our remaining days."

Jeffrey cast a glance at Gregor's own twisted form, then looked quickly away.

"I did not say we would not face trials," Gregor answered the glance softly. "I said we would always be given the strength and the protection and the guidance to see us through."

"My apology—"

"My dear boy, why should you? You didn't cause this." He sipped from his glass. "Now tell me. If these people with whom you spoke about the experience of faith did so in fullness, they shared another trait. An event equally as important as being broken. Can you see it?"

"I'm not sure."

"Remember. It is there, I assure you. Can you see it?" he asked again.

Jeffrey felt as though he was being pointed directly toward something, but was unable to identify it. He shook his head.

"Someone told them about faith. Ah, yes, now you see. Excellent. Yes, it is important for all believers to remember that faith is always teetering on the verge, always just one generation away from total extinction. There is only one way for faith to continue."

"It has to be passed on," Jeffrey said.

"Exactly. Someone has to plant the seed. The gift of witnessing has to be offered. A believer must stand and by his or her life show the power of the invisible at work." Gregor offered a smile. "And this brings us to what I would suggest as your next little exercise, my young friend. I would ask you to go out and practice illogical witnessing."

He could only shake his head.

"Choose the absolute least likely person you can find. Make sure it is someone who leaves you utterly unsettled. If possible, somebody whom you detest." He examined Jeffrey. "Am I getting through?"

"How about another assignment?" Jeffrey asked wryly.

Gregor shook his head. "This one fits perfectly."

"No, it doesn't. I'm positive about that."

"I feel utter harmony with this notion."

"So you do it. Just the thought makes my skin crawl."

Gregor beamed. "Wonderful."

Jeffrey shook his head. "Anything but."

"Listen to me, my brother in Christ. Here is the key. There is absolutely *no one* on earth whom God does not love. You need to begin to see yourself as an instrument of this love, someone through whom Christ may live and love and save. You must accept this as a part of your daily life and stop trying to keep it at arm's length.

"You want something that makes sense. Something that you can analyze and fit into a comfortable little box. My friend, God's salvation is intended to explode *every* box, to shatter *every* myth in your life. Including the one you continue to hold out in front of yourself as a shield. Do you know what that is?"

Jeffrey motioned his denial. "I'm not sure I want to know."

"Of course you do. You're upset because I speak of what you both want to hold on to and desperately seek to let go. It is the old and the new struggling for central place in your life. The myth you cling to is that you are unworthy, is it not? You fear that you are not good enough to receive God's love, to be filled with His gift of the Spirit. The mirror of your newfound faith is confronting you with the multitude of your faults and your sins, and you are wondering at how an all-knowing, all-seeing, all-powerful God can truly love someone such as you. Is that not it, Jeffrey? Is this not the question you are afraid to bring out into the open and admit to yourself and to God?"

Jeffrey remained silent.

"Listen, my brother. Your fear has power because it contains truth. It is both true and not true. True, because you are *not* worthy of God. But not true because He has sent His Son to cleanse you, to clothe you anew, to *make* you worthy. It is the greatest gift of all history, both what has been written and what is yet to come. So when you stand before this person you loathe and witness to him, I want you to remember this ultimate and undying truth. That not only is this other person eternally worthy, if only he or she will open their hearts to the truth, but *so too are you.*"

———

Their first meeting that morning took place at the Forum Hotel, a vast structure of over four hundred rooms, situated across the Vistula River from Cracow's old city. The seller was an eye doctor, in town for a symposium on new ophthalmological equipment. A tall, slender man going prematurely bald, his face was as bland as his voice, his hands the only expressive part about him.

The doctor led Katya and Jeffrey through the foyer and down a hall transplanted from any big-city Hilton—marble floor, veneered walls, decorative modern art displayed for sale, flower shop, hair salon, travel agent, Hertz. The change from the world outside could not have been greater.

The symposium took place in a hall that looked to seat five or six hundred and was filled to standing room only. Outside the hall were smaller rooms filled with displays of the latest Western equipment. The doctor led them toward a stand of microscopes mounted on what looked like a cross between a robot arm and a crane.

Through Katya he pointed to it and said, "This is what I want. A surgical microscope. Fifty-four thousand dollars the cheapest one costs, when I add up the diagnostic equipment here and here. I want you to see this and understand that I am perfectly serious. I must have this much money. Otherwise I do not sell. Do you understand? I do not sell unless I can buy this for my practice."

With the same hurried calm that Jeffrey knew from Western doctors, he led them back down the hall, through the main foyer, and into a waiting elevator. He talked the entire way, Katya using his brief pauses to translate for Jeffrey.

"Until the fall of Communism, private practice and physician-owned equipment was illegal. The only items I was allowed to use in my own office were those things abandoned by a hospital. You cannot imagine the battles we had among the hospital doctors over machines that were barely more than scrap. Even if we couldn't use them, there was still a certain status associated with having your own equipment.

"Now all this has changed, and private practices are allowed. Doctors can charge clients for their services, which before was also illegal. And now doctors want to work at Western technological levels. Myself included."

He led them out of the elevator and down the seventh floor hall to his room, still talking. "This is becoming urgent, because the hospitals are sliding into chaos. The social system has broken down. People keep going to the hospitals, but the government has no money for funding. The poor are now waiting *days* in hospital lobbies for an appointment with a doctor. I will not make you sick by describing what our emergency rooms look like. When patients are finally seen, they are inspected with equipment that has broken down and treated with drugs that are out-of-date. There is a desperate lack of needles and syringes and even the simplest of bandages. The few who who can afford it are going to private clinics for everything."

He opened his door, ushered them into a room fitted with standard Western hotel furniture, and waved them toward the two seats. He perched on the end of his bed and continued. "If you're retired, you get free medicine. Everyone else pays thirty percent for local, Polish-made pharmaceuticals. If you can afford it, however, you purchase drugs made in the West, and for them you pay the full price. The problem is, you see, there is a *huge* difference in quality."

He went to his closet and pulled out two heavily strapped cases. "The government ran out of money to pay for medical treatment, which means that the pharmacies have not been reimbursed for the drugs they distributed free of charge or sold at subsidized prices. So what happens? The state-run pharmacies are cutting back on the number of drugs they keep and dispense to match the amount they received from the government the month before. Many of the poor are going without, or having to spend what to them is a month's salary for one dose of imported antibiotics at an international pharmacy."

The doctor opened the first case and began unfolding multiple layers of burlap wrapped around an ornate silver tureen chased in gold leaf. Jeffrey took the opportunity to whisper to Katya, "Do you remember our talk about tithing together and doing something for the people here?"

She turned and gazed with eyes that seemed to drink him in. "I remember," she said quietly.

"I have a feeling this is it," he said. "Could you ask him for an introduction to a hospital that's in trouble? Maybe one that treats kids?"

CHAPTER 35

There was another snowfall that night, so the next morning they decided to take the train for their visit to the children's hospital their new doctor friend had recommended. A thaw had set in by the time they left for Wroclaw, which was good, because the heat on the train was truly feeble. It was an old Polish train, with PKP stamped on the side of each green, smut-fogged wagon.

The trip took seven endless hours. Jeffrey worked through all his notes, talked with Katya until the jouncing fatigue silenced them, watched landscapes roll by under a flat gray sky. He walked the passageway, saw young and old huddled under coats or swaddled in quilts and blankets, sitting with the patience of those who knew that however long the voyage took, it would take longer still.

With each stop, the compartments and passageways became more crowded. The train went from comfortable to overstuffed, with all seats taken and people standing in sardine-packed confinement in the passageway.

"It used to be like this all the time," Katya said. "Train tickets cost pennies, and there were always delegations traveling everywhere. Even a visit to another factory was done by committee. Delegations meant extra eyes were open and watching."

An hour outside Wroclaw, Katya told him, "Many Poles still consider this region to be a part of Germany. It didn't belong to Poland until 1945. After the war, the Allied powers agreed to redraw Poland's boundaries. The Soviet Union annexed almost a third of Poland, which was then attached to its border. In compensation, a slice of Germany, including parts of Silesia, was given to Poland on this side."

"No one complained?"

"Who listened to a defeated Germany? As for Poland, the Soviets made sure no one made an official complaint. A lot of people, like Mama, protested with their feet. They moved West in hopes of escaping the spread of Russian troops. A few managed to escape. Most did not."

She pointed out the window at a passing small village. "The architecture is very German here. You won't find structures like this anywhere else in Poland."

"Like what?"

"Wait until we arrive in Wroclaw. It's easier to describe when you see a city."

The ring of factories marking the outskirts of Wroclaw left the air tasting bitter. Within the city proper, the streets showed a hodgepodge of building styles. Communist high-rises mingled with prewar apartment and office buildings that would have looked at home in Paris or Vienna if only they had been painted. Lacy iron grillwork wove its way around breakfast balconies fronting tall French double doors. Walls were festooned with plaster bas-reliefs and stone gargoyles. Wrought-iron streetlamps from the age of gas and candles still stood guard over many street corners.

"Yes, I see what you mean," Jeffrey remarked as he looked out the window.

The station itself was tall and curved and walled in with glass, as were many European stations remaining from the steam-driven Industrial Revolution. The air smelled dry. Metallic. Sooty. It sucked the moisture from Jeffrey's eyes and mouth and throat.

"Now it's mostly Poles who live here," Katya told him as they walked through the echoing terminal. "The Germans left in waves of hungry refugees. Then Stalin forcibly resettled many families here from eastern Poland, which was incorporated into the Soviet Union after the war."

They stepped out into a wind-driven mixture of sleet and slushy rain, and settled into a taxi that stank of the driver's Russian cigarettes. After Katya had given him directions, Jeffrey asked, "What happened to the Poles who didn't make it out of those eastern lands?"

Katya gave a tiny shrug. "From one day to the next, all contact was lost. I remember asking the family I stayed with in Warsaw that same question. They had relatives still there, or so they thought. But no communication was allowed. Now we know that some survived, but many were lost. Most, perhaps. Stalin sent wave after wave of those Poles to Siberia, never to return. He wanted to make those lands totally Soviet, to silence any former claim those people might have made for their homeland."

The children's hospital of Wroclaw was a grim, square-faced building stained gray by years of soot. It was fronted by what once had probably been a formal garden and was now a parking lot paved with cinders. Grimy windows gave way to prim cleanliness within as they passed through the entrance. The waiting area was lined with hard-backed benches and filled with parents and children waiting in patient silence.

Katya gave their names to the receptionist, and they were soon joined by the chief pediatrician, Dr. Helena Sova, an attractive blond woman in her mid-thirties. "Dr. Mirnik called from the opthalmologist's conference to say you were coming," she said in greeting. "He has been very kind to consult here when our small patients have eye troubles. Please, come this way."

She was very trim, very stately, with a happy face framing a pair of huge sad eyes. "We have seventy beds for children from birth to eight years," she said, leading them down a very old yet absolutely spotless hall. She spoke excellent English with a most appealing lilt, her voice brisk and slightly breathless at the same time. Jeffrey noticed that her presence brought a smile from everyone they passed— doctors, nurses, parents, children. All smiled, all spoke, all received the blessing of a few quick heartfelt words. The process was so natural and continuous that it never interrupted their conversation.

"Our main problem is lung disease, as the air pollution is extremely bad. Poland, you see, is the most polluted country on earth, and we stand at the edge of the most polluted region in Poland. From Cracow to Katowice and up to the edge of Silesia, that area is known as the Triangle of Death." She gave them a smile in direct contrast to the look in her eyes. "Rather dramatic, don't you think?"

She ushered them into her office, made the formal offer of coffee or tea, and continued. "In the 'sixties and 'seventies, the government borrowed billions from the West, gambling that they would be able to launch Poland into the future. They constructed massive factories, with absolutely no consideration whatsoever to the environment. They were desperate, you see, to use all this capital Bfor output."

"You heard such words everywhere," Katya agreed. "Output and productivity and five-year programs."

The doctor gave Katya a closer inspection, then spoke to her in Polish. Katya's reply brought a new light to those sad, intelligent eyes. They conversed gaily for a few minutes, then Dr. Sova turned back and said, "She tells me she is your fiancée. She speaks an excellent Polish."

Fiancée. It was still a new enough thought to send shivers up his spine. "So I have been told."

"As I was saying," the doctor continued, "the government built these industrial behemoths all through Poland, but many were concentrated in this area because the Germans left behind an excellent infrastructure—roads, power stations, waterlines, and so forth. These factories were both extremely dirty and extremely inflexible, so large that they could not be adapted to a changing environment."

"And out-of-date before they were built," Katya added.

"Many of them," Dr. Sova agreed. "Poland was forced to buy Russian technology at vastly inflated prices. The Russians simply told us what we were to purchase, and what the price would be, and that was all. But in some areas, such as steel and chemical production, the industries that are concentrated in this region, the technology dated from before the First World War."

"There was a total disregard shown for worker safety and health," Katya explained, "and the consequences are just now being understood. In the Nova Huta steel works outside Cracow, the *average* time a worker holds employment in the factory is four years. The major reasons for departures are accidents and lung disorders."

Dr. Sova gave Katya the welcoming glance of a kindred spirit. "Such information has been released only in the past two years.

Under the Communists, studies of this kind were outlawed, because they feared public reaction if the truth were ever known. But we knew. We saw the result of their attitude toward pollution here in our children."

"This region has forty times what is considered to be the maximum safe level of dust in the air," Katya told Jeffrey, "and sixty times the level of lead in both the air and the water. Half of all rivers in Poland are so polluted that they are not even fit for industrial use; their water will corrode the intake pipes. Almost two-thirds of Cracow is without any sewage treatment at all; everything is simply dumped into the Vistula River. New studies show that the level of chemicals in the air has reached critical levels."

"Sulfur dioxide," Dr. Sova recited. "Carbon dioxide, carbon monoxide, heavy metals, iron, and just plain soot. This region has one *ton* per square meter of dirt fall from the sky each year, the highest on Earth."

"The effect on people's health must be devastating," Jeffrey said.

"Especially the children," Dr. Sova agreed. "Within this region, *ninety percent* of all children under the age of five suffer from some pulmonary disorder at one time or another. One half of all four-year-olds suffer from some *chronic* disease, two-thirds of all six-year-olds, and three-quarters of all ten-year-olds. Again, these figures have only in the past six months become collected. Under the Communists, all records of our children's health were classified top secret, and no such collation of data was permitted. All we could tell you was that too many of our children were ill for too long. Far too long."

She stood and motioned toward the door. "Now that you have heard a bit of the background, perhaps it is time to show you the result of all this pollution."

Rather reluctantly Jeffrey followed her into the hall. The walls were institutional orange and yellow, the floors mismatched strips of various linoleum shades. The air smelled faintly of disinfectant and soap.

"As I said, lung diseases are our single greatest problem," she said, walking them by glass-fronted rooms filled with cribs and children of various ages. "Babies are born with symptoms inherited from their mothers, such as extremely irritated mucus membranes. This makes it very hard for them to draw breath. It also makes them vulnerable to infections, especially bronchitis and pneumonia."

Many of the rooms also contained beds for adults. "This is a very new program for us," she explained, pointing to where a father assisted a nurse in bathing his child. "Under the Communists, parents were not allowed into children's wards at all. Nowadays we encourage it for all of our non-critical patients. We feel both the children and the parents are helped by being together."

She passed by two rooms whose glass walls fronting the hallway were painted over. "Cancer ward here, and next to it leukemia," she explained curtly. "I do not think we shall stop in there."

"Thank you," Jeffrey said quietly.

She glanced at his face. "This is hard for you?"

"Very."

"And yet you wish to help us?"

He felt tender relief as Katya's hand slipped into his. "If we can."

"I have discussed it with my superiors, and we have decided that it would be best if we pinpoint one particular area of need— that is, if you are in agreement."

He nodded. "Where did you learn your English?"

"Here and in America. I was able to do a year's residency at Johns Hopkins." She smiled wistfully. "It was very hard to leave there; so many new and exciting things were taking place every day. But I knew I was needed more here."

She pushed open a door at the end of the hall. "And here you see exposed the wound to my nation's heart."

The ward held a number of tiny cribs and glass-covered incubators. Dr. Sova marched purposefully toward one, seemingly unaware of the difficulty Jeffrey and Katya had in following her. When the incubator's occupant came into view, Jeffrey felt the air punched from his chest. Katya response was a very small cry.

"This baby is now in her thirtieth week," Dr. Sova said, the professional briskness unable to hide her concern for her tiny charge. "With premature births we count from gestation, as you do in the

West. This is now what we call an old lady, because she has survived the first critical ten days, and her weight is up over three pounds."

"She's so small," Jeffrey whispered.

Dr. Sova's smile was tinged with sadness. "This is a very big baby. Very healthy. She's almost ready to go home. We have many premature births with weights at seven hundred grams, or about one and one-half pounds. Those are the ones who cause us the greatest worry."

The baby was more than tiny. She was so small as to appear incapable of life. A rib cage smaller than his fist. A head that could have fit within the palm of his hand. Incredibly fragile arms and legs and hands and feet, like the limbs of a tiny china doll.

"The problem is not just one of survival," Dr. Sova went on. "The problem is the *quality* of survival. Cerebral palsy. Blindness. Mental ability. All of these are unanswered questions with premature babies at this stage of their development."

Wires and needles were taped to the baby's head and abdomen and wrist and ankle. A tiny tube was taped inside her nostril. Monitors standing on a bedside table and hung from the wall hummed and beeped and drew electronic pulses.

"Today, one in five babies born in this region are premature. In the West, the rate is less than one in twenty. Here, placentas are affected by air and water quality—this is now documented fact."

She placed a hand on the thick plastic incubator cover and stroked it, as though touching the baby within. "We are still using incubators that are extremely loud for the baby—their ears are very sensitive at this stage. Some of those from Russia, the only ones we can afford, risk 'cooking' the child—sorry," she said with a glance at their expressions, "because the temperature inside is not always the same as what is registered on the thermometer. We need new ones that both monitor the child's safety and let it grow healthily through this dangerous period.

"Some of my patients who were preemies like this one are now children of seven or eight years of age. I've watched them grow, and I love them as my own. I want to give all these children not just the gift of life, but the gift of a *quality* life. If they wish to be violinists, I want to be sure that their ears are intact and their muscle coordination is precise enough to allow them to play as a virtuoso."

"You need new incubators," Katya said.

"We need *everything*," Dr. Sova replied. "Our financial problems are crippling. We hold our doctors' salaries to two hundred dollars a month and pray that they will not be stolen away by offers from the West at twenty times that amount. With the government's finances in such disarray, we find our budgets being cut daily, while everything we require grows steadily more expensive. Light, coal, repairs to buildings and equipment—every week we wonder if next week we shall have enough to do what is required. One day we lack needles, the next syringes, another day something else, but up to now we have lost no child because of our lack. Of this we are very, very proud."

Dr. Sova guided them around the ward and its tiny occupants. Everywhere were signs of a world far removed from the wealth of the West. The cribs were prewar metal types, heavy and painted white and sided with bars that rose and lowered with screeching protests. The bed sheets all bore hand-stitched repair jobs, as did most of the blankets Jeffrey saw. Machines and wirings wore heavy bandages of silver tape. In the corner station, two nurses were using their break time to crochet miniature bonnets and booties for their patients, Dr. Sova explained.

"Basically we need to outfit an entire new ward," Dr. Sova explained. "We need Western-type incubators, which will ensure a stable environment for our little ones. IV pumps, monitors, X-ray machine, lung ventilator and compressor—all of these are desperately required."

As she walked them back down the hall toward the main entrance, Dr. Sova told them, "Across the border in East Germany, before the Wall fell, they had a policy very different from ours. We heard it from doctors we met in conferences. In their heavily polluted cities, all babies weighing less than a kilo were drowned at birth." She waited a moment after Katya's strangled little cry before continuing. "The authorities decided to spend their scarce resources on patients with a better chance of survival, you see. We have struggled with the problem in a different way, but so long as the culprit remains, so long as pollution levels continue to climb, such horrors are a real possibility in poorer lands."

She pushed open the doors, shook hands, smiled them out and away from the problems locked within those doors. "Poland has never faced so great a threat as it does now from air and water pollution," Dr. Sova said before they left. "This I believe with all my heart. The future of this very generation—the one being born today, not several decades from now, but today—lies in the balance."

t's the Amber Room," Jeffrey announced to Alexander the next evening by telephone. He made no effort to mask his own excitement. "Rokovski is absolutely certain."

"And, no doubt, most ecstatic."

"He did everything but climb the walls while we were with him," Jeffrey confirmed. "He's had three top experts examine the stuff. They've found tracings of old ink on the tissue around each piece."

"Instructions for fitting the puzzle back together."

"That's what they think," Jeffrey agreed. "And he says there is no doubt whatsoever that the amber fits the descriptions of old documents."

"They haven't made their find public in this search for authentication, I hope."

"Not on your life."

"That is good. If this truly is the Amber Room, two million dollars is a paltry sum to pay."

"Not for them," Jeffrey replied. "Rokovski is frantic with worry over how to gather together that much money without going to the central authorities and running the risk of word getting out."

Alexander was silent a long moment, then, "And he is certain that the carvings are not forgeries?"

"Rokovski estimates the suitcases' contents alone are worth over a third of what they've requested," Jeffrey replied. "He said the carvings are exquisite. That was his word. Exquisite. Like nothing he has seen in modern times."

"A lost art," Alexander agreed. "There is no longer a world of kings and queens and dukes and princes who can afford to sustain the expertise of carving jewels into entire chambers."

"He's worried that if he doesn't come up with the money soon, they may search out other buyers."

"And rightly so. Now that this German group has its hands on it, there is an enormous risk that they will either try to move it or to up the price completely beyond Poland's reach." Alexander paused, then decided to say it. "Jeffrey, I want you to call Rokovski for me. Inform him that if he is willing to use the remainder of the funds we have in his special account, I shall lend him the balance."

Jeffrey felt a surge of pride and affection. "He wasn't expecting this. I'm certain it hadn't even occurred to him."

"Yes, Pavel is that sort of man. Nonetheless, this is my decision. Tell him no papers will be necessary. His word will be sufficient." His tone darkened. "It is the least I can do, under the circumstances."

"Speaking of which," Jeffrey replied. "He said he has to travel to Rome the day after tomorrow."

"In relation to the chalice?"

"He didn't say exactly, but I'm pretty sure. I hope so, anyway." Jeffrey hesitated, then continued. "There's more, but maybe it should wait until you get here."

"What on earth do you mean by that?"

"I don't want to get your hopes up unnecessarily."

"My dear Jeffrey. I have seldom given you a direct order, but I shall do so now. Tell me everything Pavel said."

"His researchers have turned up another item. Do you remember his talking about the ancient story of the Vatican emissary who came to Poland bearing gifts?"

"Of course."

"Well, they have found records of a legend. That's what Rokovski called it, a legend. The emissary was a powerful member of the Vatican and traveled through lands totally devastated by the Reformation Wars. There was not a sense of safety nor an absence of starvation until he passed over the Polish borders. Then he arrived in Poland in time for the summer harvest, the only harvest that was still intact in all of northern Europe. All of this convinced him that it was absolutely imperative for Rome to have a man in this powerful kingdom, a man they could fully trust."

"Go on."

Jeffrey took a breath. "The legend is that the Polish king was willing to accept the Pope's man as the new cardinal. But then he told the emissary that he had heard there was a reliquary in the Vatican's possession which contained a segment from the crown of thorns. He wanted it for his kingdom in return for this agreement."

"And the emissary accepted?" Excitement crackled over the line.

"Rokovski says there are two versions of the legend, both of them written down about two hundred years ago, over a century after all this took place. In one, the king backed down and accepted the cardinal without further payment than the non-reliquary chalice. In the other, the emissary made a *second* trip to Poland. A *secret* one. Instead of the chalice the Pope had intended as the gift, he brought instead the one containing the reliquary which the king demanded. The emissary then returned to the Vatican with news of the king's acceptance of Rome's cardinal."

"So the reliquary did find its way to Poland after all," Alexander exclaimed, "and without Rome's formal approval."

"Perhaps," Jeffrey cautioned. "At least, as far as this second legend is concerned. A few years later, the Vatican supposedly discovered that the chalices had been switched. They approached the king of Poland and said there had been a mistake, that the reliquary had been given without the Pope's permission. They requested that it be returned to its rightful place at the heart of Christendom. The king replied that there had been no mistake. Poland had hundreds of valuable chalices, he said, but no such symbol of Christ's suffering and dying for mankind. The only reason he would have considered granting the cardinal the appointment was in return for this priceless gift."

"I wonder what happened to the emissary," Alexander murmured.

"Rokovski said he asked the same thing. His researchers told him there was never any further mention of him or his family's name. Not anywhere. It was as though he never had existed."

"Yet the Vatican could not complain too loudly," Alexander mused. "There was too much at stake, and the ties with Poland too tenuous."

"It appears that polite enquiries were made every ten years or so," Jeffrey replied. "With each new cardinal or king, the question was raised. How would it appear in the eyes of the world if it was learned that such a relic were no longer in Rome? In time, though, as Poland's preeminence continued, an agreement was reached. What was important to Cracow was that they had the relic. What was important to Rome was that the people thought it was still in the Vatican. So without actually saying as much, Cracow agreed never to make public the fact that the chalice they had was indeed the reliquary."

"And in the more than three hundred years since the switch was made, there has been time for the secret to be forgotten," Alexander concluded. "And now that the millennium approaches, there is pressure to bring the reliquary back to Rome."

"Again, all this could be true only if the second legend is the valid one," Jeffrey went on. "But I think it is, and so does Rokovski. At the least he said it was worth pursuing to the end. It also appeared that he was on to something else. But it was only half worked out, and Rokovski refused to tell me what he was thinking. All he would say was that he hoped to have something positive to report to you upon his return from Rome."

"This indeed is a night filled with good news." Alexander's tone sounded lighter than it had in weeks. "Find out from him when he expects to return to Cracow, if you would. I shall be there myself to greet him."

"I'll call him first thing tomorrow morning."

"Splendid. Now tell me, how are your other activities proceeding?"

"Business is great. We've picked up some excellent new pieces."

"Not new in the strictest sense, I hope," he said, smiling at his own jest.

"No." Jeffrey smiled too, then hesitated, and finally told him about Katya and his visit to the hospital and their decision to work on equipping a new premature birth unit.

When he stopped, Alexander released a long sigh. "My dear Jeffrey, I find myself deeply touched by your act."

"It was Katya's idea, really."

"Do not do yourself a disservice. Already you two are beginning to join in true union. The idea of one is given life by the actions of both." Alexander's voice softened. "And such actions. Yes, you have given me great food for thought, my friend. So. You shall speak with Rokovski and then call me tomorrow? Splendid. Then I shall bid you a good-night."

I t has taken me over a day to obtain this connection to Schwerin," Erika declared once she had Kurt on the telephone.

"I would far rather fight with operators than have to do what I have done," Kurt replied. "Which is sit on my hands."

"Waiting is pure agony," Erika agreed.

"Especially when there is nothing but doubt for company."

"I told you I could be trusted."

"Yes, you did that."

Erika paused, acquiesced, "Were I in your place, I would feel no different."

"Your honesty is most reassuring."

A muffled voice spoke from the distance. "Ferret is reminding me again."

"No doubt."

"To business, then." She kept her voice brisk, determinedly calm. "The transfer has been made."

Though expected and hoped for, the news brought with it an electric stab. He had to stop and breathe before asking, "All of it?"

"So many zeros," Erika replied. "You cannot imagine how it feels to stand in such a place, one of the grandest banks in the world, and look at a number that large."

Kurt searched as far inward as he ever allowed himself, found only doubt and worry and fear. "And here I stand," he said bitterly. "My passport is in the hands of others, and there you are, looking at all those zeros."

"It boggles the mind."

"No doubt," he agreed. For a moment, he felt the fear give way to a certainty of ruin, and in that brief instant Kurt felt a bonding with the old colonel and his tired, defeated air. "Never have I felt more helpless, or more alone."

"Such a confession," Erika remarked.

"At least you have the decency to act surprised."

"I am surprised because it is exactly as Ferret predicted," she replied. "He has arranged a suitable reply. Do you have pen and paper?"

"What for?"

"Do you have it?" A little sharper this time.

"Wait." Then, "All right. Go ahead."

"Write this down," she said, and proceeded to give him a bank's name and a Zurich address, followed by a telephone number, then two longer numbers.

"Do you have it?"

"What is it?"

"Our bank. The first set of numbers is your account. They have been instructed that you will either call or fax and request confirmation of a deposit."

"A what?"

"A deposit. A large one. Very large. Your share of the proceeds, to be exact. You are to give them this second number, which is your access code."

The flood of relief left him utterly weak. "You have done this?"

"Deliver the treasure map to Poland," Erika replied. "Then come to Switzerland. It is time to begin your new life."

Before traveling to meet Alexander at the airport, Jeffrey accompanied Katya on a stroll through Cracow's old city to the Marian Church. A placard of postcards for sale stood beside the church entrance, staffed by a smiling rheumy-eyed woman in a gray wool dress and headkerchief. The pictures were of Polish winter scenes—a heavily laden horse cart, children walking a snowy forest path, icicles growing from an ancient thatched farmhouse, mountain passes, descents into steep ravines, sunset forests lit like a stained-glass chapel. In the center was a handwritten card, the script shaky and uneven as from a very old hand.

"What does the card say?" Jeffrey wondered.

"'If you allow,'" Katya read, "'every experience will become part of the path that leads you to God.'"

Jeffrey stared into the face of the old woman and found a light in her ancient, teary eyes, a force and a sureness that left her untouched by his stare and his silent questions. She was content to stand and stare back, allow him to feed on her gaze.

"We need to go now," Katya finally said, "if we're going to have time to pray before your meeting."

Reluctantly Jeffrey followed. As he entered the immense eleventh-century oak doors, he turned to find the crone still watching him. She withdrew one hand from the folds of her wrap and pointed a twisted finger toward the card. He nodded his understanding.

Katya was waiting for him just inside the church. She asked, "Could we go sit up there?"

"No, you go on ahead."

She inspected his face. "Are you . . . is everything all right?"

"I'm fine," he replied. "I just want to stand here for a while."

"I'll be near the front," Katya said quietly, and moved up the aisle.

Although the church was ringed by vast expanses of stained glass, fifty years of soot and grime considerably dimmed the light that was permitted entry. The murky quality of this illumination was in keeping with the interior's darkened confines. Brilliant gilt work had faded over the centuries. Ceiling mosaics, once glimmering with a hundred different hues, now lay in a half-seen distance. The central cross, rising up a full seventy feet above the nave, seemed to float of its own accord. Through the gloomy light, the Christ figure gazed out and down across the eight hundred years since it first was raised.

As the afternoon faded, low-slung chandeliers were lit. Jeffrey watched people come and go, their hands clasped before them, their faces set in repose made gentle both by inward thoughts and soft lighting. The church's higher reaches became lost entirely. Jeffrey craned and searched and caught sight of lofty shadows and half-seen images, glimpses of a heaven close only to believers, visible only to the eyes of a love-filled heart.

Even in the slow afternoon hours between Masses, the church remained almost half full. Silent prayers charged the atmosphere and heightened the sense of mystery. Candles flickered before the three dozen altars tucked in side alcoves, and within stands surrounding the vast pillars. Penitents stood or knelt or sat, hands entwined in rosaries or still in laps or supporting burdened foreheads.

Jeffrey searched the faces that came and went, wishing he could somehow capture in paint the beauty he found there—their intensity of concentration, their histories of suffering, their peace, their joy. Young and old, men and women, entered and knelt and spoke to the Invisible whose Spirit filled Jeffrey's heart as he watched. In that moment he loved them all. And with the flood of caring came the realization that the love he felt was not his own.

In time, he walked forward to join Katya in prayer.

"I've never seen a church so full except for services," he said upon their departure.

"People have no place else to pray," Katya replied. "They live crammed together in apartments meant for half their number, as many as three generations in three rooms. In some families there is no quiet time, in others there is only one believer who is not given space for prayer, not even a closet. Some are scoffed at and ridiculed. The church is their island, their refuge, their place to come and sit in peace and talk to God."

===

Alexander arrived, showing his normal post-flight blues. When Jeffrey started to tell him that Rokovski had arrived the day before, he waved the words aside, saying that the situation was too important to waste upon a mind that was not yet functioning. Jeffrey bore the burden of his news in silence all the way back into town, deposited Alexander in his room, and wore a track in the downstairs carpet until the appointed hour. He and Katya arrived at Alexander's room just as the secondhand ticked into place.

Alexander opened the door with a flourish. "Excellent. The tea has just been delivered. Come in, come in."

He was wearing a neatly pressed dark suit, a starched white shirt, a discreetly striped silk tie. His color was excellent. "I hope you will excuse my concern for privacy, but I find public rooms to be no place for such discussions."

"You are looking extremely well," Katya said, taking the offered chair.

"Thank you, my dear. I must say, I am feeling better than I have in weeks. Perhaps you would be so good as to pour."

Once tea had been served, Alexander gave Jeffrey a brief smile. "You had best deliver the news before you burst."

"We leave for Czestochowa at four o'clock tomorrow morning," he announced.

Gray eyes sparked with interest. "The key to the mystery has been delivered, then."

"It better have been," Jeffrey replied, eyebrows raised.

"Rokovski is laying his professional life on the line for this," Katya explained. "If the treasure isn't there, the best he can hope for is a posting to some provincial backwater."

"You both have seen him?"

"Yesterday late afternoon and again this morning," Jeffrey said. "He hasn't slowed down since his return from Rome."

"Speaking of which," Alexander said, "did he mention what he discovered while there?"

"Only that it was good news," Katya replied, "and that his impressions about Karlovich were confirmed."

"He prefers to tell you himself," Jeffrey said. "He asks that you please have patience until after this other matter has been settled."

"But he did say that the time for worry was over," Katya added, "at least so far as the chalice is concerned."

"So there was a reliquary," Alexander said, leaning back in visible relief.

"It looks to me as if Karlovich knew there was one all along," Jeffrey said.

"I would wager that at any odds," Alexander agreed. "He was probably one of very few people alive in all Poland who did. A keeper of secrets passed down from curate to curate over three centuries."

"We played right into his hands, didn't we?" Katya said.

"Indeed we did," Alexander replied. "Our request to have a selection of Polish religious art for the gala, coming as it did through the proper channels, was the perfect way for the reliquary to depart from Poland."

"You mean Karlovich already had some deal worked out with the Vatican to return the reliquary?" Jeffrey asked.

"That would certainly appear to be a possibility," Alexander replied. "Though only Rokovski shall be able to say for sure."

"And they made the switch in London?" Jeffrey continued.

Alexander shook his head. "I very much doubt it. I would imagine that yet another emissary from Rome appeared some time ago, one who did not share the current Pope's Polish heritage, and who wanted the relic returned to its rightful place."

"Maybe even at the request of Karlovich," Katya suggested.

"That would be my guess," Alexander agreed. "A man in his position would no doubt have numerous contacts within the Vatican museum structure."

"Not priests," Katya said.

"Most certainly not. A curate such as Karlovich would consider himself a man apart and would seek people of like station and mind. No, the emissary on this occasion would probably have been the equivalent of a Vatican civil servant, puffed up with his own importance, a petty power seeker intent on furthering his own career by announcing the completion of such a coup." Alexander sipped his tea. "It is probably a very good thing for my soul that I shall never have an occasion to meet this person face-to-face."

"So the curate and the emissary met and discussed the millennium event," Jeffrey said. "And then, just as they're trying to figure out a way to get the reliquary back to Rome, up we pop. What do you think was Karlovich's motive?"

"Money," Katya decided.

"Most likely," Alexander agreed. "You see, Jeffrey, a curate is a man without power, yet charged with weighty responsibilities. He manages the church cleaning staff. He pays all bills. He handles all supplies. He arranges for all day-to-day operations such as cooking and feeding and housing the priests. He must put into effect all necessary repairs to the church. And a church of this size and age, neglected as it has been for over five decades, must be in desperate need of major repairs. So here we have a man facing financial pressures, with no one in this new capitalist regime to whom he could turn." Alexander shrugged. "And who knows? Perhaps he felt his first loyalty was to Rome, and decided that here was a means of killing two birds with one stone. So he called a colleague within the caverns burrowed beneath the Vatican, met with him and discussed the reliquary, then waited for his chance."

"There are probably records kept of all visiting emissaries," Katya presumed.

Alexander gave her an approving nod. "Which Rokovski's researches no doubt uncovered. I would imagine that he has had an interesting time in Rome."

"Not half as interesting as what's happened since he got back," Jeffrey replied. "Oh, yes. He asked me to tell you that he will not even attempt to thank you for the loan."

"Ah, the other matter." Alexander sighed luxuriously. "Such a moment comes seldom to mortal lives, my dear friends. Savor this experience, I urge you. Drink your fill. Allow it to be firmly anchored in your memories, so that you may return to it in darker hours. Here is the anticipation of triumph, the risking of it all upon a hope, a struggle, a decision to seek and if possible to *achieve*. And it is done for that most important of reasons, the type of purpose which gives meaning to the grayest of lives."

"A cause," Jeffrey said.

Alexander's strong gaze rested upon him in solemn approval. "A cause shared with friends, a quest taken on for a higher purpose. That, my young friends, is an essence strong enough to make the blood sing in your veins."

CHAPTER 39

Jeffrey would always think of it as the dawn raid.

Rokovski arrived to pick them up three hours before sunrise, as tired and frantic as a man could be after two days without sleep. He greeted them with a weary shake of the head. "You cannot imagine the problems I have had."

Alexander stood on the hotel's top step and surveyed the mass of men and equipment stretched out in front of him. "I am sure I don't want to know."

There was a trio of cars for Rokovski, Jeffrey, Katya, Alexander, two beribboned officers, a stranger in a quiet gray suit, and Rokovski's three assistants. Beyond them were two police trucks filled with silent, sleepy uniformed figures. Behind these stretched an additional half dozen open-bed trucks bearing shovels, portable lights, pitchforks, drilling equipment, ladders, rubber knee boots, parkas, ropes, and bales of canvas wrapping.

"I do not wish to leave whatever we discover there for one minute longer than necessary," Rokovski explained. "I therefore decided to bring out all the reinforcements I could think of."

"My friend," Alexander declared, "you have worked a miracle."

"I have fought many battles," Rokovski countered.

"And no doubt lit a number of fires under moribund backsides," Alexander agreed.

Rokovski managed a tired smile. "Bonfires. With blowtorches. A number of my illustrious colleagues will work standing up for weeks to come."

"And you have kept this quiet?"

"I found an ally at the highest level," Rokovski explained, leading them down to the waiting convoy. "One who has not yet decided whether to keep the entire Amber Room as a part of our own national heritage, or trade a portion of it in return for vast sums."

"Perhaps even to rid our nation's soil of the pestilence of Soviet troops," Alexander murmured.

Rokovski opened the car door for Alexander. "I see that great minds think alike."

He walked around to the other side, slammed his door shut, motioned for the driver to be away, and continued. "I have resigned myself to perhaps being permitted to keep only a few of the panels. This is to be expected. In return for allowing the politicians to place portions of this room upon the chessboard of international politics, however, I shall gain immense conditions."

"If the amber is there," Jeffrey muttered.

"I no longer have the freedom," Rokovski replied gravely, "even to permit such a doubt to surface."

Czestochowa was wrapped in sleepy silence as they ground their way through dimly lit streets. They followed the directions that Rokovski had translated and typed and kept fingering and reading and perusing. They stopped before the series of shops fronting the broad Jasna Gora lawn, where two additional police cars awaited them. Rokovski and one of the uniformed officers traveling in the second car walked over. The waiting officers snapped to attention. Papers were exchanged and examined, salutes traded. Rokovski turned and motioned for them to alight. The officers went to organize their men.

"We must act as swiftly as possible," Rokovski stressed quietly. "There are too many conflicting lines of interest, both with the treasure and with the place they chose for depositing it."

"It would be far better for all concerned to inform them of an act already completed," Alexander agreed.

"Exactly." Rokovski cast a nervous eye back to where the unloading of equipment brought the occasional clatter. He waved back into the dark as an officer softly called out, "Please go back to where my colleague waits. All of you will be equipped with rubber boots and flashlights."

When they returned, he inspected them briefly, spoke into the darkness where dozens of lights flickered and bounced and wavered up the hillside. An answering call came quietly back. "Very well," Rokovski said. "Let us begin."

They walked up the lawn alongside the cobblestone path. But where the battlements marked the road's passage through the first high portico, Rokovski motioned with his flashlight for them to descend to the base of the empty moat. "Careful here. You will need to use the hand ropes and proceed cautiously. The ground is very slippery."

One by one they grasped ropes held by soldiers and reversed themselves down the icy grass-lined slope. Jeffrey helped Alexander as he landed clumsily, then turned and assisted Katya, smiling at the excitement in her eyes. Rokovski was already reaching up and inspecting the barred window-like openings, each about four feet square, that once had delivered the medieval city's sewage and rain runoff into the moat. Suddenly he gave a muffled cry, dropped his flashlight, reached up with both hands, and wrenched at one iron-bar frame. Swiftly other hands arrived to assist; together they lifted the heavy bars free and settled them on the ground.

No more light was needed to show the fervor that gripped Rokovski as he called softly up into the darkness, then waited for a ladder to be slid down the embankment. It was propped into position, then Rokovski signaled to Alexander. "My friend, if you wish, the honor is yours."

"It is enough simply to be here," Alexander replied. "Go, my friend. Go."

Rokovski counted out several people who were to follow him, then leaped up the rungs and disappeared into the hole. The leading officer half bowed toward Alexander and motioned him forward. After him came Katya, then Jeffrey. The excitement was electric as he climbed the rungs and entered the dark, dank space. Jeffrey's feet hit ankle-deep water as he slid into the low tunnel. Rokovski was already proceeding down the depths, his flashlight illuminating tiny cantering circles of slimy ancient wall. One by one they followed him in a stooped position, craning to keep his bobbing light in view.

The floor gave an unexpected drop, and filthy water began pouring in over the top of Jeffrey's boots. He heard the squeaks of tiny animals—rats or bats or both—in nearby crevices, but had time neither for worry nor discomfort. Even Katya was hurrying forward as swiftly as caution and the mucky liquid would permit.

Without warning the tunnel joined with another and rose high enough to permit them to stand upon a dry surface. The ceiling became lofty, arched in stone and age-old brick. They paused long enough to empty their boots, then pushed on.

Another turning, yet another muffled shout from Rokovski. They rushed forward, saw him standing before an opening recently hacked from what before had been a crudely finished corner of the turning. Heaped in a half-hidden alcove was an uncountable number of human remains, now little more than bones and rags. Rokovski stood and shone his light upon them for a long moment, then raised his eyes to the waiting group and spoke solemnly in Polish. Katya translated his words. "I cannot avenge their death. But I can seek to give it meaning. On my honor, their tale will be told, and panels of what they died to keep hidden will remain in Poland, as testimony to those who come after."

"On my honor," Alexander agreed solemnly.

Rokovski bent and stepped through the opening, then emitted a long sigh. The group crowded in behind him. Jeffrey clambered through the opening and straightened to find himself facing row after row of coffin-like chests. They were stacked five and six high, lining the aged bulwark. It was possible to see in the distance where the false wall that the slain workers had been forced to build joined with the ancient original.

One chest lay open and spilled at their feet, its corroded and dirt-encrusted surface battered with shiny streaks from a recent fury of hammer blows. Fist-sized blocks of amber, still flecked with bits of yellowed paper and rotten matting, lay scattered in the grime of centuries.

Rokovski raised his arms up to gather in the multitude of chests and spoke in a fierce whisper that Katya translated.

"Behold, my friends. Behold, the Amber Room!"

They waited in the darkness just beyond the light surrounding the Cracow airport. Every breath Jeffrey and Katya took sent plumes of white into the star-studded night. He shivered, partly from the cold, more from what he knew was to come.

One moment they were alone, the next the man with the pock-marked face was standing before them. His eyes continually scanned the night as he thrust a gloved hand outward and spoke in a voice as dead as his eyes.

"He wants his papers," Katya said quietly.

Silently Jeffrey handed over the man's passport. He caught a flicker of surprise, as though the man had not expected it to be so easy, for it to come without a struggle. He riffled the pages as though unsure of his next step, then turned and started for the airport.

Jeffrey knew he was going to do it, had known since Gregor had first spoken the words. Even before, perhaps, though this he could not explain. What Gregor had told him to do was mirrored somewhere deep within, and the willingness to recognize this fact had shattered him. Left him unable to refuse. To do anything but what this new heart budding within his chest was quietly demanding.

Which was to speak. "Katya, tell him I have something else to say."

Reluctantly the man turned back toward them. Katya looked at Jeffrey in confusion, but for a brief moment he could not speak. The instant was so short as to outwardly appear as only a hesitation. But for him, in that instant, Jeffrey felt the realization rush up and up and up from a heart suddenly filled with a blinding white power that *demanded* release. "Tell him that there is an answer to his every need, to his every doubt and fear and worry." He took a breath and finished, "And that answer is Jesus Christ."

Katya hesitated before beginning the translation. When Jeffrey refused to drop his eyes to hers, her small hand shivered its way into his grasp. But there was no room just then for more than a comforting squeeze. The moment was locked in stillness. The seed was being planted. The call was being made.

When she had said the words, Jeffrey continued, "You need to confess that your ways have been the wrong ones, and that neither answers nor lasting peace have been found. You need to turn to the giver of peace and ask Him into your life."

Katya spoke, stopped. The man did not move, his gaze showing nothing but the same perpetual hostility.

In the silence of that eternal moment, Jeffrey felt his entire being struck by invisible lightning. He heard the voice of his heart well up with the power of unspoken wisdom. The power cracked open the lies of his existence like the shell of a bird now ready to emerge, and grow, and fly.

Jeffrey stood and saw the man's self-centered darkness, the dull, lightless world of suspicious eyes, the utter ugliness of all he was and thought and did. And in those eyes and in the world behind them, Jeffrey saw himself. With this moment of recognition came the gift of eternal truth, the realization that he, too, was loved. Not for what he had done, nor for the struggles he had made, nor for the searchings. Nor was he to be punished for all the missed opportunities and wrong turnings and false hopes and empty days. Or sins. All the sins of his life that were reflected in the man's empty eyes.

He was simply loved for the promise of who he was and who he could be. An eternal child of God. A man made clean and whole.

In the angry bitterness of a wounded, hateful man, in this pair of empty eyes was the answer Jeffrey had been seeking all his life. He found assurance that the Lord's offer was made to *everyone*. None were too far from the fold. None were unworthy. Not even himself.

And with this realization came the ability to love. To give, to accept, to be lost in a moment that reached out in all directions with a force that left him unable to remember what about this man had angered him before.

"As far as the East is from the West," Jeffrey said, and the calmness was not his own, nor the quietness that left him steady despite a furiously beating heart. A truth pressed upward from the deepest fiber of his being, yearning for the release of giving, the gift of passing on what was not his, yet his forever, to another in need. "That is how far you can be from all the troubles and sins in your life if only you will give yourself to Jesus Christ."

The words were more than sounds of the mouth and thoughts of the mind. They were the only way he could give purpose to the love welling up in his chest. Not love for this man. Love. Without direction and without claim and without a need to be confined or measured or given against expected return. Love.

Jeffrey listened to Katya translate his words with a voice made small and shivery by more than the cold. He looked into the eyes that squinted back in undisguised hostility. And he felt the love pour out and say with a clarity that went beyond all words, all doubt, all worry, all fear, all unworthy feelings—he stood and looked and *knew* that here was another brother his Lord yearned to call home.

And he was too full of newfound truth to feel the slightest scarring as the pockmarked man sneered and snorted and turned away.

Instead, Jeffrey reached out an open hand and called to the retreating back, "I will pray for you!"

Katya's words followed, and the man hesitated, then moved on into the dark.

———

Kurt arrived in Zurich a very angry man.

The corridor leading from the satellite terminal to the main hub of the airport was almost a quarter of a mile long. It ran beneath several runways, a gently curving tunnel of spotless white stretching ahead as far as he could see. He did not need to walk. A smoothly running automatic walkway sprang lightly beneath his feet. Classical music played soothing strains along the entire distance. Instead of windows, enormous backlit displays advertised all the things that before had remained beyond his wildest dreams, and which now were within his grasp. All of them. From the gold watch to the lakefront resort to the mountain ski holiday to the luxurious clothes to the rented sports car to the private helicopter service. All of it could now be his.

And yet all he could think of was that strange American and the insanity of his final words. It consumed him.

He felt like pounding his fists against the gleaming white walls.

Just when he should have been readying himself for the good life, a barb had been wedged in his flesh at heart level. With every step he came closer to losing control, to shouting his unexplained rage to the unseen heavens. Try as he might, he could not shake off the words. They rang in his head over and over and over, lancing at his reason in ways he could neither understand nor stop. He felt helpless, caught up in something that made no sense to him at all.

The tunnel's end appeared in the distance. Kurt picked up his single valise and marched forward, shrugging hard at the resounding pressure in his mind and heart. He would leave this barbed message behind, it and the messenger both, and enter the new life that awaited him. The life he had always dreamed of. The life he deserved.

Wait until he told the others about the crazy American.

When Jeffrey arrived downstairs the next morning on his way to Gregor's, he was surprised to find Alexander up and waiting for him. "I was wondering if you might permit me to accompany you this morning."

"It would be an honor," he replied.

Together they exchanged the hotel's stuffy warmth for a bracing dawn breeze. Clouds scuttled overhead through a sky touched with the first faintest hues of the coming sun. A silver moon hung calm and peaceful upon the horizon, touching all the world with silver mystery. "Katya does not mind your traipsing off each morning on your own?"

"A little," Jeffrey admitted. "But she knows how much it means to me, and she doesn't complain."

"An act of wisdom far beyond her years," Alexander replied. "You are most fortunate in your choice of mates, my friend."

"I'm not sure how much I had to do with it," Jeffrey said. "It's always felt like a gift from above."

"Yet who was it who endured the difficult beginning, who sought answers beyond what was evident?" Alexander strode forward with a light heart. "Who made the choice to abide despite pain and emotional hardship? Who loved in defiance of logic? Who sought answers beyond the known and the comfortable?"

"You are giving me a great honor," Jeffrey said quietly.

"None that is not deserved. I am most proud of your endeavors, both with the young lady and with your work." He pulled his scarf up around his neck. "As for myself, I seem to learn my greatest lessons in the loneliest of hours."

"As I do," Jeffrey agreed. "Some of them, anyway. I hope it's not some unwritten requirement for being a Christian."

"Oh, I think not. In my case, it is a need that I force upon myself. So long as all is well in my world, I feel little urge to struggle with uncomfortable questions." He glanced Jeffrey's way. "I have found myself comparing my own searchings with yours. I wish I had your strength of purpose."

Alexander stopped further conversation by taking a sprightly step up Gregor's front stairs and pressing the buzzer. The latch released; he pushed through, held the door for Jeffrey, then proceeded up the stairs.

Once tea had been served and Gregor was settled back in his bed, Alexander confessed cheerfully, "Your unspoken lesson has come through loud and clear, Cousin."

"It was neither my lesson nor my voice," Gregor replied mildly. "And you should not belittle the gift by failing to recognize the Giver."

Alexander remained silent for a time, sipping at his tea. "Why do I have such difficulty in accepting that I have heard God's silent voice?" he asked after a while.

"Because you are human." Gregor smiled with genuine warmth. "You continue to surprise me, my dear Cousin."

"Not nearly so much as I surprise myself."

"No doubt." He reached over to pat Alexander's shoulder. "Nothing you might say could please me more, nor make me more proud of you."

"A compliment." Alexander showed mock surprise. "I do hope you are not suffering from a fever, Cousin."

"You go against all of your worldly heritage to ask such a question," Gregor replied with a shake of his head. "Now, tell me what lesson you have learned."

"My lesson. Yes, well." Alexander sipped from his glass. "I have spent numerous sleepless hours watching helplessly as my reputation was threatened, my life's work torn asunder. And all because of a chalice that was not mine, for a gala I took on for others. Or at least, so I thought."

"Such honesty." Gregor smiled. "Go on, dear Cousin."

"I have found the hours before dawn to be a powerful mirror," Alexander said. "Most powerful. I have seen how much of what I did was for selfish pride, and pride alone."

"You cannot imagine how your words stir the soul," Gregor told him.

Alexander turned sharp gray eyes Jeffrey's way. "And then a certain young friend tells me of a project he and his fiancée have begun in a nameless children's hospital, out of sight of all publicity, in a crumbling corner of a region so polluted it is known as the Triangle of Death. He does not tell me with pride. No. He is embarrassed. Moved so deeply by the need he has discovered in an alien land that he is ashamed of his feelings. He tells me because he wishes to share his discovery with a friend. Yet he does so with shame for his own emotions, and with fear that I may scoff. He does not say so, but I hear it in his voice. And what he does not know, what he cannot imagine, is that he shames me. He *humbles* me. He *teaches* me. Not with words. No. Such a lesson cannot be taught by any means save example. He stands before the altar and honors the Father with a gift made with no expectation of receiving anything in return."

Alexander nodded solemnly. "I listened to my young friend heed the call of his Lord, and I learned. I realized that the missing chalice was part of a lesson. I understood that I might also grow through the gift of humble, nameless service. Out of the light of publicity. Away from the adulating crowds. In the lonely reaches of others' needs. Where the Father's voice might be more clearly heard."

M y friends! Come in, come in!" A jubilant Pavel Rokovski ushered Alexander, Jeffrey, and Katya into his office. "Champagne is called for, but perhaps at this hour you would prefer tea."

"Tea would be splendid," Alexander replied for them all.

"One moment, then." He soon returned and served them. "So much to tell, so very much. Where on earth to begin?"

"With the chalice," Alexander replied. "Please tell me that the mystery is solved."

"More than solved! Providence has been at work here, my friends." Rokovski pulled up a chair. "You heard of my discoveries?"

"About Karlovich, yes. But only that you discovered you were right to distrust him."

"That man." Rokovski shook his head. "He deserves to enjoy his retirement within a prison cell. He was in contact with a Vatican emissary—not a priest, however. What is the English word for niebieski ptaszek?"

"Literally it translates as a little bird," Katya replied, and exchanged glances with Jeffrey. "But it really means a peon, a scoundrel. Someone who lives off the importance of others."

"Thank you. Yes, we made several fascinating discoveries about this mysterious Vatican *aparatchik*, and these were what prompted me to travel to Rome. There I had a most interesting visit with a certain Signor Buracci, the highest official within the Vatican museum system who is not a cleric. He answers directly to the cardinal. I asked him if he might shed light on a most curious set of circumstances."

"I do wish I could have been a fly on the wall for that discussion," Alexander murmured.

"I explained to him of our careful records," Rokovski went on. "And I asked about certain things that surprised me no end. My attitude was one of requesting information, asking questions, seeking guidance."

"Most politely."

"And humbly," Rokovski agreed. "These discoveries we have made were most confusing to a simple mind such as my own, and I simply sought his lofty guidance."

"Including the confusing matters surrounding a certain curate."

"Well, yes. That was one of my questions. Why was it, I asked, that our Mr. Karlovich traveled twice to Rome in the past year, and that a certain emissary, one Signor Danilo Disertori, visited Cracow three times? The first was two months before Karlovich loaned you the chalice, the second three days after it left for display in England, and the third the day after it was returned."

"And discovered to be a fake."

"I had a further question," Rokovski continued, "about the transfer of funds from the Banco Sao Paolo to Karlovich's account here in Cracow of fifty thousand dollars. The Banco Sao Paolo, as you may know, handles the Vatican's commercial transactions."

"About this time," Alexander said, "I would imagine the good gentleman is finding his collar most constricting."

"He did appear to have great difficulty in speaking," Rokovski agreed.

"You didn't involve the Pope."

"Of course not," Rokovski answered, hugely satisfied. "It was not even necessary to suggest that I would do so."

"Everyone knew," Katya offered.

Rokovski smiled her way. "And positively trembled at the thought."

"So," Alexander nodded, the sparkle back in his eyes. "What happens now?"

"Now there will be a vast public announcement of Poland's magnificent gift, which will be displayed at the millennium celebration in Rome. It will then be returned with great fanfare to become the centerpiece of our new Museum for Religious Artifacts in Cracow, which will be officially opened in time for its arrival." Rokovski's gleam turned hard. "All the while these mysterious documents remain locked in a very safe place, and certain individuals in Rome and Cracow will be urged to consider an early retirement."

"I shall not miss them," Alexander declared.

"No, nor I," Rokovski agreed, and his vast good humor returned. "There is more. In this great central hall will be displayed three outstanding paintings, loaned by the Vatican for an indefinite time, to commemorate this wonderful new museum. A Raphael, a Da Vinci, and a Michelangelo."

"Magnificent," Alexander proclaimed, clapping his hands. "A worthy recognition of our nation's new renaissance."

"You know, of course, what will adorn the galley leading to this chamber."

"Panels from the Amber Room," Jeffrey breathed. "What an awesome place this is going to be."

Rokovski nodded his agreement. "There is still more."

"How so?"

"It appears that in their haste," Rokovski explained, "our mysterious treasure hunters miscounted the number of chests."

"Miscounted?"

"There happened to be seventy-three." Rokovski watched their reaction with immense satisfaction. "Yes. And since no one outside my office knew exactly how many the Amber Room required, this last chest remains a secret known only to me and my most trusted allies." The gleam in Rokovski's dark eyes was blinding. "This extra chest, my friends, was filled with gold and jewelry and ornaments."

"A treasure chest?" Alexander was at full alert.

"Much of secondary quality," Rokovski replied, "at least from an art collector's standpoint. Chosen in haste, no doubt, by one with an untrained eye who selected on the basis of their weight in gold and the size of the stones. There is very little that we shall want to display, but the remaining items would fetch a handsome sum on the open market. If only we might find a dealer in the West willing to represent us in the utmost confidentiality."

"We accept," Alexander replied with alacrity. "It will be an honor."

"Splendid. The proceeds shall first go to repaying your most generous loan." Rokovski stood. "Of course the personal debt shall remain with us always."

"There is no debt," Alexander replied. "Not between friends."

Rokovski nodded his understanding and extended his hand. "Or patriots."

ACKNOWLEDGMENTS

My habit of writing rather lengthy acknowledgments has grown from my desire to recognize the many people who have given generously of their time and of themselves in the development of my books. From the idea stage through research, writing, editing, and promotion, the most valuable aspect of my work is the personal contact with people willing to share, and teach, from the heart. I would like to express my sincere thanks to all those who have contributed to my books in so many ways.

In this regard, I must extend a special thanks to the readers of my books. Writing can be a rather solitary pursuit, especially in a foreign country. Your cards and letters, as well as our brief meetings at promotional events, brighten my days and encourage me more than you may know. I am absolutely thrilled to learn a particular passage has touched you deeply, or that you learned a valuable lesson, or even that you lack sleep because you proverbially "couldn't put it down." I know from you that you even read the fine print in the back of the book, the acknowledgments section, to learn how the book was developed, to seek advice from the suggested counselor, or to contribute to a named cause from helping the homeless to combatting pornography.

If you would like to write to me, please do so care of my Web site at the end of the Acknowledgements. I do try hard to answer all correspondence, but being a professional writer is much like running a small business; I always have more to do than I have hours in the day. I will try to respond as best I can.

===

As with *Florian's Gate*, this book has been enriched by the open-hearted support of my wife Isabella's family in Cracow and Warsaw. I will refrain from mentioning all of them a second time, yet a few must be remembered for a special reason. Marian and Dusia Tarka, together with Olek and Halinka Tarka, went out of their way to help me at every turn. They offered their usual hospitality and made me feel part of their extended family. Regrettably, I arrived in Cracow to do research on this book having been struck by food poisoning in Dresden earlier that week. My suffering later proved to be a liver disorder. Not only did they do their utmost to nurse me back to health, but they also took it upon themselves to become additional eyes and ears and arms and legs, helping me with much work that I was too weak to do myself. I am deeply indebted to them for this invaluable support.

Thanks must also go to Isabella's aunt in Warsaw, Dr. Teresa Aleksandrowicz, chief surgeon at one of the city's hospitals, who saw my return to a level of fitness that made traveling back to London possible. Jan and Haluta Zorawski opened their home to us during this difficult period, and laced their concern with a splendid sense of humor. Laughter truly is the best medicine.

As for all my books based within Eastern Europe, my wife's assistance has been absolutely indispensable. I remain humbled by her ability to give with such loving patience, by her wisdom, and by her love. Thank you, Izia, for enriching both my life and my work.

Much of the information that went into developing the Solidarity photographer came from my wife and her family. Isabella was traveling from Warsaw to Cracow the morning that Martial Law was declared in December of 1981, and became caught up in the heart of the army-imposed darkness. Members of her family, as all Poles, each had his own story to tell. For their patient sharing I am truly grateful.

The story of the vision within a prison cell, however, came from a businessman with whom I worked several years ago. As managing director of a major Italian confectionery company, he was kidnapped by Red Brigade terrorists eighteen years ago and held for ransom. His prison was an extremely cramped tent, erected in a dark closet, from which he was not permitted to move for almost three weeks. Three days before his release, as he was battling a despair similar to the photographer's, he had a vision of a place he had never seen before, and a gift of God's peace. The remainder of his story mirrors that of the photographer, except the vision he had was of the Island of Capri seen from the window of a friend's house on the Bay of Naples—a place he had never before visited.

Dr. Wlodzimierz M. Borkowski is the Director of the Pediatric Division of the Narutowicza Hospital in Cracow. Dr. Grazyna Gabor is a pediatrician in this department. They provided a detailed overview of both their own hospital and the general state of children's care in Poland. The conversation held during Jeffrey and Katya's visit to the children's hospital was the same one I had with the doctors during my own visit. I was most impressed with their kindness and their dedication.

Dr. Borkowski was also one of the leading authorities filmed in the BBC's "State of Europe" program on the dangers of pollution in Eastern Europe. He shared with me a copy of this program; it provided a wealth of background information that went into forming this story.

The situation within the children's hospitals in the region of Poland known as the Triangle of Death is just as it is described in this book. Premature births and pollution-related illnesses place severe pressures on their already limited financial resources. The equipment described in this book is urgently required. If any reader knows of a hospital that is upgrading their children's ward and has surplus used equipment available, please be so kind as to let us know.

The grisly stories about the former secret police in East Germany and its current status are based on true accounts and recently released German exposes. Gary Johnson, publisher at Bethany House, suggested blending some "missing Stasi spy files" into what was then just an idea for the sequel to *Florian's Gate*. As ever, I am indebted to our many friends and colleagues at BHP.

Lupoid Von Wedel, former Director for Eastern Europe of the Matuschka Investment Group in Munich, has in recent months been appointed managing director of a multi-billion dollar heavy industries conglomerate in former East Germany. Lupoid was born in the area of Poland known as Upper Silesia. He is a good friend, and has been most kind in relating both the circumstances of his early childhood and the trauma of leaving behind a war-torn Poland. I am also most grateful for his current assessment of the economic and political situation in Poland and the former East Germany.

Barbara Beck, Press Attaché with the German Embassy in London, was most helpful with background information on the search for the Amber Room. She also supplied contacts in both Erfurt and Weimar.

H. Reichmann is the new Director of Art Union Gmbh, the antique store on the Erfurter Bridge which was used as the antiques store in this novel. I am indeed grateful for his detailed chronicle of his own shop, the other nearby buildings, and the bridge itself.

Dr. Schleiff is Director of the *Erfurter Landesamt für Denkmalpflege,* which translates literally as the "Erfurt city authority for the care of memories," and means essentially the preservation of monuments and buildings. He offered very valuable insight into the current search for the Amber Room.

Joachim Vogel is Press Attaché to the Lord Mayor of Weimar, and while maintaining a professionally detached view to the whole affair is passionately interested in the Amber Room and all the interconnected mysteries. He was most kind in assisting with general information and valuable contacts.

There is only one color photograph of the Amber Room in existence today. A copy of this was loaned to me by Weimar resident Hans Stadelmann, who is involved in the current probe into the Nazi bunkers beneath Weimar's Karl Marx Platz (the former plaza for Nazi Party gatherings, soon to receive its third name change in four decades). I am indeed grateful that he offered me this picture, from which this book's front cover was painted. Poring over stacks of yellowed documents and blueprints, he provided an extraordinary account of the Amber Room's passage from the Catherine

Palace in Russia, to Königsberg in Germany, and from there into the mists of unsolved mystery.

Joachim Gommlich is currently Managing Director of Wilhelm Glaudert Gmbh in Düsseldorf. He was born in Berlin and escaped two days before the Wall was finally sealed; by this time the Russian soldiers were no longer permitting people casual passage to the West, so Joachim kissed his mother and father goodbye, and with their blessings took his camera and some pocket money and walked over the border, telling the guards he was on a school photography project. It was the last time he ever saw his parents. The war-end recollections of the Erfurt antique dealer are based on those of Herr Gommlich. I am indeed grateful for his recounting these early memories.

Reverend Seyfarth, the head of the evangelical seminary in Schwerin, granted insight into the faith of the East German people, which proved most valuable in the structuring of both this book and *Florian's Gate*.

To the numerous antiques dealers who have assisted me with both of these books, I extend my heartfelt thanks. All of you have shown remarkable patience with my never-ending stream of questions. I have been truly fortunate to meet so many people who not only know their business but love it as well.

———

I do appreciate hearing from readers. Please feel free to contact me at: www.DavisBunn.com.

THE
PRICELESS
COLLECTION

Book Three

WINTER PALACE

THIS BOOK IS DEDICATED TO

W. LEE BUNN,

BELOVED BROTHER,
TRUSTED FRIEND;

AND TO HIS WONDERFUL WIFE,
PAMELA.

"Of all the burdens Russia has had to bear, heaviest and most relentless of all has been the weight of her past."

TIBOR SZAMUELY
"The Russian Tradition"

"When the sun of publicity shall rise upon Russia, how many injustices will it expose to view! Not only ancient ones, but those which are enacted daily will shock the world."

MARQUIS DE CUSTINE
Visitor to the Russian Nobility
1839

"Everything is collapsing."

MIKHAIL GORBACHEV
In an address to parliament,
August 1991

"The situation before and after the February 1917 revolution is absolutely the contemporary situation in Russia today. There is still hatred for authorities, the same horror of hunger, the same disorder, and so on. It is the same situation."

EDVARD RADZINSKY
Russian Political Historian
In an interview with the
Washington Post, July 1992

"*The fullness of God's salvation cannot be confined to one or several historical patterns, to one or several Christological titles, to one or several doctrines; it can only be told in a varied multitude of stories which tell us what experiences to expect when trusting in Jesus Christ.*"

EDWARD SCHWEIZER

"*How good and pleasant it is
    when brothers live together in unity . . .
For there the LORD bestows his blessing,
    even life forevermore.*"

PSALM 133:1, 3

PROLOGUE

The loudest sound on the dark Saint Petersburg street was that of Peace Corps volunteer Leslie Ann Stevens' shoes scrunching along the grit-encrusted cobblestones.

There was no movement around her, none at all. Leslie Ann resisted the urge to look upward, to search the blank and darkened windows and see if anyone was spying on her. The sensation of being watched remained with her always, downfall of Communism or not.

Beside her, rusting metal latticework lined the Fontanka Canal. Once this neighborhood had been a most prestigious address, boasting winter homes for nobility from the length and breadth of Russia. Now the royal residences were split into rabbit warrens of crumbling, overcrowded apartments, and the canal itself was nothing more than a scummy pool.

As she approached the end of Fontanka, she thought she heard a murmur of voices and shifting footfalls. She stopped, her heart in her throat, and debated going back. Behind her was the safety of the relatively well-lit Nevsky Prospekt. But the other way back to her apartment meant walking almost a mile farther, and she was tired.

Ahead were the former royal stables of the czars. Once it had been a palace in itself, with quarters both for officers and members of the royal household. Now it sheltered the city's fleet of garbage trucks. Leslie Ann searched the blackness ahead of her, saw nothing, and heard no other sound. She decided to continue on her way.

═══

When President Kennedy had established the Peace Corps in the sixties, the organization was intended to assist emerging nations and to contradict the Soviets' accusation that Americans were only interested in profit, in exploitation. Volunteers had been ordered to go forth and proclaim the goodness of both the nation and the people.

In Leslie Ann's view, the survivors of Russia's Communist era were now accepting that message a little too wholeheartedly.

Her host family tended to take everything she said as coming from the mouth of God. As best she could, Leslie Ann tried to explain that not everything in America was perfect. Not everyone drove a brand-new car. Not everyone had a swimming pool in his backyard. Not all citizens could afford to eat prime beef three times a day.

In her halting Russian, Leslie Ann also tried to introduce the family members to the deeply held faith that had brought her to Russia in the first place. She shared her beliefs, led them through a prayer, and gave them a Cyrillic Bible. All the while, though, she had a nagging impression that they listened because of where she came from, not because of the message she was trying to share.

With every passing day, Leslie Ann also felt a chasm growing between her and the other volunteers assigned to the Saint Petersburg area. Some days, in fact, it seemed the only things she had in common with her companions were her age and her training as an English teacher.

As far as she could tell, none of the others who had signed up for two years' duty in Russia shared her faith. She guessed that believers joined Christian evangelical organizations instead of the Peace Corps. But Leslie Ann did not see herself as an evangelist, at least, not in the normal sense. She was an English teacher who loved God and who intended to carry her faith with her all her life, in everything she did. Yet while the Peace Corps allowed her to practice her chosen profession in an exciting foreign land, it also left her totally isolated in beliefs and motives from most of her companions.

The Peace Corps central bulletin board pretty much summed it all up. About a third of the space was given over to helpful hints on how to survive in the crumbling Soviet empire: which street vendor sold fairly fresh meat, who had a new stock of bottled water, where a trustworthy and affordable Russian language teacher might be found, who was stocking toilet paper. The remainder contained offers of parties, overnight love affairs, companions for cross-country wanderings.

Still, its irreverent humor and homegrown cynicism was one of her few connections to Stateside. Like all the other volunteers, Leslie Ann checked it daily. And just a few weeks earlier, the bulletin board had produced solid gold.

That morning she had come into the office to find a new notice pinned in the bottom left-hand corner, announcing church services in English. Although the card had been up less than twenty-four hours, already its borders had been covered with irreverent scrawls.

The pastor turned out to be an American Baptist missionary, the church a series of interconnected rooms in a filthy back-street building. For Leslie Ann Stevens, entering the newly whitewashed makeshift chapel had been like coming home. And in the space of three weeks, the church had become Leslie Ann's island refuge in a sea of bewildering confusion.

Tonight she had broken one of her own safety rules and stayed at the church until after dark. But it was hard to leave the laughter and the warmth and return to the smelly apartment house where her host family—husband and wife, three children, the wife's mother, and the husband's unmarried sister—lived crowded together into three small rooms. The fourth room had been vacated for Leslie Ann in return for the incredible sum of twenty American dollars per month, more than a professional engineer earned in three.

Saturday evenings, a trip to the floor's only communal bathroom meant struggling down a fetid hallway past clusters of teenagers playing mournful guitars and smoking foul-smelling Russian cigarettes, ignoring the slurred curses of men passing around bottles of vodka, flinching at the screams and shouts that punched through thin apartment walls. For Leslie Ann Stevens, Saturday evenings were the most difficult times for her to recall why she had volunteered for a Saint Petersburg assignment in the first place.

Her feeble flashlight beam played across the rubble-strewn street, and she walked as fast as the darkness and the irregular pavement allowed. She arrived at the end of the Fontanka, turned beside the silent royal stables, and faltered.

Up ahead loomed one of the city's numerous winter palaces, built by royal families who controlled hundreds of square miles of land and thousands of serfs. Now its hulking presence was battered by seventy years of Communism. At the front gate, several men hustled to unload a truck. Over the broad central gates, a single flickering bulb in a metal cage swung from a rusty iron rod. The dim light transformed the men into a series of swiftly moving, softly cursing shadows.

To her utter terror, all movement ceased as she came into view. Leslie Ann turned and started to flee back to the church. Then two of the shadows detached themselves and hustled toward her.

She did not even have time to scream.

Jeffrey Sinclair sat on the hard journey-bench, bracing himself against the furious jouncing and squealing turns by gripping the leather overhead strap with one hand and the cold metal edge of Alexander's stretcher with the other. Their siren's howl accompanied the racing engine as they sped through a London summer evening. The medic bent over Alexander's motionless form while flashing lights painted his tense features with ghostly hues of the beyond.

An entirely alien universe flashed by outside the ambulance. Windows tainted by the multitude of tragedies transported within showed glimpses of a hard, cold cityscape. Jeffrey craned and searched for some sign that the hospital was drawing near and found nothing familiar, comfortable, hopeful. Beyond panic, he wondered at this strange world where it took hours and hours and hours in a screaming, jouncing ambulance to arrive at the emergency room.

Several times the medic raised up from his thrusting and prodding and listening to Alexander's chest to shout in some strange tongue at the two drivers up front. The sounds were then repeated into a microphone and repeated back to them through a metallic speaker. Jeffrey understood none of it.

All he could see was the needle in Alexander's bared arm and the closed eyes and the electric voltage exploding his gray-skinned body up in a pantomime of painful exertion.

Jeffrey felt bleak helplessness wrap itself around his own heart and squeeze. And squeeze. And squeeze.

He gripped the end of the stretcher with both hands, leaned over as far as he could, and screamed out the plea, *"BREATHE!"*

No one even looked his way. His action was perfectly in order with the controlled pandemonium holding them all.

The hospital appeared, announced by a dual shout from both people in front. The driver misjudged the emergency room entrance and hit the curb so hard that Jeffrey's head slammed into the unpadded metal roof. Stars exploded in his head.

The ambulance stopped and the back doors slammed open. Impatient hands threw him out and aside with practiced motions. Through blurred eyes Jeffrey saw the stretcher slapped onto a gurney and wheeled away. He reached forward, but his rubber legs would not follow. They could not.

He did not know how long he stood there before the perky little nurse came out to ask, "Did you come with the gentleman with the heart?"

He nodded, then groaned aloud as the movement sent a painful lance up his neck. He gripped the ambulance's open door for support.

"Don't worry yourself so," the nurse said, misunderstanding his reaction. "You'll only make matters worse, going on like this. The gentleman needs your strength just now."

His eyes did not seem to want to focus. He strained, saw the young woman growing steadily more impatient, then his eyes watered over.

"You'll have to stop that, and right smart," she snapped, and raised her clipboard. "I need some information on the gentleman in there. What's his name, now?"

Jeffrey opened his mouth, tried to reply, wanted to say, that man is my boss and my relative and my best friend. But the blanket of blackness rose up and covered him.

———

Jeffrey awoke to a blinding white light.

"Don't move, please," a professionally cold female voice ordered. "Can you tell me your full name?"

"Jeffrey Allen Sinclair," he replied weakly.

"Do you know where you are?"

"At the hospital. Is my friend—"

"Just a moment. Look to your left, no, move only your eyes. Now to your right. Up, please. Can you flex your fingers? Fine. Now your toes."

"How is Alexander?" he demanded, more strongly this time.

"The gentleman you arrived with? Cardiac arrest? He appears to have stabilized." Fingers probed his head, the back of his skull, his neck, worked down his spine. "Any discomfort?"

"No," he lied. "How long was I—"

"A few moments only." She then spoke to someone Jeffrey could not see. "No immediately visible damage to skull or vertebrae. Possible mild concussion, probable muscle contusion in the cervical area. Have a complete set of spinal x-rays done, then fit him with a neck brace."

"Yes, Doctor."

"You'll be staying with us for a bit, I'm afraid." A tired woman's face came into view and gave him a brief smile. "We'll need to keep you under observation for a day or so. Anyone who passes out at our front door can't be allowed to get off easy."

The longer he was awake, the more his head and neck throbbed. Even blinking his eyes brought discomfort. "All right."

"Popped your head on the ambulance roof, did you?"

"Yes."

She was not surprised. "The casualty department's entranceway is too narrow by half. You're the third one this year who's knocked his noggin. First time we've had one delivered on a gurney, though. You must have caught it right smart. Well, not to worry. Anyone we should contact for you?"

Jeffrey gave the number for Katya, his soon-to-be wife. "Are you sure my friend—"

"He's as well as can be expected, given the circumstances. Now, off to x-ray with you." The weary smile reappeared briefly. "And, Nurse, best give our patient something for the pain he claims he doesn't feel."

CHAPTER 2

Царю небе́сний, утіши́телю, Ду́ше і́стини, що всю́ди єси́ і все наповня́єш, ска́рбе дібр і життя́ пода́телю, прийди́ і вsели́ся в нас, і очи́сти нас від уся́кої скве́рни, і спаси́, благи́й, ду́ші на́ші.

"Heavenly King, Advocate, Spirit of Truth, who are everywhere present and fill all things, Treasury of Blessings, Bestower of Life, come and dwell within us; cleanse us of all that defiles us and, O Good One, save our souls."

The newly reopened Ukrainian Rite Catholic Church of St. Stanislav sat on the outskirts of Lvov, the second largest city in the newly reinstituted nation of Ukraine. When the congregation had intoned their amen, the priest continued with the liturgy of John Chrysostom, reciting the words as they had been spoken in more than a hundred tongues for over fifteen hundred years: "Blessed be our God, always, now and for ever and ever. May the Lord God remember you in His kingdom always, now and for ever and ever. Lord, You will open my lips, and my mouth shall declare Your praise."

Ivona Aristonova stood with the others waiting before the bishop's confessional and droned another amen, her thoughts elsewhere. She did not much care for confession to the bishop, and was grateful that the man was normally too busy to perform this duty himself. Yet today he was here, and as his private secretary she was obliged to stand and wait; to do otherwise would have set a hawk among the pigeons.

It was not that the bishop would ever refer to something from the confessional in their daily life; he was too good a priest ever to suggest that he even remembered what she spoke. No, her discomfort came from the fact that inside the confessional the bishop took his role seriously. He asked questions for which she had no answer. He probed where she did not care to look.

The priest conducting Mass stood before the altar table, separated from the congregation by a frieze of ancient icons. It was one of only three such tableaus, from over two thousand, which had survived the Communist years. He droned, "Blessed is the kingdom of the Father and of the Son and of the Holy Spirit, now and always and forever."

"Amen." Ivona held the prayer book in a limp hand, the words so often heard that she could recite virtually the entire book from memory. To take her mind off what was to come, she cast her eyes back and forth around the scarred and pitted church. For the past forty years, it had seen service first as a stable for the horses that drew the streetcars, then as a garage and oil depot. Only two months earlier had it been reopened as a church.

"For peace from on high and for the salvation of our souls, let us pray to the Lord."

"Lord, have mercy." The air was awash in the incense burning before the altar, the church full to overflowing. Every seat was taken, the back area packed with those who arrived too late to find seats. A church made for a maximum of six hundred now held well over a thousand souls.

"For the peace of the whole world, for the well-being of the holy churches of God, and for the unity of all, let us pray to the Lord."

"Lord have mercy." It was like this virtually every service. They were holding seven Masses on Sunday, and still people arrived a half hour early to be sure of a place.

"For this city, for every city and countryside and for the faithful who live in them, let us pray to the Lord."

"Lord, have mercy." Every side altar was a solid wall of flickering light, fueled by countless candle flames. Worshipers were going through devotional candles at a rate that even two months ago would have been unthinkable. Locating a reliable source was yet another of Ivona Aristonova's unending worries.

"For good weather, for abundant fruits of the earth, and for peaceful times, let us pray to the Lord."

"Lord have mercy." The bishop's assistant had recently departed to study abroad, and to Ivona's mind this was no great loss. The young man was like most of the Ukrainian Rite priests who had been consecrated in secret—poorly trained and suspiciously hostile toward all outsiders, including the bishop, who had recently returned from exile. Still, his absence meant that Ivona and the bishop and the priest saying Mass today were basically alone when it came to coping with the unending problems of resurrecting a church that had been outlawed for forty-six years.

"For those traveling by land, sea, or air; for the sick, the suffering, the imprisoned and for their salvation, let us pray to the Lord."

"Lord have mercy." Ivona chanted the words as she did most things in church—by rote and without feeling. Her mind remained fastened upon the incredible changes that had taken place within the Ukrainian Rite Church over the last few years and the overwhelming difficulties that accompanied them.

When Stalin convened the 1946 Ukrainian bishops' synod and declared the entire church illegal, worship according to traditions founded in the fourth century became a crime against the state. Following the decree, the church's leaders—the Metropolitan and all bishops—were gathered and shipped off to Siberian concentration camps. Only two survived, so battered in body and soul that neither would ever walk again.

All cathedrals and churches were declared state property. Many worshipers followed Stalin's orders and joined the only church officially tolerated within the Soviet Union, the Russian Orthodox Church. Stalin and his henchmen held no special affection for the Orthodox; they simply wished to bring all believers into a single unit so that they might more easily be monitored, dominated, and eventually exterminated. The Russian Orthodox Church had the singular advantage of being based in Moscow, and thus could be more easily controlled.

Josef Stalin harbored a violent hatred for Christian churches, the Ukrainian Rite Catholic Church in particular. It was too nationalistic, and it owed allegiance to a foreign-based pope. As soon as World War II ended and the need for the church members' assistance in defeating the Nazi invaders was over, Stalin began his infamous purge.

In the decades that followed, however, the Ukrainian Rite Church did not die as Stalin and his successors demanded. Despite the harshest possible punishments leveled against convicted believers, the church survived.

It moved underground. Mass was celebrated in cellars. Priests were taught and consecrated in absolute secrecy. Weddings and christenings and baptisms were performed in the dead of night. Bishops lived ever on the run, ever watchful for the KGB, often trapped and tortured and sentenced and imprisoned. The toil and terror and tears of its priests and believers earned the Ukrainian Rite Church the title of the Catacomb Church. Within the Catholic hierarchy, the two names became interchangeable.

Through it all, the Ukrainian Rite Church still did not die. When it again became legal in 1991, four million, five hundred thousand people claimed membership.

"Help us, save us, have mercy on us, and protect us, O Lord, by Your grace."

"Lord have mercy." It was Ivona's turn to enter the confessional. She knelt, recited her rehearsed lines, and waited. She dreaded what was now to come.

From behind the intricately carved wooden screen, Bishop Michael Denisov sighed and spoke in his ever-gentle voice, "So, so, dear sister Ivona Aristonova. And have you made peace with your husband?"

But Ivona was saved from both answering and receiving more of the bishop's painful probing by shouts rising above the chanted service. She and the bishop started upright as the priest cut off in mid-sentence.

"Gone, all gone!" A chorus of voices wailed their distress through the sudden silence.

"The treasures have been stolen!"

CHAPTER 3

Jeffrey awoke to find familiar violet-gray eyes peering down at him with a worried expression. "Are you all right?"

He nodded, or started to, then moaned as the pain brought him fully awake. "How?" he croaked, or tried to, but was stopped by the dryness of his throat.

Katya reached beyond his field of vision, came up with a cup. "Don't try to raise up." She fitted the straw in his mouth and said as he drank, "You've had a neck strain and possibly a mild concussion."

He managed, "Alexander?"

"He's alive," she answered, and took a shaky breath. "It's almost ten o'clock. I went to your apartment and waited almost an hour, but when you didn't show up for dinner I went by the shop, and when I saw all the police outside the door . . ." Katya had to pause. "I never want to go through anything like that. Not ever again."

Jeffrey lay still and recalled the events. It had been almost closing time at the Mount Street antiques shop. Just another day. He had been giving the antique table on the front podium a careful polish when the sudden thump had echoed from the back office-alcove. He had called Alexander's name. No response. He had set down his polish and rag and walked back, feeling an icy touch without knowing why. Then Alexander's legs had come into view.

He remembered screaming into the telephone, though he could not recall having dialed a number. He remembered trying to resuscitate the old man for what seemed like several lifetimes, but he had no recollection of the ambulance's arriving or of anyone gathering them up or starting off. Or closing the shop.

"The shop was swarming with the security people from down the street," Katya told him. "You left the door wide open. The security cameras can't see into the back alcove, so they didn't know what had happened until the cameras showed the medics wheel Alexander out on a stretcher."

Alexander's eyes had been open when Jeffrey raced into the alcove. They had pleaded with him, even while one hand tore at the carpet and the other pressed hard to his chest, clenching the suit and shirt with inhuman strength. The power of that gaze was a knife that Jeffrey still felt.

"They almost lost him." She choked on that, swallowed, tried again. "But he's stable now. I've seen him. Twice. He's breathing okay. His heart rate is stable. They say if he makes it through the next seventy-two hours he will probably be out of danger."

"Want to see," he whispered, his voice a rasp.

"You can't move just now," she replied gently. "They've made x-rays of your neck and head. There doesn't appear to be any serious damage, but the doctor wants to check you again. And you have to be fitted with a neck brace."

She stroked a strand of hair from his forehead. "Even if you could move, there's nothing to see. He's in intensive care and heavily sedated. There are all kinds of monitors, and he's being carefully watched."

"Want—"

She shushed him, lowered her face and kissed him softly. "Pray for him, Jeffrey. Speak to him in your heart. He will hear. Now try to rest. He needs you to be strong, and so do I." She grasped his hand with both of hers. "Close your eyes. I'll pray with you."

═══

Despite Katya's entreaties and the doctor's orders, the next morning found Jeffrey making his stiff-legged way alone to Alexander's bedside. His neck was encased in a white foam vise that smelled like a rubber glove. The soreness had moved lower to wrap around his back and shoot down his legs if he made too wide a step.

Jeffrey entered the hospital room to find the Count Garibaldi di Grupello, an old friend and client of Alexander's, looming above the foot of the hospital bed. The count greeted him with a grave nod, then returned his attention to the bed's silent form. "You positively must not allow me to win our bet, Alexander. You, Jeffrey, what is the word for someone who throws in the towel too early?"

"Wimp," Jeffrey offered, immensely relieved to find Alexander's eyes open.

"Precisely. My dear old friend, listen to me. Behave yourself and do not under any circumstances permit yourself to indulge in any wimpish behavior. We must marry these young people off, then give them a proper start. How on earth do you expect me to do this alone if you insist on wimping away?"

Jeffrey cleared the burn from his throat. "The correct term is wimping out."

"Whatever. I am sure the message has been received. Yes? Nod if you heard me, Alexander. There. You see? He agrees. And now my three minutes are up. Farewell, old friend. Next time I intend to hear you argue with me once more."

He turned away with a regal half bow. "Jeffrey, be so good as to join me in the hallway for a moment."

Before following the count, Jeffrey stood a moment looking down on Alexander and feeling weak with relief to find him alive. The old gentleman's eyes held him in silent communion. Then one hand raised to point weakly at Jeffrey's collar.

"I bumped my head on the ambulance roof," Jeffrey explained.

Alexander released a sigh.

"Hard," Jeffrey added.

Alexander rolled his eyes toward the headboard, gave his head a gentle shake.

Jeffrey watched until he was sure Alexander was resting peacefully, then slipped quietly from the room.

Once the door was closed behind him, the count said, "Young man, you must be strong for our friend in there."

"I've been told that before."

"Because it is true." The count squinted at the brace and demanded, "What on earth is that ghastly thing clamped to your neck?"

"Long story."

"Not a tiff with the young lady, I hope."

"Not a chance."

"That is good, for she shall also rely on your strength for now."
The count held up his hand. "I know, I know. From all appearances she relies on no one but her God. Such appearances are not
always true, young man. She has great strength, but not the ability
to withstand such blows to those she loves."

"I don't know if I do, either," Jeffrey confessed.

The majestic nostrils tilted back as the count gave Jeffrey his
most affronted gaze. "You *must*. You are the binding force here.
Now, go in there and be strong, and bring our friend back to life.
The world would suffer too great a vacuum were Alexander to pass
out of it."

Jeffrey found it difficult to force words around the thought of
Alexander's absence. "What do I say?"

"Talk of antiques," the count commanded impatiently. "What
else? Speak about the shop. Feed to him a sense of remaining here
with the living. Tell him I have finally agreed to purchase that cabinet, although how you can manage to claim such an outrageous sum
for it and still keep a straight face is utterly beyond me."

"Are you?"

"Am I what?"

"Buying the cabinet. You wouldn't want me to lie to him,
would you?"

"There, you see? This is what Alexander requires from you. He
must feel a part of life. Now go in there and fill the empty house."
The count turned his attention to the closed door. "For a man of
years, illness brings a new meaning to the word *alone*. Let him live
through your strength, Jeffrey, until he is once again prepared to
live for himself."

Prince Vladimir Markov, last surviving member of the Markov dynasty, knew exactly what the general was thinking behind his practiced stone mask. No doubt all the former Soviet army officer saw was a beautiful Monte Carlo villa transformed into a vast sea of clutter. The general made it quite clear that he considered the prince an eccentric collector, a magpie in a foppish nest, a pathetic has-been who clung to any object even slightly scented by the past.

It was true that the prince's villa was so full of furniture and paintings and valuables that it looked more like a warehouse than a home. Several rooms had simply been stacked from floor to ceiling and then locked up. The living room alone contained sufficient articles to furnish ten chambers.

But it was not a fanatic's hoarding instinct that drove Prince Markov. Not at all. The articles represented his family's royal past, a past that included a palace large enough to hold all his precious belongings. That palace he intended to have for himself once more.

Prince Markov treated the general with polite disdain. The peon could think what he liked, as long as he helped place the means to the desired end within Markov's grasp.

These days, the prince reflected, retired Soviet army officers were eager for any work that would keep them from the shame of common unemployment. Many of the groups struggling for power and wealth within the crumbling Soviet empire found them perfect as hired hands. Retired Soviet generals, it was said, had years of experience in corrupt activities. They were utterly efficient. They were brave to the point of idiocy. They were weaned of troublesome concern for human life. And they were too dogmatic to come up with independent plans on their own.

These days, it was very easy for such a one to go bad.

General Surikov had a taste for antiques. He stopped several times in his slow meandering walk toward Markov's balcony to examine several of Markov's more remarkable pieces. Markov held his own impatience in check. Barely.

"I know what needs to be done," Markov said, ushering his guest through the doors and out onto the terrace overlooking the Mediterranean and the Bay of Nice.

"Of course you do," his guest replied, giving the spectacular view an approving glance. "You're a professional."

General Surikov was a trim, hard man in his late fifties. He would never allow himself to balloon out as some of his fellow senior officers did. Not for him the triple chins that enveloped his colleagues' collars on parade days, nor the enormous girth that required two towels knotted together in the military baths. Nor did he show the red-veined nose and cheeks of a dedicated vodka drinker. His hair was short, his face as tough as his grip.

"These new Russian politicians," General Surikov complained, accepting the offered seat. "They sit in front of the television cameras and mouth, ma-ma-ma-ma, like sheep. All their lives they've studied butterflies through a microscope or written poetry nobody can read on a full stomach. And now they're running our country."

"Accountants," Markov agreed. "Engineers."

"Civilians and dissidents." The general snorted his disgust. "They tell the people, why do we need a military power? My comrades and I must sit and watch them enact this charade called transition to capitalism. Where is the mighty Soviet state now?"

"Gone," Markov sympathized. "Lost forever."

"These buffoons will not hold on much longer," the general added ominously.

Markov straightened. "You have news?"

"Nothing definite. Nothing except the *Afgantsi* are prepared to move."

Markov nodded. With the growing governmental crisis, the danger of a hardliners' coup grew daily. If one happened, it would no doubt be led by the cabal of officers, veterans of the conflict in

Afghanistan, who were known as *Afgantsi*. "Rumor has it that now they virtually control the army."

"For once the rumors are correct," General Surikov replied with evident relish. "The new Defense Minister is one of us. Through him we have secured all but two of the top defense positions. Within the past eighteen months, we have settled the entire senior officer corps in our grasp."

"You served in Afghanistan yourself, did you not?"

"In the early days, yes, before ill health forced me to accept a posting to the Baltic. Were I only ten years younger!" Surikov sighed. "Still, at least I am now again able to stand proud and proclaim that I did my patriotic duty."

And spilled how much innocent blood in the process, Markov reflected. Aloud he commented, "How nice for you."

"Patriotism, yes. It is indeed nice to be among friends who still honor the word, while these idiots called politicians stand around and allow our empire to crumble."

"It appears to be what the people want," Markov observed.

"The people!" The word obviously left a bitter taste in Surikov's mouth. "The people are sheep, to be led astray by the lies of blathering imbeciles. The people will like what they are told to like. Where is their pride now, I ask you? Where is their direction? What has democracy brought except growing chaos and disaster piled upon disaster?"

"A valid point," Markov soothed, deciding not to mention that much of the present chaos was caused by the people who now employed Surikov—they and others of their kind. "When do you think the officers will make their move?"

"Either this winter or the next. When coal and oil run low, and food runs out, and patience runs thin, and fear runs rampant." The words came out as a chant. "Then you will hear the Russian bear howl its demand for change. And we will be ready."

Markov considered the situation carefully and decided a right-wing coup would not damage his objectives; perhaps it could even help things along. An alliance with a former prince of the realm might appeal to the new Russian dictators as a further stamp of legitimacy. "How, pray tell, does all this mesh with your current work?"

The general hesitated, then responded, "A man must eat."

"A good time to have friends, no?"

"I am not made for following a capitalist's orders," Surikov confessed.

"Or for poverty," Prince Markov reminded him. "Which is why you are here."

General Surikov gave an abrupt nod. "To business, then. I am here to report that the time has come to proceed."

Markov struggled to keep the triumph from registering on his features. "This pleases me," he said smoothly.

"As it should. It is seldom that my superiors show such confidence in an, if you would excuse me, outsider. Not to mention one of the former czarist aristocracy."

Superiors. The thought was laughable. The Russian ship of state threatened to sink any day now. Crime filled the current political vacuum, creating vast opportunities for the unscrupulous. Criminals knew sudden power and wealth, and courted those who had lost power with the advent of democracy. Out of the chaos a new alliance had been born.

"Please tell your superiors," Markov kept the irony from his voice, "that I am certain our plans will meet with great success."

"They better," the general replied. "With all due respect, let me assure you that errors of judgment are met with great harshness."

"There is no need to speak in such terms."

"Of course not. I am simply doing as ordered. They, you see, have never had the pleasure of making your acquaintance."

Markov straightened the lapel of his immaculate jacket. "Have they informed you of a time plan for the next stage?"

"Now," the general replied bluntly. "My superiors say the stock has reached capacity. And there have been further developments."

Markov raised an eyebrow. "Developments of what sort?"

"Nothing that affects our plans."

Which means they didn't tell him, Markov guessed, wondering how such developments might affect his own designs. "Then I shall make my contact immediately," Markov replied, "and inform you when events begin to unfold."

CHAPTER 5

Jeffrey arrived at the intensive care unit two days later to learn that Alexander had been moved to a private room. He rushed back down through the central lobby, hurrying because Katya and the doctors allowed him only a few minutes alone with the old gentleman. But as he passed by the main entrance, he nearly ran into his friend Andrew. The antique dealer's face was almost hidden behind a massive bouquet of flowers.

Andrew took one look at his neck brace and commented, "What a loving little company you work for, lad. One gets sick, the others all get sick with worry."

"Worry did not put this thing around my neck."

"No, of course not." He patted Jeffrey's shoulder. "How's the old gent getting on?"

Jeffrey repeated the official, "As well as can be expected." Andrew nodded his understanding. "Doctors, they all get their lips sewn together at graduation."

"He looked okay yesterday, and I just learned they've shifted him out of intensive care," Jeffrey said.

"Then trust your own gut, I say." Andrew inspected the collar more closely. "So how did you get yourself fitted up?"

"Long story. How are things with you?"

"Oh, I'm suffering a bit. Seem to have swallowed a fire-breathing dragon sometime during the night. Otherwise, I suppose I can't complain."

"Tie one on last night, did we?"

"We?" Andrew looked confused. "Were you there too?"

Jeffrey found it nice to have a reason to smile. "Figure of speech."

"Don't do that to me on such a morning, lad. Makes me worry if I pickled my marbles." He extended the flowers. "Didn't have any desire to bother the old gent. Just wanted you to pass on my best regards and these posies."

"That's very kind, Andrew," Jeffrey said, accepting the sheaf of blooms. "I'm sure he'd like to thank you himself."

"That can wait for when he's dressed in something more than a drafty gown and slippers. Just let him know that I'm thinking of him." He patted Jeffrey's arm. "Take care of yourself, lad. And do let me know if you're ever in need of the old helping hand."

———

"I believe I have caught my second wind," Alexander declared weakly as Jeffrey entered the room.

"Have you?"

He nodded. "A small breeze, at any rate."

"Your color's better," Jeffrey observed. Alexander still looked very ill, but life was back in his eyes.

Jeffrey lowered himself carefully into the bedside chair. He looked around at the four bare walls, the flickering monitor screens, the hospital bed, the tubes and wires, the starched sheets, the roll-away table with plastic tray and utensils and food. "A long way from Claridge's."

Alexander managed a shaky smile. "You should try the food."

"I already did." Jeffrey returned the smile. "You're resting well?"

"My body draws upon slumber like an elixir," Alexander replied. His voice remained barely above a whisper. "I relish it as I never have before. I slide in and out as one draws a fine silk covering over his body. Sometimes it is so delicate that I am scarcely aware of its arrival."

A gentle knock announced Katya's entry. She walked in, bringing a sense of joyous sunshine with her. She pecked at Alexander's cheek, gave Jeffrey something more substantial, and asked, "How are my two favorite men this morning?"

"Alexander is feeling better," Jeffrey said, giving up his seat and pulling over a second chair.

"Of course he is." She inspected Jeffrey's neck brace. "Did you sleep in it as the doctor ordered?"

He nodded as far as he could. "Turning over has become a major event."

"Better than having to wear that contraption on your honeymoon," she replied primly, then turned to Alexander. "After Jeffrey left to come visit you yesterday afternoon, a Mr. Vladimir Markov called you from Monte Carlo. He seemed most distressed when I said you would be indisposed for the next few days."

"Markov. Sounds more like a spy than somebody living on the French Riviera," Jeffrey commented.

"Hardly a spy," Alexander replied in his hoarse half whisper. "Quite a distinguished gentleman, actually. I believe he may even be some long-lost relative of the Romanovs."

"Romanovs, as in the Russian kings?"

"Czars," Alexander corrected. "Exactly."

"Is he a client?" Katya asked.

"I suppose you might say so," Alexander replied. "He purchased my home in Monte Carlo. I haven't seen him in well over a year."

"Monte Carlo," Katya sighed. "The name alone sounds divine. What was your place like?"

"Quite simple—well, no, I suppose that would be a bit of an understatement." He paused to cough weakly. "It was built of stone, two stories high, and tucked into the hillside overlooking the sea. It had the charm of a Provençal farmhouse, but with these marvelous arched windows."

Slack muscles pulled up in a vestige of a smile. "When Markov walked in, he threw his hands in the air and said, I'll take it. He was perhaps halfway through the entry hall. The real estate agent was as surprised as I. And Markov insisted on purchasing one of my antiques from Eastern Europe. Gave me a bit of a pang, but where was I to place the item otherwise?"

"Perhaps return it to the shop," Jeffrey murmured.

A spark of the old Alexander returned. "So that you might have the pleasure of selling it to someone else? I do so admire your logic."

"So how did this Russian become so rich?"

"It's not that he became rich," Alexander replied. "It is that he held on to a small share of what before was one of the world's largest fortunes. At the turn of the century, the Russians considered it quite chic to travel to France. They positively loved the Riviera, and those who could built magnificent villas there. They learned the language and spoke it with the most atrocious Russian accent. A number of blue-domed Orthodox cathedrals still remain today, quite at odds with the local Provençal architecture."

"But the Revolution changed all that," Katya added. Alexander nodded. His voice was gradually losing strength. "When it looked as though the Bolsheviks would succeed in overthrowing the government, those of the nobility who did not have their heads in the sand became panic-stricken. Some managed to escape at the last moment, the fires that destroyed their palaces and their heritage and many of their kinfolk lighting their way."

"So Markov's family was in Monte Carlo when the Revolution broke out in 1917?" Katya asked.

"Quite likely," Alexander replied. "He had an amazing house, a palace really, erected by his family around the turn of the century. It looked like an art-deco wedding cake by the sea. It was surrounded by elaborate gardens, with dozens of statues, Greek gods and goddesses. A most remarkable place."

"So he gave this up to buy your home?" Jeffrey asked.

"Yes, I suppose sentimentality can only hold a person for so long," Alexander replied, his eyelids threatening to close of their own accord. "I heard rumors that the place was bought by an Arabian prince for a positively staggering sum."

Katya rose to her feet. "You are growing tired. It's time we let you rest."

Jeffrey stood with her. "I'll be back as usual this afternoon."

"Thank you both," Alexander murmured, slipping away.

Katya held on to her smile until the door had closed behind them. Then she stopped and clung to Jeffrey with fierce strength, her face buried in his chest. Jeffrey stroked her silken dark hair. "Alexander's going to be all right," he said, and for the first time truly believed it was so.

===

Alexander awoke in time to watch the afternoon sun emerge from behind thunderclouds and paint his hospital room with a thousand rainbow hues. Jeffrey was dozing in the chair by his bed, his neck still protected by the foam collar. Alexander stared at him, and saw how the rain-cleansed light turned the young face into that of a world-weary king, burdened with the woes of many.

Sleep was a blanket that never entirely left Alexander's mind, a drug that demanded ever more of him. He had turned the day into a swatch of gentle breaths, was only halfway conscious as later the nurse eased him over to bathe a body that was only partly his. He had slept during the doctor's afternoon visit, dozed as Jeffrey and the doctor conferred, caught only snatches of the talk. But it did not matter. It was enough to lie in a sort of floating awareness and to see the world anew.

Alexander looked around, taking in as much as he could while moving only his eyes, seeing everything as for the first time. There was a glory to each object, a burnished quality, as though reality had been polished and set on display for him to savor. But no matter where he looked or what he saw, always his eyes returned to his slumbering friend. Always.

The sunlight inched its way across the linoleum floor as Alexander continued his inspection of his surroundings. Bit by bit, impressions came to him through reawakened senses—the sharp hospital smells, the dividing lines between pastel shadows and angled brightness, the beep of machines attached to his body, the squeak of shoes in the hallway, the sound of his own breathing, the memory of how he came to be here.

Memories. All he had to do was shut his eyes, and the past rose vividly before him. There was a clarity to his internal vision that made memories appear as real and fresh and immediate as the world outside. One world with eyes opened, a thousand worlds when the veils fell and his sight searched inward.

Monte Carlo. Monte Carlo. Alexander replayed the morning's conversation as he drifted along the edge of sleep. Monte Carlo. As a young man he had loved the place; the city had made him feel *alive*. All the loss and hunger and deprivation of the war years in Poland had been softened by the thrill of his times in Monte Carlo.

There the senses surpassed themselves. The sea was an impossible blue, fringed with palm trees and sand-castle mansions. Champagne had more bubbles. Just breathing the air made a man feel rich. Alexander had lived for himself there and made no apologies to anyone.

By 1955, Alexander's London-based antiques trade had earned him almost enough money to fit into Monte Carlo society, while his charm and his skill at the gaming tables had made up the difference. Evenings he had enjoyed racing along the lantern-lit Corniche in a vintage cabriolet, taking the scent of night-blooming jasmine in great heady draughts.

Evenings he had wound his way down the hillside to the Place du Casino. He had loved the casino. He had loved to enter late, impeccably overdressed. He had loved the acknowledging nods of the croupiers across the expanse of green felt that separated him from his winnings. He had loved to click his chips into tall stacks, concentrating on the cards and the numbers and the counting. He had loved to drink espresso and tip generously before calling it a night—or a morning, as the case had often been—usually several thousand francs richer for the experience.

When he had finally sold his villa in the late eighties, the magic of Monte Carlo had long since faded. The landscape had changed beyond all recognition. The steep foothills of the Alpes Maritimes had been gouged with dynamite, lined with concrete, and studded with apartment blocks, office complexes, and utterly charmless hotels. A high-rise skyline had been grafted along the rim of the old fairy-tale kingdom.

The people had changed as well. When he finally departed, his neighbors had included deposed African dictators, Arab billionaires, retired arms dealers, and South American drug lords. Hulking bodyguards whose coats pinched around poorly hidden machine-pistols replaced the universal sense of secure comfort. The atmosphere of discreet pleasure once enjoyed by the patriarchs and players had been exchanged for a dismal blend of ostentation and secrecy.

Alexander well understood the secrets of shared confidences between friends, of loyalty to a cause, of wounds kept hidden from the world. But this secrecy took on a conspiratorial quality, serving nothing more glorious than self-interest and bulging bank accounts. Such an atmosphere left him more and more the outsider.

But still, Monte Carlo. The very name continued to hold a power over him. He remembered the place not with regret, but with a bittersweet fondness, as for a childhood sweetheart who had grown up to marry the wrong man. He would like the chance to visit again. There were still a few places that clung determinedly to the old charm. As he drifted toward consciousness again, he wondered if the jasmine was in bloom this time of year.

Even before he opened his eyes, he was cuffed by the offensive hospital odors. This was his reality, being bound to a body that no longer leapt to his bidding. This was his fate, held by his own weakness to a starched white bed in a stark white room. Alexander knew a moment of crushing despair as he realized with the fullness of defeat that Monte Carlo might very well be beyond his reach—now and forever.

He opened his eyes once more to find Jeffrey still seated beside the bed, awake and alert now, waiting patiently for his return. He motioned with his eyes toward the cup.

Once he had drunk, he whispered, "Send for Gregor." Then he closed his eyes once again upon a world where it felt as though he no longer belonged.

———

When Jeffrey left Alexander's room that evening, he found Katya standing by the nurses' station, deep in conversation with Alexander's doctor. He waited until they shook hands and separated, then walked over and asked, "So, what did she tell you?"

"Well, it is still quite serious. But it could have been a lot worse, especially if you had not reacted swiftly and brought him here as fast as you did."

Jeffrey started to shake his head, winced and caught himself. "It felt like time was standing still."

"I'm sure it did."

"Are they going to have to operate?"

"They don't think so. They need to monitor him for a few days before making a final decision about a pacemaker. But he appears to be in good general health, they say. They are hoping it won't be necessary."

"Alexander would hate having to go through surgery. Anything that reminds him of his mortality is a hard blow."

"He'll probably be insisting that the doctor send him home this weekend." She hesitated. "Especially with our wedding coming up. But the doctors said he will have to be in for at least another ten days. Maybe more."

The wedding. The same thought that had been pressing at him since first looking down at Alexander in the hospital bed rose again. This time it almost broke through to the surface.

Katya caught his internal struggle. "What's wrong?"

"Nothing."

Early on in the planning stages, Jeffrey had learned he had very little control when it came to preparations for the wedding. Over the years, Katya had built up a very definite idea of how she wanted her wedding to be. Jeffrey had learned to look at it as her day, and to allow her a free rein in making her dream come true.

Katya searched his face, then said quietly, "You are right, Jeffrey."

"About what?"

"I think I have known it since I first walked into the shop and heard you were at the hospital with Alexander. I just haven't wanted to face the truth."

"What are you talking about?"

"You know exactly," she said. "You've known all along."

"Known what?"

"Ten days," Katya repeated. "I can't imagine Alexander not being there."

Jeffrey showed the remarkable good sense of not replying.

"With your family coming from the States, we can't put it off." Katya focused on nothing. "You know he will want to be there, but it would be risking his health for him to try and move across town."

"We can't take that responsibility," he agreed.

"But he has to be a part of this. He's supposed to be your best man." Katya focused on him. "The Bible says we need a faith that can move mountains. Why not a faith that can move weddings? If Alexander can't join us, then we'll have to join him."

"What are you saying?" He waved his arm about as far as he could. "Hold the wedding in the hospital?"

"There has to be a chapel here somewhere. Every hospital does, right?"

Jeffrey blinked. He couldn't believe what he was hearing. Not after the past few months, when an entirely new side to Katya's personality had appeared. Seeing her so happy had granted Jeffrey the patience to withstand an almost hourly barrage of wedding details. But he had wondered about it, wondered how such a practical woman, worldly wise far beyond her years, could become so totally caught up in recreating a fantasy moment dreamed up in her childhood.

And now this.

"I'm sure the chapel isn't anything fancy, but we'll just have to make do," Katya told him firmly. "At least this way Alexander could be with us."

This same woman who was now offering to move their wedding to a hospital had taken a swatch of her wedding-dress fabric to a bakery on the other side of London to make sure that the marzipan frosting was tinted just a shade darker ivory than her gown; she did not want her wedding dress to look dingy by comparison. She had then tracked down the calligrapher for the royal family to ensure that the invitations would be perfectly hand-lettered.

"Don't you think that would be better than not having him share the day with us?"

She had absolutely insisted on Peruvian lilies for her bridal bouquet. Undaunted by the fact that they were months out of season, she had persuaded the director of the Chelsea flower show to have several sprigs shipped by air from Ruritonga, a tropical island somewhere in the Pacific, the day before her wedding. She had also gone to the hairdresser twice for "rehearsals" of her bridal hairdo.

"I would so much rather have it here than have it without Alexander," Katya told him.

She had convinced the Grosvenor House banqueting manager to allow her to attend three receptions, uninvited, so that she could personally sample and *then* decide upon which selection of hors d'oeuvres to serve; despite the fact that there would only be eighteen guests at their reception.

Katya grasped his hand with both of hers. "I know you're disappointed. I am too, in a way. But could we please do it here?"

She had persuaded the Anglican minister at the Grosvenor Chapel to reschedule two christenings so that the church would be available for their early evening vows. After all, she had said, it was so much more romantic to be married by candlelight, and in a church designed by Sir Christopher Wren.

"Please, Jeffrey? For me?"

The preparations for their wedding had been a genuine test of Katya's ingenuity and Jeffrey's patience. Now this same woman was telling him she would be quite content to be married in a hospital chapel. He imagined a small room at sub-basement level, somewhere near the boiler works, painted a shade of off-off-green.

He could not help but love her.

"Whatever you want is fine," Jeffrey said, sweeping her up in a fierce embrace. He released her and started for the main lobby. "Now I have to try to get Cracow on the phone."

vona Aristonova glanced at her watch for the hundredth time that morning, counted the people ahead of her in the bread line, and decided she could still make it back to the bishop's tiny apartment in time to prepare his midday meal.

These days she was shopping for two households, both her own and Bishop Michael's. With his assistant studying in the West, there was no one else to make sure the man ate. And unless someone did the cooking and then stood over him, the man would simply forget. He gave little care to the things of this earth, especially to his own well-being. It was one of his traits that left Ivona both a little awed and a little frightened of the man. That and his ability to see much deeper than she preferred.

She took another step in line, maintaining bodily contact with the hefty woman in front. Line breakers hovered like vultures, seeking to swoop down and save themselves the wait. Beyond them rose the cries of beggars, old and young, pleading for the chance to feed themselves another day. The beggars were a recent phenomenon. The line breakers had been with them always.

For a citizen of the former Soviet empire, the everyday components of life were not to be recalled with great fondness. Standing in line for hours and hours was a daily millstone, waiting so long that the back of the man or woman in front became memorized down to the slightest flaw in the weave, the lint on a scarf, the dandruff dusting a collar like miniature snow. Feeling the breath of the person behind was the worst for some; for others, it was breathing the smell of the one before.

Statistics grudgingly released by Izvestia showed that half of Russia's population had fallen below the official poverty level.

Helpless to put brakes on the decline, the Russian parliament had reacted by lowering the official level of what it meant to be poor.

Under the Communists, capitalism had been a crime punishable by imprisonment, a stay in Siberia, or treatment at an asylum. Now it was supposed to be the answer to all their nation's ills. But the state foundered in a Communist-made dilemma. Competition remained dampened, if not stifled, for the sake of full employment. People standing in endless lines did not need a degree in business to know that something was not working. Ivona waited alongside her countrymen and felt more than mounting impatience drawing nerves to the breaking point.

After buying bread, Ivona hastened back to the bishop's apartment behind the church and let herself in. She was busy preparing soup when she heard a knock at the door. Before she could set down her work and dry her hands, the bishop answered the call himself.

"Why, my dear brother, what a pleasant surprise," she heard his gentle voice say. "Come in, come in."

The Orthodox priest followed the bishop down the hall and into his cubbyhole of a study with the fearful demeanor of one approaching the gates of hell. She recognized the young man as one of the few Orthodox priests who sought to live in peace with the Ukrainian church. He was an outcast in the eyes of many of his own brethren, but his eyes burned with the fire of abiding faith. Ivona drew back into the shadows so she could see, yet not be seen, certain that if she was spotted she would be sent away.

The young man had a bear's girth and a martyr's open-hearted gaze as he faced the bishop. "I had to come."

"You are safe here, brother. There is no need to whisper."

"I am safe nowhere," the priest replied. "But still I had to come."

The bishop sighed. He was by nature a hopeful man, but there were days when the never-ending acrimony between the various factions of Christ's church dragged down his spirit like a lead weight.

Bishop Michael had been a fresh-faced acolyte when he fled Ukraine directly after Stalin's synod. He had trained for the priesthood in Rome and from there had traveled to serve exiled Ukrainian populations in France, in Switzerland, and finally in New Jersey. He had ministered in lands where religious freedom was a fact, rather than the basis of propaganda. And then, with the declaration of Ukrainian independence in 1991, Bishop Michael had asked to be sent home.

He had arrived to find utter chaos.

More than half the church buildings had been destroyed, often to make way for apartment blocks or office buildings or plazas dedicated to the great Communist uprising. Others had been used as gas and oil storage depots, warehouses, stables, vegetable bins and compost dumps for communal farms, or prisons for the criminally insane. Many had not been touched in any way since the Communists barred their doors seventy years ago. Few remained in any condition to be used as churches.

But now Communist Party members were being tried for crimes against the people, the Soviet Union was facing gradual dismemberment, and the Ukrainian church was once more becoming active. They wanted their churches back. They *demanded* them back.

The government had responded with a paper transfer of the churches that remained. And because they had no interest in tracing the original owners, they had simply given all the properties, six thousand ruined churches, to the only church that had officially existed for the past forty-six years: the Russian Orthodox.

Yet the Russian Orthodox Church could not respond to the Ukrainian church's demands for these properties because they in truth never received anything except a letter. The legislature in Moscow and elsewhere might have acted, but the old Party officials still controlled the local bureaucracies, even within the newly formed Ukrainian republic.

These officials still harbored the same old resentment for anything stinking of church and faith.

Bishop Michael understood all this, and in understanding he was granted patience. Yet he could also understand the feelings of his brother Ukrainian bishops, the ones who had served in persecuted secrecy and who had suffered all their lives under the hands of the Soviet overlords.

These men saw the Russian Orthodox Church as part of the official power structure, the same system that had convicted them of anti-Soviet crimes, imprisoned them, tortured them, chained them into gangs of mine workers, declared them insane, loaded them with drugs for months on end, and murdered fellow believers out of hand. For those who survived the years of fear and persecution and horror, it was very hard to muster patience for anyone, most especially for an institution they viewed as a conspirator to their own oppression.

The bishop led the young priest toward the office's most sturdy chair. "Who threatens you, brother?"

"All who refuse to call you brother in return," the priest replied, his gaze scattered about the room. "All who use their eyes to watch, but not to see."

"Are we not free from such spying times?"

"You, perhaps," he replied, "but not I. Not here. Not ever."

"No, it is my heart's yearning which spoke so, and not truth," the bishop replied sadly. "And yet you came."

"I had no choice," the priest replied. "I saw them."

The bishop stilled in watchful intensity. "The thieves?"

"I was praying a vigil in the side alcove," the other said, his voice lowering to a hoarse moan. "They wore the robes of my order, but they were not of Christ's body."

"I have seen the torn robe and the cross upon the broken chain which someone left lying by the open crypt," the bishop replied. "And now you are telling me that the thieves were Orthodox priests?"

"They wore the robes. And yet, and yet, I saw their eyes. I heard their voices. Their talk was of gain and of death. Their actions were of . . ." He dropped his face to his hands. "What is happening to us?"

"What did they say, brother?" the bishop urged.

"Saint Petersburg," the young priest moaned through his hands. "They have taken your treasures there."

When Alexander's cousin Gregor passed through the gates at Heathrow Airport, most of the waiting crowd saw only a frail old Polish gentleman with a halting, arthritic walk. Jeffrey saw a treasured friend, a business partner, a spiritual teacher. With Gregor's warm embrace he felt the tight knot of anxiety in his chest begin to ease.

Once settled in the taxi into London, Gregor listened carefully to the latest reports on Alexander's condition. He advised gravely, "It is time for you to be strong, my dear young friend."

"I'm trying."

"You will more than try," Gregor replied firmly. "You will *do*. For Alexander. For Katya. And for me. We all require what we know you have."

A distant smudge gradually solidified into the London skyline. Gregor greeted it with a very quiet, "I can scarcely believe I am here once again."

"Forty years is a long time," Jeffrey told him. "The city has changed."

"Of that I have no doubt," Gregor replied.

===

"You look much better this morning," Jeffrey said to Alexander as they entered his room. A thoughtful nurse had combed his hair and helped him into his robe before elevating his bed to a seated position. The brilliant red dressing gown added to Alexander's natural dignity and lent a bit of color to his pale cheeks.

"Thank you," he said weakly, and focused on Gregor. "Hello, cousin. Welcome."

Gregor leaned over the bed, exchanged the double kiss of greeting, and said, "You must be feeling better, if you are able to act the host while in a hospital bed."

Alexander watched his crippled cousin settle carefully into the hard-backed hospital chair. "I confess to a great need for your wisdom, Gregor."

"The Lord is the One to whom you should turn at such times," Gregor said gently, reaching forward and grasping one of Alexander's waxlike hands. "Not another mere mortal."

"I would if I could," Alexander replied.

Jeffrey rose to his feet. "I'll be waiting outside if you need anything."

"Stay," Alexander said in his coarsened whisper. "Please."

Gregor's attention remained fastened upon Alexander as Jeffrey seated himself. He asked his cousin, "You are having difficulty making this approach to your Lord?"

"Never have I felt more alone," Alexander confessed weakly, "or my God more distant. At a time when I need Him most, He is not there. I can no longer find Him."

Jeffrey would often think back to that moment and wonder, not at what he saw, but at what remained unseen. He looked upon Gregor, a man crippled and bent and in pain, his body twisted back and to one side so that the chair took every possible ounce of weight from his disabled frame. Yet that was not what Jeffrey *saw*.

Gregor did not answer directly. Instead, he paused and withdrew to a place Jeffrey could not fathom. He watched a man who lived in perpetual discomfort close his eyes and know a peace so total it shone from his face.

Gregor's creases of pain and sleeplessness and bone-weariness smoothed away in a moment of silent miracle, one so calm and natural that Jeffrey could identify it only by the ache of utter yearning that suddenly filled his own heart.

Gregor opened his eyes, and immediately his features returned to their earthly set. "The sixty-third Psalm was written after David was anointed by the prophet Samuel and proclaimed as Israel's future king," Gregor said in his gently searching manner. "Yet after this promise from the Lord, David was still forced to wait. Wait and suffer and yearn and doubt, straining some forty years before his inheritance could be claimed.

"I have seen You in the sanctuary, David said to the Lord. I beheld You there. He was speaking in the past tense, do you see? It was once so, and now is no more. He saw, he beheld, then again he walked along desert ways. For David, his promised divine inheritance contained vast stretches of isolation and loneliness and want."

Gregor carefully shifted his weight forward, his gray eyes intense with understanding. "My dear cousin, I understand your pain. I too have traveled through lonely, empty stretches. Such an experience is common among believers. It is also common to misunderstand the reason for these periods and to miss the blessings that God bestows in such times.

"You must understand that what is happening to you is *not* punishment. Yes, you face difficulties which you have not brought upon yourself. Yes, you are burdened. Yes, God seems distant. But if you see this as punishment, you set yourself up for assault. Doubts will assail you, and fears, and desires to complain of how you have been unfairly treated by life. Nights are given over to anxiety, when fears chase you back and forth across the floor."

He smiled gently at Alexander's nod of recognition. "At such times, it is most important not to doubt in the dark what you have learned in the light. On the bad days, you must live by the lessons gained in the good times. Remain confident and solid upon the rock.

"The desert, my cousin, is a time of testing. In the eighth chapter of Deuteronomy, the Lord says we are taken into the desert to test our faith and to humble our hearts. He offends the mind in order to reveal the unseen. Your sense of order and balance and symmetry is shaken. You are thrown to your knees. The winds of change blast down from the heavens while darkness blankets your vision, and you *know* your strength alone is not enough.

"In such times, Alexander, you must cling to the rock and cry aloud to the unseen One for strength to cover your naked weakness. And once you return from this testing, you are called to do one thing further: to *remember*. Learn, and then hold on to this gift of learning for all your days."

He touched Alexander's hand. "A fruit tree that remains constantly in the light will never bear fruit. It is the tree that experiences the *normal* cycle of light and darkness that fulfills its divine purpose. Remember that in your trials, my dear cousin. And stay with God."

Gregor rose slowly to his feet, smiling down at his cousin. "Now rest in His glorious peace, my brother in Christ. I will come to see you again this afternoon."

====

"That was very beautiful," Jeffrey told him as they crossed through the hospital's main lobby.

"Mmmm," Gregor hummed distractedly, then pulled the world back into focus. "I'm sorry. What was it you said?"

"What you told Alexander in there. It was really inspiring."

"Oh, thank you . . ." His mind remained elsewhere. Once through the main doors, Gregor ceased his limping gait to turn and face Jeffrey. "I was wondering if I might ask a favor."

"Anything."

"It is time that I go and visit my Zosha's resting place, but I find myself unwilling to go there alone. Would you be so kind as to accompany me?"

"Of course," Jeffrey replied. Zosha was the name of Gregor's deceased wife.

Gregor offered a distracted smile. "I am indeed grateful, my young friend. This is most good-hearted of you."

Jeffrey left him isolated in his contemplation and joined the ranks struggling to find a taxi in the misting rain. Once in the cab, Gregor gave the driver their destination, then lapsed again into silence. Some moments later he emerged to say, "Forgive me, please. I am sorry for being such poor company."

"There's no need to apologize."

"No, that is the blessing of true friendship in such moments," Gregor agreed. "I was recalling the distant past. Strange how vivid memories can become at these times. I was thinking of our escape from Poland. Or rather, the time leading up to our departure."

"Alexander has mentioned your escape several times," Jeffrey said. "I'm still waiting for the whole story."

"Conversation would most certainly ease the burden of this journey," Gregor assented. There was another long silence as the world shifted slightly to reveal a door long hidden within Gregor's mind and heart. "When Alexander had recovered from his imprisonment at Auschwitz," Gregor then began, "he immediately joined the *Armia Krajowa*, the Polish Home Army, as the underground was called. Of course, he never actually spoke of it to us. The AK, as the army was known, was utterly secret. Even within the ranks themselves, the soldiers were known by code only, and each was sworn never to try to learn another man's true name. This was done so that if they were ever captured and tortured, they had less information to divulge. Of course, with my poor health, I was not permitted to join, much as I begged.

"As with most Poles, I came to know many of the activists within the local AK garrison. There were little signals you could detect if you looked carefully, such as a hint of pride and defiance against the overpowering German might, and the way they stood or looked or spoke. Alexander replaced the horror of his Auschwitz experience with this sense of secret strength, and I saw it in others. But I knew better than to speak of it, even to my dear cousin. I never had the opportunity to tell him how proud I was of him and his actions, or how much I lived through him. Or how, when he slipped away on a mission under the cover of night, he carried my fervent prayers with him. I never slept while he was out. Never. I spent the long night hours praying for his success and his safe return."

The rain stopped, the clouds scattered, the sun turned the city air dank and sweltering. Traffic held them in a fumy embrace. Gregor seemed scarcely aware of the steamy heat, the beeping horns, or their crawling progress.

"After the Nazis were defeated in Poland and the Russians swept in," he continued, "the AK soldiers began to disappear. Nothing was said, no accusations were made, no evidence was found by anyone who was willing to speak aloud. But one by one, the young men and women I knew to have been in the underground began to vanish. I watched Alexander and saw how distressed he became by this, yet I was unable to broach the subject without his speaking first. And I worried for him more than I ever had under the Nazis.

"Then one night I awoke to the sound of his moving about, the same secret movements that had woken me so often before. This time I went to him. He told me that he and two friends were going to vanish before the Russians made them disappear permanently. Where was he going, I asked. He hesitated, then told me it would be best simply to trust him, and to believe he would one day return. We embraced, and he slipped from the room, and that was the last I saw or heard of my dear cousin for seven long months."

"That must have been terrible," Jeffrey said quietly.

"It was and it wasn't," Gregor replied. "I missed him more than I thought it possible to miss another man. But it was also a time of great beauty, for that was when the Lord brought my Zosha into my life. By the time Alexander returned, I was a married man."

Gregor looked with sad fondness into the distance of his memories. "Perhaps the Lord whispered to our souls that we would only have those two short years together, and so we lost no time in lighthearted flirtation and simple chatter. Perhaps, too, we shared with such desperate openness because of who we were and what the times held for us.

"Zosha had experienced the Warsaw Uprising and arrived bearing the agony of having survived. Despite her past or because of it, we met, and we loved; that is the whole story of our lives together. We met, and the world sang with the tragic beauty of two young people loving each other in a world with little room for love. We shared all we were and all we had and all we knew, and life became so enriched that each new dawn spoke of promises too great for one small day to enclose.

"Zosha was the answer to my every prayer, even the ones which I knew not how to place into words. She drank in the lessons I had learned from my studies of faith, and in taking them so wholeheartedly taught me the heavenly delights of earthly love, of what it meant for two to join as one.

"How Zosha came to be with me, ah, to have a miracle of such joy arrive in the midst of such chaos and turmoil! The trauma of her passage—my boy, you cannot imagine what Zosha went through before she joined me." Gregor sighed and murmured, "Yet she came, my angel in earthly form. And she loved me. Ah, how that woman could love. I saw God more clearly in her eyes than ever in anything else contained within this world."

He was silent for so long that Jeffrey thought his questions would have to wait for another time. But the taxi jolted to a stop at a light, and Gregor stirred himself and continued, "My Zosha spent the war years in Warsaw, until the time of the Uprising. The Warsaw Uprising was one of many tragedies during the war years, yet it held a special bitterness because of the Soviet treachery. The Red Army had promised our underground forces that they would come to our aid and push the Nazis from Polish soil once the battle for Warsaw began. Instead, they massed across the Vistula and watched the Germans pulverize our glorious capital and decimate the population.

"They stood and watched our people die, you see, because they never intended to let Poland be free. Every Polish patriot killed by the Nazis was one less that the Soviets would have to concern themselves with. Neither the promised soldiers nor the arms ever arrived. Half-starved AK soldiers faced the modern Nazi army with petrol bombs and sharpened fence-staves and hunting guns and whatever weapons they could steal.

"The battle lasted two months and was nothing less than sheer butchery. During that time, Warsaw was a city apart. There were no supplies, little water, no electricity or oil. Then, when the city surrendered, the Germans ordered all survivors to leave their homes immediately, taking only what they could carry. Most of these people were starving and weak. They were forced to walk for two days. Along the way they were given nothing—no food, no water. There is no record of how many died in that trek of blood and tears. But my Zosha said that every step of the way was littered with the bodies of those who could not continue and were left where they lay."

Gradually the taxi made its way beyond the cramped confines of central London. Streets broadened and lawns appeared and shops

sprouted from low buildings. "German soldiers marched along either side of the road, with perhaps twenty meters between each
soldier," Gregor went on, "My Zosha was eighteen, walking with
a girlfriend, and their two mothers walked a few paces away. Suddenly a man scrambled up from the hedge and, unnoticed by the
Germans, began walking alongside them. He whispered that they
had to escape immediately, to go with him right then; there was
not a moment to lose. They of course replied that they could not
leave their mothers, that they would be all right once they arrived
at the prison camp.

"The young man whispered fiercely that they would not be allowed to stay with their mothers. Only the elderly were to be placed
in the camp. All young girls were to be sent to the bomb depots near
the front. These places were called death factories, the young man
told them, because they were being bombed so often. There was no
chance of survival. None.

"He was in the AK, this young man. He pulled them from
the road, flung them down on the earth, and ordered them to stay
there until he returned. He waited for the next soldier to pass, then
was up once again and back in line, continuing his death-defying
mission of mercy. He never came back, that man.

"Later, once we had all arrived safely in London, we learned
that what the young man had said was true. Virtually none of the
women sent to the front ever returned. My Zosha never had a
chance to thank that young man who had risked his life to save
her. She never even learned his name.

"When all the people had passed and the young man did not
return, Zosha and her friend walked to the nearest house, where a
woman came out, took one look at them, and said, you're from the
Warsaw Uprising. That was how strong an impact the events left on
the innocent. The woman took them into her house and cooked the
only food she had—rancid potatoes and black, grimy flour made
into potato pancakes. My Zosha told me it was the finest meal she
had eaten in her entire life.

"They stayed with the woman for two days, until the Germans began a house-to-house search for escapees. That resulted in

a journey from home to home, village to village, by hay wagon and horse cart and lorry, sleeping in barns or vegetable bins or cellars or open fields, until one early dawn my Zosha arrived at our own doorstep in Cracow. She was so exhausted and weak that her hold on life was a bare thread. My family took pity on the poor girl, and instead of passing her on as would have been safe, they gave her Alexander's room. And I, in turn, gave her my heart."

The taxi turned a corner, and instantly the city was exchanged for a narrow country lane. Verdant fields opened to either side. Wild flowers filled their car with the perfumes of summer. Gregor watched the line of ancient trees parade past their car.

"Alexander had been gone for seven months, as I said," he continued quietly. "He returned as silently and suddenly as he had departed, riding the winds of danger and urgency with a strength and focused power that filled our little world. We had to escape, he said. All of us. There was no time for discussion or debate. The Soviet noose was tightening and soon would close off all remaining channels to freedom.

"We did little to protest, as we could see the evidence of the Soviets' growing might all around us. So that very night we began a journey which took us the entire length of Poland, up to the Baltic Sea and across by boat to Scandinavia, and from there on to England. Every step of the way we were aided by silent, nameless friends whom Alexander had met in his time away from us. Every place we traveled, I saw how those strong men accepted my dear cousin as one of their own, a man who had fought the good fight, and I knew a pride so fierce I was sure it would burn eternal scars in my heart."

The taxi turned through great stone gates into a quiet cemetery, stopping before a tiny chapel. The driver turned off the motor and waited patiently as Gregor sat where he was and went on, "But my darling Zosha had never recovered her strength from the trauma of the Uprising. Her weakness had not been evident when we departed; otherwise, I would never have attempted the journey. But as the days of endless toil and danger wore on, that same look of haunted exhaustion which she had worn upon her arrival at my home returned to her features.

"Still, we survived, all of us. In Sweden we rested, and again I hoped that all would be well. But it was not to be. About a year after our arrival in London, my Zosha went down with a fever, and she never rose from her bed again."

With a long sigh, Gregor eased himself from the taxi. While Jeffrey arranged for the driver to wait, Gregor purchased a map and a great bouquet of lilacs and chrysanthemums from the flower stall by the cemetery chapel. Together they followed the cemetery map past progressively older tombstones, until they arrived at a carefully trimmed plot lined by flowers and bearing a simple black marble marker.

"This is Alexander's doing, bless his soul," Gregor noted quietly. "He has seen to all these details since that very day, when I was too poor and too distraught to manage."

Gregor stood for a long moment in bowed stillness while Jeffrey strolled along ways sheltered by ancient chestnuts. When he saw Gregor wave in his direction, he hurried back.

"It was good to come here once more, before—" He stopped, looked back at the grave site, and concluded. "It was good to come. I have Alexander to thank for this as well. Though I must confess to you, my young friend, that I feel no closer to Zosha at this moment than I have when seated alone in my tiny Cracow flat on many a winter's eve."

Jeffrey thought of his own new love and was brought face-to-face with its fleeting fragility. He found himself with nothing to say as they made their slow way back to the waiting taxi.

CHAPTER 8

The following afternoon Katya walked cheerfully, though somewhat frazzled, into Alexander's room, where Jeffrey was visiting. She bestowed kisses and greetings on both men and asked, "Where is Gregor?"

"Back at Alexander's flat," Jeffrey said glumly. "Packing."

"You couldn't persuade him to stay?"

He shook his head. "I got about as far as you did."

"Oh." Her cheerfulness slipped several notches. "He did warn us. I just hoped—"

"Gregor's place is not here," Alexander said kindly. "You as well as any have the perception to know that."

"But the wedding is just six days off," Katya complained, slipping into the seat Jeffrey offered.

"There is urgent relief work among the Cracow orphanages which simply will not wait," Alexander replied. "He has explained it to us in great detail. And his work here is over."

"You really are feeling better, aren't you?"

"My dear," Alexander said, "Gregor's visit has positively transformed me. This and the news that you are relocating the wedding on my account."

"Jeffrey told you, then." She bestowed the fullness of her gaze on him. "Did he tell you it was his idea?"

"I did not because it was not," he replied.

She nodded slowly. "Yes it was. You were just too smart to suggest it yourself."

"Whoever is responsible," Alexander said, "I thank you both. Your offer has done much to restore me. And I do hope that you still intend to hold your reception in my flat."

"If you really think—"

"Nothing could bring me greater pleasure, except to be there myself," Alexander pronounced gravely. "Know that I shall most certainly be there in spirit. As shall Gregor."

"Well," she said, turning brisk, "my last calm moment before the wedding was shattered by yet another call from our Mr. Markov. Whenever he phones, he seems to grow distressed by degrees. He starts off all cool and polished, ordering me in the most civilized manner to get you on the phone. When I insist that's not possible, he goes bright red."

"You've seen him?" Jeffrey asked.

"I don't need to." She smiled at him. "I'm just glad he waited to call until you had left to collect Gregor. I'd hate you to have a shouting match with somebody six days before our wedding."

"Perhaps I should give him a call," Alexander said thoughtfully.

"From the sounds of things," Katya said, "whatever he has on his mind is quite urgent."

"You do not speak French, do you, my dear?"

She shook her head. "It is a language I have always wanted to learn."

"Well, perhaps the future shall afford you an opportunity. Be so good as to dial for me, would you?"

"Of course." Katya placed the call, then handed him the phone. A woman's voice answered with, "La Residence Markov."

"*Oui. Monsieur Markov, s'il vous plaît.*"

"*Et vous êtes Monsieur . . . ?*"

"Kantor. Alexander Kantor."

A long moment's pause, then, "*Ici Markov.*"

Alexander switched to English. "Mr. Markov, this is Alexander Kantor returning your call."

"Ah, yes, Mr. Kantor. Thank you so much for responding so quickly. I understand you have had a bout of ill health. Not anything serious, I hope."

Alexander took in the bleak surroundings in a single sweeping glance, made do with a simple, "Thank you for asking."

"I do apologize for disturbing you."

"Not at all," Alexander replied. "I understood that you were under some time pressure, and I did not wish to delay you further."

"But of course I would expect nothing less than a prompt response from a professional such as yourself."

"You are too kind." For the first time since his attack, Alexander felt a surge of his old acquisitive spirit. The familiar feeling lifted him enormously. "And how are you enjoying your life at Villa Caravelle?"

"Oh, it is a most splendid place. As you know, I fell in love with it the moment I saw it."

"And you don't miss—" Alexander searched his memory for the name of Markov's former residence, one of the largest palaces along the Corniche, and was delighted when he came up with "Beau Rivage? That was certainly a magnificent residence."

"Ah, yes. Beau Rivage. No, I must say I have had quite a number of other things on my mind these past two years. Which brings me to the reason for my call. I have a business proposition for you, Mr. Kantor."

"Well, I don't know, Mr. Markov. Under the circumstances—"

"Mr. Kantor, I need a man of your discretion, honesty, and expertise. This matter positively will not wait and, I assure you, is of the utmost importance." He leaned heavily on the words.

"It is just that I am in no position to be traveling—"

"Oh, I do love the way you play at being shrewd," Markov replied. "Let me assure you, Mr. Kantor. You would find a visit to Monte Carlo most rewarding at this time."

"For any number of reasons," Alexander replied, "I am sure you are right. Regrettably, however, I am ringing you from a hospital bed."

"*Mon Dieu!* It is not serious, I hope."

"This, too, I shall survive," Alexander replied. "The doctors tell me I am on the mend."

"How excellent for you," Markov said, clearly worried. "I must say, however, this is indeed a disappointment. I am afraid my business interests require immediate attention."

"May I ask if this is in reference to buying or selling a particular piece?"

"Buying. Yes. You might say I am interested in acquiring a very special property."

"I see." Alexander hesitated, then ventured, "The only suggestion I might make is for my assistant, Mr. Jeffrey Sinclair, to make himself available to aid you."

Markov showed doubt. "Well, I am not sure, Mr. Kantor. I had hoped—"

It was Alexander's turn to press with all the force he could muster. "He is a young American. Very bright, very perceptive."

"And you trust him?"

"With my life and all my earthly goods," Alexander replied emphatically. "Like my own son."

"Could I be assured of your close collaboration with him on this matter?"

"Absolutely," Alexander replied. "It is one of the aspects of working with him that I find most pleasurable."

Markov permitted himself to be persuaded. Reluctantly. "It is true that I have no one else whom I could trust with this."

"The fact that my body chooses to remain inert," Alexander went on, "does not mean that my mind cannot remain most active. I assure you that I shall take every interest in your affairs, Mr. Markov."

"Fine," Markov decided. "Please have your Mr. Sinclair call me to make further arrangements."

"I shall do so," Alexander replied. "Can you supply me with any details about the item in question? Is this a French acquisition?"

"I believe it is best to discuss such matters in person." Markov hesitated, then continued, "But no, the item is not located here. My proposed acquisition is in former Soviet lands."

"How fascinating." Alexander made do with a minimum of formalities before hanging up.

"Thank you for the vote of confidence," Jeffrey said when the old gentleman turned back to them. "And for the kindness of what you said."

"You are most welcome," Alexander replied. "All the essence of truth, I assure you. I would suggest that you contact Markov yourself first thing tomorrow. He will be expecting your call, and promptness will assist in establishing a positive impression with such a one as him."

"What do you think he wants to talk about?"

"Whatever it is, he wants to discuss it personally. I therefore presume that it must be something quite large. Markov leans toward the extravagant."

Jeffrey smiled. "Like your villa?"

"No doubt the most discreet purchase he has ever made," Alexander replied sharply. "Now, back to the subject, if I may. He would not have contacted me unless his business concerned something out of the ordinary."

"How well do you know him?" Katya asked.

"Not at all well. Primarily from the sale of my villa, and a fair amount based on hearsay. Markov is quite the clever gentleman. Cagey would perhaps be too strong a word, but certainly very clever. The gambler in me would say that Markov is a man with an ace up his sleeve."

Alexander mused a moment, then asked, "I suppose the two of you have already made plans for your honeymoon."

"We're taking our real honeymoon in December," Jeffrey said. "Katya and I are going back to America together. That is, assuming the boss will let us have a month off."

"We didn't want to do it any earlier," Katya explained, "with so many of Jeffrey's family coming over here for the wedding."

"So for right now we are planning a few days up in Scotland." Jeffrey exchanged eager looks with Katya. "I've booked us a room in an inn built in the days of Bonnie Prince Charlie."

"Do you have your heart set on Scotland?" Alexander asked.

"What do you mean?"

"If I may, I'd like to suggest a change of itinerary. That is, if you wouldn't mind combining your days of vacation with one day of work."

"I suppose it would depend on where you want to send us."

"How about Monte Carlo?"

Katya gasped. "Monte Carlo! I hear it's just fabulous." She caught herself, turned to Jeffrey. "Oh, but maybe you had your heart set on Glasgow."

"Edinburgh," Jeffrey corrected.

"Wherever," she said, trying to hide her smile. "Of course, I would miss seeing all those men in kilts. You know what I heard about—"

"A honeymoon in Monte Carlo sounds fantastic," Jeffrey said. "But it's a little out of our price range."

"We're talking business here," Alexander said. "Plus maybe a little extra wedding gift. Believe me, if I could go, I would. As I cannot, I would be most pleased—and grateful—if you could go in my stead."

"I guess I should see to hotel reservations," Jeffrey said.

"The Hotel de Paris," Alexander said firmly. "The only place to stay in Monte Carlo, if you don't mind my saying. It is situated on the harbor, just across the square from the Casino. A marvelous old place, as grand as the Vienna opera house." He smiled fondly at them both. "It should make for a most memorable start to what I have no doubt will be a wonderful life together."

———

They went directly from the hospital to Alexander's flat. Katya bid Gregor a sad farewell, then left to resume the complex business of moving a wedding. Gregor followed Jeffrey toward their waiting taxi and asked, "When are you again coming to Poland?"

Jeffrey turned to stare at him. "You can't be serious."

"A shipment is ready for you," Gregor replied. "And the young man from Ukraine, remember him?"

"I can't leave Alexander alone. Not now."

"The young man's name is Yussef. He is ready to take you across the border. He says there are some excellent buys waiting," Gregor pressed. "This may be a major opportunity."

Jeffrey remained silent.

"I understand, my young friend. I truly understand. But you must also ask yourself, what would Alexander have you do? Who will pick up the reins if not you?" Gregor gave Jeffrey's shoulder an affectionate pat. "I shall hope to see you before the end of the month. Such urgent matters cannot wait longer than that."

"I'm sorry to see you go back to Poland so soon."

"I have been away as long as my responsibilities will allow." Gregor hesitated, then added quietly, "Not to mention my own human frailties."

"You don't want to go?"

"Want, want, want," Gregor shook his head. "So much of our thoughts hinge on that word, don't they? Especially these days. And yet I must follow the call of my Lord; that is what I *want* above all else."

"But you'd *like* to stay?" Jeffrey persisted.

"Life is very hard in my Poland just now," Gregor replied. He climbed into the taxi, waited while Jeffrey gave the driver directions, then continued, "Change has brought benefits for some, trauma to many. It is easy to forget, while living there, that such places as London truly exist."

"Conditions are growing worse?"

"Conditions, as you say, are chaotic. Robberies and violent crimes are skyrocketing. Most people who have to be out at night have bought the sort of dogs who walk their owners, rather than the other way around."

"So why don't you stay?" Jeffrey tried to keep the pleading from his voice. "Especially with everything that's happening, we'd love to have you here."

Gregor was silent for a time before replying, "Philippi was the apostle Paul's first church in Macedonia. For that and other reasons it held a very special place in his heart. When he was imprisoned in Rome, distant and powerless, frustrated that he could not continue his work, he remained utterly certain that the bonds between him and that church remained strong. No matter that he could not see his friends, no matter that he could not hear of their progress or be a part of it. Always he was sure the church was growing stronger day by day."

"This sounds distinctly like a 'no' to me," Jeffrey said glumly. "Nicely put, but still no."

Gregor smiled and continued, "Such confidence comes from a sharing of the key experiences of life, bonded through shared faith. We yearn for one another in the heart of Jesus Christ. He is the divine link which held Paul together with his distant brethren then, and He will do the same for us now, my young friend. What is more, He will unite us all on His glorious day. What we feel now for one another will then be made perfect in His glory.

"Our fragile strands of feeling are but slender threads constantly snared by the myriad of things left undone, strained by doubt and pulled by earthly hardship. They remain but a hint of what God promises to bring to completion. And this completion is not an end to itself. Not at all. It shall be for us, for those risen above all endings through their love of man's only Savior, just the beginning of all eternity."

Gregor held him with eyes that saw far beyond their earthly confines. "On that day, my dear young friend, at the dawn of our eternal day, we shall rise with the morning star, and with the angels together we will sing our endless, boundless joy."

Jeffrey returned from the airport, stopped by the antique shop to check over the day's proceeds, and read Katya's note to meet her at the church around the corner. He did that often, but he still did so with reluctance.

Katya had been making a widening inspection of the neighborhood that was soon to be her home. In the process she had discovered a church that she pronounced delightful. It served many of the local immigrant communities and held weekly Masses in several Eastern European languages. Between Masses, the rows were filled with kerchiefed women and old men bowed over canes, murmuring their prayers in a soft tide of foreign tongues.

Upon the great pillars flanking the embossed altar frieze hung two of the largest icons Jeffrey had ever seen. One of the paintings was of a Christ figure painted in the flat two-dimensional style of ancient Byzantium, the other depicted Mary and the holy Child. Both were embedded within frame after frame after hand-etched silver frame. The outermost frames were shaped as peaked medieval doorways and stood a full fourteen feet high.

Beside each of them rose ranks of flickering candles. Often when entering the church Jeffrey's eyes stung from the cloying blanket of incense, and his sense of proper worship felt offended by the sight of old women making exaggerated signs of the cross and then bowing before the icons. Masses were announced by the solemn intoning of great brass chimes hung above the main entrance.

On Sundays he and Katya attended a very evangelical Anglican church in Kensington, and Jeffrey truly felt at home among that congregation. But almost every day Katya insisted on entering this strange world of foreign rituals. She settled herself in the corner of the central side alcove, the only person in the church under sixty. She knelt alongside several dozen old women, who greeted her arrival with smiles that stretched leathery faces into unaccustomed angles. The alcove contained two smaller icons, before which burned rows of glimmering candles. The side walls were decorated with soaring marble angels whose gilded wings stretched almost to the distant ceiling.

As they had left the church after his first visit, Katya had asked him, "Well, what did you think of it?"

"I don't think I like it very much in there."

"Why not?"

He shrugged. "Too many smells and bells."

"Don't get smart," she replied sharply.

"I don't know what to tell you, Katya," he replied. "It just seemed strange to me."

"And I asked you to tell me why," she insisted, a hard light gleaming in her eyes.

"I watched an old woman kiss one of those icons, and I felt pretty sure she did it every day."

"So? Since when did you decide your own faith was so perfect that you had the right to criticize somebody else's?" He deflected her, or tried to, with, "I just don't understand why you want to go there, Katya. Doesn't the Bible say something about going into your closet to pray?"

"I pray in private," she replied, still hot. "I also like to join with fellow believers in silent worship. This place and what it represents is a part of my heritage, Jeffrey. I feel very close to these people and their lives. I like the sense of communing with them in spirit."

Jeffrey decided it was best not to respond.

She understood him perfectly. "Listen to me, Jeffrey Sinclair. Those people in there may not be doing things exactly right. As a matter of fact, they may be doing a lot of things wrong. But they are worshiping in ways that were designed back so long ago that almost no one was able to read. They were taught rituals as a way of remembering their faith. They have not had a chance to learn different ways because for the past seventy or eighty years anyone who tried to evangelize in their homeland was murdered. They have escaped, and now this church with its 'smells and bells' is the only taste of their homeland they will ever have, because they know they can never return."

"I guess I just don't understand what you see in it," he replied, wanting only peace.

"That is a grand understatement," she said, and strode forth with a full head of steam.

═══

That evening Jeffrey waited by the back wall and bowed a formal greeting to the old women who were coming to know him by sight. He had long since learned to keep his concerns about the church to himself. Eventually Katya stood, crossed herself, folded her headkerchief and stowed it in her pocket, and walked back toward him. Her eyes shone with the soft luminosity he had come to associate with her times of deep prayer. Sensing her inner glow after almost every time of communing here had done much to make Jeffrey more comfortable with the alien surroundings.

They returned to share a quiet dinner at his apartment, content to sit across from each other and drink of each other's eyes. Conversation came and went like a gentle breeze, the food more a reason to sit and enjoy intimacy than to satisfy a need. The hunger that mingled with their gazes of love was one more easily kept in control when not spoken of openly. Instead, they talked about their plans and made little jokes about the piles of boxes that surrounded them.

For the past week, Katya had spent what little free time she had, between helping in the shop and planning a wedding, moving her things into Jeffrey's flat. As a result, the minuscule living space had taken on the look of a refugee center. Every inch of formerly free space was now crammed with her things. Jeffrey had helped carry in cases and boxes and seen them as a herald of deeper changes to come. He had found himself continually inspecting his own internal vistas, discovering fear mixed in with the joyful anticipation.

By agreement, the cramped front hallway would see duty as her future dressing room. The bathroom grew new shelves, which immediately were filled to overflowing. Jeffrey freed up half the closet and all but two of the bedroom drawers, and discovered his gesture had made not even the slightest dent in her seven suitcases. A dozen boxes containing about half of her books—the ones she did not want stored in his minute cellar—were stacked by the window.

They would have to move; he could see that already. But his world would not permit yet another transition just then. Katya had shown great wisdom, and made do in silent acceptance. For the moment.

"What did you and Gregor talk about?" Katya asked over coffee.

Jeffrey found himself unable to tell her he had agreed to Gregor's insistence that he travel soon to Poland and Ukraine. Instead, he related the experience of watching Gregor's face in the hospital. "He has the most incredible eyes," Jeffrey said. "I've always thought of them as a martyr's eyes. You know, like in the paintings of the saints getting mauled or shot like pincushions, with all the fancy-robed priests standing around and watching."

"Eyes of the soul," Katya agreed.

"They aren't any bigger than anyone else's, I guess. But when I think of them, they always seem twice as large."

"Opened by the wounds of suffering, filled by faith," Katya said. "I don't see how anyone can look into Gregor's eyes and doubt the existence of our Lord."

Laughing at his own embarrassment, Jeffrey said, "Sometimes when I think of Gregor, I imagine him with this light glowing all around, like the old paintings of saints. I know it's not there; it's just this impression I have when I think of our talks. That and his eyes."

Katya was silent a long moment, then told him, "Several years ago, the BBC sent a television team to India to film a special on Mother Teresa. Later they interviewed some of the people who worked on the program, the host and a couple of the technicians. They all talked about filming the hall where the sisters worked with the dying and what an incredible experience it had been for them.

"As they were setting up, they explained, they found that there wasn't enough light for their cameras. The sisters wouldn't let them set up electric lights. There wasn't any electricity, and if they started carting in batteries and cables and stands and lights and everything it would bother the deathly ill patients. So they decided to go ahead and try filming anyway, hoping that they'd come out with at least a couple of clips they could use.

"When they returned to London they found that most of the film they had made in the hall was perfectly clear. Not all of it, though. Where there was no sister, just somebody lying on a bed, you couldn't see anything. Nothing at all. But whenever a sister moved near, Mother Teresa or any other of the sisters, it was all the same. As soon as they came up to the bed, you could see *everything*. The lighting was *perfect*."

Jeffrey fiddled with his cutlery, straightened the tablecloth, placed the salt and pepper in regimental lines, refused to meet her gaze.

"You might as well tell me," Katya said quietly. "It's written all over your face."

"What is?"

"Whatever you and Gregor talked about that has you so tied up in knots."

Jeffrey knew the time had come. Quietly he announced, "I need to go on a buying trip very soon, Katya."

"To Poland?" Her eyes opened into momentary wounds, but she recovered and hid her disappointment behind a brisk tone. "If Gregor and Alexander both agree, then I suppose you must. With Alexander in the hospital, I'll have to stay here and watch the shop, won't I? Mrs. Grayson won't be able to handle it for so long on her own." She folded and refolded her napkin in little nervous gestures. "How long will you be gone?"

"I'm not sure," he said, and forced it out. "Gregor wants me to travel on to Ukraine. The young man we met at the market in Cracow, remember? He has set up a series of buys for me."

"You'll be traveling to Ukraine by yourself?" Now real alarm colored her voice.

"With Yussef, that's the man's name. There's no other way, Katya. Gregor can't go. And you've said yourself you have to stay here and handle the business."

"I hear it's like the Wild West over there. Crime is out of control." Her voice took on a pleading note. "Surely you don't really have to go?"

"Gregor thinks so. Alexander agrees."

"How will you get there?"

"Gregor says Yussef will just drive us across the border." Jeffrey tried to make it all sound matter-of-fact. "I don't even need to get a visa anymore. I can arrange it all at the frontier."

"How long will you stay?"

"Gregor thinks about a week."

"That's not too long."

He reached for her hand. "Try not to worry, Katya."

She pulled backed. "What do you mean? Every Polish woman is born with worry in her genes. It doubles with marriage and triples with children." She continued to give her napkin a good workout. "You'll have to get all your shots."

"I'll make an appointment with the doctor tomorrow," he soothed.

"And you'll have to watch yourself every instant. Keep your suitcase locked at all times. Don't go out at night. Don't ever talk to strangers. Carry your valuables everywhere. Watch out for pickpockets. Count your money carefully every time you pay for something."

"Yes, dear."

"I hear there's a terrible drought and heat wave over there right now. You'll need to pack light clothes. And a hat."

"All right, Katya."

"And water. Don't you dare drink any water that hasn't been boiled before your very own eyes, do you hear me, Jeffrey Sinclair? And I'll have to pack you some food. There was a horrible article I saw about—"

"Yes, my beloved."

"Take your own toilet paper. With all the shortages you'll never find any. Don't smile at me, Jeffrey. This is serious." Her features were creased with worry. "Just look at how Western you are. You might as well have it tattooed on your forehead. Every thief within fifty kilometers is going to take you for an easy target. How are you going to communicate anything? What happens if you need help?"

"Yussef will supply a translator," he hoped.

"That's his name? Yussef?"

"I've already told you," he said calmly. "You're not listening, Katya."

"I'm entrusting my husband to a strange Ukrainian called Yussef?" The napkin was balled into a tight little knot. "How do you know you can trust him?"

"Gregor does."

But she was off and running. "What if you get over there and the hotel doesn't have your reservation? It happens all the time. You'll have to go sleep in the train station with the gypsies." Her voice took on a slight wail. "What if there's a coup? What if—"

"The sky falls," Jeffrey offered.

"Don't be silly. There's a drought. How could the sky—" She took on a stricken look. "Hail! What will you do if it hails?"

"Duck," he replied. "You forgot nuclear fallout."

She reached over and took a vise-grip on his arm. "Chernobyl! That's not too far from where you'll be, and it's just the one disaster they've told us about!"

"I think that just about covers it," Jeffrey said, loving her deeply. "Do you feel better now?"

The little girl appeared in her eyes. "I'll miss you terribly."

He walked around the table and embraced her. "I've not had anybody worry about me like this in a long time. Twenty-nine years old and I feel like I'm going out to the playground for the first time."

"This is not a game, Jeffrey."

"I know," he said, keeping his anticipation over the adventure well hidden. "I know, Katya."

vona Aristonova walked through the hazy dawn toward early morning Mass. The sky retained the same washed-out blue as every morning for the past four months. The drought was the worst in history, the heat a fierce animal by midday.

Ivona went to church every morning, always for the six o'clock service. Always wearing the black lace head shawl and a coat, even on the warmest of summer dawns. Always clutching a few lilacs from her garden, to be placed before her favorite side altar. And always arriving well before Mass was to begin so as to have time to light a candle and kneel and say the ritual prayers twice through before confession.

The fact that she went to church daily made Ivona Aristonova, in her own eyes, a very religious person. Her neighbors, too, considered her devout because she followed the visible pattern. There was little room in her tightly controlled world for the inner life of faith, but she valued the ritual of the church. Church ritual was understandable. It was definable. It was a visible path to follow. The knowledge that she was walking on the sure path toward eternal rest made the misery of her past bearable.

Ivona Aristonova showed great respect toward all priests, although in her mind not all priests deserved it. She bowed to each one, spoke with reverence, felt keen pleasure when one of God's chosen envoys paid her special attention.

Her prayer time involved a fair amount of breast-beating. She could not aspire to sainthood, so she settled for martyrdom. When she thought of her past, which was seldom and never for very long, she felt the stern satisfaction of knowing that her suffering had earned her God's grace.

She knew, in theory, that God was a God of love. But the reality to her was that the Lord was a wrathful judge. She lived in fear of God's judgment at all times. Forgiveness was something longed for, penance counted out with her prayer beads, salvation left for the life after this one.

After she had lit her candle and dipped a finger in the basin of holy water and crossed herself and knelt in the same pew she occupied every morning, Ivona lowered her head in prayer. But instead of beginning the chant of words that usually came without thought or realization of what she was saying, today her mind moved to the coming meeting with Yussef and the bishop. For some reason she herself could not understand, the topic of their discussion troubled her enormously.

And from there her mind flitted to the past. It was an act that she seldom permitted. But today she had no choice. The memories rose unbidden and refused to go away. Ivona knelt and fingered her prayer beads and struggled to begin her prayers, fighting the images that welled up inside her.

She remembered a white bow for her hair.

She remembered how her father had fashioned the clip from a strand of metal chipped from his saw blade. The ribbon had come from her mother's last petticoat. It had been her twelfth birthday present, a far better gift than the one from the previous year. For her eleventh birthday, the shifting tides of war and men in power had sent her on her first train ride. In an unheated boxcar. For seventeen days.

Ivona Aristonova had spent her early years in Poland, part of the large population of Ukrainians who lived in northern and eastern Poland before the Second World War. When the Russians had invaded Poland at the end of the war, most of her town had fallen victim to Stalin's program of Russification. The objective was to quash patriotism to anything but the great Soviet empire through massive relocation efforts, shifting populations about and blurring borders. Populations who might have a legitimate claim to seized property, such as the Poles and the Ukrainians and Jews, had been sent to projects in the distant north.

Ivona Aristonova knelt with eyes tightly closed and remembered how her family had been deposited about one hundred kilometers from a city called Archangelsk. This was west of the Ural Mountains, still in European Russia. But it was at the same latitude as Asiatic Russia, the region known as Siberia, and less than five hundred kilometers below the Arctic Circle.

Their village had stood at the border of a forest. And such a forest. Primeval. Virgin. Limitless. It stretched unbroken from her village all the way to where the ice conquered all. Other than the one road running from their village to distant Archangelsk, there was nothing but trees stretching to the end of the world.

Her father and mother, along with everyone else, had been put to work in the forest. It did not matter that her father had been a schoolteacher and her mother the administrator of a hospital. In that nameless village, the men had cut down trees and the women had chopped off the bark and the smaller limbs. The children had gathered what they could to supplement a meager diet, learning from those who had come earlier to spend every daylight hour searching for food.

Ivona knelt and fingered her beads and remembered what it was like to watch her parents wither under the strain of simply surviving. She remembered how each passing day became another blow pounding home the lesson that had shaped her remaining days; the lesson that love was a luxury she could not afford.

To her vast relief, the priest intoned the opening words of the Mass. Ivona rose to her feet and managed to push away the unbidden memories. For a few moments she was able to lose herself in comfortable ritual and forget all that lay both ahead and behind.

Her husband went to Mass with her on Sundays, more to keep Ivona company than as an act of faith. Yet he was glad that she went to daily services, for in God's infinite grace he also would be remembered through his wife's penance. He was an engineer, a steady man, called good by all who knew him. An honest man. Not a drinker. A man who loved her dearly and did as well by her as this chaotic world permitted. A man who never ceased his yearning to have her return his love.

The women of her circle were certain that Ivona and her husband were bound in a loveless marriage because her husband could not have children. Ivona was called a saint because she bore the martyrdom of childlessness in silence. Ivona did not contradict them. She found it best to wrap her life in layers of secrecy and deny nothing.

After Mass was completed, she hurried back to the church offices to begin her work as the bishop's secretary. Only the bishop and his questions in the confessional threatened to uncover the truth. And she hated the truth most of all.

———

"There can be no further delay," Bishop Michael Denisov told the pair. "Every day raises the risk of our treasures' having departed from Russian soil. If that happens, they shall be lost to us forever."

Ivona shifted uncomfortably. "I still do not like it. An unknown man—"

"To you he is unknown," Yussef interrupted.

"—being entrusted with the secret of our greatest treasure," she persisted. "It is too dangerous."

"Not so dangerous as leaving our treasures in the hands of the Orthodox," Yussef replied. Yussef was Ivona's nephew, her sister's son, a slender young man of fierce independence. For their extended family, his trading with the West had meant the difference between starvation and a relatively comfortable life. And now he was suggesting they use one of these trading contacts to assist with the church's most recent crisis. An American. A dealer in antiques. A man whom Yussef knew by the name of Jeffrey Sinclair.

"We do not know for certain that the Orthodox are involved," the bishop cautioned.

"We know," Yussef stated flatly. "You are too kind when it comes to dealing with our enemies."

"Not all Orthodox," the bishop replied, "are such. Not all."

"Enough," Yussef retorted. "And with our treasures most of all."

Bishop Michael waved it aside. "Be that as it may, we need an outsider. Someone who can come and go at will. Who will not be suspected. Who has reason to be asking the questions we ourselves cannot ask. Who can mask your activities as you continue your search."

"Someone we can trust," Ivona insisted.

"This man we can," Yussef replied.

The bishop asked, "And when does he arrive?"

"Nine days," Yussef replied. "We meet in Cracow."

"But an American," Ivona protested. "A Protestant and a stranger to our cause."

"A friend," Yussef countered, "who has proven himself to be trustworthy."

"For the sake of gain," she scoffed. "He does what he says he will because it pays."

"He does what he promises because he is an honorable man," Yussef countered. "I know this. In my heart of hearts I know."

"But how can we be sure?" Ivona complained. "How can we know that he will do as we ask and not work for his own profit?"

"You must test him," the bishop replied simply.

"Test him how?" she said, disconsolate. "I know nothing of such things."

"Nor do any of us," Bishop Michael agreed. "And so you shall teach him about us and our past and our ways. You are good at that. Teach, and watch his response."

"I know his response," she replied sharply. "He will be a Westerner. He will smile and nod and say, how nice. He will be naive beyond belief. He will have the face of an infant and a mind like bubble gum."

"This is not so," Yussef replied quietly. "How can you say this when you have never met him?"

"All Westerners are such," Ivona replied, not sure herself why she felt so cross at the idea. "Americans especially."

"Jeffrey Sinclair is an honorable man," Yussef repeated, without heat.

"You have trained our dear brother Yussef yourself," Bishop Michael urged. "A man who feels such a debt to you that he assists us in our quest, although he shares neither our faith nor our needs.

A trader who is also the hope of many, because of you, Ivona Aristonova. We rely on him, your very own pupil. Now he tells us that this is the man we require. Should we not give this young man a chance?"

Ivona was silent.

"Teach him," the bishop repeated. "Teach him as much as you can. Shower him with needles of truth about this land of ours. Use your gift to test, and test him hard."

"He will be the sponge I was not," Yussef predicted, grinning broadly, approving the idea. "He will show you his thirst. He will perceive beyond the veil. He will aid us all."

"Go," the bishop urged. "Go and teach and test. You both have my blessing. Only take care, and taste every wind for the first hint of danger."

Andrew arrived to fetch Jeffrey in an enormously jovial mood. "Do hope you won't be giving me trouble today, lad. Hate to have to gather our mates and drag you to the altar."

Jeffrey stepped through his front door and halted at the sight of the vehicle parked outside. "What in the world?"

"It's a boat on wheels, and if you have any doubts, wait till we take our first turning. Lists heavy to port, she does."

The car was a vintage Rolls Royce in burnished gunmetal gray. The fenders reared up and out like a lion's paws. The doors opened front to back. The seats were at a level so as to allow the passengers to look down upon all mere mortals. The hood went on for miles.

"No, no, in the back, lad, in the back." Andrew twisted the old-fashioned handle and bowed Jeffrey inside. "Room to lay back and swoon if your nerves give way."

"This is bigger than a city bus." Jeffrey settled into the plush leather seat and watched Andrew adjust a chauffeur's cap upon his head before climbing behind the wheel. "Is this yours?"

"Only for the day," his friend replied, pulling out the silver-plated handle that started the engine. "As it is, for what I paid I ought to get the Queen's Award for helping the British economy pull out of recession."

Andrew put the car in gear, pressed on the gas, and called out, "Pilot to engine room, all ahead full."

"This is really nice," Jeffrey said, clamping down hard on his nerves. "Thanks."

"Most welcome, lad." Andrew smiled in the rearview mirror. "Think of it as a hearse for your bachelorhood."

"Right. That helps a lot."

"No, suppose not," Andrew replied cheerfully. "Suppose we'll have to call it my wedding gift to the happy couple, then."

Jeffrey wiped damp palms down the sides of his trousers. The dark velvet piping of his tuxedo ran smooth beneath his fingers. "Did you have a case of the nerves before your wedding?"

"Not half. Slept a total of thirty-five minutes the entire last week before taking the plunge."

"What, you timed yourself?"

"Wasn't hard. Tossing and turning as I was, I watched the ruddy clock go right 'round for seven nights in a row. Kept getting up to make sure it was plugged in, the hands moved so slow."

"But still you did it."

"What, walk the lonely mile? Too right I did. Knew the old dear wouldn't even leave a greasy stain if I did a bonk."

"A what?"

"Bonk, lad. Bonk. Head for the hills in Yankish. Do a number. Catch a jet plane. Ride off into the sunset. Take a—"

"I get the picture."

Andrew inspected him in the car mirror. "You're not going to make me pull the manacles from the boot, now, are you?"

"You don't have to say that with such glee," Jeffrey replied.

Andrew laughed and changed the subject. "Been down working on the Costa Geriatrica, I have."

"Where's that?"

"Oh, it's what we call the region from Brighton to Hastings. Bit like your Miami Beach, I suppose. Minus the sun, of course."

"And the crime."

"Well, there you are. That's the price you pay for not enough rain in Florida. Raises a body's temperature, bound to. Turns thoughts to pillage and plunder and other such diversions."

"So what were you doing down in Brighton? Hunting down some new pieces?"

"Too right. Old dear had a houseful, too, she did. Problem was, she'd never taken much notice of their condition, said articles having been in her family since sheriffs were still lopping off heads instead of giving out parking tickets. No, if the worms stopped holding hands, her whole house'd dissolve into sawdust." Andrew permitted himself a satisfied smile. "So to keep the trip from being a total loss, I bought myself a boat."

"You what?"

He nodded. "Almost new. This Frenchie sailed it over, discovered on his maiden voyage that he hated the sight of more water than could fit in his tub. He named the ship *Bien Perdu*. Closest I could come to a translation was 'Good and Lost.' Thought I'd keep it, seeing as how that's exactly what I'll be ten minutes after untying from the dock."

Jeffrey tasted a smile, only to have it dissolve into a new flood of doubt. "Would you do it again? Get married, I mean."

Andrew nodded emphatically. "Long as there's love, lad, even the roughest days are as good as it gets."

Jeffrey felt a settling of his internal seas. "That's reassuring, Andrew. Thanks."

"Think nothing of it." He took a corner wide, gave a regal wave to a group of tourists who craned to search the car's interior for someone wearing a crown. "How's Alexander doing?"

"The doctors seem to be more confident every time I see them," Jeffrey replied. "Of course, they hedge their bets worse than bookies at the track. Getting a straight answer out of them is like trying to squeeze blood from a stone."

"Yes, well, that's why they call it a medical *practice*, isn't it. They're all still studying, trying to get it right." Andrew pulled up to the main hospital entrance and stopped. He turned around and observed with evident pleasure, "I've just enough time to pop around for the bride-to-be and make it back on the hour. If there's even the bittiest chance of your buying passage to Paraguay in the next ten minutes or so, I'll gladly chain you to the nearest tree."

"You're a big help," Jeffrey said, climbing out.

"No, suppose not." Andrew put the car into gear, then said through the open window, "Think of it this way, lad. If the old ticker gives way before you make it up the aisle, there's ever so many doctors in there who'd love to practice on you."

Jeffrey's entry into the hospital lobby—dressed as he was in tuxedo, starched shirt with studs, and silk bow tie—caused a suitable stir. Families clustered around patients in robes and pajamas ceased their conversation as though silenced by a descending curtain. Nurses and hospital staff shared smiles and hellos; clearly the news had made the rounds, and the event met with their approval. A few went so far as to offer the thoroughly embarrassed Jeffrey their congratulations and best wishes.

The closer he came to the chapel, the more his fear turned to a barrier against the world. He walked down the long Casualties hall, exchanging numb hellos and handshakes with smiling staff. He forced his legs to carry him down the main stairs and on past signs for Oncology, Radiation Therapy, Obstetrics. He turned a corner and walked by a door labeled Dispensing Chemist, briefly entertaining thoughts of stopping by for a mild sedative, something he could take by the gallon. Next was the Cardiac section—another two beats a minute faster and they'd have their first walk-in patient. A final corner and he had arrived.

Alexander was there by the chapel's closed door, seated in a wheelchair but dressed to the nines, as befitting a best man, heart attack or no. Count Garibaldi, who had agreed to push the best man's chair, was there beside him. In his severe formal wear, the count looked like a black velvet stork, with beak to match. Jeffrey exchanged greetings, shook hands, saw little, felt nothing.

Then a voice behind him said, "Here she is, lad. All safe and sound and pretty as a picture."

He turned, and knew an immediate sense of utter clarity. Of complete and total *rightness*.

Katya bathed them all in her joy. Jeffrey most of all.

Her dress was Victorian in feel, modest and alluring at the same time. The color was called candlelight, the shade of the lightest champagne rose. The fabric was antique satin and lace that her mother had found in a local Coventry market. Together they had oohed and aahed and giggled like schoolgirls as the dress had taken shape, denying Jeffrey the first glance. Until now.

He knew the terms to describe it because he had heard her speak of it in endless detail. It had what was called a princess line, fitting snugly from shoulders to hips, then belling out to a flounced skirt that ended just above her ankles. Her sleeves were tight from wrist to elbow, buttoned with tiny seed pearls, then loose and airy to where they gathered at her shoulders. Her neckline descended far enough to allow an elegant emerald necklace, a sentimental gift from Jeffrey's grandmother, to rest upon her silken skin. She held a bouquet of white roses and Peruvian lilies.

For Jeffrey, the moment was suspended in the timelessness of true love. The others cooed over her dress, her flowers, her hair. Hospital staff gathered in the hall behind them and freely bestowed smiles on all and sundry. The hubbub touched Jeffrey not at all. He stood and drank in the loveliness of her and knew that here was a moment he would carry in his heart and mind for all his days.

Alexander cleared his throat. "Although I lack personal experience in these matters, I believe it is necessary for the groom to parade down front before our festivities may proceed."

"The gent means you, lad," Andrew said, beaming from ear to ear.

Jeffrey shared a smile and a murmured affection with his bride-to-be, then turned and pushed through the chapel doors.

And stopped again.

The room was *filled* with flowers.

The two floral arrangements Katya had ordered stood on the front altar. The remainder of the room, however, was decked out in vast arrays of cascading roses, lilies, and gladioli.

"A small token of thanks," Alexander murmured from beside him, "for allowing me to be a part of this day."

From the back corner, a trio of ancient-looking gentlemen struck up a stringed-instrument rendition of Chopin's "Polonaise."

Jeffrey looked down at his friend. "Aren't they the musicians from Claridge's?"

Alexander nodded. 'They were the only ones I could locate and hire without undue fuss. Now on you go."

Jeffrey made do with a gentle squeeze of the old gentleman's shoulder. He walked to the altar and waited while the trio paused and began the Wedding March.

Then Katya descended.

That was how he would always remember it, how he felt as he stood and watched the moment unfold. Katya descended to join with him in earthbound form, bestowing upon him a higher love.

Throughout the ceremony, Jeffrey remained showered with the light and the love and the wholehearted joy that shone from Katya's eyes.

———

Jeffrey stood at the corner of Alexander's living room, amazed at how much noise eighteen people could make.

His eyes moved from one group to the next. He watched his father convulse with laughter over something the count said. He saw Sydney Greenfield chatter through a story, drinking and eating all the while. He knew a momentary pang at the wish that Alexander had been well enough to join them. But his own sense of well-being was too strong just then to grant much room to sorrow.

What had surprised him most during the run-up to their wedding was how well his mother and Katya's had hit it off. Their first contact had been one of genteel inspection, the first few days very formal. By the time of the wedding, however, they were sisters in all but flesh. His mother helped Magda to her seat, brought people over to meet her, sat and chatted with animation. With laughter. And Magda replied with a smile. Jeffrey watched to see if it would split her face.

Always his gaze returned to Katya. She flowed from group to group, and wherever she stood, the room's light shifted to remain focused upon her. She approached someone, and smiles bloomed like flowers opening to the sun. Men stood taller, women leaned forward to speak, all were richly rewarded with a moment of sharing in her happiness.

"This isn't your day to play wallflower, lad," Andrew said as he approached.

"Just taking a breather," Jeffrey replied, his eyes resting upon Katya. "And enjoying the view."

"I've never had much respect for a man who's not able to out-marry himself," Andrew said. "Glad to see you're upholding my estimation of you, lad."

Jeffrey watched as Katya spoke and laughed and positively shimmered. "I'm a lucky guy."

"You're a ruddy sight more than that. You've the good fortune of twenty men, lad. Congratulations."

Jeffrey caught sight of himself in an ancient mercury mirror. Smugness fought for place with wonder across his features. "I can't thank you enough for the car—"

"Don't give it another thought." Andrew paused, then said, "As a matter of fact, I've got a news of my own. Care for a glass of something wet?"

"No thanks. What news?"

"My wife and I've decided to adopt a little one," Andrew said, then, when Jeffrey laughed, "What's so funny?"

"You and your British calm. You'd announce the start of World War III without raising your voice."

"Having a wee one dribble on your best suit is a trial, I'll admit, but not quite as bad as that." Andrew grinned. "Life was bent on sparing us the bother, but my wife and I were never ones to rest on good sense when we were wanting something. Especially when it comes to kids."

Jeffrey offered his hand. "Congratulations, Andrew. I'm sure you're going to be a great dad."

"Wish I shared your confidence, lad. The thought is enough to give me a bad case of the shakes, I'll admit." His grip on Jeffrey's hand lingered. "I'd thought of asking you to be his godfather."

"Me?"

"Don't look so shocked. You've got all the right ingredients for a godparent, far as I can see. And in years to come, you'll be able to give the little blighter the kind of gifts he deserves, like a matching suite of Louis XIV furniture." Andrew sobered momentarily. "Seriously, lad. I'd be ever so glad if you'd accept."

"I'm honored, Andrew. Really."

"That's settled, then." Andrew dropped his hand. "You'd be amazed the things you and the little wife will get involved with when your own time comes. Never knew wallpaper coloring was a national priority." He motioned to where Magda waved at him. "You're being summoned, lad. Time to rejoin the fray."

Magda patted the chair next to her as he approached and said, "Allow me the honor of sitting next to the most handsome man in the room for a moment."

"I am only a complement for your daughter's beauty," Jeffrey replied, sitting down.

"For this moment, perhaps." Magda searched out her daughter, responded to her wave with yet another smile. "Yes, it is indeed her day."

"You have raised a beautiful daughter," Jeffrey told her.

Magda turned her attention back to him. "And granted her the good sense to choose an excellent man."

"Thank you, Mrs. Nichols."

"I was so pleased that my daughter was not artistically inclined." She sipped from her glass. "I did not wish the Lord to burden her with this passion."

Jeffrey found her across the crowded room. "She has your passion," he replied. "It comes out in other ways."

"I am glad." Magda inspected his face, then asked, "You are worried by this trip to Ukraine?"

He nodded, no longer surprised by her changes in direction or choices of topic. "Does it show so clearly?"

"No, but I know my daughter. She will have bestowed her own worries upon you. Her life and her heritage has been shaped by one view of the Soviet empire. She sees them as the oppressors. The Bolsheviks. The conquerors. The instruments of Stalin's terror." She waved the past aside. "But this nation no longer exists. Who knows what you shall find?"

"I think this uncertainty is almost as frightening as what you described."

"This too is true." Magda smiled. "Perhaps you are right to be worried after all."

"Thanks a lot."

"When do you depart?"

"Tonight we have a suite here at the Grosvenor House, then tomorrow we leave for five days in Monte Carlo. I travel to Cracow two days later."

"Know that you shall travel with the prayers of at least two women sheltering you."

"Thank you, Magda. That means a lot."

"So, enough of the future. Today we must retain the moment's joy, no?" Magda reached beside her chair and came up with a picture frame wrapped in white tissue paper. "I have made something for you."

"That's wonderful, Magda." He made to rise. "Wait, let me go get Katya."

"My daughter has already seen this," she replied. "She was the one who suggested the quotation."

Jeffrey accepted the package, folded back the paper, and released a long, slow breath.

The frame was simple and wooden. The matting was of dark-blue velvet. Set upon this cloth was a flat, hand-painted ceramic rectangle.

The picture's background was softest ivory. Upon it was painted a man cresting the peak of an impossibly high mountain. With one hand he clutched for support; the other he stretched heavenward. Above him a lamb, shining as the sun, reached down, offering a pair of wings.

Beneath were scrolled the words, "'Let us press on to know God,' Hosea 6:4."

Jeffrey's mother stepped over to where they sat. "May I borrow my son for a moment?"

"Of course."

"Did you paint that, Magda? Oh, it's beautiful. May I show it to my husband?" She lifted the picture from Jeffrey's grasp and moved off.

Jeffrey stammered, "Magda, I don't know how to thank you."

She smiled once more. "You shall make a worthy son-in-law, Jeffrey. Of that I have not the slightest doubt."

"Jeffrey?" His mother reappeared. "I do need to speak to you for a moment."

"Go," Magda said quietly. "My blessings upon you both, and upon this wondrous day."

His mother pulled him over to another quiet corner. "Katya is as wonderful as you said."

"You spent a week together and you're just getting around to deciding this?"

She gave him a playful hug. "I've told you that before and you know it."

He pulled a face. "I don't recall."

"You don't recall," she mimicked, rolling the tones. "Listen to my posh son."

Jeffrey was so completely happy he felt he could have skated a Fred Astaire dance step across the ceiling. "You know where that word comes from? In the days of colonial India, people with connections and experience chose the cooler side of the boat for their voyages out and back—port out, starboard home. Posh. Very snooty group, from the sounds of it."

She looked at him with genuine approval. "You're very happy with your life, aren't you." It was not a question.

He nodded. "Other than the odd crisis now and then, very happy."

"These bad things come," she said, her smile never slipping. "If you are strong, and if you're lucky enough to marry a good partner, and if you're wise enough to know a strong faith, the bad things go too."

"They do at that," he agreed.

"Well, I didn't pull you away to discuss the lost colonies of the British Empire."

He played at surprise. "No?"

"Your brother asked me to wait until your wedding day to pass on this momentous news. Don't ask me why. I have long since given up trying to figure out how my sons' minds work." She took a breath, then said, "Your little brother is thinking of becoming a monk."

That dropped his jaw. "Charles?"

"Unless you have yet another brother stashed somewhere which I don't know about, that must be the one."

"Charles a monk?"

"Better than Charles a drunk. His words, not mine. He is very sorry to miss the festivities, by the way. Genuinely sorry. But travel is such a tremendous difficulty for him. We discussed it and decided this was better for all concerned."

But Jeffrey wasn't ready to let that one go. "Charles is going to be a monk?"

"Not only has he convinced me and your father, but the abbot is taking this most seriously as well."

"Abbot?"

"The monastery head. Call him chief holy honcho if it makes it any easier to swallow. Your father does. He's quite a nice man, actually."

"I can't believe it."

"A fairly standard reaction. Charles says to tell you that he has finally recognized himself as a man of extremes. A born fanatic. Either he lands in the gutter, or he takes his religion thing all the way."

"That's what he calls it? His religion thing?"

She smiled, a touch of sadness to her eyes. "My dear son Charles is going to, as he puts it, spend the rest of his life doing a major prayer gig."

She walked over to the gift-laden table, extracted a long slender package, and returned. "He asked that I give you this on the big day when we're alone. I suppose this is as alone as we're going to be. It's a poem. He wrote it himself and did his own calligraphy. You'll be happy to know his poetry doesn't sound like the way Charles talks."

Jeffrey unwrapped the box, pulled out the frame, and read:

Tonight I Hear

Tonight I hear the angels sing
   With ears that never heard this earth,
A gift of grace long undeserved
   From One who longs to grant me wings.

Oh Lord, how long must I remain
   Bound to earth and earthly bonds?
Can my home your home become,
   Your love my love, my life your aims?

I seek, I seek, and cannot find
   A gift which is forever mine,
And in my frantic fury fail
   To hear His voice so softly say,
     Be still.
     Be still.
     Be still,
And know that all is here, and thine.

Salvation, grace, and guiding light
   I know are mine, yet yearn for heights
Which He Himself has called me to,
   Far beyond this clinging clime.

Yet perfection shall be never mine;
   Only His, and mine when I can die
To Him, and let Him live through me,
   And know that here indeed are wings
     That soar.
     That soar.
     That soar,
Beyond earth's stormy shore
   to Him.

Jeffrey looked back to his mother and managed to say, "Tell Charles I'm proud of him."

"Jeffrey?" Katya came over, rested a gentle hand on his shoulder.

His mother stood, shared smiles with Katya. "If I had ever tried to dream up an image of the perfect daughter-in-law, it would not have held a candle to you, my dear."

They exchanged hugs from the heart. His mother turned her attention back to Jeffrey and said, "May the Lord bless you and your wife and your lives together, with love and His presence most of all."

Then Katya took her place before Jeffrey, and looked up at her new husband with eyes that flooded his heart with their radiance. She whispered for his ears alone, "It is time, my darling."

Monte Carlo crowned a rocky promontory that descended in steep stages from the Maritime Alps to the Mediterranean Sea. The road running along the coast, the one that linked the tiny principality with such other Riviera resorts as Cannes and Antibes and Cap Ferrat, was called the Corniche. It was bounded on the Mediterranean side by a hand-wrought stone balustrade that gave way first to rocky beaches, then to a sea whose aching blue was matched only by the cloudless sky.

At the heart of Monte Carlo rested its famous port, the waters dotted with the ivory-colored yachts of the international jet set. The surrounding houses crowded tightly against one another, grudgingly permitting only the smallest of spaces for tiny, cobblestone streets. The architecture spanned the years from *La Belle Époque* to ultramodern. Yet somehow it all fit, if perhaps only because of the sun and the sea and the romantic eyes with which Jeffrey and Katya blessed all they saw.

Just off the port rose the gracious and stately Casino. Even surrounded as it was by such chrome and glass apparitions as the Loew's hotel, the Casino remained a regal crown harking back to Monte Carlo's glory days. Facing it across the stately Place du Casino was the wedding-cake structure of the Hotel de Paris, the most prestigious hotel in the kingdom.

The exterior was all honey-colored stone and liveried footmen and wide, red-carpeted stairs and grand towers. The interior was all gilt and marble and Persian carpets and crystal chandeliers. The suite Alexander had arranged for them had a view up over the rooftops to the port and the sea beyond.

It was a magical time, a sharing of happiness that knew no earthly bounds. Nights were too precious to allow for a willing descent into slumber. Exhaustion would creep upon them while one spoke and the other tried to listen, and suddenly it would be dawn. And they would still be together, opening their eyes to another day of shared joy.

They spoke of the serious, the future, the infinite. They dwelled long and joyfully upon the meaningless, the unimportant, and gave it eternal significance with their love.

"I know it's a little late to be worrying about such things," he said the fourth morning, the day of their visit to Prince Markov. "But I've got to ask. Can you cook?"

As was their newfound custom, they took breakfast in their room. They found it all too new, this beginning of their days together, to share it with others. Within minutes of their call, room-service waiters in starched white uniforms rolled in a linen-clad table bearing flaky croissants, fresh fruit, silver pots containing thick black morning coffee and frothy hot milk, and always a rose in a vase. Katya kept the flowers in a water glass on her bedside table.

Katya nodded emphatically. "I make the best gooshy-gasha on earth."

He made a face. "Sounds divine."

"It takes lots of practice. I started when I was, oh, I think maybe two and a half or three years old."

He marveled at the graceful slant to her almond-shaped eyes. "Have I ever told you how beautiful you are?"

She nodded happily. "You take a shiny new kitchen bake-pan and carry it out to the backyard. Then you mix in different things from the garden."

"For taste," he said.

She shook her head, making the dark strands shiver. "For color. Green grass, brown dirt, some water to hold it together, and as many different petals as you could find. Petals are a key ingredient of gooshy-gasha. We had a dozen fruit trees in our backyard. I remember going from tree to tree, picking handfuls of petals off the ground. I called them springtime snow, I can still remember that. It was different from wintertime snow because you could hold it in your hand and it wouldn't melt."

"When you talk like that your face gets like a little girl's," Jeffrey mused, and felt his heart twist at the thought of a child with her face. *Their* child.

But she was still caught in the fun of remembering and sharing. "Gooshy-gasha. I haven't thought about that in years. When it was thick enough you could turn the pan upside down and make what I called a *babeczka*; that means a little cake."

"A garden variety cupcake."

"A baby fruit cake," she corrected him, "with grass and petals instead of fruit and nuts. It was mostly brown, with little bits of green and pink sticking out. I'd serve it to my dolls and our pet bunnies and maybe the neighbor's dog, if I could get him to sit still long enough to put a bib on him. He was such a messy eater." She gazed with eyes so happy they rested on him with a joyous pain. "You're much neater than he was."

"Thanks ever so much." He swung around the table so that he could nestle into her lap, then said, "Teach me some Polish."

"Oh no, not now." She almost sang the words. "Nobody can learn it just like this. Not even you. It's the most difficult language in all Europe."

He made mock-serious eyes. "More difficult than English?"

She smiled. "Until you learn. It sounds a lot like Russian to the ear, though the Polish alphabet is not Cyrillic. It is a Slavic language, and all Slavic tongues have similarities, just like all Latin languages."

He traced the line of her chin with one finger, wondered at the pleasure such a simple, intimate gesture could bring. "Teach me something, Katya. Just a couple of words."

"Let's see. *O Rany Boskie* means the wounds of Christ, a favorite remark of complaining grandmothers." Happiness lent a childlike chanting tone to her voice. "*Sto lat* means a hundred years, and is used as a toast and a birthday greeting. *Na zdrowie* is a drinking salute and means to your health. *Trzymaj się* literally means hold on to yourself, but is used to mean hang in there. It's said between friends upon departure or hanging up the phone. *Słucham* means I'm listening and is said when you pick up the phone."

"You have beautiful ears," he whispered, reaching up to kiss the nearest one.

She pushed him away with the backhanded gesture of an impatient four-year-old. "Shush, this is serious. Now the word for hello is, repeat after me, *Cześcz*."

"Only if you wait until I need to sneeze," he said, twirling a wayward strand.

"Okay, then *Pa-pa*. Try that. It means goodbye, but you only say it to a close friend."

"That's one thing I never want to say to you," he told her solemnly. "Not ever."

She looked down at him with merry eyes. "*Całuję rączki*. That's thank you in the most formal, flirtatious sense, and really means, I kiss your hand."

He ran his fingers around her neck to mold with the feather-soft hairs on her nape. "How do you say I love you?"

Her eyes shone with a violet-gray light that filled his heart to bursting. She both whispered and sang the words, "*Ja cię kocham*."

=====

Late that afternoon they took a taxi along the winding Corniche to Alexander's former residence, now owned by Prince Vladimir Markov. Villa Caravelle rose from a steep hillside overlooking the azure waters of the Mediterranean. The walls surrounding the circular drive were of small, round pebbles, overlaid with great blooming pom-poms of wisteria. The air was heavily scented by flowers, especially jasmine. Everything was perfectly manicured—miniature citrus trees, bursts of bougainvillea, magnolia in full bloom. The air was absolutely still.

Jeffrey rang the bell, caught sight of Katya's expression, and asked, "Do you mind having to do this business on our honeymoon?"

"A little," she admitted.

"Sorry we didn't go to Scotland after all?"

"Of course not." She smiled up at him. "Let's just get this real-life stuff over with as quickly as possible and return to fairyland, okay?"

The door was answered by a severe-looking woman in a navy blue dress. "Monsieur et Madame Sinclair? Entrez-vous, s'il vous plaît."

They stepped into a high-ceilinged marble foyer. When the door closed behind them, their eyes took a moment to adjust to the darker confines. In the distance a voice said, "Mr. Sinclair, madame, please come in."

Electronically controlled shutters lifted from great arched windows. Light splashed into the salon with the brilliance of theater spotlights. Jeffrey was suddenly very glad that Alexander was not there to see what had happened to his former home.

The great room reminded him of a museum between major exhibitions. Antiques and works of art cluttered every imaginable space. Nothing matched. Tapestries from the late Middle Ages crowded up next to Impressionist paintings, which were illuminated by gilded art-deco lamps held by giant nymphs. Persian carpets overlapped one another, with the excess rolled up along the walls. There were three chaises longues from three different centuries, one green silk, one brocade, one red velour. A mahogany china cupboard stuffed to overflowing with heavy silver and gold-plate stood alongside a delicate satinwood secretary, and that next to a sixteenth-century corner cupboard which in turn was partially hidden behind a solid ebony desk.

Prince Markov walked toward Jeffrey with an outstretched hand. "You are no doubt wondering why a man who appears to have everything would be interested in another worldly possession."

That being far kinder than what he was truly thinking, Jeffrey replied with a simple, "Yes."

"Alexander Kantor has spoken so highly of you," Katya fielded for him.

Markov kissed her hand. "Madame Sinclair, enchanté." A slight blush touched Katya's cheeks, betraying her reaction to both her new name and to his old-world attention.

"Please be so kind as to follow me." Prince Vladimir Markov had the sleek look of a high-level corporate chairman. He was balding, even-featured, manicured from head to toe, and frigidly aloof. The results of too many overly rich meals were hidden by a chin kept aloft and by suits carefully tailored to hide a growing bulge. His lips held to a polite smile that meant absolutely nothing. Intelligent eyes viewed the world as a hawk might view its prey.

Katya stopped before the wall beside his desk and said, "Look at these wonderful pictures." They were enlarged sepia-colored prints of stern-looking men with square-cut beards and unsmiling women in bustles and trains.

Markov gave a tolerant smile. "Ah, well, they're actually what you might call family photographs."

"And is this your father?" she asked, pointing to one of the figures, which bore a marked resemblance.

"Yes, my father as a young man. He was quite a remarkable gentleman. He loved to hunt. He loved art. And he absolutely loved the classics. He understood the world through mythology. He was in his twenties when he left Russia, never to return."

"He left because of the October Revolution?"

"The Revolution, yes," Markov mused, his eyes on the picture. "The Bolsheviks and their Revolution changed everything."

"And who is this man here beside him?" Jeffrey asked.

"Ah, yes. That face may indeed look a little familiar. It is Czar Nicholas the Second. My father and he were distant cousins and quite close friends in their younger days."

"A prince of the royal family of Russia," Katya murmured.

Markov smiled dryly. "There were any number of princes and dukes in those days."

"It must have been very difficult for your family to lose all that during the Revolution," Jeffrey offered.

"At least my father was spared his life," Markov evaded. "He was passing the summer here on the Riviera, as many Russians did at the time. He stayed a few weeks longer than most, and that sealed his fate. Word came from his own father not to travel back, that the situation was becoming too dangerous. Shortly thereafter, the czar and his family were taken prisoner. The Bolsheviks had overthrown the government. Nothing more was heard from my father's father or, for that matter, from anyone else in my family."

He motioned them forward. "Shall we sit out on the terrace? Please watch your step here; these carpets were meant for my family's larger estate. As you can see, I have little space here for my remaining possessions."

He led them out through great double glass doors onto a flagstone terrace. Below, the property plunged steeply toward the sparkling Mediterranean. Jeffrey stepped to the edge and took several deep breaths, feeling as if he had been searching for air back in that cluttered room.

"Perhaps Mr. Kantor told you I sold my somewhat larger estate," Markov said, holding Katya's chair and waving Jeffrey to the seat opposite. "The palace was rather old, and required renovations that were outrageously expensive. Quite beyond the reach of an exiled prince, I assure you. What you saw inside, and of course what is contained in the other rooms, is all that I have left now of my family's glorious past."

"Certainly some of your items are quite valuable," Jeffrey ventured, wondering where the conversation was leading.

"It is not a question of price," Markov replied. "I suppose it is a matter of sentimental attachment. There are stories, some shreds of family history associated with each of these things.

"But that is all in the past," he continued, slapping his hand down on the tabletop. "And what matters about the past is the use to which it is put in the future. Which brings me to my reason for asking you here. Circumstances in Russia have changed beyond any of our imaginings. And now the time has come to act."

Markov's every action seemed to have the slightly forced quality of something carefully thought out, impeccably stage-managed down to the last detail. Jeffrey wondered whether this demeanor masked a hidden agenda, or was simply a product of an aristocratic upbringing. He had not met enough princes to know how they behaved under normal circumstances.

"What can we do for you?" he asked.

"I wish you to assist me in reclaiming what is rightfully mine," Markov replied. "The time has come for our Saint Petersburg estate, which the Communists confiscated, to return to its rightful owners."

"That is the acquisition you want us to manage?" Jeffrey asked. "You want us to go into Saint Petersburg and reclaim your family's estate?"

"That is correct. I wish for you to go and evaluate the circumstances, carefully examine and appraise the value of the estate, together with whatever may have remained of the original fittings, then report back to me."

"If you don't mind my asking, why don't you go yourself?"

Markov shook his head emphatically. "Things in Russia are not as simple as they seem. Every local government is desperate for funds. As soon as they hear that a Markov is involved, someone who wants the property for reasons beyond a commercial interest, the price would immediately skyrocket. Not to mention that there is still great animosity toward the old monarchy. I would venture that the Saint Petersburg government would not be pleased with the sudden reappearance of a long-lost prince of the royal family."

"You need a buffer," Katya offered.

"One of the utmost confidentiality," he confirmed. "To make the transaction a success, I must remain utterly unseen."

"We have experience in antiques and works of art," Jeffrey pointed out. "But none at all in international real estate."

"Who has experience in lost Russian palaces? What I need more than anything is someone I can trust." Markov was emphatic. "Your Mr. Kantor proved a most worthy business associate in the past. Since then I have made quite thorough checks into his background and his transactions. He is a man of impeccable standing. His knowledge of Eastern Europe is extensive. And he has recommended you most highly. In my humble opinion, I feel I could not ask for a more worthy representative."

There wasn't anything humble within five miles of this guy, Jeffrey thought, and asked, "So whom do I say I am representing?"

"You shall be the official representative of Artemis Holdings Limited. It is my own company, one I founded many years ago.

On its board sit some Swiss and British colleagues involved in international investments and the like. My name appears nowhere."

Jeffrey replied as he thought Alexander would have wished. "I am greatly honored by your confidence, Prince Markov. Naturally, I will have to discuss this with Mr. Kantor, but with his approval I would be happy to act on your behalf."

"Excellent." Markov fingered his tie nervously. "With the Russian economy in chaos, it is hard to say exactly how the privatization of a palace will proceed. However, I understand that approval is most likely to be given to companies planning an ongoing business activity. The documents I have prepared include a business plan for an import-export operation. Associates of mine in the Artemis group are involved in the steel trade. I shall see to details of their business from an office in my palace."

"I understand," Jeffrey said, wishing that were the case.

"Splendid. Your fees will be transferred to you as and when you require." Markov rose to his feet, their audience at an end. "I will send the dossier to London by private courier."

"I can't tell you exactly when I'll be able to travel," Jeffrey warned. "I have another trip planned to Ukraine and—"

"I shall pay what is necessary to ensure the promptest possible attention," Markov replied in his lofty manner. "This is, as you can imagine, a matter of enormous urgency."

Jeffrey called Alexander from Heathrow airport to report their safe arrival and to see if all was well. Alexander had just that morning returned home from the hospital.

"Thank you, my young friend. And the same to you. Yes, it is indeed wonderful to again be in my own flat. I cannot tell you how eager I am to return to the business of living."

"I cannot tell you," Jeffrey replied, "how great it is to hear you say that."

"I take it you had a successful journey."

"Extremely."

"I was referring to the business matters," Alexander commented dryly.

"Oh, sure. That, too. Is there anything we can do for you now?" he asked, half-wanting to check in on the old gentleman and half-hoping that they could go straight home. *Home.* The word carried an utterly thrilling new definition.

"Most certainly," Alexander replied emphatically. "There is something I have been thinking about every day since my recovery."

"What's that?"

"My dear boy," Alexander said, his tone sharpening. "You really shouldn't offer unless you mean it."

"No, no, it's fine. We both wanted to check in on you."

"Very well," Alexander replied. "Chinese."

"Chinese?" Visions of Oriental mistresses wafted through his mind.

"I have a colossal craving for a Chinese meal."

"I think that can be arranged," Jeffrey said, smiling toward a curious Katya.

"Something that will awaken my taste buds from the insensate slumber induced by hospital fare."

"What did you have in mind?"

"Be so good as to stop by Mr. Kai's on South Audley Street," Alexander instructed.

"At six pounds per egg roll," Jeffrey pointed out, "they're a bit up-market for take-away."

"Anyone returning from a stay at the Hotel de Paris in Monte Carlo has no right whatsoever to make such comments," Alexander retorted. "Now then. I presume that you two shall be joining me."

"Just a second while I ask the wife." *Wife.* The spoken word gave him thrills. He cupped the receiver and said to Katya, "Alexander wants us to join him for dinner."

"Sounds lovely," she said, then blessed him with a look that curled his toes. "Just so we don't stay too long."

"We'd be happy to," Jeffrey said to the telephone. He fished a pen and ticket envelope from his pocket. "Fire away."

"We shall start with shark's fin soup, but only if it has been made today. You must stress that. Followed by their freshest fish cooked with ginger, spring onions, and baby sweet corn. You had best order quite a lot of that."

"You've given this a lot of thought."

"You cannot conceive how much. I am quite certain hospitals make it a habit to lace their meals with mild anesthetic. It is far less expensive than preparing a decent cuisine, especially when so few of their patrons care what they place in their mouths." Alexander returned to the business at hand. "And of course we must have Peking duck. With more than an ample supply of steamed pancakes, mind. Don't allow them to skimp. And plum sauce. Make sure it is fresh as well."

"Sharpen your chopsticks," Jeffrey said. "We'll be at your place by six."

———

A cheerful fire dispelled the night's meager vestige of damp and chill, not an unfamiliar occurrence on a London summer eve.

Across the polished mahogany expanse of Alexander's dining-room table, Meissen china fought for space with an abundance of aluminum and plastic take-away containers.

"We had a wonderful trip," Katya announced, as everyone began slowing down.

"Amazing," Jeffrey agreed. "No, better than that. What comes after amazing?"

"I'm sure it would do my gradually recovering heart no good whatsoever to imagine," Alexander replied. "Would anyone care for this last pancake?"

"We can't thank you enough," Katya added.

"It was my pleasure," Alexander rejoined. "Words truly spoken from the heart."

"There's a lot to tell," Jeffrey said.

"All carefully edited for my feeble ears, I trust."

"I was speaking of the business matters."

"Naturally." Deftly he reached across the table with his chopsticks. "Neither of you cares for this last bit of duck, I take it."

"Monsieur Markov's proposition is going to require a lot of thought," Katya said.

"You can say that again," Jeffrey agreed.

Instead of replying directly, Alexander set down his chopsticks, pressed a napkin to his lips, and looked around the room. "At times I wondered if ever I would enjoy another night like this," he said quietly.

Katya reached across to take Jeffrey's hand. He found himself unable to look her way.

"There were moments," Alexander went on, a wintery bleakness to his voice, "when I grew utterly tired of it all. The bed became a holding pen, a place to keep my wasting form until it was time to depart."

"I have never prayed so hard in my life as I did for your recovery," Jeffrey managed.

Gray eyes fastened upon him. "Do you know, I believe there were moments when I could actually feel your prayers. Not in a physical sense, no. And not just yours. You were there also, my dear young lady. Gregor, too. The friends who have enriched my later years gathered there in heart and spirit and lifted the cloak of darkness and despair from me. I was able at such times to see beyond the body's defeat and realize that, in matters of greatest importance, time holds no boundaries."

Alexander returned his gaze to the room. "All this afternoon I have been content simply to sit and to drink in the beauty which this realization has granted me. Everything has taken on the most remarkable sheen. All before me is crowned in God's great glory. A shaft of sunlight through the window, the color of light against the wall, your return and our meal and the discussion yet to come. I do realize that in time this awareness will dim, clouded over by the cares of daily life. But for this moment, this glorious moment, I feel I have glimpsed the tiniest sliver of what it means to be alive. Thanks to your gift of prayers in my hour of direst need, and thanks to the Lord above for His gift of salvation, I have seen beyond the confines of my feeble realm and seen the gift of life for what it is meant to be. In this moment, this hour, I feel I have tasted what is yet to come."

A heavy rain streaked the broad patio doors as Prince Vladimir Markov ushered the general into his overcrowded study. As always, the military man unbent sufficiently to cast an acquisitive eye over some of Markov's more valuable items. Markov played the genial host, pointing out remarkable features and describing minor scandals of long-dead relatives connected to the piece at hand. General Surikov seemed unaware of the fact that the names which Markov tossed casually forward had for three centuries ruled the largest nation on earth.

Markov seated them in a relatively uncluttered corner of his study. A silver coffee service was laid out beside the French doors. Beyond his veranda, the blustering rainstorm cloaked the vista of Monte Carlo. All the world was gray and wet. The gloom outside granted their alcove a vestige of coziness.

As usual the general brought with him a complaint. Today it was related to his last posting before retirement—Estonia. As Markov poured coffee, Surikov asked, "You have heard of the Forest Brothers?"

"Of course. Will you take sugar?"

"Two. Bandits, the lot of them. Ought to be rounded up and shot."

"Given the presence of patriots from the old world order," Markov soothed, "this no doubt would be occurring."

"Freedom fighters, they call themselves," the general grumbled, slurping his coffee in the way of one used to sucking meager warmth from mugs. "Bandits using chaos as an excuse to incite rebellion."

"None of the Baltic States ever recovered from their brief spate of statehood, I suppose." Freedom had lasted only for the time between the two world wars before Stalin had gobbled up Estonia, along with its two Baltic cousins, Latvia and Lithuania. "Not to mention the fact that Russification replaced over a third of the local population with imported Russians. From what I gather, they became a state within a state. Special positions and better jobs, that sort of thing."

"I do not speak of what is behind us," Surikov barked.

"No, of course not," Markov demurred. "And of course, who could forget the fact that only the presence of our loyal comrades in arms keeps the situation from dissolving into chaos."

"It is chaos already. Unwanted guests, they call Russians who have lived in Estonia for more than forty years. Two generations born on soil they can no longer call their own. Now their so-called parliament has decided to refuse all Russians, even those born in the country, the right to vote." The thought clearly incensed him. "So now we have villages which are ninety-five percent Russian in population ruled by officials elected by the other five percent. Sheer madness."

"Not to mention the revival of the Forest Brothers," Markov offered, deciding to play at patience and let the old boy run out of steam.

"Bandits, as I said. A pity that Stalin halted his purge before the first of them were wiped from the earth."

Stalin did not stop, Markov silently corrected the general. The madman continued creating the infamous Baltic river of blood until his demise. Afterward, the Kremlin wisely gave the project up. For each death, a dozen other Forest Brothers rose to take their murdered comrade's place. "I understand they are operating more or less in the open these days."

"Three days ago they stopped a Russian convoy and demanded their papers," the general huffed. "Imagine, will you? They stood there with their ancient hunting rifles and asked for transit papers and drivers' licenses from tank commanders." Surikov shook his head. "I wish I had been there. They would have received the beating they have been begging for, that I swear on my mother's grave."

"One such attack," Markov pointed out, "and the Estonians would force the remaining Russians to make a mass exodus. And that, my dear general, would be a catastrophe."

"Only because the so-called democratic regime that is dismantling my country has the heart of a mouse and the mind of a newborn." Surikov smiled grimly. "Mark my words, they are busy digging their own graves by permitting such impossible situations to continue. My fellow officers are caught in a vise. When they demand billets inside my shrinking homeland, they are forced to stand in line with comrades stationed in Poland, Czechoslovakia, East Germany, Bulgaria, Kazakhstan, Azerbaijan, Armenia, and a dozen other states. There is no housing. There is no money. There is no government strong enough to solve these problems and rescue my country from disaster."

"A powder keg," Markov agreed. "With the fuses burning low."

"There will be trouble," Surikov warned ominously. "Of that I am certain. If the Forest Brothers are not contained, there will be an incident, and one incident is all it will take. My comrades in arms are ready to move at a moment's notice."

"Which is yet another reason for us to move swiftly," Markov countered. "In case your services are required elsewhere."

"Indeed," the general agreed, focusing once again upon the room and the present moment. "I bring a message from my present superiors. We are gravely concerned that instead of the man you told us about, we now are invited to work with an unknown."

"A better choice," Markov contradicted. "An American. A young innocent."

"A wild card," the general replied worriedly. "A loose cannon, perhaps."

"The reason we selected Kantor in the first place," Markov reminded him, "was that we wanted someone totally honest yet utterly inexperienced in such affairs."

"True, true," the general muttered. "And yet—"

"Someone who had reason to go to the East, yet who would have neither the knowledge nor the contacts to dig too deeply."

"And this man Kantor was perfect," the general agreed. "But the new one?"

"Even better."

"You have met him?"

Markov nodded. "This Jeffrey Sinclair wears his honesty upon his forehead, right alongside his inexperience. He is the naive American personified."

"This may suit us," the general conceded.

"He will go and do our bidding and return none the wiser," Markov assured him. "Wait and see."

Jeffrey carried one of the dining-room chairs into the bedroom and stationed himself by the doorway, where he could watch Katya's every move. He had protested once at the beginning that she did not need to help him pack. Katya replied that helping him was her way of placing her heart in with all that he was taking. He sat and watched her move from bureau to suitcase to closet and back. He replied with simple nods to her questions about ties and socks, and so forth, his heart too full to permit passage to many words.

He watched each movement with eyes bound to no memory, as if he were viewing her for the first time. He wanted to take this moment intact, colored by nothing which had come before. So he watched her and sought to brand his mind with the vision. The motions of his wife's lithe body. Soft, delicate hands that were never still. Violet-gray eyes so full of his pending departure they could not even look his way and continue with the packing. Hair tousled by the gentlest of motions and the faintest of breezes. A heart that filled the room with love.

As she folded one of his suits, she said, "When I was little, I thought wearing a suit made men fat. My daddy never put one on, and he was the strongest man I knew. I never could understand why any man would wear one."

He pointed at the neck brace resting beside his case. "What is that for?"

"It's for your neck," she said firmly.

"My neck is fine."

She settled it down on top of the clothing in the case. "What if it starts hurting you?"

"My neck is fine, Katya."

Reluctantly she set it aside. "Promise me you'll take care of yourself."

"I promise." Jeffrey swallowed with difficulty. "This is really hard, Katya."

"I know," she said softly. "You'll miss being with me for our two-week anniversary."

"I wish—"

"We must learn to be together even when we are apart. Remember, what's most important remains the same." She walked around the bed to settle in his lap. "We have our love," she said softly. "We have our Lord. We have a life together. In the light of these joys, the momentary fades to nothingness."

They paused for a lingering kiss. Then, "Promise me you won't do anything silly while you're away from me. You know, like three-day drinking contests to prove who's the most macho of them all."

He looked down upon the top of her head. "There's no chance of that, and you know it."

"While we're at it," she snuggled in close to his neck. "Give me your word you'll never, ever start thinking you've got to have a megabuck bank account to be happy."

He tried to back off far enough to look down on her, but she held him close. "What brought this on?"

"Have your cuticles done twice a week, a closet with thirty-six gray suits and a drawer with eleven pounds of silk ties," she said.

"Have you been lying awake at night trying to find something else to worry about?"

"Servants trained to bow every time you burp," she rejoined. "A little silver bell by your bedside for summoning Suzette with morning coffee."

"Suzette?"

"The French au pair."

He let his grin show. "As in Suzette with a too-short uniform and frilly white cap?"

She slapped his chest. "Don't even think it."

"You brought it up."

She looked up at him. "Promise me, Jeffrey."

He turned serious. "There is no one on earth for me but you. There hasn't been since the first day I saw you. I *have* to be careful, Katya. It's part of the responsibility of loving you."

Katya examined him carefully, was satisfied with what she found. She reached behind her, pulled out an envelope that had lain hidden beneath his suitcase. "Here."

"What is it?"

"Just a little something to help you on your way. You have to promise not to open it until you're on the plane." The thought of what was to come both electrified and hurt. He squeezed her close, whispered, "I promise."

===

She asked not to have to accompany him to the airport. Jeffrey found he understood. Her love was a very intense, very personal matter. She did not want this first farewell of their married life to be done in public.

A final hug, a caress, a kiss, a look, a word, and he was out on the street, flagging a passing taxi, feeling enormously excited and tremendously forlorn. Jeffrey gave the driver his Heathrow terminal, sat back surrounded by his cases, and knew a keening sorrow that left his insides as hollow as an empty well.

The driver granted him a much-needed silence until they were leaving the motorway at the Heathrow exit. Then he asked, "Where you off to today, then?"

Jeffrey cleared a rusty throat and replied, "Cracow."

The driver pushed his battered cap aside and scratched a scalp wired with a few gray hairs. "Amazing what's tucked away in odd corners of this old world, ain't it? All these places right out of the spy books, now you can just hop on over. That's democracy at work for you. Here, and all them new Russian states."

"They're not Russian anymore."

"No, well, I wouldn't put it past them Russkies to want it all back one day. You ever visited over there?"

"I'm going to Ukraine for the first time later this week."

"That so? Ukraine, Georgia, Uzbekistan—they made a right mess of the Olympics, all them new countries. And them names, enough to make a body think it's a different planet. Up till not long ago, Lithuania wasn't nothing more to me than an unlucky ship."

The driver pulled up in front of his terminal. "Here you are, then. Hope you get back safe and all in one piece. From the sounds of it, there won't be no holiday camp waiting for you."

═══

As soon as the plane lifted from the tarmac, Jeffrey pulled Katya's envelope from his coat pocket and opened it. Inside was a card featuring a solemn little girl dressed in crinoline and ribbons, her tumbling black curls framing a pair of great dark eyes. Her chubby hand offered out a single red rose.

Jeffrey blinked hard, opened the card, read, "You love me. That knowledge is enough to carry me over any time, any distance, any worry, any event. Take care, my love. You carry my heart with you. Katya."

Jeffrey pressed the card to his chest and turned unseeing eyes toward the airplane window.

═══

Gregor greeted him at the Cracow airport with, "The weather is somewhat unpleasant, I fear."

Jeffrey carried his suitcase in one hand and his jacket in his other as he followed Gregor's swaying gait out of the terminal. "It's like a steam bath out here."

"The longest and harshest heat wave Poland has seen in two hundred years," Gregor agreed. "And it's much worse across the border."

"Thanks for the encouragement." He dumped his satchel into the back of the little plastic car. "Still driving the same old Rolls, I see."

"It is adequate for my needs," Gregor replied. "As to the weather, I take it as long as I can stand, then I find urgent work at one of my country orphanages. The heat is as bad, but the air is much sweeter."

Their business in Poland progressed on the well-oiled wheels of experience and mutual confidence. Jeffrey threw himself into his tasks with single-minded purpose, using work to soothe the inner ache as best he could. Within forty-eight hours the antiques were purchased, the required paperwork was completed, and the moment of Jeffrey's departure was upon them.

That afternoon, they stood before Gregor's apartment building and waited for Olya, Yussef's wife, to arrive. Gregor told him a little of what he would find across the border. "The Soviets were even less respectful of privacy than the Polish Communists. Their internal spy network was far more vigilant, even savage. And personal wealth has been illegal for far longer."

"So I will be buying mostly small items," Jeffrey concluded.

"Items easy to secret away," Gregor agreed. "That is, unless you deal with former Party officials. They of course seized all the privileges of any ruling despot."

"What can you tell me about Ukraine itself?"

"Lvov and its surroundings were a part of Poland for almost five hundred years," Gregor explained, "but little evidence remains today. The borders have shifted back and forth, and when Stalin annexed this territory to the Soviet Union after World War II, he immediately began his program of Russification."

"I've heard that term," Jeffrey said.

"Many have, but few can fathom the horrors it involved. Entire towns were emptied overnight, Poles and Jews and Ukrainians all treated with equal brutality. These former citizens were shipped to Siberia or Samarkand or the borderlands of Mongolia, and replaced by Russians brought in and ordered to make the area their home. Any sign of their former heritage was stripped away. Patriotism to any land save the Soviet Union became a crime of sedition, punished by years of forced labor. As a matter of fact, some of Yussef's family were Ukrainians who had lived for centuries on Polish soil. Perhaps you can hear from him a little of what transpired."

"Yussef is Polish?"

"No, our young man is pure-blooded Ukrainian, as much as anyone can be in a land that has known only glimmers of nationhood for over seven hundred years. But his mother's family called Poland home for many generations. His mother has passed away, but her sister—Yussef's aunt—will be working as your interpreter, I believe. She has been someone quite important to Yussef—a sort of lifetime tutor, I gather, from the little I have been told."

"Sounds like you've spent some time with Yussef."

"Quite a bit," Gregor agreed. "The young man fascinates me. I fear I have tried his wife's patience quite severely."

Jeffrey recalled the hard-faced woman he had met at the outdoor market that previous winter. Five minutes of translating into Polish for Yussef, from which Katya had translated into English, had brought her to a boil. "That must not have taken long."

"No, Olya is not a woman given to idle talk," Gregor agreed. "In any case, Yussef has remained both independent and principled in a land which has striven to quash such qualities. He could never have been admitted to university, as he vehemently opposed the Communist Party. So this aunt has tried to teach him, and by all indications she has done quite a good job."

"I have to admit," Jeffrey said, "he did not seem so impressive when I first met him."

"Do not underestimate our young man," Gregor urged him. "He has been shaped by a world totally alien to your own. Yet he has managed to hold on to both his honesty and his personal integrity in the face of pressures you can scarcely imagine. He is also most intelligent. He reads and, what is more, he remembers."

"A scruffy intellectual."

"If you travel this world long enough," Gregor replied, "you will find that the light of learning burns in the strangest of hearts. I urge you to look beyond the exterior and take full measure of this man."

"I'll try," Jeffrey assured him. "So when do we get started?"

"It's all arranged," Gregor said. "You will stay this night in Rzeszow, then at dawn cross the border and begin your journey."

My journey. "Rzeszow is a border town?"

"No, it is a good eighty kilometers from Ukraine. But Przemyśl, the nearest town to the border station of Medyka, is no longer safe. It has become a campsite for newly arrived Russians and Ukrainians. Those who come over for the first time are said to be the most dangerous, because they do not know how to handle the sudden freedom. All the food they can afford is available. And the liquor. There are constant brawls, with some unfortunate found stabbed in the gutter almost every morning."

Gregor shook his head. "*Przemyśl* sounds like the Polish word that means to think again, or to consider very seriously. Some say it was an ancient warning given to all who crossed the border into the Kingdom of Rus."

"Sounds as if it still applies today."

"Indeed it does. So you shall stay in Rzeszow, where you should be able to have a safe night's rest."

"Should?"

The old gentleman was unnaturally somber. "Such things as should be taken for granted in this world are no longer certain. Not here. Not now."

"It's not safe to be around these traders?" Jeffrey was immensely glad Katya was not around to hear it.

"The men and women who make their living through such international trade live in a gray world," Gregor replied. "What they do is technically illegal, but at the same time the old Communist laws are dropping like trees in a forest being logged. What the traders do is too profitable and too necessary for either the Ukrainian or the Russian officials to close down, so their answer is to squeeze and squeeze and then squeeze even more. The Ukrainian border officials charge fifty dollars for an entry-exit visa. Keep in mind that the current average monthly salary in the former Soviet lands is twelve dollars. Only someone involved in a highly lucrative trading activity could afford to pay such sums just to cross a border. The border guards know this and demand even more in bribes."

"A life that doesn't attract the best kind of person," Jeffrey surmised.

"Pirates, most of them," Gregor agreed. "Our young friend Yussef is truly one of a kind."

Jeffrey caught sight of Olya driving a battered automobile up the street. She approached in a cloud of oily fumes and ratchety noise. He said, "His wife more than makes up for it."

Gregor waved in her direction and hummed a denial. "Olya chose a man with heart. There is much to be said for a person who is capable of realizing her own weaknesses. It is a rare quality, especially in such a land as hers."

Jeffrey watched as the stone-faced woman pulled into a parking space and cut off the motor. He found himself wishing for a chance to see the world through Gregor's eyes. Just once. Just long enough to know what it meant to have the man's wisdom.

"I told them you have only one week," Gregor continued. "I would rather that Yussef worked you hard for a shorter period than expose you to danger for a longer time."

"What danger?"

"Nothing certain, no specific thing you can put your finger on. Just too many problems, political and economic and social, that could become explosive without warning." Gregor saw Jeffrey's worried expression and smiled. "Take comfort that Yussef agrees both that you should be safe and that one week will be sufficient this time."

This time. "You trust them, then."

"So much that I am willing to place your life in their hands," Gregor replied soberly. "Still, I shall not cease to worry nor pray until you have safely returned."

Olya climbed from the ancient car, stomped over, greeted Jeffrey with a curt nod, and poured out a torrent of words that sounded horribly slurred to Jeffrey's ears. Gregor responded in a most courtly manner, bowing and murmuring assent every few moments.

When the woman stopped and turned in dismissal, Gregor said mildly, "You and Olya's husband will alight from the car at the Polish-Ukrainian border and cross by foot. There will be someone to meet you on the other side, I assume Yussef's aunt. Olya will cross over with the car."

"Alone?"

"The wait on the Polish side is well-patrolled and not too long. Only two days, she informs me."

"And on the other side, coming back into Poland?"

"Ah. That would depend on whether or not you are a rabbit, as they call the first-timer. A professional will know whom to bribe and how much and should pass through in six or seven days. A rabbit may wait as long as two weeks and still not pass through."

Crossing the Ukrainian border by foot did not appeal to Jeffrey in the least. "What about just taking a train?"

"The border wait would be longer than going over by foot, at least nine hours," Gregor replied. "This is another holdover from the Communist days. The tracks are different gauges, you see. The Soviets in their wisdom decided that, rather than allowing passengers to change trains and possibly escape detection, they would seal all compartments and then change the train's *wheels*."

"On every train?"

Gregor nodded. "And every international border crossing. Yussef's ways may seem very strange to you at times, my young friend, but I urge you to trust his judgment. He has had a lifetime's experience at surviving inhuman conditions."

Jeffrey risked a brief inspection of the hard lines upon Olya's face, the determined cast to her eyes, the focused tension that bordered on constant fury. "I hear you."

Gregor patted his arm. "If you will take one additional word of advice."

"Anything."

"Do not fall ill," Gregor said in utter seriousness. "You would do well to guard your health wherever possible. To test the Russian medical system with an emergency would truly be gambling with the rest of your life."

"Katya's already warned me about the water."

"Heed her words well. Drink nothing that has not been taken from a bottle opened before your own eyes or boiled twice within your own sight. And eat only what appears truly clean. And take nothing—"

"You're about to get me worried," Jeffrey protested.

"Better frightened than ill."

Olya barked out an impatient word. Gregor smiled and offered his hand. "You go with my prayers surrounding you, my boy. Take care and return as you are now, only richer. Especially in wisdom."

The road to Rzeszow was decorated with horse-drawn hay wagons and roadside fruit and vegetable stands. The villages were a stream of tired sameness. Forty years of Communist rule, and the Nazis before them, had ground out all charm and individual character. Summertime greenery added splashes of color to the occasional relic of bygone glories—a palace, a vast cathedral, a stolid ministry outpost. All suffered from universal neglect.

Yet everywhere, even in the smallest of villages, were signs of new wealth—satellite dishes sprouting from gray-faced apartment buildings like strange metal flowers, houses under construction, lighted storefronts, billboards, Western cars, fresh paint. They stuck out like beacons of hope for a tired and drained people.

Between the villages, fields bustled with haymaking. Whole families gathered for the task. Grandmothers stood surrounded by tumbling piles of happy infants. Vast spreads of food and drink anchored white swatches of cloth. Crowds of boys and girls labored around horse-drawn rigs while their elders tended machine-driven equipment. Heavily laden carts were pushed and pulled toward distant barns.

On the outskirts of Rzeszow, great black crows began to flock in the freshly cut fields. Their beaks were the largest Jeffrey had ever seen, fully as broad as his hand and almost as long. Olya noticed the direction of his gaze and said, "Russki." She then clasped hands to her throat and made choking sounds. Jeffrey recalled Gregor's words about a drought and nodded his understanding. The birds had been driven West by thirst.

Their hotel was a concrete clone of the high-rise hotels all over Poland. The foyer was vast and gloomy and lined with fake marble, the lighting distant and dim, the air stuffy and perfumed with cheap disinfectant. As Jeffrey signed in, a bus pulled up outside and disgorged a milling stream of dirty, exhausted passengers. Again Olya offered her single word of explanation—Russki. The bus idled outside the entrance, dusty and swaying in time to the diesel's unmuffled clatter. The vehicle listed to one side. The windows were cracked and stuck half-open, the curtains knotted out of the way. Passengers wearily moved toward the reception desk, free hands kneading overworked backs.

The elevator was loud and cranky and the size of a small closet. Outside his room, Yussef pantomimed for Jeffrey to wash thoroughly. Jeffrey recalled the stories of Russian drought and complied.

Dinner was taken in silence, save for short spurts of conversation between Yussef and Olya. When their food arrived, they ate with great appetite but little gusto. Jeffrey had a mental image of them storing up reserves against leaner times ahead.

When they were finished, he bid them good-night and retired to the cramped confines of his room. He lay in the darkness listening to the sounds of violent revelry that echoed up and down the hallway. Finally he fell asleep, hungry for the feel of his wife's loving arms.

══

They started very early the next morning. Each Polish village on the way to the border had its market, and at each either Yussef or Olya pointed and announced, Russki. The markets sprouted wherever space was available—on stairs leading to a church, along a wall, in tiny triangular parks, in the middle of parking lots, even on traffic islands. Each vendor sat or squatted before a patch of bright fabric and displayed what he or she had to sell. It was never very much. A few handmade sweaters. Some swatches of cloth. Bottles of shampoo or individual cigarettes or perhaps a liter or two of vodka.

Boredom fought with the heat for domination of the borderlands. A seven-kilometer line of trucks and cars sweltered under a cloudless sky. Olya drove them up to the first fencing and waited while Jeffrey and Yussef pulled their bags from the trunk. She then bid her husband a curt farewell, and deftly swung the car back around to return to the end of the line. Piles of refuse lined the roadside, and bodies sprawled wherever could be found a fraction of shade. Kerchiefed babchas tended scrawny children sucking from soda bottles fitted with rubber nipples. Little wooden huts played old disco hits and plied a booming trade in soft drinks and Western snacks. Beefy truck drivers in filthy T-shirts and shorts celebrated successful entries into Poland with beers drained in one long sweaty swallow.

The border crossing came in four stages. First was a stop at the outpost where arriving trucks and cars had to show their proper documents. Jeffrey and Yussef joined the line of heavily burdened pedestrians and walked on through. Then came the Polish station, a brief glimpse of shade and sultry breeze before the guards passed them along. As they departed, the officer who had inspected his passport muttered something to his neighbor and nodded toward Jeffrey. An American crossing the border on foot. Jeffrey felt eyes on his back as he walked toward the Ukrainian station.

Outside the Ukrainian post, the wait began. Ratty buildings displayed hastily scraped-over Soviet stars replaced by new Ukrainian flags. The air tasted hot dry, metallic, sooty, as if baked in an industrial oven. The breeze was fitful and acrid. People moved slowly to and from the border station carrying satchels and shopping bags scarce inches above the ground. They waited in lines for inspection, waited in line to have their passports checked, waited to pay, waited to complain, waited to move on to wait yet again.

There was a moment at the border when time stood still for Jeffrey. He was shuffling along in line, pressed in on all sides by reeking humanity, when suddenly the world came into sharpest focus. His mind became utterly still, caught by an unseen power as he took in all that surrounded him.

Surly border guards ignored whining pleas as they rifled bags and carry-sacks and demanded customs duties, which were simply stashed away. Other bored soldiers pushed people forward, maintained order, and kept careful watch over how much their fellow guards were pocketing.

As Jeffrey inched forward, he could sense all the wailing cries, all the dust, all the chatter and horns and blaring speakers and thousands of smoldering cigarettes all gathering together and drifting upward as a rank incense on an unclean altar.

He took another step and felt unseen vestments slip from his shoulders. His cloak of security had vanished. Jeffrey's turn came then, and he set his bag down on the long metal bench. He shrugged a reply to the guard's surly bark, heard Yussef reply for him, and thought there had never been a time when he had felt so exposed.

———

Ivona Aristonova waited beside her car within sight of the Ukrainian border station, smoldering from more than the heat.

She glanced at her watch, sighed, and swiped at a wayward strand of hair. Eight o'clock in the morning and the day was already sweltering. This was by far the hottest summer she could remember. And the driest.

In lands where summer temperatures seldom rose above the mid-eighties, and never for more than a day or so at a time, scores of days came and went where temperatures hit a hundred degrees by three hours after dawn. Weeks melted into months under blistering, cloudless skies. Crops trained to grow on little sun and regular rainfall withered and browned. First streams, then rivers, and finally lakes and seas fell below any levels known in recorded history.

And still the heat continued.

As much talk focused on the coming winter as on the present heat. Babchas told tales of other hot summers, followed by winters where unending snows fell upon an earth hard as iron. Many told stories of hunger as well. Elders argued over whether the famine winters of 1917, 1918, and 1919 had been as bad as those of 1944 through 1947. Younger people wondered if, in their own time, they would sit and argue over the winter that was to come.

Corn rose stunted, with ears the size of middle fingers. Lavender, one of the region's major cash crops, refused to bloom at all. What should now have been seas of ripening wheat were graveyards whose dried husks whispered omens in the arid breeze. Potatoes baked in the ground a month before harvest. Vegetables sent up slender sprouts that wilted and fell in surrender. Village squares became anvils where farmers gathered to be hammered by the merciless sun. They stood and searched the empty sky for clouds. They spoke of omens, and of money and the lack of it, and of governments unable to help in this hour of great need, and of possible calamities yet to arrive.

But more than the heat was troubling Ivona this morning. Something about this whole plan unsettled her, and in a way she could not identify. This unreasoning unease troubled her immensely. She did not like such challenges. Life had trained her to distrust the unseen, for here lay the greatest threats to the established patterns of her existence. She held on to these habits with the same rigid insistence that she had applied to the task of learning languages. Ivona was nothing if not disciplined.

Ivona stiffened as she spotted Yussef's slender form. She returned his wave and scrutinized the tall young man walking alongside her nephew.

The American called Jeffrey was everything she had feared. He was far too handsome for his own good. His face was as fair and fresh and unmarked as a newborn's. His bearing was overly confident, utterly untested.

At that instant, it came unbidden, like a fragrance wafted upon an unseen wind. Once again, against her will, she found herself recalling the past, and the power of that memory stripped her bare.

=

The cold was indescribable that first northern winter. That she recalled much more clearly than the snow. The week before the first frost, temperatures were as high as forty degrees centigrade. Then one afternoon, the first week in October, winds came down from the north, and overnight the temperature fell to minus fifty-two degrees centigrade, a ninety-degree shift in less than twelve hours. Overnight the ground, the trees, even the grass and leaves turned to stone.

Food was very scarce that winter. To buy it, Ivona's parents sold everything they did not absolutely need. Wives of local Communist Party leaders bought several ball gowns her mother had carried on that long train trip north. After everything was sold and the money was gone, all they had to eat was what the local canteen fed them— porridge in the mornings and in the evenings a stinking fish soup. The smell of that soup, and the rotting fish from which it was made, was so strong it stayed in their clothes and bedding and hands and skin throughout that long, endless winter.

All children were required to go to school in the wintertime. That made the polar winter seem so much longer, sitting in the room next to that stinking kitchen day after day. The sun always rose late and set very early, so they arrived in the dark and left in the dark. All they saw of the day was a line of light that traced its way across the floor. Hour after hour their teachers drilled them in Communist doctrine. Ivona found the lessons a torture as harsh as the cold.

They lived in huts of raw logs with moss stuffed in the cracks. Thankfully, there was plenty of wood, and they kept a fire burning in their little stove day and night. In their settlement were eighty Ukrainian families, over a hundred Polish families, and perhaps half that many Jewish families. Fewer than a handful of those families survived that first winter intact.

In May spring finally arrived. The river outside the village lost its covering of ice in explosions that sounded like a new war beginning. The village was there only because the river was there to float logs down to a sawmill.

Before long, berries appeared; gathering them was the children's job. Those raspberries were their only source of vitamin C. By this time, of course, the whole camp suffered from scurvy. During the winter, they followed the local villagers' example and brewed pine needles in water, letting the concoction soak overnight and then drinking a cup very fast. The taste had been beyond horrible, but it had provided enough vitamins for them to retain most of their teeth.

The children on their gathering trips also found mushrooms and sorrel, from which Ivona's mother made a lovely soup. After a winter of porridge and rotten fish stew, the raspberries and her mother's soups provided a taste of heaven.

Another winter and another spring went by before Stalin proclaimed one of his famous Friendship Treaties with local leaders in Ukraine. For no apparent reason, Ivona's family received a permit to leave the camp. Most of those who had been forcibly resettled, especially those in the far north, never returned home. Ivona never learned why her family was selected to leave, but they were.

In time Ivona and her family made their new home in Lvov, leaving behind the cold of Archangelsk. But never the memories. Never, no matter how hard she tried, the memories.

As she stood and watched the pair approach, Ivona became certain that the painful act of remembering was somehow tied to the arrival of this young man, this Jeffrey Sinclair. This utterly illogical notion shook her to her foundations. She pushed hard at the thought and the lingering pain that always accompanied her memories. Then she stepped forward to greet her nephew and his companion.

———

The car awaiting Jeffrey and Yussef as they came through the borderlands was a boxy, gray-green Lada, the driver an overly thin, gray-haired woman. She replied to Yussef's exuberant greeting with a single word. She then turned to Jeffrey. "You are Mr. Sinclair?"

"You speak English. Great."

"I am Ivona Aristonova. I shall act as your interpreter." She was a prim schoolmarm sort of lady, all angles and thin features. Despite the day's dusty heat, she remained poised and collected. She wore a simple blue skirt trimmed in hand-sewn flowers. Everything about her was old, patched, and immaculate; even her battered purse shone with shoe polish. Slate-gray hair was pulled back into a neat bun. Sky-blue eyes were encircled by deep wrinkles and bruise-like smudges. Her singsong voice, however, sounded surprisingly young. "Shall we be going? We have a long way ahead and much yet to do today."

Jeffrey stored his bag in the trunk alongside Yussef's battered bag, a hand-crocheted satchel which he assumed belonged to Ivona, a case of Pepsi, a box of foodstuffs, and canister after canister of gasoline. He sat in the front seat, and felt the car sag upon springs so weary they barely kept his backside off the road.

Yussef grinned at Jeffrey's expression and spoke his offhand guttural manner. The lady translated, "These days it is best not to draw attention with too new a car or too fresh a change of clothing. Especially with the valuables we shall be carrying."

Jeffrey shifted around to make himself as comfortable as possible. "I can't remember ever feeling this hot before."

"Afternoons are worse," Yussef said through Ivona. "Clouds gather, but it does not rain. The heat is trapped to the earth. It has been like this for over two months."

"How can you stand it?"

Yussef showed his discolored teeth. "This isn't the West. You don't find an answer to every pain here. We do what we have been taught to do by seventy years of Communism. We endure."

Yussef rammed home the complaining gears and said through Ivona, "Welcome to the great Soviet empire."

CHAPTER 17

Mostiska. Javorov. Nesterov.

All of his memories of that time, as they drove from village to village and did their trading and drove farther still, would be tinged by nightfall. Even the brightest day, when the heat was a weight under which their little car threatened constantly to collapse and leave them stranded, the eye of his memory was tinged by unseen darkness.

Just beyond the border zone, the road disintegrated. Cracked and pitted pavement barely two lanes wide slowed traffic to a tractor's crawl. Without warning the pavement surrendered to holes of bone-jarring depth, slid into gravel and dust and rutted tracks, or gave way to ancient octagonal stones that caused their car to drum a frantic beat.

Ivona translated their buying transactions with precision, then maintained a silent distance at all other times. Yussef was content with his own company. Jeffrey found the car's silence as heavy a blanket as the heat.

After their third stop, Jeffrey swiveled around in his seat so as to face her. "Your English is excellent," he asked. "Have you ever traveled in the West?"

Ivona kept her attention fastened on the open window. "I have never left Ukraine since my arrival."

"Where did you live before coming here?"

"English was my escape," Ivona continued, ignoring his question. Her voice was her finest asset, so soft and light and musical that if Jeffrey closed his eyes he could imagine its coming from twenty-year-old lips. Her only inflection was a slight singsong lilt. She spoke his name, related the best and worse of news, and translated the most mundane of conversations all in this lilting sameness.

"It was my magic carpet to other worlds. My most special moments were the days I received a new English book. Well, new for me. Old, tattered, pages missing, but still holding voices that called to me. They spoke of worlds where freedom was so normal the people could *criticize* the ones in power. Such stories lifted me above myself, released me from the captivity of my existence."

Jeffrey took in the dull heat-blasted landscape, the poverty-stricken farm hovels, the concrete watchtowers. "I can imagine."

"I love the classics especially. But I also enjoyed your modern novels. Even the trash was useful. Through their pages I watched your world hate a distant war, question God, take drugs, have free sex—make mistakes, yes, but in freedom."

Jeffrey decided he did not understand this prim, undersized woman, with her old face and her young voice, her rigid mannerisms. "It's incredible to think that you could learn such an English from books."

"And radio, of course, when transmissions were not jammed. BBC and Radio Liberty and RFE. All highly illegal. Which made even the British gardening programs exciting." She snagged a wisp of gray hair and patted it back into place. "I taught English, unofficially of course; even when the student was unable to pay still I taught. That gave me hours and hours of practice. Of escape. Of imaginary freedom. For someone imprisoned as I was, such imaginings were as real as life itself."

＝＝

Rava-Russkaja. Cervonograd. Sokal.

Every hour or so a tall guard tower sprouted alongside the road. When Jeffrey pointed one out, Ivona explained, "Before the fall of Communism, cars required transit papers to travel between towns or villages. All exits from main roads were blocked and guarded. Lookouts with binoculars manned the towers and timed the cars' passage. If the drivers moved too fast they were stopped and arrested for speeding. If they moved too slowly, it was assumed that they were trading illegally, and they were stopped and strip-searched."

The smaller villages were rows of squalid hovels lining several crumbling country lanes. Larger towns were clusters of tumble-down factories and high-rise tenements. Always there was a central square, always a squat government building with the charm of an oversized tombstone. Always a patch of parched grass proclaiming itself a park. And always a Soviet statue thrusting aggressively upward in dated fifties modernism. Jeffrey saw concrete pedestals with black iron figures ever pointing to the horizon, steel and cement rocket ships bearing proud Soviet warriors toward lofty heavens, brawny figures marching shoulder to shoulder toward a Communist future that was no more, agricultural images mocking the people's evident hunger.

From time to time the horizon sprouted factories so large they appeared as mirages dancing in the shimmering heat. The closer their car came, the vaster the buildings grew—great monoliths looming up twenty stories and more, bristling with smokestacks, but for the most part standing idle.

"There was a huge defense industry in Ukraine," Ivona replied to his question. "Now it is idle because Moscow no longer buys anything. Salaries are frozen at the old rate, less than ten dollars a month. People are urged to leave, but no one does because there is no other work to be found."

Within the homes they visited, be they spartan apartments or hovels with splintered boards for walls and newspapers for floor coverings, the hospitality never failed to humble him. The poorest of shanties still offered a standard fare of vodka reserved for guests and fresh bread obtained by waiting in line since dawn. Sometimes there were tomatoes shriveled from the heat, perhaps pickles or a plate of stunted onions. But always there was vodka.

At the first stop, Jeffrey shook his head to the invitation to drink and requested water. The stumpy, middle-aged man recovered from his surprise, went to his kitchen alcove, and returned with a battered cup filled to the brim. Through Ivona he assured Jeffrey that the water had been twice boiled. Jeffrey observed the silt making milky sworls and thanked the man solemnly. He then brought the cup to his tightly closed lips and pretended to sip.

After Jeffrey twice refused the invitation to drink, Yussef began carting in a bottle of warm Pepsi at each visit. He set it down in front of Jeffrey and explained to the curious host what Ivona translated as a vow. Jeffrey swilled the syrupy goo and did not object.

He saw no more water that first day, not even bottled. At most halts, all they had to drink was Yussef's warm Pepsi, vodka, and an orange glop that children drank and Jeffrey learned to avoid after the first sip. The heat sucked so much moisture from his body that he felt a constant thirst. He took tea whenever it was offered, which was seldom, and remained bloated from Pepsi.

In each village there was some antique or collectible on offer. Many were of considerable value, but a cheap trinket sometimes slipped through. Jeffrey was very concerned the first time it happened, conscious of all the warnings he had received from Gregor before traveling.

A man with a face as seamed as the fields outside his village offered all he had, a tiny pendant set with a few semi-precious stones. He croaked his plea with a voice squeaky from disuse. Jeffrey looked at the pendant dangling from a chain long stripped of all silver plating, held by hands that would never lose their own ingrained plating of grime and oil. Out of compassion, Jeffrey offered him ten dollars. He then returned to the car in shame for being taken.

But there was a new warmth to Yussef's voice, and a strange sense of Ivona being less sure of herself than before.

"Yussef has tried to filter out the useless," Ivona said in translation. "But these people are desperate, and sometimes they make wild promises in hopes of gaining a little something once you arrive."

"And refuse to show the product to anyone but the buyer," Jeffrey said, understanding perfectly. "They say it is too valuable to risk displaying to anyone but the person with the money."

Again Ivona hesitated, as though not sure with whom she spoke. Then, "That is correct. Your ten dollars translates into a fortune for one such as him."

The next village brought yet another worthless item, this time a mercury-backed mirror in a cheap turn-of-the-century frame. The woman watched his inspection with desperate eyes, her silent plea made tragic by the trio of quiet children gathered around her chair. He decided on honesty and told the young mother as kindly as possible why he could not offer more than a few dollars. The woman accepted the money with pitiful gratitude, and Yussef showed genuine approval. As they left, Jeffrey was struck by the thought that respectful honesty from a stranger was perhaps a rare commodity.

Then, in the next village, he encountered a find that made the entire trip worthwhile. The farmer dug up a ragged bundle from the edge of his compost heap, and offered it with hands and arms stained the color of old teak. Jeffrey unfolded the wrappings and extracted a belt of almost solid silver.

The *baldric* was a sword belt worn over one shoulder, diagonally across back and chest, and connected with rope or chain or some frilly foppery to the waist. It was long considered an essential part of a gentleman officer's wardrobe. This particular one was French and dated from the Napoleonic empire. French war-eagles of solid silver rested upon fields of aquamarine. Beside them were rubies carved into stars of rank. Then began a series of silver-framed war symbols done in semiprecious stones, separated from one another by silver family shields set upon mother-of-pearl backing. Jeffrey hefted the belt, estimated its weight at fifteen pounds.

"The spoils of war," he said.

"The French left behind more than their lives," Yussef agreed through Ivona, "when Mother Russia introduced them to a real winter."

———

Vladimir-Volynskij. Luck. Rozisce.

The people were walking lessons in endurance. Serious, heavy women wore comically colored hats against the heat—beach bonnets, undersized cotton cones, floppy straw hats with pom-poms and ribbons. Those without hats carried rusty, ragged parasols whose bright polyester colors fought valiantly against the onslaught of dust and abuse.

Old men were either bloated with layers of blubber or shrunk to skin of leather and muscles of wire cable. Everyone, even the young, had features creased by constant squints. Expressions were fixed in a variety of emotions. Anger. Suspicion. Hatred. Fear. Uncertainty. Resignation. Rage.

The children were overly small, overly quiet, overly serious. Young men, many of them strikingly handsome in a rough-cut fashion, clung grimly to seventies disco fashion—elaborate razor cuts, rayon shirts, and oversized bell-bottoms—despite the withering heat. Stunningly beautiful girls showed faces marred by permanent suspicion and hostility. By middle age, men appeared scarred and stone cold, the women faded and overweight. This rapid aging gave the young the air of hothouse flowers, brought to an early bloom that would swiftly fade.

===

Zdolbunov. Slavuta. Iz'aslav.

It began with the simplest question, the smallest observation. As they left one village, Jeffrey watched a bowed farmer and his wife struggle back from the fields under hand-carried loads of hay. Their backs were bent, their faces warped in a struggle as timeless as a Baroque painting. "I wonder why life is like this here," he murmured almost to himself.

To Jeffrey it appeared as though Ivona stirred reluctantly, drawn into something she did not wish to face. Then she began.

"Our way and yours were divorced in the dawn of modern history. Europe was saved from the savagery of the Mongol hordes, and yet still today they talk of the threat with a thrill of fear. There was no one to save Russia. Russia lived under Mongol rule for more than two hundred and fifty years. While Europe struggled to cast off the Dark Ages and enter the enlightened Renaissance, Russia remained trapped in darkest night."

"It sounds like a children's fairy tale," Jeffrey said.

"It is from such beginnings, too harsh to be told as fact, that ghouls and good fairies arise," Ivona replied. "But what you must remember is that the Russia of today, along with her sister states such as Ukraine, still bears the Mongol mark. Look deeply into our society, and you will find roots reaching back over one thousand years. The Tartars, as they were known by the Russians, willed to the people their careless ferocity and utter disregard for the value of human life. They burned into our nation the painful lesson of centralized rule. Our first governments were based upon Genghis Khan's military authority, which permitted no question or doubt or opposition whatsoever."

It hit Jeffrey then. Ever since the border, he had been trying to put a finger on Ivona's attitude toward him. She did not show hostility. Nor did she appear angry. Yet there was something, some barrier she pushed at him constantly. Finally he could name it, though he could still not say why it was there. Ivona *disapproved* of him. She radiated rejection.

"The Mongols' code of law was called the *Yasa,* and it had three underlying principles," Ivona continued in her toneless singsong. "The first was that all people were equal under the law, rich and poor alike. The second was that all citizens were bound to their position in society for life. Ambition to rise above one's station was a crime punishable by torture and death. And third, all people lived in complete submission to the Khan's absolute power."

"Sounds a lot like life under the Communists," Jeffrey observed, and wondered why she bothered to teach if she so clearly wished him elsewhere.

"The parallel continues in many different directions, like roots spreading out from a dark and gloomy tree," Ivona replied. Her quiet, lilting tone carried no sense of enthusiasm. She was like a teacher who was being paid to teach but had no confidence in her student. "All land, for example, was owned by the Khan. It was granted out by title to local princes who ruled in the Khan's name. Those who actually worked the land, the serfs, were bound to it and could not leave. When the Mongols were finally defeated, the czars and their princes continued this practice. To be a serf under czarist rule, right up to the beginning of this century, was to be a slave."

"And then came the Communist state, which owned all land in the name of the people. Whoever they were." Jeffrey shook his head. "But to back up for a moment, how did the Russians get rid of the Mongols?"

"By war," Ivona replied simply. "Three hundred years of war, during which the Russians adopted every despotic tactic of their enemy. The state became all powerful, controlling every resource and person in the country. Men appointed to the military became soldiers for life. There was no alternative except death."

Yussef interrupted with a short query. Ivona spoke to him at length. He was silent for a moment, then responded with a few words. She translated them as, "It also taught the Russians to see all the outside world as their enemy."

"Three hundred years of war would do that to anyone," Jeffrey agreed.

"It was during this period that Russia's rulers learned the power of fear as a ruling force," Ivona went on. "Czar Ivan the Terrible established the world's first political police, called the *Oprichniki*. Sight of their uniforms, with emblems of snarling dogs, became enough to instill terror in Russia's citizens. These six thousand cutthroats employed such savage punishments as impaling, flaying alive, boiling, roasting on giant spits, and frying on great skillets against any man, woman, or child declared an enemy of the czar."

Jeffrey turned around so as to inspect the woman's face. She showed no reaction whatsoever to her own words. Ivona calmly viewed the endless dry-brown vista outside her window, her barrier of rejection keeping him at bay.

The road passed through a copse of brown, stunted trees, then ran straight and true across a flat landscape as far as Jeffrey could see.

"Here begin the Steppes," Ivona told him.

Yussef pointed forward and spoke, his words translated as, "Up ahead there are hills. But beyond Kiev the road runs straight and true for two thousand kilometers. No rise, no curve, no turning. That, my Western friend, is where the real Russia begins."

They passed a cluster of huts, a meager island of humanity in an endless earthen sea. "I've never seen anything like this," Jeffrey said quietly. "Not ever."

"When the Tartars were finally pushed from Russia," Ivona said, "part of their tribe settled in the Crimea, which lies in southern Ukraine. They continued to sweep out from time to time, even traveling so far as to sack Moscow three times. But by that time they were no longer interested in conquest and occupation. All they sought was booty, especially slaves. For over three hundred years, until the seventeenth century, Tartar hordes swept out year after year, carrying off the youngest and the best, leaving death and destruction in their wake. Still today this impression of a dangerous Ukraine lingers on in many Russian minds. The name itself comes from the Russian word *Okraina*, or Wild Plains."

At a demand from Yussef, Ivona translated what she had been saying. He nodded and spoke for a time, which she translated as, "The endless land is Russia's greatest wealth and Russia's greatest weakness. There were no natural barriers to stop the foes, and towns here were too spread out to help one another against invaders. I once read a story of an official who counted the slaves as they were herded onto the Crimean boats and shipped to the slave markets of Istanbul. After one raid, the number of slaves topped ten thousand men and women, boys and girls. The official grabbed one young man as he passed and demanded, 'Did they leave anyone there for next year?'"

"It's amazing to me," Jeffrey said, "how you could take a lot of these descriptions, modernize them by three hundred years, and be talking about life under Communism."

There was a moment's silence before Yussef's barked command brought Ivona's translation. He spoke a few words, which she did not interpret. Instead, she paused for a long moment, then asked, "You have heard of Stalin's program of Russification?"

"Yes."

"This, too, came from the czars, and as you have heard, they learned it from the Mongols. In the sixteenth century, Ivan III began the rule of *pomestie*, or state ownership of all land. The czar's army forcibly relocated the princes already in place to new lands far away from their original holdings. These new lands were granted on the condition of loyal service, including delivery of a certain number of new soldiers each year. The people themselves were known as *tyaglye kholopy*, or tax-paying slaves. Their duty was to work the land so that the czarist state could support the army required for its endless wars."

Ivona translated for Yussef, who added through her, "The powerful enemy was defeated only by a powerful central government ruling a powerful army. To draw this power together, they had to learn the lesson of ruthlessness. The importance of individual human life was sacrificed to the needs of the state. It is still so today."

"Over the centuries," Ivona went on, "the same problems that later plagued the Communists choked development of the earlier czarist state. The Russian bureaucracy was staffed by people who by law could never be rewarded for good work by promotion. So they became corrupt and ruled according to who held more power and who paid larger bribes. There was little trade, since no one was permitted to make a profit. Cities remained small and distant outposts, since a serf who left his assigned place was put to death."

She paused while Yussef navigated a series of dangerously dark holes in the pitted road, then went on, "Industry had no labor until the state assigned them serfs, and then companies were forbidden by law to reward skills or performance with bonuses or advances of any kind."

She translated for Yussef, who offered, "You can see the consequences even today. The price of centralized government is death of the individual. The body lingers on, but the spirit is crushed."

"So how did you make it through intact?" Jeffrey asked him.

"By being born when people began to see the lie for what it was," Yussef replied through Ivona. "And by having an aunt who taught me from the cradle to value who I was."

"Couldn't other people see they were trapped by the same forces that held them in the past?"

"Much was made of past horrors," Yussef replied. "But Communism was always painted as the great liberator. Disinformation was a powerful weapon. With their total control over the press and the television and the schools, they could deny that all these problems even existed in modern Russia."

"To deny in such a society means that the problem officially disappears," Ivona continued. "Anyone who discusses it also vanishes. End of discussion."

"This policy dominated contact with foreigners also," Yussef added. "Suspicion of foreigners goes back to the dawn of Russian history. Under the czars, citizens were forbidden to travel outside their country. For over five hundred years, they locked away all foreign visitors who threatened to return to their homeland and criticize the Russian government. Even visiting priests who dared to criticize the czarist rule were arrested and put to death."

"More than one thousand years of serfdom," Ivona continued. "How can the world expect these people to learn new ways overnight?"

"Because there isn't any more time than that," Jeffrey replied. "Either they make the change quickly, or their attempt at democracy will fail."

Ivona was silent a long moment, then translated for Yussef. When she was done the young man removed his attention from the road long enough to grant Jeffrey a look of solid approval. Here at least there was assurance. Yussef was pleased to have him around.

—————

Sepetovka. Polonnoje. Berdicev.

Zitomir. Their evening meal took place by lantern light and was entirely of goose. Nothing else. Just goose. Their hosts, a dumpy woman in clothes hand-scrubbed to ragged limpness and a man who treated Yussef as visiting nobility, apologized continually while the goose was cooking. Jeffrey assured them every time the words were translated that goose would be fine.

While their hosts busied themselves in the kitchen, Yussef spoke in a quiet monotone that Ivona translated as, "In the stores there is nothing to buy. Nothing. Shopkeepers put nothing on the shelves even if they receive a shipment. They hold the merchandise in the back room and sell at the state price plus fifty or one hundred percent. People who can afford it either buy at these prices or travel to big cities and go to the new street markets. The others," he shrugged. "Here you see how the others survive."

Jeffrey glanced around the hovel that was to be their home for the night. He took in the scant furniture, the crude homemade trestle table and benches, the lack of any adornment save a tattered photograph of an icon hung from a cracked and pitted wall.

"Life is not as it should be in my country," Yussef spoke solemnly. "Our world should be otherwise. Someday we will learn that this is a wrongness, and one that must end."

When the goose arrived, the couple paid grave thanks to a gracious Yussef. Then they applied themselves to devouring the lot—skin, entrails, bone marrow, and all. Jeffrey squelched his aversion to so much rich meat washed down with warm Pepsi. He stuffed himself with roast goose, goose crackling, goose pâté, goose liver fried in oil—so much goose that he smelled the greasy odor in his skin.

As dinner was cleared away, the single bulb dangling from the ceiling came to feeble life. He stared in weary wonderment as it was greeted with cries of pleasure and great activity by the woman and her husband.

"Energy cutbacks," Ivona explained. "Twenty-five percent, the authorities promised, but already it is down to three hours of water and electricity per day."

The old man busied himself filling the sink and bath. The woman brought out a pile of dirty laundry, apologized with a gap-toothed smile and words that needed no translation, and hurried away.

"Cooking and washing often take place in the wee hours," Ivona explained.

"Days without light or power this winter," Yussef said through Ivona. "The thought gives voice to talk more bitter than the bread lines. Imagine a Russian winter in the dark! Word is, the stock of candles and kerosene lanterns has vanished from every city in the land."

"It must be hard for you," Ivona commented, "imagining how life is here for us."

"It is and it isn't," Jeffrey replied. "I am one-quarter Polish, and over the past year I've been coming to know a little about my own heritage. The hardships I've found here appear to be similar, only worse by degrees. I'm not talking about the system, just what the system has done to the common man."

But Ivona and Yussef were caught by what he had said at the beginning. Yussef asked a question, which Ivona translated as, "You are one-quarter Polish?"

"Yes."

"Which quarter?"

Perhaps it was the fatigue of driving and dealing in the day's heat. Perhaps it was the flickering lantern light, which remained a stronger illumination than the room's single overhead bulb. Perhaps it was the sense of calm that pervaded the crudely chinked farmhouse walls, or perhaps merely the companionable light in Yussef's eyes and the questioning doubt of Ivona's gaze.

Whatever the reason, Jeffrey found the question to be perfectly logical. And he gave what to him seemed a perfectly logical answer.

"The most important quarter," he replied. "The part centered around my heart and head."

Upon hearing the translation, Yussef leaned back and nodded slowly. Ivona, on the other hand, appeared truly shaken. Jeffrey found himself too weary and too full to be concerned any longer, about Ivona or anything else. He stood, bid the pair good-night, and made his way back to the single bedroom, which had been vacated for him. He was asleep before his head hit the pillow.

He awoke the next morning to Yussef's impatient knock. Jeffrey rolled from a bumpy mattress that smelled of sweat and cigarette ashes. He folded the ratty covering and dressed in clothes that reeked from the road; everything in his case smelled from the gasoline canisters in the trunk.

The bathroom faucets were dry. He washed in a bucket of water drawn from the brown-stained bath. He walked into the parlor, greeted Yussef and Ivona, and showed ironclad control when pointed toward a breakfast of warm Pepsi and day-old bread. He ate and drank in silence, then carried the last sip of Pepsi back for brushing his teeth.

The old couple were moving about in the room where he had slept. While Ivona and Yussef dressed, Jeffrey seated himself at the table and took out his pocket New Testament. Though he did not like reading it in public, and though he had no great desire to read at all that morning, he knew he needed to. Holding to the discipline of daily Bible time was a link to who he was, and who he had grown to be over the past few years. Within minutes of seating himself, Jeffrey was lifted away from all the poverty, all the trauma, all the difficulty, all the discomfort. He read and he spoke a silent prayer and he found a touch of home in an alien world, a taste of peace in a time of upheaval, a time of healing in this wounded land.

He felt eyes upon him and looked up to see Yussef staring. The rail-thin young man bore a look of confusion that bordered on pain. Yussef started to speak, but Ivona chose that moment to step from the bathroom. He cocked his head toward the front door. Time to go.

They drove only a few kilometers before Yussef stopped as close as he could come to a filling station. The line for gasoline was very long.

His eyes on the car in front of them, Yussef spoke in surprisingly hesitant tones. Ivona translated, "I wish to ask you something."

Jeffrey stretched as far as the car's cramped confines would allow. "Fire away."

Yussef spoke again. When Ivona did not interpret, Jeffrey turned around to find her staring at Yussef, a look of bafflement on her features. Yussef spoke to her again, but without his normal brusqueness. Still she did not reply. Quietly Yussef urged her.

Her eyes still on her nephew, she asked, "Are you a devout man?"

For the first time since passing the border, Jeffrey found himself able to ignore the heat. "I think only God can know a man's heart," he replied. "So it is for the Father to say how true to His word a man is. But I try. That much I can say. I have accepted Christ as my Savior, and I try to live by God's Word."

Something in what Jeffrey said agitated Ivona very much. Her voice seemed to tremble slightly as she translated. Yussef then asked through her, "You were reading the Bible this morning at the table?"

"The New Testament. Yes."

"You do this every day?"

"I try to. It is my time with my Lord," he replied simply.

"For this you need no church?"

"A quiet place and some privacy would be nice," Jeffrey replied. "But no, nothing special is required except a prayerful heart."

Yussef said through a very subdued Ivona, "I watched you. I think I could see this prayerful heart on your face."

"I would be happy to read with you some morning," Jeffrey offered.

"You would do this?"

"Of course."

Yussef rubbed a hand down the stubble on his cheek. "I thank you for the invitation. I will think on it."

When they finally arrived at the pumps, Yussef motioned for them to stay inside. He climbed from the car and spoke long and hard with the attendant. Money was exchanged at intervals after pleading arguments. Gasoline was doled out in twenty-liter lots. When the extra canisters in the trunk were finally revealed, the attendant replied with frantic hand waving and head shaking. Yussef made certain no other car could see and revealed American dollars. The atmosphere magically changed. The tank was topped off, the canisters filled, and the attendant saw them off with a wave.

Once they were again underway, Jeffrey said quietly, "I sure would love a cup of coffee." And a bath, he added to himself. And a bed with clean sheets. And food that doesn't have me crunching on grit. But he would settle for a coffee. "Or tea."

"Coffee is hard to find outside the big cities' black markets," Ivona replied. "Tea is a different story. The former Soviet Union grew quite a good tea in the Muslim states and imported more from China and Vietnam. But the new states are desperate for hard currency and refuse to accept the ruble in payment. Now we receive only what we can barter for, and as our industrial base falters, it becomes increasingly difficult to find things they wish to buy."

They pulled into a dusty square left breathless by the heat. There was not the first hint of breeze. A pair of trees stood with leaves glued to an empty sky. Jeffrey eased from the car, his shirt welded to his skin with a coating of dried sweat. It was nine o'clock in the morning.

Their destination was an apartment in an older building which, before the Communists chopped it up, had been a village manor. Their hostess was a small, swarthy woman who kept the night's coolness trapped within closed windows and drawn curtains. A beautiful teenaged girl ignored the visitors as well as her mother's repeated screams, sulking off to whichever room they were not using. But when the woman brought out her parcel and unwrapped the multiple layers, the teenager was immediately forgotten.

The snuffbox was dated 1782 and stamped with the royal crest of Catherine the Great. Catherine ruled all of Russia for thirty-four years, after deposing her own husband in 1762. She was a ruthless libertine who plotted her husband's assassination with a favorite lover—one of over two dozen. She was also an extremely efficient ruler who founded universities and museums with the same free-wheeling verve she applied to her private life. And Catherine loved her snuff. She was known for keeping jeweled snuffboxes in every chamber of her vast palaces and for passing them out to favorite subjects as the fancy took her. It was her habit to dip only with her left hand, so that the right would always be clean for her visitors to kiss.

This particular snuffbox depicted her predecessor, Peter the Great, mounted on a proud war horse. The box was wrought of enameled silver, the emperor and his horse were gold, standing on a boulder of mother of pearl. Thirty matched diamonds encircled the scene.

From a queen's palace to a dusty backwater village. With a silent sigh Jeffrey handed back the parcel, began the lengthy purchasing discussions, and wished that the box could tell its tale.

———

Thus was the pattern for their days established—up at dawn, a quick breakfast, a hasty wash, a brief time of prayer and study for Jeffrey. Then they would be under way, driving through scalding heat toward another gray-washed village.

Several times Jeffrey invited Yussef to read and pray with him. Yussef always responded with the same reply: he was not yet ready. And yet he continued with his hesitant questions. Ivona translated, although their discussions clearly disturbed her.

Katya's absence was a wound inflamed by every motion, every experience. Each breath of feeling that drifted through his heart was accompanied by the thought that he was incomplete without her. Life was not as it should be unless she was by his side.

Yussef had done his work well. There were very few unimportant items, very few wasted visits. He had also succeeded in reducing the number of icons offered to just one. This was a relief to Jeffrey; by now, most London antique shops had sprouted walls of ancient holy images. Russians fleeing to the West had brought them in droves, and the flood of merchandise had dropped the price to one twentieth of what it had been before glasnost.

Their icon appeared on the fourth day. It was an *Elevsa*, the form that showed Mary embracing the Christ-child, usually with their cheeks touching. The other major form, known as a *Hodigitria*, depicted Mary and the Child separate; usually the baby was painted in the act of blessing the viewer, sometimes holding the holy Book in his left hand. This particular icon was encased in three overlapping silver frames. Enameled into the silver, to either side of the central figures, were paintings of two Russian saints, their names etched in Cyrillic above their heads. The item probably dated back to the late sixteenth century and was clearly of value to a collector.

Yet another item found that fourth day would have brightened the eyes of Jeffrey's friend Pavel Rokovski, an official of the Ministry of Culture in Poland. It was a silver casket, about ten inches square and eight inches high, whose entire exterior was decorated with gold wire woven into an intricate Oriental motif. It clearly dated from the late sixteenth century, when this part of present-day Ukraine was Polish soil. The styles of that era were largely drawn from Persia, which at the time bordered the empire's southern reaches. Floral patterns twined their way about hexagonal shapes, in keeping with the Koran's prohibition against depicting the human form. Along the front, golden pillars supported a domed and sweeping roof, as found upon Persian palaces of that day. The casket was supported by four balled feet of gold-studded lapis lazuli.

After each visit, as they returned to the car and the heat and the drive, Ivona continued with her endless instruction. As the hours and days dragged on, Jeffrey found it increasingly difficult to feign an interest in her lessons. But still she continued. She hammered at him with soft-spoken chisel strokes of her tongue, pressing and pressing and pressing him to learn.

By the sixth and final day, however, Jeffrey found it almost impossible to listen to Ivona's droning lessons. He was exhausted by the heat, the constant stop-and-go driving, the unpalatable food. He was tired of wearing dirty clothes, tired of trying to do business in a foreign tongue. He missed Katya fiercely. And on top of these irritants, the barrage of bounces in a car utterly lacking in shocks had brought on a recurrence of his nagging neck pain.

That afternoon they were cruising along at a modest speed when the car dive-bombed off the end of the pavement. The road went on; the pavement simply ceased. No warning, no markings, just a razor-cut across the road and a ten-inch drop from asphalt to gravel. Jeffrey felt the jar right down to his toenails. His neck and back began complaining in the strongest possible terms.

By evening his patience was worn thin as tissue paper. They were staying in a faceless apartment block, their dinner punctuated by a continual racket from the hallways and other apartments—music blaring, babies crying, adults screaming, children shouting and playing tag up and down the stairs. No one else paid the slightest attention to the babble. The middle-aged couple who were hosting them looked too bowed down by their own internal troubles to pay anyone or anything much mind. And throughout the meal, Ivona continued her endless recital of facts and data.

Finally he had had enough. Too much, in fact. Jeffrey set down his fork and demanded, "Why are you telling me all this?"

His was the one question she did not expect, and it stopped her cold. "I—What?"

"All this information. Why are you telling me?"

"I—" She stopped again, blue eyes blinking hugely behind heavy frames. "To help you."

"To help me what? Buy antiques? That's what I'm here for, isn't it?" His neck's throbbing pain felt as though it hacked at his brain. "How does it help, can you tell me that?"

"You don't want to know?"

"Of course I want to know. But this—" He waved his arm to take it all in and winced as the movement sent a lance through his back. "You're going to all this trouble, force-feeding me information all the time, nonstop, for what reason?"

Ivona faltered visibly, and her English slipped a notch. "Is not good information?"

"Of course it's good. It's great. It's incredible. I've been given a six-day university course. But why? For Yussef, sure, it's fine, he's your nephew, you teach him. But why me? You don't know me, you may never see me again, and yet you never let up teaching me.

I can see you're absolutely exhausted. We all are, yet still you go on. Why?"

She did not reply. Jeffrey watched her face and decided he'd insulted her so badly she would depart right then and leave him to fend for himself in a foreign tongue. He searched for an apology, but could not think past the pain. He stood and left the silent room for bed.

———

"What did he ask you?" Yussef demanded.

Ivona replied, her habitual lilt muted by shock.

"Naive, you called him," Yussef scoffed. "A mere boy in a man's body. A Westerner who sees nothing but gain."

"How could an American be so suspicious?" Ivona asked.

"I'll tell you how." Yussef rose to his feet. "By being twice the man you give him credit for. Ten times."

"I was so sure you were wrong," she said.

Yussef barked a short laugh. "Go. Go and speak to your bishop. Tell him I have found the man who will help us."

Once they were under way the next morning, Ivona announced, "There has been a change of plans."

"Fine," Jeffrey said. "Listen, I need—"

"There is someone we wish for you to meet. His name is Bishop Michael Denisov. He is one of the leaders of the Ukrainian Rite Church."

"Sounds great," Jeffrey replied. "But I'd just like to apologize—"

"There is something I must first tell you, however," Ivona continued in her softly warbled drone, unwilling to hear what he had to say. "You need to know a bit of the background to what we face here."

"Fine." Jeffrey leaned back in defeat. "Let's hear it."

"During the Communist era," Ivona explained, "the Russian Orthodox Church was the only church recognized by the Soviet state. The Ukrainian Rite Catholic Church was outlawed in 1946. Stalin saw the Ukrainian church as too patriotic. Nationalism to anything but the Soviet state was in Stalin's times one of the gravest crimes one could commit. Stalin needed the Ukrainians' assistance in fighting the Germans, so he did nothing until the end of the war. But in 1946 he convened a synod of all Ukrainian bishops. He gave them two choices. Either they would disband the church and instruct all believers to become Orthodox, or Stalin promised to exterminate every Ukrainian Catholic—man, woman, and child."

"The Orthodox church was under Stalin's control?" Jeffrey asked, and swiped at his forehead. Only eight o'clock in the morning and already the breeze through the car's open windows was hot as a blow dryer. Outside, the landscape crawled by in unrelenting sameness.

"There is no way to be certain," Ivona replied. "What is sure is that the Orthodox church has been a part of the Russian state government for centuries. It was more centrally organized, and it was more controllable than something based in Lvov or Kiev and owing allegiance to a nation that would never again exist, if Stalin had his way."

Yussef gave his quiet command, and Ivona translated for him. He shook his head, gave a few sharp words in reply. Ivona translated them as, "The Ukrainian church has suffered as the Ukrainian people have suffered. And now the Ukrainian Catholic church and the Russian Orthodox are locked in a very serious struggle. That is all you need to know." She watched the young man driving, and continued, "The young have little time for discussion. The Communists fed them a lifetime of twisted words, words warped into lies. Now the young wish to act. I cannot fault them for this lack of patience."

"So Stalin tried to wipe the Ukrainian church off the map," Jeffrey said, wondering anew how she managed to stay so intact in this heat.

"The Communists tried to extinguish the fire in the hearts of Ukrainians," Ivona replied. "They sought to crush all that was great. In these many decades, people here have learned to live with the worst. Few can even remember the time when their church was not something hidden in cellars and their faith not practiced in secret. Fewer still know of any great Ukrainian saint or artist or king or poet, because the Soviets sought to erase all memory of their names. This was what it meant to live under Soviet domination. This was the punishment of the innocents."

═══

Bishop Michael Denisov greeted Jeffrey with an appearance that was the only falsehood about him. He looked so gentle, so frail, so helpless in the face of all the turmoil and hardship that surrounded him. He beamed pleasant defenselessness to all he surveyed, displaying a weakness that Jeffrey sensed was not the least bit real.

"Last year, I am letting my assistant go off for a doctorate," he said, ushering Jeffrey into a cramped little flat owned by two local church members. Jeffrey showed no emotion as Yussef planted yet another warm Pepsi on the table in front of him, then retreated to the sofa beside Ivona. "Can you believe?" the bishop continued. "Who is needing a doctorate here? But, okay, there is no excuse for me, selfishness is not a holy virtue, I have to let him go. And now I am alone."

His face was aged, yet strangely unlined. His hair was snow-white and so very soft, like his gaze, which blessed everything it touched with humble peace. He moved not with an old man's shuffling gait, but rather like a balloon tethered to an impatient hand, bouncing here and there, attracted to all it saw but returning to its original path with little jerky motions. His English was somewhat mangled, but delightfully so, and his accent strong but understandable.

Jeffrey motioned toward where Ivona translated quietly for Yussef. "You don't look too alone to me."

"Yes, friends. Thank the God above for friends, no? But I tell you, brother, what we are needing more than all else is priests. First priests, then money. We are drowning in work. Drowning! And my assistant, where is he? Studying for a doctorate in Rome. But the walls, they have all come down. How can I refuse my assistant his lifelong dream?"

"I think you did the right thing," Jeffrey replied.

"You think yes?" The bishop gave a happy shrug. "Thank you, dear brother. Maybe. Maybe. But what you don't know is my church, it is having no doctorates. Not even the bishops! The apostolic delegate, yes, he is having such a title. But my assistant, he is studying Petrology. You know what is this?"

"No idea at all."

"No, nor I!" The bishop seemed delighted by the fact. "He will return and I will be having an assistant who is knowing more than his bishop. What do you think of that?"

"I think there are all kinds of wisdom, most of which does not come from books," Jeffrey replied, liking him. "Where did you learn your English?"

"Oh, dear Jeffrey, life is so full of moments that you don't expect. I am having big experiences in Newark, New Jersey. Big experiences! I was there two years, can you believe that? After I escape from Ukraine, I am studying for priesthood in Rome. Then I am working in France, always with refugees from our homeland. Many, many people escape. So many. One million flee in 1920 alone, oh, yes, and even with so many difficulties and hardships, still there are people escaping over years, just like me. We are having our own diaspora, just like the Jews into Babylon. Yes, so many tragedies. So, I am sent to the United States for two years, and still my English, it sounds like I am learning last week."

"Your English is fine."

The bishop wagged his finger. "Now, now, dear Jeffrey. You must not tell falsehoods, are you not knowing your Bible? Look at Ivona here, never out of Ukraine since a child, and still she speaks perfect English, does she not?"

"She speaks better English than I do."

"Oh, no, no, dear, no. There you are, falsehoods, falsehoods. This will not do, brother Jeffrey. We must have truth even in compliments, yes? So. I am without an assistant, and I must use my very poor English to ask help from a brother in Christ, yes?"

"Yes," Jeffrey agreed, letting his smile loose.

"So. How to explain, how to begin." The bishop sighed happily. "The Ukrainian Rite Catholic Church is in communion with the Pope, while the Russian Orthodox is not, do you see?"

"I think so."

"Excellent, excellent." The bishop beamed his approval. "Ukrainian Catholics are therefore called Uniates, because we are united with other Catholics. But our liturgy, dear Jeffrey, our services, are very much Byzantine. Uniates, yes. And then there are the Orthodox. Ivona has told you of them?"

"A little."

"They have many problems, dear Jeffrey. Oh, so many problems. Now they are having Orthodox believers in many cities who want to make a new church, separate from Moscow, separate from Rome, separate from everybody. And not just here. Just like the

Soviet states, how they are dividing, right now, right now, this very moment the church is in explosion after explosion. Estonia, Latvia, Belarus, Georgia, Lithuania, everywhere there is problems with nationalism and patriotism and Orthodox faith."

"And with your own church, if I understood Ivona correctly."

The gentleman's gaze dimmed. "Ah, dear brother, what problems you cannot imagine. Last year, we had a synod of our bishops. You are knowing this word, synod?"

"A conference," Jeffrey offered.

"Yes, a conference of bishops. The first true synod in one hundred and one years exactly. The Synod of Lvov, pronounced *Livief* in Ukrainian. Many of my brothers, almost half, they were consecrated in hiding. You see, brother Jeffrey, in 1946 Stalin was outlawing our church. Yes. But many people did not wish to become Orthodox, they are staying to the faith of their fathers, and their fathers' before them.

"Yes. Back thirty generations, this tie to the Ukrainian church. Stalin hated this. Our church was a threat to his one great Soviet state. So our priests and bishops, they only worked in secret. Great danger, dear Jeffrey, such danger you cannot imagine. They gave Masses in cellars and they christened in trucks and they met only in night. Still there were the spies and the informers, and many died. Believers and priests and bishops, many suffered. But many still believed, dear Jeffrey."

"And now it's all changed."

"Not changed, my brother. Oh, no, no. *Changing*. All is still difficult for us. Our churches, take our churches for example. Last year, we are finally receiving our cathedral, the St. George Cathedral here in Lvov, and the archbishop-general, he is now residing there. But the others, oh, Jeffrey, you cannot imagine."

"I've seen a few," Jeffrey replied grimly.

"For seventy years they have been stables. They have been warehouses. They have been crematoriums and laboratories and homes for the insane. Whatever the state could do that was bad to God's house, they did. Then in 1991, under glasnost, all the churches are being given back. More than six thousand churches, Jeffrey, can you imagine? Six thousand churches, and most of them in ruins. But this is not the problem, dear brother. No. The problem is who *received* these churches."

"The Orthodox," Jeffrey guessed.

The bishop clapped his hands. "Precisely! And do they want to share with us? No! Will they even speak with us? No! So now the Ukrainian government, first it declared independence on August 24, 1991. Then the new parliament, it *ordered* the Russian Orthodox Church to give back our churches. And still, dear brother, still they are doing nothing. But we, dear Jeffrey, we cannot wait! We have people calling to us in the street, begging us for Mass and schools and, oh, they ask for so much, and we have no place, no place! So do you know what we are doing?"

"Taking over the unused churches?" Jeffrey offered.

"If only, dear brother. If only we could. But an unused church, what do you think of a building that was seven hundred years old, and then was a stable, and then was a garage for trucks, and then was left without doors for thirty years?"

"Rubble."

"No roof, no windows, rain and snow and dirt. Oh, my brother, you cannot imagine how it pains me to go into our churches." He shook it off. "No, we *share* churches with the Orthodox. And what sharing! We hold Masses at different times, yes, but our priests, they pass like strangers down different aisles. They do not speak, they do not see each other. And what are we teaching the people who come?"

"Not love, that's for sure."

"Yes! You understand!" The bishop cast a look back toward Ivona. "So now we decide, we call them brothers. Yes. Now we are having the freedom with the religion, with our faith, so now we must show ourselves as Christians. We begin. We take steps. We are blind to anger. We give in Christ's name and see only that they are Christians. Human, yes, but brothers in our Lord. Only the heart we see. Only the good. And slowly things change. Not with all priests, no dear brother, not theirs, not ours. But many. We see smiles. We share what we have. We *pray* together."

He stopped.

"And then?"

"Yes." Bishop Michael sighed the word. "There must be a then, no? I am here, I am asking for help, so change has come. A bad change."

"Something was taken," Jeffrey guessed.

When Ivona had translated for Yussef, the young man rewarded him with an approving look. Bishop Michael nodded. "Of course. You are intelligent man. You are *perceptive* man. But are you honorable? That is what we must know. Because, dear brother Jeffrey, this is a problem of great importance. Oh, so great. Yes, so I must ask, and then I must answer all the others who ask the same question. Is this American honorable?"

Jeffrey found himself with nothing to say.

The bishop nodded from the waist, bobbing back and forward in time to his words. "Yes, you are right, dear brother. There is no answer you can give. Not in words. Just in action. So. Do I trust you or not?" Still giving his gentle body motion, he closed his eyes, waited, then said, "I am thinking yes. So. Yes, dear brother. You are right but not right. Not something was taken, but *things*. Many things."

"Antiques," Jeffrey hazarded.

"Treasures," Bishop Michael corrected, then settled back as to begin a tale. "There is a street in Lvov, dear brother, called Ameryka. It was lined with great houses. People in last century went to the United States, they worked, they came home, and they built great houses with their money. There was a church. A beautiful church. Church of St. Ivana, yes. The Communists, they made the front hall into Party offices and the back into oil storage depot. But you see, dear Jeffrey, it had doors. It had windows. Bad smell from oil, yes, but we could start there. So what we do, we *invite* our Orthodox brothers to come with us. Yes. Come and pray, we say. There are also Orthodox who need priests here. Come and share. And they do, dear Jeffrey. They come. But some people, they do not like this."

"People in the Orthodox church complained about the two groups working closely together?"

"Their church, our church, government, everywhere there are people who like and not like. Big problems, dear brother. So big. And then, we discover the crypt. No, not discover. You know that word, crypt?"

"Yes."

"A few know of crypt. Not many. One priest now in Poland, he was told by another priest, who was told—" Bishop Michael waved it aside. "No matter. We know. The church was built on older church. No, not on."

"The church was erected on the foundations of an earlier church," Jeffrey offered.

"Exactly, dear brother. You are seeing churches here. Christianity is old here, oh, so very old. The first churches, they used for building wood and the old bricks, and they crumble. With time new churches of stone were built, yes? But the foundations, dear brother, they remain. And crypts, yes, some were old. More than old. Ancient. From the great Kingdom of Kiev. Yes. Before Mongols, before invaders from Asia. Before power moves to Muscovy. Old."

"And forgotten." Jeffrey nodded. "A perfect place to hide treasures."

"Exactly!" The bishop began his nodding motion once more. "So when the Revolution starts, you know, in the twenties, up come the stones, these heavy stones in the floor, up they come, and church treasures from all over Ukraine, those they could bring in time, they are placed inside crypts. Inside coffins. Quickly, quickly, because outside there are fires and riots and battles. Chaos everywhere, dear brother. Churches full, people pray to be taken away. People are searching sky for Christ. With so much chaos, many people are saying *must* be Second Coming. But Christ is not coming, only Communists. Battles are coming closer, and the stones, you know, they were put back and the rings were cut out, so no one could see where was the stairs down."

"And then the Communists arrive," Jeffrey said. "And you wait. Amazing."

"Yes, dear brother. We wait. All over world we wait for time to come home. And now we are here. And we have people starving and churches ruined, oh, so many problems. So we open the crypt, yes, and the treasures, they are still there. Amazing!"

"And then they were taken."

"Stolen," the bishop agreed. "The crypt is opened, and after two nights it is empty."

"Do you know who did it?"

"I know what people *say*, dear brother."

"The Orthodox?" Jeffrey stared at him. "Orthodox priests stole from you?"

Bishop Michael spread his hands wide. "Is not strange? Strange they would come in robes to steal? Strange they leave Orthodox cross on broken chain? Torn robe?"

"Those are the clues you have? It sounds almost as though they wanted you to think it was them," Jeffrey said.

The bishop clapped his hands in agreement. "So do I think also! And others! Orthodox also! We have new friends, dear brother. Friends in Christ, they pray with us, and they are friends. They look. They go where we cannot. They tell us, yes, there are whispers here and there of treasures. Big gathering of treasures in Saint Petersburg. Too great to leave Russia easy. Icons and altars and miters and oh, so many things."

"And they sound like your pieces?"

"Some, yes. Some not sound, *are.*"

"A big city like Saint Petersburg, close to the sea and having strong ties to the West; it would be a perfect gathering point." Jeffrey thought it over, glanced around the impoverished apartment, reflected on how much the bishop was struggling to accomplish with so little. He reached his decision and said, "So you want me to go to Saint Petersburg as a buyer."

The bishop weighed the air in open hands. "Is little chance they sell to you, brother. They are finding better prices in West, less problems with money. But yes, you have *reason* to be in Saint Petersburg. You go, Yussef goes as your hunter, like here, and Ivona goes too."

"As my translator, just like here." Jeffrey nodded agreement. "Where do I start?"

Bishop Michael examined him. "You are helping us?"

"I am helping you," Jeffrey confirmed. "If you like. I will have to speak with my boss in London before saying for sure, but I think he will agree."

"You take care? Great care? There is danger, dear brother. No treasure worth life."

"I have already promised my wife to be extra careful."

Bishop Michael nodded as though this made perfect sense. "Then you must know all."

"There's more?"

"Oh yes, dear brother." The bishop took a careful breath, then continued. "We are also needing help for finding what was there *before*."

———

"You're telling me," Jeffrey said, once they were underway, "that the priests found other treasure already in the crypt when they took their own valuables down?"

"It was a good hiding place when the Communists arrived," Ivona replied. "It had been so before. Long before."

They made their rocking way back toward the Polish border, the car's windows opened wide in a futile effort to reduce the heat. The air blowing in felt drawn from a blast furnace. The sweat dried as fast as it poured from Jeffrey's body.

"How long?" he asked her.

"No one knows for certain," she answered. "Perhaps as long as a thousand years. Long enough for all records and all memories to be washed away in the sea of time."

"So they opened up this ancient crypt to put in the church's valuables and found somebody else had the same idea a couple hundred years before." Jeffrey smiled at the idea. "Bet they were surprised."

Ivona translated for Yussef, who replied, "They were too busy to be surprised for long."

"So you've got two sets of treasures that have been taken to-gether to Saint Petersburg—you hope." Despite the heat, Jeffrey felt the faintest surge of adventure thrill. "Do you know what the first treasures were?"

"Not for certain," Ivona replied, "but perhaps an idea. In the ninth century, Lvov was the provincial capital of the Kingdom of Kiev. Sometimes it is also called the First Kingdom of Rus. It was a great center of learning in those days, and of tremendous wealth, especially within the house of Rurik. One of the Rurik princes ruled Lvov when the first Asian hordes swept down out of the Steppes. Khazars, Pechenegs, Polovtsys—historians argue over which tribe finally defeated the First Kingdom. But in the twelfth century first Kiev and then Lvov were sacked, and the center of power in Rus shifted to the more easily defendable Muscovy."

She dabbed the perspiration beading on her temples with an embroidered handkerchief. "The Rurik crown jewels were never recovered. Legends abounded, but nothing was ever located."

Jeffrey twisted in his seat and examined her impassive face. "Treasures have lain hidden under this church for over seven hundred years?"

She translated for Yussef, who replied, "A wooden structure burns and falls upon a stone floor. Records burn with the rest of the city. All the city's noblemen and priests are murdered." He shrugged over the steering wheel. "A river of blood and a mountain of ashes. Those were the only records the invaders left behind. It would be easy to lose a world of secrets beneath them."

———

Jeffrey Allen Sinclair arrived back at the border feeling as though he wore a second skin of grit. He climbed out of the car with the stiffness of one several days in the saddle. Yussef came around and asked through Ivona, "How is your neck?"

"Still there."

Yussef gave his discolored smile. "It shouts to you, does it?"

"Only when I blink," Jeffrey replied. "No, seriously, it's much better. And it's been worth it."

"No doubt you will enjoy a bath tonight."

Jeffrey looked down at his rumpled form. "I've probably been dirtier," he replied, "but not since I was five years old and rolled around in mud puddles."

Yussef grinned. "There is a certain flavor to friendship after a week of such work, yes?"

"Flavor and aroma both," Jeffrey agreed. "It's been great, though. Really."

Yussef spoke again. Ivona's internal struggle and hesitant voice returned. She gave Yussef an affronted stare before translating, "Can you tell me, where did you learn to read Bible?"

"I've studied with some different people," Jeffrey replied. "And I've read some books. But the most important lessons for me have come through God showing me some special message in His Word. I know that's hard to understand, but it is true."

"Yes," Yussef responded once Ivona's flat-toned translation was completed. "I see that you speak what is truth. For you."

"For anyone," Jeffrey replied. "For anyone willing to read God's Word with a listening heart."

"I have watched you," Yussef said, as though trying to convince himself. "You live what you believe."

"I have doubts," Jeffrey countered. "I have difficulties. But I try to do as He commands."

"Well said." Yussef scuffed his shoe in the dust, studied the road stretching out before him, decided, "I will think on what you say."

"And I will pray for you," Jeffrey replied quietly.

"A kindness for which I am grateful." He straightened from his thoughtful slouch. "Now, to business."

Yussef motioned toward fenced pens where crowds of exhausted-looking people stood in the dust and the heat. "Usually there are between three and four thousand people in the holding areas, waiting to cross from Ukraine into Poland. They are treated horribly by the guards because they're the poorest. They can't afford cars, so their bribes will be small. Give me thirty dollars, and I'll take care of your way out."

"All right." Jeffrey handed over the money. "How will you get the items we've purchased across the border?" he asked, and instantly regretted the question. "Sorry."

When Ivona had translated, the young man laughed. "You will not pass it on to other dealers?"

"I need no other dealer in Ukraine," Jeffrey replied simply. "Not ever."

Yussef grinned at the translation and then explained. "According to the law of today, what I take out of the country is not illegal. But yesterday it was, and tomorrow again, perhaps. Besides, such wealth is an invitation to every dishonest guard at the border, yes? So I stock heavy items that will require a large bribe. Automobile parts and wrenches are the best. Underneath is a false bottom to both the trunk and the backseat. It is too much trouble for the guards to shift all that weight, and too unlikely that a simple trader would carry anything else." He showed his gap-toothed grin. "Sometimes it is best to look the peasant, no?"

"Yes," Jeffrey agreed, and offered his hand. "These were the longest days of my life. I can't say it was fun, but I learned a lot, and I am grateful for the company."

Yussef accepted the hand. "You share your Cracow friend's honesty." Ivona hesitated a moment, then continued translating, "Bishop Michael was right to trust you."

"I will try to help."

"You *will* help, of that I am sure." Yussef pointed beyond the border station. "There is a bus just across the frontier at Medyka which leaves every two hours for Cracow. With luck, you will arrive at the Hotel Cracovia before midnight."

Making for another very long day, Jeffrey thought, and said, "Fine."

"You will travel to Saint Petersburg tomorrow?"

"If I can get a flight, yes." And if Katya doesn't mind too much, he added to himself.

"Then we shall see each other in the big city." Yussef grinned. "I will keep looking for antiques there through my contacts, and I will bring you anything I can find of value."

"Great."

"It is indeed our good fortune that you have this other business to take you to Saint Petersburg." He examined Jeffrey, added, "You would call it a miracle, no?"

"I find God's hand in almost every part of my life these days," Jeffrey replied. "Will you consider praying with me when we meet there?"

"It is so important? That I pray with you?"

"It is important that you pray," Jeffrey replied. "With or without me."

Yussef nodded and changed the subject. "You will come to Ukraine again?"

"If you like."

"I like very much. Your coming has enriched our lives as well." He clapped Jeffrey's shoulder, then said, "Wait here while I arrange your passage through the border."

When he was gone, Jeffrey turned to Ivona and began, "I can't thank—"

She handed him a slip of paper. "This is the name of a small guesthouse run by Ukrainian friends of ours in Saint Petersburg. They are people you can trust. You will be much safer there than in the larger hotels."

Jeffrey nodded his acceptance, both of the news and of her barriers. "All right."

"I will depart from Lvov by train before dawn," Ivona told him. "I should arrive in Saint Petersburg that afternoon. As the bishop explained, I will act as your interpreter whenever you need me. If anyone asks, you should explain that we worked together here and that you asked me to join you. With work in dollars so hard to come by, there should be no questioning of this."

"I understand."

"Yussef will travel as your buyer. When you do not need us, we will continue with our search for the missing church treasures." She nodded to where Yussef was motioning for him to come, and said, "Goodbye, Mr. Sinclair. Until we meet in Saint Petersburg."

Jeffrey watched his plane descend through smoggy Saint Petersburg skies and missed Katya with an ache that had settled in his bones. The very fiber of his being knew the need of her. That his heart continued to beat so steadily baffled him.

Their telephone conversation had been surprisingly smooth and intensely painful. Katya had listened carefully as he described the trip, the problem, and the need for him to travel on to Saint Petersburg immediately. "Five days," she had said quietly when he was finished. "Five days more is all I can bear."

"I miss you," he said, feeling the words carried by a wind that scorched the heart's lining.

"I woke up this morning and reached for you," she said, her voice a sorrowful tune. "When I realized you weren't there, and how far away you were, I started crying."

"Katya," he whispered.

"I couldn't help it," she said, the words trembling like leaves in rainfall. "My heart wasn't there where he was supposed to be."

"Five days," he agreed. "I'll confirm the reservation from Saint Petersburg back to London before I fly out tomorrow."

══

Only one shuttle bus was there to meet the plane from Cracow. It was too small and soon full. Jeffrey came off the plane too late to have a place. He milled about with a hundred or so other passengers until a militiaman finally arrived and escorted them to the terminal on foot.

The hall was vast, as high as it was long. On the distant domed ceiling, ornate cupolas and gilded wreaths surrounded square paintings of bombers flying overhead and releasing scores of paratroopers. Jeffrey joined the jostling throng and filled out the required currency declaration form, listing his watch and wedding ring as instructed. He fought his way through the worried passengers calling in a dozen different tongues as bags were tossed carelessly onto the single revolving band. After a wait, he picked up his bag and headed through customs.

The exit was a squeeze. Currency traders and taxi drivers jostled one another and called out offerings of business. A harried Intourist guide shouted warnings to avoid unofficial traders because many were giving out counterfeit bills. Her voice was drowned out by the clamor.

Three paces later a leather-jacketed young man approached Jeffrey and insisted, "Ten dollars, six thousand eight hundred rubles. Bank only give you five thousand nine hundred. You change, yes?"

"No thank you."

"Why you not change?" The man moved to block his progress toward the taxi rank. "This good rate. You save big. You change how much?"

"*Vsyo, vsyo!*" A driver ran up and shooed the man away, then led Jeffrey back toward his taxi, a relic from a bygone era. He was a little man with pudgy features creased into a worried frown. He accepted Ivona's slip of paper, read the address printed in Cyrillic, and said something Jeffrey could not understand. Then he gunned his motor and they sped off.

=====

Saint Petersburg wore the air of a queen in a royal sulk. The city remained dressed in the imperial finery decreed by Peter the Great, founder of the Russian empire. Yet eight long Communist decades had left her sullen and slightly wilted. Buildings cried out for a good cleaning. Filth clogged every pore. Dust erased the sea's perfume and choked the air.

The city was rimmed by water and laced with canals. Narrow cobblestone streets opened suddenly into great thoroughfares, which emptied into sweeping royal plazas, then closed again into cramped alleys. Bridges were poorly preserved works of art.

The guesthouse was located on the Nevsky Prospekt, one of the city's main thoroughfares. No sign announced its presence. The taxi driver stopped in front of what appeared to be storefront windows masked by heavy drapes and pointed down a set of stairs leading to an entrance slightly below street level. Jeffrey paid him and motioned for him to remain while Jeffrey made sure the place was open for business. The driver nodded as though he understood, but as soon as Jeffrey had pulled out his suitcase and closed the trunk, the driver was away.

Jeffrey turned to find a tall, dark-haired man come bounding up the stairs. "You Sinclair?"

"Yes. Is—"

He was about Jeffrey's age, but his face appeared to have lived through twice the number of winters. "How much you pay that driver?"

"What he asked. Twenty dollars."

The young man shook his fist and shouted abuse after the rapidly vanishing taxi. Then he turned and grinned. "Is okay. You rich American, yes? You pay four times cost for taxi, maybe ten times cost for room."

"No. That is—" Jeffrey stopped. "Four times what I was supposed to pay?"

The young man laughed. "Hey, is no big problem. He bring you where you want to go, not to place where gang wait and take everything, maybe your life." He reached for Jeffrey's case, hefted it, and said, "Welcome to Saint Petersburg, Sinclair."

The stairs led down to a glass-door entrance that still bore faint remnants of its former business. "This old butcher shop," the young man said. "We buy lease from city. First make mountain of paper. Send paper to everybody in whole world. You get your paper?"

"Not yet," Jeffrey replied.

"It come, no worry." The young man wore faded jeans and a Harley-Davidson T-shirt under a form-fitted leather jacket. "You my first American guest. This special day. I love America. So great there. So free. Can do anything, no rules. Nobody looks down your back all the time. You work hard, you make good money, you keep it. Is dreamland, yes?"

"America isn't perfect," Jeffrey replied quietly. "A lot of people have it tough there." The young man chose not to hear. He opened the doors and ushered them into what clearly had once been the main shoproom and was now a ceramic-tiled parlor, sporting thread-bare furniture and brightly colored Kazakh carpets. A waist-high stove was decorated with cheerful hand-painted tiles. Through the rear doors, Jeffrey could see a neat dining area leading into a large kitchen. A set of wooden stairs climbed the side wall and disappeared into a hole in the ceiling that appeared to be lined by an old door frame. Jeffrey squinted and decided it was indeed a door frame.

"This place is great," he declared. "A thousand times better than some faceless hotel."

The young man puffed out with pride. "I am Sergei Popov. Welcome to first Popov Hotel."

"The first of many," Jeffrey assured him.

"That is dream." He turned to a doting old lady seated by the stove. "This is grandmother," he said fondly.

Jeffrey gave a formal sort of bow and motioned toward the in-tricate hand-crocheted tablecloth on which she was working. "That is truly beautiful work."

The old lady replied with a smile that revealed a mouthful of gold teeth. She spoke to her grandson, who translated, "She asks if you are one buying old estate for Artemis company."

Jeffrey assumed Ivona had already been at work, setting their cover in order. "I won't be acquiring it myself I am just represent-ing a buyer."

"Grandmother not happy with this. She wants all old palaces to go back to proper families," Sergei translated. "My grandmother's mother used to work at palace, before Revolution. Grandmother was there often as little girl. She remember old family very well from this palace you buy."

"How interesting," Jeffrey said politely.

"My grandmother," Sergei continued, "she survives the Nine Hundred Day Siege. You have heard of this, yes?"

Jeffrey nodded. It was the name given to the Nazis' attempt to bomb and starve Saint Petersburg into submission. "It must have been horrible."

The young man translated and was given a few creaky words in reply. "'The hardest time is now.' That is what she says. That is what many of the people are saying. The hardest time is now. I tell you, Sinclair, if many more people begin to say the same, you will see change from your darkest dreams."

"My name is Jeffrey," he corrected. "The people are growing angry?"

"My people, their anger is like wave," Sergei replied. "Up and down, up and down. All their lives they wait, wait, wait for change. Now change comes, but so slow it touches grandchildren's lives, not theirs. And the new government, now they say, you must wait some more. And the people are saying, no. No more waiting."

He picked up Jeffrey's bag. "Come, I show you room."

As they climbed the narrow stairs, Jeffrey said, "I love the way so many of your buildings are painted with bright colors."

"Yes, is pretty. You see, Russian winters are hard. Many days with gray skies. Much snow and ice. Colors important then."

"I've seen a lot of buildings being reconstructed. I hope they keep to the old color schemes."

"Yes, maybe." He opened a door onto a small room equipped with a sagging bed, a nightstand, a chair, a table, a tiny window, and frayed curtains. It was spotlessly clean. "But the reconstruction, it is almost all stopped. The city has no money. The city tries to teach people to pay taxes. You can guess what the people say back, yes?"

"I sure can," Jeffrey replied.

"Sure. So the city asks bank for loan. You can guess what says the bank. So the city is broke. Police, they stop cars and say, I give ticket. People say back, no, here is money. Police say good, no salary, so I take. This new style of Russian government. You like?"

"Not really."

"No. I am also not liking. Is chaos." He set down the suitcase with a thump. "Room okay?"

"It's fine, thanks."

"Not first class Paris-style, but clean. And my grandmother, she good cook. You see." He clapped Jeffrey on the shoulder and turned away.

"Wait," Jeffrey said. "Do you think there's any hope that Russia can make it work?"

"Sure, is hope." The man exposed a stained grin. "You know Russian folk songs? Balalaika and accordion and mandolin?"

"I've heard a few."

"So many songs, they start slow, very soft and slow. Then a little fast. Then more fast. Then very fast and boots stomping and hands clapping and everyone shouting and boom! All the people are laughing and singing so fast, like storm of music. The Russian people, they are like song. Slow at start, then boom! You watch. The boom soon come. Either they race to be good capitalists, or they race to darkness. But my people, soon they race."

═══

Ivona Aristonova arrived in the early afternoon. She acknowledged Jeffrey's greeting with a brief nod and allowed Sergei to show her to her room. The stress of her long train journey was etched deep on her face, but she swiftly returned and began the trial of telephoning around for appointments.

An hour later she announced, "We are in luck. The director responsible for applications to acquire property is available this afternoon. We have an appointment to present your request. You cannot imagine how fortunate you are."

"Great," Jeffrey replied, and wondered why she sounded as if she were accusing him of something. "Could I perhaps book a call to my wife?"

Again there was the sense of unbalancing Ivona with his words, again for no reason that he could understand. "Your wife?"

"In London," Jeffrey replied. "I would just like to let her know I'm all right."

"How long are you staying?"

"Five days. Why?"

"It will not be long enough to obtain a connection." She collected herself. "Shall we be going?"

Basil Island was connected to what now was Saint Petersburg's center by the Palace Bridge. It was the largest of the forty islands in the Neva Delta that made up Saint Petersburg, Ivona explained as their taxi drove them to the meeting. Jeffrey showed polite interest, wondering if the lessons were intended as anything more than a shield. A shield against what, he could not determine.

"Originally," Ivona continued, "the region belonged to the Novgorod principality. In the time of the Tartars, that principality was the only one in all Russia strong enough to resist their onslaught. It remained a free city throughout that dark time. But in the sixteenth century, Czar Ivan the Terrible decided that Novgorod was not loyal and succeeded in doing what the Mongols could not; he slaughtered the inhabitants, then put to the torch what before had been Russia's most active port. The region was then too weak to withstand the Swedish invasion and remained under Swedish rule until Peter the Great retook the area and declared it the capital of the new Russian empire."

She pointed to a red-brick castle wall fronting the river. "Czar Peter's first residence was the St. Peter and Paul Fortress, which in later years became the most infamous and gloomy prison in all Russia. Not far beyond that is our destination, the Smolny Convent."

"We're meeting with government officials in a convent?"

"Most of the city's old winter palaces, including the one you are interested in, are the responsibility of the Ministry of Culture," Ivona replied. "The ministry's central offices are located in the convent's outbuildings."

The taxi turned into a garden fronting a vast series of Baroque buildings. Their exteriors were painted a bright robin's-egg blue and were graced with dozens of white pillars and porticos. A series of gold-decked onion domes crowned the roofs.

Ivona waited while Jeffrey paid the driver the agreed-upon fare of two dollars. As they walked toward the side entrance, she continued, "Smolny Convent literally translates as the convent of the tea warehouses. Peter the Great placed the city's main spice and tea docks on this point. When the harbors were moved farther from the growing city, the Empress Elizabeth established a convent here. Her successor, Catherine the Great, turned it into the nation's first school, and it remained a school until the October Revolution. Now the main church is a hall for city recitals and speeches, and the outer buildings house the city's Ministry of Culture."

They entered doors embossed with the standard red-and-gold Cyrillic sign denoting an official government building. Ivona gave their names to the blank-faced receptionist seated beside the hulking militia guard. Soon a heavyset woman appeared and motioned for them to follow her.

The reason for the officials' willingness to see Jeffrey on such short notice was evident the moment introductions were concluded. "It is a tremendous strain to maintain these places," the senior official explained through Ivona. She was a dark-haired matron with piercing green eyes. "We now are required to pay the going commercial rate for all materials. The cost of upkeep for several hundred such old palaces is enormous."

"So you are willing to sell us the palace in question?" Jeffrey asked, pleased with her direct approach.

"Under the proper circumstances," she replied, an avaricious gleam to her eyes. "Some of these places will be retained for state use, but there are so many of them right now that it really doesn't matter which ones are sold."

Her associate, a bearded gentleman seated beside her at the oval conference table, spoke. Ivona translated, "For what purpose did your group wish to use this building?"

"Artemis Holdings is a Swiss trading company with an international board," Jeffrey began, reciting directly from the papers Markov had supplied. "They deal primarily in construction metals. They want to use the estate as a base for business operations in Russia, and maintain residential flats there for local managers."

"Good," the woman director replied. "We are most eager to see more international companies coming in and making such investments."

"Given that Artemis proves to be an acceptable company," her associate agreed, "this should be no problem. Especially since their activities in metal trading will help stimulate our economy."

The director consulted a paper before her. "The property appears to have been well maintained over the years. The house was formerly used as office space by a government-owned company which went out of business with the advent of perestroika. Then last year a local company took a short-term lease on the ground floor." She peered at the next page. "They list their purpose as warehouse and distribution."

"With the enormous rise in costs," her associate said apologetically, "we have been forced to accept whatever offer comes our way."

"This is not necessarily all bad," the director offered. "Having an occupant means that vandalism is kept down. This has been quite a serious problem recently with vacant buildings."

"All renovation must maintain the external facades," her associate continued. "No expansions will be permitted unless they retain the original architectural style and are accepted by the local council. You would be amazed, some Western groups have wanted to transform our priceless heirlooms into warehouses."

"That won't be a problem here," Jeffrey murmured. Ivona did not translate.

"Here is a list of all the documents we require, legal and financial, before the purchase can be cleared," she said, handing him a two-page register. "And this is a translated description of the main house."

"What about the evaluation of the property from your side?" Jeffrey asked, folding the papers and sliding them into his pocket for future examination. "Can you give me some idea of the price you'll be asking?"

She smiled for the first time. "What is the value of such a property in the Russia of today? Do we take the cost of building another, the cost when it was built, the value today in rubles, the value ten years ago, or the value tomorrow?"

She shrugged. "It is up to the potential owners to make a bid, and that bid will be taken into consideration by the privatization committee. On the basis of the financial documents and proposed purpose, the committee will decide if the bid is acceptable. A formal notice will be posted in the *Saint Petersburg Gazette* and at the mayor's office, and thirty days will be allowed for any other parties to submit a competing bid. At the end of that thirty days, if no other bid is received, the notaries are instructed to draw up the lease documents."

Jeffrey sat up. "Lease?"

"Lease-purchase," the associate corrected. "The new Russian parliament has still not passed the necessary laws to allow us to sell these properties outright. At the same time, our city government is fighting off bankruptcy, and we cannot afford the upkeep."

"So we have reached a compromise solution," the director continued. "We are offering thirty-year leases with the proviso that the tenant has the first right of purchase at the stated price, with all rent payments going toward the purchase, once the ruling is made law."

"That sounds more than fair," Jeffrey said. "I guess the next step is for me to take a look around."

"My assistant will take you over immediately," the director replied, rising to her feet and offering Jeffrey her hand as Ivona translated. "She speaks some English and will be your contact here if there are any questions. I shall await word from you."

Once they were back downstairs and waiting for the assistant to locate the necessary keys, Ivona said, "If you will permit, I shall leave you here."

"Of course."

"The bishop has arranged an appointment for Yussef and me this afternoon. I know the gentleman's family, and Yussef does not."

"No problem," he said.

Ivona continued her scrutiny of the gardens beyond the door. "I shall be taking whatever time possible to continue our search. Naturally, I will be available whenever you require my assistance."

"Naturally," Jeffrey replied dryly. "I am most grateful."

"Until later, then," she said and strode away. Jeffrey watched her hasten toward the taxi rank, wondered if it was just his imagination, or if she really was running away.

The same woman who had brought them upstairs appeared soon after Ivona had departed and announced in heavily accented English, "I am responsible for your file."

"Great," Jeffrey replied.

"Come," she said, heading for the door. "We take taxi."

She led him out to the taxi rank on overly tight, high-heeled shoes, her feet crammed in so that the flesh puffed out around the edges and threw her weight forward. She slid into the taxi with difficulty, her dress being far too tight for her girth.

"Bottom floor of palace was warehouse for metal pipes," she said, propping the folder open on her knees as the taxi drove them to the estate.

"So they told me." He watched a throng of people moving slowly past a group of old ladies selling everything from cold potato pancakes to shoe polish on the street curb. "I wonder what happened to all the people who worked for the company that was upstairs."

"Who's to say?" She did not raise her head from the file in her lap. "Now is no more socialism. Now all is private initiative. Fine. Let some private initiative find people more work."

The taxi turned from the main thoroughfare onto a boulevard lined with old apartment houses and shadowed by the past. They swung around the corner and stopped beside a small caretaker's lodge. It was built into an outer wall constructed of brick and hand-wrought iron. Huge, rusty hinges, now broken and twisted, had probably once held impressive gates. Through the sweeping entrance, Jeffrey could see what once must have been a formal garden and now was little more than a jungle.

His attention was caught by the sight of a large American car parked along the curb opposite the estate. The black Chevrolet totally dwarfed the little plastic cars near it, including their own taxi. Jeffrey paid the driver and got out in time to see a tall, lanky man with a blond buzz-cut, his tie at half-mast, saunter out through the main gates.

Jeffrey's guide did not like this development at all. She clambered from the taxi and paraded toward the blond man. Jeffrey was right behind her. The woman shouted a full blast of rapid Russian.

"Sorry, lady," the man drawled in English. "I don't speak the lingo."

Jeffrey stepped forward, unaccountably irritated by the intruder's air of nonchalant superiority. "She wants to know what you're doing here," he said. "And so do I."

That startled him. "You American?"

Jeffrey nodded. "I asked what you are doing here."

The guy flicked a glance at something behind them, and sidled swiftly back into the estate. "What's it to you?"

"He official bidder," the woman answered, following the man's backward movement, her tone rising indignantly. "He have right to ask. I am ministry official. I have more right. Now you say, what you are doing here?"

"Just having a little look. No harm in that, is there?" Keen eyes flickered back from their inspection of what was behind them and rested on Jeffrey. "That right, what the lady said? You want to buy this place?"

"I don't see how that's any business of yours," Jeffrey retorted. "And you still haven't said what you're doing on this property."

He shrugged. "Maybe I'm thinking about buying it too."

Just as Jeffrey had feared. A competing bid. "Who for?"

The guy shook his head. "You first."

"This private property," the woman said sharply, almost dancing in place. "You must have proper authority to enter. Mr. Sinclair has authority. You have nothing. You leave. Now."

"I was just on my way out," he replied. "That your name? Sinclair?"

"Who else wants to buy this place?" Jeffrey demanded.

"See you around, Sinclair," the guy said, and ambled off.

"Come," the woman insisted to Jeffrey. "We go."

"I don't like the look of him," Jeffrey said quietly, watching the man's slow progress down the street.

"I am also not liking," the woman agreed. "Is much in Russia today I am not liking. People with no proper authority do much, too much. No respect for anything."

Jeffrey followed her down the drive. "Have you had other bids for this palace? Any from Americans?"

"No, no bids from anywhere. Is just another winter palace, one of thousand. More. City full of old palaces." The woman walked the rubble-strewn path on feet that clearly pained her. "We need many buyers with proper authority. Not men who walk where they like and speak without respect."

She fished through a voluminous purse and came up with a series of heavy, old keys wired to a piece of cardboard. "How long you take?"

"This afternoon," Jeffrey mused, craning to get a look at the exterior above his head, "three or four hours. I suppose I might as well start on a floor plan, then finish that up tomorrow. And I'll need a local architect to look over the foundations and the roof."

"Yes, yes," she said impatiently, climbing the rough stone stairs. "But such time I don't have. I give you keys, yes?"

"That's fine with me."

"You let no one in without proper authority?"

"Not a soul," he promised.

"I come and check on you," she warned.

"I will look forward to it," he replied.

She harrumphed, unlocked the door, pushed it open, and handed him the set of keys. "You now responsible."

"I'll guard them with my life," he replied. "Thank you."

———

Everywhere were remnants of the past, whispers of the mansion's former glory. The dual entrance halls were floored with marble mosaic, now cracked and pitted and dulled by ingrained dirt. Hallways were floored with rough-worn hardwood overlaid with cheap, peeling linoleum.

The ground floor chambers had been whitewashed, but so long ago that the paint was falling in a slow-motion snowfall upon the pipes and sheet metal and bent steel rods scattered over the scarred floors. The back garden doors had been enlarged with a sledgehammer, then fitted with a rusting warehouse-type truck door.

Upstairs the linoleum gave way to laurel-wreath carpet that smelled of damp and age. The first great hall was lined in what once had been royal-red silk wall covering and now was a dull pinkish-gray. The fireplace was large enough to stand in upright and was flanked by two ancient Greek statues. This had been a common practice in many great royal houses, when conquerors returned home with spoils that were then fashioned into their villas as decoration. The ceiling was a full thirty feet high and decorated by a hand-wrought wooden frieze, now completely covered with water stains and mold.

Opening from the hall's far end was a smaller room that testified to Russia's former love affair with the Orient; it was a gilded chamber in the best Islamic style, the intricate geometric designs on the walls rising to lofty heights, where they joined to a gold-leaf ceiling shaped like the dome of a mosque. Beside the main doors, where the family's crest had once been carved, former Communist occupants had painted crude hammers and sickles.

Beyond this chamber began, if Jeffrey correctly read the cursory description supplied by the ministry, the rooms of the head of the house, Prince Markov's grandfather. As befitted a distant member of the royal family, the suite consisted of a dozen chambers—billiards, music, library, reception, study, and so on. Across the main hall, his wife had struggled to make do with a mere seven rooms of her own. His work set aside for this first viewing, Jeffrey walked through the rooms in a reverie of what life in this great house once might have been.

The third floor was an almost endless series of connecting rooms for younger children, with separate halls for honored guests. After a brief inspection, Jeffrey returned to the ground floor. The kitchen and galleys had been stripped and filled with the warehouse's rubbish. Jeffrey went back to the central room, which clearly had been sort of a glorified waiting salon, not nearly as grand as the upstairs chambers. Leading from that was the apartment of the family's eldest son, Markov's father. It consisted of a large sitting room, a study, a dressing salon, a bath, a toilet, a second private salon, a long hall lined with closets and wardrobes, and a bedroom.

Four hours later, Jeffrey had completed the initial floor plan and seen about all he cared to for one day. He left via the front entrance, carefully locking the door behind him.

A voice from the bottom of the stairs asked, "Is the dragon lady still around?"

Jeffrey bristled at the conspiratorial tone. "Whether she is or she isn't," he retorted, "the situation's the same. You have no right to be here."

"Proper authority," the young man scoffed. "What a joke. Proper authority's sent this country to the bottom of the economic scrap heap."

"So why are you here?" Jeffrey stalked down the stairs and strode up close to the other man, trying to make him give ground. "Better still, why don't you leave?"

The man backed up a step. "Hey, did it ever occur to you that maybe we got started on the wrong foot?"

Jeffrey pressed forward. "Now."

Another step. "I got a better idea. How's about you ask me one more time who I'm with?"

"I don't care anymore."

"Hey, but you should."

"I just want you—"

From the other side of the high outer wall came the sound of several men's voices approaching. The man's casual attitude vanished. Quick as a cat, he grasped Jeffrey by his shoulder and arm, pushing him across the driveway and up against the wall. There wasn't much force behind the movement, and the contact was softened by a thick overgrowth of hanging vines. Still, the jolt was enough for his neck to give a lancing ping. Jeffrey groaned, or started to, but the man stiffened and hissed and silenced him.

The voices receded. The man released Jeffrey, craned to see through the open gates, and said softly, "You ever heard the name Tombek before?"

Jeffrey rubbed his neck. "Would you mind telling me what's going on?"

"I asked you a question, Sinclair." His attitude was casual again, but his voice was distant as last winter's frost.

"I couldn't care less. Who are you?"

A swift motion brought forth a leather ID, which was flashed open so fast that Jeffrey only caught sight of a photograph and official printing. "Name's John Casey. I'm here with the U.S. Consulate. Cultural Affairs, if you want to be technical, which I'd advise you not to be. Now, Sinclair, have you ever heard the name Tombek?"

"No." Consulate. It didn't make sense. Jeffrey felt his anger subsiding into embarrassment. "Why push me around like that?"

"A couple of their goons followed you here." He watched Jeffrey continue to massage his neck. "Hurt yourself?"

"No. You did."

"Sorry." He eased into the gateway and searched the road outside the gates. "I think it's okay."

Jeffrey remained unconvinced. And hot. "If they were already following me around, why try and hide me?"

"Can't say for sure that they were. But their car pulled up right as you and Miss Proper Authority got out."

"And?"

Casey shrugged. "Why take chances?"

His neck subsided to a dull throbbing. "So who is this Tombek?"

"Tell you what," Casey replied, leading Jeffrey over to the large American car. "Why don't we take a little drive and let the Consul General decide how much you ought to know."

"The place you've been looking over backs up on the Fontanka Canal; that's the water trough running down the middle of that street over there," Casey said as he navigated the heavy car along the rutted pavement. "Used to be one of the best neighborhoods the city had to offer. Over across the street is the former royal stable. It runs a full city block and has an interior courtyard over two acres in size. Now it houses the city's garbage trucks, police vans, and some of the smaller buses."

Jeffrey reached past his growing annoyance and confusion in an attempt to gain more information. "How do you know so much about this area?"

Casey shrugged in reply. "Boredom, I guess. Had to have something to do in my off time, so I studied some of the local lore."

"Off time from what?" Jeffrey probed.

"That's for the Consul General to say." He pointed through the front windshield at a beautifully restored church with six multicolored onion domes. "That's the Church of the Resurrection. Alexis II, the czar who abolished serfdom in 1861, was assassinated on that spot by nobles who weren't too happy to lose all their slaves. The local folk, though, they wanted to honor the guy who gave them freedom. After Alexis was killed, it became a crime to speak his name. So they always called that church the Cathedral of the Spilled Blood."

"I'm not in any trouble, am I?" Jeffrey demanded.

"You might as well save your breath," Casey replied. "Why don't we just give it a rest and enjoy the ride?"

The United States Consulate in Saint Petersburg was built to fit within the hollowed-out shell of a once prestigious city dwelling. Set upon the fashionable Furshtadtskaya, the outer stairs were as worn and pitted as the rest of the city. Beyond the double set of bulletproof doors and past the watchful Marines on guard duty, however, all was pure Americana—plush, neutral-colored carpets, warm wood-veneer walls, fluorescent lighting, decent air conditioning, color photographs of the President.

Jeffrey waited in a cramped security lobby while Casey went elsewhere and reported in. Eventually the Consul General's private secretary arrived, introduced herself, and led him into an elevator operated by a key suspended from her belt. Jeffrey tried not to gawk as he was led down a bustling corridor past ranks of bombproof filing cabinets stamped "Top Secret" and clamped with combination safe locks.

The Consul General's office had once been the house's central drawing room, and no amount of bland paint and dull-colored carpet could completely erase the chamber's former splendor. As Jeffrey was ushered inside, a vigorous-looking man rose from his desk and walked around it with hand outstretched. "I'm Stan Allbright. Good of you to stop by."

"Jeffrey Sinclair," he replied. "I didn't have much choice."

"Casey didn't get too carried away, I hope." Allbright's softly measured midwestern twang had been polished by distance and time and foreign tongues to the point that the accent seemed to come and go at will. "Why don't you take a seat over there in the comfortable chair, and let's talk it over. You like a coffee? Maybe a Pepsi?"

"I'm fine, thanks."

Even when the Consul General was seated, he appeared to be in motion. He was a wiry bundle of energy, the sort of man who brought people to attention just by turning their way. He was dressed in what Jeffrey had once heard described as diplomatic fatigues—dark suit, white shirt, black shoes, bland tie. His gaze was intelligent, cautious, measuring. "What brings you to town, Mr. Sinclair?"

"I'm working on a project."

"Mind if I ask what sort?"

Jeffrey explained the Markov estate purchase. "This is the first assessment."

"You have any idea what's behind the interest in that particular project—what'd you say their name was?"

"Artemis Holdings Limited. And no, I'm not sure what they want to use it for, besides something to do with their company's operations. Exporting metals, I think."

"The name Artemis is new to me. The international corporate community is still small enough for us to have a handle on most movers and shakers, especially somebody big enough to go for a winter palace backing up on the Fontanka. You know that's what it used to be, don't you?"

"I figured it had to have been somebody's private residence," Jeffrey hedged.

"Yeah, these royal families, they all had their estates out in the back of beyond, and believe me, you can't get farther out in the sticks than some of these places in Russia. So off they'd all go and rule their serfs and farm their lands and make their money during the summer, then hightail it back to the capital and civilization before the first snows. A winter out in the boonies meant eight, maybe nine months without contact to their nearest neighbors. Taking care of the estates during the cold, lonely days was what overseers were for, right?"

"I suppose so," Jeffrey agreed, wondering where the man was headed. Wishing he would get there.

"These people, their holdings were *big*. Twenty, thirty, even a couple of hundred square miles. Tens of thousands of serfs. Folks like these, they'd have their family castles back on the home range, then set up a second winter palace here in downtown Saint Petersburg. Most of these houses are in pretty bad shape after seventy years of Communism, but the ones that haven't been trashed would make your head spin. What's the condition of the one your people are looking at?"

"Stripped bare," Jeffrey replied. "But otherwise not too bad, considering."

"And they weren't interested in any other property but this one?"

Jeffrey shook his head and winced at the motion. "Why are you so concerned about this?"

"I'll get around to that in just a minute. What's the matter with your neck?"

"Your man Casey pushed me into a wall."

"Yes, he told me. I'm sorry about that, but he assures me it was important to get you out of view. You say you've never heard the name Tombek before?"

"Not until this afternoon. Who is it?"

"Local trouble." The tone turned deceptively easy. "How'd you get involved in this project, Mr. Sinclair?"

"My boss in London and the head of Artemis are business associates."

"Mind if I ask who's behind the Artemis group?"

"Sorry, I can't answer that."

"No, of course you can't." Long legs stretched out in a parody of calm. "I have to tell you, Mr. Sinclair, I get the impression you're not telling me everything."

"You haven't told me anything at all."

"No, suppose not. We've got ourselves a problem here, you see, and it must be kept quiet. I'm tempted to go against the grain and let you in on it, but I can't get a handle on whether or not I can trust you."

"If you mean trust me to help, I can't answer that unless I know more," Jeffrey answered. "But if you mean trust me to keep my mouth shut, I guess the way you feel about the answers I've given so far are the best response you could have."

Consul General Allbright gave a genuine smile. "You know something? I do believe if we ever had the time we could get to be friends. Mind if I call you Jeffrey?"

"I guess not."

"Fine. What we're facing, Jeffrey, is one utter mess. We had someone kidnapped a little over a week ago." Allbright opened the file in front of him, extracted a photo, handed it over. "Young lady by the name of Leslie Ann Stevens."

Jeffrey inspected the picture, saw a fresh-faced young woman in her early twenties with auburn hair, alert eyes, and a sweet smile. "An American?"

"Peace Corps volunteer," Allbright confirmed. "Picked up right in front of your little palace too, far as we can tell. A couple of neighbors didn't actually see the girl get snatched, but did spot a truck parked outside the manor late that same night. Only activity on the whole street. Crime's so bad these days, you don't see much moving after dark except on the main boulevards—which this isn't, not anymore. Everybody we talked to agreed on one thing; they were unloading something from that truck. A lot of boxes."

"Into my palace?"

Allbright nodded. "That's why I was asking, Jeffrey. You sure you didn't find anything that could have been packed inside boxes and shuttled inside?"

"Not a chance." Jeffrey was emphatic. "The place looks furnished from a jumble sale. And all the warehouse section has in it is a lot of rusting pipes and sheet metal."

"You've been all over the place?"

"Top to bottom."

"Casey's been all through the grounds, says the house must be all of ten thousand square feet. Big house like that, you might have missed a room."

"Not unless there's a hollow wall. I've already worked out a basic floor plan."

"Mind if Casey takes a look around inside?"

Jeffrey hesitated, then decided, "I suppose not."

"Thanks. Any way we might be able to get in without attracting attention?"

"I've got a key. Why would somebody want to kidnap a Peace Corps volunteer?"

"Can't say for certain. We do know she's been kidnapped, though." Allbright rubbed a hand through thinning hair. "We know because we've received a ransom note and her Bible. The pastor at the local English-speaking church identified it as hers. Seems she was returning home from a prayer service."

"And the palace was on her way home?"

"It was if she took the shorter route, which she wouldn't have if she'd showed the brains given a very small rabbit. She could have walked on down Nevsky Prospekt, which she didn't, according to one of the people who saw her off. It was twice as long that way, and maybe she was tired. Maybe she thought she'd be safe, that close to home. Maybe she just didn't think." Allbright managed a weary smile. "My biggest concern right now is whether the lady's still thinking at all."

"Have you been to the police?"

Allbright grimaced. "Any crime involving a foreigner is still the KGB's bailiwick. They're a strange bunch to work with these days, let me tell you. Always have been, of course, but before at least you knew where you stood. With the changes facing everybody these days, you can't be too certain they won't turn around and bite off the hand you're offering."

"So you're going to pay the ransom?"

"Washington is busy giving me the royal runaround, but if we could have some assurance the lady's still alive and kicking, yes, we'll pay."

"So what can I do to help?"

"That's what I like to hear. No beating around the bush, just straight up and straight out." The Consul General rose to his feet. "Tell you what. We're having a little reception for some people tonight over at my residence. Why don't you stop by? We'll discuss it then."

"All right, thanks."

"Good. What we could do is have Casey come by for you."

"At the palace," Jeffrey said, understanding. "An hour or so early, and I could just offer to show him around."

"See? Just like I said." He extended his hand. "Nothing like a man who knows how to get things done."

S t. Isaac's Square was dominated by St. Isaac's Cathedral, which had been the largest church in Saint Petersburg before the Communists declared it a museum. Its marble exterior still bore the scars of Nazi guns; it had been bombed almost daily during the Nine Hundred Day Siege. The high gold cupola had remained visible to the German gunners stationed across the Baltic even when everything else in the city had been masked beneath the smoke from bombs and countless fires.

Across the square, by the Blue Bridge, was the Marien Palace, the home of the new city government. Between them and slightly to one side was the newly renovated Astoria, one of the city's two exclusive hotels. Room prices were higher than a five-star hotel in the heart of Paris, meals more costly than a restaurant overlooking New York's Central Park. By Western standards neither was worth half its cost—especially the meals. But the hotel was clean, and visitors could be fairly assured that what they ate would not make them sick. Western businessmen kept it booked solid six months in advance.

The young man leaned across the coffee table and asked, "You're absolutely certain they can't trace this back to me?"

He wore a rumpled suit in the latest Western fashion. His hair was carefully trimmed, his shoes softest Italian leather. He looked like an up-and-coming young executive exhausted from a hard week's work—which he was, after a fashion.

He was also extremely frightened.

"You have our word," Yussef replied for both himself and Ivona.

They were seated in the lobby of the hotel's ruble section, where their language and appearance drew fewer stares. The Astoria was in effect two hotels—one for rubles and one for hard currency—with different entrances, reception desks, key systems, gift shops, and restaurants. Staff relegated to the ruble hotel were perpetually disgruntled, barred as they were from ever seeing dollar tips.

"How was trading today?" Ivona asked.

"Like always." He stood and cast off his jacket. Dried sweat stained his expensive shirt in darkened splotches. He could not have been over twenty-five years of age, but his eyes held the blank confusion of a tired old man. He lit a fresh cigarette from the ashes of his last and drank thirstily from his beer.

"Buy, sell," he rattled. "Took fifty thousand pairs of stockings in exchange for a hundred personal computers this morning. You like a pair?"

"You are very kind to ask," Ivona replied. "But no."

Before, when a Russian company needed something—anything, no matter how small or large—it would place a requisition through the Moscow-based central planning agency called Gosplan. Gosplan would then, hopefully, approve the request and forward it to the appropriate supplier, who could sell nothing unless Gosplan first approved the order. The product would inevitably arrive late and be of poorer quality than requested, but to a point the system had worked.

All that had vanished with the fall of Communism.

In an attempt to stifle an inflation rate approaching fifty percent per month, the government had dried up the source of rubles. Companies with products to sell suddenly found themselves either without buyers, or with buyers who had no hard cash. So they had begun to trade.

By the second summer after Communism's fall from grace, the government owed two hundred and twenty billion rubles in unpaid salaries. Cash-starved factories paid workers with truckloads of fresh oranges and ton-lots of clothes. Company apartments were completed by trading steel wire for concrete, then having skilled machinists work overtime as plasterers and carpet layers. The world's largest steel works, the Metallurgical Complex in Magnitogorsk, was reduced to paying workers with fifty-pound sacks of sugar and pieces of steel that their employees could then resell.

The fastest growing industry, in a country whose economy had contracted thirty percent in a two-year period, was the commodities exchange. Russia resembled a vast factory in a panic bankruptcy sale. The commodities markets sold everything from vodka to new MIG jet fighters.

Whenever the government told the commodities brokers that selling a certain item was against the law, that item was simply removed from the floor and offered on the street just outside the exchange. New laws were tossed out as easily as the floor sweepings each evening. Computerized barter houses overloaded the outdated phone systems and took a taste off the top from every deal cut.

The majority of dealers were under twenty-five. They had been born at a time when their culture was coming to realize the Communist social structure was based upon a lie. Thus the propaganda and brainwashing had not stuck so well. Initiative had not been stripped away nor traded for the promised security of socialism.

Ivona received the nod from Yussef. "Could you please tell us what you have learned?"

The frightened look returned. "I need to know I'll be safe."

"We seek only for ourselves," Yussef soothed. "What you tell us will go only to the bishop, no further. He will treat it as though it came from the confessional."

The young man leaned forward, and said quietly, "There are rumors of a *matrioshka* shipment."

"This is news," Yussef said, clearly pleased.

Russia's *matrioshka* dolls were known worldwide: a series of smiling wooden figurines in graduated sizes, each figure nesting in the next larger size. A *matrioshka* shipment meant hiding an illegal product inside a legitimate export. The technique was normally used for transporting heroin from the Asian states to the West.

"This is mafia work?" Yussef asked.

"Who knows? But that is how it sounds, and what the rumors say. The bribes are too high for anyone else to use the transport route, and the mafia controls the docks." He looked from one to the other. "It is the mafia you are up against?"

"We do not know who was behind the theft," Ivona replied.

"We know," Yussef retorted, his face like stone.

"We are not sure," Ivona insisted.

The young man flashed a weary smile. "Confusion is a sign of the times."

"What will the outer shipment be, do you know?" Yussef demanded.

"Hard to say, but my guess would be raw metal. There is more of this than anything else going out just now. One group I know does forty tons per week to Estonia. They're hooked up with Western buyers who like the Russian prices but don't want to have to bother with Russian bureaucracy. The group clears four thousand dollars a week."

Yussef whistled softly. "They're mafia?"

"Not the group themselves, but anything this rich will have the mafia circling like vultures around a kill. They take a taste, never fear." The young man stubbed out his cigarette with jerky motions and lit another with a gold Dunhill lighter worth more than the average Russian's annual salary. He snapped the top shut, and said with the smoke, "Copper, bronze, zinc, titanium, strategic metals—we see the trades every day, and we know the end buyer is in the West. The factories are crumbling, they have no money to pay salaries, and the Westerners are ready to pay in real dollars. Anything the companies can smuggle out, they do; it's the difference between life or death for many of them."

"Big business," Yussef agreed thoughtfully.

"Listen, I'll tell you how big. Estonia has no metal resources at all, and only a handful of factories. But this year Estonia became the sixth largest exporter of copper in the world. There is one trial before the courts right now, where a group was caught trying to ship *five thousand kilometers* of aluminum irrigation tubing from Saint Petersburg. One deal."

"We think this would be shipped from Saint Petersburg," Yussef replied. "Have you heard of anything here?"

"A new player?" He flicked his cigarette in the ashtray's general direction. "They come and go like the wind. But something this big would require big financing, maybe more than one shipment if what you say is correct." He thought a moment. "There is word of a new metals dealer with backing from a Swiss group. Nothing definite. Nothing on the market. But big enough to attract interest. Traders are like wolves. They sniff the wind and travel in packs."

Ivona concluded, "So you think the mafia might handle such a deal—"

"They handle nothing," the young man said impatiently. "They *control*. They falsify the export documents. They pay bribes. They frighten. They threaten. They eliminate all that stands between themselves and profit."

"And they tell the suppliers what will be hidden inside their metal for shipment," Yussef finished.

The look of genuine fear returned to the young man's face. "You now have my life in your hands."

"We will guard it well," Yussef promised, rising to his feet. "We thank you. All of us."

asey arrived at the palace exactly on time. He shook hands with Jeffrey, and said, "No hard feelings, I hope."

Jeffrey found the man's casual attitude as fake as his smile. "I still don't know what it was all about."

Casey motioned toward the door. "Mind if I have a look around?"

"That's why we're here." Jeffrey led him into the central foyer. "Do you even know what you're looking for?"

"Tell you what," Casey replied in his lazy drawl, looking over the papers jumbled on the trestle table, "why don't you just keep on with your business plan or whatever it is you've been doing and let me mosey about on my own."

Jeffrey waved a free hand. "Be my guest."

Ninety minutes later, Casey interrupted his continued sketching of the floor plans with an abrupt, "Guess I've seen all I need to. Matter of fact, we were due at the Consul General's a half-hour ago."

Jeffrey stacked up his work. "Find anything?"

"Like you said, a lot of dust and steel. Nothing else. Come on; this place's got too many dried-up memories for my liking."

Jeffrey followed the man down to the waiting car. They drove through the gathering dusk in silence.

The evening's beauty rekindled his yearning for Katya. The blankets of smog and airborne soot burnished the sky a hundred fiery hues. He wished for her to share this night, when only main streets had lights, and former palaces had their wounds soothed by soft illumination. During the day he had been sorry to be alone, yet glad she was not there. This world was too harsh. The people were drawn with jagged lines. Safety was a word with little meaning. This evening, however, as he sat in the American car's plush luxury and watched the silent orchestration of colors, he ached for her with a longing that scarcely left him room to breathe.

As they turned onto the Nevsky Prospekt, Casey interrupted his reverie with, "How's the neck?"

"Better, but still sore."

"Didn't mean to handle you so rough."

"I hurt it a while back, I guess it's not completely healed." His hand went up automatically to massage it. "Who is this Tombek anyway?"

"The bad guys."

Talking to Casey was like drilling through stone with a tooth-pick. "What makes you so sure somebody was following me around?"

"If you don't know," Casey replied, "don't ask."

"What kind of answer is that?"

"A smart one." Casey hesitated, then went on, "There aren't a lot of black and white lines to be drawn around here right now. Too much gray in this country for my liking. But Tombek's all black. Not anybody you want to mess with. Definitely not."

Jeffrey thought of Yussef and Ivona's work, then asked, "But why would Tombek want to have me followed?"

"Brother, that's the million dollar question."

"I've got another one for you," Jeffrey said. "Why does a local consulate official know this much about the Saint Petersburg bad guys?"

"Like I said, there's too much gray in this world. Not many people we can rely on. Best way to get things done is to do it ourselves."

"Consul General Allbright indicated the KGB weren't much help."

"You said it. These days, the KGB's like a dead elephant lying in the middle of the Russian road to progress. All that weight is hard to shift, and it stinks to high heaven. But it's blocking traffic something awful, and sooner or later it's got to go."

"Have they done anything for you at all?"

"Lot of paper flying back and forth, lot of telephone calls asking these double-edged questions. But we haven't seen much in the way of real results. No, this thing's gotta be baked at home." Again Casey hesitated, as though debating something internally. Then he went on, "There is hope, though. Maybe. We've made contact with a sort of subgroup, a new offshoot within the KGB that appears to mean business. They've offered to help us on this."

"And you think this guy Tombek might be involved in your kidnapping?"

"Tombek is not a person; it's a gang," Casey corrected. "They're involved in just about everything else. Might have their hand in this as well."

The Consul General's official residence was located in a short alleyway off one of the city's main thoroughfares. When they arrived, the cul-de-sac was filled with late-model Western cars and grim-faced Russian bodyguard-chauffeurs.

The residence still maintained a vestige of its former glory. High ceilings supported brilliant chandeliers whose light shone down upon chambers of vast proportions. The well-dressed crowd milling about the carpeted expanse could have been lifted from any major international community.

Jeffrey circled about the trio of rooms filled with the city's movers and shakers. He paused beside a group paying careful attention to a heavyset Russian who spoke with authority: "Step by step we make progress. It is a long voyage from Communism to liberty. Very long. No one expects to make it overnight. But if I have one criticism of my countrymen, it is that they concentrate overmuch on the unsolved and do not take hope from the successes. Yes, the positive aspects are small when taken against all that is left undone. But these are steps in the right direction, and for this reason it is most important that they be given a place in the limelight."

"I guess seeing goods on the shelves has helped reassure the people," a listener offered.

"Yes and no. Appearance of Western goods and high-priced foods is pleasing to those who can afford them, but a source of great tension to everyone else. Most people find these products completely beyond their reach. They see them, but cannot buy them. This is like one of our ancient fables." He shrugged. "We are a patient people. We are very hard to get moving, but once we are going, we are very hard to stop."

Somebody asked, "How does the situation look for this winter?"

"Difficult, but we hope not dangerous." He tossed back the remainder of his drink. "So long as there is not a coal or rail strike and the roads stay open, we will make it. Famine combined with no heat would end everything."

"At least there is some help coming from the West," another offered.

"Not enough, and too slow," he replied. "We are starving on the West's cautious assistance. The biggest lesson we have learned recently is that capitalist money is a coward. The spenders hear the word risk and they zip up their pockets. We are fed with words, when what we need is the machinery to make our own bread."

"Speaking of bread," someone asked, "is there any hope that Russia will ever be able to feed itself?"

"At the turn of the century," the Russian replied, "my nation was exporting more food to England than it consumed itself. In the years before the October Revolution, after the system of serfdom was abolished and Russians worked the land as free men, the farming villages had a higher level of income than the cities. But the Bolsheviks feared the peasants' power and smothered the villages with their policy of collectivization."

"Not to mention the pricing structure," another offered.

The Russian nodded his agreement. "A loaf of bread cost the same in 1987 as it did in 1925. The situation was so catastrophic that farmers found it less expensive to feed their pigs with fresh bread than with raw barley. Communist pricing structure was a lesson in insanity."

The Consul General appeared at Jeffrey's elbow. He pulled him away from the crowd and said quietly, "Sounds like Casey wasn't able to find anything more than you did."

"I wouldn't know," Jeffrey replied. "He made it clear he'd just as soon not have me around."

Allbright smiled without humor. "In these parts it's hard to find people to trust, and harder still to trust them once you do.

Casey's got the eyes of a hawk, though. Doubt seriously if he missed anything." He nodded a friendly greeting to a passing face and said more quietly, "I hope."

"You took quite a risk in telling me about the kidnapping, didn't you?"

"Not if you're as honest as you look."

"Still, I imagine you had some disagreement from your staff," Jeffrey ventured. "Disapproval, even."

"Comes with the job. You develop a thick hide or you retire and grow flowers," Allbright stated flatly. "Might surprise you to know that Casey felt we could trust you as well. I put a lot of value on that man's opinion."

Jeffrey hid his surprise. "I imagine you learn to trust your own judgment, too."

"Makes a lot more sense than asking the advice of somebody behind a desk in Washington, six thousand miles from the action." Allbright faced him. "What are you getting at?"

"You were right when you said I hadn't told you everything," Jeffrey replied. "I think I ought to exchange honesty for honesty."

"That's all a man can ask for." He took Jeffrey by the arm. "What say we find us a quiet corner."

They left the main suite of three public rooms and passed the central staircase where Casey stood watching everything and everyone with his deceptively easy gaze. Allbright motioned for him to join them. Together they ducked into a small guest apartment.

"We call this the Nixon Rooms," Allbright explained. "He used to stay here when he visited during his presidency."

Once they were seated in a small alcove, Jeffrey related what he knew about the stolen articles from the Ukrainian church. "One of the priests overheard the thieves say something about the treasures being headed for Saint Petersburg. There was also evidence that the thieves were from inside the Orthodox church."

Allbright mulled this over, then asked, "You're not alone on this, are you?"

"There are two others here from Lvov, sort of using me as a cover while they check things out."

"And you think you can trust these folks?"

Jeffrey shrugged. "All I have to go on is their word, but I believe they're telling me the truth. If so, the stolen items would be worth millions in the West. More."

"And the Orthodox might be behind the theft," Allbright mused.

"Nothing definite," Jeffrey replied, "but according to what I was told, there is at least the possibility."

"From the tone of your voice, I'd say you don't believe it."

"I guess I have trouble accepting the idea that one church would steal from another," Jeffrey confessed.

"Are you a believer yourself?"

"Yes."

"Protestant?"

"Baptist," Jeffrey affirmed.

"Well, there are a few bad apples in every barrel, even in a church, I'm afraid. But like you, my first reaction is to treat this with skepticism. Still, Russia's not like any place you've ever been before, and that holds true for the Orthodox church as well." Allbright exchanged a glance with Casey. A moment's silent communication passed between them, then Allbright said, "Have you spoken to anyone within the church here?"

Jeffrey shook his head. "I don't know a soul."

"Something as serious as a possible theft of another church's treasures should certainly be discussed with a senior authority. Let me make a couple of calls," Allbright offered. "Maybe I can help you out there. If so, I'll make the connection with someone who will be sure to give you a fair hearing."

"That would be great, thanks."

"Hard to tell what happens these days when you pull a string. Might come up with gold. On the other hand, so much changes every hour, you might come up with something that'll try to eat both the string and the hand that's pulling it." He gave his best effort to produce a reassuring smile. "But maybe it's time to take that chance. If not for your sake, then for the sake of our lost lady friend."

The Alexander Nevsky Lavra was surrounded by wide thoroughfares. The streetcars and trucks created a continual barrage outside the high stone gates. In his conversation that morning, Allbright had explained to Jeffrey that a Lavra was a large monastery whose enclave had been granted independence by royal decree, a sort of miniature city-state. The early morning light treated the ancient structure with a gentle hand. The roughened walls were smoothed, the flaking plaster polished, the colors restored to their brilliant past. For a brief instant, Jeffrey was gifted a glimpse of what once had been.

The high outer walls contained an area so vast that two great cemeteries, a canal, and a forest surrounded the seminary and cathedral. The walls and first line of trees muted the barrage of traffic noise to a distant hum. Pensioners and cripples lined both sides of the central cobblestone way, their chanted prayers and soft pleas a murmur as constant as the wind.

Inside the dual cemeteries rested the remains of Tolstoy, Dostoyevsky, Tchaikovsky, and other greats of Russian arts and literature. Yet what caught Jeffrey's eye as he headed for his meeting was how many of the old gravestones had been defaced, their crucifixes damaged with savage strokes. Over more recent Communist remains rose simple marble pyramids topped with a single red star, stone fingers pointed toward a heaven whose existence they eternally denied.

"Go see Father Anatoli," the Consul General had told him that morning over the telephone. "He's personal assistant to the Metropolitan of Saint Petersburg, though for how much longer is anybody's guess. The ultraconservatives are sharpening their knives. He studied in England for a couple of years, which leaves him tainted in the xenophobes' eyes. Anatoli doesn't have time for their 'Russia for the Orthodox' nonsense, and he'll say so to anybody who listens. Not a way to make friends in this town."

Jeffrey stored away his questions about xenophobia, took down the address, and asked, "What's a Metropolitan?"

"Local church leader. In the Orthodox church, the Patriarch in Moscow is the head. Metropolitans run the different regions."

"The Patriarch is like the Pope?"

"Yes and no. There's no such thing as papal infallibility in Orthodoxy. The Patriarch's called 'the first among equals.'"

"What should I tell Anatoli?"

"That's for you to decide. If I were in your place, though, I think I'd trust the man."

＝＝

Following the Consul General's instructions, Jeffrey turned right by the outer canal and followed the walkway to a tall, free-standing structure enclosed within its own fortified wall. Jeffrey walked through the copse of tall birch, entered the broad double oaken doors, and loudly pronounced the priest's name to the elderly gentleman acting as both guard and receptionist. The man rose from his stool and shuffled down the long hall, motioning for Jeffrey to follow. They passed through an outer alcove fashioned as a private chapel, where the man made a sign of the cross using large, exaggerated gestures. He opened tall inner doors and pointed Jeffrey toward a dark-haired man seated at a massive desk.

"Mr. Sinclair?" The voice held a rich depth, the eyes great clarity. As he rose, the silver cross hanging from his neck thumped against his chest. He walked forward with hand outstretched. "I am Father Anatoli, the Metropolitan's personal assistant."

"Nice to meet you." Jeffrey felt his hand engulfed in a bearlike grip.

"Please take a seat." He motioned Jeffrey toward the conference table at the room's far end. "I have spoken with Mr. Allbright this morning. He said you had something of possible importance to the church which you wished to discuss with me."

"Yes, that is, I—"

"The Consul General also informs me that you are a Christian." A peasant's hand, flat and broad as a shovel blade, began stroking his broad curly beard where it collected upon his cassock. "And a Protestant. Is all this true?"

Jeffrey listened behind the man's words and heard the same measuring tone he found in almost everyone in this alien land. The need to assess, to test for truth and strength, before trusting. "I know Jesus Christ as Lord," Jeffrey replied. "I hope and pray that on the day when I stand before Him, He will know me as well. And yes, I am a Baptist. My wife and I currently attend an evangelical Anglican church."

"This is all most interesting," the priest said, his lazy hand motions belied by the intense gleam in his eyes. "I seldom have an opportunity to meet with Protestants from the West. Tell me, Mr. Sinclair. Have you visited one of our churches?"

"I have not yet had an opportunity, but I would like to."

"You know, Mr. Sinclair, many of my fellow priests within the Orthodox faith are quite opposed to the Protestant revivals sweeping our country. I do not agree with these men, but still they are a force to be reckoned with."

Jeffrey met the questing gaze square on and replied, "In America there is room for many different kinds of churches."

"Some of us believe the same is true here in Russia. But not all, I am sorry to say. There are those who say the Orthodox way is the only way for Russians. Such men claim that the Orthodox church alone has been invested with spiritual responsibility for this nation. Such declarations in my opinion are as great an error as it would be to say that only Protestants hold the keys to heaven."

"I always thought salvation rested in Jesus Christ," Jeffrey said.

"A profound statement." A glimmer of approval showed on the heavy features. "But unfortunately, not a truth the church always remembers. The first Protestant churches arrived in Russia toward the end of the nineteenth century, established by German and English missionaries. There was horrible persecution in those early days, both by the state and, tragically, by my own church. Both saw it as an invasion of the spirit. They accused the outsiders of weakening the Russian nation. In the smaller cities and villages there were massacres. Then in 1905 the czar issued a manifesto that legalized all evangelical churches. There was a truce of sorts until the Bolsheviks swept to power. In the persecutions of 1917 to 1930, as the Communists solidified their position, the churches learned to band together in order to survive. This lasted until the onset of perestroika."

"So now that the state persecutions are over," Jeffrey concluded, "the old feuds are surfacing once more."

"And with great ferocity," Father Anatoli agreed. "You see, under the Communists every person was taught that he or she was an element of a unique social system. Their nation was destined to teach the world not the better way, but rather the *right* way. The *only* way. The entire Communist method of education for the young and indoctrination for adults is based upon this principle." He paused. "Or was, I suppose. If the beast has truly been laid to rest for all time."

"You don't think it is?"

"I see problems everywhere," he replied, "with no solutions, only empty promises from our politicians. I hear questions being raised and no answers being offered, only arguments. I do not know how much more my poor nation can take before panic drives them back to the known, to the familiar. At least under the Communist dictatorship they were granted a sense of security." He spent a moment delving inward in weary resignation, collected himself, and asked, "Where was I?"

"Conflict among believers," Jeffrey reminded him.

"Thank you. The Communists taught people to live in enmity. They taught that progress for the socialist society was possible only if all who were not Communists, all who resisted their doctrine, were eradicated. They pressed the people to live in perpetual suspicion and violent hostility toward 'the other.' You know, of course, who this 'other' is."

"Anybody who does not believe as they do," Jeffrey offered.

"Exactly. Such a mind-set does not disappear simply because the government changes. Four generations have been taught since the age of three, when public schooling begins here, to hate anyone who does not conform.

"Today, the newcomers who fill our churches may indeed be sincere seekers of truth, but many retain vestiges of the old Communist psyche. They see other people going in a different direction with their faith, and the old attitude surfaces: Is the other person correct in their beliefs? Do they worship the *true* Christ? If not, punish them. Lock them up. Declare them criminals. See them as the enemies they are."

Father Anatoli sighed with regret. "Such people insist that every letter of every page of every doctrine be checked and rechecked. Such people have a new name for the incoming Protestant ministers: 'the wolves from the West.' Such people fear that this new invasion will tear down what few walls of Russian Christianity the Communists left standing."

"But you disagree with this."

"I and a number of my fellow priests, although we are a minority and at times find our voices drowned out by the others," he replied. His gaze evidenced a grim memory of former battles. "With us, the problems are all tangled together like a ball of yarn. For example, there are one hundred and eighty parishes in Russia. Twenty of these, some the size of an American state, have no priest at all. All parishes are short-staffed. We need a minimum of twenty more priests in Saint Petersburg alone. There are not enough priests to staff even *half* of our churches. Many of the priests we do have should not be priests at all. They have little training; they have less faith. There are only seven seminaries in the entire country. There are only twelve church-run schools."

He shook his head. "Problems, problems. We drown in problems. I close my eyes and watch them dance before me in the darkness, and I find no solutions. None."

Jeffrey hesitated, then ventured, "You could ask the Protestants to take over ministries that your church can't staff."

The explosion he feared did not come. Instead, the priest sat with head bowed low. "In a perfect world," he murmured. "In a world that truly followed the teachings of Christ . . ."

He lifted his head, the gentle light back in his eyes. "You have a gift of simple speech," he told Jeffrey. "It makes the hardest challenge something I can bear to hear. For this, I thank you."

"I haven't done anything," Jeffrey replied.

To his surprise, the father smiled broadly. "No, perhaps not." He leaned back in his seat. "So what was it you wished to discuss with me?"

Father Anatoli listened carefully until Jeffrey was finished with his account of the missing Ukrainian church treasures. Then he turned away and sat in utter stillness. Eventually he murmured, "A letter. Such a simple affair. Who could think that it would create such problems."

Jeffrey showed confusion. "I don't—"

But Father Anatoli was already on his feet. "Come. Let us walk together to the cathedral. I must prepare for Mass. What are your own plans for the next week?"

"I leave for London the day after tomorrow, Monday afternoon," Jeffrey replied, rising with him. "I'm not sure exactly when I will be back in Saint Petersburg, but it shouldn't be too long."

"Then I suggest you leave this matter with me until your return. I will see what I can learn."

═══

The cathedral interior was rich with the cloying flavor of incense, and Jeffrey instantly felt a familiar unease. There were no seats within the vast hall. Icons were everywhere, rising in great gilded frames ten and twelve high upon the walls. They rested upon the central pillars, they stood on huge bronze altars in the many alcoves, they bedecked the screen before the nave. Candles burned before them all. Hundreds of people were deep in prayer—standing, kneeling, laying prostrate upon the worn marble stonework. Each began and ended their petitions with multiple signs of the cross, some resting their foreheads upon the icons' glass enclosures.

Jeffrey and Father Anatoli paused together at the high-arched entrance to the central chamber. Eyes turned their way, examining the black-bearded priest standing beside the Westerner. Father Anatoli kept his attention focused upon Jeffrey. "You are uncomfortable with the concept of our icons," he observed.

Jeffrey nodded. "It's something I just don't understand, I guess. Maybe it's my Baptist background."

"The arguments and the issues and these icons date back almost two thousand years," Father Anatoli explained, his voice pitched low. "The problems arose when some Christian first painted a picture of Christ in the catacombs and another called the painting an idol. Your word *iconoclast* came from that time and described one who destroyed icons. They also had a name for those who wished to see no picture of Christ, or even crosses. They were called puritans."

He lowered his head so that the black beard fanned out and molded to his cassock. "There was a time in the eighth century when people found with a painting or tapestry depicting the Lord Jesus, or even a cross with a man's figure carved upon it, were tortured and put to death."

"All in the name of love," Jeffrey said quietly. "The same love that drives this wedge between us today."

The light of approval was strong in Father Anatoli's eyes as he continued, "The Orthodox concentrates upon the *mystery* of faith. The *wonder* of the liturgy. Great emphasis is placed upon experiencing union with God. We seek constantly to remind all believers of their responsibility to seek knowledge of the glory that comes through complete and utter surrender to Christ."

"Everything I see here seems so alien," Jeffrey confessed.

"Icons are not idolatry," he stated flatly. "They are not the object of veneration, but a reminder. They point the direction only."

Jeffrey watched a woman complete her prayers by leaning forward and kissing the jewel-studded icon's lower frame. "I'm afraid it looks awfully like idol worship to me."

Black eyes leaned close and drilled him with their intensity. "Now who is the one who condemns with judgment?"

Jeffrey tried not to flinch under the man's gaze. He kept his
disquiet hidden until the father nodded and said, "I must go. Come
to my chambers immediately upon your return to Saint Petersburg.
I should know something by then, if there is indeed anything for
me to know."

——

Two cultures moved within the church, the tourists and the
penitents. Jeffrey felt like a stranger to both.

Those who came in prayer remained utterly blind to the others,
displaying a single-minded focus that Jeffrey found awesome. They
represented every age, every walk of life. The young and successful
in suits or fresh new dresses. The old and bowed, clinging to canes
and crutches. Mothers with children, husbands with wives, teenagers in groups and alone. And as he watched their coming and
going, Jeffrey found a trait utterly lacking in the outside world of
Saint Petersburg. Here were gentle smiles and unstrained voices.
Eyes held a simple, open quality. Hearts could be seen in many
gazes. Not all, but many.

Jeffrey stood beside a pillar, out of the way of those kneeling
in prayer. As he stood and watched, a pair of male voices began a
chanted prayer from somewhere above his head. The first, a light
tenor, sang a swift chant upon one single note. The second voice
was very deep and very rich. His words rose and fell in slow, steady,
deliberate tones, like the tolling of an unseen bell.

Jeffrey found the atmosphere utterly alien, yet comforting, like
the making of a new friend who somehow greeted him with the
ease of a trusted brother.

As Jeffrey turned and left the church, it was this feeling of calm
acceptance that troubled him most of all.

CHAPTER 25

Peter the Great housed his art collection in one small extension of his winter palace. His successor, Elizabeth, gave little thought to art, and left the collection where it was. The next ruler of Russia, the Empress Catherine the Great, found it necessary to build an entire new palace to contain her acquisitions. Yet she continued the practice started by her great-uncle Peter of allowing only a privileged handful of outsiders to view her collection. Over the years, the halls of art and treasures became known as "The Dwelling Place of the Hermits." As French became the language of royal culture, the name was translated to L'Ermitage.

Ivona entered the Hermitage museum and walked down the long Hall of Eighteen-Twelve, lined with over one thousand portraits of officers who had fought in the war of that year. Those who had died in the field and left no record of their faces had empty frames, with their names embossed beneath, to commemorate their sacrifice.

The hall gave way to the Outer Chamber, where dignitaries had waited—sometimes for weeks, sometimes for years—before being escorted into the smaller Throne Room beyond.

Ivona then entered the Pavilion Hall, and found her contact awaiting her beneath one of Russia's few remnants from the rule of the Mongol Khans. Eight centuries before, the Khan had traveled to Poland on a diplomatic mission, fallen in love with a beautiful Polish princess, and made her his fifteenth wife. The first wife, bitterly jealous of the Khan's evident love for his new bride, had arranged for the girl to be murdered. In her memory, the Khan had designed a pair of matching wall fountains where water trickled down in unending streams, from one onyx half-shell to another, representing the continual cascading tears of his heart.

Ivona strode toward the slender man who stood beside that weeping fountain. "Ilya, I bring the heartfelt greetings of Bishop Michael, as well as those of your beloved parents."

He said nothing, only took her hand and guided her away from the tourist hordes. Twice he paused and scanned the crowd while pretending to point out treasures for her inspection. The third time she asked, "Is there something wrong?"

"If there is," he replied, sweeping his hand out in a grand gesture to present a treasure neither of them saw, "you will know of it when I disappear."

The Hermitage administrator seated her in an unobtrusive corner and searched the throngs once more with worried eyes. "Tell me why you are here."

"Word has come to us of your difficulties. The bishop asks for details."

"Word?" He showed real alarm. "What word?"

"Through your mother," Ivona soothed. "She told us only after hearing of our own troubles. And only after the bishop gave his solemn word that the information would go no further."

The Hermitage administrator subsided. "You, too, have something missing?"

Ivona nodded slowly. "Tell me. Please."

Ilya was quiet for a very long moment, then said, "There are so many treasures on display here that no one thinks of what remains hidden. So much rests in our warehouses, more than you can ever imagine. The authorities just leased to us the former Military College to use as storage space. This is distant and harder to keep secure, but anything is better than the damp confines of our basements. I have six hundred thousand etchings baled together and stored in closets."

"And in the process of this transfer," Ivona guessed, "you have found items missing from your inventory."

"Not for certain," Ilya replied. "Certainly none of the most valuable articles, for which we have records in duplicate. But every day another three or four articles are not to be found—sketches, *objets d'art*, small paintings, religious artifacts, anything."

"You are sure?"

"I am sure of nothing anymore," he replied resignedly. "Even within the museum itself, the halls closed to visitors are stacked with boxes. The papers listing their contents are lost. Security is declining as the government allocates us fewer and fewer militia guards. Do you know what we are paid?"

"I know," she replied quietly.

"Twelve dollars per month," he persisted. "The most qualified museum staff in all Russia, and we can barely feed ourselves and our families. How can you blame those who turn to accepting bribes and looking the other way?"

"I blame no one," Ivona replied.

"There is more. The Golden Treasury has been closed for renovation. We are not sure," he said, then hesitated.

"Sure of what?"

"There are over twenty thousand items in this collection alone," he continued. "If it were one crown, yes, of course, we would prize it. But with seven hundred? So what if one is lost? Could we not have loaned it to a regional museum? Twice we have almost sounded the alarm for missing items, only to find records that twenty, thirty, forty years ago they were loaned to a provincial museum for some exhibition."

"And never returned," she finished.

"Why should they be, when we never asked for them back?"

"But you do think items are missing," she pressed.

"Nothing certain, and nothing of first order."

"Relatively speaking."

"Exactly."

"Their value?"

"In the West?" He pursed his lips. "Who can say? And once again, the museum is not even sure that anything is gone at all."

"We speak not of the museum," Ivona replied. "Official announcements can be kept for the press. I ask for your opinion."

"Candelabra," he relented. "Gold chains, emblems, boxes, a few icons. From the other departments, any number of items. Possibly. I repeat, nothing is certain."

She thought in silence, then asked the inevitable. "The same is occurring in other museums?"

"Rumors," he replied. "We are feeding on rumors only."

"Yet again—"

"What could they do with so much?" he demanded, his voice rising in painful frustration. "If even a tenth of these rumors are true, we are speaking of thousands of objects."

"Perhaps a bit more quietly," she cautioned.

"*Tons* of valuables," he continued. "Where could they be taking it all?"

"There is no reason to shout," she said.

Ilya sank back. "There are too many rumors for the stories to be smoke alone. There must be a fire. A hundred fires. Yet the government refuses to listen."

"They have other problems," Ivona stated. "Other crises."

He nodded. "You realize, of course, that such thefts have occurred before."

"Yes." Such stories had circulated for years.

"One of the largest collections of Impressionist paintings in the world currently occupies the Hermitage's former attic servant quarters," Ilya went on. "It was collected by two merchants. They presented these treasures to the czar as a bribe for safe passage when they and their families departed westward the year before the October Revolution."

"This much I have heard," Ivona said.

"When the Communists came to power," Ilya continued, "the paintings were condemned as degenerate and made to disappear. For decades it was rumored that Party officials had destroyed them all—Matisse, Van Gogh, Degas, Pissaro, Monet, Renoir, Cezanne, Gaugin, three *rooms* of early Picasso. Then in the late fifties the Party line changed, and Impressionists were declared to be compassionate painters of the common man." Ilya snorted. "The exhibition then reappeared without fanfare, as though closed only for cleaning. Yet dozens of the paintings, perhaps even hundreds, were not to be found. Investigators were met with unofficial warnings, and the persistent found themselves granted postings to museums in Siberia. Eventually all records of the missing pictures also disappeared."

"Who do you think is responsible?" Ivona pressed. "Not for the paintings, that is history. For your current thefts?"

Ilya shrugged, despondent.

"Are there stories to be heard on this as well?"

"Rumors," he muttered. "Of what worth are they to a custodian of Russia's treasures?"

"The Orthodox church," she demanded. "Could they be involved?"

"Of this I have heard nothing," he replied, definite for the first time that day, "although there are rumors of items missing from this quarter as well."

"From within the Orthodox churches?"

Ilya showed wry humor. "You would think they had already lost everything of value, no? Fifty thousand treasures we have here in the Hermitage alone from the churches, all listed as voluntary gifts. Very generous with the new Communist state, these churches were."

"Mafia or KGB," Ivona pressed. "Do you hear anything unofficial? Could one or the other perhaps be behind the thefts?"

He looked at her. "Why do you suggest they are separate? As far as I am concerned, nowadays they both function outside the law. Why should they not operate together?"

"So there *is* word of this," Ivona said.

"Suddenly the air in here is stifling." Ilya stood. "Come. I will walk you out."

Reluctantly she allowed herself to be led forward. "There is nothing more to say?"

As he walked he drew her closer with one hand on her elbow. He asked in a small voice, "Tell me, Ivona Aristonova. What rumor is worth getting killed over?"

"I seek information for our use only," she replied just as quietly. "Tell me what you know."

"I know nothing."

"What you guess, then."

They entered a vast chamber in the original palace, one whose ceiling and pillars were gilded with more than seven hundred pounds of gold. Excited clusters of tourists milled about, jabbering in a dozen alien tongues. Ilya slowed his pace, pointed to a chest made in the time of Peter the Great from sixteen tons of pure silver. He pitched his voice so low that it was lost at three paces. "The KGB is selling its only remaining assets."

"Information and access," Ivona offered.

Ilya nodded. "Still there are moles on my staff. Only now the KGB bosses are no longer interested in dissidents. They seek only to pad their nest. With dollars."

"These moles are making it easy for certain items to vanish," Ivona helped him with guesses of her own. "They are pointing out what articles to take, then making the records disappear."

They stopped before a massive display case containing religious artifacts appropriated from the nation's churches. A handwritten sign stated that it was a sample from the Hermitage's Golden Treasury, which was now closed for renovation. The case contained gold plates for sacramental bread, the handles fashioned like crowns. Gold and silver chalices, embossed with diamonds and rubies the size of quails' eggs. A Bible with a cover of solid gold, the depiction of Christ framed by a hundred matching emeralds. Yet another chalice, the entire exterior embossed with diamonds. An incense burner in the form of a holy shrine, an empty tomb at its heart, all in gold.

"There are several articles I know in my heart are missing," Ilya murmured, "though I can now find no record of their ever having existed. I am beginning to suspect that a drop has been arranged. Outsiders dressed as security or transport workers come for shipments, or to move a case, or to relocate a picture. All the documents are in order, all the proper answers prepared for anyone who asks."

"Mafia," Ivona repeated.

"Wolves in sheep's clothing," Ilya replied. "They devour our nation's greatest treasures. They have the pity of carnivores for their prey."

They entered the exit hallway. Ilya swept a despairing hand at the surrounding boxes. "This passage is used by thousands of visitors every day. Yet we line it with the beautiful and the valuable, the returned foreign exhibits. Why? Because we have no place else to keep them. Look at the addresses. Brisbane, Australia. Long Island, United States. Turin, Italy. Seoul, Manila, Tokyo, Sao Paulo. What you see is the smallest example of this national crisis."

She stopped at the exit doors, tried to put her own worries aside. "You are a good friend, Ilya. In the name of our bishop, I thank you."

"Bring back my treasures," he replied quietly. "Return my nation's pride."

The general arrived in a very worried state. "Your naive young American is causing my superiors great concern."

"How is that possible?" Markov seated the general at the rosewood table in the most comfortable corner of his cluttered parlor and personally poured tea for them both. "The boy has only been in Saint Petersburg for a few days. Don't tell me he's already made a drunken fool of himself in public. There is nothing more ridiculous than a young man with a bellyful, don't you agree?"

General Surikov was not amused. "He arrived in Saint Petersburg with Bishop Michael Denisov's personal secretary as his interpreter."

"Bishop who?" Markov seated himself. "I don't believe I know that name. Will you take sugar?"

"Denisov. He's one of the leaders of the Ukrainian Rite Catholic Church."

Markov sipped at his own cup, gauging the man across from him. "Please forgive me, but I fail to see—"

"Let us just say that Denisov is someone we wish to have as far removed from this entire process as possible."

Markov nodded slowly, his mind working hard. Clearly something had been taken from the Ukrainian church. Something valuable. But that the young American with whom he met might be—no, no, it was simply too preposterous. "My dear fellow, you and I both know that one reason we selected this particular individual was his established links to Eastern Europe."

"Such links as these to the Ukrainian church are utterly unacceptable," Surikov barked.

"Please calm yourself. The American mentioned that he already had a trip planned before coming to our meeting. He said this to explain why he would be unable to travel immediately to Saint Petersburg."

"He said that?" The general relaxed by degrees.

"He did, indeed. Now think for a moment. How on earth could he have planned a voyage to ally himself with such a group before he even met with me and learned of my requirements?"

"That is true," the general murmured. Still he remained troubled. "With all due respect, Prince Markov, you had best be right."

"I am quite sure it is mere coincidence," Markov declared. "Mr. Sinclair traveled to Ukraine, he worked with a good interpreter, he asked her to assist him in Saint Petersburg. Nothing more, nothing less."

"My superiors will no doubt be pleased to hear of your news. It was a most unpleasant moment when they learned of your man's choice of interpreters."

"May I ask why?"

"You may indeed," the general replied sharply. "But I am not sure you would wish for my superiors to know that such questions were being posed."

"An idle remark. Please disregard it," Markov said. General Surikov's superiors were not the type to displease with unnecessary probings.

But the general was not finished. "You have not seen, as I have, how curiosity is dealt with. And mistakes."

"I am quite sure—"

"The Chechen clan were not selected for their manners," the general pressed on. "They are the cruelest of the cruel. And they are always hungry for more."

Chosen by whom, Markov wondered. And for what? But he quashed such curiosity flat and chose the wiser course of a personal question. "Tell me, general. Why do you consort with such as these?"

For once the general did not retreat. "I was offered a job in the ministry last week," the general confessed, but without enthusiasm. "Done out of respect, however. Not out of real need."

"You are too modest," Markov protested. "No doubt they see in you a treasure trove of experience."

"It was made out of loyalty," the general countered. "A job without meaning or purpose. And the payment is paltry, made with currency that grows more worthless with each passing hour. Still, I have been considering it."

"Perhaps it would be wiser to wait until the course of events is more certain," Markov offered, and thought, or at least until our own business is concluded.

"Perhaps," the general agreed dismally. "And yet I was ordered—" There he stopped.

"Ordered?" Markov's interest overrode his better judgment. "By whom?"

But Surikov shook his head. "I have my reasons."

Could it be, Markov wondered, that the military cabal and their Party minions maintained a shaky alliance with the Russian mafia? Markov inspected the general as he sipped his tea, and decided the idea had merit. In the present vacuum, the mafia had risen faster and higher than anyone could have imagined. In such a case, Surikov would be far more valuable as a liaison than as simply another retired officer cluttering the ministry's hallways.

"A senior Soviet officer, now serving a cabal of criminals," Markov hesitated, then guessed, "perhaps with connections to the KGB—you must admit that is, well, rather remarkable."

"Former officer, former KGB, former Soviet empire," Surikov corrected. "The world has tilted on its axis."

"The KGB still exists."

"Not as it once did," the general amended. "And not as it still should." The bushy eyebrows tightened. "Nor as it shall again, you mark my words."

Absently Markov stirred his cup. If it were true that Surikov was being used as a liaison with the increasingly powerful criminal elements, that meant the general would be an even more valuable contact for himself. He ventured, "I have heard that parliament almost managed sufficient backing for a no-confidence vote. Our leaders must be quaking in their boots. No doubt you are pleased with these developments."

The general returned to his habitual bearlike rumblings. "I will be pleased when the whole circus is over, when such nonsense is put back in the only place it belongs—the theater."

Markov nodded sagely. "The delegates who would most likely support a coup are led by the Speaker of the House, are they not? A Chechen, if I recall correctly. Of the same tribe as your superiors."

Surikov responded with a stony silence, then, "Perhaps we should return to the matter at hand."

"Certainly," Markov agreed, satisfied that his guesses were correct. "Please assure your superiors of my wholehearted support."

"Your support, yes. They will be most pleased to hear of this." General Surikov's gaze was bleak. "Let us also hope that you can assure them of success. Because if not—"

"There is no chance of anything other than full success," Markov replied hastily. "We need not even discuss such a contingency."

"That is good," Surikov replied. "As to the American, my superiors are not as trusting as you appear to be."

"On the contrary," Markov countered, "I trust only myself. This American, however, is of no great account. A pawn in the great game of power and wealth. He knows nothing and understands less."

"It is indeed good to hear that you have no great affection for the man."

"Affection?" Markov lifted his eyebrows. "What has that to do with anything?"

"Because if there proves to be a problem," Surikov answered, "there will soon be no problem."

A chill wind wafted through the chamber. "What will they do to him?"

"Better to ask," General Surikov replied, rising to his feet, "what they will do to you."

ood morning, Sinclair," Sergei Popov greeted him cheerfully as he descended the stairs the next morning. "How you sleep?"

"Great, thanks."

"Your lady translator, she leave early. I have message." He handed over a slip of paper, then a second. "And this come too. American in big car. Maybe gangster, yes?"

"Doubtful."

"Yes, you right. Russia has too many already, no need to import from Chicago. You like breakfast?"

"Please." Jeffrey seated himself at one of the little tables and opened the notes. The first was from Ivona, whom he had not seen since their meeting the day before. "We meet with Yussef tomorrow before your departure. He has news and antiques." No greeting, no apology for leaving him high and dry, no nothing.

The second was from the Consul General, and more positive. "If you can spare the time, I have a conference this afternoon which you might want to be in on. If so, I'll pick you up at three in front of your winter palace. And in case you are interested, there's an English-language church service this morning at ten and a second service at twelve. If you want a seat, you'll need to get there a half-hour earlier. They fill up fast. Allbright." Below the Consul General had written an address for the service.

Sergei came back with coffee, bread, and jam. He glanced at the New Testament Jeffrey had brought downstairs with him and asked good-naturedly, "You are religious man, yes?"

"I try. I think I fail more often than I succeed, but I do try."

"That is answer of a good man," Sergei decided. "I have friend, he is religious man. He believes."

"And you?"

"Maybe someday," he replied cheerfully. "Now life too full."

"Perhaps faith could help you handle your problems more easily," Jeffrey offered.

"Maybe," he said doubtfully, then added, "Good to be religious. Give you something to fight about, now that Soviets gone. Man must fight or die, yes?"

"I hope not."

A forefinger as rigid as a broomstick poked the table beside Jeffrey's Bible. "You Christians, you talk peace and fight all same time. Go in church, shout love, love, love to everybody, yes? Then go out, shout hate, hate, hate to all other churches. Protestants, Catholics, Orthodox, all same." The finger retreated to tap the side of Sergei's head. "Christians, they smart. They know. Man needs enemies. Keeps him strong."

"I try never to condemn anyone," Jeffrey replied quietly, remembering yesterday's experience in the cathedral, wondering if he spoke the truth.

"Then you very strange man, Sinclair," Sergei declared, and changed the subject. "You know, now Russians, they go to church, but many not go for God. Before, nobody goes. Now is fashion and people with no belief, they go. But this stops soon, I think."

"Why do you say that?"

He shrugged. "Church asks too many questions. People who not believe, they don't like these questions. Soon they will stop going, and the church will be for believers."

Jeffrey shook his head. "I know a lot of people in the West who go to church, hear the questions, and just decide they apply to everybody else but themselves."

Sergei showed surprise. "This problem is in West too?"

"Maybe less than here, since churchgoing isn't such a fashion anymore. But yes, we have it."

Sergei thought it over. "Yes, is true. People turn from questions they don't like. So. Maybe churches stay full but not full of belief. What is answer?"

"I think it lies in searching your own heart," Jeffrey replied. "Searching with honesty and prayer."

Sergei turned serious. "I think maybe you know many questions. Hard questions. You know answers too?"

"Only a few," Jeffrey replied. "The most important one is Jesus Christ. You need to know that He is your Savior, to know His presence in your heart."

Sergei mulled that over in silence until Jeffrey finished breakfast. As he stood, Sergei said, "Listen, Sinclair. My grandmother, she collects things."

"What kinds of things?"

"From other lands." He gave a cheerful shrug. "What no matters. Her room a museum of all what you never want to see."

"You mean tourist souvenirs."

"Look." He reached in his pocket, came out with crumpled dollars. "I have twenty dollars. You take, buy for me. Buy things for tourists. Things so she can look and think of lands she will never see."

"No, I can't accept your money."

"Take, take. Is good money. Not stolen. You buy with this, yes? You bring back next time. Please. You do this. Friends, yes? You help me. Please."

"All right."

"Is good to help. I know. Touches heart. Gives much freedom to soul, this help of friends. You have strength, you share."

"What strength?"

Sergei showed great amusement. "You have so much, you don't understand. Freedom is strength, yes?"

"I suppose so."

"You free to choose. But to choose is hard. You learn to be strong because you learn to choose. You act. In Russia, we strong in talk, not in act."

"You can learn."

He shrugged. "Maybe yes, maybe no. Who can see? We have big experience in talk. Too big. Centuries and centuries. Action dangerous. Get you killed. Talk our only freedom. But my people, they forget how to act."

Jeffrey accepted the money. "I'll bring a little something back with me next time."

"Good, good. You earn thanks. You see, I pay. I pay back big. Someday you need, I give." He extended his hand. "You watch."

Jeffrey grasped the firm grip and agreed, "Friends."

———

The church was located in a series of interconnected storefront rooms just off a main thoroughfare and not far from the Markov palace. Jeffrey found it wonderfully refreshing to enter, be greeted in English, exchange the sort of smiles and greetings he was used to in his own church. After a few minutes, he found himself relaxing in a way that had not been possible since his arrival.

The church was *very* full. Every seat was taken. People stood four and five deep along the back and side walls. Jeffrey listened as first the greetings and then all songs, prayers, and the sermon itself were given in English, then translated into Russian. He looked around the crowded chambers and guessed that perhaps half those attending were locals.

According to the program handed him as he entered, the pastor was a Reverend Evan Collins. He was a scholarly sort, not in the least what Jeffrey might have expected in the rough-and-tumble of post-Soviet Russia. He was a middle-aged gentleman with sparse graying hair. Collins viewed the world through kindly, inquisitive eyes. There was no righteous anger, no domineering salesmanship. He spoke with a voice that invited listeners to lean closer, relax their guard, draw near. Here is safety, his voice seemed to say. Here is rest.

When the service was over, Jeffrey joined the congregation for coffee. He bided his time until the pastor was free, then walked over and introduced himself. "I have a problem I was wondering if I could ask you about."

Reverend Collins shifted over one chair and invited him to be seated. "How did you find out about our church?"

"Through the American Consul General."

"Oh, yes," Collins said, quickly sobering. "Stan Allbright has proven to be a good friend to us. We have been confronted with a very serious problem, and had it not been for his assistance, quite frankly, I don't know what we would have done."

"As a matter of fact," Jeffrey replied, "the work that's brought me to Saint Petersburg might be connected."

"How is that?"

"I'm not sure I should say." Or could, he added silently.

"No, of course not." Reverend Collins paused to greet a passing friend, then continued, "But I take it you know about Leslie Ann Stevens."

"A little."

"She was returning from a prayer meeting at our church when she was kidnapped. I suppose you know that, too. We have done everything we can think of, spoken to everyone we could approach, and the only vestige of hope we've found has been from the Consul General."

"He appears to be taking the matter very seriously."

"That girl was an absolute godsend for my wife and me," Collins said, his eyes reaching out over the crowd. "Often we feel we are trying to run a church on the outer edge of civilization. The problems have been impossible to describe, truly impossible. We are growing at an incredible rate, utterly understaffed, more crises than you could ever imagine. And then up pops Leslie Ann, always willing to help out, never complaining, always taking over at the last minute—"

A gray-haired American gentleman breezed over and cheerfully shouldered his way into the conversation. Collins introduced him as a deacon. Jeffrey shook hands and settled back to wait. Eventually the pastor turned back to him. "Sorry about the interruptions. Was your question about Leslie Ann?"

Jeffrey shook his head. "It wasn't anything urgent. I can see you have a lot of more important things to tend to right now."

"Nonsense. I'd be glad to help if I can, and now is as good a time as any. Do you mind talking about it here in public?"

"No." He related the discussion with the Orthodox priest and his feelings upon entering the church. Reverend Collins listened in silence, his eyes never wavering from Jeffrey's face, his depth of listening resembling the hidden reserves of a quiet, slow-moving river.

"Unity among believers is based on a twofold process," Reverend Collins said when Jeffrey was finished. "In the Book of Peter, we are told that all of us, once Christ has entered our lives, participate in the divine nature. Christ is in me, and I am in Him. A glorious reassurance. And throughout the New Testament, we are declared joined to each other. A *body* of believers. The bride of Christ. A hint of the divine in earthly form. I think that we owe it to our Father to behave as He commands, don't you?"

Jeffrey nodded. "In principle, I agree totally with what you say. I guess my question is where to draw the line. At what point does a practice become unacceptable?"

"Who are we to judge what is and is not acceptable? In Proverbs we are told that one of the seven things God truly despises is a man who sows discord among those whom God loves. Why on earth would anyone wish to take that risk?" He paused to sip from his cup. "The Bible says that all the world is in the hands of darkness. Conflict between believers is for me the greatest evidence of this dark presence within the earthly body of Christ."

Jeffrey took a breath. "I lost my faith a while back and only recently found it again. Or it found me; I'm not so sure about that part. What I'm trying to say is that the experience is still really fresh with me. I can remember how it felt to be without faith—boy, can I ever. And I can still feel how it was to return to the fold. Such a *powerful* moment."

"The moment of earthly rapture," the man agreed. "An earth-shattering experience."

"I think a lot of people," Jeffrey went on, "mix up the *path* that led them to this moment with the *goal*."

Gray eyes fastened him with an intensity that suspended time. "Fascinating."

"I wonder if maybe people think that because their particular church brought them to Christ, it is *the* church of Christ. The *only* church. The *right* church."

"And what, pray tell, keeps you from making the same mistake?"

Jeffrey had to smile. "A Baptist loses his faith, falls in love with a devout Anglican, and is guided back to the Lord by a Catholic brother. Who do I give the credit to?"

"The good Lord Jesus," Collins replied firmly.

"And yet," Jeffrey added, "I have these strong feelings of discomfort with the way the Orthodox worship. Actually, I guess it's the way a lot of the Eastern churches worship. It's not anything I've thought out. In fact, it bothers me to feel this way. But I do, way down at gut level."

"Their ways are different," Collins agreed. "But so is this entire world. What troubles me about the Orthodox church is their view toward evangelism here. They tend to see themselves as guardians of the country's spirituality. As a result, many are uncomfortable with anyone else coming in to do direct evangelism. They tend to identify the church very closely with their national heritage, you see."

"What about the icons?" Jeffrey asked. "Don't they bother you?"

"It's interesting," Collins replied. "One objection the Orthodox make about us is that Western religious art depicts saintly figures in contemporary form. Do you understand what I'm saying?"

"Yes." As styles of art and even fashion had changed with the centuries, Western religious paintings had done so as well. Biblical figures had been painted using local models and had often been dressed in clothing from the period in which the painter lived. Jeffrey had laughed when he first learned of this habit, until another dealer had pointed out that even today, actors in period films had their clothes and hairstyles adapted to modern styles and tastes.

"But we don't kneel before Western art and pray," Jeffrey protested.

"Certainly not in the same way," Collins agreed. "But you see, the Orthodox *deliberately* make their paintings more abstract, exactly because they are used in the worship service. They do not wish to depict people, but rather religious principles."

Jeffrey thought this over. "I still don't get it."

"Perhaps you are right," Evan agreed. "Perhaps I am trying too hard to show compassion and fellowship with people who make real mistakes in their form of worship. But so long as there is this tiniest room for doubt in my mind, I hesitate to condemn. There has been so much condemnation between Christians over the centuries."

Jeffrey recalled lessons about the Reformation wars. "And so many bloody mistakes."

"Exactly. So I tend to search for harmony rather than judgment, even if that may mean erring on the side of tolerance. I still feel more comfortable leaving the condemnation up to God."

He shrugged and added, "The Orthodox are facing problems that we in the West have enormous difficulty even imagining. Not enough priests, and those they have are often undertrained. Large numbers of believers who cannot read. And even if they could, for seventy years it has been virtually impossible for them to have Bibles."

Jeffrey struggled to understand. "So they use pictures to remind people of lessons?"

"Here again, the Orthodox would say we are making a typical Western judgment," Collins replied. "They do not see icons as pictures at all. They exaggerate hands and eyes and features because they intend to communicate truth *through* the painting. Attention should not be on the painting, but rather on what stands *behind* it. The worshiper must be pushed by the painting to see *beyond* the picture to the spiritual reality itself."

Jeffrey shook his head. "But how do you separate the concept of icons from that of idolatry?"

"Well, maybe you shouldn't," Collins allowed. "I'm not saying what is right or wrong here, you understand. I'm simply trying to understand what they think. That was a central question I had when I arrived: was I facing a nation that, like the early Israelites, had fallen away to follow other religions? As my Russian improved, I listened as best I could, and I came to believe that those who had refused to follow the idolatry of Communism had remained Christian, at least in their own eyes."

"And so?"

"And so I'm still not sure," Collins replied. "What I *think* is that it is one thing for informed priests and theologians to *know* the difference, and *maintain* the difference, and so look through an icon to the truth beyond instead of worshiping the icon as an idol. But it seems to me that maybe ordinary folks haven't been able to maintain that distinction. They end up identifying the Spirit's power with these icons and images. In the worst of cases, perhaps they do follow the idolatrous path.

"They make offerings to shrines—we see this all through the poorer lands where illiteracy is a big problem, not just here. Mexico is covered with them. The impression you get is that people identify the source of power as the object itself, not something beyond the object. So I think—and it's just one person's thoughts here, all right? But yes, I think that the way priests explain the icons is often quite different from the way a lot of the people here understand them, and the way they understand salvation. These distinctions are lost on a lot of them."

The troubled look firmed into a clear-sighted determination. "So I take it as my own personal responsibility to remind everyone with whom I have contact of the Lord Jesus' saving grace. I do *not* condemn. I simply remind. I point to the Bible. I teach from the Bible. I teach as I myself was taught. I pray with them. I encourage them in the Lord. And I hope that all who seek shall find the one true Answer."

═══

"What I'm about to tell you is documented fact," Consul General Stan Allbright told Jeffrey that afternoon when he and Casey picked him up at the Markov palace. They were driving toward an unidentified appointment, with Casey at the wheel. "But it's also highly confidential, so I want you to keep it under your hat."

"I understand."

"For the moment, we're going to assume that even if there's no connection between our two dilemmas, they are at least not in conflict, and possibly in parallel. You have any problem with that?"

Jeffrey shook his head. "Not that I can think of."

"Okay, here's the picture." Allbright crossed his legs in the Chevrolet's roomy interior. "Everything we've been able to uncover points toward the Orthodox church not being directly involved in anything going on here. The mafia clans—and they call themselves that, by the way, mafia, even spell it out like that in Cyrillic. So the mafia and the Orthodox, they occupy two totally different worlds. What makes your story interesting is the suggestion that maybe, somehow, there is a bridge between the two."

Casey spoke for the first time. "All those unemployed spies got to have something to occupy their time."

Jeffrey looked from one to the other. "You mean the KGB?"

Allbright nodded. "You've probably heard stories about how some of the priests used to spy for them. That's true. But what is not true is this assumption some people make that because a few of the priests were twisted, everybody in the church was on the take. That is plain nonsense."

"A minority," Casey interjected. "Powerful, dangerous, deadly. But still a minority."

"Now, these Orthodox priests who were controlled by the KGB," Allbright went on, "they've lost their power base. Just like the KGB itself has."

"Can't say I've ever had a chance to talk with one," Casey offered. "But I kind of doubt that they're real happy about the current state of affairs."

"What this means," Allbright continued, "is that there are two struggles inside the Russian Orthodox Church. One is between the devout and the xenophobes—that's what I call the ultraconservatives who believe that only the Orthodox should tend to the spiritual needs of Russia. You get this struggle in a lot of churches, sure, but not like here, where the lid's been screwed down tight for over seventy years. Anyway, the one point these two groups agree on is the second contest, which is in effect a major house cleaning. And guess who's on the way out."

"The priests who spied on their own church."

"Right the first time," Casey said.

"I bet that's easier said than done."

"Absolutely," Allbright said. "The KGB infiltration goes right up the ladder, although it's not as complete as you might expect. In some places, though, like in the Ukrainian Orthodox church based in Kiev, the power structure's pretty much rotten to the core. So instead of obeying the commands of the Patriarch in Moscow, they just broke away entirely."

"And where does that leave us?"

"The only people these soon-to-be outcast priests can rely on," Allbright responded, "are their old buddies over at the KGB."

"Who are in a pretty shaky position themselves," Casey added.

"Exactly. But the KGB hasn't been sitting around on its hands while its power vanished. On that point you can bet your whole bundle. Part of the organization is digging in its heels and shouting doom and gloom at the top of its collective voice. The radicals are working hard as they can to bring down the democratic government and replace it with a dictatorship. Some of these are diehard Communists, some are right-wing military fanatics, others are just out to feather their nest."

"A real mixed bag," Casey said. "They'll stay together only as long as they don't have power. Right now, though, you'd think they were all long-lost brothers."

"This faction also contains the KGB department that used to control the flow of black-market goods," Allbright said.

"Which was where the mafia gained their first foothold in the Russian power structure," Casey explained.

Jeffrey asked, "So you really think the mafia's involved here?"

But Allbright was not to be hurried. "Any place as tightly controlled as the former Soviet Union needed a safety valve for illegal goods, especially for items the bigwigs wanted, like Western radios and cameras and such. The KGB was the guy riding shotgun on the stagecoach. Only now, with their power structure in shambles, the horses are in control and the shotgun riders are hanging on for dear life."

Allbright began drumming his fingers on the car window. "Over in the Asian part of Russia there's a saying that goes, 'A man needs two legs to stand upright.' A lot of people feel like Russia's trying to make headway with only one working leg. This newest Russian revolution has made great political strides, but from the legal side there's total chaos. Economically too. The mafia's taken a long look at this situation and decided to fill the vacuum and their pockets all at the same time."

"How does this tie in with your missing girl?"

"This is pure conjecture," Allbright replied, "but I think maybe our lady just happened upon something she shouldn't have seen. They took her because she was there."

"If it's the mafia in control," Casey said, "our only hope is if they figure she's worth more alive than dead."

Allbright pointed to the blank-faced building up ahead, a concrete and glass structure not far from the Neva River. Uniformed policemen flanked the entrance, stood sentry at either corner, and arrayed themselves in silent ranks across the street.

"KGB headquarters," he said, then went on with his explanation. "There's a second group emerging in there. Been hard at work over the past few months, made a strong impression on me and some others. Real law-and-order team. They're trying to adapt to the new world order, become a sort of super-police, kind of like our FBI."

"A definite minority," Casey added. "Powerful, though, and growing stronger every day. They're about our only hope when it comes to problems like ours."

"Follow our lead here," Allbright ordered. "Don't open your mouth until we're in the group's offices and the door's locked. As far as they're concerned, their most dangerous enemies are people under the same roof."

—————

"The mafia in Saint Petersburg is just as powerful as the city government," the scruffy young man declared. "Here and every other major city in Russia."

When Jeffrey, Casey, and the Consul General had entered the main doors, their contact had been waiting for them. He had exchanged harsh words with the sullen guard behind the protective glass barrier, refused to sign his guests in, then led them down a grimy hall lined with closed, unmarked doors. The only sinister element to the entire building had been the silence.

The man led them into a large office containing a dozen battered wooden desks pushed into a trio of square groupings. A punching bag hung over the entrance. At their arrival, the other four men and two women stopped their work and gathered near. Clearly they had been expecting the visitors. The outer door was quickly shut and locked.

They were all young, all hard-faced, all armed. They listened in silence as the Consul General related his own findings in surprisingly fluent Russian. Jeffrey spent the long minutes looking around the room. It was as cluttered and faceless as any American big-city bullpen. The biggest difference was the lack of electronics. There was no trace of a computer, nor any of the normal background radio static. He saw only one prewar telephone for the entire room. It did not ring the entire time they were there.

One of the young men spoke fluent English. When the Consul General was finished and they had conferred in quiet, clipped tones, he said to Jeffrey, "There are almost three thousand gangs operating in Russia, and another thousand or so from other states that work here from time to time. The markets are coming more under their control every day. Doing business means finding the right connections and paying them a share. If somebody doesn't pay on time, the answer here is to shoot him."

"This group is Saint Petersburg's main anti-mafia squad," the Consul General explained. "I've worked with them on a couple of items before, and think you should trust them. I do."

"Hits go for about two hundred dollars these days," the young man continued. He was dressed in rundown denims and a shirt that had seen better days. He needed a shave and a month of dedicated sleep. But his voice carried the authority of hands-on experience.

"Soakings, they're called. We get seven to ten of them a day just inside this city. The Azerbaijani mafia is battling for control of the central markets, so right now we're seeing a lot of intergang killings, more than usual. The Uzbekis are big in the local hash and marijuana trade. The Chechen control most roads and harbors. The

Georgian mafia controls most of the restaurants. The Siberian clans control the flow of gold and diamonds and furs. The Ingush are big in protection and shakedowns."

"What about kidnappings?" Allbright asked.

A flash of grim humor circled the room after the young man had translated. "Everybody," he replied flatly.

"And treasure?"

A glimmer of new interest surfaced. "Stolen?"

The Consul General turned to Jeffrey and waited. This was his ball to play as he chose. Jeffrey hesitated, knowing for certain what Yussef would think of his sharing the information with the KGB. Finally, he decided to go with his gut. "In Ukraine. From a church."

Swiftly the information was translated. Then, "Value?"

"Big. Very big. Hard to say without having seen it, but from what I've heard, well over a million."

"Dollars?"

"Yes."

The group exchanged glances, and one of them released a silent sigh. "We have been hearing rumors," the young man explained. "A couple of pieces missing here, more there, little bits and pieces that alone are not too much, never too much. Never as much as what you are saying, not apart. But together?" He shrugged. "A fortune."

"Any idea who's behind it?" Allbright demanded.

"We don't know if what we hear is true at all. But we hear there is a gathering of pieces."

Allbright shot Jeffrey a quick glance. "Here in Saint Petersburg?"

The young man shrugged. "Rumors only. But we think yes."

"It would be logical," the Consul General speculated. "The ports around here have the greatest amount of traffic with the West. And Saint Petersburg is the city closest to the Finnish border."

The young man shook his head. "Something this big, I think by sea."

Casey spoke up. "What about the Tombek clan?"

The room's atmosphere instantly rose to a new level of intensity. Even those who spoke no English reacted to the sound of that name. The young man asked, "What about them?"

"Are they involved in kidnappings?"

"They are involved in everything," he replied flatly. "Especially things that make big money."

"Like kidnapping foreigners," Casey persisted.

"Maybe. Why do you think they are involved?"

"Casey thought he spotted a couple of their men following Mr. Sinclair," Allbright explained. "Near to where Miss Stevens was taken."

"Not think," Casey corrected. "Know."

Alert gray eyes focused on Jeffrey. "You were followed by Tombek?"

"So he says."

Glances were exchanged with other members of the team. "You are still alive?"

Jeffrey fought off a sudden chill. "As far as I can tell."

"Tombek is Chechen," the man said, as though that were all the explanation required.

Casey explained to Jeffrey, "Chechen is a tribe from the Caucasus region of southern Russia. They are winning the bloody gang war for control of the Moscow markets."

"Here, too, they are a problem," the young man added. "Very dangerous. Very deadly. Many killers."

Allbright asked, "Have you heard anything about them moving into stolen treasures?"

There was a moment's quiet discussion, a chorus of head shakes. "Nothing," the young man replied. "But Chechen control much of the ports and international harbor traffic."

"Like drugs," Casey explained to Jeffrey. "Raised in the southern reaches of the country, then exported to Western Europe and America."

"Big in trade," the young man continued. "Like importing stolen cars or exporting Russian factory goods. We have heard they are making big contracts with Western companies to supply steel. They have plans to make everything look legal."

"Front," Casey offered. "They have a Western group that is going to front for the gang."

"Yes. This we have heard. There is much money in such trade, especially if they can make it look all legal with such a front."

"But no treasures?" Jeffrey asked.

"Or kidnappings?" Allbright added.

"Who knows with Tombek? They are always hungry, always growing. Never enough. And always danger. There is great danger with all Chechen, but especially Tombek. Their only answer to a problem is to kill."

Allbright demanded, "So you'll check it out?"

There was a brief discussion, then, "We will see if we can learn anything." To Jeffrey, he asked, "Where do you stay?"

"A small guesthouse off the Nevsky Prospekt, near Kirpichny."

"Run by the Ukrainians, yes? It is nice?"

"It's fine."

"And if you happen to find a missing American lady while you're looking," the Consul General added, "I'd sure appreciate hearing about it."

The young man stood and motioned toward the door. "We'll be in touch."

As they passed through the entrance, the Consul General drew the young man over to one side. Jeffrey took the opportunity to tell Casey, "It looks like I've misjudged you." Casey shrugged it off, his eyes on his boss. "It happens."

"I think I owe you an apology."

"Takes a good man to be willing to change his mind." Casey turned toward him and stuck out his hand. "Pals?"

"Sure, thanks."

"Just be sure and watch your back. If the Tombeks or any other of the Chechen clans are involved here, the stakes are high. Winner takes all."

On Monday morning, Ivona stepped into the guesthouse's cramped parlor. She spotted Jeffrey Sinclair seated in the corner waiting for her, but she hesitated before approaching him. Somehow, for reasons she could not yet understand, everything about the young American was a challenge to her, a threat. Even before she had first met him, she had feared the meeting.

It was here again now, this challenge. He sat in a quiet corner of the crowded lobby, the jangling noise and the milling people touching him not at all. Amidst this clamor, the young man sat quiet and still. His attention was focused on the small book in his lap. His entire *being* was drawn into the act of reading.

As she stood just inside the entrance and watched him, once again the unbidden memories arose to add to her disquiet.

———

Her family was given transport passes to leave Archangelsk, but that did not mean they could leave the frozen north. Not yet. First they had to obtain train tickets. The very same night the passes were handed out, her parents sold whatever they did not need to wear or eat or drink. The next morning, they all went together to the station. And there they found a scene straight from hell.

Thousands of people fought and screamed and wept and pleaded for seats on the one train leaving for the outside that week. There was much fear that the policy would be overturned before the next train arrived, and so everyone fought for a ticket. Somehow her father managed to battle his way through the crowd and buy seats.

The train trip to the southwest of Russia, to near Kiev, lasted three weeks. Fifteen people and all their belongings were crammed together into a compartment meant for six. Three of these were men from the gold mines of Vorkuta, a place so awful that Ivona's parents refused to speak of it around her. They looked like walking skeletons, these men. Two did not survive the journey.

For Ivona, time simply ceased to exist. She sat and she lay and she watched the same endless landscape of mud and trees and primitive villages move slowly by. She sank into a feverish, half-awake state and came to see the train as a new prison, one from which they would never escape. They were destined to drift for the rest of their lives, with no money and little food, on tracks that led nowhere.

And then, finally, they arrived in Kiev, the capital of Ukraine. Their long journey came to an end, and the ordeal of beginning a life in a strange new land, with neither family ties nor work nor money nor a place to live, began. As Ivona struggled to disown the past and put down roots in new rocky soil, she learned the lessons of self-discipline and determined concentration and fierce independence. And the seed of love within her heart remained stillborn.

——

Jeffrey was seldom able to lose himself in the Scriptures. Most days the words remained silent upon the page. He had sometimes come upon Katya during her times of prayer and felt the silence and power that surrounded her. The intensity of her stillness humbled him and mirrored the tenuous hold he felt he held upon his own faith.

This morning he was forced to do his morning study while seated in the lobby, waiting for Ivona to arrive. He had awakened late and rushed through breakfast, only to realize he had forgotten to pray. So back he went for his Bible and, ignoring the people and the noise surrounding him, he sat down and bent over the Book.

He prayed silently, his eyes open yet not seeing the page, the words a tumble in his mind. He then focused upon the verses there before him, struggling hard to hold on to this fragment of daily spiritual discipline. Although he was unable to admit it even to

Katya, these moments were the anchors that reminded him of just how important faith was to him. He saw these brief periods as a much-needed expression of belief in a world that granted little room for anything of the Spirit.

But today, without warning, his inner world changed. Somehow, surrounded by the cramped parlor's noisy clatter, he felt an enveloping peace. The same thing had happened once or twice on his trip through Ukraine. Why this sense of gathering calm would appear in the midst of such chaos, he could not say. He just knew a sense of being utterly protected, separated from all the world by a divine sea.

He read and reread the passage, searching for something that would tell him why here, why now, why today. He found nothing.

So he let the moment go and drifted back across the sea of silence to join with the world once again.

———

Ivona circled the lobby so as to come up from beside and behind. She looked down, and saw that it was the same Bible the American had carried with him throughout Ukraine. She couldn't escape the fact that he was encircled by an immense stillness. It called to her. It touched deep. It left her troubled.

All her life she had heard the tales of holy men and women who through great trials and sacrifices had approached God. Yet here was a young man, coddled by the West, his face as smooth and unlined as a newborn babe. He followed no tradition that she could see. He practiced no ritual. He bore no marks of suffering. How was it then that even in the act of reading he knew the stillness of abiding prayer?

Jeffrey stirred, straightened, and shifted the muscles of his shoulders. With a guilty start Ivona stepped into view.

Jeffrey was instantly on his feet. "Good morning. I'm sorry, I didn't see—"

"We must hurry," she said, more sharply than she had intended. "Yussef is expecting us."

═══

The apartment where Yussef waited was located off a side street near the hotel. It was reached by passing through a long tunnel lined with the rotting blankets and newspaper padding of several homeless people. Wires sprouted from rusting fuse boxes to run in slack confusion overhead. The passage opened into a courtyard, which led to another courtyard and after that to another and then another still. All were surrounded by faceless apartment buildings and lined with dead grass and a few stunted trees. Jeffrey followed Ivona up a set of crumbling stairs. She stopped and spoke to a bloated middle-aged man who occupied a glass-enclosed room; the man waved her on without turning from his flickering television.

In contrast to Ivona's silent resentment, Yussef appeared genuinely glad to see him. He clapped Jeffrey on the shoulder as they entered, led him toward a trio of threadbare settees, and asked through Ivona, "You have had a successful trip?"

"Very," he replied. "Yesterday afternoon I completed the preliminary work. Now I have to make the presentation and have my client complete all these forms and give me a figure for the formal bid."

"And you leave today?"

"In," Jeffrey glanced at his watch, felt an electric thrill at what awaited him, "about three hours."

"We have no right to ask," Yussef said delicately, "but your presence here is our best possible cover."

"I can't say for certain when I will be back," Jeffrey replied, understanding perfectly. "I will have to discuss it with my boss and my wife."

Yussef grinned at the translation. "There is a difference between the two?"

"Maybe not," Jeffrey agreed. "I will explain the situation to them, though, and try to be back before the end of the week."

"The sooner the better," Yussef said. "We can only stay so long here without you."

"You really think there is so much danger?"

"The more I learn," Yussef replied seriously, "the more certain I become of that."

"You haven't found anything, I take it."

"Nothing definite. Only trails." He pushed the gloom aside, and went on, "Ivona has told you that I came here to visit my fellow countrymen and ask if they had anything to sell. At least, that is what everyone is hearing."

"Are you sure we should be talking about it openly?" Jeffrey warned.

"Here we are safe," Yussef stated flatly. "Within these doors you may rest easy."

"That's good to know," Jeffrey said doubtfully.

Yussef watched him with evident humor. "You are learning the lesson of distrust, yes? We'll make a Russian of you yet."

Gingerly he lifted a heavy, wrapped object from his carryall and set it on the table, then swept aside the covering with a flourish. "Tell me what you think."

The object's beauty as well as its surprise appearance caused Jeffrey's heart to stutter. The *coupe en cristal* was a sixteenth-century drinking basin that usually served a decorative purpose. The goblet, fourteen inches long and ten high, was carved from one solid piece of rock-crystal. The face elegantly concealed the stone's single flaw by incorporating the milky-white vein into a bull's head. The horns bore intricate crystal floral wreaths and were sturdy enough to be used as handles. The base was of solid silver, delicately carved as a series of matching wreaths, and the center of each held a ruby the size of Jeffrey's thumbnail.

"This is fantastic," Jeffrey murmured.

"There is more," Yussef announced, enjoying himself immensely. A smaller package was produced, the wrappings unfolded. "In the company of wolves, a hungry man needs to find those he can trust. The bishop's word has opened many doors for us here."

Jeffrey scarcely heard him. The cigarette case had a facing of a sunray pink enamel usually referred to as *guilloché*. On this background, intricate work had been done *en plein*, which meant different colored enamels had been applied in such a refined manner as to appear like carved gemstone. Along the sides was a chasing of white gold, swirling in a complicated union at the catch, which was set with a large, rose-colored diamond. Jeffrey thumbed the clasp, found a scrolled interior of *quatrecouleur*, or blue-tinted metal formed by combining gold with copper, steel filings, and arsenic. It was signed in fashionable French hand plate by Court Jeweller Carl Blanc, Saint Petersburg, and dated 1899.

"Now, one last item," Yussef announced, playing the conjurer a final time, "at least for now."

The ebony-backed case was the size of a book. Within was an early Limoges ceramic altar of the kind used in private chapels or as adornment in the houses of wealthy believers and dating from the early fifteenth century. The interior scenes were startlingly vivid, the colors made by pounding jewels and semiprecious stones to dust and mixing them with resin. The picture frames were of solid silver.

After the business was concluded, Jeffrey watched with pained reluctance as Yussef rewrapped the items and made them disappear once again. "You'll have plenty of time to enjoy them in the West," he said through Ivona.

Jeffrey nodded, offered, "I've been trying to help you with your search for your church treasures. I haven't accomplished very much, but I've done what I can."

"For this we are grateful," Yussef replied, his eyes on a downcast Ivona. "Tell us what you've learned."

All lightheartedness vanished as Jeffrey described his contacts with the Consul General. With his description of the Orthodox priest, Yussef's face became an immobile mask. By the time he had completed describing the meetings with the KGB organized crime squad, the atmosphere had turned frigid.

"You are taking risks," Yussef muttered. "Such risks you cannot understand."

"I think it was correct," Jeffrey said stolidly. "Each step felt correct at the time, and still feels right. By the way, have you ever heard the name Tombek before?"

After the translation, Yussef and Ivona exchanged glances, then, "The name means nothing. Why do you ask?"

"They are a gang. Part of a tribe called Chechen from a region in southern Russia. I was told they were following me the other day."

"Again, why?"

"That's what I can't figure out," Jeffrey replied. He related what had happened at the winter palace. "All I can say is, from the looks of things I'm doing what you and the bishop wanted. The attention is on me, not you."

"My blood runs cold at the risks you are taking," Yussef said worriedly. "Risks with our lives as well. The Chechen mobs are animals."

"I haven't mentioned your names to anybody," Jeffrey countered. "And I am convinced the people I spoke with are on our side."

To his surprise, Yussef did not disagree. Instead, he searched Jeffrey's face with a probing gaze. "I see you truly believe this."

"With all my heart," Jeffrey replied. "I am certain that they are allies to your cause."

Ivona said something sharply in Russian. Yussef did not respond. Instead, he kept his gaze centered on Jeffrey. "I cannot tell if your bravery comes only from innocence, or if you are truly guided by a greater hand."

Jeffrey could not help but grin. "Both come in handy. At least I can sleep at night."

"In four days Bishop Michael is visiting here to meet with fellow Ukrainian priests. He will help in setting up home churches, taking care of problems, serving Mass, christening newborns. He must hear of this."

"Give him my regards," Jeffrey said. "He is a good man."

"So are you, Jeffrey Sinclair," Yussef replied, "though what you have done is touched by the brush of madness."

"I don't think so."

"No, this much is clear, that you believe strongly in what you have done." Yussef pondered this a moment longer, then went on, "I would ask you something."

"Anything."

"Though I remain troubled by what you have done," he went on. "I wish to speak on something else while you are still here with us. I have thought much on what you have said to me about faith, and there is much I do not understand."

"I'd be happy to help you any way I can," Jeffrey replied. "But for answers to many questions you simply have to turn to the Father."

"You make that sound so simple."

"It is and it isn't." Jeffrey tried hard to overcome Ivona's cryptic, singsong dullness with heartfelt sincerity. "To make the turning called repentance, to admit to past errors and sins, to ask for Christ's gift of salvation, is probably the hardest step a man can take. But the *gift* of salvation, and the growing wisdom which comes through prayer and daily Bible study, is there for anyone who asks."

Yussef's brow remained furrowed with the effort of concentration. "And God speaks with you?"

"He does," Jeffrey replied. "Only not always in words."

"You have visions?"

"No." Jeffrey was surprised by the absolute clarity that filled the moment. He looked about the room and knew he would never forget any of it—not the smell of old smoke and unwashed bodies, nor the filth cluttering the floor, nor the taste of the air, nor the stubble on his companion's cheeks, nor the sense of divine presence that presided over it all. "But when I feel the Spirit, then sometimes I can read God's Word and know that it continues to live for me here. Today."

"The way you say this," Yussef shook his head. "You make it sound possible."

"A person is either willing to listen to God or he is not," Jeffrey said. "If he is, he will hear."

"Yes? You can be so sure of this? That I will have such a gift as well?"

Jeffrey nodded. "Sometimes the most powerful of messages cannot be placed into words at all."

"Yes? And then how can the impossible be stated?"

"With love," Jeffrey replied simply, awash in the reality of faith. "And the gift of peace that surpasses all understanding."

"I wonder if what you feel is truly peace," Yussef countered, "or just a resignation."

"I think it would probably depend on whether the Spirit of God was at work, or just my imagination," Jeffrey replied.

"A worthy answer. So tell me. How do you ever know the difference?"

"Only from within," Jeffrey replied definitely. "Only by personal experience. Only if you go and try for yourself." He paused, then offered, "You could try praying with me. It's the only way you'll know if God is trying to speak to you right here, right now."

Yussef shook his head. "I'm not ready yet for that."

"For myself," Jeffrey replied, "I've found that to be the best time to act."

When the flame of his homecoming had cooled to warm embers, when he could bear to loosen his embrace for an instant, when the painful release within his heart had soothed to a murmur, when he finally could accept that he was truly home and truly with Katya and truly held by arms who craved him more than anything else in the entire world, Jeffrey lay with his head nestled in her lap, his face turned upward so as to search deep into her eyes. And he loved her with the fullness of a gradual awakening.

They joined for a kiss, a lingering vow beyond words, a tasting of each other's love with their lips. The fullness of the moment left them silent for a time, until there was again the time for heart to know heart through words as well as eyes and touch and taste.

He stirred and asked, "What is your earliest memory?"

She cocked her head to one side. "Where do you come up with these questions?"

He gave an easy shrug. "I just want to know."

"Know what?"

"Everything." He reached up to caress her cheek. "I want to know everything, Katya. I want to know how you think when I can't see your thoughts on your face. I want to hear your heart speak to God. I want to know how you became this person I love."

Her touch was as gentle as the sighing music of her words. "I have missed you so much."

He sifted the silk of her hair with gentle fingers. "I want to *know* you, Katya. I want to fill myself with your love and your words and your touch, so that when I go away somewhere, I can take all these memories with me and keep me warm."

Katya held him with a strength meant to weld them together, and said, "Cherries."

"What?"

"My first memory is of getting dizzy on candied cherries."

"You're kidding."

She shook her head. "Do you remember me telling you about Chacha Linka?"

"The old woman who kept you when your mother went back to work. Sure. She taught you Polish."

"She was a real Polish country woman. Her days always started before dawn, and everything in her kitchen was homemade. She had a cellar full of canned mushrooms and jams and pickles and vegetables. Her house always smelled of fresh bread. I can't go into a bakery without being back at, oh, I must have been around two, holding myself erect with one hand on a chair leg, surrounded by the smell of baking bread."

Jeffrey let one finger trace its way around a perfect ear, then down the line of her neck. "I wish I had known you then."

"Chacha Linka kept this enormous jar on her kitchen counter, filled to the brim with fresh cherries floating in pure grain alcohol and sugar," Katya went on. "The adults would eat them for dessert, sometimes a couple with afternoon tea."

"Pure grain alcohol." Jeffrey smiled. "Must have packed quite a wallop."

"It did for me. Sometimes Chacha Linka gave me one to suck on when I was teething. I still remember rubbing that cherry back and forth across my gums, and how good it felt." She looked down at him, the little girl in her reaching across the years to gaze at him through Katya's grown-up eyes. "Sometimes I told her I had a toothache when I really was okay."

Jeffrey backed off in feigned shock. "You didn't."

She gave a little girl's solemn nod. "They tasted so good, those cherries, and I knew she wouldn't just let me have one. So I pretended."

"You fibbed," he corrected.

The two-year-old Katya thought about it for a moment, decided, "Only a little bit."

=====

"You absolutely must return," Alexander declared over breakfast the following morning. "And at the first possible moment."

The old gentleman was up and about, but at a pace markedly reduced from his earlier days. Still, Jeffrey was immensely pleased at his friend's evident improvement. In the days since Jeffrey's departure his color had improved, his voice had gathered strength, his gaze had become more alert, his hands had steadied. The doctor had expressed satisfaction with his progress and predicted that he should be able to return to a relatively normal, if somewhat reduced, routine within six weeks.

Katya had insisted that Jeffrey take this morning time alone with Alexander; the old gentleman had been so looking forward to seeing him again. Jeffrey had complained about being apart from her even for that long, but not too loudly.

"This was not exactly what I had hoped to hear," Jeffrey replied.

Alexander's gaze showed a glimmer of humor. "You must take solace from the fact that you and Katya shall have the rest of your lives to enjoy each other's company, then be prepared to go when and where the call is made."

Jeffrey reached across the table, poured each of them a fresh cup of coffee. "You really think it's that important."

"I know that it *may* be important, yes. Here you are, back from your first venture into what for you were two unknown territories. And if your descriptions are correct, you have come upon a number of world-class finds. And only because of the efforts of this one young Ukrainian and his aunt."

"All true," Jeffrey agreed.

"So your new ally finds himself in a position where he urgently requires your assistance," Alexander went on. "Of course you must return. And immediately. Certainly no later than the end of the week. You are building powerful alliances, Jeffrey. Go. They need you. Upon such actions a lifetime's trust is founded."

"Do you think there is any real hope that they will find this treasure of theirs?"

Alexander waved the subject aside. "That is immaterial. What matters, my young friend, is that this search is important to *them*. They are trying. They request your help. I urge you to give it to them. Immediately."

"Markov will be pleased to hear he's receiving such prompt attention," Jeffrey said. "It has been an interesting project."

Alexander shrugged. "A one-time deal, quite removed from our normal activities. That the gentleman agreed to my rather exorbitant fee without a whimper is surprising, but there is no accounting for the impulses of these royals. No, my young friend, the potential for future business rests not with the likes of Markov, but rather with your scruffy Ukrainian. I agree wholeheartedly with Gregor. This young man is indeed a find."

"Well, I'll talk to Katya about it this afternoon," Jeffrey promised. "There shouldn't be any problem about my traveling so soon. She figured out last night that I had to go back."

"Of course she did. You have found a woman who matches intelligence with a very keen perception. A worthy combination."

Jeffrey gave his friend a frank inspection. "It's great to see you looking so well again."

"Thank you, Jeffrey. Yes, it has been a long struggle, and far from an easy one. But I do feel as though the worst is behind me. For the moment, at least."

"What is that supposed to mean?"

"It is most distressing to confront the time pressures set by an ailment for which there is no cure," Alexander replied.

Jeffrey knew a keening fear. "I thought the doctors said everything was all right."

"I was not speaking of an affliction in the traditional sense," Alexander answered. "No, I meant the ultimate of ailments for those privileged to lead a full life—old age."

"We've been through this before," Jeffrey pointed out.

"Spare me the record-keeping when I am attempting to unburden myself," Alexander replied sharply.

"I don't like to hear you talk about this," Jeffrey complained. "It really makes me uncomfortable."

"Not half so much as it does me, I assure you. But despite our mutual loathing for the topic, we shall nonetheless have discussions. I insist upon it."

"You can't expect me to sit here and listen to you talk about growing old and whatever comes next—"

"Death, my boy. Death. You might as well say it. We all knock at death's door sooner or later."

"Alexander, can we please stop this?"

"Death is not my concern. Not any longer. Not now, when I have come to know the Savior's eternal blessing. No, what I find most distressing is a possible slow descent into permanent ill health. That prospect, I must confess, absolutely terrifies me. As far as death goes, I have busied myself seeking a peace with Almighty God. Although I admit to more confusion than illumination, I still feel a solace that is far beyond anything I could ever have offered myself. This is most reassuring, both when thinking of what lies beyond death's door and when wondering at this path I have chosen for my latter days."

Alexander crossed arms determinedly over his chest. "I do not intend to slide reluctantly into old age. I shall march into it vigorously, taking these last years of life with great strides and departing with a wealth of fanfare and farewells."

"From what you said a moment ago," Jeffrey replied, "I thought it was out with the wheelchair and shawls."

"Tears," Alexander doggedly continued, a warning in his visage. "I should like a few tears at my passage. Enough to know there remain at least a few true friends who shall remember my name with fondness and miss me at least a little."

"And a nurse," Jeffrey continued just as stubbornly. "A battle-ax with the face of a gargoyle, the sort of nurse old-timers get when they can't manage a sterling beauty."

"I shall thank you to never refer to me as an old-timer," Alexander snapped. "Not ever again."

"A nurse built like a tank and dressed in a starched white bunny cap, support hose, and marching boots," Jeffrey persisted. "Voice like a foghorn. Good for getting through when you lose your hearing aid."

"Are you quite through?"

Jeffrey subsided. "You scared me back there."

The old gentleman permitted the bleakness to show. "At least you were frightened here in a well-lit room, with a comfortable chair and a friend to keep the shadows at bay. My own fears arrive in the dead of night, when loneliness drapes itself around me like a shroud and my prayers exit as dust from my mouth to blow listlessly through my heart's empty chambers."

Alexander inspected Jeffrey gravely. "I shall need to share these fears with you from time to time. Bringing them out in the open, you see, helps mightily."

Jeffrey nodded his assent, not trusting his voice just then.

A hint of the old fire returned. "And I shall expect you to answer with your jabs and jests, young friend. Continue to remind me of the folly of self-pity."

He cleared his throat, managed, "I'll try."

"Splendid. Far be it from me to spend my remaining hours planning the one celebration which I know in utter certainty that I shall not be allowed to attend." Alexander tasted his coffee, and said, "One other item which I have found most remarkable during this entire period is how vivid my recollections have become."

Jeffrey found immense pleasure in changing the subject. "Gregor said the very same thing."

"Did he, now. When was that?"

"While he was here in London."

"And what was it that he found so riveting about his past?"

"He was recalling your escape from Poland after the war," Jeffrey replied.

Gray eyes sparkled brilliantly. "Did he, indeed?"

Jeffrey nodded. "Could I ask you something?"

"Anything."

"I was wondering what happened when you disappeared like that toward the end of the war."

"That is just like Gregor. He knows the story well, unless his memory is fading with age."

"His memory is fine. He was involved," Jeffrey hesitated, then finished, "in another story."

Alexander sobered. "Zosha?"

"Yes."

Alexander sat in reverie for a long moment, then drew the present back into focus and asked, "It was hard for him, going back to the grave site?"

Jeffrey nodded. "But he was glad he did it."

"That is good. I would not like to think I asked him back to London, then forced upon him yet another painful duty. So. What did he tell you of those days?"

Jeffrey related the story. "I was wondering what happened when you disappeared for so many months before returning home. All he said was that, with the Red Army's arrival, one by one the AK soldiers began to vanish."

"Indeed they did." Alexander settled back in his chair, his gaze centering upon the distance of vivid memories. "Our officers said nothing outright. It was all still too new, and the full extent of our betrayal during the Warsaw Uprising was as yet unknown. The Germans remained our primary enemy, and although they had been pushed from Polish soil, the battle for Berlin still raged. But within a few days the evidence was too stark; we were forced to accept that the Russians had begun eliminating the Polish Underground's survivors.

"I decided, along with three of my closest friends, that we needed to beat them at their own game. The Soviets had begun recruiting Poles to join them in the battle for Berlin. We signed on, under false names, for Red Army training."

Alexander's voice held a mere shadow of his former strength, yet some of the old determination and drive came alive through his recollections. "After just eleven days of the most rudimentary training imaginable," Alexander continued, "we heard that we were to be shipped to the front. My friends and I realized that we were meant to serve as nothing more than cannon fodder. So using that most universal of Soviet currencies, vodka, we bribed our way into the tank training school. We hoped that those six weeks of further training would be enough to see us through in safety until the end of the war.

"But it was not to be. The conditions at the camp were horrid, worse than anything I had known since my imprisonment at Auschwitz. Our food was watery gruel for breakfast, gruel for lunch, and gruel for dinner, served with whatever insects and filth happened to land in the pots while it was being cooked. Our second week, the entire camp refused to eat a particularly bad breakfast. There was no discussion; the food was simply inedible. We were then marched out onto the parade ground, where the commanding officer accused us of mutiny and ordered that every tenth man be taken off and shot.

"A few days later, or nights rather, I was waked from a deep sleep by a bright light in my face and the order to dress and follow in silence. I did not need anyone to tell me that this was the work of the NKVD, as the Soviet secret police were then known. I was taken to a metal-lined room and subjected to a most brutal interrogation. They had word that some of the new recruits were former AK, and they wanted names. I somehow managed to convince them that I knew nothing about the underground army, and I was eventually released.

"The next night, my friends and I escaped under the wire and joined up with an AK outfit operating from the forests not far from the training camp. I stayed with them, fighting the invasion of this new enemy, until it became evident that the struggle was in vain and that to remain meant certain death. I then decided to leave my beloved Poland behind. I returned home for Gregor and my family, and there I met Zosha.

"I wish you could have known her, my young friend. She was truly not of this world. The first time I met her was the night of our escape, I suppose Gregor told you that. Yes, after a seven-month absence, I arrived back to my family home in the dark hour before dawn, chased by any number of ghosts, both seen and unseen. Gregor was there to meet me, as I hoped, and with him was a woman. At first sight I thought she was an angel who somehow had hidden her wings. After all these years, I am still not sure I was wrong.

"Her face was luminous, Jeffrey. Lit from within by the love she held for my cousin. She would look his way, and the room was bathed in a light that touched the farthest recesses of my cold heart. I have never in my life felt unworthy, save for that moment. I watched them share their glances of otherworldly love, and I knew that here was something that was forever beyond me.

"Still," Alexander continued, his voice filled with gentle yearning, "I was blessed to know her as I did. The ruling force in my life at that time was a desire for revenge. Then I would speak with her, or see her with my cousin, and I would know that if I were to be worthy of even the smallest place in her life, I would have to cast my hatred aside. It was hard, so very hard, but even so I did it. For her.

"Zosha, Zosha," he sighed, his vision cast to another time, a different world. "Even to be loved as a friend by her was more than one man deserved. I suppose she was beautiful, but I am not sure. I believe her hair was somewhat dark, and perhaps a bit long, but it matters not. Even then, when I was away from her, I could not recall how she looked. Her heart gave off such a blinding light that I was unable to see anything else about her very clearly.

"When she died—" he began, and had to stop. After a moment he went on, "When she passed on, the world's light was dimmed. A candle passed from this earthbound home to burn more clearly in a heavenly sanctuary. Although we never discussed it, my cousin and I, this thought held me intact through those first dark days after her departure: that she was never meant for this world. Her place, in truth, was elsewhere. Her heart was made by heavenly hands to serve in other, more holy lands. Angels such as Zosha possessed hearts too great to ever be held for long in a fragile earthly vessel."

Ivona stopped outside the Kuznetahny Market's main entrance to button her purse inside her jacket. As she rejoined the jostling crowd, she passed a relatively well-dressed young man who stood on an empty wooden crate and called to the crowd in an official-sounding voice, "Watch out for your valuables. There are pickpockets at work in the market."

Ivona watched as men patted their pockets and women clutched tighter to their purses. Out of the corner of her eye she spotted two other youngsters who noted the motions and passed the information on to a series of runners. They in turn sped off to tell the pickpockets which newcomers looked to be paying less careful attention and where their money was kept. It was a ploy introduced several weeks ago by the Uzbeki mafia, who now controlled Saint Petersburg's largest market. She had been warned of the danger by the person she was here to meet.

There was now an alternative to the endless Russian food lines. At least, there was an alternative for those with money. Free-enterprise markets, they were called, stalls tended by greedy babushkas and unkempt men charging vastly inflated prices. An average Russian's weekly wage for a bag of lemon-sized oranges. A pensioner's entire monthly check for five kilos of beef. Meanwhile, rats feasted on refuse at the stallholders' feet.

Health regulations were becoming the source of numerous jokes, humor remaining the populace's safety valve when facing problems out of their control. Out of anybody's control, in truth. The government remained in a state of flux, with inspectors' wages set at the old levels and prices now out of sight. Most could be bought with a pittance.

Stallholders sold food tainted with salmonella, used contaminated chemicals for canning, mixed poisonous mushrooms with safe, offered botulism as a main course. Cats and dogs were disappearing from the streets. Butchers dangled lit cigarettes over their work and used ashes as a universal spice. People bought meat pies from street vendors, then waited for them to cool before taking the first bite; if it was a genuine meat, like beef or lamb, the fat solidified and became visible. Food poisoning was so prevalent in hospital emergency rooms that orderlies were taught basic treatment. Outside the major cities, epidemics of hepatitis and meningitis and amoebic dysentery worsened daily. Authorities were powerless to take protective measures.

Laws were left at the market gates. Restaurants and bars did a booming business in empty whiskey and brandy bottles, which enterprising stallholders purchased and refilled using grain alcohol colored with old tea.

The word for street market was *tolkuchka*, which translated literally as "crush." The word applied as much to the trash that formed borders around the poorly policed areas as it did to the hordes that crowded the rickety stalls. Chinese brassieres, French cosmetics, Russian T-shirts, Spanish faucets, German shoes—the wealthier stall owners offered smatterings of whatever they had managed to pick up from unnamed sources. Hunting knives glinted beside stacks of disposable diapers. Plastic cola bottles shouldered up to rat poison.

Next to the professional stallholders crouched old-age pensioners, whose social security payments no longer kept body and soul intact. With the ruble's tumble from financial power, Russian old-age support was set at forty-seven U.S. cents per day. The result was a forced sale of whatever was not desperately needed. They at least escaped the mafia's control, at least so long as not too many of them appeared.

Ivona passed an old woman crouched on the curb, offering two rusty cans of imported hot dogs. An old man sold sweaters not required in the summer heat; winter worries could be left until after today was survived. An elderly couple offered cracked flowerpots, a container of oatmeal, three boxes of matches, and a pair of expressions locked in silent desperation. A woman held up a second pair of shoes with her only pair of laces; the ones on her feet were roped to her ankles and lined with newspapers. One offered a half bottle of old hair dye, another a ratty pullover with one sleeve unfurled, yet another a battered kitchen pot. The meager possessions on display were a loud condemnation of the crumbling regime.

Years of chronic scarcity had taught Russians to barter whatever was not needed. But today was different. The tone of pleading was not one of simple need. Despair and panic overcame the shame of begging. Hunger contaminated voices. Men and women alike shouted silent accusations with rheumy eyes. Medals tarnished with bygone glory hung listlessly from lapels in a declaration that here, this person, this one who had sacrificed and risked all, now deserved better. Was owed more. No matter what the regime, they should not be left to know such shame.

The stallholder Ivona sought sold fresh fruit, the produce of fine Ukrainian orchards brought here because, even after the mafia took its share, the profit was ten times what the husband-and-wife team would earn at home. They paid the mafia's price and counted themselves lucky to have a place in the market at all. Ivona picked up and examined beautifully fresh apples. "Yours are the nicest in the entire market."

"You touch, you buy," the woman declared harshly. "Four hundred fifty rubles a kilo."

Ivona could not help but gape. "That's twenty times what the state stores charge."

"You want state produce, go stand in line," the husband said loud enough for the benefit of passersby. "Here you pay the price."

Ivona fumbled inside her jacket for her purse. "A half kilo, then. It is all I can afford."

"More than most," the man replied, more quietly now as the crowd before them thinned out. "You see what they did to Tortash?"

"Who?"

"Next stall but one. The man with the bandaged face." Ivona spotted a man bearing a heavy white gauze strip running from eye to chin. Around the edges of the bandage peeped a violent rainbow of blue and black bruises. "He had two bad days in a row, sold almost nothing, and didn't pay on time," the shopkeeper told her softly. "They have men who like that kind of work. Call them brigadiers."

Ivona accepted the package. "I understand. Your information is safe."

"Nothing is safe," his wife grumbled as she stacked fruit. "To live in these times is dangerous, to say what you know is worse. Better your eyes do not see than to speak."

"Yet I have seen," the husband said, placing a trio of pears upon the weighing machine. He waited for a shopper to pause and ask prices and shake her head and walk on, then said, "I saw a crate of paintings at the warehouse when I went for my fruit."

"When?"

"Four days ago. And another of icons. In gold. Old, or so they looked."

"And did your mind not scream danger?" His wife crumpled an empty packing crate with violent motions. "Did you not have a care for your children?"

"There were more boxes, but smaller and closed," the man went on, twisting the bag closed and handing it over. "And in the office when I went to pay there were people. Dangerous people."

"And still you speak," his wife hissed, her eyes darting everywhere. "Still you risk speaking. And for what?"

"For the church," Ivona said softly, handing over money her eyes could not even count. "For us. For our children and their heritage."

The woman faltered, turned sullen. "Say it then. Be swift."

"Southerners," the man said. "Some of them, anyway. Of the Chechen clan. From the Tombek family. Senior men."

Ivona thought of what Jeffrey had told them before his departure. "Tombek is mafia?"

"Tombek is death," the wife declared. "Even their shadows are poison."

"They are here from time to time," the man went on. "There is some agreement with the people who control the market. Transport, probably. Tombek controls the roads into Saint Petersburg."

"And the harbor?"

The man shrugged. "I have heard so, but cannot say for sure. We have no dealings with the sea."

"Better we had dealings with none of this," his wife retorted. "Not ever again."

Ivona stowed her purchases in a shopping bag pulled from her pocket. "I and all who cannot be seen thank you for this gift," she said, and turned away.

express-mailed all the completed bid documents to you yesterday," Jeffrey reported to Markov by phone. "Along with a copy of my report."

"How long have you been back in London?" The man's voice sounded decidedly strained.

"Three days. I waited to call until after I had the photographs and had worked through the documents with your lawyer. Everything looks in pretty good shape."

"Excellent." Markov was decidedly less than enthusiastic.

"The documents, I mean, not the house," Jeffrey added. "Well, the house is in fairly decent shape as well, all things considered. A group's been using your ground floor as a warehouse for the past few months. The floor's pretty badly scarred."

"You don't say."

"There was also a company with offices upstairs, but they've gone bust. They seem to have left everything pretty much intact. All the ornate fittings have been stripped, of course. And there's virtually no furniture left anywhere, so there was nothing for me to evaluate within my own area of expertise. Basically, all that's left are some wardrobes."

"What?" He turned positively alarmed.

"They're in the suite of rooms that I believe were your father's chambers," Jeffrey said, wondering where he might have made a mistake. "His dressing room has some really nice built-in mahogany wardrobes. They've been painted this awful matte white, but you can tell that they would be worth fixing up."

"I see," Markov said, subsiding.

"The garden is overgrown, and the outbuildings have pretty much surrendered to the march of time," Jeffrey persisted. "You'll probably have to gut them and start over."

"Quite, quite." Worriedly.

"I have an architect going over everything right now. Which brings us to my next question. The architect won't have his blueprints and repair estimates done for another week, maybe two. But the Saint Petersburg authorities are pressing for some kind of formal bid. They're really eager to see this manor taken off their hands. So I was wondering if you'd review the package and give me a figure I could use as an opening bid. I'll make it contingent upon the architect's finding no serious structural damage, of course."

"Fine, fine."

"You need to make your bid for the actual sales price, but they will only be able to offer you a lease for the moment. I guess you already knew that."

There was a heartbeat's pause, then a shrill, "A *lease*?"

Jeffrey explained the current legal situation. "The contract with the city authorities will state that they will sell the palace to you once the laws have been passed. Until then, you will have a thirty-year lease, with all payments going to the eventual purchase price."

There was the sound of breathing, then, "I shall look forward to receiving your report and then will come back to you immediately. Until then. Goodbye."

———

"Someone who nobody in Russia knows, you said," General Surikov told him. The man's guttural voice was flat as an empty barrel. "Somebody with a name in Eastern Europe, yet unknown in our area."

Prince Vladimir Markov shifted uncomfortably. "It could be just a fluke."

"Indeed. A fluke that the young man arrives in Saint Petersburg with Bishop Denisov's secretary, then proceeds to make contacts with a series of people who have nothing whatsoever to do with his assignment. A fluke. Indeed."

"Speaking of flukes," the prince countered, "you said that if I were to cooperate with you on this, the palace would be mine once more."

"Once more?" The general showed frosty humor. "It has never been such."

"Mine, my family's, there is no difference." Markov hated the way his voice sounded to his own ears. This was too much like begging. He hated not having the money to simply go in and purchase the palace on his own. But that was completely beyond his reach.

Almost all the family's wealth had been tied up in land and houses and possessions in Russia, every cent of which had vanished with the Bolsheviks' arrival, along with every member of his family save for his father, who had been saved simply because he had been in France at the time of the October Uprising. The same father who had squandered away almost all their remaining funds upon mistresses and drink and gambling and entertainments the family could hardly afford. The same father who had left him a crumbling Riviera palace he had not been able to keep up, along with burning desire to see his family's position restored.

Markov had been forced to accept the reality that, given his own financial situation, he would never be able to afford the repurchase of his family's Saint Petersburg estate. The sale of his current, smaller Riviera home would barely cover the cost of renovation. No, Markov had decided, the purchase funds would have to come from elsewhere.

And then the general had appeared.

"The agreement," Markov reminded him, "was that my palace would be used as a warehouse for your goods. My company would be granted your required export licenses, your shipments would be made, and I would be left in peace to restore my family's name and honor. And home."

Markov had struggled long and hard before agreeing to allow himself to be used as a front. Front for what, Markov did not ask nor care to know, but he assumed it involved drugs or something equally dangerous, illegal, and expensive.

Surikov's group had initially approached Markov solely because of his name. They had seen the prince with his gradually declining wealth as a perfect front for their export activities. Markov had then responded with the plan that was now unfolding. In return for allowing his palace to be used as a warehouse, his company as a basis for the export of their goods, Markov would be granted the return of his old home.

It was the sort of work that Markov felt was not beneath his station. All was to have been kept at arms' length, and his hardest task should have been to wait for all to unfold. Until now.

"Such loyalty is to be admired," the general said dryly. "In any case, the holdup is a mere formality. Parliament will pass the required laws any day now."

"That may well be," Markov replied. "But what of my home?"

Surikov showed confusion. "What of it?"

"Your group will pay the required lease amounts until your shipments are completed," he said bleakly. "And then you will leave me with a debt I cannot pay, for a palace I will not be allowed to keep."

"Ah. Now all is clear. Rest assured, Prince Markov, this too can be arranged in a manner acceptable to all concerned. An account opened with the sales figure deposited before the first shipment is completed."

Markov nodded his acceptance, yet somehow knew in an instant of startling pain that the moment would never arrive.

"What should concern you just now is remaining healthy so that you may enjoy it." Eyes the color of old Siberian ice plunged deep. "To whom have you spoken of our little project?"

"To no one, of course."

The general snorted his disbelief and declared, "A payment will be demanded for this error."

"I have made no error," Markov protested, his heart fluttering like a captured bird. "I did only as we discussed. As we agreed. And there is still nothing certain to indicate that the American is anything more than he appears."

"Let us both hope that nothing incriminating is ever discovered," the general said, then subsided into brooding silence.

"You will be moving your articles to another location?" Markov asked, half-hoping that it would be so. At this point, he wanted nothing more than to be rid of the general and his invisible superiors and the whole stinking mess.

The general shook his head, his eyes focused elsewhere. "Not just now. There is too much attention placed upon it. By too many. Including the Americans."

"You stole from the Americans?"

"No. Well, yes, I suppose. In a sense."

Markov could scarcely believe what he was hearing. "But why?"

The gaze sharpened. "Shall I pass that question on as well? Allow my superiors to hear that you are now questioning their judgment?"

"No, of course not. It is just—" Markov backed off, wiped a clammy forehead. "What do you wish for me to do?"

"Send your American antiques dealer back to Russia."

"That is all?"

"For the moment. My superiors have decided to take matters into their own hands."

"The American has just informed me of his intentions to travel at the end of this week."

"Excellent. Whether or not he is simply a casual bystander, a mere pawn, the risk has now grown too great. The chance that he might be other than he seems is now too dangerous to permit. This chance must now be eliminated."

"And for myself?"

"Know I shall argue on your behalf," the general assured him. "Still, if I were in your position just now, I should have long and serious discussions with whatever gods might be at my disposal."

First the United States Consulate, then the Russian Orthodox Church, and now the KGB." Bishop Michael Denisov gave his head a merry shake. "Our young American friend has proven to be quite a surprise."

It was a rare ability, this talent of his for enthusiasm. He delighted in all, showed compassion with humor, brought even the bitterest of babushkas a moment of peace. This reaction to all that the world brought his way caused Ivona equal amounts of awe and frustration.

"You cannot possibly be pleased with his actions," Ivona protested.

They were seated in the kitchen of what had been the central Ukrainian Rite Catholic Church in all of Saint Petersburg—a converted cellar in a nameless high-rise apartment block. Now that the church was permitted to work above-ground, now that Mass could be held without the threat of arrest, the cellar had been split. Half had been converted into a Bible school for children, and the other half served as a small apartment for visiting church officials.

"Well, he most certainly has been active. You must say that for him." Bishop Michael looked to Yussef. "Has he told you why he chose to disclose our loss to them?"

"He thought he could trust them," Yussef replied, and shook his head. "It chills the blood."

"Yes, quite so," the bishop agreed, although he did not appear the least concerned. "Still, he has avenues open to him that we do not."

"The KGB?" Ivona's voice had a shrill catch to it. "The Orthodox? You call these avenues?"

Yussef released the briefest of smiles. "My dear Aunt Ivona, were you not the one who refused to accuse the Orthodox church of being behind it all?"

"But to turn to them, to confess our secrets," Ivona protested. "This is madness!"

"He thinks not," Yussef countered.

"And what has he learned," Bishop Michael demanded. "Has he told you that?"

"It matches what we ourselves have discovered."

"Does it indeed?"

Yussef nodded. "And adds some missing pieces."

"You approve of the American's actions?"

"The better I know him," Yussef confessed, "the more I approve."

Bishop Michael examined him closely. "You are not speaking just of our mission."

"Not only, no." Yussef took a breath. "He has a way of bringing the impossible within reach."

For some reason his words appeared to shake Ivona to the very core. Her hand trembled as she set down her tea and muttered, "Madness."

Bishop Michael paused to inspect her face, then turned his attention back to Yussef. "You think that he may lead us to the missing treasures?"

"I think," Yussef said carefully, "that he will do his very best to assist us. And I believe that all his actions are meant to further this aim."

"Then his coming is indeed a miracle," Bishop Michael declared. The expression that flashed briefly across Yussef's features caused him to pause. "What is it?"

"He . . ." Yussef hesitated. "I do not know how to say this."

"He speaks to Yussef about faith," Ivona said bitterly, "and Yussef listens."

Bishop Michael's eyes widened. "This is true?"

"He challenges my heart," Yussef confessed.

The fragile, gray-haired man gave a faint smile. "Indeed a miracle," he repeated.

Ivona was dumfounded. "You can't possibly mean that you approve of this outrage."

The bishop gave her a long and thoughtful stare before telling Yussef, "When he returns to Saint Petersburg, share all we know with the American. Let him apply his heart and mind to solving our puzzle. And guard yourselves as best you can, both of you. Danger stalks behind every shadow."

The night before Jeffrey's departure, they held each other close and long, speaking little, sharing with their hearts. If truth be known, if night whispers were to speak in human tongue, it might be found that he wept a bit that night. For he was much in love, yet the wind called out to him, and he knew it was to sweep him away with the dawn.

He knew, but did not let the knowledge rise. He wept, and thought the tears were hers. Which they were. He gave them to her, and she accepted them with her heart and with gentle lips that tasted their saltiness and the love that lifted them from his eyes.

She cried as well, trying to lower her head so that he would not see how his tenderness opened her soul. She with a woman's wisdom could, in the moment of their first true confession of spirit, see all that was already gone from her life, all that he and his love was to change, all that she was called to leave behind. That was the price of this adventure called lifelong love.

The next morning she clung to him with bonds that went far beyond the tender caresses, the soft words, the yearning eyes. Her heart held his, filled him with a light and a joy that caused real pain as his own heart grew and expanded to accept her gift. They watched the dawn with eyes sharing an inner light more majestic than the cloud-flecked sky, more glorious than the symphony of bird-song outside their window.

"You can't just treat this as a game," she said over coffee.

"It's tempting," he confessed.

"Not anymore," she went on. "Not when my life is in your hands."

He reached for her, and said the words that seemed ever new no matter how often they were repeated. "I love you, Katya."

"There is responsibility with that, Jeffrey."

"I know."

"If something happened to you, I could not go on." Her eyes were violet wells into which he plunged and wondered at the depth of love he found there. "I'm not saying that to scare you, but just to make you understand. You have to be careful. For me. You have to take care."

"I will, Katya."

She searched his face, found enough reassurance there to taste the smallest smile. "You're too handsome by half, Jeffrey Sinclair. Don't you dare look at another woman until you get back, do you understand?"

"I've already packed my club."

"I never thought I would fall for a handsome man. Never in my wildest dreams."

"Sorry to disappoint you."

"My dreams were always of a man with pretty eyes. I indulged myself that much. Pretty eyes and a good heart. A minister, maybe, or a doctor who spent his free days working with poor children." She stared up at him and repeated with wonder in her voice, "Never in my wildest dreams."

"Are you sorry?"

Jeffrey decided hers was the way all smiles should be, beginning at the heart, brimming up through the eyes, finally touching the lips. She said, "Now you're fishing for compliments."

"A shopkeeper who sells used furniture—"

"A fine young man with the face of some famous explorer," she corrected, and traced the line of his jaw with one fingernail. "You really do, you know. Full of strength and bravery and courage."

"Makes up for a heart the size of a lemon, I guess."

"Stop it, Jeffrey," she said mildly. "I think that's what frightens me, how you take this strength so much for granted. It makes me worry you might try something foolish, not even thinking it through, just because your strength's never really been tested."

"You're beginning to get me about half-scared."

"Good." Her smile took on a hint of sadness. "You are precious to me, Jeffrey Allen Sinclair. More precious than my own life."

His eyes burned from the honesty in her words. He leaned forward, tasted her lips, whispered the promise, "I'll be careful, Katya. For you."

Jeffrey stepped off the plane to find Saint Petersburg sweltering under a mustard-yellow sky. The air stank. Each breath burned his nostrils and coated his tongue. While waiting for his suitcase, he overheard another passenger say that the city's garbage dump had been burning out of control for nine days. Because of the drought, there was no water available to put out the fires.

The streets, such as they were, belonged to the pedestrians. Few people could afford cars, fewer still the bribes required to obtain gasoline. Streetcars were jammed, the metros eternally overcrowded and stuffy. Gypsies worked the crowded pedestrian ways, surrounding their chosen victim, wailing in a dozen voices, and pressing cranky babies up to the victim's face, while nimble fingers used the confusion to pick the victim's pocket. Street kids rode buses and trams for kicks, clinging to the rear guide wires that led up to the overhead power cables. They swung by one hand, smoked cigarettes with the other, dangled their bodies over the cars behind, laughing all the way.

Jeffrey watched the street scene from the backseat of a jouncing taxi and nursed a sore neck. Perhaps because of missed sleep or anticipated stress, perhaps because of missing Katya, his back was once again complaining loudly. The taxi driver did not help matters. He drove too fast down pot-holed streets, slammed on brakes at the last possible moment, raced his motor at stoplights, wove in and out of traffic, used elevated tram tracks like ski jumps, and generally drove like everyone else. Jeffrey braced himself as best he could and hoped the pain would not worsen.

After dropping his case by the guesthouse, Jeffrey continued on to the Alexander Nevsky Lavra. When he arrived at the monastery's office building, Jeffrey was escorted immediately into Father Anatoli's office.

"I have some information for you," the priest reported, motioning him toward a seat. "But first it is necessary to explain the background. Earlier this year, the leader of the Ukrainian Rite Church wrote a letter to our Patriarch in Moscow. I suppose you are familiar with the history of the Ukrainian churches?"

"Just the bare bones," Jeffrey replied.

"In his letter, the Ukrainian wrote and said, let us be brothers in Christ's name. Let us work as one for the salvation of our Russian and Ukrainian brothers and sisters. It was a glorious moment for people within the church who feel as I do. Glorious.

"Patriarch Alexis did not wish to reply with words, but rather with deeds. He ordered the Metropolitan of Kiev, the head of the Orthodox church in Ukraine, to accept the offer and to return the Ukrainian churches that were given to the Orthodox after Stalin's infamous synod of 1946." His expression turned bleak. "You can guess what happened."

"The Metropolitan refused."

"Exactly. Patriarch Alexis used this refusal as an opportunity to convene the first synod of all Russian Orthodox bishops in over ninety years. Evidence was brought against the Metropolitan of Kiev and others who had been raised up within the church hierarchy under pressure of the former regime."

"The Metropolitan of Kiev worked for the KGB?"

Father Anatoli nodded. "This we knew for a fact. And now that the KGB no longer held the reins of earthly power, he worked for the new Ukrainian government. For the Communists turned capitalists. At any rate, the synod stripped the Metropolitan of his titles."

"Something in your face tells me the story didn't end there," Jeffrey observed.

"Indeed not. The man replied by breaking the Ukrainian Orthodox Church away from Moscow."

"Trouble," Jeffrey offered.

"Chaos and danger. Our priests within Ukraine who condemn this action are now beginning to disappear. He has the backing of the Ukrainian government, you see, who wish to have the religious ties as well as the political ties to Moscow broken." The priest looked infinitely weary. "It is a problem like that of the Communists all over again."

"The Consul General mentioned the church's tie to the KGB," Jeffrey said. "It amazes me that they could infiltrate the church's hierarchy to such an extent."

"It is indeed so easy to judge the ways of others," Anatoli replied coolly.

"I'm not judging anybody," Jeffrey countered. "I just don't understand."

He examined Jeffrey closely. "Very well, I shall explain. There can be no question that many of the clergy worked closely with the KGB. Not just from our church, but *every* church allowed to operate within the former Soviet Union, including the Protestants. The question we face today is, when did the necessary contact with the Communist authorities become collaboration and betrayal? In some cases, it is almost impossible to determine. In others, there is no doubt."

"Like with the Metropolitan of Kiev," Jeffrey offered.

"Exactly," Anatoli agreed. "You see, under the Communist system, *every* priest and *every* Protestant minister required government permission to preach, to organize a parish, and to hold church office."

"Did you also have to have permission to enter the priesthood?" Jeffrey asked.

He hesitated. "Officially, no. In practice, yes. No one could be admitted to a seminary or theological college without the government's permission. Why? Because it was necessary to apply for travel permits to journey from one city to another. And once there, it was necessary to have a residence permit in order to stay and study."

"A legal straitjacket," Jeffrey said.

"In effect," Father Anatoli confirmed. "In the first year at seminary, all students were then ordered to visit the local KGB official responsible for church activities. He was always a senior officer. The pattern was well known. At this first meeting, he would be quite kind, quite friendly. There would be no threats. He would say, there is of course religious freedom in our country. We in the government are merely anxious to see that the church function in its proper way.

"But, the KGB officer would continue, there are some elements within our society who are opposed to the great Soviet system. They seek to use the church for ulterior motives. It is essential that we identify these people and protect our nation from harm. If you see among the staff or students at the theological college any anti-Soviet attitudes, we would be grateful if you would inform us. Just to ensure that the church functions smoothly, you understand. Such people can do a lot of harm to everyone."

"It chills the blood," Jeffrey declared.

"As it did for many students, especially those young ones from small villages who had no way of preparing for this contact," Anatoli replied. "Now in the second year, the interview would be much tougher. The KGB agent would say, we were looking for your co-operation, but you haven't offered it. This does not bode well for you. It is a dangerous direction to take, and it makes me question your patriotism. Here, I have a list of names. We want you to report back to us in two or three months with any information you might be able to gather on them."

"And there it starts," Jeffrey said.

"If you were a person of strong moral character," Anatoli continued, "you could get through your four years of training without giving anything of great importance away. But even so, the seeds of distrust and fear were sown among the clergy. There was never any assurance that someone might not inform on you, if ever you were to speak too openly or trust someone too deeply."

"And those of weaker character?"

"Exactly. Inevitably, among two hundred students or so, there were some who were unstable."

"Or scared," Jeffrey added.

"Or who fell into moral difficulty," Anatoli finished. "The KGB were most eager to use honey traps on any of the weaker priests. This granted them a weapon they could wield against the priest for his entire life. And so a network of spies was established within each seminary class."

"And once that first step was made, the next step was much easier."

"The downward path quickly became very steep," Anatoli agreed. "Among my own classmates there was the saying, give the KGB the first knuckle of your little finger, and they will soon take the entire body, the entire mind, and the entire soul. Once the weaker priests were hooked into the KGB machine, the state used its influence to push forward these people's careers."

"Through these permits."

"For a start. No priest or bishop could serve anywhere without first receiving permission to live there. Then, of course, once a person they controlled was in a position of responsibility, the KGB would instruct them as to which priests they should bring in or assign elsewhere."

"The way you describe it," Jeffrey said, "it seems amazing that any believers at all were brought into senior positions."

"It is indeed a miracle," Anatoli agreed. "A testimony to the power of God that despite these pressures, the majority of priests and bishops remained steadfast in their refusal to compromise their faith and their church."

"So where does that leave us in regard to the missing treasures?"

His manner turned grim. "Some of those who compromised themselves under the old regime continue to do so today. They have either chosen to do so willingly or have been forced to continue their unholy service. Their masters have simply traded one cloak for another."

"They told the KGB about the treasure hidden in the Ukrainian church crypt," Jeffrey said.

"Who in turn sold it elsewhere," Anatoli finished. "To some group who, in my opinion, has also been responsible for thefts of church treasures and artifacts from museums all over the country."

"You mean the government is involved in repeated thefts?"

"The government is involved, but not involved. Just as six thousand churches taken from us by the Communists are returned, but *not* returned. The laws offer the bureaucracy room to abuse us."

"Which they do."

"Which they have done, and continue to do at every opportunity. This was a favorite Communist trick. Now it is a favorite trick of Communists turned capitalists. The deal is done, but not done. The church property is returned on paper but not in fact. So there is a vacuum. Museums which supposedly have released church artifacts show us directives to return confiscated treasures and icons, but the church has never received them." He spread his hands in resignation. "We are forced to grasp a double-edged sword by the blade."

"You believe treasures from your own church have also been stolen in this way?"

"We know, but we have no proof. When we question others about this, we receive no help. The bureaucrats recall the orders of their former Communist masters and shun us. The police pocket the mafia's bribes and offer only words, never action. The museum directors stand under leaking roofs and shrug their lack of concern."

"I have a friend I would like you to meet," Jeffrey said. "That is, if he's still in Saint Petersburg. And if you wouldn't mind meeting someone from outside the Orthodox fold."

"He is Ukrainian?"

"A bishop," Jeffrey agreed. "Actually, while we're discussing this, there's a Protestant minister here in town whom I'd also like to introduce. Has the Consul General told you about the kidnapping of Miss Stevens?"

Father Anatoli nodded. "A tragedy. I continue to pray for her safety."

"Reverend Collins is the minister at her church and has spent a lot of time in the search. He probably won't be able to help with your thefts, but he could possibly assist with some of your other problems. From what he told me, I'm pretty sure he would like to try. Plus, I think you'd enjoy meeting him."

"Enjoy," the priest mused. "I can scarcely imagine using such a word when describing such a meeting." He focused his attention on Jeffrey. "But I agree. It is an opportunity to express my own feelings with more than words."

"So where does that leave us as far as the thefts in Lvov are concerned?"

"I have alerted my friends throughout this region," Father Anatoli replied. "They shall speak with our brothers, and they in turn with those they trust. So it shall spread, in ever wider circles, reaching out through the faithful until, I hope, an answer is found. It is by far the safest road for us to take, and one that has brought great results in the past."

He rose from his chair and extended a broad peasant's hand as he added, "You must take great care, my brother. There are wolves who hunt under the darkness of our nation's gathering night. They are without mercy. Do not fall into their clutches, I urge you. Do not relax your vigil for an instant."

——

As before, when Jeffrey left the priest's office, he walked back through the monastery grounds and entered the main cathedral. Mass was being celebrated, and the cathedral was packed. Jeffrey found a spot near the back and looked out over the throng.

Upon the ceiling, a burnished sun rose above an earth-bound cloud, and golden light streamed out from the all-seeing eye of God. From every wall, at every height and angle, flattened two-dimensional figures within ornate frames stared down at him. Their hands held open Bibles, or pointed toward a lamb wounded on one side, or beckoned for the beholder to look up, up, up toward a bejeweled city descending from on high.

Each worshiper in that vast, chairless space appeared intent on his or her own inner world. They converged, yet remained separate, each wholly involved in the individual act of worship. Even the priests, when intoning prayers, turned and faced forward with all the others. There were five priests in all, chanting prayers and moving about in ancient formality. Yet attention did not remain on them. No person held center stage. Attention was *elsewhere*.

Signs of the cross were grand gestures, often utilizing the entire body. Up to the forehead went the right hand, then below the heart, then shoulder to shoulder before clasping the other hand in an amen. Sometimes they genuflected, bending and touching the floor before repeating the gestures again and again and again.

Aspects of the church still disquieted Jeffrey. The icons remained alien presences to his mind and heart. Yet as he stood and felt the peace of worship pervade him, surrounded by the incense and murmured prayers and beautifully chanted verses, he made a conscious effort to set his judgment aside. For the moment. For this instant of seeing an unknown culture. He shut his eyes and prayed that he be able to see as he should, to understand with compassion, to witness the lives of others who struggled under burdens he could not fathom.

Jeffrey stood and watched, and for the moment was content in the enigma of all that remained unknown. And in that moment when judgment was suspended, there came a gift. A mystery. He stood in this alien world and became somehow united. Not to the others gathered here, not directly. Simply joined. His body no longer seemed to mark the boundaries to his life.

He listened, and for a brief instant he felt his heart to be listening also, hearing a voice not spoken to his ears. He heard the choir intone prayers his mind could not fathom and felt a union with the mystery of the sacrament. A communion.

The prayers rose to a crescendo, the priests' deep basso drones punctuated by lofty calls thrown heavenward by the choir. Jeffrey stood isolated within the glory of this moment and yet felt less alone than ever before in all his life. He prayed, and felt his words rising as incense to the heavenly throne room above, and truly felt as though his heart soared upward with his words.

Boundaries he had not even known existed suddenly melted to reveal vistas that called to him, challenged him to rise beyond the confines of logic and realize the deeper mysteries of living in faith. Of following the commandment, to *love*.

The Hotel Moskva was an enormous structure designed to process tourist groups with factory precision. Built in the early seventies, this hotel of a thousand rooms stretched out rather than up. Because the city rested on what formerly had been swampland and marsh islands, buildings were restricted to nine floors or less. The hotel made do with seven, but extended around a full city block.

Outside the main entrance, Yussef pushed through a crowd representative of Russia's progress to capitalism. Beggars in rags and crutches skirted the parking lot. Police mingled with illegal money changers. Crowds of hard-faced men gathered and smoked and talked and eyed passersby with the gaze of carnivores. Western tourists huddled in tight clusters and tried to hide their fear.

Directly in front of the entrance doors, dealers had pulled up four full-sized Cadillacs and two Lincolns. They dwarfed the plasticized Ladas and Muscovites parked to either side. The eventual buyers would be after symbols of the American good life as much as transport, an important fact in a land where legal gasoline purchases were limited to four gallons per month.

The crowd shoving good-naturedly about the cars consisted of the traders who filled the hotel's third and fourth floors. By day they bribed the mafia for market space; by night they filled the city's *Valuta* bars, which took only American currency. These traders came mostly from southern lands—Kazakhstan and Georgia and Uzbekistan and the Crimea—and were flush with sudden wealth. All their lives they had dreamed of the day when their fists would close around dollars, and now that day had come. They paid more than a month's average Russian wage for one night in the hotel, then spent five times that amount each night on food and vodka.

They bought the most expensive items they could afford—radios, televisions, suits, jewelry, cars, prostitutes—giving not a thought to the days to come. The barriers had come down. Their years of waiting were finally over.

Yussef took one of only four elevators to the third floor. Narrow hallways extended the length of a football field. Carpets bunched and threw out nylon tentacles. The walls were falling apart, with panels simply propped up against their frames. Lights were dim and intermittent. The sound of drunken revelry floated from nearby rooms.

Like all Russian hotels, the front desk did not issue keys, only a hotel ID card. This was taken to the appropriate floor, where a hefty woman known as a key lady inspected all arrivals. In the past, all comings and goings had been carefully noted in a multitude of books—part of the continual surveillance of all foreigners. Now, she sat alone and bored behind her desk, her power lost with the gradual dismemberment of the KGB.

Beyond the key lady's desk was a small, poorly lit lobby with a "dollar bar." Its prices were slightly lower than those of the main downstairs bar, and it attracted a crowd of hard-drinking guests.

Kiril was there waiting for him, along with a trio of his associates. To Yussef they seemed so *young*. Barely escaped from their teens. Wiry with the unfinished lightness of youth. Yet their eyes bore scars of seeing too much too soon.

"I bring greetings from your father," Yussef began.

Kiril was clearly their leader. When he showed no reaction to Yussef's greeting, the others remained mute. All four smoked their cigarettes to nubs. No paper-tube *papyrosi* cigarettes for them. They pulled Dunhills from a communal pack in never-ending turns.

Yussef drew up a chair, seated himself beside Kiril. He reached over and fingered the young man's shirt. Silk. "Very nice," Yussef said. "And is that a gold Rolex? Business must be booming."

Kiril puffed a series of casual smoke rings toward the ceiling and asked in bored tones, "What do you want?"

"Information."

"I sell cars. You want information, the KGB has opened their files. Go talk to them."

Yussef made no complaint over Kiril's attitude. Anyone who had survived what he had survived deserved the right to choose whatever attitude would see him through.

Changing borders and conquering armies had struggled over Kiril's birthplace for centuries. Lithuania, Russia, Poland, and Prussia had all at one time or another dominated his home region. And through it all, Kiril's family had declared allegiance to only one country, one that had rarely existed save in the hearts and memories of its citizens—Ukraine.

When Stalin's army drove through what before had been a border village of East Prussia, the entire population had been collected—Poles, Ukrainians, and all the Prussians who had not fled westward—and sent off to a city on Russia's southeastern border. Semipalatinsk, the largest city in Kazakhstan, had earned its first notoriety in the last century, when Fyodor Dostoyevsky had been exiled there. Then, as Stalin had continued his Russification program, Semipalatinsk had become a favorite dumping ground for Poles and Ukrainians taken from the newly Sovietized western lands.

Kiril's parents had been shipped to Semipalatinsk in the late fifties. By the time Kiril was born ten years later, Stalin had selected the area as the testing site for the Soviet Union's nuclear weapons. As a result, that city became the only place on earth where the majority of its living population witnessed a nuclear explosion with their naked eyes. Not just once, but as many as one hundred and twenty-four times.

Semipalatinsk pharmacists had experienced the same trouble stocking up-to-date medicines as the rest of the Soviet Union, but they had always managed to keep Geiger counters in stock. Families had used them daily to test their bodies and their food. By the late seventies, when even more acute shortages had hit the nation's medical system, Semipalatinsk hospitals had begun turning away all terminally ill radiation patients because of a lack of essential medicines, including anesthetics.

In the eighties, the biggest killer had been a wasting disease that locals called Semipalatinsk AIDS. It was a radiation sickness with all the symptoms of sexually transmitted AIDS. Around that same period, the region had earned the highest suicide rate in the world; the victims had mostly been young men rendered impotent through radiation. A large number of local babies had simply disappeared at birth.

Kiril's father had been one of the fortunate ones, an engineer whose skills had required resettlement in Lvov when Kiril was fourteen years old. Kiril's father and mother had returned with the faith that had sustained them through all their difficulties. But the years Kiril had spent in Semipalatinsk had left him unable to believe in anything save the cruelty of man toward man.

"I need your help," Yussef replied quietly. "Not the government's. I talk to you."

"Then we talk cars. You like a nice Audi? How about a Renault?"

"I saw the Cadillacs parked out front. Are they yours?"

Kiril cast a lazy eye down Yussef's scruffy form. "You're not the Cadillac type. Too expensive. Maybe a Lada."

"Thanks. I have one." Yussef leaned forward. "Have you—"

"Cars," the young man stated flatly. "That is all I know. How about a Skoda? You like a souvenir from Prague?"

"I come with a request from your family," Yussef persisted.

Kiril stood, lifted the trio with his eyes. "My family is a thousand kilometers and a thousand years from here."

Yussef willed himself to nod acceptance. "You were good to see me. For this I offer thanks. I will tell your family I found you well."

A flicker of something else passed in the flat depths of the boy-man's gaze. Kiril slowly drained his glass as the other young men moved a few steps away. Then he shrugged on his doeskin jacket, allowing the cigarettes to slip from his grasp and fall to the floor. He reached to the floor beside Yussef's chair and asked with the motion, "What?"

"Treasure," Yussef murmured. "Are the big men moving any? Your bosses, or anyone else's clan?"

"I am my own boss," the young man said loudly, slipping the cigarettes inside his jacket. As he turned, he quickly whispered, "Kazan Cathedral. Midnight."

I t was late afternoon when Jeffrey arrived at the United States Consulate, and the long day was taking its toll. Jouncing taxi rides from the airport to the guesthouse to the Lavra to the consulate had left his neck and back complaining loudly. Casey arrived to find him rotating his head, trying to work out the kinks.

Casey stuck out his hand, and asked, "Hope you're not still suffering from our run-in with the wall."

"No," Jeffrey said, shaking hands. "Still having problems from that earlier accident."

"Sorry to hear that. Well, the Consul General's got a free minute or two, so let's go on up."

In the elevator Jeffrey asked what he had been wondering since their first meeting, "Are you with the CIA?"

"My brief says I'm assigned to the cultural attaché," Casey replied with a perfectly straight face. "And there are some questions you just don't ask. Not ever."

Allbright tossed his reading glasses onto the pile of papers scattered across his desk as the pair appeared in his doorway. "Good to see you again, Jeffrey. Come on in."

"I tried to call you from the guesthouse when I arrived," Jeffrey apologized, accepting the man's firm handshake. "But all I got was the sound of a war zone."

"Yeah, this city has a phone system that would do Beirut proud. Have a seat in the comfortable chair there by the window." He motioned Casey into the seat alongside his desk. "When did you get back?"

"This morning." Jeffrey related what he had learned from Father Anatoli. "Have you had any word about the missing girl?"

"No, afraid not. But I may have picked up a little something for your Ukrainian friends. Have you seen them yet?"

"They weren't at the guesthouse when I went by, so I left a message."

"Casey's buddies over at the KGB," Allbright began, permitting himself a small smile. "Boy, I can hardly believe I'd ever say such a thing. Anyway, they've been scouring the earth. Came up with a lot of evidence—nothing solid, mind you, but enough to convince them that something big is going down."

"Like what?"

"Like an organized effort to make a fair-sized killing in one fell swoop," Casey replied. "Appears they've been skimming bits and pieces from a lot of different museums. Probably churches as well. Small pieces, mostly. No centerpiece, no pride of the collection, nothing that would attract too much attention, except in your case. The anti-crime squad say the thieves probably figured your Ukrainian treasure wasn't supposed to be there in the first place, so they'd be fairly safe just taking it all."

"Who are they?"

Casey shrugged. "The lines separating the KGB, the mafia, and the old Party bosses are pretty much nonexistent these days. Looks like they've pooled their muscle and knowledge and gone for the big one."

"That's what these people are saying, anyway," Allbright added. "And others, too, some of whom I would tend to trust when it comes to observations like these."

"There may be some kind of holdup with the transaction," Casey went on. "Exactly what, nobody seems to know. But something's kept the thieves from moving the goods out of the country, or so everybody's hoping."

"It appears they decided it would be safer to stockpile everything here," Allbright explained, "instead of exporting it in dribs and drabs."

"And risk having a small consignment be discovered and alert the authorities," Jeffrey guessed.

"Exactly. They have supposedly collected everything at a safe house here in the Saint Petersburg area. From there they were planning to make one massive shipment."

"Only they haven't done so yet."

"Not according to rumors. Which is all we've got to go on right now."

"My friends will be glad to receive this news," Jeffrey said. "Thanks."

"Don't mention it."

Allbright leaned forward. "Two things, Jeffrey. First, I think it is time you told them about Leslie Ann Stevens and ask them to keep an eye out. If the big boys are involved here, her disappearance may somehow be connected with the thefts."

Jeffrey nodded, then winced as the motion sent the familiar lance of pain up his back. "Sure."

Allbright was immediately solicitous. "What's the matter?"

"Nothing."

"Man's still got trouble with his neck," Casey explained.

"I'm all right, really," Jeffrey protested. "It's just been a long day."

"Well, let's finish this up so you can get back to your hotel. The second thing is, tell your friends to be careful. You, too. These boys don't play by the book."

"I understand," Jeffrey said. "So what do we do now?"

"Wait. Patience is a virtue in this business, and a necessity if you're going to work in Russia." Allbright rose to his feet. "Go get some rest, son; you look done in. As soon as we hear anything more, we'll be in touch."

——

When Jeffrey arrived back at his hotel that evening, he found that his message for Ivona and Yussef had not been collected; Sergei had not seen either since early morning. Jeffrey went to his room, lay down, found himself too wound up to rest. The pain in his neck pounded in time to his heartbeat, and he was not quite weary enough to sleep through the discomfort. Jeffrey rose from his bed, opened his case, swallowed a couple of aspirin, and drew out the pair of gifts he had purchased with Sergei's money.

Back downstairs, the grandmother beamed her toothless thanks when Jeffrey presented her with the pint-sized copperplated model of Big Ben and the Beefeater guard doll. Sergei was moved beyond words, making do with a series of shoulder pats and handshakes. Then he went into the kitchen and returned with two heavily laden plates. He set them down, moved behind the bar, and pulled out a bottle of vodka.

"Come, we drink to your return."

"Thanks, but I'm not a drinker."

"Usually, yes, this is fine. But tonight very special."

"No, really—"

"You new in Russia. Vodka old Russian tradition. You take."

"No, I—"

"Yes, yes, Yussef explain vow. Make sure we have much Pepsi. But this good Russian vodka. Best in world. You—"

The grandmother lashed out with a shrill volley of words. Sergei raised his hands in submission. "Grandmother, she say more Russian men should take such vows. Wait. I get you Pepsi."

He went out to the kitchen, and handed Jeffrey the warm drink. "Take. Please. Friends, yes?"

Jeffrey took the glass, agreed, "Friends."

Sergei motioned toward the gifts, and said, "Thank you, friend." He drained his glass and gestured to the food. "Is for you. Another thanks. Good Russian food. People come now, easy to see only bad—bad people, bad danger, bad food. But Russians have art of food. Very old. Very good. Here. You try."

The plates held a variety of miniature cold cuts, Russian style. Caviar and sour cream on cold *blinis*, or thin potato pancakes. Salty fish on dark bread, smoked fish on light, both with heavy dollops of butter. Thinly sliced nuggets of roast beef with homemade mustard. Mushrooms, both fresh and pickled. Tiny cucumbers, spring onions, and baby tomatoes sliced and served in iced vinegar and pepper. Jeffrey tasted one of the fish, pronounced it delicious.

The grandmother said something which her grandson translated as, "You are again here for work on the winter palace?"

"Yes." He reached slowly toward the plate—gradual, deliberate motions were easier on his back. He then sat and ate and held his head carefully still as he listened to them go back and forth in Russian.

"Politics and romance," Sergei said suddenly.

Jeffrey worked to focus his attention beyond the pain. "What?"

"My grandmother, she used to visit Markov palace. Back when a little girl. Her mother was Markov's number-two chef." Sergei poured himself another shot. "Once she even saw the czar."

He took another miniature sandwich, this one containing a slice of smoked sausage topped with fresh horseradish. Chewing made his muscles ache more, but the food was delicious. "I've got enough romance in my life just now, thanks."

The grandmother laughed like an old woman, a dry remnant of what once probably had been light and musical. "Young prince Markov," Sergei translated. "So handsome. And so naughty."

"You mean the current Prince Markov's father?" Jeffrey asked.

The young man's interest sparked. "You know Markov?"

"I've met him," Jeffrey replied, deciding there was no harm in discussing it among friends. "Once."

Sergei turned to his grandmother, who chomped her toothless way through one of the delicacies. When Sergei translated the news she became even more voluble. "Yes, this was in 1916, so must be father. The young prince," Sergei said for her, "he was engaged to girl from big family. Girl very nice, but Markov, he have other girlfriends. Many, many girlfriends. He, how you say, make wedding wait?"

"Postpone," Jeffrey said, massaging his neck with one hand.

"Yes. But father old, sick. He worried about family. Then girl's family start saying they stop wedding, young prince never marry. So they make day. But young prince, he still have many girlfriends, only secret. Except servants, of course, they know everything. They know of secret stairs to cellar, and door from cellar at back of garden."

Jeffrey smiled politely, sipped at his Pepsi without raising his head.

The grandmother misunderstood his lack of interest. "She thinks you not believe," Sergei reported.

"That's not it," he protested. "It's just that my back—" But she was not listening, and the grandson did not dare stop with his translation. "I know exactly where was secret stairway. They go from young Markov's chambers down to cellar."

Jeffrey played at wide-eyed interest while his nerves continued to throb.

"Grandmother spent much time there when she was little girl. Servants showed her everything," Sergei continued, drinking and translating with equal verve. "Markov chambers have long hall for clothes. Doors have paintings. Paintings were from old Russian fairy tales. Box with lever for stairs was behind one of troika. You know troika, sleigh with three horses?"

"Yes," Jeffrey replied, and decided he had sat as long as he was able. "Please thank her for me and say how fascinating it was to hear of Markov's father as a young man. But I think I need to get a breath of air."

Gingerly he stepped outside, climbed the six stairs, and stood leaning on the metal banister. He could go no farther. His pain hung like a veil across his brain, and through it he suddenly felt danger everywhere.

He gripped the railing and breathed metallic-tasting air. The pollution turned passing headlights into gleaming pillars as solid-looking as the cars. Jeffrey felt the same sense of descending into agony that had marked his dinnertime confrontation with Ivona back in Ukraine. For the moment, it dominated his world.

Impurities hung so thick in the air that streetlights wore golden globes twenty feet across. As he watched, these globes seemed to pulse, driven by the unseen beat of the city's heart, pacing in time to the late-night trucks and cars thundering by. He seemed to see shadows coalesce into dark shapes that slipped among the throngs of hard-faced people to whisper words of rage and hopelessness into unprotected ears. He stood there helplessly, his mind too foggy to pray, as the lights coalesced and clustered around him as well, mocking him with words that pierced his heart and mind.

We are the legacies of centuries past, they chanted, and in his deepening gloom Jeffrey knew the words to be true. Look and see those for whom you pray, they cried. And he did, and he saw the chains of history and the manacles of fatigue and the shackles of darkest despair. Go home, the shapes mocked. Your place is not here. We are many, and you are nothing. Go home and leave us to our work. Pray not for those already lost.

Jeffrey turned and fled as fast as leaden feet would carry him, through the lobby and up the stairs and into his room and away from their mocking tones. As he carefully lay his head upon his pillow, he knew an instant's gratitude that at least this time he had managed to suffer through the moment of pain alone.

Under the Soviet regime, the Kazan Cathedral had been renamed the Museum of the History of Religion and Atheism, a suitably bulky Communist title. Yussef remembered seeing its graceful colonnade in his childhood textbooks, the same books that had classified Christianity as a dangerous Western cult.

Only two of Saint Petersburg's multitude of churches had been allowed to remain open as houses of worship during the Soviet years—serving a population of five million people. A few had been closed and then reopened as meeting halls or recital chambers or museums—always with great fanfare and, according to the propaganda releases, always at the request of the Soviet people. Others had been used for less noble purposes; the Cathedral of the Holy Trinity, for instance, had become one of the city's three central storehouses for potatoes. The Cathedral of the Holy Spirit had been razed to make way for the Finland train station. Most others had faced with a similar fate, blown up and bulldozed and rebuilt as apartments or offices in the blockhouse style known as Stalinist constructionism.

Yussef kept away from the romantically entwined couples and the home-going revelers and paced impatiently along the colonnades, waiting for Kiril, the car dealer, to appear. Overhead the sky was cloudless, yet so laden with pollution that the stars remained lost behind a copper-colored veil.

The kid slid from the surrounding shadows and sauntered toward Yussef. He was perhaps nine years old, but it was hard to tell. Despite the heat still trapped and held firmly to the earth by the pollution, the kid wore a man's sweatshirt that fell to below his knees. Beneath that were threadbare jeans and ancient sneakers secured with binder twine around his ankles. The outfit made him look more undersized than he already was. His scrawny face had the unwashed leathery cast of a full-time street kid, and he took Yussef's measure with a professional gaze.

His appearance made his words even more startling as he recited in English, "Postcards, you buy postcards, yes? Look. Leningrad, Hermitage, Fortress. Twenty postcards, one dollar. You buy?"

Yussef was genuinely offended. He replied in Russian, "Do I look to you like a rich foreign tourist?"

"You look to me like the trader Yussef from the Wild Plains," the kid retorted. "And the price is now five dollars American."

"For postcards?"

"You buy, you see." The kid was having a good time. "You know somebody who likes silk shirts?"

Yussef reached into his pocket. "One dollar. No more."

"Ten."

He peeled off three, punched the air between them. "Add this to what Kiril already paid you."

The kid grabbed the money, tossed over the cards, retorted, "Go back to the country, peasant. City streets are dangerous for the likes of you."

Yussef nodded. "His words?"

"And mine." The kid added a rude gesture and scampered off.

Yussef strolled carefully back along the lighted way until he was well and truly lost within the nighttime crowd. He then flagged a taxi, gave his address, and released the postcards from their band. A tiny piece of paper fluttered free. He picked it up, read, "The storage point is a winter palace somewhere in Saint Petersburg."

CHAPTER 37

Jeffrey awoke to the glory of no more pain.

His neck and back remained stiff and quietly complaining as he washed and dressed and prepared for the day, but the overbearing discomfort of the evening before had vanished with the night. Gone, too, was the depression that the pain and the city had visited upon him.

As he shaved, a tiny cymbal jangled in his mind, nagging him that something important had been overlooked. But the internal voice was not strong enough to disturb his great good humor. Jeffrey descended the stairs, resisting the urge to break into song.

He accepted a note Sergei gave him from Ivona, saying that she and Yussef would be coming by soon and that he was to wait for them. He made sympathetic noises over Sergei's ashen expression, watched Sergei gingerly set his coffee cup down on his saucer and wince at the noise it made. He asked, "What did you do to yourself last night?"

"Vodka," Sergei whispered hoarsely, measuring the coffee out with bloodshot eyes. "Too much vodka."

The grandmother moved over from her customary position by the ceramic-lined stove and chattered away. Sergei translated dully, "Grandmother, she wish to thank you once more for her gifts."

"Tell her it was my pleasure."

Sergei shuffled back to the kitchen. While he was gone, Jeffrey found that the language barrier between him and the grandmother had begun to dissolve; he understood a surprising amount of what she had to say. He sat and sipped his coffee as the old woman first described her vast collection of memorabilia, then bemoaned the sad state of affairs in her fair city, before launching into a detailed analysis of her own aches and pains, then finishing off with a rip-snorting dissection of the present government.

When Sergei returned bearing breakfast, Jeffrey told him, "Your grandmother is a truly fascinating woman."

Sergei struggled to exhume a smile, set down the platter at Jeffrey's elbow. "Here, friend. Eat. You need, believe me, you need."

During breakfast Jeffrey continued to be pestered by the sensation that there was something which he had overlooked. It occurred to him that he had not contacted the Protestant minister, Evan Collins, so after breakfast he made the call. Jeffrey explained the reasons behind his meetings with the Orthodox priest and the Ukrainian bishop. The preacher showed the same quality of patient listening he had displayed in person.

"Any time, any place," he replied when Jeffrey asked if he would be interested in such a meeting. "The sooner the better, as far as I'm concerned."

"That's great, thanks."

"No sir, I thank *you*. This is an opportunity I've been wanting ever since I arrived. You're to be congratulated."

"I haven't done anything."

"If nothing else, you've allowed yourself to be used as the Lord's willing servant," Reverend Collins replied. "And I appreciate your filling me in. I don't suppose there has been any further word about Leslie Ann."

"Not that the Consul General mentioned to me."

"She is a very fine young lady. We all miss her terribly, and her parents are beside themselves with worry. You be sure and let me know if there's ever anything we can do to help you out."

"I will, thanks."

"Fine. And give me a call when you've fixed the meeting, Jeffrey. Like I said, any time, any place. I will look forward to hearing from you."

Jeffrey set down the phone, still beset by the feeling that there was something important he had left undone. He searched his mind once more, came up blank, then returned upstairs for a Bible reading and prayer time while he waited for Yussef and Ivona.

Yussef entered the miniature hotel lobby, greeted a subdued Sergei, and sat down to wait while Sergei went to tell Jeffrey of their arrival. Ivona sat beside him, consumed by the unease she habitually showed around Jeffrey. He understood the reasons, yet could find nothing to say that might improve the situation, so he remained silent.

Yussef had never had time for religion. It had called to him, but he had not responded. He had not cared to. Until now.

Yussef was too honest to ever deny the interest in his heart. But not every hunger was good for a man with goals, not every craving a call to be answered.

During his younger years, religion had meant guilt and fear and danger. It was laced with mumblings in old Russian, intoned by bearded strangers dressed all in black. He found the incense suffocating, and loathed the taint of superstition. In faith he saw only a prison of memorized prayers and endless Masses and feast days and hopes that if he did as the priest wanted, as the rituals demanded, he would be granted some poorly defined eternal release. No, religion was not for the likes of him.

His desire for a doorway to God was not so great as his demand for freedom. He had fought too hard, sacrificed too much, to accept chains from heaven.

Yet this baffling Westerner challenged him. Not with words, however. With silence. He pointed a way Yussef thought could not exist, and he did so not with demands, but rather with his life. Here was a man who spoke directly with God. Not through a church or a ritual or a chant or a priest. By himself. For himself. Jeffrey was strong in the world of business, yet somehow he also remained above the world. He demanded nothing of Yussef. Yet by his life he pushed Yussef to question everything he had ever assumed of belief in God. He was a *man*. Yet he was also a man of *faith*.

Jeffrey clattered down the stairs, looking both relaxed and happy. He patted Sergei on the back, and said something that made them both smile, giving the young Russian a gentle push up the stairs and pointing toward his room, as though urging him to go lie down. Then he turned and greeted them both.

As soon as they were reseated, knowing he needed to do this while his resolve still held, Yussef took a breath. "I wish to speak with you about your Christian faith."

———

"Nothing could bring me greater joy," Jeffrey replied.

"I wish to know God. Yet I find no comfort in ritual," Ivona translated, her voice a dull monotone. "I find no hope in tradition. Only chains."

Jeffrey winged an instant of prayer upward and spoke from his heart. "Since beginning my travels in Eastern Europe, I've seen a lot of church rituals that are totally different from what I was brought up with. I suppose a lot of the people I've met here would find the rituals in my own Baptist church pretty strange, too. What I think it comes down to, though, is that everyone needs to make an honest examination of his own heart. If the ritual itself is their way of earning salvation, then the Bible says this is wrong. Ritual empty of living faith is dead religion."

He waited as Ivona concluded her shaky, hesitant translation and marveled at the intensity with which Yussef listened.

"But every church I've ever been to has ritual," Jeffrey continued. "We come at a certain time. We stand. We sit. We greet others. We sing from a book. We hear the minister pray for us. We listen to our preacher give a sermon. And so on.

"When we follow this pattern," Jeffrey went on, "I think we are trying to give definition to the Invisible. We are setting a form to the formless. We are giving an earthly structure to our worship of the Almighty Lord. So long as the ritual remains just that, nothing more than a means of guiding us and focusing our attention on Him, then what we do in the form of rituals is probably okay. Maybe necessary. It is part of being human. But I like to think that when we reach heaven, we will find that all ritual vanishes, because we won't need it then. We will be part of God's eternal home."

Yussef continued to nod slowly as Ivona reluctantly completed her translation. "Then what is the purpose of your worship?"

"The central purpose for all Christian worship," Jeffrey replied, "is salvation."

"And how is this mine?"

"By accepting Jesus Christ as your Savior," Jeffrey replied. "By accepting that you are a sinner who has fallen short of God's glory, and then by recognizing Jesus as the Son who came to die in your place, so that you might have eternal life."

"That is all?"

"It is the bridge of salvation. It is the first step of a walk leading toward the Father, a walk that will continue all your life." Jeffrey searched his face, and asked, "Do you want to pray with me now?"

Yussef thought a moment, then decided, "No. This first time I would like to do so alone. It is not required for me to do this with another, yes?"

"Just you and God," Jeffrey replied. "Nobody else is necessary."

"Then I shall do it," he said, his voice as determined as his expression. "I shall speak with God as you say. Perhaps later we can pray together, yes?"

"I would like that," Jeffrey said, "more than I know how to put into words."

Yussef released an explosive breath. "I thank you, Jeffrey Sinclair."

"It is my honor," Jeffrey replied, "and my greatest pleasure."

"It would be good if we could now speak about other things."

"To business," Jeffrey agreed.

Their discussion took the better part of an hour as they compared notes and revealed their discoveries. Ivona never returned to her habitual singsong, however. She remained locked within some internal struggle that left her with barely the strength to translate, much less join in the conversation with her own ideas.

Yussef checked his watch and rose to his feet. "I have to check with someone before he begins his lunchtime work. There is only a very slim chance that I shall learn what I need to know, but it is the only other possibility I can think of just now."

"Perhaps the anti-crime squad will come up with the missing link."

"Perhaps," Yussef agreed doubtfully, "but it would be far better to bring them in once we have the answer ourselves, rather than wait at the door and beg for crumbs. If they find the treasure first, we have no guarantee that what was taken from us will be restored to us."

"Good luck, then."

Yussef extended his hand. "You are a good friend." Jeffrey saw him through the door, then felt an invisible hand drawing him back toward where Ivona sat downcast and silent. He lowered himself into the seat and asked, "Is something wrong?"

"I do not understand you," she said, exasperated almost beyond words. "The church is a sacred place. Yet you never even mention it. But this is where we have a relationship with God."

"I really believe our relationship with Jesus should be contained in every hour of every day," Jeffrey said quietly, "not restricted to a certain time and place."

"Christ established the church to be the center of worship," Ivona replied heatedly. "Over the centuries it has been the church that has drawn men to God."

"The church as a body of believers," Jeffrey asked calmly, "or the church as a building?"

"It is in the church that we have priests who can assist us in understanding spiritual matters," she said, so angry the words tumbled out upon one another. "In the church we have traditions handed down over centuries that maintain our sense of community and of faith. Where would the church be if everyone was like you? You pray at the table, you pray in the car, you pray on the street corner. Where is the sacred place where you go to meet God?"

Jeffrey responded calmly, "Ivona, the ritual will never save you."

"I—" She stopped in midsentence. "What?"

"Jesus Christ does not reside in ritual. He resides in your heart."

The faltering confusion returned to her eyes, but not the hostility. Now there was only naked anguish. "You are wrong. Simplistic and wrong."

He shook his head. "This truth is both simple and eternal. You either have a personal relationship with your Savior or you do not. If you don't, no ritual on earth will bridge that gap."

He leaned forward, filled with a certainty that surprised even him. "Unless your ritual is done for Christ and toward Christ, unless it is truly Spirit-filled, it has no meaning. If not . . ."

Jeffrey stopped, searched her aching gaze, wished there were some way simply to give her the peace himself. "If not," he continued softly, "then you need to go before the Lord on your knees. In solitude. In humility. You must ask Christ to fill your life with His everlasting love. And meaning."

Sadko's was a restaurant favored by the city's underworld bosses, a smoke-filled din of imitation Western elegance and outrageous prices. Hard-faced men in tight-fitting suits cut deals in quiet voices while dining on Frenchified dishes. Hired muscle slouched around the room's periphery, decked out in dark colors, sporting a variety of weapons, and holding their bosses' portable telephones like badges of honor.

Yussef pulled his rusting car up at the far corner of the street, away from the early arrivals' Mercedes and BMWs and Volvos. He hustled down the filthy alleyway leading to the service entrance and hoped that he was not too late.

The average Russian wage was 450 rubles per month, less than one American dollar at current exchange rates. With the new power of *green money*, spoken in English and denoting dollars, all rules were off. When one dollar could buy eleven pounds of fresh meat in a starving land, and two dollars could purchase an air ticket from Moscow to Saint Petersburg—farther than from Boston to Washington—all barriers were down.

The result was visible everywhere. A surgeon became a doorman at a restaurant catering to foreigners. An avionics engineer became a hotel bartender. Bars and restaurants and nightclubs sprouted leather luxury, were guarded by former KGB officers dressed in evening wear, and over their door bore the single word *Valuta*. It was a world within a world, open only to those who found a means of obtaining *green money*.

A *valutnaya*, a currency girl, earned four years' average earnings in one night. A black-market tout gained eighteen months' salary with each scalped ticket to the Kirov or Bolshoi. Taxi drivers

shunned anyone who did not dress in Western style. Eyes on the
street hunted out wandering tourists and hungered for the immea-
surable wealth they carried in their pockets.

Yussef opened the restaurant's back door, spoke in most respectful tones, and asked if he might have one word with a friend
about a most urgent matter. Then he waited, the scarfaced back-
door bouncer watching him with eyes the color of a very dark pool.

His friend blanched when Yussef came into view, recovered
quickly, came forward with hand outstretched, and said loudly,
"Yussef, so kind of you to bring word personally. How is my
brother?"

Yussef allowed the man to guide him back outside into the
alley. He answered quietly, "Your brother the bishop needs your
help. Badly."

"So badly that he would wish to see me dead?" The man hissed
his words through teeth clenched in fear. "What is it that could not
wait for a more private meeting?"

"I tried your apartment," Yussef replied. "I was told you had
moved, and I knew nowhere else to go."

"This is true," the man subsided slightly, but his eyes continued
to dance their nervous gait up and down the narrow way. "Business
has been good. The pay is nothing, but the tips are sometimes in
dollars. I have been able to take a larger flat."

"I am happy for you," Yussef replied, and lowered his voice
even more. "The Tombek clan. They come here still?" At the name
the man's face turned the color of old bone. "Do not ask, Yussef."

"I must."

"Horrid things happen to people who ask about such as them.
Things from your worst nightmares."

"Still, I must. Have you ever heard mention of a winter palace?
It would be a place where things are stored."

The man wiped a face damp from more than just the day's
gathering heat. "I waited on them three nights this week. Enough
to make me wish for a government job that paid in rubles. I hold
my breath and pray unceasingly whenever I approach their table."

"And you heard something," Yussef said, tensing in anticipation.

"It is a place on the Fontanka," he replied, the effort of forcing air through over-tensed muscles causing his whispers to rise and fall in power. "Near the old royal stables."

Yussef jerked as though slapped. Hard. "It can't be."

"People like that can't be," the man hissed. "But they are. Now go. If the walls have ears, my children will starve."

Jeffrey was out the door, his hand raised to flag a taxi, when he realized what it was that had kept nagging at him. He dropped his arm, turned, and raced back into the hotel.

Sergei was less than excited to see him again. His eyes resembled eggs fried for several hours on a very hot stove. But Ivona was nowhere to be found, and Jeffrey knew no one else to translate. So he grabbed the young man by the shirt-sleeve and dragged him complaining to where his grandmother sat knitting by the little parlor fireplace.

"What, what," Sergei complained, then raised a hand to the side of his head. "Ah, too loud. I speak too loud. What you want, Sinclair?"

"Your grandmother," Jeffrey puffed, suddenly out of breath. "She said something last night about a cellar in the Markov palace."

With a martyr's long-suffering expression, Sergei translated, listened to her reply, told Jeffrey, "She say, of course there is cellar. What you do in that house for so long?"

"How big a cellar," Jeffrey demanded.

"Size of whole house," he translated, as puzzled as the old lady. "Bigger. Run back under garden."

Jeffrey smacked the table beside him. "It's there," he breathed. "It's been there all along."

"Of course it's there," Sergei replied, misunderstanding. "Big house like that, have cellar for food, wine, heat, maybe treasure room. How you miss such a thing, my grandmother wants to know."

But Jeffrey was already moving. He ripped a sheet from the note pad by the telephone, scribbled furiously, flung it at Sergei. As he raced for the door, he shouted over his shoulder, "Give this to Ivona or Yussef, whoever shows up first. Tell them to meet me there as soon as they come in. Tell them I think I know!"

=

The architect was bent over his blueprints when Jeffrey arrived. He had made a trestle table by taking a door off its hinges and laying it across two sawhorses. The entire front hall was awash in partially uncoiled drawings. Jeffrey flung a greeting toward the bespectacled man as he raced on past.

First the kitchen, just to be sure. He tore through the main scullery, scrambled down the feeble stairs, carefully searched the cramped storage room. The walls were filthy with the dirt of ages. If anyone had erected a false barrier it was impossible to tell. Tapping on the walls yielded nothing but a shower of dust.

Back up the stairs, down the hall connecting to the ground-floor parlors, scrambling over the pipes and steel sheeting and rod-iron, thinking all the while how easy it would be to disguise a former cellar entrance under all this junk. Just as Yussef had said about hiding contraband in his own car; it was all too heavy to lift unless there was a very good reason.

Through the smaller private parlor, the one formerly belonging to the young prince, Vladimir Markov's father. Through the dust-blanketed study, his footsteps skidding as he took the turning into the hallway leading to the bath and the bedroom and the dressing salon. And the wardrobes.

There were six of them, lining both sides of a chamber made into a hallway by their size. They rose from floor to distant ceiling, each door a full four feet wide. Jeffrey opened each door in turn, the massive hardwood frames groaning with disuse but swinging easily, testifying to the quality of their original workmanship. Even through the heavy white-wash, it was possible to trace the wood's grain, to see where the full-length mirrors had hung, to see how the drawers had been fitted and the shelves made to swing out so that even the item farthest back could be easily retrieved. It was also easy to see where the framed paintings had been placed.

Jeffrey searched each of the small shadow-frames in turn, his heart beating a frantic pace. Not until he had worked his way past the first wardrobe did he realize that in order to have a box behind it, the painting Sergei's grandmother had spoken of would have to be set upon something other than a door.

There were four painting-shells not on the doors themselves, two set at either end of the long chamber. Jeffrey struck gold on the third try. At his gentle pressure the wooden block squeaked aside on hidden hinges, revealing a hiding space perhaps a foot square. His hand scrabbled in and back, his lungs chuffing like an ancient locomotive as he found the knob. And pressed. And felt the wall beside him tremble as something unseen gave way.

He pulled his hand out, looked into the closet next to him, and saw that the back section had swung out and away. Leading down into the gloom was a set of ancient stairs.

A shout from the front hallway made him jump two feet in the air. Carefully he sealed the little box, then spent a frantic minute trying to figure out how to close a door that had no handle. The shouting continued unabated as he settled on a hairsbreadth of breathing space, sealed all the closet doors, and raced back to the front hall.

Sergei was dancing a full-throated, panic-stricken two-step when Jeffrey appeared. "They come! They come! My grandmother, she speak with them. I escape through kitchen! They know your name! They come for you!"

Jeffrey fought for meager breath and asked, "Who has?"

"They! They! Who needs a name for terror?"

His heart tripped into a higher beat than he thought possible. "You mean the mafia?"

"Mafia, KGB, who knows the name these days? They seek you, Sinclair. That is all you need to know."

His mind froze, unable to move beyond the point of, I've found it! "But what for?"

Sergei turned, exasperated. "What do you think for, to dance? They come to make you disappear!"

His legs grew weak. "What do I do?"

"You wish to live? Yes? Good. Then leave, Sinclair. Go to consulate. Run. Fly. Go now."

A car scrunched on the gravel lining the main entryway. Sergei swung around at the sound, backed away from the door, groaned, "My head hurts too much to die."

Jeffrey's mind raced into high gear. He turned to the panic-stricken architect. "Tell them this. You let yourself in with your own keys, as usual. You were here alone. You haven't seen me since yesterday."

The architect yammered in fear, "But I—"

Sergei hissed a soft scream at him in Russian. Footsteps sounded along the drive.

Jeffrey grabbed his friend's arm, pulled him back through the main hall and into Markov's private salon. Jeffrey moved in frantic haste as Sergei scrambled and drew short chopping breaths. Together they raced back through the private rooms. Sergei stopped at the dressing chamber, saw a bathroom with barred walls, a shuttered bedroom, moaned, "We shall soon be corpses."

"Not yet," Jeffrey urged. He flung open the closet, pushed out the back wall, and asked, "Do you have any matches?"

"What?"

"Never mind. Come on, come on, down the stairs."

Sergei took in the secret doorway and the darkened depths beyond with eyes the size of dinner plates. "What this is?"

"Compliments of your grandmother. Down the stairs."

Jeffrey followed him in, pulled the closet door closed behind him, stepped down three stairs he could not see, fumbled and pushed the back wall-door shut on muffled voices.

As quietly as they could in utter blackness, they hustled down the stairs. When they stepped off onto cold concrete flooring, Jeffrey heard Sergei fumble about. There was a click, a spark, and a small flame pushed the gloom back three paces. What stood revealed was enough to rob Jeffrey of his last remaining breath.

Treasure.

———

A lifetime's experience had trained Yussef for this moment.

The instant he spotted the car outside the guesthouse's front entrance, Yussef hunched his shoulders and continued steadily around the corner. There he parked his car, weighed his choices, and decided he had no alternative but to see if there were any chance, any chance at all.

He made his way through the interconnecting *dvurr*—the cramped apartment-lined courtyards—until he arrived at the back of the guesthouse. He glanced through a ground-floor window and was both reassured and mightily worried. The guesthouse kitchen was empty save for the old lady, who sat in a chair by the unlit stove and wailed a constant note of wordless pain.

Yussef glanced about, tapped softly, then raised the glass farther and stepped through. "The American. Where is he?"

"Gone," she keened. "First I tell him where to dig his grave. Then I send my grandson to join him."

"Where? Where did they go, old woman?"

"The palace, the palace," she moaned. "Had I never opened my mouth, oh, my beloved grandson."

"Markov's palace?" Yussef resisted the urge to shake her. "He's been working there for more than a week. What could you tell him that he did not already know?"

But the old woman would say no more. She simply held out an arthritic fist, which clutched a crumpled, tear-streaked paper. Yussef pried open the fingers, saw the writing was English. He shoved it in his pocket.

Quietly Yussef moved forward at a crouch, peered through the doorway, saw nothing, no one. This was a guest-house for citizens of the former Soviet empire. They could smell such trouble a world away and knew precisely when to be away. Anywhere would do. Just away.

He raced through the lobby and up the stairs, then stood at the landing, wishing he had thought to ask which was her room. "Ivona," he hissed. Then louder, "Ivona!"

A door opened to reveal a rumpled Ivona, a cold compress applied to her forehead. "What is it?"

"A day for pain," he replied, grabbing her arm. "You have on shoes? Good. We go. Now."

"What? Why?" But something in his tone and tension made her follow without question.

Straighten up here, now, yes, calmly reaching the landing and walking past the window that looked out over the idling car where two hard-faced killers waited, waited, like carnivores tracking their prey. Back through the kitchen, pause for a word of comfort to the old woman, a pat on her shoulder, a promise he hoped he could fulfill. Open the window and help Ivona through, then himself. Now straighten and hurry and hope that ever-curious eyes would just this once be searching elsewhere.

When they were back in his car and underway and both were able to breathe again, Ivona said, "Tell me."

"First read this." Yussef plucked the note from his pocket and handed it to Ivona, who translated, "It is all in the palace. I know where. Jeffrey."

She looked at him askance, demanded, "He has found the treasure?"

"And perhaps his own death. We must hurry."

She repeated, "Tell me."

He did, in the fewest possible words. "I will drop you by a taxi stand. Go to the bishop. Tell him our only hope is to gather at the palace."

"Who should gather?"

"Everyone. Any call that can be made must be made. Any friend who is near must come. *Must* come. Our only hope, our only safety, is in numbers."

"But we know nothing for certain." Softly. Without the strength to truly protest. "And he has been working there for over a week. How could he have missed something so important until now?"

"This I feel in my gut to be the place and the time," Yussef said, pulling up to a rank of taxis. He turned to Ivona. "I have no answers to your questions, no way to be sure except to go back and ask the men sitting out before the guesthouse. Shall I do that, Ivona Aristonova? Shall I?"

Ivona remained silent.

"No, I thought not. Go. Tell the bishop. For the life of my new friend, tell him to hurry."

Ivona climbed from the car and asked, "And you?"

Yussef put the car into gear, spoke through the open window, "Do you remember if Jeffrey said the American Consul General speaks Russian?"

———

Stacked from floor to an arched ceiling lost in darkness were boxes and sacks spilling treasure. Piled in careless heaps. Tied in frantic bundles. Wrapped in packing blankets and sealed with tape. Spilling from overstuffed crates. Jeffrey and Sergei did a dual open-mouth spin of the room until the lighter heated up enough to burn Sergei's finger. Then a stifled curse, a clatter, and darkness.

"You dropped it," Jeffrey moaned, immediately on his knees and fumbling in the utter black.

"Here, I have." A rustling, tearing sound, then light once more, with Sergei's hand protected by a segment of his shirt. Jeffrey looked about, spotted the remnants of several candles, plucked them from the jutting stone shelf. He held the longest shred up for Sergei to light.

"What now?" Sergei asked.

"Your grandmother said something about another exit at the back of the garden," Jeffrey said, concentrating as he struggled to get his bearings, then pointing down a shadowy passage that mawed before them.

Sergei hung back. "That was long ago, Sinclair. Seventy, eighty years."

"So what would you rather do?" Jeffrey was growing frantic. Now was not the time for debate. "Sit around until we're hungry enough to eat gold? Maybe form a two-man reception committee for the next crew that comes down here?"

Sergei nodded. "You are right. We go."

They made their slow way through chamber after treasure-strewn chamber. Jeffrey struggled against his professional training, managed not to spend too much time cataloguing what he was passing. But he couldn't help giving out the occasional gasp or groan, yearning to pick up and carry along. Now it was Sergei's single-minded scramble that urged them along. The man knew much better than he what loomed behind them.

The long passage finally narrowed, then narrowed once more, until they left the treasure behind and moved into a dank, foul-smelling tunnel lined with the slime of ages. The tunnel then dead-ended, the solid rock wall before them offering no clue, no hope. To the right was a small door with an ancient iron clasp rusted shut. To the left a second door, this one bearing a newer padlock.

A thought struck Jeffrey hard enough to overcome any natural logic. His heart in his throat, he knocked softly on the left-hand door.

Behind him Sergei hissed a question, warning, and curse all in one.

"Hello," Jeffrey called softly, sweating heavily. Then he waited.

From behind the door a very small, frightened female voice said in English, "Who's there?"

===

Yussef had no idea whatsoever how to address a man of the Consul General's rank. So he chose to rely upon haste.

"Jeffrey Sinclair is my friend." Or was, if he was too late. In which case there remained no harm in hurrying for the treasure's sake.

"I would like to call him a friend as well," the Consul General of the United States replied solemnly in good Russian. "He has spoken of his friends from Ukraine as good people, people upon whom I would be confident to rely."

Yussef nodded, taking the measure of the man's tone, deciding now was the time to go with the feelings of his friend. "Jeffrey Sinclair is in danger."

"Ah."

"Possibly worse." In a few words Yussef related what had transpired that day. The Consul General stood alongside a tall, lanky, blond-haired young man who listened with singular intensity. When Yussef had finished, the Consul General turned and spoke in quick, sharp bursts to the man, who was already dialing furiously on the security desk's telephone.

Yussef felt himself draw his first full breath since driving by the guesthouse. The Americans reacted with the speed and precision of which he had heard. Here indeed was hope.

The Consul General turned back to Yussef. "I must return to my office for a moment and give instructions to my staff. We will try to call in further assistance. I must ask you to wait here. There is a strict policy of not allowing non-screened personnel beyond this point. You wish for something?"

"Go," Yussef urged. "I have a lifetime to drink and eat. My friend has perhaps only a few moments."

===

It was indeed the strangest gathering in Yussef's entire existence. But he would be forced to wait several days before realizing fully what awaited him and the Consul General as they drove into the Markov palace's main gates, followed by two carloads of marines. Taking all but one of the consulate's contingent of soldiers off duty and into civilian clothes was why they had been slightly delayed in arriving.

Standing on the palace's front steps was an Orthodox priest in flowing black robes and long, gray-flecked beard; a gray-haired gentleman in Western suit with a small gold cross in his lapel, and Ivona with Bishop Michael Denisov. Below this group was a phalanx of hard-faced men, some in uniforms, others not. Yussef stiffened at the sight, suddenly terrified for all concerned, but was stilled by the Consul General's calm explanation, "Some of these are friends of mine from the KGB. We called and asked for their assistance. The others I do not know."

"Friends and allies," Yussef replied, knowing a flood of relief as more and more familiar faces came into view. Crawling around the house's vast perimeter, leaning from upper-story windows, calling out to others unseen, were a number of allies, Ukrainians all. Those along the perimeter had armed themselves with short iron rods taken from the warehouse collection. They watched all who arrived with dangerous eyes. But there was no sign of Jeffrey Sinclair.

The Consul General climbed the stairs alongside Yussef, made brief introductions, heard the report from the architect, which confirmed both Jeffrey's arrival and the Chechen thugs' empty-handed departure. The KGB chief and the Ukrainians' appointed head man then reported that the house had been thoroughly searched. Numerous times. And nothing had been found. No sign at all.

An alarm sounded by watchmen at the front gates sent forth a score of running, shouting men. A pair of cars roared away on screeching tires, followed by racing figures, weapons held high. The KGB gathered at the base of the steps watched with evident approval, offered applause when the grinning men returned through the gates.

Yussef held out the crumpled note, and said, "Jeffrey claimed to have found the treasure here in the palace."

"Impossible," the young KGB officer replied. "I have personally been all through the manor. The grounds as well."

Yussef asked the officer, "Could your men escort me back to the guesthouse? There is an old woman who just might know the answer. But there are men outside the doors who will wish to keep us forever apart."

═══

The rust-frozen old clasp was proving infinitely harder to pry open than the newer padlock.

Jeffrey's hands were slippery with sweat as he hacked at the stubborn bolt lock with a two-foot-long, jewel-studded Byzantine cross. The floor at his feet was flecked with gold chips and thumbnail-size rubies shed by the impromptu tool.

Behind him, Sergei held their last remaining candle stub aloft and nursed a serious gash on his other arm, the result of a misplaced blow. Farther down the passage, a violently shivering Leslie Ann Stevens, wrapped in a packing blanket taken from a group of late Renaissance silver goblets, sat on a chest holding a set of ornamental medieval daggers chased in solid gold. She was supposedly keeping guard, but Jeffrey guessed the young lady was so deep into shock and sheer exhaustion that she was scarcely aware of anything about her.

He was growing increasingly frantic. The hammering was proving both futile and extremely painful. His hands ached, his fingers were so lacerated by the sharp-edged jewels that his blood formed a sticky glue under his grip. And he was making no visible progress at all.

In anger and frustration, he slammed the cross down with all his might and broke it in half. He was almost glad to see it over and done with.

Then the last candle flickered and died.

Leslie Ann Stevens let out a low moan.

He was standing in the darkness, listening to Sergei fumble with his lighter and wondering what on earth they could do to get the blasted door open when a sound at the far end of the tunnel stopped his heart. Sergei hissed a Russian oath. Leslie Ann gasped a series of terrified oh-oh-ohs.

Jeffrey closed the cell's door, fumbled with numb fingers for the shattered padlock, set it in place as best he could. Knowing it was futile. Knowing they were trapped in a dead end. Knowing they were facing death, but not knowing anything else to do. "Move back behind the bales. Quick. Sergei, give us light. Hurry."

Then the ringing voice of hope and freedom. "Jeffrey! Jeffrey Sinclair! It's Stan Allbright! Are you down here, son?"

Father Anatoli glanced at the floor and said quietly, "My brothers, we do not stand upon treasure."

"What rests beneath us," Bishop Michael agreed, "is a powder keg. A bomb ready to destroy us all."

It had been the Consul General's idea. Why not, he had suggested, place the three churchmen as joint administrators over the task of storing and dividing the treasures? The other groups, he had continued, could take joint responsibility for guarding it.

The groups had agreed with an alacrity born upon relief. After all, they had experienced decades of enmity and distrust and bloodshed, and only a few hours of this new fragile peace. It was a peace, they realized, based upon a most urgent need. A stronger and more solid footing was required for so great a treasure.

"The truce that surrounds and protects us," Father Anatoli said, "is more fragile than a single thread. It remains only because of the greater threat that still lurks outside. We must work to cement it while we still can. A quarrel between us would therefore be disastrous."

The three of them—Father Anatoli of the Russian Orthodox Church, Bishop Michael of the Ukrainian Rite Catholic Church, and Reverend Evan Collins of the Saint Petersburg Gospel Fellowship—sat together on upturned packing crates in the upstairs formal parlor of the Markov winter palace. Their conference was lighted by a pair of naked bulbs set to either side of the great mahogany entranceway.

"If we cannot work in trust with one another," Bishop Michael agreed, "how can we hope to stem the tide of conflict that will soon rise among the others?"

"And which already threatens the very life of this nation," Reverend Collins added.

"It would be a horror," Father Anatoli declared, "to see our returned fortune become the reason for further bloodshed. Better we had never found the treasure at all."

"But we have found it," Bishop Michael countered. "And with it has come a great responsibility."

"But the risk. There is wealth enough to destroy us all if we cannot unite."

"Or to heal many wounds," Reverend Collins said, "if we can."

"It is as you say," Father Anatoli acceded. "Yet our churches are so different, and conflict so familiar."

"Then let us look beyond the churches," Bishop Michael urged, "and join as brothers in Christ."

Down the hall from their own chamber, the moods of the other leaders were being shown in great bellows of argument and discussion as guard stations and duties and schedules were hammered out. The three church leaders sat in silence for a moment, listened to the shouting men and their strong oaths, and knew how easily the oaths could become curses, the words become blows.

"Too many of my people search for the salvation of a past that never was," Father Anatoli declared. "Some want the monarchy, which they declare was benevolent and beloved by all the people. Others want the Communists back in power and say they really didn't do so badly after all. Others say the church must rise back to the power of old, be the *only* church and the soul of the Russian nation." He sighed. "Such lies we tell ourselves. Such fables we feed our hopes upon."

From outside the manor came watchmen's shouted reports, ringing around the yard every three or four minutes, echoed from within the palace by their fellow guards. And for now, within their chamber, all was quiet, all was honest, all was openhearted harmony.

"At times I feel that running a church here is like fishing in heaven," Reverend Collins confessed. "Not a week passes that I don't have at least a couple of people come in and ask, can you help us grow? Can you teach us more?"

"Yet how many of them come to you because of the Gospel," Father Anatoli countered, "and how many because you are from the West?"

"I would be the first to admit," Reverend Collins agreed, "that many of those entering our doors do so because they associate us with *success*. With *wealth*. They assume we Westerners have all the answers because we have made our system work while their own has failed. But that, too, is a problem. They see no wrong in our Western society. They accept the New Age cults and the get-rich ministries just as hungrily as they do the Gospel."

"My people also drift very easily," Bishop Michael confessed. "Today it is Mass, tomorrow a Protestant revival, the next day a liter of vodka."

"When I am faced with this in my own congregation," Reverend Collins offered, "I remind myself that a newborn baby cannot be expected to stand up and run. It is still in diapers. It makes mistakes. It needs to be held and fed and loved and coddled."

"There is great wisdom in what you say," Father Anatoli murmured. "Great wisdom."

"When Hezekiah was a twenty-five-year-old king," Bishop Michael interjected, "he reversed a two-hundred-year-long trend by demanding that the Israelites return to worshiping their Lord. The priests, under this young king's instructions, tore down every heathen shrine in the country. They cleaned the pagan altars from the high places. They purified the nation. Hezekiah then declared a seven-day period of worship. And so many came with sacrifices that at the end of this time the priests returned to the king and said, we must have more time; give us seven days more. The people donated so much money that it was left in heaps outside the temple."

He looked at each man in turn. "In my heart of hearts, I believe that the same miracle could occur here, if only we were to join together and offer the Lord's message in a spirit of His divine love."

"And yet, and yet," Father Anatoli murmured, his gaze sorely troubled. "What can I say to those of my church who do not agree with the concept of brotherhood among Christians?"

"What we should say to everyone in every church who thinks this way," Reverend Collins replied. "Tell them that throughout the New Testament, we are declared joined to one another. A body of believers. The bride of Christ. A hint of the divine in earthly form. I think we owe it to our Father to behave as He commands, don't you?"

"Indeed," Bishop Michael agreed. "And yet, within my own church at least, the greatest problem is where to draw the line between Christian and heretic."

"But who are we to judge what is and is not a part of the body?" Reverend Collins replied. "The Book of Proverbs states that God truly despises someone who sows discord among those God loves. Who here on earth has been given such perfect judgment that he or she can say who in God's eyes is among the fold? And if there is not the power of perfect judgment, why would anyone wish to take such a risk?"

His dark eyes filled with penetrating strength, Father Anatoli observed, "You have thought of this at length."

"I have had to face within myself the desire to judge," Reverend Collins replied somberly. "To be perfectly honest, I don't agree with many of your practices, or in some respects even with your concept of Christ." Evan Collins shook his head. "But to argue about it, or judge you, is just to make matters worse. As soon as the battle is started, even by thoughts that are never uttered, the war is lost."

"I feel I have waited all my life to hear such words spoken," Bishop Michael said.

But Reverend Collins was not finished. "The truth of Jesus Christ I would defend to my dying breath. My whole life is based upon His gift of salvation. But I must continually be on guard to separate my own restricted perspective from His divine and eternal truths."

"And how do you do that?" Father Anatoli asked.

"By remembering three things at all times: that I am human, that I could be wrong, and that I most certainly don't know everything."

"My brothers," Bishop Michael told them, a gentle smile playing upon his features. "Last night I dreamed that the white roses of heaven were unfolding and sending their petals down to fall in invisible drifts upon this scarred and hurting earth. People were being healed, shadows were being banished, and hope was being restored."

"Our people need our help," Father Anatoli declared. "And there is only one answer we can show them. Love and harmony in the name of Jesus Christ. Unity beneath the glorious banner of our Lord."

There were sober nods around the circle. "If we are to concentrate on the ones in need and not on the problems of an earthly existence for our churches," Reverend Collins agreed, "then we must show in our lives what we promise they will find within their hearts. The everlasting peace of Jesus Christ."

"We must build a shelter for our people's suffering hearts," Father Anatoli went on. "We must work as one to erect a home filled with light and hope, a palace large enough for all believers. One strong enough to withstand the bitterest of winter winds."

"The only answer," Bishop Michael urged, "the only way forward, is mutual forgiveness."

"By living the teachings," Father Anatoli agreed, "of our Lord Jesus."

They stopped at that, shocked into stillness by the boldness of their words.

P rince Vladimir Markov put down the telephone receiver, and was pleased to find that his hands were not shaking.

From his place at the desk, the same desk which had passed from father to son for seven generations, Markov gazed at the blue-upon-blue of cloudless sky meeting deep Mediterranean waters. The sweet scents of jasmine and lemon blossoms drifted in through tall open windows. Beyond the glass-fronted French doors, the veranda table bore a sterling silver coffee service, a gift to his grandfather from the czar himself. A brilliant white umbrella protected the wrought-iron table from the afternoon's warmth. His chair, from which he had been drawn by the general's telephone call, was at its customary place by the outer wall, so that Markov could sip his coffee while watching a bustling Monte Carlo prepare for evening.

Markov did not return to his coffee, however. He looked out toward the horizon with eyes that saw nothing, took in nothing, and reflected upon all that was lost. All that was placed beyond his grasp, and would remain so forever.

It was good of General Surikov to telephone. He had called to report personally about the developments, and to say that they were coming. Despite the man's many faults, Markov decided, Surikov had the mark of a gentleman.

Prince Markov unlocked the bottom right-hand drawer to his desk. His hand hesitated over the box containing his great-grandfather's set of matched dueling pistols, then settled upon the letter resting beside it. Gently he pulled out and flattened the single sheet. Although the page was yellowed and brittle with age, the Cyrillic handwriting was fresh and strong and certain, as though written only the day before.

The letter had been sent by his grandfather, universally known as the old prince, to Markov's own father, several weeks before the Bolsheviks overran Saint Petersburg and overthrew the czarist government. It was the last word his father had ever received from any of the family:

My dear son:

I know it is not your habit to listen to advice, especially from me. I also know that you shall go your own headstrong way no matter what I say. Yet I beg you to honor an old man's request on this one matter, if on nothing else: Do not ever collaborate with the enemy, no matter what they may offer.

From what I can see of the gathering storm, these thieves are attempting to hide within the cloak of legitimate authority. They intend to steal all we have—our lands, our homes, our titles. They may then find themselves robbed of their own power to govern. When they realize this and show weakness, you may be tempted to negotiate with them in hopes of restoring yourself to power. Do not do so, my son. Do not forsake your soul to these evil ones. They will repay you with nothing but empty promises.

If you were to try and collaborate, the day will come when you shall displease them. Make no mistake, my son. With such people, it is inevitable that displeasure or jealously or enmity will occur. When that happens, they will kill you.

Understand this, and you understand an essential difference between a man of honor and such men as these—they have no respect for human life. None whatsoever. Their only answer to a problem is to kill. To destroy. To annihilate.

Do not allow yourself to be sucked into the maelstrom, no matter how strong the temptation. In the end it will destroy you, unless you choose to become like them, which is itself a destruction worse than death.

As the Good Book says, you cannot serve two masters. Remain loyal to who you are. Do not taint our family's great name with the walking of false paths. The thieves will never return us to power, nor offer you the glory they might claim. Even when everything earthly is lost, hold steadfast to the truth. And so, my son, may the good Lord keep you and yours.

Farewell

Carefully Markov refolded the letter and drew out the embossed teakwood box. He hefted the cold metal, was mildly surprised to find it far heavier than he expected, and knew a moment's regret that he had never been granted an opportunity to meet the old man.

CHAPTER 42

That night Ivona returned to her room, exhausted by the day and defeated by the internal voices that called to her with deafening intensity. Once in bed, her mind would not cease its restless searching.

She wanted so much to condemn Jeffrey. He and his ways went against everything she had ever known or believed. Yet she could not. The bishop had accepted him since the very beginning, despite her strongest disapproval. And Jeffrey had returned this trust by accomplishing the impossible.

Ivona had accepted work on this investigation because the bishop told her to. It had been her duty to set aside her doubt, no, more than that, her *certainty* that the church's treasure was lost and gone forever. To do the bishop's bidding was her life's work, even when doing so had been an exercise in dangerous futility.

Here again, Jeffrey had proved her wrong.

Then there was Yussef. *Her* Yussef. He had turned to this Western stranger with questions she had waited a lifetime to hear him ask of her. Why? Why had he turned to Jeffrey and not to her? Why was it so?

Even more disturbing, why did she herself feel this answering call within her own heart?

The very foundations of her world were being shaken with violent intensity, and she felt utterly helpless in the face of such a storm.

Always before, she had simply assumed that the bishop and the priests, the *good* priests, were the ones to have a close relationship with God. They read all the holy books. They lived holy lives. They worked in holy service. They acted as God's holy emissaries. She *expected* them to have such a deep spiritual life.

How was it, then, that such a divine spirit dwelled within Jeffrey when he prayed? He was none of these things, not even a part of the holy church. Yet her own basic honesty would not allow her to deny what she had seen, what she had felt, both within the man's actions and within the man's words. And to admit that this spirit existed within him challenged her to find it also for herself.

====

Finally she slept, and dreamed of a funeral. A funeral long over, yet still continuing. The friends and the mourners and the incense and the priest and the flowers and the tears were all gone, yet still the funeral went on. Still she was there, and somehow she knew she had been there for a very long time.

The funeral van sat in an empty field under a leaden sky. It was nothing more than a rusted hulk, without wheels or windows or doors, locked into place by an anchor of weeds.

There beside the coffin sat her husband. Only it was not he, but rather a young boy who looked sadly out through the hearse's window frame. At the sight of her, he started guiltily and turned back to his place beside the coffin. As he turned, he aged, resuming what she knew was the position she had forced him into for the past forty years, forced to sit and wait with her without ever understanding why, or what she herself was waiting for. Yet he loved her too much to leave. So he continued to sit, trapped in a funeral that had lost all meaning to everyone, including herself. And in the process he had become an old man, stooped and bent and defeated.

Her attention was caught by another person standing a few paces away, and with a shock she recognized herself. Her back was to the hearse and her husband. She stood in such rigid, unbending anger that vines had wound their way up around her legs and body and bound her to the earth, just as they did the ancient van. With her anger blinding her, she had not even noticed that she too was trapped.

Ivona walked around to the side of the van, but the distance was great, so great that even as she walked her husband continued to shield her from seeing the coffin. Faster she walked, and faster still. Still she could not see around her husband. Suddenly she was running, and as she ran she realized she was fleeing, pursued by all the wasted years and all the chains of anger.

With that flash of realization the coffin came into view.

And it was empty.

She stopped, shocked into frozen stillness by the sight of that vacant coffin. Ivona understood then. She *understood*.

She mourned years lost, and hurts caused her by an uncaring world. She was angry with the apathetic way life had treated her. She had used her sorrow as a weapon to punish the world for her loss. Especially her husband. And her God. And herself.

And for nothing.

There was only one answer. Only one solution. She flung herself down before the empty coffin, and she wept. She wept for the youth which was no more. She wept for the years that had been lost. She wept for her husband, and for herself. She wept for the anger she had harbored against her God.

A hand came to rest upon her back. The hand of her husband. And somehow, at the same time, the hand of her Lord.

The calm, gentle motion was enough to awaken her. And as she sat upright, her face washed by the same tears she had sobbed in her dream, she realized that, somehow, all was forgiven.

Ivona rose from her bed, knowing a wisdom and a need that left no room for slumber. It was time to extend the hand of forgiveness here on earth.

CHAPTER 43

The next morning Jeffrey arrived at the American consulate to find Casey waiting for him at the front door. "How are the paws?"

Jeffrey raised two bandaged hands. "Not bad. Your doctor did a great job."

"Good to hear. Come on up, the CG's waiting for us."

As Jeffrey entered the Consul General's office, Allbright rounded his desk as usual, hand outstretched, only to drop it and say, "Guess that's not such a good idea."

"They're a lot better than they look," Jeffrey said. "Mostly just scratches."

"What about your friend Sergei?"

"Fifteen stitches in his arm, and almost hugged to death by his grandmother when he got back home."

Allbright smiled. "The old lady's given me and Casey a standing invitation to come and eat with them any time we like."

"You should take her up on it; she's a great cook," Jeffrey said. "How is Miss Stevens?"

"Left for Berlin last night as scheduled. Sedated, of course, but otherwise in good shape, all things considered. Our base doctors should have her back on her feet in short order. They've unfortunately had quite a bit of recent experience treating released hostages and kidnap victims."

"A tough sign of troubled times," Casey offered.

"You said it. Here, take a seat, both of you. Can I get you anything?"

"I'm fine, thanks."

"Your reservation took a bit of arm twisting. As you know, most planes to and from the West are booked solid these days. But we managed to get you onto the midday flight for London." Allbright glanced at his watch. "We'll drive you out, of course. Probably should plan to leave here in a half hour or so; that'll give you time to pack."

"Thanks a lot," Jeffrey said, his spirits lifting dramatically.

"Don't mention it. The least I owe you is help with moving up your departure date and maybe an explanation."

"You don't owe me anything," Jeffrey replied. "As a matter of fact, it seems to me I'm the one who owes you a life."

"Well, let's just put it down to one friend helping another, how's that?"

"Fine," Jeffrey said. "Thanks."

"I'd still like to fill in a few gaps," Allbright added. "But before we start with that, would you like to call anyone and let them know you're coming in early?"

"If it's no problem."

"What's the use of being a Consul General if you can't throw your weight around every now and then? Just give Casey as many numbers as you can think of. It improves your chances. Sometimes the operator hits with one, sometimes with another."

"Modern-day Russian roulette," Casey offered.

"Right. In the meantime, let me give you some of the background to the situation we've been facing here."

Situation. Having almost been killed by one gave the word an entirely new meaning. Jeffrey handed three telephone numbers to Casey. "Thanks a lot."

"No problem. Be right back."

"Okay, let's back up about six months," Allbright began. "Early this year, a senior KGB official was accused of staying in office after he was offered retirement, not out of patriotism or some misguided fervor for Communist ideology, but to get rich. He used the only existing network of contacts the nation had, the Party power structure, to swing assets and deals his way. His efforts came to light when one of his former KGB associates, now working with our buddies in the new anti-crime squad, linked his activities to one of the most powerful mafia clans in Russia."

"Your friends and mine," Casey said, reentering the office. "The Tombek clan."

"Word has it that this is just the tip of the iceberg," Allbright continued. "As the scent of wealth grew, so did the number of KGB bosses clamoring for a piece of the action."

The phone chose that moment to ring. "That'll be your call," Allbright said.

Jeffrey sprang from his seat, accepted the receiver, shouted a hello, and heard Alexander's voice through the static.

"Jeffrey, what a delightful surprise. I hope you are not calling because of bad news."

"Everything's fine," Jeffrey said, looking down at his bandaged hands, thinking back over the previous twenty-four hours, feeling weak with relief. "Really. How are you doing?"

"I am very glad to report that I continue to progress on almost a daily basis. The doctors are quite pleased, so much so that they are actually puffing themselves up with pride, as if they were solely responsible for my recovery and I was simply along for the ride. But there you are. Human nature, I suppose."

"Are you at your flat?"

"Yes, of course. Where did you think?"

"I gave the operator a string of numbers, and yours was the one that came up. I was just wondering if you were already back in the shop."

"Ah, I see. No, my dear boy, I am still taking my leisure at home. Although I must admit that I have begun strolling down to the shop as part of my daily constitutional. Not to interfere, you understand. Your lovely young bride has managed things quite well in your absence, I am happy to say. Even the count has granted her his official seal of approval."

Jeffrey turned toward the back wall so he could hide his tired smile from the two gentlemen. "I hope I still have a job when I return home."

"Don't even joke about such matters. There is much awaiting you. Gregor called this very morning to ask if you might be able to arrange another trip to Cracow in the near future. When do you expect to return?"

"That's why I called. My work here was completed early," Jeffrey replied. And, he added to himself, almost permanently. "Please, if you would call Katya and tell her that my flight should be arriving late this afternoon."

"She will be delighted to hear this," Alexander assured him, "as am I. But you sound quite exhausted. Are you certain everything is all right?"

"Everything is fine," Jeffrey replied. "I have a lot to tell you."

"I shall look forward with great anticipation to hearing every word."

"I can't get over how much better you sound."

"Yes, and grateful for every moment of life and relative good health left to me," Alexander replied, then added, "And for the pleasure of good friends."

"Good friends," Jeffrey agreed, and hung up.

=====

"Our buddies in the anti-crime squad are averaging a new discovery every other day," Casey told Jeffrey as he drove them toward the airport. "The latest was a state research institute that set up a private company, then placed the former local KGB leader as president. The institute sold this new company one hundred state-of-the-art computers for pennies. The company then turned around and re-sold the hardware for three thousand times the purchase price. The senior directors of the institute split the profits."

"People on the street call such deals 'nomenklatura privatization,'" Allbright explained. "Who has money these days to buy the factories going up for sale? The list is limited to only three groups—foreigners eager to buy on the cheap, Russian mafia seeking to go legal, and the old Communist Party elite using funds they stashed during their heyday."

"And it is looking more and more like the lines separating the Party and the mafia are disappearing," Casey said.

"Exactly. Now that their Communist Party power base is dissolving, the former bosses are scrambling like rats from a sinking ship, grabbing for anything that might keep them on top. The mafia is making money hand over fist right now, what with the breakdown in laws and security. Maintaining connection with the old Party bosses is a logical step to becoming legitimate."

"In other words," Casey summed up, "It's a real mess."

Jeffrey sank back into the cushions, interested in the discussion but distracted by thoughts of the last few hours. The farewells with Yussef, Sergei, and Sergei's grandmother had proven more difficult than Jeffrey had expected. There had been a few tears from the old lady, a round of back slaps and numerous farewells from both men. Jeffrey had found himself making promises of another trip very soon just to get out the door.

But nothing could have prepared him for Ivona's goodbye.

She had taken him aside and with downcast eyes had solemnly thanked him for his gift of wisdom. Those had been her words: a gift of wisdom. Jeffrey had been so surprised he had actually kissed her cheek.

"Right now," said Allbright, "this collection of KGB, former Party bosses, and mafia is gathering power with auctioned factories, and the people are again being crushed under the same old weight, now bearing a new name. And that means there are lots of angry, disaffected people out there. Every day, the public's hatred for all this chaos is mounting. It is a powder keg with the fuse tamped and burning."

Jeffrey asked, "So why doesn't the government do something?"

"Because their hands are tied. You see, the current parliament was elected under the old Communist scheme, where the local Party dominated everything and opposition was outlawed. Given the circumstances, it is amazing that even a third of them are backing the government's proposed reforms, which they are."

"Which leaves two-thirds of the parliament against them," Jeffrey deduced.

"Not necessarily. One-third, yes; the hardliners go all purple at the sound of the word reform. But another third, the pivotal group, is made up of the people smart enough to realize the old Communist system doesn't work, but frightened by the thought of change."

"It's sort of like driving with one foot on the gas and the other on the brake," Casey explained.

"Which pretty much sums up the government's position right now," Allbright agreed. "In order to keep the hand-wringers from bolting, they have been forced to give up control of several key ministries, including defense."

"And security," Casey added.

"So, in regard to a lot of things, the government is simply powerless. This is one of those cases where we just have to hope that the tree of democracy will take root, and with time a good pruning of all these dead branches will be possible."

"And you think that will happen?"

"I'd sure like to think so. Right here, right now, we're watching the biggest economic upheaval the world has witnessed since the Industrial Revolution. The largest country in the world is trying to go from complete anti-capitalism to capitalism in one fell swoop. And they're doing it! But people keep pointing to unsolved problems and shouting out gloom and doom with these great voices, while the grass of change grows quietly.

"Look," he continued. "Eighty-five percent of Saint Petersburg's economy depended on the military-industrial complex. Now the military isn't buying *anything*. So local companies are trying to go from tanks to toasters without investment capital. I've seen the result. You want to buy a three-hundred-pound toaster?

"But you know," he went on, "nature can take a squirmy little worm and turn it into a butterfly. So can they. They've just got to close things down, break them up, then rebuild. And it is happening."

"But how fast?" Jeffrey asked.

"Yes, that's the million-dollar question," Allbright agreed. "Can they do it before the people lose patience?"

"What do you think?"

Allbright was a long time replying. "After the Germans were defeated in the First World War, the country suffered this awful time of economic hardship. When historians look for reasons why the Nazis came to power, they point to this horrible depression and hyperinflation, and they say, 'Look, see how bad things were? The Germans would have accepted just about anything to get food back on the table.' But for a few people, myself included, this just doesn't hold water. A lot of other places have suffered bad economic times and held on to democracy and basic principles of human justice. No, I think it was a bad economic struggle tied to something else, something just as big. The people faced a *vacuum*."

"In leadership," Jeffrey suggested.

"Not just leadership. Deeper than that. You see, the first World War didn't just destroy the country's industry; it defeated an entire value system. In those chaotic days after the war, the Germans had nothing to cling to, no basis for hope or confidence. Then the Nazis came along and filled this vacuum with hate. And on that hate they rebuilt a nation's pride."

Jeffrey thought it over. "Seventy years of Communism swept out overnight could produce a pretty good vacuum."

Allbright nodded grimly. "Our biggest hope is the Russians' own patience. They just might be able to see this through. Watch Russians standing in line for bread in the dead of winter, and you get some idea of how much patience these people really do have."

"Seems to me there might be a better source of hope than that," Jeffrey said quietly.

Allbright grew still. "You're talking about religion?"

Jeffrey shook his head. "I'm talking about faith."

"Hard to see how," the older man replied doubtfully. "It would be nice, I admit. I even have enough hope left myself to have asked the three churches to oversee the distribution of that recovered treasure. And maybe, when we are talking about just a few people, it might work. But with all the nation's churches?"

Allbright gave his head a doubtful shake. "The Protestants argue with one another, and some accuse the Orthodox of not being Christian at all. The Orthodox respond by urging all Russians to treat the incoming Protestant missionaries as heretics. Then they both look down their noses at the Catholics. And the Catholics don't like much of anybody except themselves. Long as you see these different churches at one another's throats, I doubt you'd find many people around here who'd agree that religious leaders could find their own hats, much less answers to a nation's problems."

"I wasn't talking about religion," Jeffrey repeated, his voice still quiet. "I was speaking about faith in Jesus Christ. The one hope eternal."

Allbright examined him for a long moment before replying, "Something tells me it's a shame we don't have more people like you around here. People able to look to the heart of the matter and lay it out in plain words that plain people can understand."

═══

The plane lifted up through the layer of clouds and on into the endless blue. Jeffrey leaned back in his seat with a very tired sigh, extremely glad the Consul General had made the travel arrangements for him. He wanted nothing more at that moment than to be home.

He picked at the bandages wrapped around his hands and looked out on the brilliant cloudscape. Tracers from earlier aircraft stretched out like long white ribbons across the sky.

Fatigue turned the previous hours and days into a jumble of conflicting memories. He drifted into sleep, only to be jolted awake. He opened his eyes to find the stewardess leaning over him, asking if he cared for food. He did not, but accepted anyway. He thanked her as she set down the tray, refused her offer of something to drink, and turned his face back toward the window.

His eyelids drifted downward once more, weighted by the stresses and strains of the past days. This time he slid smoothly into welcome rest. His final waking thought was of Katya.

"The mind-set of the times threatens to strip our faith of symbols, rituals, dramas, mystery, poetry, and story, which say about life and God what logic and reason and rationalism can never say. Instead, we attempt to analyze and explain God. Scripture becomes mere religious information, and faith simply the progressive realization of moral or 'religious' goals. From this perspective we cannot expect anything but flatness. One-dimensional faith, like a tent with only one peg, easily collapses. Yet, we Americans tend to secure our faith primarily with the one peg of logical thought."

> Reverend Lynn Anderson
> (Church of Christ)
> *If I Really Believe, Why Do I*
> *Have These Doubts?*

Throughout the journey of this novel, I have been constantly humbled by the gentle hospitality of people whose hearts were open to our Lord, and by the smallness of my own world. I hope I have managed to convey some of this spirit in my work. The writing of this book has coincided with Isabella, my wife, beginning graduate studies in theology at Oxford University.

Despite the strains of studying in this area for the first time (her previous studies have been in law and international relations), Isabella has continued to walk with me through the formation of this book, helping out at every turn. Truly, this work was completed in large part because of her loving assistance and bountiful wisdom.

＝＝

Because of the importance of these dialogues among churches, all discussions on matters of doctrine and faith were taken verbatim from interviews I had with respective priests, bishops, and ministers. I have done this in hopes that people interested in becoming more involved in evangelistic efforts within the former Soviet lands—and make no mistake, help is desperately needed—might perhaps gain a bit more insight into the current religious culture.

United States Consul General to Saint Petersburg, Mr. Jack Gosnell, has spent more than twelve years serving his country in Russia and China. His knowledge is simply immense. It was a great privilege to work with him. His overview of the political and economic situation facing Russia today was both succinct and extremely perceptive. We are indeed fortunate to have a gentleman of such talents representing us in this volatile region. I would also like to thank his lovely wife and most talented staff for their gifts of assistance and hospitality.

While in Saint Petersburg, I was granted the opportunity to speak at length with a member of the nation's Foreign Ministry. I did so with the understanding that I would not name him. But I would nonetheless like to offer my very sincere thanks for the perceptivity and depth of analysis he granted me.

Vladimir Gronsky is editor of the International Department of the *Leningrad Daily News*. At the conclusion of my visit to Saint Petersburg, I was faced with the daunting task of pulling together the results of almost fifty interviews. Mr. Gronsky assisted me in rising above the mass of facts and related experiences, and searching out the overriding themes. With his honest advice as guidance, I was able to establish certain tenets that became central points in this story's development. I am indeed thankful for his patient aid.

H. Kozyritskiy is the Mayor of Sestoretsk, the region running from northern Saint Petersburg to the borderlands. In a discussion that was slated for fifteen minutes and ran to over two hours, he outlined with frightening honesty the economic trials facing his region. If Russia is able to overcome the challenge facing it today, it will be in no small part due to the unsung efforts of men like him.

Reverend Allen Faubion and Reverend Larry Van Tuyl are pastors at the International Church of Saint Petersburg. For those traveling over, Sunday services are located inside the Concert-Theater Complex at 39 Nevsky Prospekt. (This was altered in this book to a location used by another Western group giving services only in Russian, as the story required a more permanent location.) I would like to offer my heartfelt thanks both for the excellent information granted to me in our discussion prior to the service, and for the most inspiring sermon. May the Lord richly bless them and their work.

Dr. Karl Keller, pastor at the Walnut Grove Lutheran Church in British Columbia, was a leader with Christian Embassy, and traveled with a group of Canadian Christian businessmen on a goodwill mission to Moscow and Saint Petersburg. They had high-level meetings within the national and city governments, and with military officials. I am very grateful that Dr. Keller was willing to take the time from his mission work to stop and share with me both his experience and his findings. Several of his observations have been worked into Reverend Collins' discussions.

The story of Alexander and Gregor's escape from Poland at the end of the war was drawn from the experiences of my wife's uncle, Marian Tarka. He was a member of the Polish Home Army, or AK, and when the Russians arrived and fellow members began to disappear, he had the idea of escaping into the Red Army. The story is his save for one fact; he survived his interrogation, and remained with the Red Army until discharged, while his friends made their escape into the woods and joined the AK and eventually left Poland. The route up through Scandinavia to London was one used by a large number of escapees in the turmoil before the Soviet's Iron Curtain was firmly fixed into place.

The story of Zosha's escape from the trek headed from the Warsaw Uprising to the German concentration camp is also true. It is the story of my wife's aunt, Dusia Tarka, who escaped due to the courageous efforts of one young man, who slipped in and out of the line of German soldiers to save as many young people as he could. She never even learned his name.

Ryszard Litwicki was taken from his home in Lvov by the Germans to work at forced labor in Berlin, where during the bombing campaign he worked in a bomb depot. I am grateful that he survived the experience, and was willing to speak of his upbringing in what now is western Ukraine, and then was the area of Poland known as Galicia.

Eugenia Krajewska is secretary to the Father Superior at the Marian Fathers monastery outside London. When she was eleven years old, she and her family were deported from Poland to a logging village just south of the Arctic Circle in European Russia. This life story made the chronicle of Ivona Aristonova's tragic past. It is very hard for us as Americans to fathom the suffering caused to literally millions of people by Stalin's policy of amalgamation and relocation, what was commonly referred to as Russification. Her story is in no way exceptional, and stands as a testimony to a tragedy that we as free men and women must strive never to permit to surface again.

=

Some time ago, Reverend John Wimber spoke to the Holy Trinity Church in Brompton, England, on the desert experience. The section in this book that began with a reference to the sixty-third Psalm was drawn from his magnificent teaching.

Each year, bookstore owners from across the nation join together for the Christian Booksellers Association annual convention. This year, Dr. Joe Aldrich spoke at the Sunday service. His address was on the need for harmony among the body of believers. Great inspiration, as well as considerable material for this book, was drawn from the gentleman's well-spoken wisdom.

Reverend Alec Brooks is formerly President of the Bethany Fellowship, with responsibility for their worldwide missionary program as well as the Bible college. Currently he is teaching Theology, Marriage and Family, and Developing a Christan World View at this same college, and remains a member of the advisory board. He was most helpful in gaining a solid perspective on how an evangelical missionary pastor might view the Orthodox church—his words formed the discussion Jeffrey had with Reverend Evan Collins on the issue of icons. Alec has been a good friend and most helpful guide over the years. I am grateful for the opportunity to grow from his wisdom.

The gentlefolk at Christies auction house continue to show remarkable patience with the presence of an author with no possibility whatsoever to purchase any of the items he hovers around. I am especially grateful for Amelia Fitzalan-Howard's surprising eagerness to offer hospitality, wisdom, insight, and answers to what I am sure appeared to be an unending stream of questions.

Her Majesty Queen Elizabeth recently opened an exhibition in Buckingham Palace of antiques and paintings collected by one of her forebears, King George III. I would like to extend my thanks to the staff who prepared both the exhibit and the excellent brochure. They proved an invaluable source of information for the period from which many of the antiques in this book were drawn.

The story of Communist Party and KGB bosses secretly attempting to establish a Party-controlled mini-economy for no other reason than greed is true. I would like to thank the BBC's Panorama news team for their excellent coverage of the story, and for supplying me with most helpful documentation as this book was being developed.

A very special thanks must be extended to two leaders of the Russian Orthodox Church, Metropolitan Anthony in London and Metropolitan Ioann in Saint Petersburg. They were most kind in their offers of assistance and contacts. In both cases, I was an unknown American Protestant who simply wrote and asked questions. In both cases, I was answered with open-handed kindness. Thank you.

Bishop Kallistos, of the Ecumenical Patriarchate in England, is author of numerous books and articles on Orthodox faith. I found his book *The Orthodox Church* to be a wonderful introduction both to the history and the present-day status of this church. I am also most grateful for the hours he so willingly shared with me. His kind assistance went far beyond discussing with me such painful subjects as KGB infiltration into the Russian Orthodox hierarchy. He was also most open in sharing what Christian faith means to a Russian Orthodox, where it parallels the Protestant faith and where it diverges. He is a kind and Spirit-filled man, whose assistance added greatly to the work on this book.

Diakon Vsevolod Chaplin, personal assistant to the Patriarch of the Russian Orthodox Church in Moscow, outlined a number of current issues facing the church in Russia today. He was open and frank about the trials besetting the church, both from within and without. He discussed the church's historical perspective to evangelical movements and the impressions of today. He then made introductions for me, both with the senior bishops and Metropolitans in Russia and with the Orthodox community leaders in Great Britain. This book's attempt to portray the Orthodox church's position with authenticity stems in large part from his very kind assistance.

Father Archimindrit Simon is personal assistant to the Metropolitan Ioann of Saint Petersburg. He was an extremely erudite individual, who helped to place the current problems and issues facing the Russian Orthodox community in simple, understandable terms. This was no small feat, as everything besetting the church today is a legacy of that which has come before. He and all his staff were burdened with the work of ten. I am indeed grateful that he would nonetheless take an entire morning to educate me.

Bishop Michael Kuchmiak is head of the Ukrainian Eastern Rite Catholic Church for all of England, Wales, Scotland, and Ireland. I was humbled by his willingness to rearrange extremely busy schedules to talk with me in depth about his church and the crisis it faces today as it emerges from forty-five years of illegality and persecution.

Marina Karetnikova is a deacon and lay minister in the Baptist church of Saint Petersburg. She is also a teacher at the newly opened Bible college in that city. She was extremely helpful in granting me a living history of the Russian Baptist movement and of the courage and faith demonstrated by its believers through these tremendously difficult times.

Father Graham Woolfenden was trained as a "Biritual" priest, meaning that he was most familiar with the Eastern Rite churches, as well as with the differences between them and the Catholic liturgy. He was most helpful in granting me this essential overview required before in-depth research could be started.

Valerie Morozov served as Director of Education of the Bibles for Everyone Society of Russia. Their primary purpose was two-fold: to supply Bibles in modern Russian and other Soviet tongues and to teach Bible classes to school-age children. Their number of classes increased from ten in 1989 to one hundred thirty in 1992. They operated classes in foster homes, orphanages, hospitals, and reformatories. I am very grateful for his taking the time to discuss the situation facing them as they tried to set up classes inside former Communist-run school systems, and for the overview of Christianity in modern Russian society.

═══

I do appreciate hearing from readers. Please feel free to contact me at: www.DavisBunn.com.

Davis Bunn has been a professional novelist for over twenty years. The author of numerous national bestsellers with sales totaling over six million copies, his work has been published in sixteen languages, and critical acclaim includes three Christy Awards for excellence in fiction. Formerly an international business executive based in Europe, Africa, and the Middle East, Bunn writes full time except for lectures in creative writing, and he is the Writer in Residence at Regent's Park College, Oxford University, Britain. He and his wife, Isabella, divide their time between the English countryside and the coast of Florida.